COME
HOME
&
KEEP
QUIET

Also by Lisa Scottoline

After Anna

One Perfect Lie

Most Wanted

Every Fifteen Minutes

Don't Go

Save Me

Look Again

Daddy's Girl

Dirty Blonde

Devil's Corner

Running from the Law

Final Appeal

Rosato & DiNunzio Novels

Feared

Exposed

Damaged

Corrupted

Betrayed

Accused

Rosato & Associates Novels

Think Twice

Lady Killer

Killer Smile

Dead Ringer

Courting Trouble

The Vendetta Defense

Moment of Truth

Mistaken Identity

Rough Justice

Legal Tender

Everywhere That Mary Went

Nonfiction (with Francesca Serritella)

I See Life Through Rosé-Colored Glasses

I Need a Lifeguard Everywhere but the Pool

I've Got Sand in All the Wrong Places

Does This Beach Make Me Look Fat?

Have a Nice Guilt Trip

Meet Me at Emotional Baggage Claim

Best Friends, Occasional Enemies

My Nest Isn't Empty, It Just Has More Closet Space

Why My Third Husband Will Be a Dog

COME HOME

&

KEEP QUIET

Lisa Scottoline

ST. MARTIN'S
GRIFFIN
New York

Published in the United States by St. Martin's Griffin,
an imprint of St. Martin's Publishing Group

COME HOME. Copyright © 2012 by Lisa Scottoline.
KEEP QUIET. Copyright © 2014 by Smart Blonde, LLC.
All rights reserved. Printed in the United States of America.
For information, address St. Martin's Publishing Group,
120 Broadway, New York, NY 10271.

www.stmartins.com

The Library of Congress Cataloging-in-Publication Data is
available upon request.

ISBN 978-1-250-84237-4 (trade paperback)

Our books may be purchased in bulk for promotional,
educational, or business use. Please contact your local
bookseller or the Macmillan Corporate and Premium Sales
Department at 1-800-221-7945, extension 5442, or by email
at MacmillanSpecialMarkets@macmillan.com.

First Edition: 2021

10 9 8 7 6 5 4 3 2 1

COME HOME

This novel is dedicated, with deepest gratitude, to Jen Enderlin, my amazing editor and friend.

Physician, heal thyself.
—*The Holy Bible,* Luke 4:23

It is an old maxim of mine that when you have
excluded the impossible, whatever remains,
however improbable, must be the truth.
—Sherlock Holmes in *The Adventures of the Beryl Coronet*
by Sir Arthur Conan Doyle

Chapter One

Jill stopped on the stairway, listening. She thought she heard a voice calling her from outside, but she'd been wrong before. It was probably the rushing of the rain, or the lash of the wind through the trees. Still, she listened, hoping.

"Babe?" Sam paused on the stair, resting his hand on the banister. He looked back at her, his eyes a puzzled blue behind his glasses. "Did you forget your phone?"

"No, I thought I heard something." Jill didn't elaborate. She was in her forties, old enough to have a past and wise enough to keep her thoughts about it to herself.

"What?" Sam asked, patiently. It was almost midnight, and they'd been on their way to bed. The house was dark except for the glass fixture above the stairwell, and the silvery strands in Sam's thick, dark hair glinted in the low light. Their chubby golden retriever, Beef, was already upstairs, looking down at them from the landing, his buttery ears falling forward.

"It's nothing, I guess." Jill started back up the stairs, but Beef swung his head toward the front of the house and gave an excited bark. His tail started to wag, and Jill turned, too, listening again.

Jill! Jill!

"It's Abby!" Jill heard it for sure, this time. The cry resonated in her chest, speaking directly to her heart. She turned around and hurried for the entrance hall, and Beef scampered downstairs after her, his heavy butt getting ahead of him, like a runaway tractor-trailer.

"Abby who?" Sam called after her. "Your ex's kid?"

"Yes." Jill reached the front door, twisted the deadbolt, flicked on the porch light, and threw open the door. Abby wasn't there, and Jill didn't see her because it was so dark. There were no streetlights at this end of the block, and the rain obliterated the outlines of the houses and cars, graying out the suburban scene. Suddenly, a black SUV with only one headlight drove past, spotlighting a silhouette that Jill would know anywhere. It was Abby, but she was staggering down the sidewalk as if she'd been injured.

"Sam, call 911!" Jill bolted out of the house and into the storm, diagnosing Abby on the fly. It could have been a hit-and-run, or an aneurysm. Not a stroke, Abby was too young. Not a gunshot or stab wound, in this neighborhood.

Jill tore through the rain. Beef bounded ahead, barking in alarm. The neighbor's motion-detector went on, casting a halo of light on their front lawn. Abby stumbled off the sidewalk. Her purse slipped from her shoulder and dropped to the ground. Abby took a few more faltering steps, then collapsed, crumpling to the grass.

"Abby!" Jill screamed, sprinting to Abby's side, kneeling down. Abby was conscious, but crying. Jill reached for her pulse and scanned her head and body for signs of injury, and there were none. Rainwater covered Abby's face, streaking her mascara and blackening her tears. Her hair stuck to her neck, and rain plastered her thin sundress to her body. Her pulse felt strong and steady, bewildering Jill. "Abby, Abby, what is it?"

"You have to . . . hold me." Abby raised her arms. "Please."

Jill gathered Abby close, shielding her from the rain. She'd held Abby so many times before, and all the times rushed back at her, as if her very body had stored the memories, until that very moment. Jill flashed on the time Abby had fallen off her Rollerblades, breaking an ankle. Then the time Abby had gotten a C on her trig final. The time she didn't get picked for the travel soccer team. Abby had always been a sensitive little girl, but she wasn't a little girl anymore, and Jill had never seen her cry so hard.

"Abby, honey, please, tell me, and I can help."

"I can't say it . . . it's so awful." Abby sobbed, and Jill caught a distinct whiff of alcohol on her breath and came up to speed. Abby wasn't injured, she'd been drinking. Jill hadn't seen her in three years, and Abby had grown up; she'd be nineteen now. Abby sobbed harder. "Jill, Dad's dead . . . he's dead."

"*What?*" Jill gasped, shocked. Her ex-husband was in excellent health, still in his forties. "How?"

"Somebody . . . killed him." Abby dissolved into tears, her body going limp, clinging to Jill. "Please, you have to . . . help me. I have to find out . . . who did it."

Jill hugged her closer, feeling her grief and struggling to process what had happened. She couldn't imagine William as a murder victim, or a victim of any kind, for that matter, but her first thought was of his daughters, Abby and Victoria, and her own daughter, Megan. The news would devastate all of them, Megan included. William was her stepfather, but the only father she'd ever known. Her real father had died before she was born.

"Babe, what are you doing? Let's get her into the house!" Sam shouted, to be heard over the rain. He was kneeling on Abby's other side, though Jill didn't know when he'd gotten there.

"William's been murdered," Jill told him, sounding numb, even to herself.

"I heard. We're not calling 911, she's just drunk." Sam squinted against the brightness of the motion-detector light. Raindrops soaked his hair and dappled his polo shirt. "Let me take her arm. Lift her on one, two, three," he counted off, tugging Abby's arm.

"Okay, go." Jill took Abby's other arm, and together they hoisted her, sobbing, to her feet, gathered her purse, and half walked and half carried her toward the house, sloshing through the grass, with Beef at their heels.

Jill tried to collect her thoughts, which were in turmoil. She'd always dreamed of seeing Abby again, but not in these circumstances, and she dreaded telling Megan about William. But as agonized as she felt for the girls, Jill wouldn't shed a tear for her ex-husband. There was a reason she had divorced the man, and it was a whopper.

And evidently, not only the good died young.

Chapter Two

"Come in and sit down, honey. Here, right here." Jill helped Abby to the kitchen island, catching Sam's eye. "Sam, I'll take her from here; can you get us a glass of water and some towels?"

"Sure." Sam eased Abby off his arm and hustled to the sink, while Beef danced a circle around them, wagging his tail, missing the point entirely.

"I can't believe . . . Dad's really *gone*." Abby slumped heavily into the seat, covering her face with her hands, her body wracked with sobs. "It's so . . . *horrible* . . . I don't know what to do . . . I'm not ever . . . going to see him again."

"I know, sweetie, I know." Jill sat down next to Abby and held her while she wept, and all her love for the girl came flooding back, coursing through her system, flowing warm and sure as lifeblood. "I'm so, so sorry."

"I don't know . . . *who* did this to him . . . or *why* . . . I still can't even . . . believe it's true." Abby wept, bereft and broken. "I won't talk to him . . . ever, *ever again* . . . that's not possible, that's not even . . . *possible* . . . and I don't know what to *do*."

"I know, I understand." Jill hugged her closer, trying to warm her with her body, feeling every inch like her mother, all over again. Abby's real mother had died when she was only four years old, and Jill had been her stepmother for eight years, raising Abby and her older sister Victoria for most of their childhood.

"I live at home and . . . even though Dad was, like, away a lot . . . I knew . . . I could call him . . . and ask him stuff."

"You poor thing." Jill looked up when Sam brought her the water glass and set it down on the island.

"Here we go," he said quietly, meeting her eye with concern. "You okay, babe?"

"Yes, thanks." Jill nodded, but she was fighting her own tears. It killed her to hear Abby's hoarse, choking sobs, echoing in the quiet house.

"Okay, I'll get the towels, be right back." Sam patted Jill's shoulder, then left for upstairs.

"And he took care . . . of the bills . . . and *everything* in the house . . . and I don't know how . . . to do everything . . . all by myself . . . and now . . . I'm all alone . . . like, there's no one."

"There's me, Abby. You have me," Jill said, without a second thought, and the next few words arrived unbidden, as if they'd been waiting offstage for their cue. "I love you, honey, and I always will."

"Oh, God, I love you, too." Abby looked up in Jill's embrace, her eyes brimming with tears. Mascara marred her cheeks, and the fair skin on her cheeks was mottled with emotion. "Jill, I love you, so much . . . you're my *mom* . . . and you always will be and you *always were*."

"It's okay now, honey. I'm here." Jill wiped tears and makeup from Abby's cheeks, comforting her. "Don't cry, it's okay."

"I don't know why you still even . . . love me." Abby shook her head, bewildered. Tears spilled from her eyes. "I don't even *deserve* . . . to be here, with you."

"Of course you do, honey." Jill's heart broke for her. "What a thing to say. Of course you do."

"No, I don't . . . I don't . . . you called and called . . . and I didn't even call you back . . . I wanted to, I did, but Dad said not to . . . I was afraid to . . . he'd go ballistic if he found out . . . that's why I didn't." Abby cried, her gaze on Jill, pleading. "I'm so sorry . . . I feel so *guilty* . . . and I'm so sorry . . . I had nowhere else to go . . . I feel like such a jerk."

"It's okay, honey." Jill's throat caught, and she hugged Abby again, cradling her. "You know if I had it my way, we would've talked all the time." Jill had done everything in her power to stay in touch with the girls, but William had demanded she stop trying to contact them, even threatening her with a restraining order. She'd hired a lawyer to see if she had any legal recourse, but she didn't, and the lawyer had advised her that opposing a restraining order would mean that the girls had to testify, and she couldn't bring herself to do that to them.

"I don't know . . . how you could still love me . . . after so long, like *three years*."

"Love doesn't go away, not this kind of love." Jill hadn't seen the girls since that awful night, but the rupture still felt as fresh as yesterday.

"I know . . . I'm the one who did the bad thing . . . the way I treated you . . . you tried so hard to talk to us."

"Don't worry about it for a minute. Divorce is hard and weird, and it's not your fault, at all." Jill felt Abby's body shudder with each sob. William would have done anything to get her back for the divorce, even if it meant hurting Abby and Victoria, but she didn't want to think about him now, just Abby.

"How can you forgive me . . . I'm such a terrible person . . . and I knew if I came here, you'd be so nice."

"Honey, of course I would, and I'm glad you did, even on this sad day. Especially on this sad day. You've come . . . to the right place." Jill stopped just short of saying, *you've come home.*

"Thanks, so much." Abby burrowed her head in Jill's shoulder. "I really do love you . . . and I really missed you . . . so much . . . and I'm sorry I didn't call you back . . . I hoped you knew . . . I didn't forget you."

"I did know, and that's why I stopped, too. You know that I thought of you and Victoria, all the time."

"I never stopped loving you . . . Jill, or wishing . . . I could see you."

"I know, sweetie. I always loved you, too. You know that." Jill felt her chest tighten, her anger like a fist at the ready. She hoped William was burning in hell right this minute. It felt strange to have such hate for him and such love for Abby, both at once. "Breathe, honey. Just breathe, and I have Kleenex here. Want some? That'll help."

"Okay . . . yes . . . good idea." Abby released her, and Jill reached for the box of Kleenex, pulled out a few, and handed them to Abby.

"Here we go. Blow your nose, then have a sip of water."

"Yuck, I'm so snotty . . . I always cry like such a . . . dumb baby." Abby took the tissues, mopped her eyes and cheeks, then blew her nose noisily. "Gross."

"Here, take some more." Jill took the dirty tissues, handed Abby a bunch more, and Abby blew her nose again, then surrendered the soiled ones to Jill.

"Sorry."

"Don't worry about it." Jill handed her another few tissues, and Abby sniffled, wiping her eyes, her tears subsiding.

"I feel like such a . . . little kid."

"Everybody feels like a little kid when they cry. Ready for some water?" Jill handed Abby the water glass, and Abby took it with two hands, her fingernails polished dark purple.

"Thanks." Abby drank thirstily, and Jill appraised her with a maternal eye. Abby's eyes were bloodshot and sunken, as if she hadn't been getting enough sleep, and her dress was too thin for the weather, clinging wetly to a body that was shapely, if a little too skinny. Her dark blonde hair dripped with rainwater.

"Need more water?" Jill looked over as Sam returned with the towels.

"Here we go, babe."

"Thanks." Jill took the towels and set one on the island as Abby put the water down.

"No more water, thanks."

"Take a towel." Jill placed the towel around Abby's shoulders, rubbing her upper arms to warm her. "Better, honey?"

"Yes, thanks." Abby's chest heaved once, then again, and she sniffled.

"More Kleenex?"

"No, thanks. Whew." Abby seemed to be getting her bearings, straightening up in the seat, blinking to clear her eyes. She dried her face on the towel's edge, leaving streaks of pinkish blusher and lip gloss. "Oops. Sorry."

"It doesn't matter." Jill handed her the other towel, and Abby flopped it onto her head and twisted it into a turban.

"I just can't believe Dad's really gone." Abby sighed deeply, her lower lip trembling.

"I know, I'm so sorry, honey."

"Sorry I lost it like that." Abby shook her head, her lovely eyes shining, brown as earth itself.

"Don't be. It's an impossible thing to go through."

"Well, I'm not buzzed anymore, that's for sure."

Jill patted her arm. "Let me get you some coffee, okay? Warm you up?"

"Great, thanks."

"Still take it black?" Jill got up from the island and went around to the coffeemaker.

"Yes, like you." Abby brightened, adjusting the towel on her head. She had matured into a natural beauty, but looked more like her younger self without the makeup; she still had her large, round eyes, a small, straight nose, fair skin, and lips shaped like a Cupid's bow.

"Okay, hang in." Jill plucked a coffee pod from the bowl and popped it into the machine, then took a mug from the cabinet, slid it under the spout, and hit BREW. "How about something to eat?"

"I'd love that, if it's not too much trouble."

"Great." Jill felt better at the prospect. If she couldn't cure something, she'd cook something. "Why don't I make you some French toast?"

"My favorite." Abby managed a shaky smile, her eyes glistening. "You remember?"

"Of course." Jill smiled, then went to the refrigerator and retrieved a carton of eggs, bread, and a plastic bottle of two percent. "But the days of white bread are over. I have only whole wheat."

"That's okay. Jeez, I miss your cooking."

Jill felt her heart ease, seeing Abby recover her composure. She brought the food to the counter, and the coffee brewed behind her, filling the air with a delicious aroma. "Sam, you want some coffee or French toast, too?"

"No, thanks," Sam answered. He was leaning against the sink, his arms crossed over his chest, with Beef sitting at his side. The rain was beginning to dry on his polo shirt. They both were still dressed from their run, in polo shirts, gym shorts, and sneakers.

Abby sighed, heavily. "Dad died four days ago, on Tuesday. The cops said it was a heart attack, caused by alcohol and prescription meds."

Jill blinked. "I thought you said he was murdered."

"I think he was."

"You do, but the police don't?"

"Right." Abby straightened up, her tone newly firm. "I think they're wrong. Rather, I *know* they're wrong. You're a doctor, and you know Dad. He didn't take any prescription meds. He was murdered, no matter what the police say."

Jill cracked some eggs into a bowl, hiding her confusion. She'd never known William to take prescription meds, but she'd never known the real William Skyler. He was the ultimate con man, fooling her, Megan, and even his own daughters. "So the police say it wasn't murder. What do they think it was?"

"They say it was an accidental overdose. The cocktail, whatever that means."

"It means that certain drugs can kill you, in combination with alcohol." The coffee was ready, and Jill set the full mug in front of Abby. "What drugs did he take?"

"He didn't take them." Abby picked up the coffee and held it in two hands, warming her fingers. "The report came back today and said he had the drugs in his body, but I know he didn't put them there. He never would have, and I went on the Internet and it doesn't say those are lethal drugs, anyway." Abby sipped some coffee, then set it down, sniffling. "The cops found pill bottles in his bedroom, but I never saw them before, and they didn't dust for fingerprints like on TV, to see how they got there."

"What pills did they find?" Jill retrieved a fork and beat the eggs.

"Three bottles. Xanax, Vicodin, and one other, T-something."

"Temezepam?"

"Yes. I *knew* you'd know." Abby brightened a little.

"They're common drugs for anxiety and pain, honey." Jill drizzled a dash of vanilla into the egg mixture, veining the light with the dark, then beat it again.

"Not common for Dad." Abby shifted forward, and water dripped from a curling tendril that had escaped from the towel turban. "Plus, there was a bottle of whisky in his office, but no glass. When did you ever know Dad to drink out of a *bottle*? Never, and the drugs had to be planted there, by whoever killed him."

"What does Victoria say?" Jill picked up a pan that had been drying on the counter, cut in a pat of butter, and set it on the stove, firing up the gas.

"She says I just don't want to accept that Dad's dead."

Jill could have guessed as much. Victoria was always the sensible one to Abby's free spirit. "Couldn't she be right? It's a hard thing to deal with—"

"She's wrong, they all are. I know it, and we'll prove it." Abby looked down as Beef trotted over, wagging his tail, sending droplets flying. She rested her hand on his coppery head, where his wet fur spiked at the crown, like a doggie punk rocker. "I missed Beef, too. Remember the day we got him?"

"Sure." Jill did. It had been a cold, sunny afternoon at a golden retriever rescue in Delaware County. The three girls cooed over a passel of fluffy golden puppies, and Abby scooped up the fattest one, naming him on the spot. *This one is Beef on the hoof!*

"Where's Megan?" Abby asked, adjusting the towel.

"At a sleepover." Jill opened the bread and dunked a slice into the eggs.

"Aw, I wanted to see her. I miss her, too."

"You'll see her in the morning. Stay over with us. Right, Sam?" Jill realized with embarrassment that she hadn't introduced them, at all. She abandoned the slice of bread. "Yikes, I'm sorry. Abby, this is my fiancé, Sam Becker. Sam, Abby Skyler."

"Hello, Abby." Sam smiled at her, with sympathy. "I'm sorry about your loss, and of course you can stay here tonight."

Abby seemed to be leaning away from Sam, almost recoiling, though she said, "Nice to meet you, Sam."

"Yes, thanks, Sam," Jill chimed in, trying to smooth over her own awkwardness. It struck her as odd that Abby and Sam had never met, as if her life had been hacked into pieces, not only the Before and After of two marriages, but the Before and Before and After, of three. She had been a widow when she'd met William, and Sam would be her third husband.

Abby kept an eye on Sam. "Not gonna lie, Sam, I feel like you're mad at me or something. Are you? Don't be mad at me, okay?"

Jill tensed, and she could smell the butter starting to burn in the pan. She hated burned butter. She turned off the gas for a moment.

"I'm not angry at you, Abby, I'm concerned," Sam answered, gently. "You drove here, drunk. That concerns me, for your sake and for the sake of others."

Jill turned to Abby, puzzled. "You drove? I thought that SUV dropped you off."

"What SUV? I parked around the corner. I looked up your address online but couldn't find the street." Abby looked down as Beef nudged her with his muzzle, his bid to keep getting petted. "I'm sorry, I won't do it again."

"I know you won't, sweetie." Jill didn't have the heart to lecture Abby, not tonight. "What did you have to drink?"

"Just some vodka and orange juice."

"Hard liquor?" Jill hid her dismay. Abby used to be so wholesome and healthy, a competitive swimmer. All the girls swam, Jill had taught them.

"I'm sorry, I know, I was upset, because of Dad." Abby stroked

Beef, who rested his big head on her lap. "It's so good to see Beef again. I was worried he died."

"He's not that old, is he?"

"Sure he is." Abby patted the dog, and her wet dress gapped at the neckline, revealing a flowery tattoo above one breast. "He'll turn ten, this Valentine's Day."

"Really?" Jill tried not to stare at the tattoo, lost in time, for a moment. *When did Abby start drinking, or get old enough for a tattoo? When did Beef get so old? Where did all the time go?* Abby had arrived out of nowhere, and it was as if Jill's past had crashed her present like a house party, leaving her disoriented.

"You said you remembered, Jill. We picked him out on Valentine's Day. It was Dad's present, for you."

"Oh right." Jill had forgotten that part. She let the moment pass, eyeing Sam's back as he turned around, tore off a paper towel, and wiped his face and glasses.

"This is such a pretty room." Abby was looking around the kitchen. "It's so you, Jill."

"Thanks." Jill glanced around, too, proudly. The house was still a work in progress, but the kitchen was warm and homey, ringed by white cabinets and countertops of ivory granite veined with butterscotch. The walls glowed a golden hue, which set off a cherry dining table and kitchen island, where they all ate, used the laptop, or did their homework, like the sun to their family solar system.

"I'm really sorry about the drinking, Jill."

"I understand." Jill was curious where she got the liquor, but didn't want to torture her, not now. "I saw on Facebook that Victoria's in law school, at Seton Hall. How's she doing?"

Sam looked over, but he didn't say anything, and Jill read his mind. He was surprised that she followed the girls on Facebook. She had never told him that.

"Victoria loves law school, which isn't surprising. She was doing great, until Dad." Abby paused. "You know how she is. She'll be fine."

"You both will, in time, but don't rush it. Grief takes all the time it needs, no matter what you do." Jill knew that Victoria would internalize her grief, much like Megan would.

"She lives with some roommates, near school. I was living with Dad in town, but now I don't know what's going to happen."

"Why aren't you in college, honey? You're so smart." Jill kept her tone non-judgmental, but Abby still avoided her eye.

"I'm waitressing. I guess you saw, I started at art school but I broke up with Santos and that kind of messed me up. I'll go back someday, I know it's a good thing." Abby seemed to deflate again, her shoulders sloping and her turban sliding to the side. "Anyway, Dad's memorial service is tomorrow. They already cremated him. Victoria arranged it, I couldn't deal." Abby sighed. "Can you come to the service, Jill? And can Megan?"

"We'll see. I have to ask her. I know she'll be so sad about your Dad."

"Afterwards I can take you over to the house, and you can see what I mean. Dad was murdered, I know it."

Jill felt torn. "I can't do that, honey, especially not with Megan."

"But I'll prove it to you, I'll show you Dad's medical papers. You'll see he didn't take those drugs, there's no record of it. You know Dad used to save all his medical stuff in one place, because of his cholesterol."

Jill returned to making the French toast, while Abby talked. William had always taken excellent care of himself. It was everybody else he disregarded, even his daughters.

"He never would have taken those pills on purpose. So he had to have been murdered, and you can help me figure it out."

"No, I can't. I'm a pediatrician, not a detective."

"You're a doctor, and Sherlock Holmes was a doctor. You told me that, remember, for that English paper? I got a B plus, because of you."

Jill felt touched. "What I said was that the author, Sir Arthur Conan Doyle, was a successful doctor, and Dr. Watson was as important as Sherlock."

"But you said that the way they solved a murder case was the same way you diagnose a disease." Abby leaned over, urgent. "Please, will you help me? We can do it together."

Sam cleared his throat. "Ladies, I'll let you two spend some time alone." He came over and kissed Jill lightly on the cheek. "Love you. Call me if you need anything." He turned to Abby, straightening. "Goodnight, Abby."

"Goodnight." Abby gave him a little wave, and Sam left the kitchen. When he was barely out of earshot, she leaned over and said, "He's kind of old for you, don't you think?"

"No. Hush." Jill saw Sam turn around, but she knew it was the liquor talking. "Now, drink your coffee."

Chapter Three

"I think a shower might be a good idea for you, before bed, don't you?" Jill climbed the stairs with Abby, who was still in her turban and towel.

"Yes. Clean me up and tuck me in, huh?"

"That's the idea." Jill put an arm around her, and Abby looked over, her expression sad and soft.

"Dad never got serious with anyone after you, Jill, you know. We met a few of his dates, but he didn't have a girlfriend."

"That's too bad." Jill kept her thoughts to herself. They took a left at the landing, past a lineup of candid photographs of her and Megan. "Come this way. We have a guest room you can sleep in, with its own bathroom."

Abby stopped on the stair, at the photographs. "These pictures are so nice. Did you guys go to a photographer or something?"

"No, Sam took them. It's a hobby of his."

"This is the best one, of you alone." Abby lingered at one photograph, a candid taken at the Jersey shore, and Jill was laughing, her hair curling in the salty air. Sam had been trying to get her to relax, pretending that he'd dropped his camera in the sand, and Jill loved the photograph because she loved the photographer.

"Ah, I was younger then."

"You're still young, and your hair is so sexy, that way. You should wear it down all the time."

"Please. I don't have time, and it's not doctor hair."

"Remember when I was little, we looked so much alike, people thought I was your daughter? I mean, your real daughter?" Abby gestured at the photo, waving her dark fingernail up and down. "See, your nose is little and straight, like mine. Our eyes are the same shape and almost the same brown, only yours are lighter. Our hair is more different, I don't have the reddish brown like you, but we have the same exact smile. I think our smile is our best feature."

Jill managed a smile, but couldn't ignore the wistfulness in Abby's tone, and put an arm around her. "You know, I kept track of you, on Facebook. Your Dad asked me not to write you there or post on your wall, but I read your feed, all the time."

"I bet you were, I knew it." Abby smiled at her.

"I know about your cat, Pickles, and your ancient car, and how sad you were over your breakup with your boyfriend." Jill didn't add that the boyfriend looked a little rough around the edges.

"I *love* my cat." Abby smiled, more easily, and Jill warmed at the sight, happy to lighten her heart, if only for a moment.

"I can see why. He's the cutest cat ever."

"Did you see that photo of him in the laundry basket?"

"Yes, of course, and orange tabbies are my favorite."

"I know. Dad told us to unfriend you, and Victoria did, but I didn't. I just made my settings private, so he didn't know." Abby's smile faded. "I feel bad saying that about him, now."

Jill gave her a final hug. "Let's get you showered up, girl."

"Okay." Abby hugged her back, and they went to the guest room, where Jill switched on the overhead light. It flickered off, and the room went dark.

"Damn. I'll get a new bulb and some clean sheets. The last time this room was used was when Sam's son Steven visited. He's an architect, in Austin."

"So Sam lives here, with you and Megan?"

"Yes. I bought this house after the divorce, and he sold his condo in Philly and moved in."

"When are you guys getting married?"

"This summer, in July." Jill felt suddenly uncomfortable, telling her the details, and Abby smiled, shakily.

"So Steven's going to be your new stepson? Does that make this the steproom?"

Jill smiled, then the bedroom brightened from a flash of lightning, with a loud thunderclap.

Abby made a nervous face. "Do you think I could sleep in Megan's room tonight? Since she's not here?"

"Sure." Jill didn't think Megan would mind, in the circumstances. "Follow me."

"Thanks." Abby walked down the hall with Jill, and Beef stayed between them, panting and trembling, because of the storm. "He still hates thunder, I see."

"You have such a good memory, honey." Jill stopped at Megan's door and flicked on the light. "Here we are."

"*Sweet* room." Abby stood in the threshold, taking in the large room, with its white canopied bed and a pink-patterned comforter. The far wall had a panel of windows with a padded windowseat, next to full bookshelves and a matching oak desk. A bulletin board hung above the desk filled with swimming awards, team photos, and stills from the school play, as well as glossy pictures of Michael Phelps, the Phillies, and the *Twilight* crew, which Megan had cut out of magazines.

"Bathroom's to the right." Jill gestured, but Abby was already walking there with Beef.

"She was always so neat."

"She still is." Jill went to the threshold of the bathroom, and Beef settled down on the bathmat. She pointed at the shower stall, where overpriced shampoos and conditioners were lined up. "Put the caps back on, you."

"You remember the orange juice?" Abby smiled, sheepishly.

"How could I forget? It was funny." Jill smiled back. She'd taken a jug of fresh-squeezed out of the refrigerator and shaken it, but Abby hadn't put the cap back on and the walls were orange for a week. "You take a nice, warm shower, and I'll bring you some clean towels, okay?"

"Okay, thanks." Abby leaned over and kissed her suddenly on the cheek, and Jill felt a rush of emotion. It felt right to be taking care of Abby again, and at the same time, it felt strange to be taking care of Abby again. She left the bathroom, went to the linen closet, got the towels, then stopped to see Sam.

"Still up?" Jill asked, entering his home office, which was small, lined with bookshelves filled with medical textbooks and teaching awards. Sam taught at Penn's medical school and was also a researcher in diabetes.

"Just waiting on you." Sam looked up at Jill, with a worried smile. He was sitting at his old wooden desk against the window, raking his floppy hair with his fingers as he read a book online. "How's the kid?"

"Okay." Jill looked at him anew, after what Abby had said. His tortoiseshell glasses reflected two white pages with tiny footnotes, and behind them were sharp blue eyes, full of intelligence and humor. Sam was only eight years her senior, and his deep crow's feet and laugh lines only made him more handsome to her, in a lived-in sort of way. The gray in his hair reminded her of the weathered cedar of a comfy rocker, and Jill felt lucky to have him. "Thanks for being so nice to her."

"No need for thanks."

"She's upset tonight, obviously. She's really a sweet girl."

"I'm sure." Sam slid off his glasses and set them on his desk, which was clean except for his laptop and iPhone. He touched her arm. "I'm sorry about your ex's death. How are you feeling, really?"

"Honestly, it's upsetting, mainly because of the girls." Jill set down the towels and looked behind her, to make sure Abby wasn't within earshot. "Megan will take it hard, because she was so conflicted. She loved him, but after the divorce, he didn't answer any of her calls or texts. That killed her, and now she'll never get the chance to ask him why, or understand."

"I'll be there for her. We'll get through it." Sam buckled his lower lip, pained. "I was supposed to meet Lee tomorrow, he's coming in from Cleveland. But I can see him after the memorial service, if you want to go."

Jill felt touched. "But Lee's flying in just to meet with you, isn't he?"

"Yes, but I can delay meeting him. It's a death in the family, more or less."

"No, don't. Thanks for the offer, but you don't have to come. If Megan wants to go, I'll take her."

Sam frowned. "You sure?"

"Totally."

"Okay, thanks. But please, promise me you won't get sucked into this murder business. It's absurd. We both know the Internet is full of idiocy about which drugs can kill you."

"I won't get involved. The cops are experts, I'm not." Jill picked up the towels and gave him a kiss. "Gotta go back now."

"Come to bed, soon. It's late."

"I know." Jill smiled, straightening up, then left the office and went back to Megan's bedroom. The bathroom door was closed, and she knocked. "I have fresh towels, honey."

"Don't need them." Abby opened the door. Steam clouded the air, and she was wearing one of Megan's nightgowns, a red-striped Lanz, of worn flannel. "Is it okay I'm wearing this nightgown? Remember, it used to be mine?"

"How could I forget? It was so nice of you."

"It's even better than it used to be, it's so soft. Megan kept it, huh?"

"She wears it all the time." Jill smiled, remembering when Abby had given Megan the nightgown. Megan had coveted it for so long, and they'd tried to find one like it in Nordstrom's, but they couldn't. So Abby had folded her own, put it in a box, and gift-wrapped it for Christmas, and Megan had been delighted.

"God, I'm so tired." Abby padded past her and climbed into Megan's bed, and Beef bounded up behind her. The dog settled down, stretching out his tufted front paws while Abby ducked beneath the comforter. "It's so cozy here."

"Good." Jill went over to the bed and tucked Abby in, on mom autopilot. "I remember when you and Megan would get into the same bed, even though you barely fit."

"I know." Abby smiled, her breath minty from the toothpaste. "It was fun, and we would whisper so you and Dad couldn't hear. Beef used to get in bed with us, too, especially when it rained." She stroked the wavy fur on the dog's back. "I bet Megan misses those days."

"I'm sure she does." Jill sat down and moved Abby's wet hair away from her forehead, noticing a stray streak of electric blue. "You want a towel for your head?"

"No, thanks." Abby paused. "Can I ask, what happened with you and Dad? I know what Dad said, but I want your side of the story. Why did you guys get divorced?"

"Let's not talk about that tonight, honey." Jill felt her chest tighten. If she told Abby the truth, it would make William look terrible, and she knew from her practice that kids who felt terrible about their parents somehow ended up feeling terrible about themselves. "Maybe someday, but not tonight." Jill brushed Abby's hair back again. "Blue, huh?"

"Yeah." Abby smiled softly. "Do you like it?"

"Yes, but the tattoo is another story." Jill mock-frowned. "No more tats, please. I don't have my mom powers anymore, so it's just a request."

"You'll always have your mom powers, to me." Abby raised her arms for a hug, and Jill embraced her.

"I'm sorry about your Dad. You shouldn't have to go through this."

"It's just that he looked so horrible, lying there. I found him."

"Oh no." Jill hadn't realized.

"I came home, and the house was so quiet and the cat was meowing, which she never does. I went upstairs and he was lying in bed, with the TV on. His face was all, like, slack."

Jill imagined how traumatic that would be, at Abby's age. Jill had dissected cadavers in medical school and she never got used to it. It took her months to shake the images, and some never left her.

"His mouth was open, but just hanging there." Abby emitted a new sob, her body hiccupping. "His eyes were open . . . stiff, like they were cold . . . but they weren't looking *anywhere*."

Jill held her close. She knew the unfixed gaze of the dead, but it was one thing when it was clinical, and another when it was eyes you had loved, in life. She had been there, too. One minute she'd been in anatomy class, locating the trigeminal nerve in the cheek, and the next minute, she'd come home to find another body, dead. This one, of someone she had loved, with a cheek she had kissed.

"I was . . . calling him . . . I put myself right up to his face . . . trying to get him to see me . . . but he couldn't see *anything*."

Jill was the one who'd found Gray, her first husband, lying dead on the kitchen floor. She'd tried CPR and heart massage, but he was gone, from a brain aneurysm. A week later, she would learn that she was pregnant with their child, Megan.

"I grabbed him and held him . . . and his mouth was, like, hanging open . . . and his head hung back like his neck was *rubber* . . . like he didn't even have a . . . neck bone."

Jill felt tears come to her eyes, her thoughts immersed in the past, reliving every emotion of finding Gray, the agony and the shock and the surreality. She felt terrible, mourning her first husband while Abby was mourning her second, but she couldn't help herself.

"Please, Jill . . . help me figure out who killed him . . . I can't do it alone."

"Let's not talk about it now, honey."

"Please . . . just think about it? Please?"

"I'll think about it, but just breathe for now, just breathe." Jill held Abby until she stopped crying and finally dozed off. Then Jill eased out of bed, covered Abby with the comforter, and turned out the light.

Plunging herself into darkness.

Chapter Four

Jill answered email from her patients, working in bed, her laptop warm on a pillow she'd set on her lap, an improvised desk. Sam slept with his back to her, Beef slumbering near his feet, and the room was quiet except for the snoring of man and beast. She felt tired but she couldn't sleep until she'd answered the questions that came in before the weekend: *how many drops in a teaspoon, do I give it again if he throws it up, it's finally yellow and that's good, right?*

She answered them all, but her thoughts kept straying to Abby, William, Megan, and Victoria. She remembered back to the beginning, the very first day when they all began, a sunny flash of beach and sand and boogie boards at the Jersey shore. She had been seeing William for a while, having met him when she worked at her old pediatric group. All but one of them were women, and William was the handsome pharmaceutical sales rep who called on them every Friday, the one they all buzzed and joked about, and some of them, like Jill, nursed secret crushes, none of them immune despite their advanced degrees, so that even their happily married office manager put up a sign in the ladies' room that read, TGIW, THANK GOD IT'S WILLIAM. He charmed them all with his dark good looks, breezy confidence, and easy smile, but more than that, he was a widower, alone with two little girls.

The hearts of every woman in the office went out to him, they all wanted to hold him, comfort him, and ease his pain, and what they didn't know about him, they filled in with their imagination, projecting onto him all kinds of qualities he'd never showed, assigning to him all of their own values and emotions, fleshing out their fantasy. He began to pay special attention to Jill, the only single doc and a widow to boot, and he struck up conversations about their mutual daughters, listening thoughtfully to her answers until his sales calls became a sort of date, with Jill putting on a little extra eye-makeup, making up a story of her own about a lonely widow and a lonely widower meeting for a last chance at love, like an announcement in the wedding section of the Sunday *New York Times,* so that by the time she and William had the girls meet each other for a day at the beach, she was stone in love.

With a fantasy.

William played his character to the hilt, and Jill marveled at how rough-and-tumble he was with Abby and Victoria, letting them jump off his broad shoulders into the crashing surf, diving under the biggest waves with them, even dunking them underwater, so different from the way Jill played with Megan, which was protective and careful, mindful always of the undertow. Megan watched William and the girls for a long time, hanging back, taking in the scene of the laughing daughters and the hunky, handsome daddy, so that by the time William turned around to grin at the fatherless girl, jerking his head back to flick his wet hair from his forehead, twisting his strong body from his tapered waist, reaching out to her a tanned and muscular arm ending in a large hand with its fingers extended, offering her a chance to be with him, the shy little girl would have begged to go.

Come on, come in, I won't bite!

Jill had watched delighted, seeing her daughter thrilled in the company of this unusual and exotic creature known as a man, and the five of them bobbed into the water together, Megan migrating to William, who played the father she had never known, and for her part, Jill took naturally to being a mom to the motherless Abby, who clung to her like a girl barnacle. Victoria took her time coming to Jill, always the closer daughter to her father, not wanting a rival for his attention, but she had no such problem that day with Megan, who carried with her the promise of a sibling without the rivalry.

Looking back now, Jill could visualize all of them in the water, seeing their heads from the back so that they were faceless, as if she were watching her younger self from the shore, which was exactly the vantage point her mother Conchetta had had that day. Her mother was her best friend, and the three of them—Jill, her mother, and Megan—had been on vacation when William and the girls had joined them. Her mother had always come to the beach after the hottest part of the day, sitting in her plastic lattice chair, and she'd read a book under the yellow-striped umbrella.

But this time, when Jill went back to check on her mother, her book remained unopened in her lap. Her mother had frowned up at her, her gnarled hand shading her hooded eyes, an uncharacteristic scowl replacing her usually welcoming smile, her lined features collapsing into deep, unhappy fissures, as if her very face had folded up as tight as her beach chair.

I don't like him, her mother had said.

Jill had been astonished. It didn't occur to her that her mother still hadn't warmed up to William. Everybody liked William, and her mother liked everybody, so it should've been a natural. Jill had asked her why.

I don't trust him. Don't trust him. He's no good for you. He'll do you wrong.

And Jill knew now, her mother had been right. Her mother had looked at the scene and had seen what was really happening, not the projections and the roles and the acting that had fooled Jill. Jill would turn out to be William's sucker, not his wife, and the only saving grace was that when it all came to light, her mother had already passed away. Because it would have broken her heart.

Jill blinked away tears that she hadn't realized were there, looking down at the laptop, and she found herself opening her My

Pictures file and navigating to the older files. She clicked, and a photo of Abby popped onto the screen, one Jill had taken on the front steps of another house, in another town, in another time. Abby had just gotten her braces adjusted, and other kids might have whined, but Abby made the best of it, sporting red rubber bands in honor of the Phillies. She was thirteen, the same age Megan was now, still what Jill's mother used to call a tomboy. Her hair was in a messy braid, and she had on her swim-club jersey, its white letters forming a half-circle, Strafford Strokers.

Jill had encouraged her to join the school team and had loved teaching her to swim, and Abby had run to her with open arms, willing to learn anything, needing a mother like a wildflower needs sunshine. Victoria had come around only slowly, and Jill had built a relationship with her during silent car trips to the mall and awkward greetings after school plays, the cameo appearances of the suburban stepmother. Jill had saved every greeting card the girls ever gave her, and the dearest to her was a Mother's Day card from the both of them, given the first Mother's Day after she and William were married. Victoria had handed the card to her, and it was covered with pink lace, so Jill knew Victoria had picked it out. Jill had opened it up, and she'd never forget the message, written in Victoria's perfect penmanship:

It's official. You're our Mom now.

Jill felt a pang at the memory, bittersweet because it had been so hard-won, and now was lost just the same, and the wound still felt acute, defying the very powers of nature, to heal. Jill knew there was no stronger bond than between mother and child, and she didn't feel like an ex-mother, nor were the girls her ex-children. She had lived long enough to learn that families didn't dissolve or reconfigure neatly, but left debris lying everywhere, and it was human debris. And sometimes, like tonight, she felt as if she were tripping over the bodies.

She pressed a key and advanced to the next photo, taken after Megan had mugged her way into the picture. She was eight years old at the time, and she and Abby had become best buddies. They could have passed for big-and-little sisters because Megan had big brown eyes and dark blonde hair, too, which she wore in a copy-cat braid.

Jill thought ahead, to having to tell Megan about William's death. Megan was a year old when she met William, and he'd been in her life until the divorce, when she was ten. He hadn't been especially doting or attentive, never fulfilling the promise of that day on the beach, but he'd been there, more father figure than father, and sometimes for kids, that was enough. Even now, Jill could remember trips they took as a family, one to Linvilla Orchard to pick pumpkins, or another to Great Adventure, screaming down the roller coaster. It looked like family fun on the surface, but you didn't need a microscope to see what was really going on. Jill would be having fun with the girls, and William would be off to the side, on the phone, or complaining about the long lines or the cold French fries, or withdrawn, lost in his own thoughts.

Jill hit Start Slideshow and watched Megan, Abby, Victoria, and William flash by in a continuous stream of swim meets, DQ Flurries, and guinea pigs. The divorce ended the pictures of the five of them, and the following photos were of her and Megan, like leftovers, only of family. It hadn't been an easy transition, then Jill met Sam, who turned out to be real in all the ways that William was false, and in time, the three of them had moved forward as a new family, with a second stepfather stepping into the shoes of the first stepfather, who'd stepped into the shoes of the father who had died.

Jill froze the slideshow on a photo of Sam, Megan, and Steven, who looked like a younger version of his father. Tall, lean, and brainy. Steven wouldn't replace Abby and Victoria, because nobody was ever replaced in life, no hole completely filled or loss totally healed. You didn't need a medical degree to know that the human body really wasn't stronger in the broken places. Like any bone, the cracks would always show if you looked hard enough.

"Babe?" said a voice, and Jill looked over, startled. Sam had turned over and was propped up, squinting against the lamp light. His brow furrowed, and his fine nose had two permanent pink indentations from his glasses. "You all right?"

"Sure, yes." Jill hit a key to stop the slideshow.

"What are you up to?" Sam lay back down, his eyes a calm blue now, like the sea without waves, and he regarded her with an un-hurried air that told her he really wanted to know. "You upset about your ex? Or the kid?"

"Both, but mostly, I was thinking about my life."

"What about it?"

"Just that there's so much of it." Jill felt oddly embarrassed. "I have a lot of past."

Sam chuckled. "Not as much as I do."

"But my past is so much messier than yours. Two marriages, and two ex-stepdaughters. It's a mess, isn't it? Have I made a hash of things?"

"No, it's life, that's all." Sam smiled. "Is that what you're fretting about? I was worried that you'd been looking up Temezepam in the PDR online."

Jill hadn't been, but she'd thought about it. "I feel for her."

"I know you do."

"And it does seem strange, about the drugs. Not like William."

"You don't know what he's been up to the past few years."

"True."

"So?" Sam lifted an eyebrow. "If they found drugs on his tox screen, he took them."

"They could all be dissolved and put in a drink. Temezepam is a capsule." Jill knew because she had teenagers in her practice on various meds.

"You think somebody made him swallow the drugs, in a drink? He'd taste it." Sam ran a hand through his hair. "If you really want to help the kid, I'll call Sandy. She owes me a favor and she's the best psychiatrist in town."

"Thanks," Jill said, grateful. "Also, I think we might go to the memorial service, after work. Abby's the one who found William, dead. That's a trauma, and I can't just send her on her way tomor-row, alone."

Sam pursed his lips. "What about Megan?"

"She'll want to go."

"How do you know?"

Jill felt awkward, spelling it out. "I just think she'll want to go."

"Is going the best thing for her? She's only thirteen, and she'll be hurting, too."

"We should go."

"Then go, if you want to." Sam shrugged, and Jill touched his arm.

"Do you mind that she didn't invite you? I guess she felt that she didn't know you as well."

"No, I get it." Sam shifted back down onto the pillow. "Whatever you want to do is fine with me."

"Thanks." Jill leaned down and gave him a light kiss.

"It's late." Sam smiled, softly. "Come to bed."

"I am." Jill closed the laptop and set it on the cluttered night-table, edging aside her to-be-read pile of books, a jar of Cetaphil, and her gold hoop earrings, linked together like Venn diagrams in a math textbook. She remembered helping all three girls with their math, especially Abby. She would sit with her at the kitchen table for hours after practice, their heads bent together, working the practice problems in the textbook, with a king-size bag of M&M's at hand. By the end of middle school, they'd both hate M&M's.

I'll never understand geometry!

"I won't get fresh," Sam said.

"Huh?" Jill asked, confused a moment, caught in mid-thought, betwixt and between.

"Trust me."

"I do." Jill smiled and switched off the lamp, and just before it went off, Beef raised his head, his eyes clouded at the edges. It struck her that the golden had lived through more of her lives than Sam had, and she couldn't imagine losing him. She reached over and patted his ample butt. "Let's have Beef in our ceremony."

"Fine with me. I thought you didn't want to."

"I changed my mind. If he jumps up on people, they'll have to deal. He's family."

"Done." Sam smiled, tugging up the covers. "He can be my best man. He's better looking than Mort."

"Aw, Mort's a sweet guy." Jill slipped under the sheets, which felt cool on her bare legs.

"Agree, but he never grew up. Not like me. I was born grown up."

Jill smiled. It was part of Sam's charm, to her. She'd felt an ease with him from the start, which was a blind date set up by an endocrinologist they both knew, who thought Jill's bookish side would find common ground with a doctor in academic medicine like Sam, and she'd never felt more herself with any man, except Gray. She shifted over and rested her head on Sam's chest. His cotton T-shirt was soft against her cheek, with the iron-on Penn faded out of existence.

"Okay?" Sam held her close.

"Okay." Jill grew still, listening to the sounds of his heart. She listened differently since Gray had passed, hearing not the beats but between them, trying to pick up the tiny, subtler sounds that made the difference between life and death. She didn't know whether she did it because she was a doctor or a widow, or both.

"Everything's going to be all right," Sam said, reading her mind.

"How do you know? What's your proof?"

"You're asking me, seriously?"

"Yes. You're a scientist. Talk facts, not belief."

"Well, then." Sam gave her another squeeze, in the darkness. "My proof is, right now, and right here. Just *be* a minute, and you'll see."

Jill smiled uncertainly, then tried just to be, and came to understand what he meant. They were happy, really in love, a grown-up love that came from knowing and really appreciating the other person. Sam was her best friend, and she was his, and they had great kids and many other blessings. Their bedroom was large, quiet, and still. The darkness around them was as soft as black velvet, and a breeze billowed through the sheers, the aftermath of the storm. The burglar alarm was on, and the dishwasher thrummed downstairs. They lived on a pretty street lined with pin oaks, in a suburb outside of Philadelphia, which was just like all the suburbs outside all the cities all over the world.

Sam gave her another warm, cottony squeeze. "See?"

Jill felt the exact same way. "Yes. I love you."

"I love you, too. And you're stuck with me, forever."

"You, too," Jill said, after a moment.

"Now, let's get some sleep." Sam let out a final sigh, and in time Jill could feel his arms begin to slip, loosening his grip. He turned over in the next minute, and she pulled up the comforter, wondering. She'd believed in forever in her twenties, when Gray had said it, meaning every word, and she'd believed in forever in her thirties, when William had said it, lying through his teeth. But she'd lived long enough to know that forever couldn't be guaranteed to anyone. Even tomorrow couldn't be relied upon.

She closed her eyes, feeling suspended in time, between past and present, here and there, now that Abby was sleeping across the hall. Jill had thought that Abby and Victoria were a part of her past, her ex-life, that followed behind her, like a shadow, but Jill wasn't so sure of that, anymore. She was beginning to think that the past was an overlay on the present, like a transparent page in an old-school anatomy textbook. That Abby and Victoria hadn't really left her life, but had been lingering like ghosts in a familial limbo, waiting until she found them. Waiting until now.

Jill thought about getting married for the third time. She didn't have the heart to lose again, and neither did Megan. She was betting for them both, on forever. She wanted it so badly this time, and she wanted it with Sam. He was the last great love of her life. On impulse, she slid out of her T-shirt and panties, then shifted over and pressed herself against his back, feeling his warmth against her breasts, through the thin cotton. Her arms found their way around his waist, and she nuzzled his neck, kissing the hollow behind his ear, where his whiskers were rough, out of a razor's reach.

"Baby?" she breathed, a question that Sam didn't need words to answer. He stirred and came to wakefulness, shifting onto his back and reaching for her when she climbed onto him, kissing him. He tasted still of toothpaste, and his breath came quicker when she wrangled off his T-shirt and boxers, leaving the both of them naked, together, skin against skin, until they were nothing but each other, and all the clothes, eyeglasses, stethoscopes, and employee IDs had been stripped away, and the roles they played for the rest of the world had ended, and she felt as if she had been broken down like a stage set, finally becoming herself. And in that moment, she was no longer a mother or a doctor, but simply a woman, his woman.

And that was not only enough, that was everything.

Chapter Five

"Mom!" Megan whispered, loudly. "Abby's here! What's going on? Mom, *Mom*!"

Jill woke up to find an astonished Megan, shaking her awake. It had to be before dawn because the bedroom was still dim, quiet except for Megan, who was dressed for swim practice in her yellow Valley West hoodie. Her hair was pulled back in its doubled-under ponytail, its dry ends sprayed out, stiff from chlorine.

"Mom, *Abby's* here! In my bed! Oh my God, did you even know that?"

"Yes, I do, hi, honey." Jill rose slightly, propping herself up on an elbow. The clock read 5:15 A.M., and she didn't have to be up until seven, for work. "I didn't expect you this early. What's going on? Did Coach call a practice?"

"Yes, I have to get my stuff, but Mom, Abby's in my bed. What's she doing here? It's so weird! You know, right?"

"Yes, remain calm, and let me explain." She sat up with the grim realization that she'd have to tell Megan about William, right now.

"Why? Why is she here? I have to get in my room, Courtney's mom is picking me up in twenty minutes, but Abby's sound asleep, in my bed! In my *nightgown*. How weird is that? So weird!"

"Relax, please." Jill inhaled, bracing herself as Sam began to stir and Beef stood up in bed, wagging his tail. Megan looked over at Sam, bewildered.

"Sam, hi, did you meet Abby, my stepsister? She's sleeping in my *bed*. In my *nightgown*."

"I met her." Sam smiled sadly, knowing that the news about William's death was coming.

"Megan, sit down, would you?" Jill patted the bed, next to Beef, who wagged his tail so hard his butt wiggled. "I need to talk to you."

"What's going on? Why is she here?" Megan sat down, petted the dog, and set her omnipresent phone beside her. "You're scaring me, Mom. Why do I have to sit down? Is she sick or something?"

"No, but I have bad news, about William." Jill prepared herself to break her daughter's heart. Motherhood was not for the weak. She put her arm around Megan's shoulders. "Honey, I'm sorry, but Abby came here to tell us that William died, a few days ago."

Megan gasped. Her hand flew to her mouth, and her eyes filmed. "Oh my God," she said, hushed.

"I'm so sorry, sweetie." Jill hugged her closer, and Megan wilted in her embrace, holding back her tears, her lips going tight over her braces. Jill's heart broke for her. "I'm so very sorry, honey."

"This is horrible," Megan whispered, stricken.

"I know, I'm sorry."

"Really, is it true? Are you sure?"

"Yes."

"I don't believe it."

"I know, I'm sorry." Jill hugged her close and nuzzled her hair, breathing in her young-girl smells of vanilla oil and strawberry-scented conditioner. "He had a heart attack, because of some medication he took."

Megan looked over, her eyes wet with tears, her brow furrowed with pain. "Like, he was allergic?"

"No, he had a bad reaction to prescription medication, which he mixed with alcohol."

"Like he had a drink and that was *it*?" Megan's lower lip trembled.

"Yes."

"Can that even *happen*?"

"Yes, it can." Jill didn't mention Abby's suspicions. It was pointless and would hit Megan like a double whammy. Beef settled down and put his head on Megan's leg, evidently getting the message, for a change.

"That's so *random*." Megan's cell phone chirped on the bed, signaling a text, but she didn't even hear it, which told Jill how upset she must be.

"Honey, I think I should call Coach Stash and tell him what happened. I'm sure he'd let you stay home from practice."

"No, don't, I can't, Mom." Megan shook her head, wiping her eye, though it quickly filled again. "I'm captain, I can't let the team down. Coach Stash is counting on me, they all are. We have qualifiers for states this weekend, remember?"

"But he'd understand, there's a death in the family."

"No, no, I can't," Megan shot back, her voice quavering. "I have to go. We were lucky to get the pool at the high school, that's why he called the practice. We have doubles today. This is our year, Mom."

Jill could see the pressure on Megan's face, and it killed her to think that her daughter's life was so scheduled that she didn't have time to cry. "Honey, I know, but this is a big deal, and you can stay home and we can talk about it."

"You have work, anyway, and I can't miss, I never miss. The team's counting on me."

"This is an exception, something he'll understand." Jill felt the conversation going in the wrong direction. They were talking about practice instead of Megan's feelings, and Sam must've had the same thought, because he shifted over and touched Megan's arm.

"I'm so sorry, kitten. This is terrible news, and I know it comes as a terrible shock."

"It is, it's so weird and horrible and random." Megan pressed her lips together, making a hump over her braces. "I know I shouldn't be upset, I mean, I hadn't seen him in so long, like, *years*."

"Of course, you're upset," Sam said, gently, stroking her arm, and Jill gave her a squeeze.

"Right, of course you feel upset and sad, sweetie."

Megan hung her head, and a tear fell on the comforter. "I shouldn't be, not really. He didn't want to see me. He didn't answer my emails, and he's only my stepfather, anyway." She caught herself, shooting Sam a teary look. "I'm sorry, I didn't mean it that way."

"I know you didn't." Sam rubbed her arm. "This is random, as you say. Nobody knows how to react."

Megan turned to Jill, blinking wetly. "How's Abby? She must be so upset. Is that why she came here? She doesn't have any parents anymore. Now she's an orphan, right?"

"She is," Jill answered, touched that Megan would even think of Abby at a time like this. Jill gave her another hug. "She invited us to a memorial service this afternoon, if you feel up to going. We can go after practice. It's at three o'clock."

"I can go, I'll go." Megan looked uncertainly from Jill to Sam, wiping her eyes. "Right? Okay? Do you guys think that's okay, or weird?"

Jill stroked Megan's cheek. "I think it's okay, and it makes sense."

Sam nodded. "Agree. I don't think it's weird, at all. I can't go with you, I have a meeting with a colleague. Your Mom said you guys can go alone, but I'll cancel if you want me to come with you."

"No, thanks, okay." Megan turned to Jill, keeping tears at bay. "Mom? Right? Do you want to go? I mean, I know you didn't love William anymore, and you got mad at him, from the divorce."

Jill gave her a squeeze. "That doesn't matter now. Of course I want to go, and I'll take you."

"I don't really know why I want to, exactly." Megan rubbed her cheeks, covering her braces with her lips again. "I just think that it's the right thing to do. Like Grandma would say, I should pay my respects."

Jill felt pleased, thinking of her mother, who had passed away five years ago. Jill still missed her, every day. "I think Grandma would be so proud of you, right now."

Megan turned to Sam, with a sniffle. "I feel so bad about what I said, it was dumb. I love you, Sam, even though you're my stepfather—oh, Jeez, you know what I mean, right?"

"Yes, and I love you, too." Sam opened his arms, and Megan threw her arms around him. He gave her a big bear hug. "I love you very, very much. We love each other, and nothing else matters."

Jill felt tears spring to her eyes. She couldn't wish for a better stepfather to Megan. Sam's calm manner was the perfect antidote to their mother-daughter drama, and he helped Megan with her homework, drove her to practice when Jill couldn't, and was even teaching her photography. Suddenly Megan's phone rang, a new Lady Gaga ring tone, and its screen lit up with a photo of Megan's best friend, Courtney.

Megan let go of Sam. "Oh, no. Mom, can I get that? She's calling to tell me they're on their way."

Jill hesitated. "Sure, get it."

"Thanks, I'll go into your bathroom. I won't be long, I have to get ready." Megan grabbed the phone, pressed a button, and left the bedroom, saying, "Court, you wanna hear something totally weird and horrible?"

The bathroom door closed, Beef went back to sleep, and Jill eyed Sam. "That was okay, to let her take the call, I figure."

"Sure. Let her talk it over with Courtney." Sam put an arm around her, and Jill felt a twinge.

"She's upset, but she's keeping it in."

"She'll process it her own way. She'll talk to Courtney and her pals on the team. Isn't that what girls do?" Sam made a talking mouth with his hand. "Yakety-yak?"

"Is it wrong to miss the days when she yakked about it with me?"

"No." Sam put an arm around her. "She's reached that age, honey. I saw it with Steve, too, but I know it's not the same as a mother and daughter. You guys are closer than we were, because of all those shoes."

Jill smiled. She knew he was trying to cheer her up.

"And to her credit, that's why she chose to go to the memorial service. She's growing up, and you take the good with the bad." Sam gave her a squeeze, and suddenly Jill realized that it had gotten quiet in the bathroom. Megan had stopped talking on the phone.

Jill rose. "Did she hang up?"

Sam looked over, and Jill heard a noise in the bathroom and knew what it was, instinctively. A muffled sob. The loss of William had just hit Megan, and she'd started to cry.

"Mom?" Megan called out, her voice choked with sobs. "I need you."

"Sure, honey," Jill called back, already on the way.

Chapter Six

Jill and Megan moved quickly and quietly around the bedroom, packing a swim bag for practice, while Abby made a sleeping mound in the bed. Megan was shaky and crestfallen, still recovering from her crying bout, and Jill's heart went out to her, having to function when she felt so raw.

"Megan," she whispered, by the bureau. "Did you eat? I can get you a breakfast bar, or some yogurt."

"No, thanks, I'm gonna be so late." Megan was digging in her drawer. The room was growing lighter, and they could see without a lamp. "Where are my new sweats?"

"Still in the laundry room." Jill had seen them on the top of the hamper. She hadn't gotten to the wash yet. "I'll wash them tonight, okay?"

"Okay." Megan took a bunchy set of old sweats out of the drawer, stuffed them in her gym bag, then hurried to her bathroom. "Oh Jeez," she said softly.

Jill went to the bathroom, which had been left in disarray. The shower door hung open, the shampoo lay on its side, and a pile of wet towels sat on the floor. "Sorry, honey."

"It's okay. She must've been so upset." Megan grabbed her

conditioner and shampoo and tossed them into her bag, then looked over at the bed, with wet eyes. "Uh-oh, we woke her up."

Jill turned around to see Abby sitting up in bed, raking back her long hair, and Megan heaved a little sob, dropped her bag, and hurried over to the bed.

"Abby, I'm so sorry about your Dad." Megan reached for her, and Abby raised her arms, equally teary, and the two embraced, crying and hugging each other, like two halves of the same, broken heart.

Standing to the side, Jill felt her throat catch, sad and happy, both at once. She loved seeing the sisters reunited, but not on the worst day they could share, and she thought of all the times they had consoled each other, growing up. When Megan hadn't gotten a speaking part in *Annie,* Abby threw her a pity party with a pint of vanilla Häagen-Dazs, chenille bathrobes, and an "I Will Survive" mixtape. And when a mean girl had teased Abby about her low PSAT scores, Megan had treated her to sundaes at Friendly's, with money she had earned babysitting. *Ice cream fixes everything,* Megan had said, and they had laughed through their tears. But not this morning.

Jill could hear the tremor in Abby's voice as she buried her head in Megan's neck. "I'm sorry, too, for you. I know you loved him, too."

"It's so horrible. I can't even believe it."

"That's just what I think. I can't believe it." Abby released Megan, wiping her eyes. "I just tell myself, this isn't really happening. It's not. It's not even possible."

"I know, you must be so sad, I'm so sad for you." Megan looked stricken all over again, but was trying to compose herself, wiping her eyes. "I'm so sorry, I don't even know what to say."

"I love you, Megs." Abby sniffled, sad again. "Sorry, I'm such a crybaby."

"I love you, too." Megan frowned, her lower lips trembling, seeming to cry and smile, both at once. "It's hard, I mean, he's your *Dad.*"

"I know, and your Mom was so nice." Abby stifled a sob. "And you, thanks for the nightgown. It's my old one, remember?"

"Yes, sure." Megan tried to smile again, straightening up. "I still wear it, it got softer."

"I know, right?" Abby managed a smile, too. "You look so awesome, you're so skinny. Can't call you Mega anymore, huh?"

"No." Megan smiled at the old nickname.

"You have braces now? I thought you didn't need them."

"I know. My teeth shifted, doesn't that suck?" Megan touched her mouth, self-conscious. "Two more years, and this is so lame but I have to go, I have practice."

"It's okay, I know. I hated those early morning practices." Abby rubbed her forehead, and she seemed a little pale, even in the dim light. "God, I feel lousy. My head is killing me."

Sam appeared at the doorway, in his bathrobe. "Hey, ladies," he said, smiling, but it vanished when he sized up the scene. "I thought I would make banana pancakes, if anybody wants some. Abby, want to try my specialty?"

"Pancakes, yuck. I feel so sick." Abby leaned over, and before anybody knew what was happening, she was vomiting on the bed. Megan recoiled, and Sam blanched.

"Here, honey." Jill snatched up a wastebasket and rushed over, but Abby heaved again, spewing vomit on the bedclothes.

"Ugh, no, sorry, guys."

"Come on, sweetie, let's get you into the bathroom." Jill set the wastebasket down, took Abby's arm, hustled her out of bed, and got her to the bathroom just as she heaved all over her nightgown, the used towels, and the tile floor. Jill got her to the toilet, where she dropped to her knees, and Jill held her hair back.

"Mom, I'm gonna be late!" Megan called out from the bedroom. "Sorry, Abby, I have to go!"

"Hold on, honey!" Jill called back, torn. She wanted to say good-bye to Megan, to make sure she was okay, but she couldn't leave Abby. She felt ripped in half, with both girls grieving and needy, but she couldn't be in both places at once. "Just hang on one sec! I want to see you before you go!"

"I'm late, Mom, and Courtney's mom is waiting! I can't wait! Bye, I love you!"

"Oh, no." Abby began to retch into the toilet, and Jill couldn't leave her, holding her hair.

"I love you, too! Take it easy this morning! Call if you want to come home!"

"She will!" Sam called back, and Jill felt a wrench in her chest, knowing it meant Megan had left.

Abby coughed, spitting. "Please, close the door. This is so embarrassing."

"Don't worry, wipe your mouth." Jill handed her some toilet paper, then closed the bathroom door. "Be still. Let your stomach relax."

"Thanks," Abby said, thickly. She wiped her mouth. "I'm so sorry."

"Make sure you're finished. Take your time." Jill rubbed her back. "There's still some things you haven't thrown up on."

Abby smiled and let the paper drop in the toilet. "I'm done."

"Good. Let me help you up." Jill steadied Abby, flushed the toilet, and put down the lid, with a *clunk.* "Sit here until your head clears."

"Thanks." Abby sat down and put her head in her hands. "Sorry, I ruined our nightgown. Can you help me take it off? It reeks."

"Reach for the moon." Jill lifted the nightgown off and dropped it on the floor with the soiled towels. She took Megan's bathrobe from the hook and handed it to Abby. "Here, stay warm."

"I'm not a drunk girl, I swear. If I were, I wouldn't be this sick."

"I know, honey." Jill eyed Abby, straightening up on the seat. "Okay, wash up and I'll be right back."

"Okay."

Jill left the bathroom and went into the bedroom, where Sam was balling up the comforter on the bed. "How was she? Was she crying when she left?"

"She'll be fine. I gave her a big hug. I say we throw out this comforter and buy a new one."

"No, don't. She loves it, and I'm not sure they make it anymore. It'll have to go to the Laundromat. I'll take it when I get back."

"I'll do it, and by the way, Sandy emailed me to say that she'd squeeze Abby in next week, anytime."

"Jill!" Abby called from the bathroom. "Help!"

"That's great, thanks," Jill said, already hurrying back to the bathroom.

Chapter Seven

"How are you doing, little guy?" Jill smiled at little Rahul Choudhury, an adorable one-year-old she was about to examine. She'd spent the morning treating a leaky procession of sniffles, fevers, and sinus infections, all the while worrying about Abby and Megan. They say a mother is only as happy as her happiest child, and it applied to stepmothers and ex-stepmothers, too.

"He's such a good baby," said his mother, Padma, steadying Rahul as he sat on the examining table, wobbly in his thick diaper. She was a pretty woman with a ready smile, dressed in a blue cotton sweater, khakis, and clogs. Jill would have normally worn a similar outfit, but she was dressed for the memorial service, in a dark jersey suit. Like most pediatricians, she never wore a lab coat, because children tended to associate them with needles.

"Rahul, hello, what a good boy you are." Jill wiggled her stethoscope, and Rahul's round, dark eyes focused on it so intently that they crossed slightly, under a sloping fringe of eyelashes that any woman would kill for. She kept it wiggling, initiating a tug of war with the baby, and felt satisfied when he reached out, made a swipe for the black rubber tubing, and caught it in his tight little fist. "Good for you! You're strong, Rahul. You work out?"

Padma smiled. "I hate when he's sick. I don't have time for him to be sick."

"I know just what you mean." Jill was thinking of Megan, with no time to cry. She tickled Rahul, and he giggled, drooling. "It's so easy to make a baby laugh. I should do standup, for infants."

Padma chuckled. "All my sons are fans of yours. Roy loves it when you ask him if he brought his heart today."

"Aww, good." Jill didn't add that joking around was part of her exam. The first thing she did with a patient was to engage him, to see if he was sick or not. One of her pediatrics professors had called it the *gestalt,* or the big picture, and her *gestalt* about Rahul wasn't good. "Now, how long did you say he'd been sick?"

"Since Thursday. It's another ear infection. He tugged at his ear most of last night, and I know, I was up, on the phone with my mother, in Mumbai. She's not feeling well."

"Oh no, I hope she feels better. You have your hands full." Jill had read the notes from the nurse, who had taken Rahul's vitals. Nothing was remarkable except a fever, at 101 degrees. Anything between 97.5 and 100.3 was normal. "When did Rahul get the fever?"

"This morning, it's new. I wanted to get him on amoxicillin before it gets worse, because I have the week from hell coming up. Two field trips, one for Roy and the other for Devi."

"Yikes. Got Xanax?"

Padma laughed, and Jill realized she'd made the joke because she must have been thinking of William. It was odd that he was taking prescription drugs, but she tried to put it out of her mind. She offered Rahul a finger in trade for her stethoscope and listened to his lungs, hearing transmitted upper-airway sounds. She checked his ears, and there was purulent fluid, or pus behind the drum.

"How's Dave?" Jill asked. Padma's husband Dave was in the Army Reserves, serving in Afghanistan.

"Fine, and he says hi and thanks for those books you sent. They all shared them. Thanks so much."

"Please, it's the least I can do." Jill looked in Rahul's nose, mouth, and throat, and they showed redness, irritation, and post-nasal drip, all consistent with a viral URI, or upper respiratory tract infection. "I give you so much credit, doing all that you do, on your own."

"Sometimes it gets to me, but most of the time, I do okay."

"I'm sure, but you can always vent to me, you know that. Email or call, I mean it."

"Thanks." Padma smiled, but Jill knew she wouldn't take her up on the offer.

"Tell me, how are the boys?" Jill palpated the lymph nodes in Rahul's neck, both the anterior and the posterior chain, and the anterior were slightly enlarged, also consistent with a URI and ear infection.

"Doing well in school, and they're brown belts, both of them."

"Wow, that's great!"

"But they miss their father, so much."

"I'm sure, poor things." Jill found herself thinking of Abby and Victoria, and how much they would miss William. She'd have to get Abby to the therapist to deal with her grief, instead of talking about murder. "I bet it's been hard on them."

"It has been, but we email and Skype, so that helps."

"That's good." Jill lay Rahul down gently and palpated his belly, liver, and spleen, all of which were also slightly enlarged, again, consistent with his little body trying to fight the infection. But for some reason, he was losing the battle, too often. It was Rahul's fifth ear infection this year and he'd also had a pneumonia, which worried her.

"How old is Megan, now?" Padma cupped the back of Rahul's head with her hand. "In middle school?"

"Yes, if you feed them, they grow. Right, handsome?" Jill spoke to Rahul, and he broke into a smile, with wet lips, which showed he wasn't dehydrated. To double-check, she pinched him gently on the arm, and his skin didn't tent. "What a tough guy! No crying, huh?"

"He's the third. They learn."

Jill smiled, stroking Rahul's soft cheek, noting his color. His Indian ancestry gave his skin a glow, but she'd trained at D.C. Children's, where she'd seen kids of all races, and she thought he was febrile, feverish. "He look flushed to you, Dr. Mom?"

"He always does when he gets an ear infection. So, do you have a wedding dress yet?"

"I'm thinking a lab coat. It's white, right?"

Padma laughed. "Come on, tell me everything. It's fun to talk girly stuff. I love being a boy mom, but I wish for something with ruffles at times."

"Well, I do have a suit, a nice one." Jill palpated the axillary lymph nodes under Rahul's armpits, which were also swollen. "Megan's addicted to *Say Yes to the Dress,* so I'm failing her as a mother."

"I know that feeling. It comes with the territory."

"Ha!" Jill peeked inside Rahul's diaper, which was clean and dry. "They'll grow up and realize how lucky they were, but by then, we'll be dead."

Padma laughed.

Jill's last stop was to examine Rahul's skin, and she noticed a tiny patch on his right arm, which reminded her of something about his older brother, also a patient. "Roy has hay fever. Do you or Dave?"

"Yes, I do. Why?"

"Look at this." Jill showed her the patch. "This is eczema."

"Really?" Padma peered at it, frowning. "I thought it was a rash, or maybe poison ivy. He was playing in the grass yesterday while I weeded."

"It's not uncommon in babies, and it's nothing to worry about. But we call asthma, allergies, and eczema, the allergic triad. It runs in families, and several of them can be in the same child."

"They do, I know, in my family."

"Let me see the rest of you, Rahul." Jill examined the skin on his chest, legs, neck, and back, with its tiny scapula, like the nubs of angel wings. There were no other eczema patches. "How's he eating?"

"Not great, but not terrible."

"Drinking?"

"Okay."

"Sleeping? You said he tugs at his ear?"

"Yes, off and on, at night."

"Poor little guy." Jill looked up and met Padma's eye. "I think you're right, it's another ear infection, but he gets a lot of ear infections for a baby who's not in day care. On the other hand, he has older brothers, so I bet he gets all the colds they bring home from school." Padma's eyebrows sloped down unhappily. "Do you think he should get tubes? My brother does, and they helped my nephew."

"No, I wouldn't do that for Rahul. We used to do that more often, because of language impairment, but he isn't showing any delays. You can dress him, now." Jill went to the computer on the desk, typed her password into Epic, opened Rahul's file, and typed in her notes. Pembey Family Practice had EMR, or electronic medical records, but Jill always waited until after the exam to record her findings. She liked to look the mom in the eye and stand in front of a child, not a keyboard.

"So no tubes?" Padma asked.

"Not yet. Let me check one last thing in his file." Jill navigated to Rahul's weight chart, with its line climbing up a hill, until six months ago. He'd started life in the thirtieth percentile, but now was down to the fifth, which meant he fell off his curve. That wasn't good, either.

"So, amoxicillin?"

"Yes, since it's been over a month since the last time he'd used it, and Tylenol, too." Jill closed out the file, leaving the screen waiting for the password of the next doctor. She'd coded it as a URI for insurance purposes, but she wasn't 100 percent sure why it kept happening. The saying in medicine was, if you hear hoofbeats, don't go hunting for zebra, but Jill knew better. Zebras existed, and pediatrics was full of them. She stood up. "Let's see him again on Wednesday. I know you're busy, but I want to keep an eye on him."

"Okay."

"Also, before you leave, I'd like to take some blood." Jill didn't elaborate because she wasn't about to alarm Padma. There was a chance that Rahul had an autoimmune problem, leukemia, or lymphoma, but they were only remote possibilities. "The lab's just down the hall. It won't take long."

"Blood?" Padma's dark eyes flared. "For an ear infection?"

"Yes, I want to know why he keeps getting them, and a blood test will give me a complete picture of what's going on in his system and see what type of infection his body is fighting." Jill didn't add that the blood test would tell her how many and what type of white blood cells Rahul's body was producing, whether lymphocytes, neutrophils, or monocytes, and that would eliminate the more serious diagnoses. "You only have to take him down the hall, and I promise Selena will make it easy."

"Okay, if you think it's really necessary." Padma pressed a strand of dark hair into her short ponytail.

"I do, and I'll call you when I get the results, probably on Tuesday. Please let me know if anything changes." Jill printed out a script for amoxicillin, signed it, and handed it to Padma. "Here we go."

"Thanks." Padma picked up Rahul's little jeans, and Jill placed a reassuring hand on her shoulder.

"I mean it, don't hesitate to call me."

"Will do. Thanks again." Padma smiled, and Jill gave her a hug.

"Love to the boys and Dave. Rahul, bye-bye." Jill caressed the baby on the cheek and left the examining room, checking her watch on the fly. Pembey Family Practice had office hours until one o'clock on Saturdays, and it was 1:15, so she wasn't as behind as usual. She needed to spend time with the patients, but it put her in constant conflict with their office manager, Sheryl Ewing. Jill hoped to leave today without seeing Sheryl because she didn't need the lecture, with the memorial service ahead of her.

She bustled to her office, thinking of William, and anger flickered in her chest, an ember that didn't need fanning. She felt hypocritical going to his memorial service when, in her darker moments, she had actually wished him dead. And if she were really honest, she wouldn't be surprised if it turned out that someone had murdered him.

Because in her very darkest moments, she would have done it herself.

Chapter Eight

Jill drove down Route 202, heading east toward Philly, with a somber Megan in the passenger seat, her face turned to the window. Even her phone was quiet, and Jill wondered if she had silenced it or turned it off. Rain pounded against the windshield, and they passed a strip mall that used to have a huge Circuit City, which was now vacant. The only sound was the rhythmic beating of the wipers and the low rumble of the road.

"You look nice, honey," Jill said, looking over. Megan looked grown up in a simple black dress she wore for choir concerts, with low-heeled black shoes. Her hair was still wet from the shower and gathered in a black velvet scrunchy.

"Thanks." Megan turned to her, with a brief smile, but the strain showed on her face. "Is this service gonna be weird?"

"A little, but we'll get through it."

"Will it have an open casket like Grandma's?"

"No." Jill felt a pang, thinking of her mother's wake, in the funeral home. "This isn't a Mass, it's a memorial service, in a church. An historic church."

"William didn't go to church."

"Sometimes they hold services in church, even if the person didn't go there."

"Is there something after it, like with Grandma? Do we all go to a restaurant?"

Jill realized that Abby hadn't mentioned a reception. "I don't know."

"Who else will be there, besides Abby and Victoria?"

"I don't know. I guess William's friends and maybe someone from work."

"Where did he work?"

"I don't know that, either."

Megan shook her head. "We don't know anything about him anymore, and he used to be my *Dad*."

Jill felt stricken. She knew the feeling, albeit from the other side. If it was impossible to be an ex-parent, it was impossible to have one.

"It's like he just forgot we were in the same family. Like he never even knew us, and we didn't matter to him at all."

"He didn't forget you, honey." Jill's fingers tightened on the wheel. They'd talked about this many times, but it was all coming back now, with William's death.

"Yes, he did. He didn't answer any of my emails or texts, not one. He didn't call me, not even when I got into National Honor Society." Megan's tone stayed matter-of-fact. "You tried to talk to Abby and Victoria, but he didn't even try to talk to me. He didn't even answer me, when *I* tried."

"That doesn't mean he forgot you."

"Yes, it does."

"No, not necessarily," Jill said, wanting to comfort Megan, even though she could never forgive William for cutting Megan off the way he had. If Jill hated him for one single thing, it was that, and she always would.

"Then why didn't he answer my email?"

Jill tried to think of an honest answer. "Maybe because he couldn't face his hurt, or yours. We'll never know now. But I know nobody could forget you. You're a wonderful, wonderful girl." Jill patted her leg, and another silence fell. Megan looked out the window again, her head moving slightly with the motion of the car.

"Look, a padiddle." Megan pointed at the window. "Remember when we used to play that game in the car, with Abby and Victoria?"

Jill did. A padiddle was a car with only one headlight, and whoever saw one on the road got a point. "I do remember that, but I don't see a padiddle."

"Look in your mirror. There's a padiddle behind us, one car back."

Jill glanced in the rearview, and a black SUV with one headlight was behind them. She flashed on the scene outside the house last night, when Abby had come staggering down the sidewalk. She'd been visible in the beam from a black SUV, with one headlight. A padiddle. Not that it meant anything. The world was full of black SUVs, with or without headlights, which was why Jill drove a white Volvo.

"Do you think they think about us, when they play padiddle?"

"I bet they do." Jill was remembering that the headlights on the SUV last night were boxy, but all SUVs had boxy headlights. SUVs were boxy, in general. They were practically boxes on wheels.

"Except they probably don't play padiddle anymore. They're too old."

"They still might."

"I think Abby thinks about us, but Victoria doesn't, as much. Abby loved us more." Megan turned back to Jill, her dark eyes troubled. "Victoria doesn't let herself love people a lot, you know what I mean?"

"Yes, exactly."

"Victoria doesn't love enough, and Abby loves too much. Isn't that funny?"

Jill looked over, impressed. "Well said."

"Which is better?"

"The middle. Let yourself love. Love is good. Just choose the people you love wisely. They have to deserve you." Jill heard herself pontificating, but she'd learned it the hard way. "You'll make mistakes, but that's okay."

"It is?"

"Yes, of course, it's human."

"You mean because you can always get a divorce?"

"Well, yes," Jill answered, pained. "It's not ideal, but it's the best choice, if your marriage is terrible."

"Except I didn't divorce William," Megan said, again, matter-of-factly. "I didn't divorce anybody. Neither did Abby or Victoria. The kids don't get a choice."

Jill felt a wave of guilt. "I know, sweetie, and I'm sorry."

"I didn't mean it in a bad way, I'm just saying."

"I'm still sorry, for the way it all turned out."

"It's okay." Megan reached for her phone at the sound of an incoming text.

"Don't forget to turn that off at the service."

"I won't." Megan checked the text, and a new smile flickered across her face.

"Is that Courtney?"

"No. A boy."

"Really?" Jill brightened, happy to change the subject. "Can I know more?"

"Well, he's really cute." Megan smiled, warming. "He's in one of the other clubs, the Hornets. He's one of the fastest freestylers on the team."

"Good for him. What's his name?"

"Jake Tilson."

"Did you start doodling Megan Tilson in your notebook?"

"No, Mom, you weirdo!" Megan laughed, which was the desired effect.

"What does he look like?"

"He has blond hair and it's curly, and he has blue eyes and he's a little short but I don't care. And he's really cut."

Jill laughed. "Everybody's cut at thirteen."

"No, he's *cut,* Mom. He's *ripped.* He's *shredded.* You can see his abs from across the pool. And he plays guitar. Real guitar, not Guitar Hero."

"How did you meet him?"

"I've seen him at meets but I talked to him at Courtney's party. He knows her twin brother from swim camp. He friended me after the party, and now we're texting."

Jill felt delighted. Megan needed more fun in her life. "Sounds like a modern romance."

"And guess what else?"

Jill smiled, looking over. "What else?"

"We *kissed*!" Megan covered her face with her hands, laughing.

"Good for you. So, was it fun?" Jill knew this was big news, because Megan hadn't had a boyfriend yet. She felt happy, and sad, that Megan had her first kiss, but counted herself lucky that Megan was slower than her classmates, judging from the stories she'd heard from other swim moms.

"No!" Megan slid her hands down, flushed. "It was scary and I was bad at it. He has braces, too. We were like Iron Man!"

"Aw, no you weren't."

"We *were*." Megan moaned. "It's me. I'm a bad kisser."

"You want a tip?"

"*Mom*." Megan recoiled. "It's not like the backstroke, you can't *teach* me."

"Why not? Just relax your mouth. Don't pucker up."

"Oh, this is so *random*." Megan giggled. "You have to be kidding me, right now."

"No, I'm a pretty good kisser. I've been kissing boys for a long time. I've kissed thousands. Millions." Jill's heart eased when Megan giggled again.

"Stop, no. This is gross."

"No, it's not. It's okay to like a boy, and it's okay to kiss a boy, too. Just don't lose your head."

"I won't, Mom." Megan snorted. "I'm not *Teen Mom*."

"I know that, but still." Jill knew that any teen could become *Teen Mom*.

"You're so *wacky,* Mom."

"I know, I get it from you."

Megan laughed again, then resumed texting, and Jill hit the gas, keeping her eye on the road. Traffic picked up, and she took the on ramp onto the Schuylkill Expressway with most of the traffic. She checked the padiddle, and it was still back there, behind a white pickup, too far away to tell the make. They reached the West River Drive, and she lost the padiddle in the traffic. The rain finally stopped, and they parked in a garage, where Jill cut the ignition.

"Remember, stay with me," Megan said, looking over.

"I will, don't worry." Jill managed a smile, shooing the black SUV out of her mind.

Chapter Nine

Jill and Megan got to the church early, entered through the arched doors, and found themselves milling in the back among a small, well-dressed crowd, talking in low tones before they went to their seats. Jill didn't recognize anyone, which didn't surprise her, because after the divorce, their few friends had sided with her. She caught a glimpse of a teary Abby, accepting condolences from the guests, standing next to the rector, in his red-and-white vestments.

"Poor Abby," she said to Megan.

"I know, she looks really sad," Megan whispered back. "I feel so bad for her."

"Me, too." Jill felt a deep pang, seeing how Abby looked, lost and heartbroken in an ethereal boho dress, with heavy makeup. It made her worry about Victoria, whom she couldn't see through the crowd. "Megs, do you see Victoria?"

"Yes, you'll see her when that old lady moves. She's doing better than Abby. Look, Mom, she looks so pretty. She got highlights."

"Really?" Jill craned her neck and spotted Victoria, standing tall in a black linen dress with pearl drop earrings. Her newly honeyed streaks were pulled back into a sophisticated twist, and her lovely face had elongated as she'd gotten older, enhancing the prominence of her cheekbones. Light, perfect makeup emphasized her hazel eyes, and she projected grace and poise, though she was only twenty-three. Jill felt a bittersweet rush of emotions, feeling love at seeing her again, happy that she'd grown up so well, but loss at all the years they could have been in touch, and pain for how she must be feeling.

"I think that's her boyfriend," Megan whispered, and Jill noticed a tall, good-looking young man in a dark suit and wire-rimmed glasses, who stood behind her.

"Think she has a boyfriend?"

"Yes, I see him all the time, on Abby's Facebook page."

Jill blinked, not surprised that Megan was checking Abby's Facebook page, too. "Let's find our seats. They're going to start the service."

"Mom, Abby just saw us, she's coming over." Megan stiffened. "What do I say to her? I already said I'm sorry."

"Say what you feel." Jill looked over to see Abby walking toward them, wiping a tear from her eye. It struck Jill that no one else was crying, or even upset, except for Abby, and that didn't surprise her, either. William had lots of acquaintances, but no real friends, which was only one of the red flags Jill had ignored. Love was not only blind, it was colorblind.

"But what *should* I say?" Megan asked, worried.

"You can say you're sorry again, that would be nice."

"Like, 'I'm sorry'? Or, 'please accept my . . . sorrow'? Or what?"

" 'I'm sorry' will do, sweetie," Jill answered, as Megan met Abby and gave her a hug.

"Abby, I'm so sorry, again, I really am."

"Thanks." Abby squeezed Megan tight, her eyes brimming with tears, then she let Megan go, turned to Jill, and practically fell into her arms. "Jill, thanks for coming."

"I'm sorry, honey." Jill embraced her, trying to will the strength from her body into Abby's.

"This makes it so real, doesn't it? Like he really is gone, and all these people I don't even know them."

"I know, sweetie, I'm sorry." Jill released her when she spotted Victoria heading for her, with a deep scowl.

"Jill, what are *you* doing here?" Victoria's eyes flashed with anger. "You have no right to be here. This is a private ceremony."

Jill froze, stricken. "I'm sorry, I thought—"

Abby interrupted, "I asked her to come, Victoria."

"Are you *crazy*?" Victoria shot back, then turned to Jill, infuriated. "How *dare* you! You should be ashamed of yourself. You know what you did to Dad. To all of us."

Megan gasped, teary. Heads turned. The rector's mouth fell open.

"Victoria, wait." Jill put up a palm, stunned. She'd never seen Victoria so angry, especially not at her. They used to be so close. "Listen to me—"

"No, *you* listen to *me*." Victoria's fair skin flushed with barely controlled rage. "You didn't love Dad, and you didn't love us, either. You threw us out!"

"No, that's not true." Jill edged away, mortified. Her face felt like it was on fire, her mouth had gone dry. She wouldn't stay another minute if it upset the girls. The crowd murmured. The rector grasped Victoria by the arm, but she pulled it away.

"Now it's my turn to throw *you* out, Jill. Leave. Go!" Victoria pointed to the door, but Jill was already in motion, turning to catch up with Megan, the two of them fleeing, their pumps clattering on the colonial floorboards.

"Jill, no!" Abby shouted, and just when Jill thought it couldn't get worse, she realized that Abby was running after them.

"Megan, wait!" Jill called out, but Megan blew through the glass doors into the church's courtyard. Jill ran through the doors after her and reached Megan, who was crying, full bore, in the rain.

"Mom, what did I do? What did I do?"

"Nothing, honey." Jill hugged Megan just as Abby came flying out, her cheeks tear-stained, her mascara dripping black.

"Jill, I'm sorry." Abby ran headlong toward her, and Megan backed off. Jill caught Abby as she burst into new tears. "I'm so sorry."

"Abby, what's going on?"

"I'm sorry, it's my fault, I messed up. I didn't tell her, but I didn't think she'd freak out in front of everybody." Abby sobbed, shuddering. Megan stood aside, wiping her eyes, but Jill couldn't go to her, because she was comforting Abby. "Dad said you cheated on him, that you wanted a divorce, you met another man."

"*What?*" Megan blurted out.

"No, that's not true." Jill released Abby. "Abby, go inside. This isn't the time or the place—"

"Was he lying?" Abby wiped her eyes, leaving mascara smudges. "You didn't really cheat on Dad, did you?"

"My Mom would never do that!" Megan shouted. "She cried, I heard her, lots of nights! He probably cheated on *her*!"

"No, he didn't!" Abby shouted back.

"Yes, he *did*!" Megan yelled louder, veins bulging on her neck.

"Stop fighting, both of you." Jill took control, horrified. "Abby, we have to leave. Go inside. Take care. Good-bye."

"No, wait, don't go." Abby grabbed Jill's arm, her tears abruptly stilled. "Can't you just come over, like I asked? Please, after the service? Somebody murdered Dad, and we have to find out who."

"No, Abby, I can't." Jill pulled her arm away.

"Mom, was William *murdered*?" Megan asked, her voice breaking.

"No, he wasn't," Jill answered firmly, taking Megan's hand. She could see Victoria inside the church, hurrying toward the glass exit doors. "Let's go."

"Yes, he was, Megan!" Abby called out, and behind her, Victoria was opening the door, followed by the rector. "Somebody killed him, I know it! Jill, please, help me!"

Jill hustled a weeping Megan away just as Victoria emerged with the rector.

"Please, Jill, I need you!" Abby called again, but Jill kept going. Running from one crying child, with another.

Chapter Ten

Jill sat across from Megan in a restaurant near the church, a small, quiet place that seated them at a table in the back. Megan had stopped crying in the ladies' room, though her eyes were still puffy and reddish, and she'd cut her lip on her braces. "Are you okay, honey?" Jill asked Megan, worried.

"Yes." Megan drank some water, crestfallen. "Victoria was so mad, I didn't mean to upset her."

"Honey, stop, you didn't do it. Victoria didn't expect us, and we caught her by surprise. She's a little crazy right now, is all."

"What's Abby talking about, that William was *murdered*?" Megan's eyes rounded, a bloodshot brown. "Was he, Mom?"

"No, sweetie."

"Why does Abby think he was?"

"She's wrong, honey." Jill shook her head. "People say and think strange things in grief. She's too upset to think straight. They both are."

Megan sniffled. "I know you didn't cheat on him, Mom."

"I didn't. I never would."

"I know, you're honest." Megan managed a weepy smile. "You don't let me sign your name to anything, *ever*. Even absence notes."

Jill smiled.

"Did he cheat on *you*?"

Jill sighed, inwardly. A couple of tourists got up from a nearby table. "I'm not sure we should get into this here and now, honey."

"Mom, I can take it. I'm not a baby."

"Frankly, it's not your business. Or Abby's. Or anybody's but mine." Jill wanted to stand her ground. It wouldn't help for Megan to know more, and it was too emotionally charged a day. "I had to divorce him, and I did, and we're better for it."

"Mom, tell me, please?" Megan leaned forward, putting her hands on the table, palms down. "William told Abby and Victoria. He thought they could handle it."

"William lied to Abby and Victoria."

"Trust me, Mom. Trust me enough to tell me."

"It's not a matter of trust." Jill tried to shift gears. "I wish we would use this day, and the fact that he's gone, to put this chapter behind us and go forward."

"We can't go to the next step until we understand this one."

Jill blinked. Either Megan had read that somewhere, or she was getting smarter.

"You told me that, last week. When you were helping me with equations. You said you can't go to the next step until you understand the last one." Megan leaned over, bearing down. "Now tell me what happened. Why did you and William really break up?"

Jill felt her resolve weaken. She spotted their waitress, coming toward them with their meals. "Hold on."

"Here we go, ladies," the waitress said, setting salads in front of them, filling the air with the tang of balsamic dressing. They both thanked her, and Jill waited for her to leave before she spoke.

"Honey, I don't know if he cheated, and it really doesn't matter to me."

Megan's eyes flared. "Of course it does. It *should.*"

"Let's keep the drama to a minimum," Jill said, though she doubted it was possible. Mothers and daughters were automatic drama, and if you add dead ex-husbands, it rose to operatic levels.

"So what went wrong?"

"We were happy for a while, but then the trouble started, and I didn't notice it at first. I ignored things, like symptoms you minimize when you don't want to change your initial diagnosis. Classic confirmation bias."

Megan nodded, used to medical analogies by now.

"You remember William, right? What was he like, to you?"

"Fun. Silly. He liked to do things." Megan smiled. "Like when he got the bouncy house, and the trampoline."

"And the red convertible. Remember that day? He took you all for rides?"

"Right. The Mustang." Megan smiled more broadly, and Jill hoped she hadn't made a mistake, having her recall such happy times, but that was the point.

"Well, somebody had to pay for all that. William made money, but not as much as I did, and he wanted that lifestyle. He wanted to buy cars and trampolines, whatever he wanted, you name it."

Megan frowned. "So what's wrong with that?"

"Nothing, but he began to run up huge credit bills and wanted to take loans against the house. I'm not a big spender, and married people are supposed to agree on things." Jill tried to explain, but it was impossible to explain divorce to a teenage girl, with a head full of *The Bachelor.* "He wanted more money, so he was always investing in things. He wanted to buy into a biotech start-up, and when I gave him that, he wanted to buy a title insurance company. He was all over the place."

"So it was only about money?"

"Not only about that, but money matters."

"He was trying to follow his dream, Mom."

"Not exactly." Jill wasn't surprised by Megan's defending William, because she always did, which was why these conversations were no-win. "It's not 'follow your dream,' like *American Idol.* You can follow your dream, but you have to be practical, too."

"So he couldn't afford to pay for his dream."

"No, he didn't really have a dream. His only dream was being rich, and that doesn't count as a dream. That's just plain greed."

Megan blinked.

"Pretty soon I could see a pattern, and I knew it would never end. No matter how much money I gave him, it would never be enough. If I let him, he would bankrupt me."

Megan frowned. "So that's *it*? That's *all*?"

Jill felt her chest tighten. "One day he asked me for a lot of money, for another business venture."

"How much did he want?"

"$325,000."

"Wow." Megan's eyes flared, though Jill knew she had no idea how much or how little that was. If it was as much as an iPhone, it was a lot.

"I said no." Jill wouldn't tell her that the money William asked for had belonged to Megan. It was her inheritance, since Gray's parents had established a small trust for her after his death. Gray hadn't had any life insurance; they both thought he was too young to die, and in fact, he was. "And when I said no, he asked me to take out a loan for it, and I refused. Then he did something that broke the camel's back."

"What?"

Jill hesitated, but maybe it was time. "He used to come to the office at night and bring you. He'd wait for me, and you'd play with the toys in the waiting room, then we'd go out to dinner."

"I remember, it was fun."

"I thought he came by to see me, but he didn't. It turned out that he was stealing from my office."

Megan's lips flattened, and Jill could see hurt flicker across her face.

"Petty cash went missing, and drug samples. It took us a long time to notice, because we weren't talking to each other about it, with all the work we had to do. He did it in small amounts, especially the pads."

"He took pads? Like school supplies?"

"No, prescription pads. People sell them to other people so they can get prescription drugs, illegally."

"Really?"

"Yes. You can get as much as fifty dollars for a blank prescription, and they're usually bought by people addicted to pain meds, like Oxycontin and Vicodin. We didn't know who was stealing ours, but it was William."

Megan fell silent, wounded, for William, and Jill kicked herself for starting the story. She decided not to tell Megan about the money William had taken from her purse, or his trick of using her ATM card before she was even awake, withdrawing amounts too small to notice, until too late.

"You okay, sweetie?" Jill reached across the table and rested her hand on top of Megan's.

"How do you know he stole the pads? You could have been wrong."

Jill sighed inwardly. "No, actually, we caught him in the act."

"Really?" Megan asked, hushed.

"He was caught in the basement, taking old pads out of the box. We left them down there, out of the locked cabinet, to catch the bad guy. We even set up a hidden video camera, which was my idea. I never thought the bad guy would be my own husband."

Megan set down her fork, stricken.

"It was a terrible thing he did, embarrassing to me, and worse, it could have ruined me and all of the docs in our group. My colleagues, my friends. We could've lost our licenses."

"He didn't have to go to jail, did he?"

"No." Jill felt touched, and saddened, that Megan was still concerned for William. "The group didn't report it, out of kindness to me, but I had to leave the practice and I paid back every penny he took. I was lucky to get work anywhere else, after all the gossip. That's why I took the job at Pembey Family. They were the only ones who made an offer."

Megan blinked. "Do you think he cheated on you?"

"I don't know, and I don't care."

"*Really,* Mom?"

"Really." Jill squared her shoulders. She didn't bother to explain that the betrayal was worse. The deception was worse. That she hadn't known what was going on under her own roof, under her very nose, that was worse. "I want to be with a man I can trust and believe in. So I took some time alone, and finally met Sam. End of story. Or beginning."

Megan cocked her head, mulling it over. "I think William had a dream, but it wasn't the dream you wanted."

"Okay, we can agree to disagree on that one." Jill swallowed hard, knowing it was time to stop, if only to save Megan's feelings. The unsayable thing, the thing she was about to say next, the real truth of the matter, was that Jill didn't think William ever really loved her, he just married her for her money and to have a mother for his children. But if Jill told Megan that, then Megan would conclude that William had never really loved her, either, that he had only acted as if he had, that she had been used, too. And Jill sensed that Megan couldn't handle hearing that, despite her middle-school savvy. She was only thirteen, and inside, just a kid.

Megan was eyeing her. "What's your dream, Mom?"

Jill was happy to change the subject, and almost laughed with relief. "You," she answered.

Megan laughed, unexpectedly. "No, really."

"What? It's true. My dream is having a wonderful daughter, like you." Tears came to Jill's eyes, surprising even her, and she blinked them away. "I never dreamed I'd be so lucky. I don't know how I got so lucky."

"But for *you,* what's your dream? Like they say, your passion?"

"Other than you?"

"Yes." Megan rolled her eyes, but Jill wouldn't let go.

"Honey, someday you'll understand this, but every mother's passion is her children, and there's nothing wrong with that. People don't say it enough. I see it every day at work, in all the mothers doing everything they can to help their babies get well, in all the panicky calls and emails, in all the things mothers do for their kids." Jill thought of Padma and her three sons, and her own mother. "Women sacrifice every day for their children, and they love it. They do it without question, second nature. *That's* passion."

Megan smiled, but still looked searching. "Okay, but before

me. Before I was born, what was your passion? Did you have a passion then?"

Jill thought a minute. "Okay, well, I guess I would say that my passion was helping kids. That's why I became a pediatrician. I'm a professional mother now."

Megan grinned. "Uh-oh. Watch out."

"I know, right?" Jill smiled at her, happy they were back on an even keel. "Let me ask *you* now. What's your passion? What do you love doing?"

Megan frowned, slightly. "I don't know. Is that bad?"

"No, not at all. You're still young, and you'll know when you know. Like love, because it is a form of love. It could be swimming, or becoming a vet. You're great in the school plays, and your passion can be acting or singing. *That* will be your life's work. Money isn't a life's work. Love is."

Megan sighed. "So what are you going to do about Abby?"

"What do you mean?" Jill had to switch gears.

"What if she's right that William was murdered?"

"She's not. The police say it's not murder, just a reaction to the drugs and alcohol. He had some whisky that night, and you can't mix those."

"I remember he liked whisky sometimes, he let me taste it. Ugh." Megan wrinkled her pretty nose. "I didn't know he took drugs, though. What drugs?"

"They found drugs for anxiety and painkillers."

"Was he on them when you guys were married?"

"No, I didn't think he was, but he was stealing samples and pre-scription pads. When I confronted him, he said he sold them, so I didn't think he was taking drugs himself. I was wrong, I guess."

"Were those the samples he stole?"

"No, he stole ADHD drugs, like Ritalin." Jill didn't have to explain because Megan knew about a scandal at the high school last year, with kids arrested for selling their Ritalin as a study drug.

"If you took those drugs with alcohol, do you get a heart attack?"

"Yes, you can." Jill picked up her fork and stabbed her salad. "It's possible, and it's not suspicious that they did."

Megan looked down at her food, untouched, and Jill could see she was struggling.

"Honey, this talk of drugs and murder is Abby's way of not accepting that William is gone. The police say it wasn't murder, and Victoria agrees."

Megan looked up, her eyes glistening again. "But I still wish you'd do what Abby wants. Help her figure it out."

"Why?" Jill asked, dismayed. "She's wrong. She doesn't know what she's talking about."

"Then help her figure that out, too. Don't you love her, anymore?"

"Yes, I do."

"She loves you, Mom. She always did. She acted like you were her real mom. She told me once, she doesn't even remember her real mom."

Jill didn't know what to say. Abby's real mother had died when she was only four, in a car accident. She'd had money, too, but Jill didn't want to go there, and this conversation was supposed to be about Megan. "Did that bother you?"

"No, not at all. You always love it when people love what you love." Megan smiled. "Like when people say Beef is cute, I love that. I hate people who say he's old or fat. Abby's a sweetie, and you know how she is when she gets an idea in her head. She's like Beef, with his sock, she never lets go. She needs us, Mom. We're her family."

"Are we?" Jill asked, feeling surprised and validated, both at once.

"Yes, sure, you can't just kick somebody out of your family. She's in my family, so she has to be in yours."

Jill smiled. She still thought of herself as Abby's mother, but it came as a revelation that Megan thought of her as family, too.

"Mom, you say your passion is helping kids. Right?"

"Yes," Jill answered.

"So how can you *not* help Abby? She's *ours*."

Chapter Eleven

Back at home, Jill had changed her clothes and was putting fresh sheets on Megan's bed, in a house that was empty and felt that way. She had dropped Megan off at Courtney's to work on an English project until their afternoon practice, and Sam was still in town with his colleague Lee. Jill was doing laundry and other chores, trying to put the memorial service and its aftermath out of her mind, without success.

Why did you guys really break up?

Jill felt a twinge, missing Megan. It was too soon to be an empty-nester, but you didn't have to be a pediatrician to know that the baby birds left before they could fly. She tucked in the flat sheet and made a lousy hospital corner. She had worked in six different hospitals and couldn't make a decent hospital corner. Even hospitals didn't make hospital corners anymore. The irony was lost on Beef, who watched her from between his paws, resting his head on his dirty tube sock.

She's like Beef, with his sock. She never lets go.

Jill reached for the duvet cover, an old one she'd gotten from the closet. It usually took her two or three tries to put on a duvet cover, and it was a chore she hated. She'd rather change a bedpan than a duvet cover.

Brrring! Her cell phone rang, and she slid it from her pocket and checked the number, in the Philly area code. She answered it, "Jill Farrow."

"I'm so sorry about what happened." It was Abby, her voice thick, and Jill set down the duvet cover, feeling for her.

"How are you, honey? How was the service?"

"Um, okay. I'm okay." Abby sniffled. "I'm glad you didn't change your phone number. Am I still A on your speed dial?"

Jill felt a stab of guilt. "You were until I got a new phone, but that erases all the speed dials. Where are you, honey?"

"Home."

"Alone?"

"Pickles is here."

Jill sank onto the bed, hating that Abby was all by herself after William's service, sitting in the house they'd shared.

"Jill, I'm so sorry for what I said, accusing you of cheating on Dad. I know, deep inside, that you didn't, but Dad said it and Victoria went along, and I didn't want to think he'd lie. I mean, he's all I have. Had."

"I know, don't worry. Did you have a reception afterwards?"

"We did, but I left. Victoria's so mad at me. She's still at the restaurant. It was Brian and all her friends anyway."

"Who's Brian?"

"Brian Pendle. He was at the service. Tall and cute, with glasses."

Jill remembered. "Megan said he was her boyfriend."

"Not yet. He has a girlfriend studying abroad, but Victoria's working on him. He's a lawyer in New York, and she's crushing like crazy on him. The more unavailable the guy, the happier she is."

Jill let it go. "Did you eat?"

"Not yet. I'll get take-out, I'm obsessed with this Chinese place near us. The one time I didn't call and order, they called me to make sure I was okay. It was the day Dad died."

Jill shuddered.

"What are you and Megan doing?"

"Everybody's out, and I'm making the bed somebody barfed on." Jill was trying to make Abby laugh, and she did, chuckling.

"Oh no, yuck, sorry. Does Megan hate me?"

"No. Megan loves you, and so do I."

Abby fell silent. "I don't mind being here alone. I have Pickles and I decided I'm going to live here on my own, from now on. Victoria says I can't do it, but I know I can. She wants to sell the house, but I want to stay."

Jill knew it was the grief talking. "It's too soon to make any decisions, sweetie. See how you feel in time."

"I can't, Victoria's already talking to the lawyer. We're in a fight."

Jill sank onto the bed. "Well, maybe she's right, honey. It costs money to live in a house. You have to pay the mortgage, every month."

"No, there's no mortgage. The house is paid for."

"That's not possible." Jill and Sam were a decade away from paying off the house, and together, they made good money.

"Yes it is, Dad told me."

Then Jill figured it had to be a small mortgage. "But you'll have living expenses. Can you afford them, waitressing?"

"I quit."

"What?" Jill checked her tone. Criticism was the last thing Abby needed today. "Why?"

"I want to find out who killed Dad. I'm going to do it, whether you help me or not."

Jill let that go, too. "What will you do for money? Did your Dad have life insurance?"

"Yes, Victoria said there was a policy for a million dollars, and we're the beneficiaries, and I saved about three thousand dollars, so I'll be fine."

Jill relaxed, reassured. She'd made William get life insurance when the girls were young, though they hadn't had a million-dollar policy. It seemed odd.

"Jill, can you tell me how to set up a budget? How to run the house, like Dad did?"

Jill saw room to strike a bargain. "Yes, but if I do, you have to do something for me. I want you to meet with a psychologist, a really great woman. "

"A shrink?" Abby moaned.

"You've had a terrible loss, and there's no shame in therapy. I had plenty after my first husband died. Give it a chance is all I ask. She'll see you anytime this week."

"Okay," Abby answered, after a moment.

"Thanks, sweetie." Jill felt a wave of relief.

"So wanna come over? You said you were alone. We can order Chinese."

"Tonight?"

"Why not?"

Jill felt her mood lift. She had answered all her patient email, returned all their phone calls, and done the laundry. She was going to take a swim, but she could do that anytime. "Okay, sounds good," she said.

But Jill didn't know what she was in for.

Chapter Twelve

It was almost dark by the time Jill got to Philly, surprised to find that William had lived in one of the best parts of Society Hill. His house was a stunning contemporary column, with a concrete-and-glass façade, and she climbed the steps in astonishment, ringing the bell. Abby opened the door in her flowing boho dress, sweeping into Jill's arms.

"Jill, I'm so glad you came."

"Me, too, sweetie." Jill let her go, gesturing at the modern façade. "This is your house? It's amazing."

"Now you know why I want to stay. Come in." Abby moved aside, and Jill followed her through an all-white entrance hall to a dramatic living room, with walls of massive glass sheets and beige leather sectionals, arranged around a state-of-the-art TV and entertainment center.

"Abby, where did your Dad work?" Jill asked, mystified. She set her purse down on the couch. "He wasn't still a drug rep, was he?"

"No, he was doing really well on his own, making investments with his friend Neil." Abby smiled, with pride. "Dad has a Mercedes, and he bought Victoria a BMW, so she could drive back and forth to visit us. He got me the old Datsun, you saw, but it was all I wanted. She's a rescue car."

Jill didn't get it. "But even if you have the money, are you sure you want to live here, by yourself?"

"I already do. Dad was on the road, sometimes four nights a week."

"Why, if he wasn't a rep anymore?"

"For business." Abby shrugged. "He went lots of places, to New York and other cities. You know how Dad was, he kept his business to himself."

Jill bit her tongue. William kept everything to himself. "So you would be here alone?"

"No, my boyfriend was here. Santos." Abby's face fell. "He helped me a lot with the house, he was older."

Jill had guessed that the boyfriend was older. Santos must have been the raggedy-looking guy on Abby's Facebook page. "How old was he?"

"Thirty."

Jill masked her disapproval, worried at how vulnerable Abby was, especially now. "Honey, I don't know if you're safe, living here alone."

"Sure I am. We have a burglar alarm, and Dad had a gun."

"He did?" Jill blinked, surprised. That would have been a new thing for William. They'd never owned a gun, at least she didn't think they did, but there was so much about William she never really knew. "But you, in this big house, honey? It's too much for you."

"Why does everybody keep telling me I can't do things, even you?" Abby's eyes turned pleading. "You never did that before, Jill. You were the one person, all my life, who told me I could do whatever I set my mind to."

"It's not that I don't think you can, it's that I don't know why you want to."

"Why *wouldn't* I want to find out who killed my Dad?"

Jill let it go, for now. "Okay, now, where did your Dad keep his bills and things?"

"Upstairs, in his office. It's really his man cave. Come this way." Abby turned and led the way to a transparent staircase leading to a light-filled hallway on the second floor, then opened a door. "Here's my bedroom. The other is Victoria's room, but only Pickles sleeps there. He likes it in the daytime."

Jill looked inside Abby's bedroom, speechless, for a moment. It was a replica of the one she'd shared with Megan, traditionally decorated with a blue hook rug, a comforter covered with forget-me-nots, and matching curtains.

"I know, it's crazy but I wanted to make it feel like home, so I wouldn't miss everything so much."

"Did it work?" Jill asked, pained.

"Kinda."

"Good for you." Jill touched her arm, realizing that the divorce had cost Abby her family and her home, neither of which could be replaced by an empty glass column, a veritable house of air.

"Here's Dad's office." Abby walked ahead, and Jill found herself in a stark, masculine office with a dark-patterned carpet. There was a black leather sofa and a side chair with lacquered end tables, and a sleek walnut desk with a black Herman Miller chair. "He paid all the bills in here, and I have to learn about that stuff if I'm going to take over. The file cabinet has lots of the old bills."

"Okay, but I have an easier way." Jill went over to the laptop. "When we were married, we used Quicken, which is a program that pays all the bills. Mind if I check the laptop?"

"Go for it." Abby stood aside, and Jill sat down at the desk and tapped a key, feeling odd about intruding into William's life. The laptop came to life with a vacation photo of a grinning William, Abby, and Victoria, and Jill cringed, looking up at Abby, to see if it upset her.

"You okay, honey? We can do this another time."

"No, I'm fine, go ahead. I already checked his email but I didn't see any hate mail, psycho girlfriends, or anything suspicious." Abby pointed to the side table. "That's where the police found the bottle of whisky. It was Glenfiddich, but there was no glass. If Dad had the killer up here, whoever it was took both glasses when he left."

Jill let it go. She scanned the Programs, found Quicken, and clicked the icon for Household Expenses, which brought a virtual check register onto the screen. "Here we are. This will tell you your fixed expenses each month, and we can make you a budget. Easy-peasy. Where did you say the old bills were, just in case we need them?"

"Here." Abby went to the file cabinet and rolled open the top drawer. "This is all the bills. I went through it, looking for clues, but I didn't find anything."

Jill let that go, too. She crossed to the cabinet and skimmed an array of files that started with AT&T Mobility and ended with Verizon. There was a file labeled Important Documents, and she slid it out and opened it. On top was the deed to the house, which was in William's name. "So the house is in your Dad's name, it will have to go through the estate. Let's check out the other drawers."

"They're empty now. Victoria took it all, for the lawyer." Abby closed the top drawer and opened the second, which was empty. "They used to have bank statements and financial stuff."

"Okay." Jill straightened up. "Okay, why don't we bring the files and the laptop to my house, and you stay with us a few days, while we get you up and running? If you have a bag or a suitcase, we'll pack it and go."

"Great, thanks." Abby brightened, then hesitated. "But don't you want to see Dad's room, where he died? Please?" She gestured at a closed door off the office. "I kept it closed after the police left."

Jill sighed. "Why, Abby?"

"To help me." Abby begged Jill with her eyes. "I need your help, Jill. There's no one else."

"But honey, I'm not an expert. Why don't we hire a private investigator? I'll even pay for it, how's that?"

Abby shook her head. "Why? No stranger will care as much as I do. Jeez, aren't you even curious if he was murdered? You loved him once, didn't you?"

"Of course I did, but—"

"Jill, please." Abby grabbed her arm, urgently. "I just want to understand, that's all. My life turned upside-down all of a sudden, and I didn't see any of it coming. Can't you just take a look in the bedroom and tell me if you see anything suspicious?"

How can you not help her, Mom?

Jill sighed. She always had trouble saying no to the girls.

"*Please,* Jill?"

"All right, but just one look, then we go."

"Thanks." Abby whirled around, and Jill followed her into the bedroom, which was large and modern, with white walls and a navy blue accent wall, a navy oriental rug, and a walnut headboard that matched the nighttable and a long, low bureau. On the bureau was a posed photograph of William and the girls, all of them in matching white shirts with him in the middle, his grin cocky and his eyes flashing darkly under a spray of jet-black bangs.

"Abby, I don't see anything suspicious. Can we go now?"

"Wait, listen." Abby turned, newly animated, her gaze focused. "I know there are no signs of a struggle, nothing out of order or searched, but that's not the way I think it happened."

"What do you think happened?" Jill asked, trying not to sound like she was humoring her.

"I think he'd been in his office with the killer, and they had a drink, then he came in here and . . . died. I found him here, on the left side of the bed, nearest the office door." Abby gestured, dry-eyed. "I didn't see any marks on him, like he was hit or anything."

"I understand." Jill felt her chest tighten, looking at the bed. The navy sheets were in disarray, and there was a large stain on the left. It was urine, and she shuddered.

"Here's why I think it. He had on his jeans and his white dress shirt, like he'd been out or met someone. You remember how he used to change his pants, but not his shirt?"

"Yes." Jill remembered, but she didn't want to. She just felt sad that Abby sounded so convinced.

"If he was going to stay home, he would have had on a T-shirt or something more relaxed. But he had on a white shirt, which tells me he had a meeting." Abby walked over to the nighttable, which held two pens, a car magazine, and an empty phone charger. "Also, there were three bottles of pills here and his cell phone.

The police took them, but I know they weren't his pills. Look." Abby dug in her dress pocket, pulled out a yellow Post-it, and handed it to her. "I wrote down the doctor's name and number. He's not our doctor, and he's not returning my calls."

Jill took the Post-it and read it:

Dad's meds:

Vicodin, 5 mg, once a day

Xanax, 10 mg, once a day

Temezepam, 10 mg, once a day

Dr. Raj Patel # 9483636

(215) 555-2923

All were filled same day 4/12

Broad Street Pharmacy, 1200 N. Broad Street

(215) 555-9373

Jill thought a minute. "These could have been prescribed by a psychiatrist, and if your Dad was seeing one, he might not have wanted you to know."

Abby scoffed. "Please, he wouldn't've cared. I tried to Google the doctor, but you know how many Dr. Raj Patels there are? Also, I went to the drugstore and showed the pharmacists a picture of Dad, but they hadn't seen him before, and they were all women." Abby lifted an eyebrow. "Now, I ask you. What woman would forget Dad, only a week later?"

"It's possible, Abby." Jill didn't press the point. She was trying to forget him, years later, but not in a good way. She handed the paper back to Abby. "Here."

"Keep it. I have a copy."

Jill stuck it in her purse, which was still on her shoulder. "You said he had a gun. Where is it?"

"Right here." Abby slid open the drawer on the nighttable, revealing a black revolver. "It's loaded."

Jill didn't get it. "Honey, if someone was trying to kill him, why didn't he use the gun to protect himself?"

"What if they drugged him? What if he didn't know it was happening, and by the time he did, he couldn't do anything to help himself?"

"He could have pressed the alarm button." Jill spotted a burglar alarm panel on the wall, near the bed. She knew it would be there because they'd had one there at their old house, at William's insistence.

"Not if he was drugged."

"But the room is in perfect order. Didn't he fight back, at all? Your Dad was a big, physical guy."

"What if he did, and the killer put it back together, afterwards? Without fingerprints, how would you know?" Abby's tone grew stronger, more confident. "The police refused to call the mobile crime unit because they said there was no sign of a murder, so I'll investigate it myself, whether you help me or not. No matter what it takes, or how long. I'll do it."

"Why would anybody kill him?" Jill asked, trying to reason with her. "There's no sign of a robbery. Look." She walked to the bureau, where a lacquered box was open and in full view, with an array of watches on a velveteen stalk. Then she remembered that William always kept cash in his sock drawer, so she opened the top drawer, and under his balled-up socks nestled a stack of wrinkled twenties. "This money isn't hard to find, all anybody would have to do is open the top drawer. He wasn't robbed, even after the fact. Where was his wallet?"

"In his back pocket. The police took that, too." Abby frowned, frustrated. "Maybe it wasn't about money. Maybe it was personal."

"Do you know of anybody who had it in for him?"

"No. Neil called him The Mayor. Everybody loved Dad, he had tons of friends."

Jill let it go. She hadn't seen "tons of friends" at the memorial service, and there hadn't been a tear in sight. "Who's Neil?"

"Neil Straub, his business partner."

"Oh, right. Did he get along with your Dad?"

"Totally. Neil would never do anything to Dad."

"Where does he live?"

"New York, but he travels with Dad a lot."

"Okay, now, can we go?" Jill had indulged this long enough, and Abby was getting riled up, with all the encouragement.

"Wait, one last thing." Abby went to the bathroom and opened the mirrored medicine chest. "Here's Dad's Crestor. This is where he keeps his meds, not on the nighttable. Also, this prescription was filled at our CVS. Dad chats up the pharmacists, and they all love him. Proves my point." Abby turned at the faint sound of a hip-hop ringtone. "Wait, that's my phone, downstairs. I should get that." She headed out the bathroom door, then the bedroom. "I'll be right back."

"I'll come with you."

"No, wait, stay." Abby rushed out of the room, leaving Jill lingering unhappily by William's bed. She and William used to have a brass bed, and she flashed on a Sunday afternoon long ago, when they were driving in the car, dropping off the last daughter at her friend's. It was early on in their marriage, still happy times, and as soon as the car door closed, they both looked at each other across the console and realized, in the same moment, that they would have the house to themselves, like a sort of suburban miracle.

Are you thinking what I'm thinking? William had asked her, with a grin.

Totally. Food-shopping can wait.

William had hit the gas, and they raced home, flew from the car, then ran inside, not stopping to let Beef out, and William chased her upstairs to their brass bed, shouting, *Let's make some noise!*

"Oh, well." Abby was entering the bedroom, teary again, and the expression on her face brought Jill back to earth. She went over and gave Abby a warm hug.

"What's the matter, honey?"

"That was Victoria on the phone. I can't go to your house, tonight." Abby sniffled in Jill's arms. "She says I'm taking sides, or switching to the wrong side, or whatever."

"Aw, there's no sides, there never was, not to me." Jill let her go, and Abby wiped her eye.

"I know, but still, I don't want to upset her anymore. It's a hard time for her, too, and she's right, I'm not being very considerate."

"I understand." Jill used to mitigate Victoria's tendency to boss her little sister, but those days were gone. "Don't worry about it, honey. Whatever you're comfortable with, I'll do."

"I'll stay here tonight, but please, take the laptop and the other stuff. I do want to try and live here, make a go of it, no matter what Victoria says."

"Okay." Jill hated leaving Abby alone, but there was no choice. "What's in your refrigerator, sweetie?"

"Bottled water." Abby managed a smile. "And half and half, for Pickles."

"How about I go to the store for you, pick up some groceries, and drop them off? Then you can at least make yourself a bowl of cereal in the morning. You still like Special K? With strawberries?"

"You remembered." Abby smiled, more broadly. "You're such a *mom*."

An hour later, Jill was back in the car in the rain, having dropped off groceries for Abby and picked some up for herself. The traffic on the expressway heading out of the city was congested, and she inched along, using the time to return phone calls and emails from her patients. Padma hadn't called her about Rahul, and Jill hoped he was improving, but the bloodwork would be definitive.

She stewed behind the wheel, her thoughts all over the map. So much had happened, she couldn't absorb it quickly enough.

What woman would forget Dad?

Jill couldn't shake the question, and it wasn't the kind of thing that would get the attention of the police, even if they had followed up. You had to know William to know it was fishy. She fed the car some gas, then braked again in traffic, and the reflective letters of a sign on the overpass caught her headlights. BROAD STREET, ½ MILE.

She remembered that William had filled his scripts for the drugs at a pharmacy on Broad Street, and she wondered if she should stop in and ask. She was curious about the scripts, and Broad Street was on the way home.

You're a doctor, and Sherlock Holmes was a doctor.

She thought of the lesson she'd taught Abby, that all deductive reasoning was the same, a process designed to find the truth. When Jill ran a differential for a patient, she would systematically cross off diagnoses that weren't supported by the data and keep those that were, testing as she went along, until she understood what was really going on. That was the reason she'd ordered the blood test for Rahul; if his results came back normal, as she expected, she'd have ruled out the more serious diagnoses.

Jill thought about it in traffic. If she could go to the pharmacy and rule out anything being wrong with the scripts, she could put to bed Abby's murder theory. So she reached for her purse and felt around for the yellow Post-it.

Chapter Thirteen

Jill cruised down Broad Street, going north in the driving rain. The boulevard bisected the city, and this stretch was lined with check-cashing agencies, empty storefronts, and used-car lots. Streetlights were broken, leaving entire blocks in darkness, and Jill tried to understand why William would have come here to fill the scripts. She saw the BROAD STREET PHARMACY sign ahead and scanned in the darkness for a parking space. One opened up suddenly, and she braked to pull into it, but when she checked her rearview mirror, something strange caught her eye.

Mom, look in your mirror. There's a padiddle behind us, one car back.

She blinked. There was a padiddle, two cars behind her. To double-check, she squinted at her outside mirror, and she could see the padiddle clearly, though raindrops dotted the mirror. It was two cars back, and it was also a black SUV, with the left light out and the same boxy grille, which was quite coincidental.

Jill's mouth went dry. She hit the gas, drove past the drugstore, and turned right off Broad Street. The sidestreet was skinny and even darker, lined with rundown brick rowhomes and plenty of parking spaces. She pulled over, shut off the engine, and slid down in the driver's seat to see if the SUV would follow her.

Her heart started to pound, and she felt scared and silly, both at once. Her eyes were glued to the outside mirror. A few minutes later, the padiddle appeared, driving fast. She ducked deep into her seat, let it pass, and popped up again. She couldn't see the driver, but she caught the beginning of its license plate, and the first letter was a T.

Jill told herself to calm down, trying not to jump to conclusions. There would be no reason for anybody to be following her, and it would be dumb to follow anybody in a padiddle. Then she thought again. The driver might not know he had a headlight out, and maybe he'd started following Abby, then more recently started following her.

Jill started up the car, drove out of the space, took the next right, and backtracked three blocks, heading for the drugstore. She parked, chirped the car locked, grabbed her purse, and checked around her before she got out, but the SUV wasn't anywhere in sight. She climbed out and hurried through the rain into the drugstore, more than a little spooked.

She hustled inside the bright-lit store, which was cold, empty, and dingy, with a tile floor that felt gritty under her pumps. She spotted herself on a security monitor, then hustled to the back where the pharmacy would be and got in line at the counter behind a young blonde mother, with a crying baby wrapped in a thin receiving blanket. There wasn't a pharmacist on duty, just a young male clerk with gelled hair, whose pallor wasn't helped by the fluorescent lights overhead.

"Is this a drop off?" the clerk asked the young mother, who was jiggling the baby while he cried.

"Can I see the pharmacist?"

"No, she's gone for the night."

"Then can you help me?" The woman held the baby close, but the crying didn't stop. "My little boy's teething, and my aunt said to rub brandy on his gums, but it doesn't help."

"You gotta go to the doctor. I'm not a doctor."

"I don't have one. I went to the ER, but it was too crowded. Can you just answer a question for me?"

"No, I just work here, sorry."

Jill felt torn, knowing she wasn't supposed to step in. The baby wasn't her patient, and the Good Samaritan didn't apply. But she wasn't about to let a mother and child suffer, even if the system would. "Miss, maybe I can help you. I'm a pediatrician."

"You, a doctor?" The young woman's eyes lit up, an exhausted blue, and she had a neck tattoo with her name written in curlicued script. "He kept me up all night with his crying, and I can't calm him down, no matter what."

"Let me see his hand a second." Jill checked his tiny hand, and he had a telltale rash. She didn't even have to take the baby, because when he cried, he opened his mouth wide enough for her to see a blister on his tongue. "How did he sleep and eat, today?"

"Not much."

"And he has a fever, I bet."

"Last night it was 101, and he's still warm, for sure."

"Is he urinating, wetting his diapers?"

"Sure, all the time. I keep him changed, though. Nice and fresh, all the time."

"Good for you, and it's good that he's not dehydrated. He's not teething, he has coxackie virus."

"Cock-a-what?" The mother frowned, understandably.

"It's a virus that babies get in their mouth, and it's also called hand, foot, and mouth disease. It'll go away in ten days, but don't give him any more brandy. Popsicles are great to give him fluids, and he'll feel comfier on Tylenol. How old is he, eight months or so?"

"Yes, eight months."

"How much does he weigh?" Jill couldn't tell, he was so bundled up

"Twenty pounds."

"Okay, then give him infant's Tylenol. Use the dropper inside, and give him one full dropper."

"I ran out," the young mother answered, averting her eyes.

"Let me treat you to a bottle, okay?" Jill slipped her hand in her purse, pulled out her wallet, then handed a ten to the clerk. "This is for her Tylenol."

"Okay." The clerk pointed left. "It's right there, top shelf."

"Thank you." The young mother smiled gratefully, at Jill. "Thank you so much, ma'am."

"You're welcome. He'll be fine. Hang in with him."

"Thanks again." The mother hugged the baby and hurried down the aisle.

Jill faced the clerk. "Now, I need to see the waiver book."

The clerk smiled slyly. "You a real doctor, lady?"

"Yes, now can I see the book?" Jill put down another twenty, and the clerk scooped it off the counter, then slid over the red plastic binder.

"You got it."

"Thanks." Jill flipped the pages, slowing when she got to the fifteenth, then scanned the printed names next to each customer, with their signatures. None were William, so she flipped one more page, and his name leapt out at her. **William Skyler.** Three script stickers were pasted in a row beneath the label, all filled at 12:03 A.M. The signature was so messy she couldn't even tell if it was forged. William's handwriting was more slanted, but he could be sloppy, too, in a rush.

"Okay?" the clerk asked.

"You have a surveillance camera back here, don't you? Most pharmacies do, and you have one at the front of the store. I saw it when I came in."

"Yes, what about it?"

"I need to see the tape. For fifty bucks."

"Sweet! Meet me in aisle eleven, near the soda. The office door is right here."

"Thanks." Jill turned right, headed back toward aisle eleven, and waited by the office door. Five minutes later, Jill had paid the clerk his fifty dollars and was standing with him in a cramped, filthy office stuffed with boxes. Video equipment sat stacked on an unpainted plywood shelf, under a small security monitor. The clerk aimed a remote control at the equipment, and the screen showed people zipping around in reverse. Their faces were small, but visible, and Jill was hoping that William had filled the scripts, so she could tell Abby and end this thing.

"Keep going?" the clerk asked, turning to her.

"Yes, all the way back to the twelfth."

"You're lucky, Doc. It only goes back a week, then it erases."

Jill watched the people walking backward, at speed. The numbers of a digital clock were spinning on the screen, too fast to read. The pace of the surveillance film slowed, and the clock wound back from 2:00 A.M. to 1:00 A.M. The onscreen clerk was an attractive woman. Jill asked, "Is the clerk a pharmacist?"

"No, that's Trisha. We don't have a pharmacist on that late at night. We stay open for pickups only. The CVS down the block is twenty-four-hour, but we're not. Okay, I'll stop the tape now." The clerk pressed a button on the remote. "Is that the dude?"

The screen froze, and Jill squinted at the grainy image, unsure if it was William. His face was obscured by aviator sunglasses, and a black ballcap hid his hair and forehead. He had on a nondescript windbreaker, and he was tall and broad-shouldered, like William and five million other men. Jill gestured at the screen. "I can't tell, but how can you dispense narcotics to someone you can't see? It looks like an obvious disguise."

"You don't know the wack jobs we get in here, Doc. They don't look half as good as him."

"Can you play the film slowly back and forth, one more time?"

"Sure." The clerk did, and the man in the black ballcap went to and from the counter, in slow motion. He didn't seem to talk to the clerk more than was necessary, and he kept his head down the entire time. It wasn't the way William behaved, and it was no wonder that Trisha hadn't remembered him when Abby had asked.

Jill had another thought. If William had wanted these drugs, he could have gotten them as samples, because he knew reps at all the drug companies. So maybe the man in the ballcap wasn't William at all. Maybe he drove a black SUV, license plate T something, and didn't know his headlight had burned out. She eyed the screen, thinking of yet a third possibility. That the man really was William, but for some reason, he was disguising himself.

"Uh-oh." The clerk pointed at the small window in the door. "Customer's out there. I gotta go."

"One more sec." Jill reached in her purse, took out her Black-Berry, and snapped a picture of the monitor's screen. "Thanks."

"No problem." The clerk grinned. "Come back anytime."

Chapter Fourteen

Jill closed the front door, dropped her keys in the bowl, and lugged two food bags inside. Beef ran barking to greet her, sniffing the bags, but the house was otherwise quiet. Sam's maroon Lexus was in the driveway, so she knew he was home.

"Babe?" she called out, and Sam came in barefoot from the family room, rubbing his eyes with a tired smile. He looked comfy in his T-shirt and baggy jeans, and he tucked his book under his arm as he took the bags from her and kissed her lightly on the lips.

"How are you, honey?"

"Good."

"How's Abby?"

"Fine." Jill would have to figure out when to tell him about the pharmacy. "How about you?"

"Catching up on my reading. Lee's well and says hello, and I washed the comforter, so Megan's back in business." Sam headed into the kitchen with the bags, and Jill fell into step beside him, dropping her handbag on the chair.

"Thanks. Was it gross?"

"Nah. Did you know that Laundromats have video games these days? I watched a ten-year-old save the planet." Sam set the bags on the island. "Before I forget, Katie called you. She said she left a message on your phone, too."

"Oh, thanks." Jill hadn't heard her phone ring. Katie Feehan was her best friend, and she lived nearby, with her husband Paul and three boys. "Did she say it was important?"

"She needs your help with a recipe. Something for the kids."

"Uh-oh." Jill smiled. Katie was a better friend than a cook.

"Are there more bags in the car?"

"No, just a box, with a laptop and some papers."

"Whose laptop and papers?"

"William's. I'm going to help Abby do a household budget. She's going to live on her own."

Sam shrugged. "Good for her, but with what money?"

"More than we have. It looks like William finally hit the jackpot." Jill rummaged in the shopping bags, found the ice cream, and put it in the freezer. "And she agreed to see a therapist."

"Great." Sam broke into a relieved smile. "I'll call Sandy and we'll make that happen. Where's Megan?"

"Courtney's, doing her English project." Jill unpacked the bagged vegetables and stowed them in the fridge. "I think she's milking it, don't you?"

"I don't blame her if she needs some time with Courtney. She can't be delighted with Abby after last night."

"Because of the comforter? It wasn't Abby's fault. She got sick."

"Not only that, but the way she kind of barged in, and all of a sudden, she's taking up your time. Like tonight."

Jill looked at him, surprised. "That's harsh, don't you think? I was alone, so I went over. I wanted her to come and stay a few days, but Victoria bullied her out of it."

"What do you mean, a few days?"

"I mean hang here for a little, so I could help her with the budget, and she could spend time with Megan."

"She works, though."

"She quit."

Sam frowned. "I don't know if her coming here is a good idea. Do you?"

"Sure, why not?"

"Is it a *fait accompli*?" Sam's eyes flared briefly behind his glasses. "Do I have a say? Does Megan?"

Jill didn't get it. "Megan was really close to Abby and she'd be happy to have Abby stay."

"I'm not sure you're right about that."

"I know I am. Megan told me she thinks of Abby as family."

"Megan may not understand the implications of that for the future, and anyway, do I count? Abby's not in *my* family. I don't know her. Steven never even met her."

Jill felt a tug at her heart. She couldn't say he was wrong, and she couldn't agree with him, either. "Abby's a great kid, Sam. Give her a chance."

"May I be honest, or are you going to bite my head off?"

"Be honest," Jill answered, meaning it. She hadn't seen this coming.

"You're thinking of the Abby you raised, not the Abby I met. The Abby I met drove drunk, was rude, and took over Megan's room. Is that the same Abby you remember?"

Jill felt stung, for Abby. "You can't judge someone on the worst day of their life. Her father just died."

"Isn't it likelier that she's changed? She's grown up without you, or any mother, in her life, and it hasn't done her any good."

Jill felt a wave of guilt. "That's not her fault, and I really think you're being harsh. You talked to her for fifteen minutes."

"I can tell. You can't. You're not objective. You love her."

"So what are you saying?" Jill asked, puzzled. "You don't want her here this week?"

"I think you should slow this relationship down, between you and Abby. Even between Megan and Abby. You're responding to a need, automatically, which is what you do so well. It's as if Abby's an acute wound and you're rushing to stop the bleeding." Sam kept his tone reasonable, his gaze steady. "It's what makes you a great mother, and physician, too. But you have competing needs here, and you have to weigh them carefully."

Jill couldn't agree. "You're making too much of it. How does it hurt Megan if Abby spends time here?"

"Megan's gotten used to living without her, and it took a long time. I know, I remember that time. Do you?"

"Yes." Jill nodded. Megan had gotten a little lost after the divorce, weepier and more sensitive than usual, with the familial rug pulled out from under her. "But it wasn't only about Abby."

"Either way, you're inviting Abby back into Megan's life, but it won't be the same as before. Abby isn't the same girl, and neither is Megan. Megan's grown up a lot, and these girls won't fit so well together." Sam leaned on the gleaming counter, which reflected him in a murky outline. "In fact, if you ask me, Megan's gotten stronger, and Abby's only gotten weaker."

"I don't get it." Jill couldn't deny a growing irritation, like having something in her shoe. "Abby needs a hand now, so can't we give it to her? She's so vulnerable, and anything can happen. I'm scared for her, Sam. Can't we just see her through this patch?"

Sam blinked. "How long is the patch?"

"I don't know."

"Then how do you know it's a patch?" Sam raked his hand through his hair. "I don't know where this road ends, or if it ends. This is a kid who'll need help for the foreseeable future. She'll need therapy, love, a family, and a home. You name it, she needs it, she's a *bolus* of need." Sam cocked his head, blinking thoughtfully behind his glasses. "How will you cut her off, babe? When? It'll only get harder, you know. You're taking on a problem you don't own, and where will we be, down the line? Megan goes off to college, and we're at home with Abby? I don't want the problems of a problem child, at this point in my life."

Jill recoiled. "Slow down. We're not there yet."

"But we have to think about it, now. You know me, I'm a researcher. I know that what I do now will pay off years from now. In fact, it won't pay off *until* years from now. Everything's long-term, Jill. *Life* is long-term."

Jill had heard him say this before, to Megan. "So what's your point?" she asked, impatient.

"My point is, let's not start this process without thinking. You have a triage mentality. You see a problem, you fix it. You go. You act."

"It's not because I'm a clinician, it's because I'm a mother. That's what all mothers do, Sam. We're practical."

"But whose mother are you? Don't slip so easily into the role of being that kid's mother."

"I used to be."

"But you're not, anymore."

"Really?" Jill's chest tightened. "What's a mother, or a step-mother? What's a family? Isn't it forever? The love doesn't stop when the legal relationship does."

"No, but the obligation does. The responsibility does."

Jill tried a different tack. "Okay, think about it this way. Your son Steven is going to be my stepson, after we get married. I love him, and he's a great young man. Let's imagine that, God forbid, something happens to you, and I remarry, and your son Steven gets into trouble. Medical, legal, whatever. Do I turn my back on him because my new husband says so?"

"Steven's thirty years old, busy as hell, down in Texas. He doesn't need us anymore, he barely even visits."

"But he could need us, or me."

"Then you can't be there for him, not forever and ever."

"Love isn't finite, Sam."

"No, but time is. Money is. Resources are. Energy is."

"I know, but is that the world you want to live in?" Jill thought he was missing the point. "Wouldn't you want me to take care of Steven?"

"No, I still come down the same way." Sam's lips flattened to a firm line. "I'd understand it if your husband felt the way I do, which is that I didn't sign on for this. I love you and I love Megan, but I don't love your troubled ex-stepdaughter, and I don't want another kid. I'm getting out of the kid business."

Jill felt her heart sink, listening to him and seeing his adamancy.

She could tell the way it was going, and it wasn't good. If she wanted her family with Abby in it, then she'd have to fight for it. And the person she'd have to fight was Sam.

"I'm older than you, and I see the light at the end of the tunnel. Steven's gone, and Megan's on her way. She'll be in college before you know it." Sam leaned over, urgently. "I'm looking forward to you and me, being alone together. No more blow dryers or swim meets."

"I think exactly the opposite." Jill felt heartsick. "I'll be sad when Megan leaves. I'm sad that she's already growing up, so fast. I never want to be out of the kid business."

"We'll be fine, you'll see. You'll love it."

"You never talked this way before," Jill said, hurt.

"I never had to."

"Are you unhappy?"

"No, I'm happy, and I'm trying to stay that way. We were fine before Abby entered the picture, just last night. We were great." Sam smiled and tried to touch her arm, but Jill found herself backing away, wishing she had a sounding board.

"You know what, I'm not that tired, so maybe I'll drop by Katie's and see if she still needs me."

"Really, babe?" Sam looked disappointed, puckering his lower lip.

"Well, she is cooking."

"Fair enough." Sam managed a smile. "She could burn down the neighborhood."

"Right." Jill picked up her handbag, gave Sam a dry kiss on the cheek, and left the kitchen. "I should be back in an hour, or so."

"Okay, drive safe," Sam called after her.

"Love you." Jill called back, and it wasn't until she reached the front door that she realized she hadn't told Sam about the pharmacy or the padiddle.

But he wasn't exactly a willing ear.

Chapter Fifteen

"Sorry I missed your call." Jill followed Katie into her kitchen, which was in disarray. Flour dusted the butcherblock counter, and grated potatoes made a lopsided snowdrift on a plate, next to a lineup of cracked eggshells, chopped onion, and a Pyrex bowl of batter. The air smelled like something good was cooking. "Yum. What's going on here?"

"Paul took the boys out to dinner, then the bookstore." Katie hurried back to the stove, her blonde ponytail swinging. Like Jill, she had on a light cotton sweater, capris, and clogs, the uniform of suburban moms. Katie picked up the spatula. "I was having an I'm-gonna-kill-my-kid moment."

"Why?" Jill asked, though she knew Katie was kidding. They'd been best friends since Penn State, and Katie had gone on to become a teacher, then an at-home mother of three sons, all under twelve years old. She always said humor and a cattle prod were her only weapons.

"Monday is International Day at school, and Robbie tells me this an hour ago, when we're gone all day tomorrow." Katie rolled her large, cornflower blue eyes. She was wholesomely pretty, with no makeup, an easy smile, and a turned-up nose under a sprinkling of soft freckles. "We're moving my mother-in-law to a retirement village. With her, it'll take a village."

"Yikes." Jill set down her purse and came over to the stove. The big Viking oven gave off a homey warmth, and she started to relax, after the talk with Sam. She felt lucky to have a friend like Katie and she could only imagine how Katie would react when she found out about William's death.

"You want soda or coffee? Or a margarita? Feel free."

"No, thanks. So what are you making? It smells great."

"Irish potato pancakes."

"Ambitious."

"*Insane.*" Katie flipped the pancake. "He has to bring in a typical food that represents his family, and you have to *make* it, so no Entenmann's."

"Uh-oh."

"Am I screwed or what? Can I just say that not all moms can cook? And what kind of time do they think we have? Should I thatch the roof next? Jeez! You know, the joke is, I assigned all this crap when I taught, too. Payback's a *bitch.*"

Jill smiled. "How can I help?"

"Just keep me company. It's good to see you. I called you to get an old family recipe of yours, for anything, but then I found this old family recipe on the Internet."

"How many do you have to make?"

"Too damn many." Katie flipped the third pancake. "There are twenty-three kids in the class, and I figure some kids will eat two, so that's thirty-three. Plus I have to suck up to the teacher, the aides, and the secretaries in the office, so that makes fifty. I bribe everybody. Elementary school is a banana republic, without the limos."

Jill smiled. "It's nice to include the office. I always did. Nobody makes them anything. They'll never forget it."

"I know. Great minds, right?"

"Here, let me help."

"Okay." Katie waved the spatula at the base cabinet. "Get another pan going. We'll get it done twice as fast."

"On it." Jill went into the cabinet, got a heavy skillet, and set it on the stovetop, then reached for the butter, glancing over. "You need to let them cook longer."

"No, I don't. This is for eight-year-olds. They eat crayons."

"You'll give them salmonella."

"You get what you pay for." Katie flipped another pancake. "I'm so glad you came over. What's shakin'?"

"Brace yourself. I have big news." Jill held the pan's handle, turned on the heat, and waited for the butter to melt, a spreading pool of gold. "You're not going to believe this, but William's dead."

"*What?*" Katie gasped. She looked over, her eyes wide, in disbelief. "William, your *ex-husband*? Are you *kidding*?"

"No, it's true."

"Hallelujah!" Katie broke into an incredulous smile. "Was it painful? Please tell me it was painful."

Jill felt torn. "I admit, I'm not crying over the man, but—"

"Look, a jig! Kiss me, I'm Irish. Happy International Day!" Katie put down the spatula and did a dance, shaking her butt. "Lordy be, what goes around really does come around. Hey, can we go dance on his grave?"

"He was cremated."

"He did that for spite." Katie made a face, scrunching up her nose.

"Come on, stop. Be nice. Abby came over with the news last night, and she thinks he might have been murdered."

"Abby was at your house?" Katie asked, suddenly growing serious. "Aw, I love that girl. How was it to see her again? How is she? Tell me everything."

"I will, but your pancake's burning." Jill gestured with the ladle, then poured some batter into the pan. "I feel terrible for the girls."

"Oh, well, okay, that *is* sad, only because they're hurting." Katie's face fell, and she picked up the spatula. "But they're better off without him, they just don't know it. He didn't really care about them. Narcissist, crook, thief, liar, sleaze, cheater."

"Cheating was unproven." Jill reached over and flipped one of Katie's pancakes. "Now, don't speak ill."

"You can't talk about William Skyler *without* speaking ill." Katie shook her head, disgusted. "I'm sorry, Jill, but he almost ruined you, and he kept those girls from you, too, after the divorce. He punished you, and he punished them, too. He used them like pawns to hurt you, and he straight-up *abandoned* Megan. I'll *never* forgive him for that, ever."

Jill tasted bitterness on her tongue. "Well, he's gone now. You want to hear what happened or not?"

"Yes, please," Katie answered, calming down, and while they cooked, Jill told her the whole story, from Abby's visit to the surveillance film at the pharmacy. Katie asked questions, Jill elaborated, and sixty-two pancakes later, the story was finished.

"You want to see the photo from the drugstore?" Jill went to her purse, slid out her BlackBerry, thumbed her way to the photo, and showed it to Katie. "Think it's him?"

"I can't see it, it's too small. Email it to me." Katie went over to her laptop on the counter near the chopped onions, and Jill emailed her the photo. They huddled around the computer while Katie opened the email, saved the photo, and enlarged it. Katie shook her head. "It could be William, but I can't tell."

"Me, neither. He could be disguising himself."

"Why would he do that?"

"I don't know." Jill dug in her purse. "Hold on, let me check something else on the web."

"What?"

"The prescribing doctor." Jill found the paper with Abby's notes, logged onto the Internet, Googled *licensing authority in Pennsylvania,* and got the website. "I have his license number, so I should be able to find his address."

"How?"

"Anybody can check the status of a doctor's license, online."

"I didn't know that."

"Most people don't. Luckily, Abby didn't." Jill found the Pennsylvania Department of State website, typed in Medicine, then supplied the doctor's name and license number from Abby's paper. She had to add a location, so she plugged in Philadelphia, then hit Search. The screen switched to a single line of text:

Dr. Raj Patel, Lic. No. 9483636, DEA # 393484, DECEASED, 3/9/09

Jill felt her heart sink. "The prescribing doctor is dead, so Abby's right about one thing. This script is a fraud."

"Whoa."

"And it's not even recent, so it's not like the doc wrote the script, then died."

"Are you sure it's the same Dr. Patel?"

"Yes, it has to be. Only one doc is given that license or DEA number. They're unique." Jill shook her head. It meant that she couldn't put the matter to bed, not yet. "If it's William, he's up to his old tricks, using stolen prescription pads. But I don't know why he'd fill them himself, if it wasn't his meds."

"Wonder where he got Dr. Patel's pads?"

"He could have called on the practice in the old days, or got them from the office trash." Jill opened the enlarged photo of the man in the black ballcap, eyeing it in confusion. "None of this makes sense. William knew enough about drugs to know not to mix them with alcohol."

"Is there life insurance?"

"Yes, for a million bucks. The girls benefit."

"We're worth more dead than alive, too."

Jill blinked, thinking. "That's funny. What if he took the pills intentionally? What if it really was suicide, but insurance companies don't always pay off for suicides. He wanted the policy to pay off, so he made it look like an accidental death? What if he staged the whole thing?"

"Why would he do that?" Katie's eyes narrowed, sharply blue. "He had money, so he didn't need it from the insurance company. Unless he doesn't really have the money, and it's all a sham."

"True, but I can't find that out. Victoria and the lawyer took his financial info, but some of it should be in Quicken."

"Definitely, if he pays his bills online."

"He didn't, at least when we were married. He said he didn't trust it."

"The pot calling the kettle." Katie snorted. "I don't see him killing himself for them. It would be a supremely unselfish act."

Both women fell silent a minute, thinking, and Jill picked at the pile of rejected potato pancakes. "I wonder if I should call the cops. Tell them about Patel and the faked script. They can check out the surveillance video."

"No reason not to call, but why would they care? It's not evidence that he was murdered, and they don't care if he committed suicide."

"The insurance company does." Jill thought of the implications. "But if it's suicide, and I start raising questions, I could do the kids out of their benefits."

"Right." Katie looked over, her brow wrinkling with new concern. "Can I ask you a question? Why do you care?"

Jill smiled, but Katie wasn't kidding this time.

"Who cares why or how William died?"

Jill answered, "I told you, Abby thinks it was murder."

"I'm asking why *you* care."

"I don't care, I'm just exploring it."

"It sure looks like you care. You're running around to drugstores and researching licenses online."

Jill realized she was right. She valued so many things about Katie, and her honesty, above all. "Okay, good point. I care because of Abby. She believes it was murder and she's going to try to figure out who did it. She reached out to me, after so long." Jill knew it now, she felt it inside. "I care because Abby does, and I can help her. She needs to get her life back on track, and she won't do that as long as her father's death is a question mark."

Katie shrugged. "Okay."

Jill smiled. "That easy?"

"It was such a good speech."

"So glad we had this little talk. Do you think I'm wrong to help Abby?"

"I don't judge you, honey. I understand why you'd want to help, and why you feel you have to."

"Sam doesn't."

"He didn't know her, and he's not a mother."

"He's a father."

"It's not the same. Sorry to be politically incorrect, but it's true." Katie ate a piece of blackened pancake. "Paul is a great father, but he got to take the kids out while I stayed behind, and I guarantee, he'll read the computer magazines while they pick out their books. He won't sit with them, helping them pick one like I would, and he won't worry if they get out of his sight. Men don't worry like we do, but we know, things go wrong."

"True." Jill saw it in her practice, when a child's eye got injured by a paintball gun, or an arm sliced with a fishing knife. She knew things went wrong, and some made wounds you couldn't suture.

"My real worry is my godchild. Megan." Katie's features softened. "You're talking about Abby's loss, but Megan lost a father, too, and William's death comes at a bad time for her, with you about to get married. And now Abby's back in the picture. Even if Megan's happy about it, it's a change. Megan's got a lot going on, for a kid."

"You're right." Jill felt a guilty pang. "It's like the King is dead, long live the King."

"Exactly."

"I guess I haven't been paying enough attention to Megan, with Abby so needy."

"It's understandable. Like my mother says, you give to the kid who needs it the most."

"What if they all need it the most?"

"Margarita time."

Jill smiled. "Sam wants to get out of the kid business."

Kate scoffed. "Gimme a break. Moms never get out of the kid business. Last time I checked, motherhood had no expiration date."

Jill laughed. "How'd you get so smart?"

Katie smiled. "Hanging around you, except for the padiddle part. First off, can I just say, I hate all car games?"

"Do you think the black SUV is following me? Or Abby?"

"No, that's totally paranoid. Don't worry about it."

"But what if the driver is the man in the black ballcap?"

"The man in the ballcap had the worst disguise ever, and anyone who would follow you in a padiddle is the worst stalker ever." Katie snorted. "Come to think of it, maybe it is the same guy, but he sucks."

"If he killed William, he doesn't."

"Tell me about it." Katie raised an eyebrow. "If he killed William, he deserves a medal."

Chapter Sixteen

Jill pulled into her driveway and cut the ignition in the dark. She hadn't seen any padiddle on the way home, and she was starting to think Katie was right about her being paranoid. She got out of the car, breathing in the cool night air, damp from all the rain. She closed the door behind her, looking down at the end of the street where she'd seen the black SUV.

What SUV? I parked around the corner.

Jill thought a minute. She had first seen the SUV in front of the Bakers' house, but they didn't own an SUV, so on impulse, she walked down the street to the Bakers'. The lights were on inside the house, a Dutch colonial, and a flickering TV shone through the curtains in their living room, so she walked to the front door and knocked. It was answered in a minute by Janet Baker, an older woman with a round, sweet face.

"Hello, Janet," Jill said. "Sorry to bother you."

"It's okay." Janet smiled, pleasantly. "What brings you here?"

"Last night, during the rainstorm, did you have a visitor who drives a black SUV? I saw one pull away from the front of your house."

Janet frowned, shaking her head. "Why, no. We were home alone. Just us."

"Do you know if the DiLorios did, or the Jacksons?"

"I have no idea."

"Thanks. Sorry to keep you. Goodnight." Jill backed off the steps, wondering, then put it out of her mind. It had to be nothing. She walked back down the street to her car, retrieved the box with William's files and laptop, then closed the door and went into the house, juggling her house keys, purse, and the box to open the door, which was when her cell phone started ringing, with Megan's ringtone.

"Arg." Jill clambered into the house to the sound of Lady Gaga, plunked the box on the console table, and slid her phone from her purse, pressing ANSWER. "Honey, aren't you home?"

"No, I'm at Courtney's. Can I sleep over?"

"Again?" Jill sat down in a ladderback chair, and Beef came over, wagging his tail and sniffing the box, which had a paper plate of pancakes on top, covered with tin foil.

"I know, but we're working on our English project, and we're not finished yet."

"What is this project, anyway?" Jill could hear the sound of the TV, playing in the family room.

"We're studying *Romeo and Juliet,* and we have to memorize a scene and do it for the class, so we have to practice together. I'm Juliet."

"How much longer will you take to finish?"

"A while, Mom," Megan answered, with theatrical impatience, and Jill let it go, trying to take it easy on her.

"You can come home after you finish it. I'll pick you up, whenever."

"Why can't I just stay here? Her parents are home."

"But I was hoping to see you tonight. I know it's been a tough weekend for you, and I'm worried about you."

"I'm fine, Mom." Megan sighed, and in the background, Courtney was saying something.

"I have fresh potato pancakes," Jill offered, though the days of food bribes had gone. Pizza bagels used to be her trump card. "Wait, don't you have a meet tomorrow?"

"Yes, but I'll sleep, I promise."

"Okay, you can stay, but don't make it a habit."

"Thanks. Courtney's mom will take me to the meet, if you can bring my bag. It starts at noon, at the high school. Also, did you order that book for my report?"

Jill had forgotten. "No, but I will. When do you need it by?"

"Next Monday. Courtney orders online all the time, by herself, from her iPhone. Why can't I do that?"

"Because you don't have an iPhone."

"That's not funny, Mom."

Jill laughed to herself. "I'll take care of it, honey."

"Thanks, I gotta go. Love you, too. Bye."

"See you tomorrow. Sleep tight. Love you." Jill hung up, set the phone down, and petted Beef on the head, his brushy tail awag. Sam hadn't greeted her, which wasn't like him, and she owed him an apology. She got up and went into the family room, but he'd fallen asleep on the couch, his book open on his chest and his glasses pushed onto his head, so his hair puffed through the nosepiece. The TV played on low volume, and Jill thought of the scene that Abby had described, when she found William lying in bed with the TV playing.

Dad never filled those scripts. They were planted there by the killer.

Jill shuddered, going to the kitchen, where she slipped Beef a piece of pancake and put the rest in the fridge. She went out to the entrance hall, got the box with the laptop and files, brought everything back into the kitchen, set it on the island, then sat down and dug in.

The manila folder on top was labeled MEDICAL INFO, and she opened it and skimmed through. It contained William's lab reports for his bloodwork, and the results were normal. The only drugs William reported as taking regularly were Crestor, 10 mg, and Co Q 10, commonly taken with statins. There was no mention of any other prescription drugs, so either he wasn't taking them or he was lying.

Jill went through the rest of the files, determined they were nothing but old bills, so she closed the box and opened the laptop, plugging it into the island outlet and getting busy. An hour later, she'd gone through William's laptop, but had found nothing unusual. His email was between his golf buddies, Abby, Victoria, Neil Straub, and various women, a sharing of blog posts, articles, YouTube links, and plans for golf dates or dinners. The email was more significant for what it didn't contain rather than what it did. There was nothing about his business investments, which had to be what was paying for his house, lifestyle, and the girls.

She navigated back to Quicken and skimmed the entries, which were equally mundane, and he still wasn't paying his bills online, so she couldn't connect to his bank files. It only took her twenty minutes to make a spreadsheet for Abby, because the household expenses were so routine, and there were no other financial files. She went back to the Programs files, but the laptop had only the programs the computer came with, and not much else.

She eyed the laptop, in thought. It was almost generic, as if it had been sanitized or kept purposely clean. She went online, clicked on the online history, and it was empty, erased. She went to the deleted email file, and it had been completely emptied, too. So either William had cleaned out this laptop or someone had done it for him.

Jill tried another tack. If she worked under Abby's theory and assumed that somebody killed him, it had to be someone close to him, since there had been no sign of a struggle or break-in at the house. So all she had to do was figure out who was close to him. She went into My Computer, scanned the list of programs, and found My Pictures. She clicked to open the file, and there were three file icons, the oldest dating only from a year ago: **London trip with girls, Victoria's graduation weekend, Neil at Pebble Beach**. She skipped to the folder with Neil, to see if he was a viable candidate for the man in the black ballcap, despite what Abby had said.

Jill opened the pictures folder, and there were photos of William on a golf course with Neil, who was wearing a white Callaway ballcap and aviator sunglasses similar to those worn by the man in the black ballcap. The outfit obscured some of Neil's features, but he had a winning smile and a strong, jutting chin and he was tall and well-built, about William's height and weight. Jill clicked, and more of the file photos flashed by, but they were all taken outdoors and Neil wore sunglasses in every one, and so did William, in a few shots. She clicked a photo of them together and hit PRINT.

She went online and Googled Neil Straub, but there were no listings. She checked him on Facebook, and he was on, but he'd blocked his profile except to his friends and had no picture. She logged onto www.whitepages.com for his address and plugged in New York, but no address came up, so it must have been unlisted. Neil Straub kept a low profile, and Jill wondered why.

Just then her phone rang, and the screen flashed a number she didn't recognize. It was almost eleven o'clock at night, and it could have been a patient. She answered the phone. "Jill Farrow."

"It's Victoria. Let me speak to Abby."

"Victoria," Jill repeated, startled at the sound of Victoria's voice. She had heard it so many times before that she could've picked it out in a choir, and had, at so many school concerts, when Victoria was growing up. Victoria sang in a clear, strong alto, ringing with certainty, always pitch-perfect, more than a match for the showy top notes of the sopranos in the Stafford High Select Chorale, and her voice stood out so much for its clarity that the choir director had given Victoria a solo, even as a freshman, which had terrified the reserved young girl. That night, Victoria had called Jill from backstage, in a panic before she went on.

Jill, I can't do it, I'm going to forget the words. I can't solo!

Victoria, relax, you can do it, I know you can. Jill answered the call, sitting in the audience with Abby and Megan, at another concert that William had missed, supposedly working late.

Where are you guys sitting? Are you in your regular seats?

Yes, stage left, front row. We'll be right in front of you. Just forget everything and sing, honey. Sing it out. Let everybody hear your voice. We know you're wonderful, and it's time to show everybody else.

And after the concert, Victoria had come running, her eyes alive with pride and happiness, her arms reaching for Jill.

I sang it to you, Jill. I sang it to you.

"Jill, put Abby on," Victoria was saying, her voice now so cold that the disconnect left Jill shaken.

"First, Victoria, let me tell you how sorry I am about—"

"Put Abby on, please. I need to speak with her."

Jill swallowed hard, recovering. "Listen, she's not here, and I'm so sorry about your father's death, and about what happened at the memorial service. I know this is an impossibly difficult time for you, and I wouldn't have come if I had known—"

"Save it, okay, Jill? I need to speak to Abby. I know she's there. I also know you were at the house with her tonight, and I told her not to go home with you, but once again, she didn't listen. Put her on, please."

"She's not here, Victoria. She didn't come home with me, after your call." Jill moderated her tone, trying to open the door between them. She couldn't accept that Victoria was a stranger, when she used to be her daughter.

"You're incredible, you know that? Let me talk to my sister, now. Stop lying for her."

"I'm not lying. I never lied to you, honey." The term of endearment just slipped out of Jill's mouth, and she knew it was the wrong thing to say before Victoria raised her voice.

"Don't call me *honey*! That works on Abby, but not on me. Put her on, now."

"I swear to you, Abby's not here." Jill's thoughts shifted from Victoria to Abby, and she started to worry. "When did you see her last?"

"None of your business. She's probably at work, but they don't pick up the phone."

"She's not at work. She quit her job."

"She *quit*? How do *you* know?"

"She told me. Could she be on a date? She might have been last night. She was drinking when she came over."

"There's a shocker," Victoria said, dryly.

"Do you know who that was? Was it Santos? Could they be back together?"

"Again, how do *you* know about Santos? Boy, you don't waste a minute, do you?" Victoria snorted. "My father just died, Jill. Can't you hold your horses before you try to worm your way back into my family?"

Jill didn't want to fight. It was bad enough that she and Victoria were so far apart. "Do you have Santos's phone number?"

"No, he moved back to Brazil. She could have picked somebody up at random. She does that, you know. She goes out a lot, she likes to party."

Jill cringed. "On the night of her father's memorial service? She didn't seem like she was up for a party when I left her. Did you call any of her friends?"

"I don't even know her friends. They didn't even care enough to show up at the memorial service."

"Are you going to the house to check on her?"

"No, Jill. I'm not her mother, and here's a news flash, neither are *you*. Good-bye."

"Wait, please call me if you hear from her, or ask her to call me."

"Like you care?"

"I *do,* Victoria. I care about you both. Please, call me or—"

Victoria hung up, leaving Jill holding the phone, and she pressed END. She scrolled back to her phone log, found Abby's phone number, and pressed CALL. It rang and rang, then the voicemail came on, with Abby saying, "I'm having too much fun to take your call! Leave a message!" The beep sounded, and Jill said, "Abby, I'm worried about you. Please call me and let me know how you are. Victoria called, looking for you, too. Call me anytime, no matter how late. Love you."

Jill hung up, worrying. It seemed odd that Abby wasn't home tonight. Abby would have no reason to go out, and she didn't seem strong or stable enough to party. Jill thought of the padiddle. The man in the ballcap. The surveillance video. The sanitized laptop.

Suddenly, Jill didn't think it was completely outlandish that

William had been murdered, then something else dawned on her, with a shock. If William had been murdered, Abby could be in danger, too. Abby lived in the same house as William. Maybe she had seen the killer and didn't know it, or overheard something or saw something else, or maybe the killer merely thought she did. Whatever William was up to could destroy Abby, as well.

I love you, Jill.

Jill felt a bolt of fear at the notion. She couldn't bear it if anything happened to Abby. She jumped up like a shot and went running to the family room.

"Sam!" she called out, stricken.

Chapter Seventeen

Jill sat in the chair across from Sam, having told him about the surveillance tape, the forged script, and the black SUV, at warp speed. Beef slept on the rug, his back legs twitching in a doggie dream, and the TV was playing a late-night talk show, on mute. Sam had calmed her down, listening carefully to her, looking over the top of his glasses, sitting forward on the couch, resting his arms on his thighs, his concern etched into every line on his face.

Jill asked, "So what do you think, honey?"

"I think a lot of things." Sam raked a hand through his hair. A glass of soda with melted ice sat next to him on the oak end table. "I must admit, it does seem strange, especially that the prescribing doctor was dead."

"I know, right?" Jill felt a rush of validation, but an equal measure of worry for Abby.

"It's what William did to you, stealing the pads, so it suggests it was him filling the script."

"Why would he disguise himself?"

"In case someone found out it was a phony script. To avoid prosecution."

"Right. I didn't think of that." Jill rubbed her face. "My brain must not be working, I keep thinking about Abby. Where could she be?"

"Anywhere." Sam's expression cooled, and he slid off his glasses.

"What if she's in danger? Or trouble?"

"I doubt that she is." Sam checked his watch. "It's one o'clock in the morning, and we know she likes to have a good time."

"She wasn't having a good time last night, Sam. She was in pain."

"Okay, fair point."

"I wish she lived close, I could go check on her." Jill tried to suppress her fears, but failed. "Anything could have happened to her, even in the house. She could have had too much to drink and fallen down the stairs. She's so alone. She has no one looking out for her."

"She has a sister."

"Who's in disapproval frenzy."

Sam lifted an eyebrow. "Maybe she deserves it."

"Nobody deserves it, Sam."

"People who drink and drive do."

"Don't judge her, help her."

"Stop." Sam put up both hands. "We are. I am. Could we change the subject and talk about you, instead of her? The black SUV following you, that concerns me. It might be nothing, but I'd prefer it if we played it safe."

"And did what?"

"Stay out of this. Who knows what William got himself into?" Sam frowned, deeply. "I don't think you should get further involved."

"I didn't mean to, it's just happening."

Sam pursed his lips. "The drugstore didn't just happen, Jill."

"I didn't expect the answer that I got."

"Understood. So stop, now. Tell the cops, and let them handle it." Sam shook his head. "I don't want you in harm's way. Or Megan."

"I would never endanger Megan."

"You may have, already. You're worried about Abby's safety, what about hers or yours?" Sam gestured at the door. "You're saying the SUV was on our street, for God's sake."

"I didn't realize it." Jill felt defensive, her thoughts confused. "It might not have been the same car."

"Is it or isn't it? Why take a chance? Do you really want to bring trouble to our door, and for what? It's police business, not ours." Sam raised his hands slowly, palms up. "Why am I so involved in your ex-husband's life's, all of a sudden? Why are you?"

"I don't think of it as his life, honey. I think of it as Abby's life."

"It's the same result, isn't it? It's all about him. You're on his laptop, reading his email, trying to find his business partner. Until yesterday, your ex was dead to you. And now that he's dead, he's come back to life."

"Don't be that way." Jill could see he was hurt, even jealous, which was so unlike him. "I can't just give up on Abby."

"She's not yours to give up."

"It's a figure of speech."

"No, it's not." Sam sighed heavily, and just like that, they were at an impasse.

Jill looked around the family room, with its cheery, red-checked couch and white ginger lamps. She had picked out new furniture after she was divorced, and this house was smaller than the one she'd lived in with William and the girls. When Sam had moved in, they'd added a picture rail for his photographs and book-shelves for his collection of first editions. They'd worked together on the room, and they'd succeeded in making a new home and a new family, until now. The family room didn't define the family anymore, and Jill knew they needed to find some middle ground.

She met Sam's eye. "You're right about the police. I'll call them tomorrow. I'll tell them about the forged script and the SUV."

"Good, thanks." Sam rose stiffly, offering his hand. "Why don't we go to bed and hope that Abby's back in the morning?"

"Honestly, I know I won't sleep. I can't rest until I know every-body's safe, all under one roof."

"She has a different roof, babe." Sam let his hand drop to his side, and Jill wanted to clear the air, once and for all.

"I know that, but it seems like a technicality, doesn't it?"

"No."

"Really?" Jill didn't understand. "What if she's injured, Sam? Or missing? Doesn't that change your analysis?"

"No." Sam stood firm, straightening up. "Did it occur to you that her disappearing act could be a bid for attention? It's inconsiderate, at best. You're back in her life, and she loves it. She loves you. You heard her last night."

"I love her, too. That's real, honest emotion, not manipulation."

"Is it, on her part?" Sam cocked his head. "What was she thinking, inviting you to the memorial service and not telling her sister? She had to know there would be a scene."

"She didn't expect that reaction."

"Come on, Jill. If you ask me, the kid's acting out to keep you involved with her, taking your attention away from Megan and me."

"You? That's crazy, Sam."

"No, it isn't. I'm the guy who replaced her father. She was downright hostile to me last night."

"She was drunk, and she doesn't even know you."

"Okay, enough. I'm out of gas. I'm going to bed. Wanna come?"

"No, not just yet." Jill felt torn, betwixt and between, again. She loved having Abby back in the fold. It made her feel whole again, filling the Abby-shaped hole in her heart, like the blank cutout from a sheet of cookie dough. "I'm not tired, and I just can't go to sleep like nothing's wrong."

"One last thing, babe. Ask yourself whether you're getting involved with Abby because Megan's pulling away."

"Do you believe that?"

"Doesn't matter. What I said was, ask yourself." Sam put his hands on his slim hips. "You don't have to answer to me, you have to answer yourself. Maybe you're getting what you want, in Abby. A kid to worry about, a kid to raise. Because Megan is growing up, the way she's supposed to. Maybe you want to have a baby forever, to replace her."

Jill opened her mouth to object, then shut it. She knew he was wrong, but he had a working hypothesis, and she couldn't talk him out of it, tonight.

"Either way, I love you. Goodnight." Sam leaned over, placed his hands on the arms of her chair, and gave her a dry kiss on the lips. But when he pulled away, he didn't meet her eye, and his expression looked troubled. "I'll let the dog out."

"No, I will. You've done enough today."

"Thanks." Sam flashed her a tired smile, then turned to go.

"Love you, too," Jill called after him, listening to the sound of his footfalls disappearing. She didn't like the distant look in his eyes, one she'd never seen before, and she could feel a new rift between them, as if suddenly they were on two separate ice floes, drifting apart on a vast and frigid sea.

Jill, I love you, so much, you're my mom.

Jill got up and hurried into the kitchen.

Chapter Eighteen

Jill crossed to the coffeemaker and popped in a pod, then set a mug underneath and hit BREW. She couldn't ignore the sensation that Abby was in trouble. Abby's drinking worried her, and it was possible that she was passed out in a club or an alley somewhere.

Jill picked up the phone and checked her messages, but Abby still hadn't called her back, so she called her again and left another message, saying the same thing. On impulse, Jill called the University of Pennsylvania Hospital in Philly, transferred to the emergency room, and asked for Abby Skyler or a Jane Doe with Abby's age and description. No luck. Meanwhile, the coffee had brewed, and Jill slid it out, took a hot sip, then called Temple and Hahnemann hospitals, but Abby hadn't been at either of their ERs or admitted.

Jill took the mug back to the laptop and moved the mouse. There was nothing more she could do for Abby right now, so she told herself to be patient. She stared at the screen for a moment, feeling the weight of Sam's words and wondering if she'd been giving short shrift to Megan. Katie had said almost the same thing, and Jill was beginning to sense a consensus. She'd have to make sure to take care of Megan, too, and even that seemed a familiar balancing act, from her days as a mom of three.

She had to get Megan that Lincoln book, so she navigated to an online bookseller, plugged *Lincoln's Ghost* into the search, and waited for the book to come up. It appeared, and she clicked SEND TO CART, but then realized she might have to rush it to make sure it got here in time, so she reviewed the order form, changed the shipping preferences, and looked at the shipping addresses, which was when it struck her.

The list contained all the people who were closest to her, both past and present. She'd never deleted the older addresses, and it still had her mother's home address and Sam's old condo address. William could have had a list like that, too, online. He used to shop online and was always sending gifts to doctors, nurses, and secretaries whose offices he called on, to grease his sales calls. Jill even knew his passwords, but she didn't need them. She had his laptop.

She palmed the mouse, went online, and plugged in the website. The flash screen came up, offering an array of new and upcoming books, and at the top, it read, **WELCOME, WILLIAM!** She navigated to My Account, which had all of his account settings, including Addresses, and the Default Address was the house on Acorn Street in Philadelphia. She clicked Manage Addresses, and a list of old addresses popped on the screen, some twenty odd long.

Jill shifted onto the edge of her seat. William had sanitized his laptop, but he'd forgotten to erase information that was stored online. The second address on his list was an apartment in Philly, to which he and the girls moved after the divorce, and after that was their old home address. Next was a string of doctors' office addresses, with the names of office managers, followed by a few women with addresses in and around Philadelphia, presumably girlfriends. There was a group of men on the list, but all of them were doctors except for the one she'd hoped to find: **Neil Straub,** with an apartment address on West 11th Street, in Manhattan.

Jill picked up her phone, called information in New York City, and asked for the phone number, but the automated voice said they didn't have the listing. She pressed 0 for an operator and reached a supervisor who looked up the number, then came back on the line, saying, "I'm sorry, we can't give out that number."

Jill hung up, with a growing suspicion that Neil and William had been up to no good. She'd found out as much as she could about Neil for now, but she could find out about the others on the address list, and maybe they would yield information about him or lead to something else. Maybe there would be some connection to Abby, or at the very least, it would give Jill something to do until she could call Abby and the hospitals again.

She printed the address list, then got to work.

Chapter Nineteen

Jill woke up in front of her laptop at the island, with a shaft of sunlight coming through the windows over the sink. The kitchen was bright and still, and the wall clock read 6:15 A.M. Her first thought was of Abby, and she prayed that she'd called or texted. She picked up her BlackBerry and checked her messages, but there was nothing from Abby, or Victoria. None of her patients had called either, including Padma, but Jill wouldn't rest until Rahul's bloodwork came in.

Beef came over from his dog bed, wagging his tail slowly, and she patted him on his soft head, scrolled to her call log, found Abby's number, and pressed CALL on the way to the back door, to let him out. The call rang as she unlocked the deadbolt, and Beef trotted outside, with Jill behind. It was a clear Sunday morning, the neighborhood quiet and peaceful, because it was too early for leaf-blowers and lawnmowers. Their backyard was large, a full, flat acre with a pool, bounded by a tall privacy fence. Pin oaks shaded the left end of the property, which was Beef territory.

Jill stood in the sunshine, letting it warm her and hoping Abby would pick up the phone. She listened to the ringing, but there was no answer, so she left another message, then pressed END. She scrolled back to her call log, pressed in the number for the Penn ER, and asked again about Abby. Still no luck. She called Temple and Hahnemann, but Abby hadn't been in there, either.

She checked her phone for the time, and it was 6:35. She wanted to go to Abby's house to check on her, but she'd have to leave soon to be back in time for Megan's meet. She found Victoria's number in the log and pressed CALL.

"Jill?" Victoria answered, groggy. "Why the hell are you calling me so early?"

"I'm sorry to bother you, but I didn't hear from Abby. Did you?"

"No. You woke me up."

"I'm sorry, really. She hasn't returned my calls, and I want to check on her, but I don't have the keys. Do you know if any of the neighbors have a set?"

"I don't know, and are you *nuts*? What's your problem, Jill? Stay out of it, would you?"

Jill had expected the reaction. She kept her tone conciliatory. "I'm worried she fell down the stairs, hurt herself, or can't get to the door somehow."

"She didn't fall. She's not an old lady. Jeez!"

"If she was drinking, she could have fallen and aspirated her own vomit. It happens, Victoria. People die from that."

Victoria scoffed. "I thought you said she wouldn't go out partying last night."

Jill bit her tongue. "What if I was wrong? Do you have keys?"

"Yes."

"Will you meet me there?" Jill asked, hoping against hope. She couldn't drive to Victoria's apartment in Central Jersey and still get back in time for Megan's meet.

"Why would I do that?"

"Because you love your sister."

"Right," Victoria shot back. "I love her enough not to enable her."

Jill wasn't getting anywhere, so she went for it. "Victoria, I think a car might have followed her to my house the other night, and I think it's been following me. It's a black SUV, and the license plate was T something. Do you know it? Does she date anybody who drives a black SUV?"

"No." Victoria scoffed. "How do you know it was following her?"

"I don't, for sure, but it had one headlight. I noticed it because it was a padiddle, that game we used to play."

"You think a *padiddle* is following her? Really? Did you spy it with your little eye?"

Jill didn't know how to convince her. "Besides that, the pills that were found in your father's bedroom were prescribed by a doctor who's been dead for years. It was a forged prescription."

"Are you saying Dad *forged* his prescription?"

"Either he or someone trying to—"

"He would *never* do that. Are you crazy? Really, are you? None of this is your business."

Jill wanted those keys. "Victoria, you don't know this, but if you meet me, I can explain. He did it once before—"

Victoria gasped. "Stop it right now. Did you wake me up to trash Dad? What's the matter with you? You're a sick woman."

"Please, meet me and give me the keys, for Abby's sake."

"No, this is all about *you*. She's fine, you're the *freak*." Victoria hung up, and Jill pressed END, agitated. Beef came trotting forward, wagging his tail, and she turned to see Sam coming out the back door with a soft smile, in his T-shirt, running shorts, and bare feet. He met her and gave her a big hug, holding her close.

"Sounds like that went well," he said, sadly, and as Jill hugged him back, she felt that the tension of last night had diminished, and they were reconnecting, almost back to themselves again.

"I'd kiss you, but my breath stinks."

"Kiss me, anyway."

Jill went on tiptoe to give him a kiss. "Tastes like stale coffee, right?"

"No." Sam smiled. "Tastes like wife."

"I love you." Jill smiled back, but her thoughts returned to Abby. "Are we allowed to talk about Abby?"

"Yes." Sam smiled, crookedly.

"She's still not answering, and I want to go downtown and check on her. Megan has a meet today, and Courtney's mom is taking her. It starts at noon but I can be back in time, don't you think? She won't swim until one o'clock or so."

"Yes, and I'll go downtown with you."

"No, thanks, I can go alone."

"I wish you wouldn't." Sam's expression darkened. "I slept on it, and though I don't think your ex was murdered, I'm worried about this SUV."

"I'll keep an eye out for it. On a Sunday morning, I'd spot it a mile away, there's no traffic. Besides, Megan needs her swim bag, and if I run late, I can't get it to her."

"We can drop it off on our way out."

"And wake up Courtney's family? Their dogs bark like crazy."

"Then we can leave it at school."

"The meet's at the high school. It won't be open, and where would we leave it? They don't know her there." Jill gave his arm a squeeze. "Thanks, but it's best if you stay. If there are any problems, I'll call the police."

Sam pursed his lips "You're supposed to be calling the police today anyway, correct?"

"Yes, I will, after I check on Abby." Jill gave him a final hug and patted Beef good-bye. "I'll pack Megan's bag before I go."

"I can do it. But be careful in Philly, will you? Any sign of that SUV, call 911, then call me. Text me when you get there."

"Will do."

"Wait. What are you going to do if Abby doesn't answer the door?"

"I'll knock until she does, or I can see if her car is there, so I'll know she's home."

"You don't have a key to the house, do you?"

"No, but I hope a neighbor does. We always used to do that, just in case."

"By 'we,' do you mean you and William?" Sam lifted an eyebrow, but he smiled.

"Yes. Sorry."

"We're going to stop talking about him by our wedding, no?"

"Promise," Jill answered, and took off.

Chapter Twenty

Jill zoomed into town and didn't see any black SUVs as she hit the on-ramp toward Society Hill. She made it in no time and found a parking space on Acorn Street, cut the ignition, texted Sam that she was fine, and got out of the car. The sun slashed through the trees along the street, and a breeze disturbed the leaves of the trees, but it was too early on a Sunday morning for anyone to be out, even tourists.

Jill made a beeline for William's house, hustled up the steps, and rang the bell. She rang it again, then again, but no answer. She knocked on the door, rapping hard with her knuckles. "Abby?" she called out, loud enough to be heard without waking the entire block. "It's me, Jill! Open up!" She waited, then called out again, knocking, but there was no reply.

She peeked in the front window, edging over on the stoop, but she couldn't see anything. The window was too high in the wall, and a massive shade covered the bottom. There were no lights on inside the house, and she didn't know if Abby was home, but she knew a way to find out. She climbed down the front steps and continued down the street until she came to the break in the rowhouses. She'd lived in the city during her residency and she knew that alleys usually ran behind the rowhouses.

She took a right and hurried down the alley, which changed to a stone walkway that led to a pocket parking lot. Each house had two parking spaces, and the lot was full. There was a cheap orange Datsun parked right behind a black Mercedes sedan, and they had to be Abby's and William's cars. Jill worried anew. So Abby was home, but she wasn't answering the door? Was she hurt inside the house? Or had she gone somewhere, with someone who had driven her? Jill went over to Abby's car and peered inside. Balled-up Trident wrappers dotted the passenger's seat, next to an empty water bottle and a hairbrush. On impulse, she went over and looked inside William's car, and it was predictably immaculate.

She straightened up, then noticed something. The house had a back door, painted dark blue. She walked around the cars and down another stone walkway that ran along the back of the houses, stopping at the door with house number 363. A recycling container sat outside it, next to a galvanized trash can. She banged on the door, and called, "Abby, Abby!"

"Hey! What are you doing?" said a stern voice behind her, and Jill turned around to see an older man in a green track suit, with a newspaper tucked under his arm. He was standing in the lot, his lined brow furrowed and his hooded eyes glowering behind bifocals.

"Hello, I'm Jill Farrow, Abby's stepmother, and I'm looking for her. Are you a neighbor?"

"It depends." The man frowned, but his tone softened. "Abby's the girl who lives here?"

"Yes, that's her car." Jill gestured at the Datsun. "She's home but she doesn't answer the door. Her father, who lived here, died last Tuesday, and I'm worried about her."

"Oh, I didn't know that." The man's forehead relaxed. "My condolences. Name's Ernie Berg."

"Hi, Ernie." Jill walked over and shook his hand. "Where do you live?"

"Two doors down, on Acorn." Ernie pointed at a black Lincoln. "That's my car."

"Have you seen Abby recently?"

"No, not recently. Pretty girl, and she always waves. I'm retired, so I'm home, and I see most things on the street. I'm on the Town Watch, too."

Jill knew it was a lucky break. "How about William, then? Her father? Do you see him much? The Mercedes is his."

"I know who you mean, but he's not around that much. That night, guess it was a few days ago, the street was full of police, even the medical examiner. Quite a to-do." Ernie shook his head. "He was too young, wasn't he? What did he die of?"

"A reaction to a prescription drug."

"That's too bad. I didn't know him, but a man that young, that's too bad. I asked him to be on the Town Watch, but he said no. Said he was traveling all the time."

Jill made a mental note. "Do you know the neighbors on either side? I'm wondering if they've seen her or if they have a key to the house."

"You can forget about that. The Wilsons and the Eraskos. The Wilsons are skiing, and the Eraskos are on some college tour, with the son. He plays basketball. Heavily recruited."

Jill felt defeated, momentarily. "I'm worried that Abby's in the house and fell or something. She lives alone now that her father died."

"I'd worry, too." Ernie buckled his lower lip. "Most fatal accidents occur in the home. Might be time to go to the police. We discourage the use of 911, when it's not an emergency, and our precinct house is just a few blocks away. We're in the Sixth District."

"You think I should go?"

Ernie shrugged. "How many daughters you got?"

Jill was about to answer "three" when she realized it was rhetorical.

Chapter Twenty-one

Jill hustled toward the police station, which was an aging, low-rise building of nicotine yellow brick, shaped like a grocery-store sheet cake. It had a stop-time blue sign with art-deco letters that read POLICE 6TH DISTRICT, and a parking lot beside the building held a handful of white cruisers bearing the distinctive yellow-and-blue stripe of the Philadelphia Police. There weren't any cops on the street or out front, and she hurried inside the smudged stainless-steel-and-glass entrance.

She found herself in a hallway of dingy tile that ended in a forbidding steel door, obviously locked. To the right was a pay phone, and to the left was a poster that read CURFEW CRACKDOWN, then a small sliding window in a blue frame. She crossed to the window, which revealed a rectangular room barely large enough to fit four old desks of gray metal, arranged cheek-by-jowl, each with a black swivel chair. Two of the chairs were occupied by a female and male police officer, and the female looked up, rose, and came to the window.

"Good morning, I'm Officer Mendina," she said, pleasantly. Her nameplate read Veronica Mendina, and her blue shirt matched the earnest hue of her eyes. Her thick brown bangs were held off her forehead by a bobby pin. "May I help you?"

"Hi, I'm Jill Farrow, and I'm worried that my former stepdaughter is hurt in her house, or missing. Her name is Abby Skyler, and she lives on Acorn Street. Her car is there, but there's no answer at the door."

"How old is she?"

"Nineteen."

"When was the last time you saw her?"

"Around seven o'clock last night, and she hasn't returned my calls or her sister's. Her father just died, and she believes he was murdered."

Officer Mendina's eyes flared. "She believes he was? Was it ruled a homicide or not?"

"No, it wasn't, but she still believes it was." Jill realized something. "Would you be the ones who investigated it, when the police were called? His name was William Skyler."

"No, that's Central Detectives, up on 21st Street. So you say she's missing, but it's only been one night. Does she usually stay out all night?"

"I don't know, I don't live with her. I'm a mom, so I worry."

"I hear that." Officer Mendina reached under the window and pulled out a form, revealing a black Glock holstered on one hip. On her other hip was a radio, its stiff antenna sticking up like a black spire. "Now what did you say your daughter's name was? Also, I'll need to see an ID."

"She's not my daughter."

"I thought you said she was."

"No, she's my ex-stepdaughter." Jill went into her purse, got her driver's license, and slid it across the sill. "I used to be her stepmother, and both of her parents are dead."

Officer Mendina examined the driver's license. "Are you her legal guardian, Dr. Farrow?"

"No."

"Then what exactly is your relationship to the girl, again?" Officer Mendina returned the driver's license, but withheld the form.

"I'm her ex-stepmother. I was married to her father, who died last Tuesday."

"Then you don't have standing to file a missing persons. Sorry." Officer Mendina put the form away.

"Does it matter who reports it? She's hurt or missing, that's all that matters." Jill pulled a photo from her purse that she'd printed from William's laptop before she left the house. It showed all of them together, down the Jersey shore. "Look, this is us, from when I was married to her father. The long-haired one is Abby."

Officer Mendina scrutinized the photo. "Who's this other girl, the tall one?"

"Her sister, Victoria. Can she file a report?"

"No, she can't. You say the girl's over eighteen, so she's legally an adult, and it's not against the law to want to be left alone. It's only one night."

"But can you check the house? She's been so distraught since her father died, and drinking."

"I'm sorry, I can't help you. Our manpower is limited, and we can't go chasing down every nineteen-year-old who has a few beers." Officer Mendina pursed her unlipsticked lips, and Jill saw empathy in her eyes.

"But she's just been orphaned, and that's hard at any age. Are you a mother? Can't you just check on her?"

Officer Mendina paused. "Wait here. I'll talk to my supervisor."

"Thank you, I really appreciate it." Jill watched her walk back to the office and disappear out of view, and she returned a few minutes later with a shortish, African-American police officer in a white shirt. He had wire-rimmed glasses and a serious expression, and he walked over to the window with Officer Mendina, then took the lead.

"I'm Sergeant Destin, and I'll tell you what we can do for you. I'm going to send Officer Mendina and another officer of mine to do a walk-through of the house. Make sure everything's okay."

"Thank you so much," Jill said, grateful.

"You can't file a report, but we can make sure nothing's going on inside. We can also talk to the neighbors, see if any of them saw her, and put your mind at ease. You say you don't live with her, though?"

"No, I don't."

"You have keys? We don't break in."

Jill had assumed they would, unfortunately. "I don't, but I can get you some. Gimme an hour."

"Do it, and we'll meet you there. What's the number on Acorn?"

"382."

"Okay." Sergeant Destin checked his thick watch. "Wait for us at the house."

"Thanks so much." Jill turned, slid out her cell phone, and scrolled down for Victoria's phone number as she hurried out of the police station. The call rang twice, then connected. "Victoria, it's Jill."

"Don't tell me, let me guess. Abby's over your house. Does she have her own bedroom yet?"

"She's not with me." Jill hurried toward her car, which was parked in front of the Vietnamese restaurant next door. "I need you to meet me at your father's house, with the keys. The police are going to go inside and—"

"The *police*? What do they want?"

"They're coming to the house to check it out and—"

"What are you doing? This is none of your business, Jill."

"Victoria, please don't give me a hard time. I'm worried that Abby is inside and may be hurt. Her car is there but she doesn't answer." Jill got her car key, then chirped the door open. "Just come with the keys. Please."

"I can't, I have to study."

"It can't be helped." Jill climbed inside her front seat, keeping a lid on her temper. "I know you love your sister, so please come."

"I don't need you to tell me whether I love my sister or not. I have a life, Jill. I'm not my sister's keeper."

"Victoria, if you don't come open the door, they'll break it down." Jill would tell a white lie, if it saved Abby's life. "You have to come with the keys, as soon as possible."

"Damn you! This is a total and complete waste of time." Victoria hung up.

Jill pressed END, set the BlackBerry down, and slid the key into the ignition. The engine and dashboard clock came to life, glowing a digital 8:03. She had time, but she had to hustle.

She hit the gas, took a right onto Vine Street, then headed back toward Society Hill.

Chapter Twenty-two

Jill stood in front of William's house waiting for Victoria, while Officer Mendina and a heavyset male cop were knocking on the neighbors' doors, asking about Abby. The block was waking up, and young couples, groups of tourists, and runners eyed the police and their two cruisers, their presence causing a commotion. Suddenly a white BMW steered onto the street and drove toward them, and Jill spotted Victoria in the passenger seat. Her friend Brian was driving, and Jill hustled toward the car.

Victoria got out when the BMW slowed to a stop, double-parking to drop her off, and her lovely hazel eyes glittered as they surveyed the street. She must have dressed quickly, but still looked put together in a white sweater, skinny jeans, and ballet flats. Her makeup was perfect, and her blonde hair twisted into a tortoise-shell barrette.

"What the hell is going on, Jill?" she asked, angrily. "This is a circus."

"I'm really sorry to take you from your studies." Jill kept her tone even, still hoping to reconnect. "If you give your keys to the cops, they can do a walk-through—"

"Hell to the *no.*" Victoria turned away, hoisted her purse to her shoulder, and stalked off toward the police, and Jill fell into step beside her.

"Victoria, look, I'm sorry, but—"

"I told you, you can bulldoze your way into Abby's life, but keep out of mine. Now, don't speak to me."

Jill took it on the chin, and they both walked to meet Officer Mendina, who was climbing down the steps of a rowhouse and slipping a long white pad into her back pocket. She strode toward them, frowning under the patent bill of her cap.

"Dr. Farrow," Officer Mendina called out, with a wave. When she got closer, she said, "No one's seen the girl this week, or seen anything else suspicious at the house or on the street, except the day her father passed. Do you have the house keys?"

"Right here," Jill answered, gesturing at Victoria. "Officer Mendina, this is—"

"Jill, excuse me, I can introduce myself." Victoria edged Jill aside. "Hello, Officer, I'm Victoria Skyler, Abby's sister. I'm also a law student at Seton Hall, and I object to these tactics by the police. You have no right to break down the door to my father's house."

"Hold on a minute, Ms. Skyler." Officer Mendina raised a hand. "I'm sorry about your loss, and you have my condolences. Unfortunately, you may be misunderstanding our procedure. We're not breaking down any doors. We don't do that unless we know a crime or a medical emergency is in progress."

"I *thought* so." Victoria turned to Jill. "You told me they'd break down the door."

Jill's mouth went dry. "I'm sorry, I told you that to get the keys."

"So you lied to me." Victoria nodded, her lip curling. "You disgust me, you know that? Didn't you say on the phone last night that you'd never lie to me? Wasn't that you? You're the one who called me 'honey,' right?"

Jill felt her face flush, embarrassed. She'd started off on the wrong foot with Victoria and she felt heartsick, wondering if they'd ever be close again. "Only because I was worried about your sister."

"She's *fine,* Jill. I know her a helluva lot better than you do. Butt out."

"Ladies," Officer Mendina said, toughening her tone, "if you want us to do a walk-through, we will. If not, we won't. Make up your mind. What's the decision?"

"No," Victoria answered.

"Yes," Jill answered at the same moment.

Officer Mendina looked from Jill to Victoria and back again. "We're here, we canvassed, so we might as well finish what we started. May I have the keys, Ms. Skyler?"

"Oh, fine." Victoria dug in a huge black purse, stuffed to the brim with a hairbrush, flowery makeup case, and an orange EpiPen, for her allergies. The sight of it took Jill back to a spring day when the girls were little and she'd taken them on a picnic to Valley Forge. Victoria had been stung by a bee, and before Jill even realized what happened, the self-possessed little girl had slipped her EpiPen from her pocket and was injecting herself with the calm assurance of a surgeon.

Honey, you did that perfectly, Jill had told her, afterwards. *You'd be great in an emergency.*

Victoria had grinned up at her. *I'm going to be a doctor, like you.*

Jill banished the memory as Victoria found the keys and handed them to Officer Mendina.

"Ladies, you both wait outside." Officer Mendina slid out the printed photo from her back pocket and handed it to Jill. "Dr. Farrow, before I forget, here's the photo you gave us."

"Thanks." Jill took the photo, and Officer Mendina left for William's house, meeting up with the other officer on the sidewalk in front.

Victoria frowned. "Jill, where did you get that picture? It's Dad's."

"Here, please take it, then. I didn't mean any harm. It was in his laptop." Jill didn't want to fuss anymore, especially now that the police were walking up the steps to William's house. She found herself in motion, her gut tensing at the thought of what they might find inside.

"Where did *you* get his laptop?" Victoria dogged her steps.

"Abby lent it to me. She asked me to help her set up a budget." Jill kept walking, and the officers were unlocking the front door.

"She had no right to give it to you, and you had no right to take it. It belongs to Dad."

"I'm only trying to help her." Jill stopped at the sidewalk outside the house, her heart in her throat as the police vanished inside. It killed her not to follow them.

"Please stop telling me about my own sister, whom you haven't seen in, like, forever. You're not our mother anymore."

Jill felt cut to the quick, but sucked it up. She glanced back at the house, and the front door was closed partway, with the officers inside. "Victoria, just so you know, Abby came to me, not the other way around."

"Of course she did, because she's a drama queen, and it's the only way she knows to get attention. She can't do anything right, so she does everything wrong. She can't live on her own. She's a mess, and you have yourself to thank for that."

Jill took it on the chin, wondering again, what was going on inside the house. Passers-by were beginning to stare, making a pedestrian gaper-block. "Then maybe I can help her now."

"Too little, too late." Victoria shook her head. "She's manipulating you, and you're too full of yourself to know you're playing into her hands."

"That's not true." Jill edged over to peek in the window, but couldn't see a thing. "Victoria, your sister really could be in there, hurt or injured."

"No way, she's only gone one night, and she sleeps around, don't you get it? She's the crazy chick that men love." Victoria stepped closer. "All that talk about Dad being murdered is for attention. He wasn't murdered, Jill. I'm really not shocked, the way Dad died. He worked all the time, and he took meds, so what? I take them, too. It's not that bizarre."

"No one's saying that it is." Jill could hear that Victoria was feeling criticized, and it reminded her that Victoria was just as sensitive as Abby, maybe more, but would never let it show. Jill turned to her, trying to make peace. "Is that why you're so angry?"

Victoria's face flushed. "No, I'm angry because you and Abby are turning my father's death into yet another drama, and it's all about her. You should've seen her at the memorial service. She made that scene of running after you, and when she came back in, every man in the church was standing in line to console her."

Jill ignored the jealousy in Victoria's tone and pictured the memorial service, intrigued. "Does that include Neil? Did he say anything to you at the service?"

"I don't know Neil, and the service was chaos. I didn't see him or half of my friends, because of you." Victoria threw up her manicured hands. "You're making everything worse, Jill. You're making *Abby* worse. We're not yours anymore. Go home to your own family. Leave mine alone. In fact, leave now. *Go.*"

Jill felt slapped. "I understand how you feel, and I'm sorry, but I'm not going, not this time. I want to make sure Abby's okay."

"She's not, and she never will be. You should've thought about that before you ditched us." Victoria's tone changed slightly, her anger giving way to the pain, beneath, and Jill realized, like an epiphany, that Victoria was feeling as betrayed by her as she was by William.

"Victoria, I didn't ditch you, I want you to know that. I never ditched you. If I had my way, I would have seen both of you, anytime, but your father told me not to—"

"Shut up!" Victoria shouted, as if newly provoked. "Can't you leave my father out of it? Will you ever stop hating on him? He's *dead,* Jill!"

Jill felt stricken. Between fighting with Victoria and worrying about Abby, her head was about to explode. She looked back at the house. She didn't know what was taking the cops so long. The crowd was gathering. Suddenly, Jill took off for the stairs to William's house. She couldn't wait another minute to know if Abby was safe. She was going in.

"Jill, no!" Victoria shouted. "Don't go in! The cops said to stay here."

Jill hit the stairs just as Victoria's friend Brian came hurrying up the street.

"Brian!" Victoria called to him. "You're not going to believe this woman! She's driving me nuts!"

Jill hurried inside.

Chapter Twenty-three

Jill scanned the living room, relieved to see that Abby hadn't fallen down the stairs, and everything looked as it had last night. She could hear the police walking around on the second floor, and they were talking and joking with each other, their voices echoing in the large, open house.

Jill felt a wave of relief wash over her. If the police had found anything wrong, they wouldn't be joking around. But she didn't hear Abby's voice among theirs, which left her more confused than ever. Abby's car was here, but she was gone, and Jill wondered what had happened after she'd left that night, after dropping off the groceries.

She sneaked into the kitchen, which was large and ringed with gray enamel cabinets and black marble counters. Sunlight emanated from a window that overlooked the car park, and the kitchen was clean to the point of being unused. She wondered if Abby had ordered her Chinese take-out for dinner, so she opened the chrome trash can with a step-on lid, releasing the odor of a scented garbage bag. The can was empty, and there was no take-out debris.

Jill turned and opened the refrigerator door, but it was full of the food she'd bought—salmon, cold cuts, even blueberry yogurt.

None of it had been opened or eaten, and it suggested that Abby had left before dinner.

She closed the door and looked in the dishwasher, but there were no used tumblers. She noticed two bowls on the floor, one filled with triangle-shaped kibble. She remembered that Abby's cat drank half and half, but she didn't see the cat anywhere.

He always hides when people come over.

Jill went over to the bowl. It was full of half and half, and its surface had thickened, leaving a yellowing ring around the bowl. The bowl of kibble was also full. Just then she heard a commotion in the living room, and it sounded like Victoria and Brian entering the living room, and the cops, coming down the stairs, so Jill left the kitchen to meet them.

"What were you doing in there?" Victoria asked, frowning. She stood next to her friend Brian, who was tall and good-looking in wire-rimmed glasses, a starchy white oxford shirt, pressed jeans, and Gucci loafers, looking every inch the Manhattan lawyer, on the weekend.

Officer Mendina turned to Jill, disapproving. "Dr. Farrow, I asked you to wait on the sidewalk for your own safety."

"I know, I'm sorry. What did you find?"

"Nothing. She's not up there, and there's no sign of anything to worry about."

"Is the bed slept in? It's the blue one."

"No, it's made and didn't look slept in."

"Is there a suitcase out, or anything?"

"Nothing like that. It all looks normal, nothing out of place."

"When you were upstairs, did you see a cat?"

"No, she has a cat?"

"Yes, but it hides."

"Then it hid." Officer Mendina took out her long pad and slid a ballpoint pen from her shirt pocket. "Our procedure is to leave a 48A, an incident report, in plain view. It says we've been here, so when she comes home, she knows. But that's the most we can do."

"It just seems odd. She didn't eat last night, even though she told me she was hungry when I left. I went to get her groceries."

Victoria rolled her pretty eyes. "Oh, brother," she said, under her breath.

Officer Mendina cocked her head, her expression sympathetic. "Dr. Farrow, I have a twenty-year-old daughter, myself. She doesn't cook. Nobody cooks. Mom-to-Mom, don't worry about it. She'll be home when she gets home."

Jill wanted to believe her. "I'd agree if it weren't such strange circumstances, with her father."

Officer Mendina shrugged. "You still got questions, I'd take them over to Central Detectives. If there's a body on a floor in Philadelphia County, a detective gets called. Two, usually, and they work it up. Central Detectives has jurisdiction over the Sixth District, and they're the ones who decided it wasn't a suspicious death."

"Do you know which detective I could ask for, in particular?"

"No." Officer Mendina scribbled on a pad. "Whoever caught the case when the daughter called. That's what happened, right?"

"Yes, I believe so." Jill glanced at Victoria for verification, but Victoria only looked daggers at her.

"Then ask them." Officer Mendina tore off the sheet of paper, set it down on the coffee table, and gave the keys to Victoria. "Ms. Skyler, thanks for your cooperation. Looks like your sister isn't here, and I didn't see anything suspicious. Just the same, you're lucky to have somebody like Dr. Farrow worrying about you two."

"Thank you." Victoria dropped the keys into her big purse.

Jill caught Officer Mendina's eye. "Thank you for your help."

"You're welcome," she said, and the police left for the front door.

Victoria turned to Jill, frosty. "Leave. Go. Stay out of my life, and Abby's."

Jill composed herself. "I'm sorry for what happened, for everything. I was trying to help Abby, and I'd do the same for you, if you needed it."

"I won't need it." Victoria's eyes narrowed. "So now what? You're going to the police station? You're investigating my father's alleged murder? You're buying into Abby's craziness?"

"I'm going to see what I can find out in the hope it will shed some light on where Abby is. I'm not investigating any murder, I'm looking for your sister. Good-bye now, and please call me if Abby calls you." Jill started to walk to the door, but Brian caught her by the arm.

"I'm Brian Pendle, and I don't believe we've met." His blue eyes flashed behind his glasses, and his grip on her forearm felt oddly firm.

Jill pulled her arm away. "I'm Jill—"

"Oh, I know who you are." Brian's tone was calm and controlled. "Let me break it down for you, Dr. Farrow. Victoria's been through hell since her Dad's death. It's hard enough for her to deal with that and her sister, while she's in law school. I don't know what your agenda is, but you need to step off."

Jill felt taken aback. "I don't have an agenda, except helping Abby."

"Nevertheless, you don't belong. I'm an attorney, and if you keep this up, calling Victoria at odd hours and taking property that is part of her father's estate, I'll file for a restraining order against you."

Jill bit her tongue. "Good-bye, now," she said, going to the door. She wasn't afraid of restraining orders anymore. She was afraid that something had happened to Abby.

Not even a lawyer could stop a mother.

Chapter Twenty-four

"I'm Jill Farrow, I'm wondering if you could help me," she said to the affable detective sitting at the front desk. She'd never been inside a real squad room before, and it looked distinctly less photogenic than on network TV. Two detectives worked on outdated computers at old gray desks stacked high with files and papers, and the sun struggled through dirty windows on one wall, barely illuminating a panel of mismatched file cabinets and a cork bulletin board cluttered with Wanted posters, official memos, wrinkled cartoons, and an old March Madness office pool.

"Yes, hi, I'm Detective Pitkowski." The detective extended a hammy hand over a half-eaten Egg McMuffin, which filled the air with the aroma of steamed sausage. He was in his fifties, completely bald, with an unusually bumpy head and steely glasses that perched atop a bulbous nose. "What can I do for you?"

"It's about my former stepdaughter, Abby Skyler. She's nineteen, and she didn't come home last night. I'm worried it has something to do with her father, William Skyler, who was found dead in their home on Acorn Street, last Tuesday."

"Skyler? I know that case." Detective Pitkowski nodded, pushing up his glasses from the bridge. "It wasn't a homicide."

"Abby thinks it was. Were you the detective on the case?"

"No. And you are—"

"His ex-wife."

"Is this a joke?" Detective Pitkowski chuckled, and his pot belly jiggled, straining the buttons on his shirt, above his belt. He had on a striped tie with his white, short-sleeved shirt, and an old-school tie clip. "I got an ex who'd throw a party if I kicked the bucket."

Jill managed a smile. "No, it's not a joke. I'm trying to find Abby. Can I talk to the detective who worked on the case? Do you know who it was?"

"Detective Reed, but he's not in, and he couldn't meet with you, anyway. You're not immediate family."

"But I was."

"You're not now. Sorry."

Jill felt momentarily stumped. "My problem is that Abby has been gone all night, and she was raising questions about her father's death, so I'm worried that something bad happened to her."

"Like what?" Detective Pitkowski asked, cocking his shiny head.

"Worst case scenario, some form of foul play." Jill shuddered at the very notion. "She thought there was something fishy about the prescription painkillers that killed her father, and it turns out that they were gotten via a forged script, and the guy who filled the script was in disguise."

"Whoa, whoa, whoa." Detective Pitkowski put up his hand. "Let me ask you something. How did you find this out?"

"I went to the pharmacy and checked. Also, I think there's been a black SUV following her lately, and maybe even me. The license plate starts with a T."

Detective Pitkowski frowned. "How do you know it's following you?"

"I saw it, twice." Jill saw his expression change to skepticism. "What do you advise I do, if she's missing?"

"She's not a missing person after only one night."

"I would agree with you, if not for whatever happened to her father. She lives with him, and if he was murdered, maybe she saw something or knows something, or the killer *thinks* she does, and that's why she's gone."

"You're speculating wildly here." Detective Pitkowski eyed her. "Tell you what, when she comes home, and I bet she will, have her come in. Detective Reed will sit down with her, talk to her, and answer any questions she has. You can come with her, if you like."

"Let me ask you this. Detective Reed took her father's cell phone, wallet, and the pills. Would he give them back to her?"

"The phone and wallet, yes."

"Would he show her your file, your investigation of her father's death, if she had questions about whether it was really a murder?"

Detective Pitkowski shook his head. "No, not even immediate family sees our files. It has crime scene photos and the like. We show that to no one."

"If she got a lawyer, could he see it? Or if she hired a private investigator?"

"No. No charges were filed, so it should never come to light."

Jill took a flyer. "Do you happen to know if Detective Reed spoke with any of my ex-husband's business associates about the case? There's a man in New York named Neil Straub whom he should call. I have Straub's address."

"Hold up, I suggest we do it this way." Detective Pitkowski slid a ballpoint from a Phillies mug on the desk. "Give me all the information you have, and I can pass it on to Detective Reed. The prescription, the SUV, the whole kit and caboodle. He'll look into it."

"Will he get back to me?"

"Only if he has a question, he will. Otherwise, he's not gonna discuss this case with you. If the daughter calls, he'll discuss it with her."

"Okay, thanks." Jill told him the story, and Detective Pitkowski listened in a professional way, taking notes and asking questions. It took about twenty minutes, and when she was finished, she hurried from the police station, checking her watch on the fly. She'd make it back just in time to see Megan swim.

She hustled to the car, chirped it open, hopped in, and started the engine, but couldn't stop worrying about Abby. Jill remembered what she'd said to her, only last night.

There's me, Abby. You always have me.

Chapter Twenty-five

Parents and kids filled the pool area, and their cheering, talk, and laughter echoed harshly off the tile walls and deck. The air was warm and thick, and the meet was already underway, but Jill had five minutes before Megan swam. She scurried up the stairs to the bleachers and spotted Sam sitting with the other swim moms and dads, Len Wynn and Rita Cohen, the McGraths, and Bill Roche and Jenny Zeleny.

"Sam!" she called out, and he turned, breaking into a grin.

Sam motioned her to come over, and Len and Rita looked up, smiled, and shifted aside to make room as Jill picked her way down the row. She sat down on the hard wooden bleacher and kissed Sam lightly on the lips.

"Hiya, honey." Jill was already sweating under her shirt, and she could practically feel her hair curl. "I made it."

"Way to go. What happened? Was Abby there?"

"No, but her car was. I went to the police, and they checked the house."

"Good." Sam nodded, his face shiny from the humidity.

"I told the police everything, but I'm still worried that she hasn't called me back."

Sam patted her leg again. "I gave Megan her swim bag."

Jill could see he was over talking about Abby. "Was Megan bothered that I wasn't there?"

"If she was, she didn't say so. I told her you went to check on Abby, and she seemed fine with it."

"Good." Jill turned her attention to the pool, which was new and Olympic-sized, to accommodate the high school. Navy-and-white tiles rimmed the edge, in Sequanic High colors, matching the floating lane dividers. The far wall was a panel of glass, and it flooded the pool area with indirect light, making bright shadows of each ripple, illuminating the chop churned up by a hundred arms and legs, like a restless sea.

Sam craned his neck at the starting blocks, where the girls clumped together, a noisy flock of yellow bathing suits and swim caps, like so many baby chicks. "Which one's Megan? I can never tell. They all look alike."

"There." Jill pointed at Megan, standing near the front and swinging her arms to keep them warm. The yellow spandex of her bathing suit outlined her skinny little body, and Jill could see her hips and breasts, formed but not fully mature, somewhere between girl and young woman.

"How can you always tell it's her?"

"It's like penguins. You know your own."

Sam gave her a sweet nudge, and they both watched Megan, who was looking up at the bleachers, trying to find them in a way that wasn't obvious.

"Hey, honey!" Jill called out, raising her hand, but Megan was still looking for her. "She doesn't see us."

"Yes, she does."

"No, she doesn't, I can tell." Jill stood up, waving her arms, but Megan had already turned away and was talking to Courtney, their yellow caps close together. Jill shouted, "Megan!"

"Down in front!" called a man behind her, and Sam turned around and shot him an annoyed look.

"It's okay." Jill sat down, and on her other side, Rita leaned over. "He's from the Plymouth Meeting club. Want me to hit him?"

Jill smiled. "It's okay, I just like it when Megan knows I'm here.

We always make eye contact before she gets on the block. It's our thing."

"She saw you." Sam patted her leg. "It's okay, relax."

Jill thought Megan looked worried as she walked toward Coach Stash. Jim "Stash" Stashevsky was only in his thirties, short but powerfully built in his yellow polo shirt and sweats. He bent over to talk to Megan, tucking his clipboard under his arm, and she listened intently, nodding as he spoke, her dark eyes looking up at him and her mouth making a stiff little line, like a dash.

Sam shifted forward on the bleachers. "You can do it, Megan!"

Jill made a megaphone of her hands. "Go, Megan, go!"

Megan climbed onto the third platform, swinging her arms, then slipping her yellow goggles down over her eyes and adjusting them on her head, her cap, and her nose. Jill knew all of Megan's swim rituals, and the time for making eye contact with Mom was over. She'd be visualizing the race, ignoring the other swimmers as they climbed onto the blocks, shaking their arms and fidgeting with their goggles.

"Go, Megan!" Jill shouted again.

"Come on, Megan!" Sam hollered, and Rita, Len, and the others cheered for Megan, because they all cheered for each other's kids. The parents from other clubs added to the chorus, hooting and hollering for their own kids.

Megan and the others took the positions on the blocks, bending at their bony knees, tucking their heads, and curling their toes around the edge. The electronic beeper sounded, barely audible above the crowd noise, and the girls shot into the air, stretching out their lithe bodies and extending their fingers and toes. For a split second, they were all knifing forward through thin air, transformed from girls into something that could fly. But Megan didn't get her typical smooth start, and she hit the water behind the others.

"Sam?" Jill heard herself say, her gaze on Megan. "Did you see that? She's off."

"She'll catch up."

"No, it's not that." Jill had been a competitive swimmer, but she didn't care about Megan's time or if she won. Megan's skinny arms started to bend and extend, but they were churning more than usual, and she didn't move through the water the way she always did. Her hands slapped the surface, and her kick was too low, not her distinctive flutter. "Am I crazy, or is something the matter?"

"No, she's fine."

"Go, Megan, go!" Jill yelled. The other swimmers stroked ahead, kicking hard and picking up the pace, and Coach Stash shouted for Megan, holding his clipboard to his mouth, to amplify the sound.

Megan fell behind two lengths, then three, and the other girls reached the wall, straining for the tiles with outstretched fingertips. Megan only seemed to slow down, losing ground.

Jill leapt to her feet. "Go, Megan!"

Sam rose. "Go, Megan!"

The man behind them yelled, "Sit down!"

They both ignored him, and Jill started to worry as Megan took a few more feeble strokes, then stopped in the middle of her lane. Coach Stash hustled poolside past the cheering teammates, and before Jill knew why, she found herself in motion, climbing down the bleachers toward the pool, pushing past the other parents.

"Yo, watch it!" one man said, as Jill moved him aside. The race continued fast and furious, the crowd kept cheering, and the teams on the pool deck jumped up and down with excitement.

"Megan!" Jill cried out, just as Megan's yellow cap disappeared beneath the water. Glare from the windows reflected on the chop, whiting out the water's surface, obliterating everything.

"Help!" Jill reached the bottom row of the bleachers, threw herself over the rail, and half stumbled and half slipped toward the pool.

Megan was gone.

Coach Stash dropped his clipboard and dove into the water. Jill dove in behind him. The water muffled the cheering, and she opened her eyes to see Megan sinking to the bottom of the pool, her eyes closed and air bubbles leaking from her mouth.

Coach Stash reached Megan first, grabbed her by the waist,

and raised her head up and out of the water. Jill grabbed her other side, pushed aside the floating lane markers, and they all popped together to the surface.

"Megan!" Jill shouted, terrified. Megan remained unconscious, her head flopped over. "Get her to the side!"

Coach Stash nodded, his eyes wide with fear. The race stopped, and the cheering silenced. Kids and parents watched in shock, and a stricken Sam came running.

"Megan, Megan!" Jill shouted, swimming with Megan, and they reached the edge of the pool. The coaches grabbed Megan and lowered her onto the pool deck. One flipped Megan onto her back and started to administer CPR, but she coughed and gasped.

"Megan!" Jill climbed out of the pool and scrambled to kneel beside her on the watery deck.

"Stay back!" shouted one of the other coaches, stiff-arming Jill, but she brushed it aside.

"I'm her mother and a doctor," she said, turning Megan onto her side, letting her cough out the water. Coach Stash, the other coaches, and all the swimmers gathered around while Jill kept a hand on Megan, who was spasming with coughs. "Honey, let it come out. Cough it out."

"Mom?" Megan said, weakly.

"I'm here." Jill held her steady. "You're okay. Everything's okay."

Megan expelled the pool water, inhaling deeply.

"Just breathe, honey." Jill sent up a silent prayer of thanks, and Sam came through the crowd of coaches, horrified.

"Is she okay?"

"Yes," Jill answered, holding back tears of relief.

Later, Jill, Sam, and Coach Stash stood at the exit of the high school, where the ambulance was driving around to pick Megan up. A healthy pink had returned to her cheeks, and she was breathing normally, sitting wrapped in a yellow team towel. She'd taken off her swim cap, and her dark blonde ponytail hung down her back, its tip wet, like a brush dipped in black paint. She sipped water from a bottle, and Courtney sat next to her in a wet bathing suit and towel, providing moral support.

Jill touched Megan's shoulder. "Feel better, sweetie?"

"Yes, I'm fine." Megan glanced over her shoulder at the pool, where the other swimmers were visible through the windows. "I don't have to go to the hospital, do I, Mom?"

"Yes, it's a good idea to have you checked out."

"But can't you guys drive me, please? An ambulance is so embarrassing."

"It's safer this way, just in case."

"Do we have to? I'm fine, now, I really am."

"Let's do it this way, honey." Jill patted Megan on the shoulder.

"It won't have the siren, will it?"

"I don't hear one."

Megan set down the water bottle, then glanced back at the other swimmers again. "Court, is he there?"

Courtney nodded, and Jill realized that Megan was embarrassed in front of her new crush.

Megan looked up at Coach Stash, her eyes baleful. "I'm sorry, Coach. I let you down, and the club."

Courtney shook her head, her goggles around her neck. Her cute little mouth tilted down at the corners. "No, you didn't, Megs."

"Don't worry about it." Coach Stash shot Megan a wink, his team towel over his soaking sweats. His wet hair was a shiny black helmet. "Nice warm water, big-time pool. I felt like a swim, and so did your mother. Right, Jill?"

"Right." Jill smiled, grateful for his kindness to Megan. "You're fast, Coach."

"If I'm not, I'm fired."

Megan looked up at him. "Will we lose now, Coach? Because of me?"

"Just focus on getting better." Coach Stash patted her on the shoulder. "You're our star, Megster. You'll always be our star."

"I warmed up so well." Megan shook her head. "All of a sudden, my heart started beating real fast. It felt like I was going to die. Like it was going to jump out of my chest."

Courtney looked over at Megan. "Was it like that time we had the triple shot at Starbucks?"

"No, worse. A lot worse."

Jill already had a diagnosis, and it wasn't a difficult one. "Honey, when did it start, your heart beating so fast?"

"Before the race. My hands got sweaty, too. My palms." Megan showed her hands, palms up. "At first I thought it was pool water, but when I wiped it off on my suit, it kept coming back. It got worse when I got on the block. I thought it would go away, but it didn't."

"Could you see okay?"

"Yes."

"Hear any weird sounds?"

"No."

"Dizzy?"

"No."

"Any headache?"

"No, and when I dove, I couldn't catch my breath and my heart wouldn't stop, and then I just, I don't know, went unconscious." Megan looked down. "I drank my water, Mom, I did."

"I know, honey." Jill didn't think it was dehydration, and Megan had no history of heart problems or low blood sugar. Suddenly, an orange-and-white ambulance reversed into the driveway and braked, then the back doors opened and a paramedic sprang from inside, rolling out a gurney on wheels. The kids at the pool pressed closer to the window, and Megan groaned at the sight.

Jill helped her to her feet. "Let's go, sweetie."

Megan rose. "Thank God there's no siren."

Courtney got up, too. "I've never been inside an ambulance. I think it's awesome, Megan."

"Mom, can she come with us?"

"Sorry, I don't think that's allowed. You're stuck with me." Jill motioned the paramedics over with the rolling gurney, and Megan lay down so they could strap her in.

And just then, the ambulance's siren went off.

Chapter Twenty-six

Jill sat in the hard chair in the examining room, her damp clothes sticking to her body. She'd dried off as best as she could with some paper towels, and she and Sam were alone together while Megan had been taken off for tests. A fluorescent panel overhead shed bright light, and the pastel blue walls were covered with inspirational posters and state-of-the-art equipment. The air smelled of an antiseptic that did little to stop bacterial infections, many of which were spread by doctors who didn't wash their hands between patients. But that was one of the profession's dirty little secrets.

"So, what do you think?" Jill asked. "Panic attack?"

"Agree." Sam was leaning against the wall with his arms crossed. "It's been tough for her, lately."

"Yes, it has." Jill shook her head, kicking herself. "And all I could think of on the way here was Abby. I even called back a bunch of patients, and I worried about one of them, Rahul, a baby waiting on a CBC. I worried about all of them, not Megan. You can say I told you so, anytime."

"No, I wouldn't, you know that."

"Thanks." Jill appreciated him being so kind. "Panic attacks are symptomatic of anxiety. All in one weekend, she lost her stepfather, got thrown out of a church, and was reunited with her ex-stepsister, who puked on her bed."

"Don't beat yourself up." Sam straightened up, walked over, and stroked her hair, which was finally drying. "After all, you're the mom who jumped into the pool to save her."

Too little, too late.

"Honey?" Sam asked, and Jill realized she'd lost focus, remembering what Victoria had said, this morning.

"Sorry."

"You were in that pool before I knew she was going under. I thought you were going to dive on top of Coach."

Jill knew he was trying to cheer her up, but it wasn't working. She felt so guilty, first over Abby, then over Victoria, and now over Megan. She'd been trying to mother all the girls and failing each of them. She didn't know how she had managed being a mother of three before, or how any mother did it, with more than one child. It wasn't just a juggling act, it was a *magic* act.

Sam touched her shoulder, gently. "Maybe we should think about making an appointment with Sandy, for Megan. Let her talk it out, explore her feelings about William's death."

"I'll think about it." Jill groaned. "I'm not only a bad mother, I'm a bad ex-stepmother."

"It's okay." Sam rubbed her back. "You want some coffee? I saw vending machines in the hall."

"I would, thanks." Jill smiled up at him, and Sam bent down and kissed her on the cheek.

"Be right back. Hang tight."

"Thanks. I really love you, you know that?"

Sam lifted his eyebrows, surprised. "What did I do right?"

"Everything. Sorry it was such a difficult weekend."

"No apology necessary." Sam flashed her a reassuring smile, then left.

Jill tilted her head backwards, against the wall. She wondered if Victoria had been right, and she had blown everything out of proportion. Maybe Abby had met a cute guy and stayed out all night. Maybe William wasn't murdered but filled the scripts in disguise, for the reason Sam had said. Maybe Abby was in denial, and Jill had jumped at the chance to get back into her life, to have a permanently needy child at home.

We're not yours anymore.

Jill swallowed hard. She thought of the Venn diagrams again and pictured herself stuck in the intersection of circles, a member of both families at once, conflating past and present. Katie had said that motherhood had no expiration date, and Jill had agreed, believing to the bone that that it transcended everything—biology, law, even time and space.

Abby's in our family, Mom. You just can't kick someone out of your family.

Jill thought of what Megan had said that day, feeling the weight of her words and their truth. Jill resolved to fight harder, for her family, and she couldn't neglect Megan just because Abby was missing, especially because Megan was probably worried about Abby, too.

Jill slid her BlackBerry from her purse, relieved that she hadn't had it in her back pocket when she'd jumped into the pool. She checked it, but there were no new messages from Abby.

I'm glad you didn't change your phone number. Am I still A on your speed dial?

Jill scrolled to her phone log, found the last time that Abby had called her from her cell phone, and saved the number to her speed dial, under A.

Now all Abby had to do was call.

Chapter Twenty-seven

Jill set the swim bag and purse down in the entrance hall while Beef met them all at the front door, wagging his tail and sniffing all the strange new smells. "Hiya, Beef," she said, dropping her key into the bowl.

"Hey, pal." Megan scratched the golden behind the ears. "Guess what? We lost."

Jill looked over. "Don't let it bother you, honey."

"Right." Sam closed the door behind them, muffling the noise of a neighbor's lawnmower. "Dogs don't care about winning and losing. They're too smart for that. They love you, no matter what."

"I love you, too, boy." Megan bent over and kissed Beef on the muzzle, and Sam whistled for the dog.

"Come on, Beefsteak. Wanna go out?" Sam went to the back door, and Beef trotted after him, his nails clicking on the hardwood.

"Let's eat," Jill said, going to her comfort default. "Anybody else hungry?"

"I am." Megan flashed a game smile. She looked like herself again, her eyes bright and her hair dry, in its messy braid. She'd changed into a gray hoodie and jeans at the hospital, and the ER doc confirmed that she'd had a panic attack. She hadn't asked any questions, and if it'd bothered her, she hadn't let it show. Jill was wondering if that was part of the problem.

"Megan, I'm going upstairs to change, and I'll be right back."

"Okay. I'll get a drink."

"Oh, wait, I'll get it for you." Jill started into the kitchen, but Megan waved her off with a smile.

"Mom, I can get it myself. You don't have to baby me."

"Okay." Jill checked herself. "Be right down."

"Good. Love you."

"Love you, too." Jill gave her a quick kiss, then went upstairs to her bedroom and peeled off the clammy shirt, then her jeans. She was about to toss them in the hamper, but they felt heavy, and she realized she'd left her BlackBerry in her pocket. She pulled it out and checked the messages, but there were none. She slid into her go-to jeans and a thin white T-shirt under a navy cotton sweater, then found a barrette and clipped up her wet hair. She slid the phone into her back pocket and went downstairs to the kitchen.

"Hi, Mom." Megan was writing in her binder, already doing her homework at the kitchen island. The pink troll doll that sat atop her pencil wiggled with each stroke, and her phone rested near her right hand.

"Hiya, sweetie. Why don't you put your notebook away and take a break, until after dinner?"

"I can't, I have to finish this dumb worksheet." Megan wrote in her notebook while checking her phone.

"Honey, no phones at the table, okay?"

"We're not eating yet, and everyone's texting. They want to know how I am." Megan looked up, eyes pleading, pencil poised. She had spent most of the ride home answering text messages, and Jill was guessing that the mystery boy was one of them.

"Okay, just for today."

"Thanks. Can we have grilled cheese?"

"For dinner? I could make salmon, and we have brown rice."

"Nah, I'm hungry, and I have to finish my homework."

"Do you need more time? I can probably get you an extension, if we show them the ER doctor's note." Jill realized it was the wrong thing to say as soon as she'd said it, and Megan winced.

"No, I can do it, and I don't mind grilled cheese. Is that okay?"

Sam came into the kitchen, with Beef trotting behind. "Grilled cheese is fine with me, too," he said, going to the island.

"Grilled cheese it is." Jill went to the fridge, feeling a warm rush of love for Sam. He'd eat anything to make Megan happy.

"Mom, can we put the tomato inside, like last time?"

"Sure." Jill rummaged in the fridge and retrieved a block of cheddar cheese, bread, and two tomatoes.

"Awesome." Megan filled in a blank on her worksheet, and Sam looked over her shoulder, sliding his reading glasses on.

"What're you working on, kitten?"

"Health. It's so dumb."

Sam eyed the worksheet. "Ask me about fallopian tubes, go ahead. I'm an expert. I have five."

"Eeeww!" Megan squealed, giving him a playful shove, and not long afterwards, the kitchen was filled with the delicious aroma of grilled cheese sandwiches, the merry noise of talk and laughter, and the sweet snoring of an overweight golden. Not to mention the occasional beep of a text message.

In other words, a family.

Or at least, most of one.

Chapter Twenty-eight

Jill took her time tucking Megan into bed, because that was when they usually talked things over. She knew Megan had a lot on her mind, because she'd grown quieter as night fell. "How you doing, sweetie?" Jill asked, sitting on the edge of the bed.

"I'm okay, I guess." Megan pulled her covers up, watching Beef circle a few times before assuming his customary curl on the bed. "He's making his glazed doughnut."

"He's beyond cute."

"What a good dog." Megan patted Beef's back, where his coat curled in waves.

"He sure is." Jill moved some hair back from Megan's face, and her eyes glowed in the warm light from the lamp, on her night-table. White dots of acne medication made a constellation on her chin.

"Did you throw my other sheets away?"

"No, Sam took them to the Laundromat. The comforter, too. Wasn't that nice of him? So I didn't have to."

Megan grinned. "Gross, right?"

"I'll say. What a guy."

"You don't always have to tell me how great Sam is. I know he's great. I love him."

Jill's throat caught. She hadn't realized she did that, but Megan was right. "I love him, too," she said, simply. "So what's on your mind? I can tell those wheels are turning."

Megan frowned, her smooth forehead creased by one tiny line. "Like, I don't know what comes after you die. What do you really think happens?"

"Really?" Jill guessed Megan was talking about William, and maybe Gray, too. "I think your spirit lives on, with God. I think all your emotion and thought and heart can't just vanish."

"Do you think somebody killed William? Courtney says there would be more evidence, like *CSI*."

Jill hoped to ease Megan's mind, not upset her before bed. "I don't know, but I told the police about it, and they're looking into it."

"You did? When?"

"Today. That's why I was late to the meet, and I'm sorry about that."

"It's okay, Sam told me. Do you think Abby's okay?"

"I'm sure she is."

"But she still hasn't called you. I saw you checking your phone, after dinner."

"I'm hoping she will soon."

"I sent her a message on Facebook, but she didn't answer yet. I sent one to Victoria, too. She didn't answer, either."

Jill hid her annoyance at Victoria. "When did you do that?"

"When I was doing my homework."

Jill let it go. She didn't like the multitasking that Megan did, but she knew it couldn't be stopped. Her own mother used to say, do one thing at a time, but those days were long gone.

"Abby has lots of guy friends on her Facebook page. I was thinking that she could be with a guy friend. Maybe she's not really gone, or missing."

"You're right, that's what I'm hoping. Don't worry about Abby. Leave that to me." Jill tugged the comforter up, and next to Megan, Beef lowered his head onto his paws, closing his eyes. "You need to get a good night's sleep."

"Am I lame because I had a panic attack?" Megan asked, after a moment.

"No, of course not." Jill kissed her warmly on the cheek. "It's been a hard weekend, with the news about William. On top of that you have homework, the meet, Abby, and your Guitar Hero. There's a lot of emotion, all at once. It's too much for anybody to deal with, even somebody as strong as you."

"I thought I was having a heart attack."

"I bet. You weren't, it just felt that way."

"I thought I was going to die. You can't die from a panic attack, can you?"

"No, of course not." Jill stroked her cheek.

"I mean, what if I die tonight? In my sleep?"

"Honey, no, that can't happen." Jill was about to launch into a medical explanation, but stopped when she read Megan's expression. Her brow wrinkled deeply, and her lips clenched over her braces, in what was becoming a nervous habit. Megan was an anxious little girl in the body of a young woman, and she didn't need a pediatrician, she needed a mom. Jill gathered her up and gave her a big hug. "Everything's going to be okay, honey. Don't worry about a thing."

"Wanna lie down with me a while, Mom? Like we used to?"

"Good idea." Jill released Megan, then reached up and turned off the light, leaving them both in a soft, velvety darkness. "Move over, okay?"

"Sure." Megan shifted over in bed, and so did Beef, which left a skinny strip for Jill at the edge of the bed, only as wide as a balance beam, but familiar to mothers everywhere.

"Perfect," Jill said, meaning it, and she hugged Megan close, feeling her body relax.

"You sure I won't die?"

"Positive." Jill hadn't realized that when Megan was asking about death, she was asking about her own. "It's impossible. Don't worry about it, at all. Okay?"

"Okay." Megan paused. "Did you really kiss thousands of guys, Mom?"

"*Millions.*" Jill laughed, and so did Megan.

Sam's silhouette appeared in the door. "What's going on in here? Sounds like you two girls need adult supervision."

Jill was about to answer, but Megan beat her to it, opening her arms to him.

"Sam," Megan called out. "Come in! Kitten needs hugs! Hugs!"

"Talked me into it." Sam walked over, piling into bed and giving Megan a big hug, and Jill watched Megan cling to him. Sam was a true father to her, not just the father figure that William had been, and it would kill Megan to lose him.

Jill had to find a way to make it work, when Abby came home.

If Abby came home.

Chapter Twenty-nine

It was Monday morning, and Jill walked from the parking lot to the office, trying to switch mental gears. She'd worried about Megan and Abby all night, tossing and turning, but she'd have to put them to the back of her mind today. Flu season was like tax time for germs, and she'd need to focus at work. She'd called Padma about Rahul, and he was still feverish. She wished she'd ordered his bloodwork stat, just so she'd have the answer.

PEMBEY FAMILY PRACTICE, read the carved wooden sign in front of the large stone home, one of many on the street that had been converted to offices for doctors, lawyers, and accountants. Pembey was the town next to Jill's, only twenty minutes from her house, and a suburban practice had been just the ticket while Megan was still young.

Jill opened the door onto the waiting room, greeted by its freshened air and soothing blue décor. Big bay windows made it feel cheery, homey, and bright, even on an overcast day like today. Patients occupied most of the comfy blue-patterned chairs, reading magazines or typing into BlackBerrys, but none of the patients was hers. She didn't have anybody for half an hour, and she'd come in early to catch up on her charting and insurance paperwork, which was endless. Pembey Family took fifteen types of insurance, and Aetna alone was four of them.

Jill headed for the door leading to the doctors' offices and examination rooms, then spotted Elaine Fitzmartin standing at the intake window, signing in her elderly mother, Mary, who was an Alzheimer's patient of Dr. Thoma's. They were in all the time, and Jill liked them both. "Hi, ladies, how are you this morning?" she asked.

"Fine," Mary answered, turning with a sweet smile. "You look nice today."

"Thank you," Jill said, though she only had on her usual cotton sweater, khakis, and clogs. "How are you feeling today?"

"I did the crossword this morning, in pen. Do you do the crossword?"

"Not in pen, my dear. Good for you. Keep it up." Jill turned to Elaine, because she knew from taking care of her own mother that caretakers needed caretaking, too. "And how about you, Elaine?"

"We're fine, thanks. Much better now that Mom's on Memoril."

"Great." Jill didn't know much about Alzheimer meds. "And you, are you living on the edge, too? Doing crosswords in pen?"

Elaine smiled. "No, but I'm loving that book you lent me, the mystery. I can't put it down."

"Great." Jill noticed Sheryl, their office manager, eavesdropping from the file cabinets, but she ignored her. "You won't guess the ending, so don't even try."

"I always try, and I think I know who did it."

Jill smiled. "Don't skip ahead, like last time." She turned to Mary. "You're her mom. Tell her not to skip ahead."

"Oh, she never obeys me. She never obeys anybody."

"Then you raised her right," Jill said, and they all laughed. Behind them, Sheryl was motioning to Jill to finish the conversation.

"Excuse me, ladies, I've got to go. Take care." Jill opened the door into the hallway, and Sheryl swooped out to meet her, short and stocky in her blue scrubs, with bristly, short hair that was prematurely gray, from trying to control the universe.

"I need to speak with you in your office, right away."

Jill didn't break stride. "Okay, I have an idea. Why don't I invite you into my office to speak with me, right away?"

"That's not funny." Sheryl clutched a file folder to her chest.

"By the way, good morning." Jill opened the door into her office, a windowless white box that held her diplomas, licenses, reference books, and a neat desk with a struggling ficus plant. She spent as little time as possible here, preferring the examining rooms. She loved her patients, but didn't love working at Pembey Family, mainly because of Sheryl. "So what's up?"

"I need to speak to you about your stats, again. I know you're part-time, so I accounted for that." Sheryl pursed her thin lips. Her eyes were dirt brown, and she had the doughy features of a baby, without any of the charm. "I sent an email to John, showing that last quarter, you saw only between eighteen and twenty cases a day." Sheryl whipped out a printout of numbers, from the folder. "That's ten to twelve fewer than the average of all the other docs. Each doc needs to keep the schedule, and you need to see more cases a day."

"They're patients, not cases, and if you want to talk averages, their average age is two." Jill had explained this many times before. "I'm the only pediatrician here. I take longer because babies can't tell you where it hurts."

"Don't be funny."

"I wasn't being funny, just now. I was being funny, before." Jill gave up on the humor thing, and Sheryl's eyes hardened.

"The numbers don't lie. You take too long with the cases. You have to draw the line. Five minutes with each case, ten at the max, and twenty only if it's an annual. You're consistently running twenty minutes or longer, with each case."

"Sheryl, come on. Pediatricians don't work the same as adult docs, we can't." Jill had said this before, too. "Each visit, I have two patients, a parent and a child. I use the time it takes to give my patients the best care possible, and no more."

Sheryl gestured at the door. "Like with Mrs. Fitzmartin, you chat them up, don't you?"

Jill almost laughed. "Guilty as charged. I'm friendly with the patients."

"She's not your patient."

"I *like* her, is that okay with you? If I were keeping patients waiting, it would be different, but John wanted me to build a pediatric practice. The best way to grow is to provide quality care, including the relationship side. The statistics aren't the same for me."

Sheryl arched an eyebrow. "You don't follow *any* of the rules of Pembey Family, whether they pertain to a pediatric practice or not."

"Of course I do. Which rules don't I follow?"

"For starters, you answer questions by email."

Jill blinked. "How do you know that?"

"We monitor it."

Jill recoiled. "You *read* my email?"

"It's not your email, it's Pembey Family email. We own it, it's proprietary, and it's my job to monitor it."

"Since when?" Jill should have guessed as much, but somehow she hadn't. "Why do you care if I answer by email? We lose the exam fee?"

"It's a business, Jill. We don't encourage uncompensated phone or email advice. You're the only doc who gives out her intraoffice email, Jill@pembeyfamily.com, which you're not supposed to do, either. All patient email has to go to me, at info@pembeyfamily."

"Then it gets to me three days later."

Sheryl frowned. "Also, you're exposing us to lawsuits if your orders are misunderstood, or if a misdiagnosis is made because the case wasn't seen."

"I would never prescribe anything unless it was a patient I'd seen, and I don't use it for acute medical issues." Jill was so sick of hearing about lawsuits. Pembey had layers of CYA paperwork in case they got sued, and that was on top of the insurance-company paperwork. "I have to be available by phone and email. You can't tell Mom to chill out when her baby's sick."

"You're only hurting yourself, you know. Your bonus would be higher if you were more productive."

"Seeing more patients isn't necessarily more productive, and if money were all that mattered, I'd do cosmetic surgery for a living."

Sheryl's eyes narrowed. "You think everything is a joke, don't you?"

"No, I don't. I take my patients and my practice very seriously. I'm using humor to keep the mood light, and I'm failing, evidently."

"I have a sense of humor."

"Where?" Jill smiled, and Sheryl frowned.

"You act as if you're the exception."

"I am, because of what I *do*."

"Not so. You're the only part-timer we have. Why? That doesn't have anything to do with what you *do*."

"Yes, it does." Jill felt taken aback. Of all of Sheryl's complaints, she'd never heard this one before. "I do it to be home with my daughter. I love kids, even if they're mine, as absurd as that sounds."

"Megan's *thirteen,* Jill. I don't think she needs you to take her to playdates anymore. You'd be working full-time if you were committed to Pembey Family."

"I'm committed to *my* family, okay?" Jill felt herself flush. "I made a part-time deal when I got here, and I still don't get home some nights until eight."

"Every doc here works long hours."

"I'm sure," Jill said, though she never saw any of the four other docs. They all ran separate practices, and there was no time to interact with anyone except Sheryl. "But I'm the only woman, the only mom."

"So again, you're the exception."

"Yes." Jill wasn't getting anywhere. "Look, I have to do some charting, then get ready for Carrie Bryson, who'll be here any minute. She has a two-year-old and she emailed me last night, about his rash. She called the office first, for the after-hours program." Jill caught herself. "But I guess you knew that."

"Yes, and you told her that you could squeeze her in this

morning. You have to stop doing that, too." Sheryl frowned. "She has to go through Donna. Donna is the appointment secretary."

"I emailed Donna and told her myself."

"That's not Pembey Family procedure. These procedures serve a purpose. If we don't know Carrie's coming in, we can't pull her file, and we can't make sure that the case is properly logged, coded, and billed."

"Donna wasn't available at midnight, when I answered the email. I know we have procedures, but they can't get in the way of the patients and the medicine. That's why we're here."

Rring! Jill's cell phone rang in her back pocket, and her heart leapt up. It had to be Abby; it wasn't the ringtone for Megan or Sam. "Excuse me." She reached for her phone and checked the screen. She didn't recognize the number but she wasn't taking any chances. "Sorry, I have to get this."

Sheryl was already stalking away. "Don't be long," she called over her shoulder, closing the door behind her as the call connected.

"Jill, it's Victoria, calling from home. Have you heard from Abby?"

"No," Jill answered, surprised. Victoria sounded less angry. Not warm exactly, but not as hostile as yesterday. "She hasn't returned my calls."

"Mine, either." Victoria paused. "She usually calls me back, eventually. She would have called by now, especially after the last message I left."

"Why? What did you say?"

"I yelled at her."

Jill could imagine. "Did you check the house again?"

"Yes, and I don't think she's been home. The car is there."

"How about the cat?"

"I don't know, I didn't check. I never see that cat."

Jill sank into her chair, her gaze wandering over the things in her office, ending with the miserable ficus. "Do you have any idea where she could be?"

"No, none."

"Is there anyone she would turn to?"

"Not that I know of, in particular."

"What about Neil Straub? Would she call or contact him?"

"I guess that's possible," Victoria answered, sounding encouraged. "It makes sense she'd contact him, but I don't have Neil's number or address."

"I have his address. It's in Manhattan. I can go see him tomorrow, on my day off."

"No, I can go. I'm going into the city tonight, for dinner."

"I don't think you should. It might not be safe." Jill caught herself before she called Victoria "honey." "If Neil had anything to do with your father's death—"

"That again?" Victoria scoffed, cold again. "Enough. Stop with that."

"Please, let me go instead. It can wait a day."

"Dad wasn't murdered, and Neil is his best friend. I can go see if she's there, I'm a big girl. What's the address?"

Jill told her. "Let me know what happens, okay? You have my cell number."

"Good-bye," Victoria said abruptly, hanging up.

Jill hung up. If Victoria was going to see Neil Straub, now Jill was worried about *her.*

And just like that, Jill was a mother of three, again.

Worried, times three.

Chapter Thirty

"What happened?" Jill said into her cell phone, when Victoria called back. It was after dinner, and she was in the kitchen, returning calls from patients and charting on the laptop. Sam was reading in the family room, and Megan was upstairs in the shower.

"Neil wasn't home. The guy at the desk buzzed. It's a doorman building."

"They called the apartment from downstairs?"

"Yes. It's 4-D, but he didn't answer." Victoria sounded cool, almost businesslike. But not angry, so Jill counted that as progress.

"When were you there?"

"I made them try when I got there, around six o'clock, then I went for dinner and came back later, at eleven. Neil still wasn't home, and I still haven't heard back from Abby. Have you?"

"No." Jill rubbed her forehead, slouching behind her laptop. It had been a long day at work, and she'd seen a slew of flu, colds, and sinus infections that didn't respond to antibiotics. If she could bottle the resourcefulness of a sinus infection, she could find Abby in no time. "Did they tell you when Neil's expected back?"

"No, they don't know."

"When did they see him last?"

"They didn't say."

"Did they see Abby?"

"They didn't say that, either."

"Did you ask?"

"Yes, but they said they don't give out information about the residents. They blew us off."

"Who's us?"

"My friend Brian came with me, after dinner."

"Did you tell them it was an emergency?"

"Yes, but they still wouldn't tell me anything about the residents."

"Understood." Jill felt momentarily stumped. Her gaze shifted restlessly around the kitchen. The dishwasher thrummed, and the granite countertops glistened. "The fact that Neil isn't there doesn't mean much. He could be elsewhere with Abby. So the issue is if the doorman has seen Abby, or if anybody else around the building has, like other tenants."

Victoria snorted. "They for sure won't let me ask any other tenants."

"You don't have an office address for Neil?"

"No."

"Do you know the name of his company, if he has one?"

"No."

Jill didn't like what she was thinking. Even if Neil wasn't a suspect, he could be in danger, too, if he and William had been involved in anything crooked. Either way, Abby could be in danger if she was with him.

"Jill—" Victoria hesitated.

"What?"

"I'm worried she could do something to herself, if you know what I mean."

"No. What do you mean?"

"I mean, like, suicide."

"Don't be silly. She'd never do anything like that."

Victoria fell silent a moment. "She already has. She tried it once, before."

Jill thought she'd heard Victoria wrong. "*What?*"

"Abby tried to kill herself, before."

"No!" Jill cried out, reeling. "When? How?"

"A while ago, about three months after we left the house. I was at school, and she called me and told me that she and Dad had a big fight." Victoria hesitated. "She was telling him that you guys should get back together. He said no, that the marriage was really over, and never to answer your emails. The next day, she tried to, you know, commit suicide."

Jill's heart broke. "How?"

"Pills. She took the whole bottle."

"What pills?"

"Lexapro. She was on it, for depression. She still is, that's why she shouldn't drink."

Jill didn't have to ask when Abby's depression had started, because she could guess.

"I found her. Dad had left that morning on business. I stopped home, just by chance. I thought she was taking a nap, but she wouldn't wake up. If I hadn't come by, she'd be . . . gone."

Jill visualized the scene, horrified. After a bottle of Lexapro, Abby would be almost comatose. It wasn't a suicidal gesture, it was a bona-fide attempt.

"That's why I've been so mad at you." Victoria's tone softened, just a little. "I blamed you for her trying to kill herself, and deciding to be a screw-up, the rest of her life. If you hadn't left, she'd be fine, and I wouldn't have to act like her mom all the time."

Jill listened, and her head dropped into her hands. She never would have believed Abby would do anything like that. Abby's pain must have been so deep, like an agony.

"So that's what's worrying me, now. I try not to worry about her, and I don't want to worry about her, but I do, all the time, like if she does it again, it'll be my fault . . ." Victoria's sentence trailed off.

"I'm so sorry, Victoria." Jill's head was still in her hands, and she let all of her regret and anguish flow. "I'm so sorry for what happened to Abby, and for what you had to deal with. I never wanted it to be—"

"Whatever," Victoria interrupted, cool again. "You see the

problem now. I'm not worried about somebody hurting Abby. I'm worried about *Abby* hurting Abby. That's why we need to find her, fast."

"Okay, right." Jill rubbed her face, straightening up. She willed her emotions under control. "I know what to do. I need to go back to the police and light a fire under them. It's been another whole day, she's still missing, and they should know all the facts, especially this one."

"No, I'll go instead. I can do it. It's my place."

"Can we go together?" Jill asked, hopeful. "I've been there before, and they know me. I can meet you there, it's Central Detectives, on 21st Street."

"No, I'd prefer it if you didn't go. I'll go with Brian." Victoria's tone was final, and Jill could feel her maintaining the wall between them.

"Why don't we just go together?"

"Jill, you have to respect what I'm saying. Can't you do that, please?"

"Okay, fine, if that's what you want." Jill surrendered, tired of fighting and getting nowhere. "Ask for Detective Reed. He's the one who handled the investigation of your father's death. Detective Pitkowski is the one I spoke with, because Reed wasn't there."

"Got it."

"Please call me and let me know how it went?"

"If I have time. I have a brief due, for legal writing."

Jill bit her tongue. "Please let me know if Abby calls you then, okay?"

"That, I'll do."

"I think I'll go up to Manhattan tomorrow and stop by Neil's apartment, to see if they'll tell me anything they wouldn't tell you."

"Okay, whatever. Knock yourself out."

"Thanks, bye. Love you," Jill said automatically, hearing herself end the call the way she always used to, with Victoria.

Love you.

"Babe, you okay?" Sam asked, from the threshold of the kitchen.

Jill pressed END. She didn't know if Victoria heard her, or how long Sam had been standing there.

And she didn't like the look in his eye.

Chapter Thirty-one

"Did you say that Abby tried to commit suicide?" Sam asked, quietly.

"Yes, a while ago, after William and I broke up."

Sam padded over barefoot and cupped her shoulder. "I'm sorry, honey."

"Thanks, but it's not about me, it's about her."

"You feel guilty."

"As I should." Jill shook her head, slumping in the chair. "When we find her, I'll make sure she goes to Sandy, I swear. It's a way for me to make amends."

"You don't need to make amends."

"Yes, I do." Jill straightened up and met his eye. "She suffered after the divorce."

"They all did."

"It doesn't mean that she didn't, and in some ways, it was unique."

Sam frowned. "Was it really?"

"Yes." Jill could sense the tension growing between them, as if the kitchen had developed an atmospheric pressure of its own, brewing a domestic storm. "She tried to kill herself. Victoria didn't. Megan didn't. That's unique."

"Everyone suffers in his or her own way."

"True, but that's beside the point." Jill stood up and walked past him to the sink, where she grabbed a tumbler from the cabinet and let the door close with a *bang* that woke Beef up, blinking.

"I'm sorry," Sam said. "I don't want to fuss."

"Me, neither. Sorry." Jill ran water into the glass, turned off the faucet, and took a sip. It was warm and tasted like nothing. She tried to move past the moment. The air felt too thick to breathe. "Anyway, the problem is we don't know where Abby is, and time matters. It doesn't make sense that she's disappeared of her own volition. If she would try to commit suicide because I wasn't in her life, why would she vanish now that I am?"

"Because now she knows you're watching." Sam came over and leaned against the counter, on his elbow. "It's how she keeps your attention. It's consistent with the drunk-driving, the phone calls, the requests for help. You stay if you're needed, so she acts needy."

"I wouldn't keep ascribing so much bad motive to her, honey." Jill felt her chest tighten. "Her father, he was a schemer, but she isn't. If I can separate the two, so can you."

"But you're seeing her suicide attempt as a game-changer, and it isn't. This isn't new news, not really. We knew she was troubled."

Jill couldn't hide her irritation. "Anyway, you heard, I'm going to New York to find her, tomorrow."

"Why *New York*?"

Jill thought he said it like *Neptune,* even though they went up there all the time, for the museums. "Neil Straub is a guy who was in investments with William. He lives in an apartment in the West Village. Victoria couldn't find out much about him, but I hope I can."

"Why do you think so?"

"Because I don't take no for an answer."

"That's for damn sure."

Jill looked over, then let it go. She dumped out the water and set the tumbler in the sink since the dishwasher wasn't through with its cycle. "Abby could have gone up to be with Neil. Or he could have taken her in, even. Or he could be in danger, too."

Sam lifted an eyebrow. "Then it's not a great idea, your going there."

"I'm just going to ask a few questions, like if the doorman has seen Abby with him recently. If it seems dangerous, I'll go to the police."

"In New York?"

"Yes. They have cops there."

Sam's lips flattened. "Do you want to fight? It seems as if you do."

"No, I don't, but I just don't want to be"—Jill paused, searching for the right word—"*resisted,* at every turn. To get pushback when I'm trying to do the right thing."

"But what if I disagree that it's the right thing? I'm supposed to be a yes man?"

"No."

"Then what?"

Jill leaned on the counter, suddenly weary. "Abby is still missing, Sam. She's a suicidal girl. I'm not making something out of nothing."

"Still, it's not your problem."

"Yes, it is. I can't unknow something. I helped create the problem and I can't deny it."

"No, you didn't," Sam said, firmly.

"Then we don't agree, and in any event, who's going to look for her? Her parents are dead."

"What happens to Megan, when you're in New York?"

Jill thought it was a low blow. "What does she have to do with it? She's in school tomorrow, then she has practice. Manhattan is two hours away. I should be home by five at the latest, even if I take the train."

Sam shook his head. "I would think that after yesterday, you'd let go of this Abby thing, but you're just getting in deeper."

"I can't let it go, now." Jill raised her voice, though she knew Sam wouldn't. Whenever they fought, she felt like a screaming meemie. The angriest he ever got was a sort of scholarly consternation.

"You have to let it go. Megan needs you."

"During the day, for what? I'd be running errands, making calls, or answering email while she's at school." Jill didn't add that she'd been feeling more and more useless on her days off, like she didn't deserve to work part-time anymore, especially after what Sheryl had said.

"So we're in for the duration, are we?" Sam took off his reading glasses and tossed them to the counter, an uncharacteristic gesture.

"What's that mean?"

"It means we're going down this road. You're fully on board with Abby, and we're left behind."

"Who is?"

"Megan and me."

Jill moaned. "Oh, come on, that's not fair. I'm paying special attention to Megan after what happened, but I don't have to choose, I can multitask. Nobody's where they are anymore. I have to return calls while I make dinner. I have to answer email when I'm in the car, waiting for Megan. Every mom does it, every day. *I* do it every day."

"And what about me?" Sam's blue eyes pierced her. "Where are my wishes in your plans? Where are my concerns? Do I even factor in, or do I just keep the home fires burning while you go off on your own?"

"Do I have to get permission from you to go to New York?" Jill asked, incredulous.

"No, but you're not thinking this through, you're just reacting."

"Yes, because it's an emergency. I'm trying to find Abby. She could kill herself."

"Let's say you find her. Does she come with us to Austin, or did you forget?"

Jill had forgotten. They were due to visit Steven, this weekend. "I haven't gotten that far."

"Well, you should. You have a stepson. When did he stop counting?"

"He didn't."

"Explore this with me, then." Sam opened his hands, palms up.

"Assume you find Abby. Then what? You help her live on her own?"

"I suppose so," Jill answered. Her thoughts hadn't gotten that far on that issue, either.

"You don't want her to move in with us, do you?"

Jill blinked, and Sam eyed her fixedly.

"Well?"

Jill felt her heart tug.

"Please tell me it's impossible."

"I can't."

Sam winced. "You're kidding."

"No."

"I knew it." Sam shook his head, looking away. "Why not? It's your house."

Jill didn't want to go there again. It was an old wound. "You moved in here because we didn't want to uproot Megan. You resent that now?"

"No, not at all. I'd do anything for Megan, but not for Abby." Sam's lips went tight. "Does Abby take Steven's room?"

"What do you want from me, Sam? Just forget about her? You're making me choose, her or you, is that what you want?"

"Tell you what I *don't* want. I don't want another kid, and I don't want *that* kid, in particular. You're simply ignoring my wishes, no matter what I say or do, and I don't want to be in a marriage in which my wife gets what she wants, no matter what I want."

"So don't marry me!"

"Then I won't!" Sam shot back, and for a second, the words hung in the air between them.

Jill was too angry to appease him, and their eyes met without seeing each other.

"I'll sleep at the lab." Sam turned around and left the kitchen, and Beef lifted his ears and looked bewildered at him, then back at Jill.

Jill felt anguished tears come to her eyes, but blinked them away.

Chapter Thirty-two

Jill stood in the backyard with Beef, her arms folded across her chest, trying not to think about Sam. He hadn't called or texted, and neither had she. She didn't know if he'd really meant what he said, and she didn't know if she did, either.

Then I won't!

She bit her lip, wondering if they were going to fall apart, dreading she'd been right, that forever was impossible. She found herself back on the night her marriage to William had ended, when she'd confronted him about the theft. They were alone upstairs in their bedroom, and she'd hoped to ask him about it calmly, but as soon as she mentioned the script pads, he'd flown into a rage like she'd never seen from him before.

How dare you accuse me! How dare you! You disgust me!

Jill had gasped, frightened. His face had gone bright red. Veins bulged in his neck and forehead. He was spitting mad. She didn't know what he would do. *We have a videotape,* she said, and that was all she got to say. William had raced from the bedroom and down the stairs, Jill terrified at his heels, not knowing if he'd hurt the girls or what he would do. *No, William, stop, please, we can talk about it!* She hadn't seen this coming, this violence. *Don't hurt them, don't hurt them!*

William had raced into the family room, where the girls were watching TV and doing homework on their laptops, in sweats and flannel pajamas, bowls of microwave popcorn at their sides, with Beef eating fallen kernels off the rug. They looked up as their parents ran into the room, crazed and screaming, Jill pulling at William, the three incredulous girls, their mouths horrified circles, like silent screams.

William yelled, *Abby, Victoria, get up, get your coat, we're leaving! Right now! Get the hell up!*

Dad, what? Victoria shook her head, terrified and stricken. *No! Is this a joke?*

Abby burst into tears. *No, I won't, I can't! No, Daddy, no! Jill, Jill? Why? We live here!*

GET UP, GIRLS! NOW! William grabbed Abby by her shoulder, ripping her pajama top, her favorite pair, covered with cartoon tabby cats.

DADDY? Abby shrieked, terrified, and Victoria fled the family room, her laptop falling to the floor.

Mommy, Mommy! Megan had run howling to Jill's arms. *Mommy!*

William, no! Jill had shouted at him, shielding Megan with her very body, wishing she could run after the girls but Megan was shaking, clinging to her, screaming and screaming. William had yanked Abby away, dragging her, hysterical, to the entrance hall, throwing his daughters out of their own house, grabbing the car keys on the way, slamming the front door.

BAM!

In a matter of seconds, the family had been blown apart, like a bomb exploding in the family room, and all that was left was Jill and Megan weeping, collapsed together on the floor, and Beef barking and barking, running back and forth, alarmed and not knowing why, so freaked out he ignored the popcorn, spilled in bowlfuls on the rug.

Jill wiped a tear from her eye, coming back into the present. She refolded her arms, hugging herself, breathing in the night air. It was cool out, and the darkness above took on a softness, with the stars obscured. Crickets kept up a constant chirping, and bats squeaked noisily behind the louvered shutters of the house.

Beef lifted his muzzle, turning toward the pool, and she looked over, but couldn't see what had drawn his attention. The flagstone deck was slick from the humidity, and the pool looked black, without the light on. She always opened the pool early and heated it because she loved to swim, but she hadn't gone for a night swim yet. She could use one, now. Her last was last summer, with Sam.

I'll sleep at the lab.

Jill went over to the pool, found the outlet hidden near the steps, and flicked on the light. It transformed the pool into a glowing turquoise rectangle, like a blue topaz in an emerald cut, a "dinner ring" her mother used to called them, wistfully. She remembered the day she'd bought the house, happy to be able to afford an in ground pool. She'd grown up using the public pool, in much humbler circumstances, her father a draftsman and her mother a nurse.

On impulse, she slid out of her sweater and khakis and let them drop to the flagstone, which left her in a bra and panties. It was the same thing as a bathing suit, and nobody could see through the privacy fence. She stepped into the pool and stood on the top step, getting used to the cold water, like the old Italian grandmas at the Jersey shore. Beef trotted over, standing on the deck and wagging his tail, and she petted his head, staying in the moment. Just her and a dog and the water. No men, no kids.

She waded into the shallow end to her waist, gasping at the sudden chill, then she plunged underneath, stretching her fingers ahead of her, feeling the cold everywhere at once, as she held her breath and plowed under the water, driving a wedge, then she was off.

She swam freestyle, her favorite stroke, and tried to focus on technique, bending and extending her arms, keeping her elbows high, holding her head down, in line with her spine, then rolling to catch her breath and pointing her toes to the back of the pool. She was breathing hard in no time, her body remembering its job even though her lungs weren't as able, and she reached the wall and did a flawed flip-turn, then slipped through the water again, rolling left, then right with each stroke, trying to streamline her body, ignoring the raggedness of her breath and the ache in her arms. Her college coach used to say that nothing trains you for swimming but swimming, and he'd been right, though she kept on anyway.

Jill swam, letting her body feel its own way and find its natural rhythm. She heard the gasp of her own breathing, and she tried to maintain the pace, taking the fewest strokes because it would make her faster, striving for economy of effort, matching the gliding motion she visualized as she swam. She focused with all of her being, exerting muscle, heart, and mind, feeling the sheer physical pleasure of the water sliding against her breasts and tummy.

She hit the wall again, did a better flip-turn, and powered forward, fingertips reaching and legs fluttering until her body finally found its stride, slipping through the water at speed, her brain focused only on her swimming, like a meditation in motion, and she hit the wall again, then again, swimming one lap, then the next, effortless as a jet at cruising altitude, until she exhausted herself, when she stopped, her heart thundering, floated suspended in the pool, then holding on to the jagged edge of the thick flagstone and climbing out, gasping for breath but feeling better. Cleansed, relaxed, new.

Beef barked at the fence, standing up, his tail straight out, and Jill hoisted herself out of the pool, turning to see where he was looking, but there was nothing there. The neighbors, the Weitzes, weren't in their driveway, and the neighborhood had gone to sleep.

"Quiet, Beef, no!" she said, her chest heaving from exertion.

Beef ignored her, barking and bounding to the privacy fence, as if someone were on the other side, and Jill rose to a crouch, dripping wet, beginning to wonder.

Beef barked and barked, the hair rising on the back of his neck, and before Jill understood why, she was scooping up her clothes, instinctively covering her body with them, feeling exposed and vulnerable.

"Beef, come!" Jill shouted, hurrying toward the house. Maybe she was being paranoid and maybe she wasn't, but she had to get inside.

Jill tore open the door and scooted into the house, dropping the clothes and hiding behind the door, but she couldn't leave Beef out.

"Beef, *come!*" she called, with fear in her voice, and Beef came running to her, his tail between his legs as he bolted inside the house.

Jill slammed the door closed behind him, locked it, and twisted the deadbolt, then hurried to the burglar alarm pad and pressed STAY, listening to the beep of its exit delay, staying close to the wall, trying to hide from the windows, dripping water onto the hardwood floor, spooked.

And wishing she knew what was on the other side of that fence.

Chapter Thirty-three

"Megan, hurry." Jill didn't want to miss the train to New York and hurried to the car under a clear, morning sky. Megan inched along, texting with her head down, her knapsack and swim bag hanging in the crook of her arm and banging against her legs. Jill unlocked the car, put her purse inside, and climbed in, starting the engine. "Megan, *today*."

"Chill, Mom." Megan opened the passenger door and tossed her bags onto the floor, then climbed into her seat, phone in hand. "We've got plenty of time."

"No, actually, we don't." Jill could have launched into a lecture, but Megan had already returned to texting, absorbed. "What's going on, if I may ask?"

"Just Courtney," Megan answered, head down, and Jill steered down their street, waving to Janet Baker, who was leaving for work.

"Oh. I thought it was Guitar Hero."

"No." Megan looked over, frowning. "Mom, is Sam coming home? I heard you guys fighting, last night. Then he left."

Jill almost braked in surprise. Megan didn't need that kind of stress, especially now. "He slept at his lab, and he'll be back tonight," Jill answered, though she wondered if that was true. She hadn't heard a word from Sam, nor had she sent him one.

"He doesn't like Abby, does he?"

"He will when he gets to know her."

"No, he won't. I get it. She's changed." Megan checked her phone, which chimed to signal an incoming text. "I like the old Abby better than the new one, too. But I know the old one's in there, somewhere, if that makes any sense."

"It does." Jill cruised down the street, joining the line of traffic heading to work, all the drivers sipping travel mugs of fresh coffee and making their first phone calls of the day, like a parade of distraction.

"I don't want anything to happen to her."

"Me, neither, and it won't."

"Do you think she's, like, a runaway?"

"Honestly, no. It's all right." Jill patted her leg. "Tell me about you. What's up today?"

"I have a French test."

"Oh, Jeez." Jill was a little out of touch. Normally they went over her French vocab together. "You ready?"

"Did Abby run away because of Sam?"

"No, not at all, and she didn't run away. Like we said, she could be with a date, and we're doing all we can to find her. Victoria went to the police, and they're handling it. Don't worry about Abby."

Megan fell silent, looking down at the phone. "She was embarrassed that she barfed on the bed. Maybe if I was nicer about it—"

"No, that's not it," Jill interrupted, to nip that thought in the bud. "It was nothing you did, and she didn't run away. I don't know where she is, but she'll turn up. Honey, please try and put her out of your mind."

"But if she's like a missing person, like on TV, we have to hurry." Megan's forehead wrinkled. "They say you only have forty-eight hours, Mom."

"Don't worry," Jill said, with more confidence than she felt, and Megan's phone chimed again, but she ignored it, her gaze searching.

"I went to the stair, I listened. What if she hurt herself?"

Jill sighed inwardly. "Okay, she tried to do that once, a long time ago, but there's no reason to think she will again."

"You think she could. You told Sam you're worried."

Jill tensed, busted by her own daughter. She wasn't sure what to say. "Just because I worry doesn't mean you should worry. You know I worry too much."

"But remember Josh's sister?"

"Abby won't hurt herself, not again." Jill cringed. A classmate of Megan's had a sister in ninth grade who'd committed suicide, and it had generated a candlelight vigil, an assembly, and a memorial garden, the public-school protocol for grief-management.

"But she *could* do it. She's drinking too much, and her Dad just died."

"Stop, enough, she'll be fine, and the police will find her," Jill said firmly. She had to get this out of Megan's mind, but she knew that wasn't possible.

"If the police will do it, then why are you going to New York?"

"I can do my part, too." Jill honked the horn. The car in front was going too slowly. "A friend of William's lives there, and he might know where she is. Now, tell me about this French test. Is it vocab?"

Megan's phone chimed again, another text coming in, but she ignored it. "Mom, I heard what Sam said last night, that he'd sacrifice for me but not for Abby. Did he say that?"

"Basically, yes." Jill hit the gas, hiding her dismay.

"I love him." Megan checked the phone as another text came in, then she thumbed in a response. "You guys are going to make up, right?"

"I hope so." Jill looked over, and a frown crossed Megan's downturned face. "What's going on?"

"Nothing." Megan pressed her lips over her braces, typing away. "When William was the dad, Abby was the first choice. But now that Sam's the dad, I'm the first choice. I kinda like being the first choice."

Jill hid her dismay, wondering if she'd ever be able to navigate the waters of her own family. She could swim in a pool, but they were an ocean, where the currents crossed and collided with each other, flowing too deep to be seen from the surface.

Megan halted her texting and looked over. "Is that a bad thing to say? That I like being first?"

"No, not if it's true," Jill answered, eyeing the red light.

Chapter Thirty-four

Jill looked through the smudgy glass window of the cab, and a warm day in Manhattan whizzed past. Cars, vans, and bicycle messengers clogged the streets, and filling the sidewalks were Asian tourists, a pierced gaggle of hipsters, and a brace of bright young men, puffing away on acrid cigars, their ties flying. Mostly everyone talked into a cell phone or a Bluetooth, all of them hurrying, smoking, and eating on the fly, their lives lived in fast-forward. A cacophony of honking, shouted epithets, random laughter, and the throbbing bass from a passing radio wafted through the window, though Jill had silenced the news video that played in the cab, hoping to be alone with her thoughts.

I went to the stair, I listened.

Jill checked her BlackBerry for the umpteenth time, for a call from Abby. There were no red asterisks by the phone icon, indicating a missed call, and she put her phone back into her purse. She hadn't heard from Sam, either, though she'd thought about calling him, but didn't. On the train, she'd ended up in the quiet car by accident, but it gave her time to think. She didn't know what she would say to him, nor what she wanted to hear. She was old enough to know that soft words wouldn't smooth over the situation, and a very real disagreement divided them.

That's no way to run a marriage.

Jill shooed Sam's voice from her head, eyeing the sky, where a pale sun hung like an afterthought, nature herself taking a backseat in the city. The cab turned onto the West Side Highway, the six-lane highway that ran along the Hudson, and a helicopter flew over the river, pitched forward like a top-heavy bug. On the New Jersey side, the old-school painted LACKAWANNA sign contrasted with the stylish neon W HOTEL sign, glowing red even in daylight. Air thick with garbage and gas odors blew inside the cab, and the humidity made Jill uncomfortable in her navy linen blazer, khaki pants, and a white shirt, with her hair pulled back into a simple ponytail. She was dressed to talk her way past the doorman, a mom on a mission. More accurately, an ex-stepmom on a mission.

What if she hurt herself?

Her gut tensed as the cab left the highway, made a few more turns through a fashionable warren of West Village streets, and pulled finally onto West 11th. They bumped over the cobblestones on the street, which was lined with ritzy apartment buildings, many modern, and all glass. Tall, skinny trees, boxed in by wrought-iron fences, threw scant shadows on sidewalks that had been hosed clean, still drying in spots.

"This is it," the cabbie said, and Jill grabbed her purse, slid the money from her wallet, and handed it to him through the plastic window.

"Thanks, keep the change." Jill got out and took stock of the building. It was shorter and smaller than the modern ones, classy in an old Knickerbocker way, with art-deco fluting over the entrance. She walked to the door, pushed through, and scanned the lobby, which was long and narrow, with a black and white tile floor. Brass sconces flanked a black security desk, and the doorman looked to be in his sixties. He was tall and lean, with frizzy gray hair, wire-rimmed bifocals, and a navy blazer that looked unfortunately like Jill's own.

"Nice jacket," she said, walking over.

"It looks better on you," the doorman said with a polite grin.

His black nametag read MICHAEL, and a *New York Post* lay on his desk, open to the sports page. "How can I help you?"

"I'm looking for a man who lives here. Neil Straub."

"Mr. Straub? He's not in."

Jill was ready for that. "When did you see him last?"

"Sorry, but we don't give out that information."

"I know, but this is an emergency. I'm Jill Farrow, and your name's Michael?"

"Mike Moran, yes."

"Mike, please help me, if you can. Neil is a good friend of my ex-husband, who just passed away last Tuesday, leaving two daughters. One of them is missing, and I'm trying to find her."

"That's too bad." Mike frowned, with genuine sympathy.

"Her sister Victoria came here yesterday, looking for her and asking about Neil Straub. Do you remember her?"

"No, I wasn't here. It was my day off."

"I see." Jill reached in her purse and withdrew two photos she'd printed. The top one was a recent one of Abby, from William's computer. "This is my stepdaughter, Abby Skyler. Have you seen her? She could have come to visit Neil."

"Hmm." Mike took the photo, eyeing it. "I haven't seen her. Mind you, I see a lot of people in this job, but I tend to remember."

"So you don't remember seeing her?"

"No."

"Who covers the desk on your day off?"

"There's three of us, and we rotate. I'm day shift, Tuesdays and Thursdays, and we split the night shifts, plus we got the weekends."

"So when would the night-shift doorman come on?"

"Leon comes in at five."

"Do you have his phone, so I can call him?"

"No can do, sorry."

"How about his address, and I'll look up his phone number?"

"No, sorry." Mike buckled his lower lip. "I'd like to help, but I can't give that information out. If you stop back at five o'clock, you can ask him then."

Jill thought a minute. It made sense that the day-shift doorman hadn't seen Abby. She'd gone missing on Saturday night, and maybe that was when she'd come up. "Okay, maybe I will. Do you think Neil, Mr. Straub, will be back by then?"

"I doubt it. He travels a lot."

"What does he do? Something financial, right?"

Mike hesitated. "Yeah, but you didn't hear it from me. I shouldn't have said what I did. Keep it to yourself, okay? I need this job."

"Sure."

"Mr. Straub is a nice guy, and rules are rules. The board takes them very serious."

"The board?"

"The co-op board. They run the place." Mike handed her back the photos, but the bottom one fluttered to the desk. It was the one of Neil and William in sunglasses, on the golf course in Pebble Beach. Mike picked it up. "Oh, there's Mr. Straub. Musta been younger then."

"Yes, by a few years, I think."

"Looks that way." Mike chuckled, handing her back the photo. "But he's gotta lose that shirt. I mean, pink?"

Jill didn't get it. In the picture, Neil was wearing a navy blue polo shirt, and William had on a pale pink one. "What do you mean? Neil's not wearing pink."

"Sure he is." Mike pointed to William. "I'm not colorblind, and this is pink."

"Yes, the shirt is pink, but that's not Neil."

"Yes, it is." Mike tapped William's face with a bitten-off finger-nail. "This here is Mr. Straub."

Jill didn't understand. Mike was pointing at William's face. "That's not Neil Straub. The other guy is."

"I know Mr. Straub when I see him, and the guy in pink is Mr. Straub."

Jill put it together, hiding her astonishment. "You mean Neil Straub is William Skyler?"

"I don't know what you're talking about." Mike handed the

photo back. "All I know is, the man in the pink shirt is Neil Straub. I know the man, I talk to him all the time. He's lived here, like, three years, in 4-D."

"Thanks." Jill put the photo in her purse, struggling to get her bearings. So William had another identity, a double life as Neil Straub. She wouldn't have guessed as much in a million years. William was a con artist, but this had to be his sickest scam ever, because he'd deceived his own children. Abby couldn't have known or she would have told Jill. Jill's next thought was that William's double life could be connected to Abby's disappearance.

"Excuse me, hold on." Mike's attention shifted to the elevator as it *ping*ed, and its doors opened, revealing an attractive woman, well-dressed in a white pantsuit, carrying a purse, a cell phone, and a large cardboard box.

"Mike, honey," the woman called. "Can you give me a hand, please?"

"Sure thing, Belle," Mike called back, coming around the desk and taking the box.

"Wait, Mike, please." Jill followed him. "Who's the other guy in the photo, wearing the navy shirt?"

"I have no idea," Mike answered, over his shoulder. "Belle, where do you want the box?"

"On the desk, temporarily." The woman eyed the lobby, annoyed. "My client isn't here yet? Sheesh! I hate it when people are late."

Jill couldn't let it go. "Mike, please, just one last question."

Mike walked back and set the box on the desk, then turned to Jill with a frown. "What?"

"Is there anyone who runs the building, like a super I could speak with?"

"Only residents speak with the super," Mike answered, his tone newly official, but the woman lifted a perfectly-penciled eyebrow.

"Why, dear? Are you interested in a unit? It's wonderful building, and I used to live here myself. I can show you an apartment that's very special. In this market, it's a steal." The woman thrust out a manicured hand. "I'm Belle Kahan, with Prudential."

Jill had nothing to lose, and everything to gain. "You know, I *am* looking for an apartment in this building."

Mike turned, pursing his lips tight. But he said nothing.

Chapter Thirty-five

Jill walked into a large, empty apartment, with two tall windows that overlooked the Hudson River. She scanned the view, her thoughts in tumult. It boggled her mind to think that William had lived in this very building, as Neil Straub. She had a zillion questions, but the only one that mattered was Abby.

"Quite a view, eh?" Belle asked, gesturing at the windows. "It doesn't get better than this."

"It's great." Jill managed a smile. "What can you tell me about the building?"

"It's a co-op, very exclusive, very fiscally responsible. It's well-run, and smaller than others on the street, only forty units. Are you working with a Realtor?"

"Not yet."

"I'd be happy to work with you. I know this building and the entire West Village, like the back of my hand. I live on Horatio now."

"I like this building." Jill remembered the doorman saying that William's apartment was 4-D. "Have you sold other apartments in it?"

"Tons. What do you do?"

"I'm a doctor," Jill answered, and Belle's eyes lit up.

"Wow! Who doesn't want a doctor in the house? You'll pass the board with flying colors."

Jill was wondering how William had passed a co-op board, with a false identity. "I've never applied to a co-op building before. What information do you have to show them?"

"Everything and then some. Tax returns and bank statements, and you need to get two recommendations and references, besides a letter from your landlord saying you're paid up. Are you currently renting in the city?"

"No." Jill still didn't get it. If William had to show that much information to the board, he'd have a whole separate identity set up with a bank. "How careful is the board? Not just anybody can get in here, can they?"

"No, but you'll do fine. This board isn't as power-crazy as the ones on the Upper East. It's much more laid back, downtown." Belle flashed a lipsticked smile. "You're engaged, I see. Nice ring. Are you scouting for both of you?"

"Yes." Jill managed a smile.

"Good for you. This building has a really nice group of residents. Very chummy, because it's so small. They have parties on the roof deck every Fourth of July, to watch the fireworks."

Jill got an idea. "Funny, I saw someone in the lobby the other day, whom I think I know from college. Neil Straub. Tall, good-looking. I think he lives in 4-D."

"4-D?" Belle paused, thinking. "Oh, right, he's a subletter. I don't know him, but I sold that apartment a few years ago to a couple from London, and they moved back home. There's only a few subletters in the building, and the board likes it that way. Don't have the same controls, with a subletter."

"Do subletters have to get board approval?"

"No."

Jill thought it explained how William had gotten past the board.

"I know who you mean." Belle leaned over, in a cloud of flowery perfume. "He's quite the ladies man. My best friend still lives in 4-A, and we see what goes on with him. He keeps busy, if you know what I mean."

Jill did, unfortunately. "He hasn't changed since college, huh?"

"They never do, girlfriend. Like the kids say, he's a *playa*."

"I guess he never got married."

"I've see him with the same girl a few times, but I doubt she knows about the others."

Jill doubted it, too. "What does she look like, this one?"

"Thin, blonde, and young. What else?"

"What does he do for a living, do you know? He used to be in the pharmaceuticals business."

"Don't know, but it's something that makes a lot of money. He drives a big Mercedes. Silver. I know because he took my parking space once."

"Doesn't the building have parking?"

"Yes, but it costs extra. He was out front, unloading."

"Where's the garage, and how does the parking work? Are there numbered spaces?"

"Yes, all marked by the apartment number." Belle gestured behind her, to the north. "The garage is at the back of the building. Sometimes it's easier to drop off your bags, then go park. Now, shall I show you the kitchen?"

"Yes, thanks." Jill learned nothing more and spent the next half-hour being led around an apartment she didn't want, trying to piece together a puzzle she hadn't seen coming. She bid Belle good-bye, left the apartment building, and stood on the sidewalk, revising her plan. It wouldn't make sense to come back at five to see the night-shift doorman. He wouldn't recognize Abby because she undoubtedly hadn't been here.

The garage is at the back of the building.

Jill walked to the end of the street, heading for the garage, curious if William's car was there. Runners trotted past her toward the river. She took a right onto the West Side Highway, and traffic had picked up, *whoosh*ing loudly in both directions, uptown and down. She turned right onto the next street, a skinny sidestreet of cobblestones, and kept walking.

Midway up, Jill found a gate over a driveway, which had to be the garage to the building. There was a door next to the entrance, and she made a beeline for it. She tried the knob, but it was locked. She glanced behind her, to make sure no one saw her, when suddenly, she spotted a black SUV, parked at the curb behind a row of others, on the West Side Highway.

Jill froze. The SUV hadn't been there before, or she hadn't seen it. It looked like the same model as the padiddle that had been following her. The headlights were off because it was daytime. She couldn't see the license plate. Sunlight glinted off its chrome grille, and a man sat behind the wheel, a still figure in shadow.

Jill told herself to stay calm. It would've been impossible to follow her here, so it probably wasn't the same car, but there was only one way to find out. She turned on her heel and walked toward the car. Suddenly the black SUV's engine roared to life, the SUV reversed, cut the wheels, and started to wedge itself out of the parking space.

Jill broke into a run, almost tripping on the cobblestones. It couldn't be a coincidence. The SUV had to be leaving because she was coming. She reached the line of parked cars just as the SUV pulled onto the West Side Highway, heading uptown. It had a Pennsylvania license plate that read TJU-something.

"Wait!" Jill yelled, on the run. "Stop! Help!"

And before she realized what she was doing, she was running down the West Side Highway after the SUV.

Chapter Thirty-six

"Stop that car!" Jill screamed, frantic. Heads turned. Runners stopped running. A cyclist braked, putting down his cleated shoe.

Jill ran as fast as she could. Her legs churned. Her arms pumped. Her flats slapped the sidewalk.

The SUV veered to the middle lane but couldn't go forward. The cars ahead of it were stopped at a red light. Crosstown traffic flowed onto the highway, in force. There were traffic lights at almost every block, and it was the only thing that gave Jill a fighting chance of catching him.

She ran harder, almost colliding with an older man walking a poodle. She kept her eyes glued to the SUV driver. He was looking this way and that, his head swiveling left and right. He was blocked in and knew it.

A moving van pulled out of the cross street and stopped, blocking traffic. The light turned green, and the SUV and the other cars started honking.

Jill raced ahead, gaining ground. Only half a block separated her from the SUV, then less. The moving van would go any second, pulling onto the far side of the highway, heading downtown.

Jill tore down the sidewalk, glanced behind her, and ran into the street like a madwoman. "Don't hit me!" she screamed, putting her hand up.

The red Saturn behind her braked, then started honking. Van and limo drivers looked over, angry. "Honk!" blared a tractor-trailer, startling her.

Jill struggled to keep up her pace. Her breaths were ragged. Her thighs burned. She closed in on the SUV. Eight cars, then seven, then six. She was almost there. The Saturn hung back, honking.

The moving van inched forward. The SUV honked and honked, still blocked.

Jill tried to run into the middle lane, but a battered pickup wouldn't let her in, roaring past her as if she'd been in a car.

"Stop that car!" Jill shouted. The SUV still couldn't go. Her lungs were about to explode. Sweat poured into her eyes. Her purse swung wildly at her side. She clamped it down with a hand.

She burst ahead, closer to the SUV. There were three cars left between them, then two, then one.

Suddenly the moving van cleared the lane. The SUV accelerated and switched into the fast lane.

Jill couldn't keep up. The SUV found open road and was getting away. Her heart thundered. Her legs wobbled. She stumbled, almost falling.

The Saturn driver leaned from his window. "Get outta the street!" he hollered, waving at her.

Jill threw her purse at the SUV in frustration, hitting the back just as the driver took off, cut the wheel, and jumped the median, making a daring U-turn and zooming down the other side of the highway, going downtown.

"Move, lady!" the Saturn driver yelled.

Jill hurried to the curb, then doubled over, trying to catch her breath. A police siren blared behind her, but it sounded too far away to get here in time. She straightened up and watched a mini-van run over her purse and BlackBerry.

Cars and trucks *whoosh*ed past her, and the police siren sounded closer. She blinked sweat from her eyes and spotted the NYPD cruiser, driving toward her.

She stuck out her hand to flag it down.

Chapter Thirty-seven

Jill sat in a hard chair beside Officer Mulvane's desk, and he was just finished typing his report on an old computer, with a grimy keyboard. The Greenwich Village precinct house had the same desks, mismatched file cabinets, and cluttered bulletin boards as the police station in Philadelphia, except for the moving tribute in its entrance hall, where six gleaming bronze plaques on a tan marble wall memorialized its six officers who gave their lives on September 11, 2001. Jill had paused at the memorial, saying a silent prayer.

"Okay, that's about it." Officer Mulvane hit a key and the form printed at a cheap desk printer with a Yankees sticker. He was a beefy cop in his thirties, with bright blue eyes, a ready smile, and thinning blond hair. He extracted the form, picked up a pen, and handed both to Jill. "Wanna give me your John Hancock?"

"Sure." Jill skimmed the typed portion, which was her account of what had happened, then signed it at the bottom. Her flattened purse sat on her lap, and her BlackBerry was road kill, but she felt more like herself, having washed up in the ladies room. "So what do you think, Officer? Can you help me find Abby?"

"Here's how it goes." Office Mulvane eyed Jill, pursing his lips. "I'd like to help you find your kid, I mean, your ex's kid, but we don't have jurisdiction. If your ex was murdered in Philly, it's a Philly case. If the kid went missing in Philly, it's a Philly case. Here, take this back." Officer Mulvane handed over the photo of William and the mystery man in the blue shirt. "Neither of these guys are known to us, much less a Known Wanted. I can't run a check on them using the images alone."

"Thanks." Jill stuffed the picture into her broken purse. "But here's what I don't understand about jurisdiction. My ex is renting an apartment a few blocks from here, under a fake name, with fake identity. Doesn't that give you jurisdiction?"

"No. Your ex-husband could be guilty of fraud in connection with the apartment, but not all fraud is criminal." Officer Mulvane nodded hello at another cop passing his desk, a radio attached to the cop's thick belt and flopping against his side. "If your ex-husband entered into a contract with the co-op membership under a false name, it's not enough to involve NYPD."

"But what if he's impersonating someone? Isn't that criminal?"

"Criminal impersonation is somebody pretending to be somebody famous, to get favors or money. Like we got a guy, he's in here all the time, pretends he's Robert De Niro to get a free meal." Officer Mulvane picked up a Styrofoam cup of coffee with two thick fingers, as if he'd crush it otherwise. "Your ex-husband isn't doing that."

"So you need jurisdiction—"

"No," Officer Mulvane interrupted, setting down his cup. "I don't *need* jurisdiction. I can't act unless I *have* jurisdiction. I'm not looking for things to do, I got plenty."

"Okay, what about the fact that I think I'm being followed by a black SUV, on the West Side Highway?"

"You don't have any real evidence that you are, and you don't know it's the same car."

"The license plate has the T, and he drove away when he saw me coming."

"Dr. Farrow." Officer Mulvane smiled, sympathetically. "Don't take this the wrong way, but I saw you, and you looked drunk and crazy. No wonder the guy hightailed it. And lots of plates start with T."

Jill tried another tack. "What if I were a friend of Neil Straub's, and I come to you and tell you that he's missing. I tell you he lives a few blocks away and I'm worried about him. What if he's dead in his apartment, right now? That would be criminal, and you'd have jurisdiction, right?"

"Right, but that's not what you said."

"It could be." Jill saw her opening, but Officer Mulvane frowned, shifting heavily away from her, in his chair.

"It isn't. I stopped for you because I thought you were a knucklehead about to get run over."

"Now you know I'm a knucklehead trying to find my daughter." Jill managed a smile. "You want me to go out, come back in again, and tell you the new story?"

"It's not a game, Doc."

"I know, and I'm not playing. I really need help. No one's looking out for Abby but me. You understand, you have a child." Jill gestured at the photo on his desk, of an adorable little boy in a blue baseball uniform, resting a bat on his shoulder. "What if your son were out there on his own, after you were gone?"

"Oh, don't do that to me." Officer Mulvane looked pained, and Jill thought of the 9/11 memorial in the entrance hall. She realized that cops went to work every day, knowing that they might not come home. She flushed, feeling terrible.

"I'm so sorry, Officer. That was thoughtless of me."

"Don't worry about it." Officer Mulvane sighed. "Okay, you win. There's one thing I can do for you, in these circumstances."

"Thank you so much," Jill said, grateful.

Chapter Thirty-eight

"They've been up there forever, haven't they, Mike?" Jill paced the lobby in William's building, waiting for Officer Mulvane and his partner, who were upstairs with the super, a bald and surly little man named Ivan Ronavic.

"No. You need to relax." Mike peered at her over his glasses. He was sitting at the desk, turning a page of the newspaper. "It's only been twenty minutes. They'll be down soon."

"I wish I could've gone with them."

"You heard them. No way. The cops aren't even allowed in the apartment, they gotta wait in the hall while my boss checks it out."

"Is Ivan your boss?"

"Yes." Mike chuckled. "You asked him so many questions, I thought he was gonna hit you."

Jill snorted. "I've met surgeons with less ego."

Mike laughed. "He didn't like you much, either."

"Ask me if I care. I should fix him up with *my* boss, Sheryl."

Mike cocked his head. "You're a doctor. You shouldn't have a boss."

"That's what *I* think." Jill let it go. "You've seen the apartment, right?"

"Yes."

"What does it look like?"

"Not for me to say. You've gotten me in enough hot water for one day."

"Sorry." Jill felt a guilty twinge. "I can write Ivan a letter, apologizing."

"Nah, don't worry about it. It's good to shake things up. Get's so quiet around here."

"I wonder what's going on up there." Jill sank onto a cushioned bench, suppressing her anxiety. She felt so out of touch without her BlackBerry and wondered if Abby had called her or Victoria. Or if Sam was home from the lab, Megan had had another panic attack, or Rahul's bloodwork had come back. Jill stood up and started pacing again.

"Here they come." Mike rose, and the elevator *ping*ed. Jill got to the elevator as its stainless steel doors slid open, letting out Ivan, Officer Mulvane, and Officer Yokimura, his talkative young partner.

"Well?" Jill asked, and Officer Mulvane smiled in a reassuring way.

"Nothing to worry about, and your kid isn't up there. It's all in order. Clean as a whistle."

"What did you see? What does it look like?"

"It's a typical guy apartment."

Officer Yokimura added, "A typical *rich* guy apartment."

Officer Mulvane didn't comment. "There was nothing suspicious. Ivan did a walk-through, answered all our questions, and told us what we needed to know. Neat and clean. Refrigerator empty except for water and beer. Stack of newspapers and bills on the table."

"What name's on the mail?"

"Neil Straub."

"No other?"

"No."

"Except for Current Occupant," Officer Yokimura deadpanned.

"Any mail from a business, like one he owned?" Jill asked.

"Not that Ivan noticed."

"What's the oldest date on the mail, do you know? Or the oldest newspaper?"

"About a week ago, that Ivan saw."

Jill turned in frustration to Ivan, who had walked to the front desk. "Can't you please tell me more about him, like what you have on file, from when he subletted?"

"No, I can't." Ivan's thin lips made a flat line. His wiry frame seemed lost in his blue jumpsuit, and he had mournfully dark eyes. "Like I told you, I do what the board president tells me. He's not givin' out any info without a warrant."

"But Neil Straub is only a subletter."

"Makes no never mind."

Jill turned back to Officer Mulvane. "We can't get a warrant?"

"No. No probable cause. No crime. No nothing."

Jill knew when she'd lost a fight. "Was there any sign of a woman living with him, like things in the bathroom, medicine chest? Or stray jewelry? He has a young blonde girlfriend, and it would help if I knew her name."

Officer Yokimura grinned. "Hell hath no fury, eh?"

Jill turned to Officer Mulvane. "Well?"

"Ivan did see some things that belonged to a woman. Clothes in the closet, that sort of thing." Officer Mulvane crossed to the front desk. "Hey, Mike, how does the mail get upstairs?"

"When the resident is out of town, we bring it up every few days. We always do that for Mr. Straub because he's usually gone so long, it clogs up his mailbox. About ten percent of the building is absentee; they got second and third homes in Florida, or they're foreign. We're white glove here. Bring up the dry cleaning, water the plants, too. Whatever they need, we do."

Officer Yokimura smiled. "Must be nice."

Officer Mulvane asked, "When was the last time Straub was here?"

Mike consulted a log book on the desk. "I found the entry, when you were upstairs. Last Monday, he left at 10:20 A.M. I was on the desk, I remember, because I filled in for Enrique. He didn't say when he'd be back."

Jill felt her gut tense. Monday was the day before William died. Neil Straub wouldn't be back, because William Skyler was dead. "Was he alone?"

Mike hesitated.

Officer Mulvane asked, "Was he?"

"Yes," Mike answered.

Officer Mulvane patted the desk, as a farewell. "Thanks for your trouble."

Jill came over. "Officer Mulvane, can we check out his car, too? I just want to see if it's here." She'd asked before, but maybe he'd forgotten. "He has a silver Mercedes, but we can't get into the garage unless they let us in."

Ivan looked over at Jill, annoyed. "You're an instigator, you know that?"

Jill smiled at him. "Hardly, but are you single? Because I've got the girl for you."

Chapter Thirty-nine

Jill felt her eyes adjust to the darkness as she walked past one expensive sedan after another, their chrome fenders gleaming under the low lights in the garage ceiling. Reflective numbers painted on the concrete floor behind each car bore an apartment number, and they were at 4-B.

"Hey, Doc." Officer Mulvane turned to Jill as they walked together with Ivan and Officer Yokimura. "You understand, we can't search his car without a warrant."

"I know. I just want to see if it's here."

"Fine. Then we're done."

"This is it." Ivan stopped, gesturing with his jingling keyring at a silver Mercedes that sat in one of the parking spaces assigned to 4-D. The other space was empty, and William's car had a New York license plate, JU 5359. Jill took a pen out of her bag and scribbled the number on a scrap of paper, since she didn't have her BlackBerry to take a picture.

"We done here?" Ivan scowled.

"Yes, thanks," Jill answered, but she stepped over and peeked inside the car, which had a light, clean interior. William always kept his cars clean, then Jill remembered that he also always kept a spare key under his car's back bumper.

Officer Mulvane peered into the car, too. "Looks kosher to me."

Officer Yokimura snorted. "Looks *awesome* to me."

Jill's thoughts raced ahead. "Well, thanks, Officers. I really appreciate your time."

"No worries." Officer Mulvane put a hand on Jill's shoulder. "I wish you luck with your kid. She'll be fine, you'll see."

"Thanks, I hope so."

Ivan gestured. "Come on, folks. Wild goose chase is over, I got things to do," he said, and they all turned to follow him, with Jill a step behind, pretending she'd gotten something in her shoe.

"Oops, a stone," she said, but she hooked a finger inside her flat and pulled out the small innersole in the back of her heel, which had an adhesive bottom.

Ivan led them to the exit door, which he opened, and Officer Yokimura went through. Jill hung back, expecting Officer Mulvane to go next, but he turned to her.

"Ladies first," Officer Mulvane said, with a smile.

It caught Jill off guard, and she had to think fast. "Damn, I was trying to check out your butt."

"I still got it, eh?" Officer Mulvane burst into easy laughter. "Tell my wife that."

"She already knows it. Now, work it!"

Officer Mulvane wagged his butt in a comical way as he went through the door, and Jill stuck the gluey bottom of her innersole on the doorjamb, blocking the lock, then closed the door.

"Thanks for all your help, Officer Mulvane," Jill said, as they walked together down the street toward the West Side Highway.

"Sure thing. I'm sure your kid will show, sooner or later. Hell, at that age, I was up to no good. Take care, Doc." They reached the West Side Highway, where Jill waved good-bye to them.

"See you. Thanks again!" Jill raised her hand to hail a cab, standing in almost the same spot where she'd seen the black SUV. The shards of her BlackBerry couldn't be far away.

"Take care!" Officer Mulvane called back, and the three men took a left, walked back down the street, and disappeared around the corner.

Jill kept her hand out, stalling until the police cruiser steered around the corner and took a right onto the highway. She waved to the police as they drove past, and when they were out of sight, she turned around and scooted back up the street to the garage. She yanked on the door, which opened easily because of the innersole, then she ripped it off the jamb and hurried to William's Mercedes. She didn't know what she'd find, but she wasn't going home without trying.

She reached the car, ducked down to feel under the bumper, and found the spare-key box. She slid open the tin lid, took out the big black key, and aimed it at the trunk, chirping it unlocked. She opened the trunk and looked inside. Nothing. It was massive and looked clean as new. She felt around the black interior to make sure, but there wasn't anything inside or hidden. She closed the trunk, then hustled to the driver's side and slipped into the seat. It was dim inside the car, but she didn't want to turn on the interior light, in case someone saw her.

She eyed the interior, and it was immaculate, smelling faintly of Armor All, a car fetish of William's. She looked in the door's side compartment, but there was nothing in it except a pack of gum. She opened the lid of the center console, and it contained only a pack of Kleenex and a navy plastic envelope, which she picked up and looked inside. It held the car's registration and proof of insurance. NEIL STRAUB, both read, and the address was the apartment building. She looked down at the signature on the registration. *Neil Straub,* it read, but it was clearly William's handwriting. Jill stuck the papers into her flattened purse, then reached over and pressed the button to open the padded glove compartment, where she spotted the glint of a gun.

Jill reached inside and pulled it out, dismayed. She'd never held a gun before, and this one was black, compact, and lethal, with cross-hatching on the handle and a small trident on the side. Beretta, it read underneath. She'd never known William to have a gun, but now he had two, and she wondered why he felt the need for so much protection. Her gut told her that his double life had to have played a role in what happened to him, and she prayed that whatever he was doing hadn't jeopardized Abby, too.

Jill put the gun back in the glove compartment, which contained nothing else but a thick owner's manual, so she shut the compartment's door. She turned around and checked out the backseat, which was clean. There was nothing on the floor in back, either. She turned back, eyeing the dashboard, which had an array of smooth buttons, giving her an idea. She plunged the car key into the ignition and twisted it on, and the dashboard came alive.

NAVI, read one button, the navigation system. She pressed it, and it brought up a list that started, ADDRESS ENTRY. She scanned the list until she got to ADDRESSES FROM MEMORY, scrolled to highlight the selection, then pressed. There were no listings, not even HOME.

Jill didn't believe it for a minute. William loved gadgets, and it seemed unlikely that he'd never used the GPS system. She glanced at the odometer, which glowed 30,393 miles, a lot of driving to not use a GPS for. She strolled down to LAST DESTINATIONS and pressed the button. NONE, it read.

Jill thought about it. There must have been a way to wipe the memory from the GPS system, and if so, William must've done so. She wondered why, stumped. She inhaled, thinking. Then she breathed in again. Armor All wasn't the only smell in the car. There was a sweeter scent, then Jill remembered his girlfriend.

She shifted over the console, climbed into the passenger seat, and flipped down the makeup mirror. There was nothing stuck underneath. She checked out the compartment on the passenger side door, and hit paydirt. The compartment had stuff in it, but she couldn't see what it was in the poor light.

She scooped the stuff out and arrayed it on her lap: a Laura Mercier lipstick, an eyelash curler, a black tube of violet-scented hand cream, and a white plastic bag from Sephora. She opened the bag, but it was empty, and she assumed it had contained the makeup, bought on the run. In the bottom of the bag were receipts, and she pulled them out and read them. One showed cosmetics and beauty supplies, for a total of $136.98, and the other was the thin receipt from a Visa customer copy.

Jill's gaze shot to the bottom of the receipt, where it had been signed by the customer.

Nina D'Orive, it read, in a lovely, flowing script.

Chapter Forty

Jill emerged from a cab at Penn Station, eyeing the rush-hour crowds. If the black SUV had followed her to William's apartment, it could follow her here, and she scanned the cabs, limos, vans, and cars all around her. She spotted three black SUVs but couldn't see the drivers, and it made her nervous. Worse, she wasn't any closer to finding Abby, and what she'd learned about William made her heartsick, for Abby.

Jill hustled to the curb, threaded through the commuters flooding into the station, boarded the escalator on the run, and kept moving. She hit the ground floor running and made a beeline for the ticket booth in the back, but the line was too long. She hustled to the ticket kiosk, eyeing everyone around her with suspicion; the burly man in a suit that strained at the seams on his upper arms, the sleepy hipster with the oversized black glasses and guitar case, the young woman in an unseasonably heavy sweater, who seemed to watch her every move.

Jill didn't know whom to suspect, so she suspected everyone, then it dawned on her that there could be more than one person following her. They could be working together as a team; in fact, they had to be. There was no way one person could have followed her from her car to the train to the apartment building. She glanced over her shoulder as the ticket printed out, but suddenly people starting surging in three different directions, regrouping as quickly as a school of tropical fish.

"Acela to Washington, D.C., with stops in Newark, Princeton, North Philadelphia, Philadelphia," blared the loudspeaker.

Jill joined the crowd surging forward, then squeezed her way into a human funnel as each passenger showed his ticket to the conductor. She filed in behind an older woman as the escalator carried them down to the bowels of the station, where she hurriedly boarded the train and took the first empty seat, next to another older woman, who immediately pulled out her knitting.

Jill set her purse on her lap and looked out the window. The train was still boarding, and all she saw on the platform was darkness broken by an array of shifting shadows. She closed her eyes, and a wave of exhaustion washed over her, born of anxiety and fear. She flashed on Abby's face and prayed she had called her phone or Victoria's, or had finally come home.

Jill kept her eyes closed as the train started to move. She didn't feel safe enough to fall asleep, but the car began to rock slowly back and forth. She forced her eyes open and found herself resting her cheek in her hand while the noise and chatter of the other passengers grew distant. In her mind's eye, she could see Abby, younger and grinning until her rubber bands showed, then Abby morphed into Megan, who morphed into Rahul, and all of the children became one, and they were all happy and whole and healthy, living without danger, disease, or death, rocked in her loving arms, back and forth, forever and ever.

And in the next minute, Jill had fallen asleep.

Chapter Forty-one

Jill got home to a house quiet except for Beef, who barked his way down the stairs, in excitement. She knew Sam was home because his car was in the driveway, but he didn't greet her. "I'm home!" she called out, hopeful.

"Up here!" Sam called, from upstairs.

"Be up in a minute," Jill called back, relieved they were on speaking terms. She set down her purse and keys, patted Beef on the head, then hurried into the kitchen to check her messages.

She went to the wall phone, picked up the receiver, and pressed the number code for her messages, but they were all telemarketers, not Abby, Victoria, or any of her patients. She hung up, went to her laptop and moved the mouse to wake it, then logged onto her email, skimming it quickly. Again, there was nothing from Abby or Victoria, but there were two emails from patients. She read them quickly, but they could wait for an answer. She checked for Rahul's results, but they hadn't come in yet, which concerned her. Her appointment with Padma and Rahul was tomorrow.

Jill went to the stairs, anxious to see Sam. She didn't know how he'd react to her knowing about William's double life, or how she would tell him. It struck her that she hadn't felt so awkward about seeing him since their first date, years ago. She climbed the stairs, thinking about it. She'd finally felt ready to go out again, but had been on one bad blind date after another, putting herself out there, keeping her chin up through the heavy drinkers, the men still in love with their exes, and men who expected her to sleep with them on the first date, since they were both adults now. She'd almost lost heart the day she'd arrived at the restaurant, early as usual, and spotted Sam already sitting at the table, wearing the plaid tie he'd told her he'd have on, and the thing that gave her a spark of hope was that he was reading a book.

Sorry I'm late, Jill said reflexively, slipping her shoulder bag on the back of the chair and extending her hand like it was a job interview.

Sam smiled, rose, and shook her hand. *You're not late, I'm early. I'm always early.*

Jill smiled, sitting awkwardly, then she noticed the title of the book. *Angela's Ashes,* by Frank McCourt, which was one of her favorites. *I love that book.*

Me, too. I'm re-reading it. It's so beautifully written, and it reminds me of how lucky I am in my life. How much human beings can endure and still survive.

Jill felt exactly the same way, but didn't say so, thinking it would sound too cute. *So, well, hello, Sam Becker. You're in diabetes research? How wonderful.*

Thank you. Sam closed the book and set it aside. *But I don't think of what I do that way. That permits the disease to define me and my work, and I concede nothing to the disease. I'm trying to beat the disease.*

So then what do you do? How do you define your work? Jill felt awkward again, like she'd stuck her foot in her mouth, though Sam's smile was even warmer.

I'm not in diabetes research, I'm in people research. I research people, to help them fight disease, so that someday they'll live happy and healthy lives. They deserve that chance. At the very least, to survive.

Jill nodded. *Like the book, I guess.*

Yes, right. Sam blinked. *I never made that connection, before now. Thank you.*

Jill smiled, flattered. *That's what books do, isn't it? That's why I love to read. They bring us closer to ourselves.*

And closer to each other. Sam smiled, then laughed, flushing. *Wait, hold on. That's not a line or anything. I hope it didn't sound that way.*

No, not at all, Jill assured him, meaning it, but she didn't add that she'd liked the sound of it, and when he'd said it, she'd felt a little thrill, a flash of emotion too small to warm her heart, but enough to fill it with light, and that was how she came to think about Sam himself, after she'd gotten to know him and had fallen in love with him, that his soul filled hers with light, and always would.

Jill was standing at the threshold of their bedroom, and Sam was packing his black rollerbag, which lay open on the bed like a thick book, one side filled with folded shirts and slacks, and the other with shoes. She stood at the threshold as if it weren't her bedroom, too. "What's this?" Jill asked, her mouth dry.

"I'm going to Cleveland." Sam looked up, his eyes cool and distant behind his reading glasses. He was still dressed from work, in a blue shirt, loose striped tie, and Dockers. "Lee got sick and I have to help present his paper."

"Oh." Jill wasn't sure what to say. "It's a conference, so you'll be back when? A day or two?"

"No." Sam picked up a sneaker from the floor and wedged it inside the bag. "I thought I might get a jump on it and go see Steve."

"But that's this weekend."

"Come on, Jill." Sam stopped fussing with the sneaker and met her eye. "We both know you're not going to Austin if Abby's still missing, and I assume she's still missing or you would have called me. Am I right?"

"Well, it's true, if she's still gone, I'd feel funny leaving—"

"That's what I thought. So why should I fly home for one night, then leave for Austin alone?" Sam zipped the black netting over his shoes. "Megan's at Courtney's, and she's fine. She called you, but you didn't call back, so I told her it would be okay to sleep over. I thought it made the most sense for tonight, since I had to leave."

"I dropped my phone, sorry."

"Don't worry about it." Sam closed the top of the suitcase, then zipped it, which for some reason, was never a good sound.

"Sam, I'm sorry. This is so crazy what's going on, with Abby gone. I found out William had a double life, a secret identity in New York."

"Really." Sam picked two novels and his electronic reader off the bed, then slid them inside the exterior flap of the suitcase and zipped it closed.

"I went to the New York police but they—"

"Stop." Sam picked the suitcase off the bed, set it on the floor, then brushed off the comforter. "I have to catch a plane, and I'd prefer it if our last words to each other weren't about your ex-husband."

"Okay." Jill sighed, resigned. "So you're still angry."

"No, I'm not angry, I'm unhappy." Sam hesitated, softening. "This conference comes at a good time, doesn't it? Let's use the opportunity to go to our respective corners and think things over. We're in trouble, the two of us."

Jill hated to hear him say it. "No, we aren't."

"Yes, we are." Sam picked up the bag and walked to the door, giving her a dry peck on the cheek. "Abby came to us out of the blue, a curve ball. Let's see what we both want from the future, given the new normal."

"What's that supposed to mean?"

"Babe, we've gone over and over this." Sam set down his bag.

"Are we still engaged?"

"Honestly, I don't know. You should answer that for yourself, and I'll answer it for myself, and we'll talk when we get back."

Jill felt like crying, but she couldn't pinpoint why. Heartbreak. Anger. Fear. Sadness. All of the above. "Really?"

"Really."

"But what about Megan?"

"She doesn't have to know. Don't tell her."

Jill tasted bitterness on her tongue. "We can't disagree without breaking up?"

Sam picked up the bag. "We can't go forward without agreeing."

"And you're punishing me until I agree."

"How am I punishing you?"

"Withdrawing, leaving."

"No, no." Sam shook his head. "I have a job to do, just like you do, and this makes the most sense to me. I don't want to hang around like a puppy dog, waiting for you to come home."

"But you're not."

"Yes, I am." Sam started to go, and Jill felt a twinge of anger. "This isn't what I want."

"Yes, it is." Sam turned at the head of the stair, in front of his lineup of photographs, all of them taken in happier times. "It must be, because it's the logical result of what you're doing. You couldn't have set it up any better."

Jill was suddenly tired of his research jargon. "Not everything is a controlled experiment, Sam."

"Then choose."

"What?"

"Choose now. I can tell you, now, that I don't want to parent Abby, in any way, shape, or form."

"She's *missing*, Sam. Can't we stay in the present?"

"Can't we plan, for the future?" Sam frowned, deeply. "Think ahead to when she comes back, or you find her. Tell me how you're going to replace the father and mother she lost. Explain how you're going to shore up a troubled kid who's already tried to kill herself once. Choose, now. Last chance. Pick that family, or this one."

"Why do I have to choose?" Jill asked, agonized.

"You just did," Sam answered, turning away.

Chapter Forty-two

Jill felt empty and hurting, disconnected, loosed from her moorings. But she had to make herself act, given that Abby was still missing. She changed quickly into comfy jeans, a sweater, and loafers, and went downstairs. She thought she should go back to the Philly police or touch base with Victoria, but she wasn't sure which to do first.

She went to the phone in the kitchen and pressed in Megan's number. The phone rang, and she sat down at the island, tugged the laptop over, and moved the mouse to wake it up. Her email server popped on the screen, and she scanned her email again to see if Rahul's results had come in, but they still hadn't.

"Mom?" Megan said, when the call connected. "Why are you calling from the house phone?"

"My BlackBerry's broken."

"Is that why you didn't get back to me? I called and texted, so don't get mad."

Jill could hear the attitude in her tone. "So what's up? You guys having fun?"

"No, working on this dumb project. Did you find Abby?"

"Not yet, but don't worry about that. Did you eat?"

"Yes, Courtney's mom made lasagna."

"Yum." Jill's stomach growled. "Wish I were there."

"Sam said I could stay over, even though it's a school night."

"I know, but let's make this the last time, okay?" Jill knew she had said the same thing, just yesterday or so.

"What's the big deal? We're working, Mom."

"Don't be fresh. How will you get to school?"

"Carol can take me."

"Since when do you call her Carol? Call her Mrs. Ariz." Jill adored Courtney's mother, Carol, and they'd been friends since the girls made the club swim team, years ago. "Be sure to thank her for me. She's doing a lot of the driving lately."

"She doesn't mind."

"Why don't I take you both to school, then she can pick up, since I can't?"

"She's *fine* with it, Mom."

"Okay, but what are you going to do for clothes? I can bring you some fresh ones, then take you to school."

"Mom, no." Megan sighed, in an exaggerated way. "I borrowed some from Courtney, and Sam brought me some, too. He was coming home early to pack for his trip, so he brought over my stuff."

Jill rubbed her face, sick at heart. She couldn't imagine telling Megan that their engagement was off. "I really wish you were home."

"I'm fine here."

Jill sighed. "Goodnight, then. I love you."

"Goodnight. Love you, too."

"Fine, and don't forget—" Jill started to say, then the line went dead. She pressed END and called information for Victoria's phone number, because it was in her BlackBerry, now defunct. She waited for the call to connect, and while it rang, she logged onto whitepages.com and plugged in Nina D'Orive, then New York.

"Jill?" Victoria answered. "Did Abby call you?"

"No, didn't she call you?"

"Oh, no." Victoria still sounded remote, but distinctly worried. "Now, this is really scary."

"I agree. I'd have called your cell, but my BlackBerry's broken."

Jill read the laptop monitor, and the website had found three Nina D'Orives. She clicked on the first one, and it showed a Nina D'Orive at 335 Winding Way, Scarsdale, but her age was listed as sixty-seven. Jill eliminated her, surprised the website even gave ages. "What happened last night, at Central Detectives?"

"Nothing. Neither Detective Reed or Detective Pitkowski were in, so we left a message to call me."

"Did they?"

"No."

"We have to go back there."

"I'll go again, but what's new? Nothing."

"Not exactly." Jill had decided on the train that Victoria was old enough for the truth about her father. "I did learn a thing or two in New York that might help them."

"Like what?"

"It's a long story, and I'd rather tell you in person." Jill clicked on the next Nina D'Orive, who lived at 701 Young Street, Albany, and she was forty-five. It was unlikely that William would be dating somebody who lived so far upstate, so she eliminated that one, too. "Just meet me at Central Detectives, would you?"

"Sure. I'll leave now."

"Good. See you there, out front." Jill hung up and clicked the final entry. Nina D'Orive, Apt 2F, East 94th Street, in New York. Her age was thirty, which would be more William's taste, and Belle Kahan, the Realtor, had said that the girlfriend was young.

Jill felt her heart beat faster and clicked on the highlighted name. A grid popped onto the screen, showing D'Orive's last known work addresses. The most recent was Pharmcen Pharmaceuticals.

Jill hit PRINT, jumped up, and went to get her bag.

Chapter Forty-three

Jill, Victoria, and her friend Brian Pendle sat across from Detective Ronald Hightower, who was a tall, fit, African-American in his forties, with short hair, knowing brown eyes, and a brushy mustache. Detective Pitkowski wasn't in, Detective Reed was on vacation, and Jill was starting to think that Central Detectives was a group practice. She asked, "So if Detective Reed is on vacation, do you handle the case?"

"No, I don't. There's no case to be handled. We investigate homicide, and William Skyler's death wasn't ruled a homicide." Detective Hightower had retrieved the file, and it lay open in front of him, on a desk that looked neat, with squared-off stacks of notes, files, and papers. His phone messages slips were arranged in layers, each overlapping the next, like napkins at a reception, and his manner exuded professionalism as he turned to Victoria. "Ms. Skyler, I'm sorry about your father's passing. Don't think me hardhearted, but it's not police business."

"But Detective, doesn't my sister being gone make a difference to you? It's not like Abby not to return my calls for this long." Victoria leaned forward urgently, looking more dressed-up than usual, with a black blazer over her white sweater and skinny jeans. Her hair was in its usual twist, her makeup was perfect, and she had on her pearl earrings. "Abby thought Dad was murdered, and I didn't agree, but now I'm wondering. What if Abby found out something, or saw something? They lived together, and who knows?"

Jill knew it was time for the truth about William's double life. She hadn't told Victoria and Brian outside, when they'd met, because it hadn't seemed like the place and time. Now it was, and Jill wished she could soften the blow for Victoria, but there was no way. "Detective Hightower," Jill began, "I have new information for you. I'm concerned that Abby's disappearance is related to a Neil Straub, whom William said was his business associate, in New York. Well, he isn't. Today I learned that Neil Straub and William Skyler are one and the same person."

"*What?*" Victoria turned to Jill, her bright eyes narrowing. "What are you talking about? That's a *lie!*"

"Are you crazy?" Brian frowned, stiffening in his striped tie and gray suit as if he'd come from the office.

"Dr. Farrow, what do you mean by that?" Detective Hightower asked, so Jill told them everything and showed them the photo of William with the man in the blue shirt, his Mercedes registration, and Nina D'Orive's home address. Detective Hightower took notes, and Jill could see his concern growing. Victoria's expression went from disbelief to disillusionment when she saw William's signature on Neil Straub's car registration. After Jill finished, she looked over at an anguished Victoria.

"I'm so sorry you had to hear all this, honey. I know it's confusing, and strange."

"Dad would never—" Victoria started to say, stricken, then stopped herself, her expression darkening. She shook her head, aghast. "I just don't understand. This makes no sense. I don't know why he would do this."

"I know, I'm sorry." Jill felt the urge to touch her but didn't know if it would be welcome. "I'm as shocked as you are. We can't know everything about our parents, Victoria."

"But *this*? A secret life? An apartment in the city? Double cars and everything?" Victoria's manicured hand flew to her forehead, rubbing it and leaving pinkish streaks. "*Dad* is *Neil Straub*? That's *unreal*!"

"I'm sorry, Vick." Brian reached over and touched Victoria's shoulder, his eyes an agonized blue behind his wire-rimmed glasses, and Jill could see how much he cared about her, which made Jill like him better.

"Victoria," Jill said, softly, "your Dad must've gotten mixed up in something that made him want to disguise his identity, but let's not dwell on that, now. The important thing is getting Abby home." She turned to Detective Hightower. "I'm hoping that William's girlfriend, Nina D'Orive, might have some idea where Abby is. Will you go and question her?"

"Correct, or NYPD will. We'll have to iron out the jurisdictional issues." Detective Hightower's dark eyes softened. "Given these circumstances, I agree that Abby's disappearance is concerning, and we'll take it up with Missing Persons."

"Thanks so much." Jill almost cried with relief.

"Yes, thanks, Detective." Victoria nodded, still upset. "I appreciate it. Abby's my only sister, and we're all we have . . ." Just then, a cell phone started ringing, and Victoria reached, embarrassed, into her large black handbag. "Sorry, I forgot to silence my phone." She pulled out an iPhone, and her eyes widened when she saw the screen. "Oh my God, it's Abby!" Victoria held up the phone, which showed a photo of a grinning Abby. "What do I do? What if she was kidnapped or something?"

"Answer it." Detective Hightower rose and hustled around the desk. "Put it on speaker."

Jill's heart started to pound. "Can you trace it somehow, Detective Hightower?"

"No." Detective Hightower waved at two other detectives, who were talking near the file cabinets in the back. "Guys, quiet a minute!"

Victoria hit the ANSWER button. Jill leaned over to listen from the left, and Brian leaned from the right, with Detective Hightower in the back.

"Abby?" Victoria answered the phone, uncertain. "Is that you? I have it on speaker because . . . my hands are full."

"Hi, girl!" Abby said. "What's up?"

Jill couldn't believe her ears. It was Abby, and she sounded happy and carefree.

Victoria frowned, shaking her head in confusion. "Abby? Are you okay?"

"Oh, I'm fine, sorry."

"Really, you're fine? No one's making you say this?"

Abby laughed. "What? Are you kidding?"

Victoria's mouth dropped open. "This is really you? And you're fine? I've been worried sick about you! Why didn't you call me back?"

"I know, I should have called, I'm sorry." Abby groaned. "But I knew what you'd say and I didn't need you to yell at me."

Jill sat, stunned. It didn't sound as if some bad guy was holding a gun to Abby's head, making her say these things. Brian leaned back, pursing his lips. Detective Hightower straightened up, waved the other detectives back to work, and strode to his chair, his lips tight.

Victoria said into the phone, "Where are you? What are you doing?"

"Jeez, sorry, I met someone."

"Who?"

"A guy. His name's Brandon, okay? He's in the TV business and he was in town, scouting locations. He has an *amazing* apartment here, so we flew out and—"

"Flew where?"

"L.A."

"*Los Angeles?*"

Jill couldn't process it all fast enough. Brian folded his arms, his annoyance plain. Detective Hightower bent over his desk, writing notes in the file.

Victoria's fair skin flushed with new anger, and she set the iPhone down on the desk. "Abby, are you *kidding* me right now? I thought you were dead."

"I'm really sorry, I am." Abby sounded genuinely regretful. "I've been so upset since Dad died, and I think I need a break, you know, to sort things out. Brandon said he can get me a job as a P.A., which means production assistant. I might come home in a week or so. I can't decide when—"

"I cannot *believe* you played me this way. What the hell is the matter with you? We're at the police station, they're about to call Missing Persons. Jill's here, too."

Abby gasped. "*Jill,* for real? Oh, no. I'm so sorry, Jill!"

Jill leaned toward the phone. "Abby, what's going on? Why didn't you return my calls?"

"I did, today. I left a message, but you didn't call me back."

Jill flashed on her mashed-up BlackBerry. "My phone broke."

"Jill, I'm so sorry, but you'd love Brandon. He doesn't think I should live alone in the house, either. He says I need to start over and take responsibility for myself. That's what you said, too."

"I'm just trying to understand what's going on with you. This is such an about-face. And how old is Brandon, anyway?"

"Older than me, but don't worry about it. I feel so much better now, and you helped me, too. I'll see you when I get back, and we can catch up. Please don't be mad at me."

Victoria snatched the iPhone from the desk. "Abby, *I'm* mad at you. When are you gonna grow up? Dad *died,* then you vanish? Do me a favor, will you? Stay in L.A. *Live* there with Brandon. You're a selfish *bitch*!" Victoria hung up, jumped to her feet, and turned to Jill, red-faced. "You got me into this! I told you, I told you, I *knew* it! I should have listened to myself!"

"Honey, please, relax." Jill reached for her arm, but Victoria edged away, holding up both hands.

"Back off! And for God's sake, I'm *not* your 'honey'!" Victoria shook with anger, and Jill thought she might faint.

"Let me get you some water."

"No!" Victoria shot back, then exhaled, seeming to catch herself. "I'm sorry, Jill. I'm sorry. I know better. I *knew* better." She balled her fingers into tight knots, like a tantruming child. "I hate my sister. There, I said it. I *hate* my sister." She exhaled once, then again, her gaze taking in the other detectives and finally coming to rest on Detective Hightower. "Detective, I'm so sorry about all of this. I'm sorry to have wasted your time."

"It's all right." Detective Hightower's tone had gone cool again. He rose, gesturing behind him. "Sure you don't want that glass of water, or a soda? I'm buying."

"No, thank you." Victoria turned to Brian, bristling with emotion. "Time to go, don't you think? Have I caused you enough embarrassment?"

Brian rose, his expression sympathetic, and he shook his head. "Don't worry about it, Vick. It's not in your control."

Jill rose, too, looking at Detective Hightower, in confusion. "I'm sorry, I guess we thought she was missing, but still."

"Still what?" Detective Hightower frowned. "I think that takes the wind out of your sails, don't you?"

"Not necessarily. It doesn't mean anything with respect to William." Jill tried to collect her thoughts. She was thrilled that Abby was safe, but what she'd learned today about William's double life only made her more sure that he had been murdered. She found herself thinking like a doctor, deciding that the new data didn't change her differential, but only confirmed it. "In other words, the fact that Abby's not missing doesn't mean William wasn't murdered."

"Oh please, Jill!" Victoria whirled around. "Do you really think even Abby thought Dad was *murdered*? She wanted you back in our life, and after Dad died, she saw a way to get it." Victoria still shook slightly, but the redness was finally leaving her cheeks. "It's totally weird that Dad had some kind of secret identity, but you know what, I shouldn't be surprised, and now that I think about it, I'm not. I know he was no angel. He played fast and loose with things. He and Abby, they're two of a kind. That's why they're so close."

Jill felt pained to see the jealous twist to Victoria's lips.

"Yes, Jill. Dad paid for art school for Abby, but not law school for me. Can you believe that? He had the money, but he wouldn't give it to me. He said he likes artists, but he hates lawyers. Funny, huh?"

Jill hadn't heard any of this before.

"I don't know what Dad was up to, but he wasn't murdered. He took one too many chances, sometimes with the wrong things. Didn't he, with you? Whether he cheated or you cheated, it all comes down to the same thing. He wasn't careful with anything, including *people*."

Jill couldn't say no.

"Dad could charm anything and anybody, but he met his match in a pill. You can't take chances with them, or they kill you." Victoria picked up her purse from the chair, threw her phone inside, and turned to Detective Hightower. "You don't think my father was murdered, do you?"

"No, I don't." Detective Hightower closed the manila file. "I'll talk with Detectives Reed and Pitkowski, but right now, I'm standing down."

Jill wasn't sure they could put it to bed so fast. "Just like that? So quickly? You're sure?"

"Dr. Farrow, I listened to you, as did two other detectives. We've given this matter more than enough of our time and resources." Detective Hightower touched his mustache. "Tonight was a fiasco. A murder investigation isn't a spigot you turn off and on."

"But you were convinced until Abby's call."

"Incorrect." Detective Hightower gathered the photo of William with the man in the polo shirt and slid it into the manila file. "I said I was going to follow up with Missing Persons. What you learned in New York isn't sufficient evidence to overturn a coroner's finding, or convert this case to a homicide. But I'll leave it to Detective Reed. He caught this case, and he's stuck with it." Detective Hightower handed her William's car registration. "Please, take this back. I made a note that I saw it."

"Thanks." Jill put the registration in her purse, and Brian moved toward the door, with Victoria behind.

"Good-bye, Jill," she said. "I wish you the best."

Brian nodded at Detective Hightower and Jill. "Thanks again for your time, Detective. Nice meeting you, Dr. Farrow. Sorry I was so rough on you, before. Occupational hazard."

"Good-bye, take care, both of you." Jill watched them go, torn between pressing the matter and letting it lie, stuck between here and there. Suddenly she didn't know where she belonged, because she didn't belong anywhere.

Detective Hightower cleared his throat, in a pointed way. "Dr. Farrow, I've done all I can do."

"How will I know if they follow up with the girlfriend?"

"Call them. Not me." Detective Hightower softened again. "But, please, don't go chasing any more cars, and for what's it's worth, I don't think you're being followed. That SUV could've been anything."

"Like what?"

"He coulda been a guy waiting for a woman who's not his wife. He doesn't want to get caught by you, you could be one of her friends."

Jill tried to believe him, listening hard.

"You know, I've learned a few things, in twenty-two years on the job. People do strange things, every day. You meet them at different times in their lives, under the influence of whatever. Most of the time, people are straight-up *nuts*."

Jill nodded. "I guess."

"They're not criminals, they're idiots. Like your ex. The man's an idiot, I can tell you that, if he lost you."

Jill thought of Sam, bittersweet. "Thanks. I do appreciate all you've done."

"You're welcome." Detective Hightower extended a hand, and Jill shook it. "While I'm on a roll, you want some advice? Don't get caught between those two sisters. My wife has a younger sister, and I know how it goes. The baby of the family stays a baby. Period."

Jill wondered if he was right. She was an only child, with an only child.

"Now, go home."

"I will, thanks." Jill's heart went heavy in her chest. She turned and left, then realized suddenly where she could go.

Chapter Forty-four

Jill told Katie the whole story, and she listened while she made a diorama. Magic Markers, construction paper, and overpriced modeling clay cluttered the kitchen table, and a shoebox sat on its side. Jill missed a lot of things about elementary school, but making dioramas wasn't one of them.

"I don't know what to think, anymore." Jill rested her chin in her hand, behind a mug of cooling decaf. "Why did William have a secret identity, and who the hell is the blonde with the Sephora bag?"

"She has no kids, this we know."

"How?"

"The eyelash curler. Really?"

Jill smiled. "I'm trying to talk about a murder."

"I bet she's young, like, an egg." Katie kneaded brown clay with her hands. "William was dating an egg."

"Still, Katie, not the point."

"Yes it is. You're the one missing the point." Katie held up the clay, which looked like a Tootsie Roll with pink spots. "How'm I doing?"

"What is it?"

"I told you, I'm making Winn-Dixie from the book *Because of Winn-Dixie*. It's a dog, named after the store."

"Oh." Jill was so distracted, she didn't remember Katie telling her.

"This is the body, but I can't get him skinny enough. Story of my life."

"What are the pink spots?"

"Bald patches, remember? Winn-Dixie had bald patches."

Jill didn't remember, and she was thinking of Megan, whom she should have called to tell her about Abby. She checked the clock—10:45. Megan should still be up. "Mind if I use your phone to call Megan? I can't believe I didn't when I first came in."

"Tell her I said hi, and don't beat yourself up. No teenager hopes her mom will call." Katie stuck brown legs on the dog body. "I don't know how they expect a second-grader to read a book and make a diorama, in three days. Why not ask him to juggle or take the SATs?"

Jill went over to the phone, picked up the receiver, and pressed in Megan's cell number. The call rang a few times, then went to voicemail, so she left a message. "Hey honey, just wanted you to know that we found Abby and all is well. Hope you're having fun. Love you. Call anytime, I'm at Katie's. Bye." Jill hung up. "Now what point did I miss?"

"Sam. Sam is the point. You love that guy, and you're about to lose him. Call him. Say you were wrong and you're sorry."

"But I wasn't wrong." Jill felt her gut wrench. "Abby behaved badly, but she'll be back, and I was right about the principle."

"Oh, okay, like *that* matters." Katie rolled her eyes, kneading the clay. "Abby was jerking you around, and her sister has her number. I'm with that detective. Call Sam and say, come home. You can use the phone in the living room, if you want privacy."

Jill put a hand on the receiver, but didn't pick it up. "I don't know."

Katie lifted an eyebrow. "You're really not going to call him?"

"I don't know what to say. He doesn't want Abby in our lives, and I don't like him telling me who I can love and who I can't." Jill felt her gut wrench. "I love Sam, I do. But I love Abby, too, and she's not in L.A. forever. She's just latched on to another, older guy."

"But Sam loves you, and he's worried about you. Call him and tell him the cops don't think you're being followed, at least." Katie frowned, her tired eyes pleading. "Tell him Abby's safe, too. He probably even cares about her. He's a caring guy."

Jill flashed on what Victoria had said, about William. *He wasn't careful with anything, even people.* "You're right. Sam is caring."

"So call him."

"All right." Jill pressed in Sam's cell number, and the phone rang. He didn't pick up, so she waited for voicemail to leave a message: "Hi babe, I just wanted to let you know that Abby turned up in L.A., and the cops don't think I'm being followed, so don't worry."

Katie was motioning to her. "Say you're sorry," she mouthed.

Jill said into the phone, "I'm sorry, and call me when you can. Try me at Katie's or later at home. Love you, bye." She hung up.

"Good girl!" Katie beamed. "Even if you didn't mean it, you sounded convincing, and that's all that matters."

Jill smiled, her mood lighter, which is what girlfriends were for. "Do you think the detective was right, that the baby of the family stays a baby?"

"Absolutely. Jamie is my baby, and I do more of his homework than the others. And don't think he didn't read *Because of Winn-Dixie.* He did, all of it. I'm the one who watched the DVD."

Jill's thoughts turned to Nina D'Orive. "Wonder how I can find out what his girlfriend does at Pharmcen? I know a Pharmcen rep and I could find him and call him, but it's a big company."

"Try Facebook."

"Right." Jill rallied. "Mind if I use your computer?"

"Go ahead, I'm already logged in."

"You use Facebook that much?" Jill went over to Katie's laptop, which was on the countertop, nestled among a stack of bills, catalogs, and school notices.

"Of course, don't you read your feed?" Katie flattened the dog body, but a leg dropped off. "I'm the Queen of Farmville."

Jill logged onto Facebook, went to the Search function, typed in Nina D'Orive, and there was only one result. "Got her. Good thing she has such an unusual name."

"What's her profile picture look like? I bet she's skinny. A skinny, skinny egg."

Jill clicked Nina's profile picture, which was a Welsh corgi puppy. "No, it's a really cute puppy."

"So she's either eleven years old or Barbie herself."

Jill clicked to Nina's wall, but the privacy settings must have been on the maximum. "Damn, I can't see her page. I'm not her friend."

"No, you're definitely not." Katie stuck the clay leg back on. "You're the psycho ex who's stalking her."

"Can I friend her, as you?"

"Sure, but why would she accept it?"

"I can send her a direct message with the friend request, right?" Jill thought a minute. "I'll say I work in a doctor's office. If she's a drug rep, she'll say yes."

"You can't do that, you're logged in as me." Katie walked over with Winn-Dixie. "My profile says I'm an at-home mom."

"I need to write something that will make her want to accept me." Jill found herself staring at the clay dog in Katie's hands. "We know she likes dogs. I'll say I'm looking for a corgi puppy for my daughter."

"You mean your sons. You're me."

"Oh, right." Jill got excited. "I'll tell her I thought her puppy was cute, and I'm curious who her breeder is. People love to talk about their dogs, and you don't see many corgis."

"It might work." Katie molded Winn-Dixie's other leg. "She's so young, she has a practice dog. Remember when you thought a dog was just like a baby, then you found out a dog is nothing like a baby?"

Jill clicked the box to send a friend request and typed a direct message: **Dear Nina, I think your puppy is supercute. My boys would love a puppy like that. Who is your breeder? Best, Katie** She clicked SEND MESSAGE. "Think she's online?"

"Of course. Everybody's online at night, especially the hot girls. They talk to the men while the moms talk to each other."

"She is hot, the Realtor said."

"You jealous?"

"Of course not. I feel bad for her. God knows what scam he's running on her. She could be another drug rep, but if that's true, he's taking a big risk not using his real name. Someone could recognize him as William Skyler." Jill thought a minute. "I bet she doesn't know he's dead. She's probably wondering where he is."

"Unless she killed him."

"Aren't we dark, Winn-Dixie?" Jill glanced over, surprised, then her attention returned to the screen. "It can't be a coincidence that she works for a drug company. William targets women to use them."

"You know, I worry about you, girl. You fell out of love, but you need to fall out of hate."

"What?" Jill looked over again, and Katie's pretty features had fallen into troubled lines.

"I know you're not in love, but are you in hate? Because that's no good, either."

"What do you mean?"

"You didn't get closure on William, not really, because of the way it ended. You didn't see it coming. You're still emotionally involved with him."

"No, I'm not." Jill scoffed.

"Then why are we looking up Nina the Egg?" Katie cocked her head, and her reddish blonde bangs fell into her eyes. "You told me you cared if he was murdered because Abby cared, and I bought that. Well, now what? Abby's out, but you're still in."

Jill had to admit that it was true. "You're right."

"I know I am. I always am." Katie smiled. "So the question remains. Why do you care whether William was murdered or not?"

"I guess I do care, and maybe you're right." Jill shook her head, considering it. "I know I'm not in love with him anymore, but maybe I'm in hate. I'm not sure. But I *do* know that today, I got all the way up to New York, and I found all this out about his double life, and I felt like I was getting to the *real* him, like finding out what he was really up to."

"Yeah, so? Why does it matter to you, what your ex-husband is up to?"

Jill thought harder. "I guess that all this time, since what happened with the script pads and the way William left that night, I never knew what he was up to, in my own marriage. Under my own roof, under my own *nose.*"

"Aww, honey." Katie's face fell into sympathetic lines. "Finding out what William was up to in New York isn't the same as finding out what he was up to in your marriage. That time has passed."

"Has it?" Jill looked up, questioning. "I'm still the same person. He's still the same person."

"Except for the dead part."

"It doesn't matter. Time doesn't matter. I want to know who William really is, or was. The *truth* of who he is, because I think it will help me understand the truth of who I am, or who I was in that marriage, and how I'll be the next time, if Sam comes around." Jill was finally getting some clarity, and she felt like it was her heart talking, now. "You can't go forward to the next step without figuring out the last one, right? It's like I'm trying to diagnose what went wrong in my own marriage, and part of me feels this will help. Because I really want my next marriage to last, Katie. Whoever I marry, Sam or no. I want it to work. I want forever, too, and I'm scared that this is my last chance." Jill felt tears in her eyes, and Katie put a warm hand on her shoulder.

"Okay, then. I get it, and I'll help you, whatever you need."

Suddenly the monitor screen changed, and both women turned to the laptop. Nina D'Orive had accepted the friend request, with a direct message: **Dear Katie, My puppy rocks! Check out my photo album to see more of her and her littermates! I love my breeder and she ships. Do you want the address? Thx for asking! Sincerely, Nina ox**

"Oh my God." Jill felt her heart pound. She couldn't believe she'd just made contact with William's girlfriend, when this morning she didn't even know he had a girlfriend.

"She uses the ox for someone she doesn't even know? She's definitely Barbie." Katie set down the clay dog. "What's the *matter* with women?"

"I'm writing her back. I want to start a conversation with her, to see where it will lead." Jill clicked COMPOSE MESSAGE. "She could know everything about William, about what he was doing and why."

"Or, like I said, she could be the killer."

"Killers don't have corgis." Jill typed, **Dear Nina, I'd love the breeder's address and anything else you can tell me about your dog. I never had a corgi before and I'm on the fence. Are they good with kids? Best, Katie** Jill hit SEND MESSAGE. "See, I want her to convince me. I need to engage her."

"You sure this is safe?" Katie asked, her tone worried.

"Yes. Now, let's see what else we can find out about our new friend." Jill navigated to Nina's Info page, and her listed address was Hoboken, New Jersey. "That's funny. I had a Manhattan address for her. She must have moved."

"Jill, do you see what I see?" Katie pointed to PERSONAL INFO, and under STATUS, it read, **Married.** "Barbie's cheating on Ken."

"Whoa. That must be what happened with the address. She moved and married, but didn't change her name." Jill read down, noticing that Nina listed her employer as Pharmcen, but didn't specify her job. The page showed that she had sixty-three friends, twenty-nine in the Pharmcen network, and five others were family, including her husband. His profile picture was of an overweight guy in a sweatshirt, and his name was Martin Dunwilig. "See, the husband's last name is different."

Katie squinted at the husband's photo. "Dude. Unfortunate fashion choices. Also, hit the gym. Wifey's skinny for a reason."

Suddenly another message from Nina popped onto the screen: **Dear Katie, I see from your FB page that you don't live that far from me, and your sons are adorable! If you want, you can bring them to meet my puppy Ruby! We can meet at the park! They'll fall in love! Sincerely, Nina Xo**

"Wow." Jill grinned, but Katie recoiled.

"You're not going to meet her, are you?"

"What do you think?" Jill hit COMPOSE MESSAGE. "Don't worry, I won't bring the boys. I'll just tell her I will."

"You shouldn't go alone, honey. Want me to go with you?"

"No, how can you? I'm you."

"I'll be me, and you be you." Katie screwed up her face. "Wait. I'm confused."

Jill laughed. "No thanks, I'll go alone. You don't know which questions to ask."

"She'll see that you're not me. We don't look alike."

"Damn." Jill paused, thinking. "What's your profile picture?" She plugged in Katie's name, and her Facebook page popped onto the screen. Her profile picture was of her boys, as was every other picture on the page. "No worries. The least-photographed person in the world is a mother."

"Wait, I think I have a shot of me in there. Let me check." Katie palmed the mouse, navigated to an album, and found a vacation picture that had a photo of her, but in a Phillies hat that covered her features. "Just one."

"Perfect. You can't see your face at all."

"Thanks. Also my hips are wider than yours."

"No, they're not, and she's a girl, so she won't notice."

"That's who *does* notice." Katie leaned over. "I don't think you should meet her."

"Why not?" Jill went back to Nina's page. "You don't mind that I'm using your name, do you?"

"No, but maybe it's dangerous. I think you should let it go."

"Luckily, you're not my mother," Jill said, typing away.

Chapter Forty-five

The house phone started ringing almost as soon as Jill got home and closed the front door behind her. She dropped her purse on the console table and ran to the kitchen for the call, with Beef trotting after her, wagging his tail. "Hello?" she said, picking up.

"Hi, how are you?" It was Sam, still sounding cool, so Jill dialed down her expectations, like putting on jeans you knew wouldn't fit.

"Fine, thanks. You?" Jill flicked on the kitchen light and stretched the cord to take a seat at the island. She hit the mouse on her laptop, and the screen came to life, displaying her email inbox. She scanned the new messages to see if Rahul's bloodwork had come in, but it hadn't. The lab must've lost it somehow.

"Good. Busy. Met with Lee, then have to prepare for tomorrow. I'm glad they found Abby. I cared, even though it sounded as if I didn't."

"I know." Jill softened at the sentiment.

"Are you safe?"

"Yes."

"Good. I'm sorry, too, about everything," Sam said after a moment, but he wasn't as convincing as she had been.

"Thanks." Jill petted Beef, who put his head on her lap.

"I have to say, the past few days have been an eye-opener, in some ways." Sam sounded sad and, finally, like himself.

"In what ways?"

"In just how much Abby meant to you, and where Steven and I fit in with that."

"I see," Jill said, surprised at the chill in her own tone. She didn't want to have to choose anymore. She was sick of failing tests she didn't want to take.

"Will you do it again?" Sam asked, calmly. "When Abby comes back from L.A., do we all have to jump around? The entire house in an uproar, as we're led around by a child?"

She's not a child, Jill thought but didn't say, because he was right, in part. Abby did act like a child. "I can't say I have it all figured out. I can't plan everything that far ahead. But I know I don't want you to tell me that I can't love her, either."

Sam fell silent, on the other end of the line. "You can love her all you want, but what you do for her impacts me."

"Then we'll have to work it out as we go along."

"I'll have to think about that, for a bit. I don't know if that's feasible. I can't speak to that now, and I would like not to."

"Okay, thanks." Jill felt resentment calcifying in her chest.

"So you're finished then? Back to business, no more looking for your ex's murderer?"

"Not exactly." Jill petted Beef's soft head, watching the Microsoft flag flap across her laptop screen. She knew the answer Sam wanted to hear, but she couldn't give it to him. She knew what she had to do, and she needed the freedom to do it.

"What then? What's going on?"

"If I tell you, it'll sound worse."

"What is it?"

"William was seeing someone. She's married, and I'm going to meet her."

"Why?" Sam asked, his tone astonished.

"To find out if she knows anything about his murder."

"Why on earth would his girlfriend agree to meet with his ex-wife?"

Jill usually admired the way Sam asked questions, each one leading to the next, as if challenging and testing a scientific theory. But this time, with each answer, she felt as if she were hammering another nail into her own coffin, sealing the lid over her face. "She doesn't know I'm his ex-wife."

"You didn't tell her?"

"No."

"Then how did you get her to meet with you?"

Jill didn't know what good it would do to explain. "Honestly, you don't want to know."

"You're right, I don't." Sam sighed. "Are the police involved, at all?"

"No, but I did tell them everything I know."

"So why aren't they involved with this meeting?"

"They don't think William was murdered."

"But you do."

"That's what I'm trying to figure out. And what he was up to, and who he was, and who I was, too." Jill noticed that Beef had fallen asleep sitting up, his head still in her lap. The sight made her smile, even as tense as she felt, which was the special gift of a pet. Love, devotion, and no difficult phone calls.

I'm not alone, I have Pickles.

Jill remembered, all of a sudden. It was Abby talking, in their phone conversation after that first night. Abby had a cat, Pickles, but she hadn't mentioned him to Victoria, on the phone call at the police station tonight.

"Jill, are you there or did we get cut off?"

"Sorry, I was just thinking. Abby didn't ask Victoria or me to take care of her cat until she came back from L.A. Doesn't that seem strange to you?"

"Stop, please." Sam's voice went cold. "I can't talk about that girl or your ex-husband anymore. We're back where we started, but worse. I have to go."

"No, wait, Sam—"

"We'll talk later. Good-bye."

Jill hung up after a moment, wondering. She and Sam had been so happy, less than a week ago. She would never have believed they'd come apart so quickly, snapped apart like a suspension cable on a bridge, undone by winds unseen, pressures uncalculated, and stresses neither measured nor accounted for.

You didn't see it coming.

Jill didn't want Sam to leave her life the way William had, but she didn't know how to stop him. She hadn't known Abby would come back, William would die, or Victoria would both love and hate her. She didn't know that the past would come back to the present and obliterate the future. She'd thought she'd moved on, stepping over the human debris, but it turned out that her life was a morgue, and all the time she'd been surrounded by bodies, hidden away, to be dealt with later.

Some not even dead, but still very much alive.

Chapter Forty-six

Jill bustled past the eye chart toward the lab, on the run. She still hadn't received Rahul's bloodwork and knew that something had gone wrong. She felt exhausted after a sleepless night, plus she'd had to be at the phone store early to buy a new BlackBerry and had stood in line forever. She'd listened to Abby's message on the way in, but it hadn't mentioned her cat.

Jill opened the door to the small lab, where their phlebotomist, Selena Grant, looked up from a full tray of blood samples, each standing like a soldier in its wire separator, with its rubber stopper labeled in her characteristically neat print. "Hi, Selena, did we get results for Rahul Choudhury? They should've been in yesterday, but I got no email."

"Choudhury?" Selena blinked, her dark eyes worried under a stiff curl of black bangs. She was small and slim, dwarfed in boxy scrubs covered with kitten faces, because she was a cat fancier. "I don't remember that name."

"He's a baby, a one-year-old? I ordered a CBC with differential. Mom is waiting for me in Exam Room B. He was in on Saturday."

"Oh no. I remember the baby, now." Selena's face fell into long, gaunt lines, and she looked much older than her forty years. "I messed up on Saturday. I forgot to send it in. I realized it late

Monday, and I was going to tell you, then I forgot that, too. I'm so sorry, Jill."

"That's not like you," Jill said, surprised. "You're our rock."

"I know, but my mother, they moved her to hospice." Selena's eyes filmed. "They called me Saturday, and I left work, upset. I forgot everything." Her hand went to her cheek, pressed flat against it. "I'm at such a loss, I can't keep track of anything. They say she has only a week or so."

"I'm so sorry." Jill felt terrible for her and touched her shoulder. She had known that Selena's mother had stomach cancer, but not that she'd declined so quickly. "Is there anything I can do?"

"Pray."

"I will, but you don't have to be here. Go and be with her. Take the time off."

"I can't." Selena sighed, shaking her head. "I'm out of vacation days and all my other leave. I used it up, on her. Sheryl says I have to stay until Monday, when Linda comes back."

Jill knew that could be too late. She remembered the last week she'd spent with her own mother. It had been hell, and she still wouldn't have traded it for anything. "No, you don't have to wait until then. Go, now. You're finished for the week."

"For real?" Selena looked up, hopeful.

"Yes, go." Jill turned to the cabinet, found a cube of Post-its and a pen, and on the top paper, wrote LAB CLOSED. "I'll deal with Sheryl when she gets back from lunch."

"Thanks so much, Jill. But what about your patient?" Selena grabbed her bag, and Jill picked up a phlebotomy kit.

"I'll take his blood. I've kept up my qualifications. We can all collect our own samples or send patients to LabCorp for a week."

"The docs will take their own blood?" Selena's penciled eyebrows flew upward.

"Yes, we're smarter than we look. Come on, let's go." Jill followed Selena out of the lab, stuck the Post-it on the door, and took off down the hall with the kit.

"Thanks again, Jill. So much." Selena waved good-bye, and Jill opened the door to Exam Room B, went inside, and set the phlebotomy kit on the counter. She faced Padma and Rahul, who sat on the examining table in his diaper, playing with a set of Acura keys.

"Padma, I'm sorry, but we lost Rahul's blood sample." Jill hated watching Padma's face fall, and there was new tightness around her lips. "That's why we didn't get his results yet. I'm so sorry. I'll take another sample myself, after I examine him."

"Oh no." Padma ran a hand through her glossy hair, stopping at the ponytail. She looked more stressed than usual, and her sweater was unusually wrinkled, for her. "I hate to do that to him again. He cried so much."

"I know, and I'm very, very sorry." Jill slid her stethoscope from around her neck and went over to Rahul. He'd been weighed by the nurse, and he'd lost another half a pound. Jill thought his *gestalt* wasn't any better, even after three days on amoxicillin. "How is your mother? Any better?"

"Yes, thanks. My brother thinks taking a blood test is overkill for an ear infection."

"I know, but I think it's important. Hey, Rahul, what do you say there?" Jill tickled his bare tummy, which felt warm to the touch, and he didn't smile as much as before, though another tooth nugget was popping through his pale pink gums. "Two teeth now? Good for you, big boy!"

"Gsmssm," Rahul said, producing bubbles, so at least he wasn't dehydrated.

"Let's get a listen." Jill warmed the stethoscope on her palm and placed it against the baby's tiny chest, then put it in her ears and listened to the stepped-up pace of his heart, then the noises of the infection in his chest. His temperature was 101, and he'd had it for too long.

"My nephew, he gets them all the time, that's why they had tubes put in." Padma tucked a glossy strand of hair into her ponytail. "You're positive that this is necessary, to take blood from him, twice now?"

"I'm sorry, but I do." Jill looped the stethoscope around her neck, then felt his glands at his throat, which were still swollen.

She looked into his ears, nose, and throat, and it was still purulent. Most pediatricians would say that Rahul was failing the amoxicillin, but Jill hated that jargon. The medicine was failing the baby, not the other way around. "He's as sick as he was Saturday. I'd like to switch him to another antibiotic and see if that helps."

"Whatever you think."

"We'll put him on Augmentin then." Jill lay him down and palpated his belly, spleen, and liver, then sat him up and felt the glands under his armpits, all of which were swollen.

"My sister-in-law was over to dinner last night, and she said we should just get the tubes, too."

"Let's discuss it after we get the results, okay? I'll order them stat, so we'll know tomorrow." Jill checked his skin, and his patch of eczema was the same, no worse. "Is he drinking and eating?"

"Yes, but not so much."

"Sleeping?" Jill checked inside his diaper, which was dry, so she sat him up, and Padma took over, steadying him.

"Same as before."

"Let me write that script." Jill went back to the laptop, logged into Epic with her password, and found Rahul's file, then printed out a script for Augmentin and handed it to Padma, who slid it into her back pocket. "Okay, I'll need to take some blood. This time, I swear it won't go missing." She went to the kit and prepared a syringe. "Would you hold him or would you prefer that I get a nurse?"

"No, I'll hold him." Padma picked up the gurgling Rahul, cuddling him protectively, and he shook the keys. "He cried so hard, last time. I hate to do it all over again, for no reason."

"I understand, but we're doing it for a reason. It's good to be thorough." Jill knew that Padma was trying to do what was right for her child. "I'm trying to get to the cause of these infections."

"They all get ear infections, some more than others, isn't that so?"

"Yes, but it's the frequency of his that concerns me, and don't forget that he had pneumonia."

"My nephew got *eight* ear infections his first year. He was on amoxicillin all the time. They called it his bubble-gum drink."

"Your nephew isn't Rahul. We know that it's an ear infection, but it's always important to ask, what's behind this? We can't stop at the short answer."

Padma shook her head, holding the baby. "I just hate to do this to him again."

"Isn't it better to be on the safe side? We don't want to call off the search just because we have an answer, if it's not the right answer." Jill met Padma's dark eyes and could see that she was getting through to her. "We call that diagnosis momentum, which is a fancy way of saying that once you arrive at a possibility for a diagnosis, it sticks, when it shouldn't. Okay?"

"Okay," Padma answered, satisfied. "I know my family influences me, a little."

"That's okay, that's what family's for. Hold Rahul, and I'll make this fast." Jill wiped antiseptic on Rahul's arm, tied a tourniquet, attached a butterfly needle to the syringe for use with babies, and inserted it into a vein.

"WAAAAHHH!"

"I'm so sorry, Rahul." Jill pulled back the plunger, collected the blood, then loosened the tourniquet, extracted the needle, and put a cotton gauze on the wound. "Good boy!"

"It's all right, honey." Padma held Rahul close as he cried.

"Padma, well done, and thank you for assisting." Jill stuck a stopper on the test tube, labeled the sample, and set it down, then took a piece of adhesive tape and put it over the gauze on his arm. "I'll see you back here tomorrow, and I'll have his results. When can you come in?"

"The morning is best, while his brothers are at school." Padma wiped Rahul's tear-stained cheeks, and his little chest heaved a baby sob.

"Poor little guy." Jill touched his cheek, wet with tears. "Okay, see you at nine. I'll tell Donna you have an appointment. Thanks so much."

"Thank you." Padma smiled.

"See you tomorrow." Jill left the room and went down the hall to the appointment desk, where Donna was just hanging up the phone, pushing back a puff of dark hair. "Donna, can you please put Rahul Choudhury in at nine tomorrow? I'll come in specially to see him."

"You mean the cutest baby ever?" Donna hit a few keys on the computer. "Of course."

"Thanks, that's my girl." Jill smiled, and Sheryl came striding over from the office. The staff must have seen that Selena had left, because they were all sneaking glances from their computers, files, and phones, waiting to see what would happen between Jill and Sheryl.

"Jill, did you really close the lab?" Sheryl asked, her voice low, so that the full waiting room couldn't hear.

"Yes." Jill matched her soft tone. She didn't want to make a scene, and she'd never get along with Sheryl if she embarrassed her. "Selena's mother is very ill, and they should be together. I know you must feel the same way."

"I do, but we have a business to run."

"I'm not trying to interfere with that. I can take blood, and so can any doc who's kept up his qualifications. Let us do some work for a change, eh?" Jill smiled, and so did the staff.

"I'll take this up with John." Sheryl edged backward, frowning. Donna studied her desk, hiding her smile, and so did everybody else.

"Great, thanks." Jill turned on her heel, went back down the hall, slid the file of the next patient from the holder, and went into Exam Room A. It took only two colds, another ear infection, and a broken toe for John Gilbert, the senior partner, to find her between patients. He was a preppy internist in his fifties, in horn-rimmed glasses, a red-and-blue rep tie, and a pressed lab coat with his name embroidered on the breast pocket. He took her aside in front of his office.

"Jill, can I see you inside, a sec? This'll be quick." John opened his door, and Jill followed him into his office. "Jill, what happened with Selena?"

"Her mom's in hospice, and I sent her home. We're doctors, and if we don't have compassion for suffering, then who does?"

"This isn't about compassion." John frowned. "Sheryl handles personnel matters, not the docs."

"I know, but Selena is so distracted that she lost a sample for one of my patients. Do you want to make Sheryl happy or do you want to get sued?"

"Good point, but I'm not about to take blood myself. I haven't taken blood in nine years, I don't have time. None of us do, you know that."

"Then send your patients to LabCorp. It's not far."

"They're not accustomed to that inconvenience."

"It's the suburbs, John, nothing's *that* inconvenient. They probably have drive-through blood." Jill thought of Rahul. "Listen, please, help me get my new bloodwork stat, would you? You have privileges at Phoenixville, don't you?"

"It's not that easy."

"It has to be. I'm worried about this patient, and with babies, you don't get the margins that you do with adults. They go downhill fast."

"Enough, okay." John put up a hand. "Tell Donna to call Charlotte. She'll make it happen."

"Thanks. Gotta go." Jill hurried out to the door, with no time to reflect on whether she'd pissed off her boss. She had a slew of patients, and she had to be out of work on time tonight.

To go see about a corgi puppy.

Chapter Forty-Seven

Jill stopped on the main drag of Hoboken, where low-rise apartment buildings and older brick townhouses stood with storefront bodegas, gourmet coffee shops, Greek restaurants, and hip boutiques. A constant stream of people filled the sidewalks, heading home from work or bubbling up from the PATH station, like a people geyser.

"You have reached your destination," said her GPS.

Jill spotted a parking space, slid into it, and cut the ignition. She'd never pretended to be anybody else before, and she wondered how William had done it, maintaining two identities at once. She retrieved the Phillies cap and popped it on. Oddly, it helped her play her part, like a costume for a role. Jill got out of the car and spotted Nina D'Orive across the street. She was a pretty, petite blonde in pink sweats and she was standing with her husband, in running clothes. A fawn-colored corgi puppy was tugging on his sneaker laces.

"Hello, Nina!" Jill waved, thinking of a way to get Nina alone. She crossed the street and extended a hand. "I'm Katie Feehan, from Facebook."

"Hiya!" Nina shook her hand, flashing a pretty smile. "This is Martin, my husband."

"Thanks for meeting me." Jill shook his hand. "I know I said I'd bring the boys, but I had second thoughts. I want to decide about the dog on my own, then make it a surprise."

"Oh, too bad." Nina glanced at her husband. "Martin wanted to meet them. He's all about kids."

Martin grinned. "I want my own baseball team. Go Mets!"

"Go Yanks!" Nina said.

"Go Phils!" Jill chimed in, and they all laughed.

Nina said, "Sorry we have to meet here, on the street. Martin didn't think we should meet you at home, since we don't really know each other."

"I get that, and you have to be careful." Jill bent down to pet the puppy, an adorable round-eyed little dog, with ears as floppy as a baby bunny. "She's so cute! I love that face."

"Isn't she something? Corgis are actually dwarf dogs, bred to herd sheep. Let's go for a walk before it rains." Nina and Martin started walking, and Jill fell into step with them.

"So, Nina, tell me a little about yourself. I saw on your Facebook page that you work at Pharmcen."

"Yes. I'm in Pharmacovigilance."

"Is that even English?" Jill knew what it meant, but she wanted to get Nina talking.

"I know, I get that a lot." Nina smiled. "Pharmacovigilance keeps track of adverse events of drugs, for reporting to the FDA. There's almost fifty people in the department, and I just became second-in-command. I'm a VP now."

Martin snorted. "They gave her a title, but no raise."

Jill let it go. "Congratulations, Nina. A promotion counts for a lot, in this economy."

Nina beamed. "I think so, too. If they have to lay people off again, I won't be one of them, I hope."

Martin checked his watch. "What do you need to know about the dog?"

"Right, of course." Jill didn't want to arouse suspicion. "Was she hard to housebreak?"

"She's almost housebroken," Nina answered, warming to the

topic. "I crate her, but she hates it. Sometimes she cries in her crate at night, which breaks my heart, so I take her out, love her up, and put her back in. Martin doesn't want her sleeping with us."

Martin rolled his eyes. "I'm the bad guy."

Jill held her tongue. She could see the fissures in their marriage easily, though she had missed so many in her own.

"I keep the feedings and walks regular, and I crate her when I'm not playing with her. I walk on a schedule, three times a day. She even pees in the same places."

Jill smiled. "You've got this down to a science."

Martin laughed. "That's Nina to a T. She's the one who wanted the dog, not me, but I went with it. Only problem, it sheds like crazy."

Nina elbowed him. "Don't tell her that."

Jill saw her opening. "Martin, what other bad stuff can you tell me? I want the truth."

"You got it!" Martin turned to her. "She bites your heels when you walk."

"She *bites*?" Jill feigned worry, and Nina gave him a playful shove.

"Honey, go for your run, get! You're giving her the wrong idea."

"Does she really bite?" Jill asked, with ersatz concern. "I don't want a dog that bites."

"She doesn't bite." Nina turned to Martin, nudging him again. "You, get going!"

"Okay, okay." Martin shook Jill's hand. "I only do one lap, or I have a heart attack. Nice meeting you."

"Nice meeting you, too. Thanks for the tips."

"Take care." Martin gave Nina a kiss on the cheek, then took off, jogging, and Jill waited until he was out of earshot.

"Nina, I really came to ask you about someone we both know. Neil Straub."

"What? Who?" Nina blinked, and recognition flickered through her lovely blue eyes. "I don't know any Neil Straub."

"I know you do. I'm his ex-wife and I knew him as William Skyler."

"I don't know what you mean." Nina glanced down the sidewalk, where Martin was lost in the crowd.

"Yes, you do. I saw your Visa receipt in his car, from Sephora. Please talk to me before Martin gets back."

"No, really, I don't know any Neil Straub."

"I'm sorry, but I have bad news for you. Neil died last Tuesday in Philadelphia, and I think he was murdered."

Nina gasped. "What? How? That can't be true."

"So you do know Neil Straub."

"Wait, no, yes." Tears sprang to Nina's eyes, and her tone turned pleading. "Please don't tell my husband. He can't suspect a thing. He gets so jealous."

"I won't. The coroner says Neil died as a reaction to a mix of prescription painkillers, anti-anxiety drugs, and alcohol. But I don't think so."

"Drugs, Neil?" Nina asked, bewildered. "He never took anything like that."

"Do you know anybody who would want to kill him, and why?"

"Is this really true? He's really . . . gone?" Nina's eyes brimmed with tears, but she wiped them away, and Jill's heart went out to her.

"Yes. I'm so sorry."

"I haven't heard from him in about a week." Nina sniffled, trying to stay in control. "I called and called, but he didn't return my calls. I was so hurt, so angry. Oh my God, I thought he was ditching me, but all this time, he was . . ."

"I'm sorry." Jill wanted to be sympathetic, but she didn't have much time until Martin came back. "He hasn't been back to the apartment, but they don't know he's gone, either. They don't know him as William Skyler. They know him the way you do, as Neil Straub."

"He *is* Neil Straub."

"You didn't know he had a double identity?"

"No, of course not." Nina flushed.

"Do you know why he did?"

"No."

"What did he tell you he does for a living?"

"He's a real-estate investor." Nina wiped her eyes with a shaky hand.

"How do you know that?"

"He showed me buildings he owns, in the city."

"He lied."

"No, this can't be. I *love* him." Nina's voice broke, and Jill knew exactly how she felt.

"I know, I'm so sorry. I loved him, too, but he used me. I don't mean this to sound hurtful, but I suspect he might have been using you, too. Can you think why? Did you give him money—"

"He wasn't using me, he *loved* me." Nina's eyes spilled over with tears, and she wiped them away again as a young couple passed.

"How long have you been seeing him?"

"Why should I tell you?"

"If you loved him, it can help find his killer."

"What do the police say?"

Jill didn't have time to go through everything. "Please, just tell me. It could help, and your husband will be back soon."

Nina paused, weepy. "Four years."

Jill reddened. Another thing she hadn't seen coming. She'd only been divorced for three years. So cheating was proven. She masked her shock. "Where did you meet him?"

"At a Starbucks." Nina frowned, recovering. "Wait a minute. Were those little boys on your Facebook page his sons, with you?"

"No, we had no children together. Did you give or lend him money?"

"No. He had plenty of money."

"Did you introduce him to anyone important?"

"No, of course I didn't. We kept everything on the down-low. It was just the two of us, always."

"Did you help him contact people at Pharmcen, like higher-ups? Give him names of people he could call, to sell them something or take something from them? He used to be a drug rep."

"Neil wasn't a drug rep." Nina shook her head, recovering her composure. "He doesn't know anything about the drug business."

"He told you that?" Jill was trying to piece the puzzle together.

"Yes, he told me that, and he used to listen when I talked about my job. He cared about me. He *understood* me."

Jill guessed that cheating wives felt as misunderstood as cheating husbands, and maybe they were. "What else did he tell you about himself?"

"None of this makes sense." Nina forced a smile for a woman pushing a stroller across the street. "Wait, stop. That was my next-door neighbor. We can't talk here."

"Look at this." Jill dug in her purse, pulled out the photo of William with the man in the blue polo shirt, and pointed at William, just to double-check. "This is the man you know as Neil, right?"

"Yes, that's Neil." Nina's eyes filled anew. "Oh my God, it's so hard to see him, now. I can't believe this. I don't believe it."

"Who's this other guy, do you know?" Jill pointed at the mystery man.

"I think that's Joe Z."

"Joe who?"

"Neil's friend, Joe Zeptien."

"Did you know him?"

"Not really. Neil talked to him on the phone all the time, and I met him once." Nina wiped tears from her cheeks, getting her bearings. "I was leaving the apartment one night, but I forgot my earrings, so I went back, and he was going in. Neil introduced him to me."

"So who is Joe Zeptien and what did he do? Did he have any reason to want to hurt William? I mean, Neil?" Jill slipped the photo back into her purse. "I'm wondering if Joe Zeptien is the man who killed him."

"No, never." Nina shook her head, tears returning to her eyes. "They were tight."

"How do you know?"

"Neil told me, and like I say, they talked all the time."

"How do you know he was talking to Joe Zeptien? You only know what he told you. It could have been anyone."

"No, I knew it was him. I answered Neil's cell once, by accident, when we were together. We both have BlackBerrys and we kept them by the bed, because I had to answer in case Martin called, and Neil always had to answer his email. I picked his BlackBerry up when he was in the bathroom, and it was Joe calling."

"What did they talk about, usually?"

"Hold on, here comes my husband." Nina looked left, stricken, and Martin was running down the block, breathing hard. She wiped her eyes, cleared her throat, and backed away. "End of discussion. I have to go. You have to go. We can't talk here—"

"What did they talk about?"

"I don't know. He always took the calls out of the room, so Joe wouldn't hear that he was with me. Neil was careful that no one find out about us, to protect my marriage."

Jill figured that William must've been protecting himself, so Nina couldn't hear his calls, not the other way around. "Where does Joe live?"

"I don't know. In the city, I think."

"New York? What did he do for a living?"

"I don't know that, either." Nina panicked as Martin got closer. "Stop. We're done. I want to know more, but we can't talk here. Did you get the police involved? Do they know my name? Are they going to contact me?"

"I can explain it all, but you have to meet me. Tell me where and when, tomorrow."

"I can't. I have work."

"I'll meet you there. How about noon, for lunch?"

"No, the only time I'm free is in the morning. I'll message you a place to meet me, on Facebook." Nina tensed as Martin got closer, panting and puffing, his T-shirt dark with perspiration. "Go now. I'll tell Martin I cried because I twisted my ankle."

"Wait, what time in the morning should I meet you?"

"Ten o'clock. I'll say I have a doctor's appointment."

You do, Jill thought, but didn't say.

It was until she was back in the car that she remembered: *Rahul.*

Chapter Forty-eight

A thunderstorm broke on the way home, the rain pounding on the roof of the car, and Jill struggled to hear on the cell phone. "Padma, are you there?"

"Yes, hello?"

"I'm so sorry, but I have to cancel our appointment tomorrow morning." Jill cringed. She hated doctors who canceled, and now she was one. "I'm so sorry. Can you meet me later in the day? How about noon tomorrow?"

"I can do that."

"Good, let's make it then. I'll have the bloodwork. How is Rahul?" Jill switched lanes, keeping an eye on the rearview. Behind her was a FedEx truck, and the traffic was heavy, moving fast despite the fact that visibility was poor, the sky prematurely dark, and everything grayed out with rain.

"About the same. He's sleeping now."

"Fever?"

"Yes, but low."

"Eating and drinking?"

"Still not so great."

Jill made a mental note. "Okay, hang in. See you at noon. Again, my apologies."

"Good-bye," Padma said, hanging up.

Jill fed the car gas and checked the rearview, but the truck be-hind her had moved, showing a gray sedan. She pressed END, then M, to call and check on Megan, who would be home from prac-tice by now, probably foraging in the refrigerator. Jill kept her eye on the road while the call connected, then said, "Hi, honey!"

"Hey, Mom, I was just about to call you."

"What's up?"

"I'm not home, I'm at Courtney's. We have to do our scene to-morrow, and we're almost ready, but I need to stay over one more night."

Jill groaned. "No. Megan, it's too much. It's an imposition on Carol."

"I knew you'd say that, and she's right here. She wants to talk to you."

"Good, put her on." Jill heard a shuffling on the other end of the line. "Carol, that you? Don't you need a break?"

"No, not at all." Carol sounded bright and cheery. "How have you been?"

"Fine, busy, and thanks for letting my daughter take up resi-dence."

"Not at all. She's a dream, you know that. Let her stay here to-night. They're working so hard, you'd be proud of them, making costumes and all."

Jill felt so guilty. "But you're even doing the driving."

"You've done your share, plenty of times before. Don't worry about a thing, I swear. I'll be out of town next week, and you can be the chauffeur then."

"Okay, thanks." Jill felt grateful. "You're a saint."

"Aren't we all? Take care, and here's Megan. See you." There was a pause, and Megan came back on the line. "Okay, Mom?"

"Okay, honey. Don't forget to thank her for everything, and get some sleep tonight, okay?"

"I will. Love you."

"Love you and miss you, too. Bye-bye." Jill pressed END and set the phone aside, spotting the gray sedan, still behind her. Its driver was a shadow of a man, and the sedan stayed to her left, on her bumper.

She accelerated, and a minute later, so did he. She didn't like to drive fast when it was raining, so she decelerated. So did he. She switched to the slow lane and let her speed decrease to fifty miles an hour. So did he, which set her heart thudding. She hit the gas and picked up her phone, in case she had to call 911.

Suddenly a sign came up for the service area, and the gray sedan split off, taking the ramp leaving the highway. Still, Jill didn't let off the gas, her hand holding the phone, and she sped all the way home in the storm.

Chapter Forty-nine

It was dark by the time Jill got home, and she let Beef out in the backyard and lingered at the door. She scanned the privacy fence for anything suspicious, but there was nothing, and Beef was acting normal, burying his muzzle in the wet grass. Mist wreathed the air, which smelled musty and thick, and steam curled from the pool. It had stormed here, too, leaving the night sky oddly bright in patches, with particles of light hidden in the dark clouds, like vermiculate in potting soil.

Jill stood in the doorway, and her silhouette stretched across the lawn, a human taffy pulled out of shape, taut enough to be dangerously brittle. Sam hadn't called her, and she thought about calling him, but she still couldn't tell him what he wanted to hear. Her head was swimming since her meeting with Nina. Beef trotted out of the gloom, his movement fluid as a daisy-cutter, even at his age. Jill opened her hand at her side, and he slipped his head under her palm, which was their secret routine. His skull felt furry and damp, and she scratched behind his ears, where there was a knot.

Suddenly her phone started to ring, and she reached for her pocket and slid out her new BlackBerry. The screen showed KATIE FEEHAN, and Jill picked up. "Hi, girl."

"What happened with Nina?" Katie asked, nervous. "Are you okay? Why didn't you call?"

"I had to talk to a patient, and the rain was bad all the way home, so I stayed off the phone." Jill was about to start the story about Nina when the boys started yelling on the other end of the line, at Katie's house. "What's going on over there?"

"Fight Club at the Feehans'. The two little ones are overtired, and they both want to be on the computer at the same time. It's not pretty."

"Uh-oh." Jill remembered when her house was full of girls, fighting over eye makeup and borrowed sweaters. She never thought she'd miss those days, but she did.

"God, these kids," Katie moaned, exasperated. The background noise surged, and the boys yelled louder. "I'm trying to let them work it out themselves. How long does sibling rivalry last? Oh, right."

Jill smiled. "Katie, if it's a bad time, I can call back."

"No, I'm dying to hear, and I got a Facebook message from Nina, saying to meet her at the Starbucks on 60 Weehawk Avenue at ten o'clock tomorrow. I'll email it to you, so you have the address. Hold on, Jill. Boys, take turns!" Katie covered the receiver, muffling her voice. "Jamie, let him use it, then you can get back on. Log out. Log out right now, okay, honey?"

"You have your hands full."

"Tell me about it. They use the same computer, so one has to log out before the other gets on, but Tommy isn't being patient. Hold on a minute." Katie covered the receiver again. "Tommy, give him a second. You know he's not that good with the mouse yet."

Jill imagined the two tow-headed Feehan boys, pushing each other out of the way, in front of the kitchen computer. She knew the log-in, log-out system because they used it at work, for the Epic program. The docs and nurses shared the computers in the examining rooms, and each had his own user account, with a separate password. Jill's was Megan0112, because January 12 was Megan's birthday.

"Hold on, Jill. Tommy, he's logging out, right now. Tommy, he's littler than you are!"

Jill's mind raced ahead. She didn't know why she hadn't thought of it, earlier. She had searched William's laptop before, and it had been clean, suspiciously so. Back then, she'd thought he had only one identity, but now she knew he had another identity. She wondered if there was also a user account for Neil Straub, set up in the same laptop.

"Okay, Jill, I'm back. Whew! I'd buy each kid a computer, but a week later, they'll be obsolete. I mean the computers, not the kids."

"Let me ask you something." Jill felt newly energized. "Do you have different user accounts in that computer, one for each boy?"

"Yes, three for the kids, plus Mike and I each have an account. So we have five user accounts."

"In the same computer?"

"Yes. Mike also has his own laptop for work, but I use the kitchen computer all the time, like for Facebook. You saw. It was logged in for my account, and it has all my settings."

Jill didn't care about the settings. "When the computer reboots, does it show all the user names? And then you choose yours and log in as yourself?"

"Yes, sure."

"Ours don't do that, at work. The screen is blank, and we log in with a password."

"It depends on the software, I'm sure. The interface. They all work the same way, it's just a question of what you're shown on the screen at start-up."

"I see, so it's just programmed differently." Jill had rebooted William's laptop when she got it home from Abby's, but hadn't seen any choices of user accounts. "Katie, who set up those user accounts for you?"

"I did."

"You?"

"Sure, it's easy. I'm the administrator. Who better?"

Jill smiled, with admiration. Never underestimate the power of a mother. "Let me ask you this. Could you hide those user accounts, do you think?"

"You mean so they wouldn't show up on the start-up screen? Sure, if I wanted to. I could probably set it to show only a few of the names, or just the boys."

"And if you can hide them, can you find them?"

"Sure. Why?"

"I'm thinking of William's laptop. If he had a secret identity in life, couldn't he also have one on his laptop?"

"He could," Katie answered, catching on. "If he has a secret user account as Neil Straub, I can tell you how to find it on his laptop."

"Really?"

Katie snorted. "Did you forget, I'm the Queen of Farmville?"

Half an hour later, Beef curled up on his bed, and Jill was sitting down at the kitchen island in front of William's laptop, next to a cup of hot coffee and a print out of Katie's instructions. She got busy, and after one more phone call to the Queen of Farmville, Jill was ready to reboot the laptop and see if William had a second user account, for Neil Straub.

She turned off the computer, hit RESTART, and waited, and the screen came to life, first with the Microsoft logo, then a dizzying array of spinning numbers, like a slot machine. They finally stopped, the screensaver went black, and the screen read, PASSWORD.

Jill felt a frisson of excitement, as well as fear. She remembered that all of William's passwords were a combination of exotic cars and his birthday, because he always said he wanted an exotic for his birthday. His go-to shopping password was P9110701, for a Porsche 911 and his July 1 birthday, so she plugged that in. The message came up, PASSWORD INVALID. Jill knew he used JAG-XKE0701 for their joint bank account, so she plugged that in, but the message came up, PASSWORD INVALID, again. Next she tried MB6000701, for the top-of-the-line Mercedes-Benz he coveted, but it came up PASSWORD INVALID, too.

Then she remembered the exotic that he always called his holy grail, and what he'd always said about the car: *I want to be buried in an Aston Martin DB9.*

Jill typed in AMDB90701 and hit ENTER. Instantly, the screen changed to the default screensaver, an idyllic sky and grassy hill, Microsoft heaven. Her heart beat faster as she moved the mouse, clicked, and read the screen:

WELCOME, NEIL!

Chapter Fifty

Jill clicked on the list of William's Microsoft Word files, and the first two were RESEARCH and NOTES, created the same date, September 9, three years ago. She clicked RESEARCH and almost fell off her chair. The file contained hundreds of files, each with a drug name, in alphabetical order: Abata, Akasin, Aormil, Aritil, Aresta, Aromytec, all the way to Zertax. She recognized many of the drugs, and they all treated different maladies: headaches, hypertension, gout, bipolar depression, skin cancer, psoriasis, nausea, aplastic anemia. There was no logical link between them that she could see.

She clicked on the first file, for Abata, which she knew treated asthma in children. The subfile was a PDF of the drug circular, with prescribing information for physicians and a description: "Abata is a hydrochloride salt of quinapril, the ethyl ester of a non-sulfhydryl . . ." She looked through the rest of the Abata file. One subfile was labeled PRESS, and she clicked on it, revealing a list of newspapers and blogs, next to dates and links. She clicked on the first link and it opened to an article in *The Oregonian*, dated June 3, some eight years ago:

Moise Yakowicz, 6, of Portland, almost died today at the Young Pioneers picnic, as a result of anaphylactic shock, which his parents claim was attributed to Abata. The drug, manufactured by Pharmcen . . .

Jill thought a minute. Abata was made by Pharmcen, where Nina worked. She didn't know if it was coincidence, but it didn't feel like one. She navigated out of the article and clicked the next, which was from the *Bucks County Courier Post,* in Pennsylvania:

Today was a tragic day for the family of Paulina Ma, 10, whose memorial service was held at Kaybock's Funeral Home, in the driving rain. Ma died last week, the result of anaphylactic shock that her mother claims was caused by Abata, a drug marketed by Pharmcen . . .

Jill went to the next drug file, Akasin, and it followed the same pattern: the prescribing information for physicians, then articles about the drug and its side effects, from sources all over the Internet. She clicked the next three, for Aormil, Aritil, and Aresta, and discovered a common thread. All five drugs were manufactured by Pharmcen.

She minimized the Word document, went to the web, and clicked BOOKMARKS. The list stretched the length of the screen, again, it was entirely drug names, starting with Abata. It looked as if William was making himself an expert in the adverse side effects of Pharmcen drugs, and she put that together with the fact that he was in a relationship with Nina, who worked in Pharmacovigilance at Pharmcen, a department that collected complaints about the adverse side effects of Pharmcen drugs.

Jill sensed she was getting close to the bottom of his scheme. Drug manufacturers had a legal duty to collect complaints about the adverse reactions of their drugs and report them to the FDA if the reactions were serious, life-threatening, or unexpected. The complaints could come from anybody, most came from doctors. Pembey Family probably over-reported because of Sheryl and her lawsuit phobia, and Jill's old pediatric group was more typical, in that they didn't report as often. They couldn't always be sure if the drug had caused the adverse reaction, and it took time to fill out the paperwork, even electronically.

Jill logged out of the Internet and back to START, looking for an email server. She spotted the email account and opened to the

Inbox, only to discover the oddest emails ever. The list of senders and recipients were all the same: Neil Straub, and the subject lines were all drug names. It was easy to see what was happening; William had been emailing himself about various drugs. Jill scanned the dates the emails were received, and the email stopped the day before William died, on Monday, and she opened it.

The subject line was Memoril, and she knew she'd heard about that drug somewhere, then she remembered. It had been in the waiting room at work, when she'd run into Elaine Fitzmartin and her mother, Mary.

We're fine, thanks. Much better now that Mom's on Memoril.

Jill figured that Memoril was an Alzheimer's drug, and she opened the email, which read in its entirety:

2, tot 4

Jill wasn't sure what it meant. She clicked the previous email, also with the subject line Memoril, and it read:

total 4 or 5, will check

Jill went to the earlier email, also with Memoril in the subject line:

1 more

Jill went to the previous email and the one before that, and they were all only numbers, as if William were counting. She went back further and found one that read:

One more. E worried

Jill didn't get the "E." It sounded like an initial, and she made a mental note, then closed the email and checked the times and dates that William had sent them to himself. Some were two days apart, some three. Then she realized something. Not one was sent on a weekend.

He always had to answer his email.

Jill put it together. The timing of the email must have corresponded to William's meetings with Nina. He must have been getting information from her about the number of complaints coming in on Memoril, then emailing the count to himself, so he kept track. He'd told Nina that he was answering his email, but really he'd been emailing himself.

Jill took a gulp of cold coffee and tried to understand why. If she assumed that William was counting Memoril complaints, she had to ask, how could that benefit him, or pay off? Then it hit her. Jill played a hunch, went back to the folders, and scanned the list. STOCK INFORMATION, read one folder, and she clicked. The file opened into another long list of folders labeled ANNUAL REPORTS, FINANCIALS, STOCK CHARTS, DIVIDENDS, SPLIT HISTORY, SEC FILINGS, CEO/CFO CERTIFICATIONS, ACQUISITIONS, and so on.

She clicked through one, then the next, confirming her suspicion. It was information about Pharmcen stock, only. Pharmcen was publicly traded, and if William knew which of their drugs had the most complaints, he could predict which, if any, would be recalled. Drugs got recalled, or safety letters issued, more often than the public realized, and it could easily affect the manufacturer's stock price, especially in today's volatile market. Even a minor recall, a Class III, would affect stock price, and a Class I recall could send stock prices plummeting.

Jill felt her heartbeat quicken. If William knew that a major drug was about to be recalled, he could make money by selling Pharmcen's stock short, betting against its value. It would explain how he could afford his homes, cars, and double life, and it was just what he had done with her, except on a bigger scale.

She navigated back on the Internet to confirm her theory, but William hadn't bookmarked any stock-trading sites like etrade .com, schwab.com, or tdameritrade.com. It shot her theory. She looked elsewhere in the computer, for some sort of trading files, but the omission was obvious. William had inside information but wasn't trading on it, which made no sense, especially for a man like him.

Jill felt stumped. She navigated out of PROGRAMS to the START menu, to see what other programs William had. The only one she hadn't seen yet was Excel, for financial spreadsheets. She clicked, and the program opened to a list of spreadsheets, dating from three years ago. She clicked on the first one, and it blossomed into a sheet that showed dollar amounts, in large chunks: $20,000 on June 6, $20,000 on June 22, and another $20,000 on June 29.

Jill's eyes opened wide. Somebody was paying William for something, and it had to be inside information about Pharmcen drugs, and which were potential recalls. He wasn't trading on the information himself, but he must have been selling it to someone who did, and Jill bet that man was Joe Zeptien.

She sat back, amazed. She had figured out his plan, and all of it was contained in his laptop, hidden in his secret identity, behind his stupid little password, AMDB90701. Then a thought struck her, like an epiphany. Her own passwords were about Megan and Megan's birthday, like Megan 0112, or Megan and her old nicknames, like Miggy0112, or Megan and Beef, MGBF0112. Jill's passwords were about what she loved the most, and that's why she'd remember them the easiest; they were what came first to her mind, at all times. Jill guessed that lots of mothers, and fathers, were the same way, and a password could speak volumes about a person, like a modern-day key to the soul.

Jill blinked, eyeing the screen. William's passwords were about himself and cars, not Abby, Victoria, or anyone else he loved, because deep in his soul, he didn't really love anyone. So it wasn't that he didn't love Jill, it was that he simply wasn't capable of love. It simply wasn't in the man. She had wanted to know what he was really up to, and the answer had been before her all along. It was right in front of her face now, on his laptop.

Money. He had wanted money, not for what it bought, but for what it said about him, as a man. It was as simple as that, because the wish itself was nothing, as substantial as an electronic transaction. Money was nothing but a construct ultimately, a collection of paper and ink, printed at will, no longer backed by anything, and signifying nothing. We all agree that money has value because we all agree that money has value, and William was the same way. Inside, he felt valueless. And so, he was.

And suddenly, as soon as Jill thought about him that way, she understood William a little better. She wasn't as angry at him, or as hurt. She just felt sorry for him, going through his life, so hollow, so empty, feeling absolutely worthless. Oddly, the fact that he was dead now was beside the point. He was dead to her, beginning right this minute. It had taken Jill a long time to heal, but she had done it, finally.

Physician, heal thyself.

Jill smiled at the revelation, then set up a plan. She'd work all night to get this information together, and she'd meet with Nina tomorrow to fill in the details, tell her what was going on, and answer her questions. Then Jill would turn it all over to the police, and they could decide whether to talk to Nina, find Joe Zeptien, or figure out if William had been murdered, why, and by whom. Something must have gone wrong with William's scheme, and the police would figure it out. Jill had figured out what she wanted to know.

The truth about William.

It was awful, but it had set her free.

Chapter Fifty-one

The next morning, Jill waited for Nina at the Starbucks, dressed in her sweater, jeans, and loafers uniform, feeling surprisingly fresh after an all-nighter spent going through William's laptop. Her theory about William's scheme had proved correct, and now she had the financial details. He'd had had two big paydays with Deferral and Riparin, equaling about $1 million over the last three years, and he'd also been paid another $500,000 for a stream of smaller insider tips. Memoril looked as if it was going to be his biggest score of all, and he'd already been paid $1.1 million for information about it. Jill had with her a manila folder that contained printed emails and spreadsheets, in case Nina needed convincing.

She checked her watch. It was 10:15 A.M. Nina was running a little late, although Pharmcen's sprawling complex in Parkertowne was just down the street, a series of brown brick buildings with a campus that boasted a man-made pond, a walking track, and an employee parking lot surrounded by manicured hedges. Jill had never been to central New Jersey before, but she could see the appeal, with lovely horse farms still managing to coexist with strip malls and corporate centers.

Jill checked her email for Rahul's bloodwork, but it wasn't in yet. She sipped her coffee, which was strong and hot, and looked around. The baristas worked quickly behind the counters, amid the squishy noises of espresso machines, and a long line of customers stood waiting to order, business people wearing laminated corporate IDs, young girls in black yoga pants, and moms with strollers, negotiating around kiosks with breakable logo mugs.

I met him at a Starbucks.

Jill wondered if this was the Starbucks where Nina had met William. It would make sense. He could have met Nina, started the affair, and after all that pillow talk, realized there was money to be made from the information and hatched his scheme. Or maybe he had even preyed on Nina, choosing to hang at a Starbucks near Pharmcen, hoping to meet a young girl who worked there, knowing he could charm her out of anything, including inside information.

The door of the Starbucks opened, and Jill looked up, expecting Nina, but it was two van drivers in Pharmcen blue uniforms, laughing and talking. She checked her watch—10:30. Maybe Nina had trouble getting out of work. The door opened again, and Jill looked up. Two young women, more Pharmcen employees, entered the Starbucks, but they were distraught, their eyes puffy and makeup streaky. Customers in line turned at the sight, and baristas craned their necks.

"I can't believe it," the one woman was saying, as they both sank into the first empty table. "It's so sudden. It's crazy."

The Pharmcen truck drivers walked over, and one asked, "What is it? Another round of cuts, in Corporate?"

"No," the woman answered, rubbing bloodshot eyes. "A girl we work with was killed. Her husband shot her, then committed suicide."

Jill felt thunderstruck, in shock. Her hand flew to her mouth.

"Jeez, that's awful," the driver said, taking off his blue cap. "Was she a friend of yours?"

"Yes, and she was really sweet. Nina was the best girl ever."

"No, no, it can't be," Jill blurted out, stunned. She stood up, but went weak in the knees, and the Pharmcen employees turned to her, astonished.

"Miss, you okay?" asked the truck driver, in confusion.

"No, sorry, this can't be." Jill tried to recover, walking over, stricken. "Was it Nina D'Orive who was killed?"

"Yes," the woman answered, teary. "Did you know her?"

"Yes, I know her, I knew her. What? How? When did this happen?"

"Late last night," the woman answered, her throat thick. "She didn't come in today, and she's always on time, so Elliott called her at home, and the cops told him."

"Elliott?"

"Elliott's our boss, in Pharmacovigilance. He just called us all into the break room and told us."

Jill thought of the E in the emails, fighting a wave of nausea. Her mind reeled. She prayed she hadn't been responsible for Nina's murder. That Nina hadn't been crying over William's death and Martin had caught her. Or maybe Nina had confessed to the affair, and he killed her for it. It couldn't be a coincidence, after last night.

Jill felt her gorge rising, panicked at the frowning faces and puzzled stares, then grabbed her purse and manila folder, bolted for the door, and ran out of the Starbucks, reaching the edge of the parking lot just in time.

She bent over and vomited.

Chapter Fifty-two

Jill hit the gas and steered out of the Starbucks parking lot onto Weehawk Boulevard. Traffic was light, which was good, because she was in no shape to drive. Tears filled her eyes, bile coated her teeth. She felt wretched and horrified, and wherever she looked, she kept seeing poor Nina, so happy to show off her cute little puppy.

Corgis are dwarf dogs, bred to herd sheep.

Jill stopped at the traffic light, across from the blue-flagged entrance to Pharmcen's campus, with its PHARMCEN sign and globe logo, in trademark blue. She thought of the laptop in her trunk, full of information about how Pharmcen's confidential information had been bought, and after what had happened to Nina, she felt the need to talk to someone at Pharmcen, find out whatever she could about Nina, tell them what was going on in their own company, and show them the laptop.

The traffic light turned green, and Jill took a left into the parking lot, followed the signs to the visitors' parking lot, and parked the car, cutting the ignition. She blew her nose, wiped her eyes, and grabbed her purse, then got out of the car, retrieved the laptop, and hurried to the glass entrance. She went inside and walked to the reception desk, a massive granite banquette with a panel of telephones and computer screens.

"May I help you?" The pretty young receptionist smiled, but Jill was too upset to smile back.

"My name's Jill Farrow and I'd like to see Elliott, the head of Pharmacovigilance. It's important."

"Do you have some kind of appointment with Mr. Horton?"

"I'm a friend of Nina D'Orive's. I need to see him, about her."

"My condolences on your loss. It's a terrible tragedy." The receptionist gestured at a seating area on the right, which held a group of well-dressed businessmen and -women. "Please, have a seat in the waiting area, and I'll call Mr. Horton."

"Thanks." Jill went over to the waiting area and sat down in a blue-patterned chair. She put the laptop and her purse on her lap, composing herself. The receptionist picked up the phone receiver, pressed in some numbers, and started talking in a low tone, then hung up, gesturing to Jill, who walked back to the desk with the laptop. "May I see him now?"

"I'm sorry, but Mr. Horton is unavailable at this time."

"Can I see someone in security, then?"

"What's this in reference to?" The receptionist glanced past Jill, to a black security desk on her right, at the back wall of the lobby.

"I'd rather not say. Can't I please speak with someone in security? This is a matter of corporate security."

"Please, relax." The receptionist motioned to the security guard, who was already on his way.

"Hello, may I help you, Miss?" The security guard had a soul patch, which looked out of place with his Pharmcen blue uniform and billed cap. He wore a laminated ID, but his embroidered patch read BARRY RONAT.

"Yes." Jill introduced herself again. "I need to talk to your boss. It's a matter of corporate security."

"And what would that be?"

"Can I just see him?" Jill could feel the heads turning, the men in ties and women in low heels eyeing her. "It's not for public consumption."

"I'm sorry, I can't do that."

"I'm a friend of Nina D'Orive, and I was supposed to meet her this morning, about an important matter."

"I'm sorry, Miss. May I escort you outside, to your car?"

"No, thanks." Jill could see it was useless. She didn't know what she was thinking anyway, coming here. She'd let the police handle it. "I'll go myself."

"I'll escort you, Miss," the security guard repeated.

"Okay, thanks." Jill walked to the entrance, sticking her hand into her purse for her cell phone. She went through the doors, found her BlackBerry, and walked to her car while the security guard stopped in front of the entrance and folded his arms. By the time she was in the driver's seat, she was already pressing 411, for information.

"In Philadelphia, Pennsylvania," Jill said into the phone. "Please connect me to Central Detectives."

Chapter Fifty-three

Jill stopped at a red light on Weehawk Boulevard, holding her cell phone to her ear, waiting for the call to connect to Central Detectives. She felt sick at heart and flashed on Nina, smiling up at Jill, with pride at her new promotion.

I just became second-in-command. I'm a VP now.

The phone call connected, and a male voice said, "Detective Ramallah speaking."

"My name's Jill Farrow, and I'm calling about my ex-husband's case, William Skyler." She had to remember which detective to ask for. "I spoke last with Detective Hightower."

"Wait, I just saw him. I'm going to put you on hold."

"Thanks." Jill waited for Detective Hightower, still upset about Nina. The traffic light turned green, but the cars barely moved because of a commotion, up ahead. White municipal trucks were on the scene, and water bubbled from the street, sloshing from a broken water main. Cops were diverting traffic off Weehawk Boulevard, using a trio of parked cruisers as a blockade, their lights flashing. Jill heard a click on the cell phone.

"Yes, this is Detective Hightower."

"Detective, thanks for taking the call." Jill fed the car gas as the traffic eased up, and she turned left in front of the waving policeman, driving slowly through the spreading water.

"Dr. Farrow, I thought we understood each other."

"I need to bring you some new information. How long will you be there?" Jill didn't have time to see Detective Hightower before her noon appointment with Padma and Rahul, and she couldn't postpone that again. "I have to see a patient first, but that won't take long."

"I'm here all day unless we get a job, you know that we closed the case on William Skyler. Correction, we never opened one."

"No, please, listen. My ex-husband was selling inside information on Pharmcen drugs, to the tune of two-and-a-half million dollars." Jill followed the traffic left, then right, and the scenery changed almost instantly, from corporate campuses to wide open spaces.

"Do you have proof of this?"

"Yes, I do. He was using his girlfriend, who works there, and I have proof, in his laptop." Jill passed a white clapboard farmhouse, with bay horses that grazed in a pasture near the road, their heads down and their black tails switching at unseen flies.

"Who is this woman? Is she coming with you?"

"No." Jill swallowed hard. She drove straight on the road, but everyone else turned right. She would have followed them if she hadn't been upset and distracted, on the phone. "She was just murdered, last night."

"What are you talking about? Who said it was a murder?"

"The Hoboken police, I assume. She lived in Hoboken. Her husband killed her, then shot himself."

"Oh, no. My apologies." Detective Hightower paused. "Dr. Farrow, where are you?"

"Parkertowne, New Jersey." Jill's thoughts raced ahead. It did seem coincidental that Nina was killed the night after her visit. What if it wasn't what it seemed to be? What if it had to do with the scheme? With William's murder? What if somebody else had killed Nina and made it look like Martin did it?

"Dr. Farrow? Did we get cut off?"

"No, sorry, I was just wondering if her murder wasn't what it seemed and—" Jill didn't finish her sentence. She didn't have any evidence and she didn't know if she believed it herself. "I'm on my way back home and I'll see you as soon as I can."

"Fine. I'll see you this afternoon, please, hang up the phone. Drive safely."

"Thanks." Jill hung up, then put the phone on the passenger seat. She didn't know the route to Philadelphia that well from here, so she started the GPS, selected FROM MEMORY, and pressed HOME, because it was quicker and close enough. She drove straight while the GPS calculated the route, and the farms spread out, surrounded by sun-dappled pastures. Tall oaks lined the street, which narrowed to one lane, the yellow line vanishing.

The GPS said, "Turn left in fifty feet."

Jill drove on a back road, and her fingers gripped the wheel, her body understanding something before her brain did. If Nina and Martin were murdered by someone else, it could mean that she had been followed to Hoboken. It could mean that she was being followed, even now. She checked her rearview mirror, and there were two cars behind her, a gray sedan and, behind that, a silver one.

The GPS said, "Turn left in twenty-five feet."

Jill drove with her eye on the two cars. The gray sedan looked like the one she'd seen the other night, but she couldn't be certain. The cars were driving in tandem, one close behind the other, as if they were together. She told herself it didn't mean anything. Many drivers tailgated, and people got confused when there was a detour.

The GPS said, "Please turn left."

Jill turned, and so did the silver and gray sedans. Her heartbeat picked up, but she told herself to stay calm, that all the cars had to turn, there was nowhere else to go. The GPS was taking them all back to the main road, with her in front.

The GPS said, "Continue on the road for five miles."

Jill felt her mouth go dry. The road ahead was a long straight stretch of asphalt lined with old trees. She told herself that it was a beautiful drive in the country, that there was nothing to worry about. That nobody got killed in broad daylight, in New Jersey horse country. Suddenly the silver sedan sped up, closing in on her rear bumper, with the gray car, right behind.

Jill's heart leapt to her throat. She reached for her BlackBerry. The silver and the gray cars were trying to run her off the road. She pressed 911 and hit the gas, going sixty-five miles an hour, then seventy.

The silver car accelerated, almost on her bumper. The gray car pulled up beside it. They both raced after her, riding her bumper, spraying gravel from the roadside.

Jill sped up to seventy-five, then eighty. She needed both hands to drive. She held the BlackBerry against the steering wheel with a thumb. The call connected, and she yelled, "Help me! I'm being chased by two cars! They're trying to kill me."

"What is your location?" the emergency operator asked, calmly.

"I don't know!" Jill looked frantically for a street or route sign but there wasn't one. She checked the GPS screen but couldn't read it this fast. "I'm near Parkertowne, in Jersey! Can't you find me? I have GPS! I'm in a white Volvo. Help!"

Jill whizzed past cows and horses. The steering wheel jerked and bobbled. A tractor in the field stopped as they flew by. She gritted her teeth and squeezed the wheel to keep the car on the road. One slip and she'd crash into a tree.

The silver and gray sedans formed a solid wall, racing to meet her.

"Help!" she screamed. She needed her hands and dropped the phone. She couldn't hear the emergency operator. Whatever happened was going to happen in the next five seconds. The cops couldn't get here fast enough.

She sped up to ninety-five, then 100. Her heart was in her throat. She began to scream and didn't stop. She'd never gone this fast in her life. The road swallowed her alive. Everything was a blur. She squeezed the life from the steering wheel. She aimed straight ahead with all her might.

The silver and gray sedans rode her bumper at lethal speed.

She floored the gas pedal, screaming at the top of her lungs. She couldn't hear the operator. No one could help her now.

Help me, God, I have a child who needs me.

Chapter Fifty-four

BOOM! Suddenly Jill's car was rammed from behind. The impact whipsawed her against the shoulder harness. She screamed and lost control of the steering wheel. Her car went spinning and spinning down the road. Her tires screeched in her ears. She whirled and whirled forever, like a nightmare amusement ride.

WHAM! The front of her car slammed into a fence. Her air bag exploded, shoving her back into the seat. She couldn't see anything but plastic. Couldn't smell anything but rubber. Felt dusted by a smelly powder of some kind. Her air bag deflated as rapidly as it had exploded. The car kept spinning in crazy motion, whirling off the road backwards, skidding sideways. A low-lying branch punched through the window on the passenger side.

"No!" Jill screamed, flattening herself against the seat. Glass flew everywhere. The end of the branch stopped inches from her head. Twigs and leaves raked her face. The car skidded, finally stopping.

The GPS said, "Please, make a U-turn. Make a U-turn."

Jill sat in the seat, stunned. Her skull throbbed with pain. Blood dripped from her forehead. She put up a shaky hand to stop the flow. Warmth leaked between her fingers. She shuddered as adrenaline dumped into her bloodstream. Her heart thundered. She scanned her legs and arms. Nothing was broken. Her left hand bled from a cut. Blood and broken glass lay everywhere. Her head hurt like hell, but she couldn't see any other injuries. She was alive.

Thank you thank you.

The engine shook, then went silent. She couldn't see through the leaves and the shattered windshield. She looked around to orient herself. The car was facing backwards on the road. She heard people shouting, then realized with a jolt that the drivers could still be after her.

She twisted wildly around, ready to get out and run for her life, but she didn't have to. The silver sedan was disappearing down the road. The gray sedan had crashed into a tall oak on the other shoulder. Its passenger side was buried in the tree trunk. Broken branches fell onto its roof and hood. The fence around the pasture lay in splintery pieces. The horses galloped away toward a barn on the hill.

Jill could see the driver of the gray sedan, slumped over his deflated air bag. The sight brought her to her senses. He didn't look like he was moving. The impact must have been horrific. She had to save him. He'd tried to kill her, but she couldn't let him die.

"Miss, are you there?" said an urgent voice, emanating from somewhere. "Miss?"

Jill realized it was the emergency operator. She was still connected to 911. She didn't see the BlackBerry. She moved the air bag aside, spotted it on the floor, and picked it up. "Hello, yes?"

"Miss, can you speak to me?"

"Yes, I'm fine. The other driver is still in his car. Please send an ambulance right away. I'm going to check on him now." Jill edged out from under the air bag. Shards of glass fell off her forearms. She reached for the door handle and pushed, surprised to see that it still worked.

"Miss, please don't attempt to treat the other driver. Wait for the EMTs. I have your location, and an ambulance is en route."

"I'm a doctor, it's fine." Jill eased herself out of the driver's seat. Glass tinkled as it dropped to the asphalt. She smelled gas and burning rubber. It hurt her arm to hold the phone to her ear. "I have to go."

"Call if you need me. I'll hang up and clear the line. Thanks."

Jill hung up and slid the phone into her pocket. She hustled to the sedan, almost falling, but kept going. Blood dripped from her forehead. She reached the sedan and opened the car door.

The driver lay face-down on the air bag. She could only see the back of his head, and his neck wasn't broken. A gash split his scalp, and he bled profusely from the wound. Blood soaked his hair and ran in rivulets down to the front of his face.

"Sir?" she said, reaching for him. His hands were pinned under the air bag, so Jill probed his carotid for a pulse. "Sir, are you all right? Can you move? I'm a doctor."

"Ooh," he moaned, slumped over.

"Can you move your legs, sir?" Jill didn't try to wedge him out of the driver's seat because the dashboard had crumpled, pinning his knees. She couldn't tell if his legs were broken, but it looked possible. His eyeglasses lay cracked on the deflated air bag. Shards of windshield littered the seat. Oddly, he had on a suit.

"Sir, can you move?"

"No," the driver answered weakly, turning to her.

Jill gasped. Blood leaked from cuts on the driver's face and pooled around his nose, but she recognized him instantly. It was Brian Pendle, Victoria's friend.

"*Brian?*" Jill said, aghast, just before his eyes rolled back in his head.

Chapter Fifty-five

"Thanks," Jill said, shaken, as the brawny EMT helped her step up onto the shiny, corrugated floor of the ambulance. Two more EMTs were on the scene, extricating Brian from the gray sedan. Another ambulance idled near him, ready to go, and the police stopped traffic, staking the street with smoking flares and flashing cruisers.

"Please, sit down slowly." The EMT steadied Jill as she sat on the gurney. "Now, lie back."

"Okay, got it. Thanks." Jill leaned back, and the EMT eased her shoulders down, lifted her feet, and placed them on the gurney.

"Good job." The EMT fastened wide orange straps over Jill's body. "We need to get going. I'll get your vitals and stop that bleeding on your forehead. You have a wound there, but it looks superficial."

"Thanks, I agree, I'm a doctor." Jill tried to collect her thoughts, but flashes of the high-speed chase burned into her brain. She was still sweaty from sheer terror. It boggled her mind to think that Brian was trying to kill her. She had no idea why he'd do such a thing, or who he was in cahoots with. Was he the one in the black SUV? Was his cohort? Jill didn't know, but she was damn sure going to find out.

"Robbie, here's her belongings," called a police officer, hustling to the ambulance. He tucked Jill's purse against the gurney, then turned to her. "Miss, somebody will come to the ER to take your statement. The tow truck is on the way for your car. I kept the ignition key and I'll give it to them."

"No, wait, my laptop." Jill tried to get up but could only lift her head. "I have a computer in my trunk. I can't leave without it. Can I go get it, or can you get it for me?"

"No, you have to get to the hospital. Your car is a wreck, your trunk won't open, anyway. You're lucky to be alive, Miss."

"But I need it, I can't leave it here. It contains evidence of a crime." Jill struggled to get up, straining against the straps, but the EMT pressed her back down.

"Please, stay down. We have to leave, and I have to treat you."

The police officer leaned in. "Miss, you can claim your laptop later, don't worry. Nobody can get inside that trunk. Robbie, you're good to go." He closed the ambulance doors, and the EMT rose and hurried to twist the handle into a locking position.

"Jenny, locked and loaded!" the EMT called to the driver. He turned and fetched a Rowbotham dressing kit from a cage in the wall, then the ambulance lurched off.

"I'm sorry, I have to make a call." Jill freed her hand and managed to reach into her pocket for her BlackBerry. "Somebody has to meet me at the hospital. Where are we going?"

"Shood Memorial, in Parkertowne." The EMT zipped open the kit, yanked out some cleanser, and swabbed the wound on Jill's forehead, applying pressure to stop the bleeding. "You okay?"

"Yes, thanks. Excuse my rudeness." Jill scrolled for Victoria's number, pressed CALL, and tried to gather her wits while the call connected.

"Hello," Victoria answered the call, testy. "What now, Jill? I can't talk, I'm driving to class."

"I have some bad news, very bad." Jill watched the EMT tape gauze to her forehead, then he rose and took a blood-pressure cuff and thermometer from a wire basket on the wall. "It's about your friend Brian. He was injured in a car crash when he and another car tried to run me off a road. They were trying to kill me."

"*What?*" Victoria gasped. "Are you serious? Is this a joke?"

"It's no joke. I'm in an ambulance now, and so is he."

The EMT didn't bat an eye as he checked Jill's blood pressure, and in any other circumstance, she would have remarked on his professionalism.

"Jill, what are you talking about?" Victoria answered, her tone still disbelieving. "You mean my friend Brian Pendle? It's not possible."

"Victoria, tell me, why would Brian try to kill me? How long have you known this guy?"

"A year, but it can't be him."

"He's a lawyer in New York, right? What firm does he work for?"

"Creed and Whitstone, but what's the difference?" Victoria asked, insistent. "You must be mistaken. It can't be Brian."

"It is, I saw him. Victoria, what does he do there, what's his field?"

"He's a securities lawyer. You could be wrong. It wasn't him. You barely know him."

"I *recognized* him, Victoria." Jill was trying to think, she still felt upset. The ambulance didn't use its siren, but it seemed louder inside than she remembered from when she went to the hospital with Megan. Its powerful engine seemed to roar, its wide tires rumbled, and the cab in back creaked mightily, the scrape of metal against metal. "So Brian works as a securities lawyer. Does that mean he knows stockbrokers and guys like that?"

"Yes, but—"

"Did he know a man named Joe Zeptien?"

"I don't know, why?"

"Did he ever mention anything about Pharmcen or Memoril?"

"No, is this real? Is it really him? He was in an accident?"

"Come and see. We're being taken to Shood Memorial in Parkertowne. He has a head wound and was unconscious at the scene."

"My God!" Victoria cried. "I'm turning around. I'll be there in half an hour, max."

"Let me ask you, did Brian know your Dad?"

"They met once or twice. Jill, what's going on? Why are you asking me all these questions? What's going on?"

"Hell if I know. I'm trying to figure it out. Did you ever hear Brian and your father talk about the drug business or Pharmcen?"

"No, of course not, just golf," Victoria answered, in bewilderment.

"Then what is Brian up to? Why would he try to kill me, do you have any idea?"

"He didn't do that, he would never. I have to go, I'm driving, and there's traffic. I'm on my way."

"Okay, good-bye." Jill hung up, more confused than ever, and her gaze fell on a digital clock embedded in the stainless steel side of the cab, which read 12:30. She thought of Padma and Rahul, and her heart sank. "Oh no. I was supposed to see a patient, half an hour ago."

"Hey, accidents happen." The EMT held the thermometer bulb to her ear. "Please, stay still a sec."

"Okay. One more call, sorry." Jill waited a beat, then pressed P for Pembey Family.

"I'm done here, your vitals are good." The EMT put the thermometer and cuff back in its basket, then stowed the dressing kit and flashed Jill a thumbs-up.

"Thanks," Jill said, as the EMT climbed up to the passenger's seat, and her phone call connected.

"Pembey Family, may I help you?" It was Donna, and Jill warmed to the friendly voice.

"Hi, it's Jill, and I'm calling because I was just in a car accident, in New Jersey. Is Padma still there with Rahul?"

"Oh no! Are you okay, honey? We tried to reach you."

"I'm fine, but I'm going to the Shood Memorial ER, in Parkertowne. Is Padma still there, with Rahul? Can I talk to her?"

Donna hesitated. "She left, but don't think about work now. Take care of yourself."

"No." Jill felt awful. "What time did she go?"

"You missed them by five minutes, but, well, Padma asked for

Rahul's file, and I had to release it. She's leaving us. She said her family wasn't very happy after we lost the baby's bloodwork. But, Jill, but don't think about that now. Just get better."

"Oh no." Jill felt like kicking herself. She hated losing Padma and the boys, and she wouldn't rest until she checked Rahul's results. "Did Rahul's bloodwork come in? I need to see it."

"Yes, the hospital emailed it to us. I printed it out and put it in the file."

"Would you forward me the email?"

"Sure, right away."

"Thanks. I'll call Padma when I get the results. Can you email me her cell number, too?"

"No problem."

"See you tomorrow."

"Jill, you can't come in after a car accident. I'll start calling your patients."

"No, don't, please. It's nothing. I'll be in."

Donna lowered her voice. "Okay, but just a heads-up, Sheryl wants to talk to you when you get in. I think it's about Padma leaving."

Jill figured as much. "I'm *so* looking forward to that conversation."

Donna laughed. "Take care, Jill."

"You, too. Bye." Jill hung up, navigated to email on her Black-Berry, and scanned the senders, who were all patients. Donna's forwarded email about Rahul's bloodwork wasn't there yet. She felt a pang, thinking she wouldn't see Padma or the boys again.

But she wasn't worried about Padma.

She was worried about Rahul.

Chapter Fifty-six

Jill waited for the police in the examining room and eyed her re-flection in a wall mirror. There was a new gauze bandage taped to her forehead, and tiny red cuts on her cheeks glistened under Neosporin. Another bandage covered her left palm, wrapped around the back of her hand. She smoothed her hair back into its ponytail and felt almost normal, except for the dried blood spat-tering her sweater.

Jill checked her BlackBerry for the third time, and the email with Rahul's results had finally come in, so she pressed OPEN AT-TACHMENT. The attachment downloaded, but when she opened it, the numbers were too small to read. She pressed the button to magnify them, but it was still impossible to see.

"Dr. Farrow, here we go." The nurse slipped past the privacy curtain, returning with an Advil packet and a paper cup of water in hand. She looked young, with an easy smile and a long brown braid. "Your discharge papers will take a bit, though. We just got super busy. You slipped in right in time."

"Thanks." Jill took the Advil and cup, swallowed the pill, and tossed the cup. "Can I ask you a big favor? I need to get some blood-work results printed out. May I email them to you and you print them out for me? It's important."

"Sure thing. Want my email?"

"Thanks. Go ahead, tell me." Jill typed in the email address while the nurse told it to her, then she forwarded Donna's email. "Thanks again, so much. Also, how's the other driver, with the head injury?"

"I probably shouldn't say. You know, it's confidential under HIPA."

"Please, just give me the headline. I want to prepare his friend, and she'll be here any minute. She's my stepdaughter."

"Oh." The nurse blinked. "Well, I can tell you that he's in the OR, and they called in the best docs."

"When will the police come for me, do you know? The cop at the scene said to expect them."

"I heard they're on the way, and I'll bring them in when they get here. I guess I can open this now." The nurse swept the privacy curtain to the side, revealing a modern ER unit ringed with examining rooms around an octagonal station. Doctors, physician's assistants, nurses, and orderlies scurried this way and that, bearing meds and paperwork. Jill used to dream about working in a place like this but dedicated to children's emergencies.

"Don't mind me, I'm having ER envy."

The nurse smiled. "I'll be back with the printout and your discharge papers."

"Can I make a call?" Jill gestured at the NO CELL PHONES sign. "I have to arrange for my daughter to be picked up."

"Okay, but you didn't hear it from me." The nurse winked, then left the room.

Jill sat down, and the movement made her realize how much her neck and back ached. Megan would be in school, then practice, so she texted Katie. **Can u pick up Megan at the pool at 5:45 and take her to your house? Fill u in later.** It only took a second for Katie to answer: **OK. Love you. Making funfetti cupcakes. Shoot me now.**

Jill smiled, then thought of Sam, feeling a sudden urge to talk to him, whether it was mutual or not. She pressed S and waited for the call to connect, eyeing the bustling ER. "Honey?" she said, when she heard a clicking sound.

"Hi, how are you?" Sam asked coolly, and Jill felt her throat thicken. She hadn't realized how upset she was until she heard his voice. She almost felt like crying, the stress and the fear hitting her all at once, but she kept it together.

"I'm okay, but something bad just happened. I was run off the road by two cars. One got away, but the other was driven by Brian, Victoria's friend."

"*What?* Where are you?"

"An ER in New Jersey. The cops are on the way."

"How *are* you?" Sam sounded like himself again, full of concern. "My God, honey!"

"I'm really fine." Jill stifled a sniffle. "The car's totaled."

"I don't care about the car. You could have been killed."

"I think that was the general idea."

"What the hell? Why does Brian want to *kill* you? This is insanity!"

"God knows."

"And so does Victoria."

"What do you mean?" Jill asked, surprised. Just then she noticed Victoria, entering the ER area, standing out in a fashionable cropped jacket, skinny jeans, and fancy boots, with her hair in its sophisticated blonde twist. She was looking around for a nurse, but there was only one, talking on the phone at the station, behind her monitor.

"Jill, think about it," Sam was saying. "Victoria must be the one who wants you dead, not Brian. He doesn't even know you. He must be acting at her behest."

"What are you saying?" Jill recoiled at the very notion, even on the phone. She couldn't believe what she was hearing. "Victoria is my *daughter,* or, at least, she's like my daughter. We may not be getting along that great now, but she still—"

"Babe, follow the money. William had a huge insurance policy, and maybe Victoria killed him for it, or had her friend Brian kill him for it."

"Victoria kill William? That's absurd." Jill watched as Victoria waited for the nurse to get off the phone, drumming her fingers. "She would never, ever do such a thing."

"No, it isn't. Think about it. Abby got you involved in solving William's murder, and you wouldn't let it drop. Victoria and Brian could have been worried that you were going to find them out, so they wanted you dead."

"That's *impossible*."

"Jill, you don't know Victoria anymore, not the real her. You thought Abby didn't drink, remember?" Sam's tone grew more urgent. "Babe, you have to see these girls for what they are today. You said two cars ran you off the road. Who was driving the other car? Could it have been Victoria?"

"Sam, no, that's crazy. We drove a *hundred* miles an hour." Jill motioned to Victoria, to catch her eye at the nurses' station. "It wasn't her car anyway. She drives a white BMW."

"We know she has anger issues, from the scene she made at the memorial service. What if she got angry enough to kill him? I don't know how she got those drugs in his blood, but she has keys to the house. I'm getting on the next plane. This ends *now*."

"Thanks, so much." Jill felt a rush of gratitude and love for him. "But nothing in the world will make me believe anything that awful about Victoria."

"Jill, think without emotion." Sam's voice rose, alarmed. "You sound like those news reports where they interview the mother of the murderer, and she says her son was a good boy."

"I know what I know, Sam, and I know that child." Jill spotted Victoria waving back, her pretty face frowning with anxiety. "I can't talk anymore. Victoria will be here any minute."

"No. Stay away from her, honey."

"I hear you, but I'll be fine. Don't worry." Jill watched Victoria hurrying toward her exam room, bypassing the nurse.

"Please, stay away from her, honey. Don't be alone with her."

"I'll be careful. I have to go. Love you. Thanks, bye." Jill hung up the phone just as Victoria entered the examining room, distraught.

"Jill!" she cried, throwing open her arms. "Are you okay?"

Chapter Fifty-seven

"What's going on? Are you sure you're okay?" Victoria released her, and up close, Jill could see that her eyes were bloodshot, and her mascara had been reapplied, so she'd been crying. "You look okay, kind of."

"I am, I'm fine." Jill managed a smile, warmed by her concern. "But I can't figure why Brian did that. It's appalling, I'm shocked."

"I know." Victoria swallowed, hard. "And they won't tell me anything about him. I called his parents but they're in Europe."

"The nurse said he's in surgery, and they have the best docs working on him."

"Oh God, please." Victoria sank into the chair. "Would he really do this? Is he going to be arrested?"

Suddenly Jill and Victoria turned as the nurse came into the examining room, leading two middle-aged men in dark suits. The taller man stepped forward, seeming to take the lead, and he was well-built, with a lined, craggy face and dark hair in a short brush cut.

The nurse gestured to him. "Dr. Farrow, this is Special Agent Donator and his partner, Special Agent Cohz, of the FBI."

"Thanks for coming," Jill said, surprised. "I was expecting the local police." She extended her good hand, and Special Agent Donator shook it, firmly.

"Dr. Farrow, nice to meet you." Special Agent Donator glanced at the nurse. "Nurse, would you excuse us for a few minutes, please?"

"Of course. I have one last thing." The nurse handed Jill her paperwork. "Here's the bloodwork you requested and your discharge papers, to be signed."

"Thanks, I know the drill. Any headaches, go to my local ER." Jill accepted the envelope, scribbled a signature on the discharge papers, and handed them back.

The nurse turned to go. "Please don't stay long, folks. We need the bed."

"Understood, thank you." Special Agent Donator nodded as the nurse left, closing the privacy curtain, then he turned to Jill, with a stiff smile. "You've had quite a day, Dr. Farrow. Do you feel well enough to be standing up?"

"Yes, thanks." Jill gestured to Victoria. "This is Victoria Skyler, my stepdaughter, uh, my former stepdaughter."

"Hello." Victoria shook each agent's hand, but her manner gave off a chill. "I'm a friend of Brian Pendle's, and I have already called him a lawyer from Creed & Whitstone. So don't even think about questioning him when he gets out of surgery."

Jill felt taken aback, and Special Agent Donator stopped smiling.

"Ms. Skyler, excuse me, but you don't have all the facts—"

"I have all the facts I need," Victoria interrupted. "I'm not a lawyer yet, but I know that attempted murder is a state law crime, not federal. The FBI is federal. So what do you have to do with this?"

Special Agent Donator pursed his lips. "Ms. Skyler, the attempt on Dr. Farrow's life was part of a dangerous, active criminal enterprise, involving the breach of federal securities laws and other illegalities. We explained to the local police that we have jurisdiction, and they agreed after some discussion, hence the delay." He turned to Jill. "You have some idea of what I'm talking about, don't you?"

"Yes," Jill answered, finally validated.

"But you were wrong about one thing, Dr. Farrow." Special Agent Donator seemed to soften, his face falling briefly into sharp lines. "Brian wasn't trying to kill you. He was trying to protect you. He's one of us."

Chapter Fifty-eight

"Pardon me?" Jill asked, uncomprehending. "Brian is with the FBI?"

"No, he isn't," Victoria said, incredulous. "He's a lawyer, not an FBI agent. He went to Georgetown Law Center."

Special Agent Donator faced Victoria, his expression grim. "Ms. Skyler, Brian has been a federal agent since he graduated from Georgetown. His law degree makes him invaluable to us in the field, and he's been working undercover. He blew his cover saving Dr. Farrow's life."

"Save me? What do you mean?" Jill flashed back to the silver and the gray cars, riding side-by-side, like a moving wall. "He was trying to run me off the road, with another car."

"No, the silver car was trying to run you off the road. Brian was in the gray car, trying to run *them* off the road. We were in communication with him during the chase, right up until the crash."

Jill blinked, shocked. "Then who was following me?"

"The man in the silver car, and we were following him. We have been, for some time. Successful prosecutions don't get built overnight, no matter what you see on TV, and they don't happen without dedication. Brian is one of the best young agents we have."

Jill couldn't process it fast enough. "He was trying to stop them? Why didn't he try to shoot their tire, or them?"

"Shooting a tire in a residential area is too risky, at speed, and we can't authorize the use of lethal force where non-lethal force can be employed. Brian trained in defensive driving techniques at the academy, and he assured us he could handle it. Unfortunately, he lost control of his car."

Jill remembered the scene, just before she was hit. Special Agent Donator was right. "The silver car *was* the one tailgating."

"Yes, and the silver car was the one that hit your bumper. It may have looked as if the two cars were working together, but they weren't. Brian risked his life to save you, and by all accounts, he behaved in an exemplary fashion. We're all pulling for his speedy recovery." Special Agent Donator glanced down, working his jaw, and Special Agent Cohz cleared his throat. He was shorter, but equally fit-looking.

"Is Brian going to be okay?" Victoria asked, stepping over. "What do you know about his condition?"

"Not much we can share, at this point." Special Agent Donator answered. "We'll discuss it further after he gets out of surgery."

Jill felt a wave of guilt. Her head throbbed, and exhaustion swept over her. She prayed that Brian would recover, quickly and completely. She couldn't bear it if one more person died because of this scheme, or because of her. Then Jill realized that Sam had been wrong. If Brian hadn't been trying to kill her, it meant that Victoria wasn't involved with William's death.

"Dr. Farrow, we'll need to debrief you and take a complete statement. The investigation is being run out of D.C., but the team is waiting to meet us in New York. Please, get your things and come with us."

"Sure." Jill picked up her bag and slid the envelope inside, to look at in the car.

"I'd prefer to stay here," Victoria said, flatly. "I'd like to see Brian when he gets out of surgery."

Special Agent Donator turned to her, his brow knit. "Ms. Skyler, there are two special agents detailed to protect Brian as soon as he gets out of surgery, and he won't be having any conversations, with you or anyone else. Countless manpower hours, federal dollars, and hard work went into this investigation, much of it from Brian himself. He's going to get a commendation. He's been undercover for a year."

"Wait, hold on." Victoria frowned. "That's when we met. Is that a coincidence?" She faced Jill, in bewilderment. "Why did you ask me when we met, and how?"

Suddenly a minor commotion arose next door, on the other side of the patterned curtain, billowing to accommodate a wheelchair. "Oooh, my leg, help me, oooh, please," wailed an elderly man in distress, as nurses tried to calm him, wheeling him into the examining room and lifting him onto the bed.

Special Agent Donator turned to Jill and Victoria. "Ladies, let's go."

"But, this is so awful," Victoria said, shaken. "Brian lied to me? For a year?"

"Ms. Skyler, we'll debrief you at the office." Special Agent Donator pushed aside the curtain, Special Agent Cohz led the way, and Jill led Victoria out of the examining room.

"We'll figure this all out together, honey." Jill put a gentle arm around Victoria, but the girl didn't reply, avoiding Jill's eye as they fell into step, walking down the glistening hallway. Jill wanted to know the whole story about William, Zeptien, Nina, Martin, and Brian, though she felt terrible that it would bring Victoria's world crashing down on her head.

But first, Jill wanted to know about Rahul.

Chapter Fifty-nine

Jill opened the envelope as soon she got in the backseat of the car, and Rahul's bloodwork confirmed her worry. His white-blood-cell count showed a major bacterial infection, at 18,000 when it should have been between 5,000 and 15,000, and his smear explained why. Rahul didn't have cancer or leukemia, but he had an immune deficiency that made him unable to fight infection properly, which was why he got so many ear infections and the pneumonia. Normal babies had four immunoglobulins, IgG, IgM, IgA, and IgE, but Rahul was missing IgE, which governed allergies, consistent with his family history.

"Oh no." Jill moaned, scanning the rest of the results. The numbers showed that Rahul's neutrophils were already shifting left, which meant they were leaving his bone marrow to fight infection before they were even mature cells. Jill felt a bolt of fear for the baby she adored, but went into emergency mode. Her plan was to hospitalize Rahul immediately and treat him aggressively with IV antibiotics, or the ear infection could spread to his bloodstream and turn septic.

Victoria looked over. "What's the matter?"

"I have a very sick patient." Jill caught the eye of Special Agent Donator in the rearview mirror. He was driving, and Special

Agent Cohz was in the passenger seat, looking at some papers. "Gentlemen, I have to call the office now. We can talk afterwards."

"Go right ahead." Special Agent Donator nodded. "I'd rather wait until we get to the city to take your statement, anyway. The team needs to hear it, and you won't have to tell it twice."

"Good, thanks." Jill was already scrolling through her Black-Berry. She found Donna's email, pressed SELECT on Padma's cell number, and hit CALL. It rang and rang, then went to voicemail. "Padma, it's Dr. Farrow. I need to speak with you right away. It's about Rahul's bloodwork. Please call me immediately." She left her cell number, then hung up and called the office.

"Pembey Family," answered a woman's voice. It was Sheryl.

"Sheryl, it's Jill. I can't reach Padma on the cell, and I see a major problem with Rahul's bloodwork. I need her emergency contact numbers. Her husband's in Afghanistan."

"I know why she won't take your call, I spoke with her. She fired us today. Is this how you grow the pediatric practice?"

Jill bit her tongue. "Now, I need—"

"I heard you were in a car accident, but I'll have to dock you if you don't come in tomorrow. I told Donna to tell you to call me, to discuss this."

"She did. Sheryl, please give me the numbers." Jill tried to keep her temper, glancing out the window, where the traffic was congested. They were approaching Newark Airport, and a line of silvery planes hung in the sky as if suspended on an invisible string, their wings glinting in the sun.

"Padma's switching to Dr. Benson's group. She asked that all future results be sent to him."

"I don't have the time to discuss this, Sheryl. This is an emergency. Get me numbers."

"How dare you speak to me that way!"

Jill couldn't take it another minute, and she raised her voice to say, "Tell you what, give me the numbers, and I won't speak to you ever again."

"You have to. You're an employee."

"I'm not an employee, I'm a *doctor*. And I quit. Now give me the numbers."

"Fine. You're required to give two weeks' notice—"

"Give me the damn numbers!" Jill shouted. Victoria jumped, startled, and Special Agent Donator's eyes flared in the rearview mirror.

"Be that way, Jill. I'm emailing them to you right now. I have an office, home, and cell for her father-in-law in Seattle. His name is Frank McCann. But I don't know if he can reach Padma, because she left for Mumbai with the kids. Her mother had a heart attack."

"Oh no." Jill felt her heart race. "Mumbai, India?"

"No, Mumbai, Ohio. Yes, of course, India."

"When did she go?"

"She left from here."

"She can't go to Mumbai with Rahul, that's a twenty-four-hour flight. His system can't take it, he's already weak."

"Really?" Sheryl asked, suddenly hushed. "She was worried it would hurt his ears, but she said she had to go. She said she'd give him some Tylenol."

Jill thoughts raced. "The problem isn't pain, it's sepsis. In that amount of time, he could go into shock. They won't be able to treat him on the plane, and he needs to be admitted. He could die."

"Oh my God, oh my God," Sheryl said, panicky. "What do we do?"

Victoria looked over, her hazel eyes wide. Special Agent Cohz glanced back at Jill. Special Agent Donator slid on aviator sunglasses.

"Sheryl, get a grip, and we'll both call. We have to stop Padma. She can't get on that plane. You hear me?"

"Oh my God, this is awful. What if he dies? What do I do? I don't know what to do! The nurses are all gone, they're all gone! I'm the only one here! What do I do?"

"Do what I say. Do it now. I will, too. Go and do." Jill hung up, scrolled to email, found Sheryl's, selected the father-in-law's cell number, and pressed CALL. The cell rang and rang, then voice-mail connected. "Mr. McCann, this is Dr. Farrow, Rahul's pedia-trician. Please tell Padma *not* to get on the plane to Mumbai. Your grandson has an infection that could prove fatal. This is a medical emergency. Please call me immediately." Jill left her cell number and hung up, as Victoria turned to her.

"Jill, can I help?"

"Yes, you have your iPhone with you, don't you?'

"Sure, yes." Victoria started digging in her large black bag, bulg-ing with stuff. "It's in here somewhere. I use the same bag for classes, so I travel heavy."

"Look on the Internet. See which airline has direct flights from Philly to Mumbai this afternoon. Get the flight while I try to get Rahul's grandfather."

"Okay." Victoria pulled out a round hairbrush, a white earphone cord, and a zipped makeup case. A stick of cream blusher rolled out like a shiny black log, then a hot pink tube of mascara, her EpiPen, and her iPhone. "Here we go." Victoria started tapping the touch screen. "Then what do I do, when I get the airline and flight?"

"See if you can find a phone number for the airline, then give me the phone." Jill pressed Frank McCann's work number, since that was a better bet than his home number at this hour. Out-side the car, the traffic inched along, and a plane flew so low over-head that Jill almost ducked, reflexively.

Special Agent Donator leaned over to Special Agent Cohz. "We'll never get there, this traffic keeps up," he said, in low tones.

Special Agent Cohz shook his neat head. "Mick, take the way I showed you, to the tunnel. The exit's up ahead."

Jill held her phone while the call rang twice, then connected. "Is this Granger Accountants? My name is Dr. Jill Farrow, and this is a medical emergency. I need to speak with Frank McCann."

"Sorry, he isn't in," a receptionist said. "What's the nature of the emergency?"

"I treat his grandson Rahul, who I understand is flying with his daughter-in-law Padma to Mumbai, today. Rahul could go into septic shock during the flight, and I need to reach Padma as soon as possible and tell them not to get on the plane. Can Mr. McCann be reached? I tried his cell but he didn't answer."

"Oh no," the receptionist said, alarmed. "He's at a conference. All I can do is try his cell, too."

"How about the hotel? Is he staying at a hotel? Where is the conference held?"

"I can't give you that information, but I can try and get a message to him. I'll try, I swear, but I can't promise anything."

"Please try, right away. Have him call me if he has any questions, but it's imperative that he stop Padma. It's a matter of life and death, for his grandson." Jill left her cell number and thanked her, then hung up.

Victoria looked over at Jill, with strain showing all over her young face. "Jill, I have the flight, but it's boarding in half an hour. It's Continental, Flight 440."

"Oh no." Jill felt her pulse pick up. "Got a phone number?"

Victoria tapped away on the touch screen. "I see phone numbers for reservations and customer service."

"Call reservations, press 0, and give me the phone when you reach a human being."

"Okay." Victoria pressed a number, then held the iPhone to her ear. "Damn it. I'm on hold, a ten-minute wait."

"That's too long." Jill shifted forward toward the front seat. She had to try something else, fast. "Special Agent Donator, can you help me? The plane is about to board at Philadelphia airport, Continental Flight 440. Can you call TSA? Or can you call the Philadelphia police, or the airport police, and tell them not to let Padma Choudhury and her son board? Or can they hold the plane?"

"That's not procedure, Dr. Farrow." Special Agent Donator pursed his lips, and his sunglasses obscured his thoughts.

"Please, a baby's life is at stake." Jill leaned forward, ready to beg. "It couldn't be more important."

"Understood." Special Agent Donator steered off the turnpike at the exit, then turned to Special Agent Cohz. "What do you think, Pete? It's not kosher, but we could always call Sean, at the Philly bureau."

Special Agent Cohz nodded. "It's a baby, for God's sake, and the Dad's in Afghanistan. Call Sean. He'll know what to do."

Jill's heart leapt with hope. "Yes, please. Call Sean. Do it, please!"

"All right." Special Agent Donator reached his hand to the backseat, palm up. "May I use your phone, Dr. Farrow?"

"Sure." Jill handed over her phone. "Thanks so much."

"You're welcome." Special Agent Donator took her BlackBerry, but instead of pressing in a phone number, he slammed it against the dashboard, where it splintered with a loud *crak*!

"What are you doing?" Jill asked, horrified.

But the next thing she knew, Special Agent Cohz had twisted toward her, and his fist was heading straight for her face.

Chapter Sixty

Jill regained consciousness in the backseat, slumped against the corner of the car, her head lying on its right side. She tried to understand what was going on. The two men in the front seat weren't FBI agents, they were killers. They were going to kill her and Victoria. Rahul was on the plane to Mumbai. He might already be dead.

Jill fought to suppress a rising terror. Her face and head throbbed with pain. Her nose was bleeding. She heard a soft bubbling sound, her own blood leaking from her nose. Her right eye felt loose, warm, and wet, so she knew her orbital bone had been hit, maybe broken. She heard the sound of quiet whimpering.

Victoria.

Jill felt the sensation of movement, a slight jostling. There were no other car sounds, no passing trucks. The rate of speed was low, maybe fifty miles an hour. There was only road noise, and weeping.

Jill lay still, forcing herself to think, and function. If her right orbital had been hit, her eye would look like a sunken and bloody mess. Nobody could tell it was open. The two men would think she was still unconscious.

She kept her left eye closed and looked around through her right eye. It wasn't easy but she could see well enough. Victoria was hunched over, crying and shaking. Her hands covered her face. Blood dripped through her slender fingers. Her phone and purse were gone. Her blusher and hairbrush lay scattered on the backseat.

"I gotta take a leak," said one of the men, up front, and from the direction of the sound, Jill guessed it was the driver talking, Donator or whatever his real name was. He must have shown ID to somebody at the hospital, but it must have been fake. Jill hadn't even thought to ask, she'd been so preoccupied.

"Make it fast," said Cohz, or whoever. "This chick is making me mental, with the boohooing."

"So pop her again."

"It just makes it worse. Hurry up."

Jill felt the car slow down. She couldn't let anything happen to Victoria. She felt a rush of love and terror, in almost equal measure.

The car pulled over to the side of the road, and Jill could see thick woods. No houses. No people. No cars. No help. She and Victoria wouldn't get far if they ran for it. The men had to be armed, and there were two of them. It was late afternoon, still daylight. One man would go after her, and the other would hunt Victoria down.

"Be right back," Donator said, braking. There was movement on the floor of the car as it stopped. Something rolled out from underneath the seat, an orange color that caught Jill's attention.

Victoria's EpiPen.

Jill knew it was a syringe of epinephrine, or adrenaline. In case of an allergic reaction, it would restore breathing, but injected into the muscle of a healthy person, it would have almost no effect. It would only increase the heart rate, cause nausea and tremors. It would have no effect in a vein.

Unless it was the right vein.

Jill didn't know if she could do it, but she and Victoria were dead, otherwise. She heard the sound of the car door opening, then a beeping that signaled that it had been left open. She couldn't see the driver, but she heard the crunch of his foot on the gravel road, then his footfalls disappeared.

She imagined him walking up a distance, then turning away

from the car. His back would be to the roadside. She'd have to wait until then. It would buy them extra seconds.

It would be her only chance. *Their* only chance.

She stilled her heart, listening. Counting.

One, two, three.

Go.

Chapter Sixty-one

Jill swooped down, grabbed the EpiPen, tore the cap off with her teeth, then lunged forward and plunged its long, thick needle directly into Cohz's carotid.

His eyes flew open. His lips parted in shock and pain.

Jill clamped her other hand over his mouth to stifle his cry. The EpiPen wouldn't kill him, but it would immobilize him long enough to give them a head start. "Go, go, go!" she hissed to Victoria.

"Oh!" Victoria sat upright, teary and shaken, then reached for the door handle and shoved the door open with Jill right behind her, pushing her outside.

"Run to the woods! Go!"

"Help!" Victoria screamed, but Jill didn't have time to tell her that screaming was the worst thing to do.

"No, stop!" Donator shouted, from up the road, behind them.

Jill grabbed Victoria's hand. They crashed together into the woods, running as fast as they could. They tore through the trees, tall and thick. They ducked low branches. The trees grew denser. There was no room to run in between. They let go of each other's hands, running together, racing with all their might. Bark scraped their legs. Their hair caught on branches. They leapt over dead limbs. The temperature cooled. The sun vanished.

Victoria panted as she ran, her arms pumping. Her legs churned. Her jacket caught on something and ripped.

Jill's breath went ragged. She put up her hands to shield her face. She was too adrenalized to feel pain. They twisted and threaded through the trees, trying not to trip on vines and undergrowth. Twigs, stones, and dry leaves covered the ground. There was no path or trail. No room to run side-by-side.

"HELP, HELP!" Victoria screamed.

Crak! a gunshot fired, close behind them.

Jill ducked, on the run. A jolt of sheer horror shot through her system. Donator was after them now. She knew what she had to do. They couldn't keep this up. She turned to Victoria.

"Go left," Jill shouted, gasping for breath. "You go left, I go right."

"What? Why?"

"Go and shut up. I'll draw him."

"No!" Victoria reached for her, but Jill slapped her hand away, though it killed her to do it.

"Listen to me! Go left! Do it! We have to separate! We can't both make it!"

"No, I'm not going!" Victoria met Jill's eye for a split second, panting hard, tears streaming down her cheeks, as heartbroken as she was terrified, and in that instant, Jill could see that they had become mother and daughter, once again.

"I love you, honey. Now, go! Get help!"

"No!"

"Yes!" Jill turned right and bolted away from her, screaming at the top of her lungs, to draw Donator. "Help! Help, police! Somebody!"

Crak! went the gunshot, closer.

Jill knew it had worked. She was on her own now.

She put her head down and ran for her life.

Chapter Sixty-two

Crak! went another gunshot, even closer.

"Help!" Jill put on the afterburners, running faster. Raising her hands to clear her way. Keeping her knees high so she wouldn't fall. Ducking when the branches got too low. She sweated and bled. She had no idea where she was. She didn't know if she was running straight or in a circle. She knew only that she was running *away*.

Her chest heaved with each breath. Her legs ached, and she started to stagger. Thorns sliced her palms and forearms. She tripped on a vine, yanking it to free herself. She didn't know how much longer she could keep going. Donator would catch up with her. Cohz would regain consciousness and join him.

Then she saw it. Up ahead, through the trees. It looked oddly lighter, like a clearing. She didn't know what it was, but she ran for it. Civilization lay ahead.

"Help!" she hollered, with hope.

Crak!

Jill felt the heat of the bullet, whizzing past her head. She bolted in terror through the woods toward the clearing. She had to get to help before Donator got to her. She didn't know how many bullets he had. The promise of the clearing gave her new strength. She got a second wind.

She raced ahead. She cried out when a branch sliced her cheek, its end pointed like a steak knife. She ran and ran, knocking dead limbs out of the way with her arms. Beyond the trees was a brightness. The sun shone through. She spotted rooftops and glimpsed houses.

"Help me somebody!"

Crak!

"No!" Jill cried out. Her left shoulder burned like it had caught fire. She'd been shot. Her arm flew instinctively to grip the wound, but it slowed her pace and she let go. She reached the clearing like crossing a finish line.

It was a housing development, unfinished. The trees had been cut down, making a circle of dirt and clay around a few Cape Cod houses, then a row of bare wooden frames for houses. They sat on an unfinished paved street, part of a larger asphalt grid. Tattered orange flags marked the building lots. RUNNING HORSE REALTY, read the faded sign, with a peeling overlay that read MODEL HOME.

"Help!" Jill yelled. Tears of relief ran down her face. She sprinted toward the model home, then noticed something, on the run.

There were no people, no cars. No toys in the front yards, no swingsets in the backs. No trash cans or recycling bins. Everything was quiet and still. It was a suburb that never happened.

Her heart sank, her hope vanished. Still, she ran on and on. The development had been abandoned. The Cape Cods stood empty and unoccupied. The unfinished houses were skeletons, their Tyvek skins flayed by the elements, their plywood bones bleached by the sun.

She ran past the model home, guessing it would be locked. She scanned on the fly for a place to hide. There were no open garages. No gardening sheds. No sewer pipes.

She ran down the street past the finished houses. They had to be locked, too. She felt exposed and vulnerable. Donator could pick her off here with ease. Her breath came harder and harder. She couldn't keep going much longer. Her shoulder was killing her. Her heart pumped hard, she was losing blood fast. She had to get out of sight.

She gulped for breath. She ran for the last frame house in the row, which was almost complete. Plywood sheets formed its front wall. She tore through the rubble and red clay to the threshold. It had no door.

She whirled around, looking for a place to hide. It was a see-through house. Wood frames stood where the walls would have been, their studs at regular intervals. All the rooms were open except one in the back, intended to become a garage. A cinderblock wall blocked her view.

She raced for the cinderblock wall and ducked behind it. The garage was open to the back, facing the woods. The floor was poured concrete.

She looked around for something she could use for a weapon, left by a construction worker. A two-by-four, a hammer. A box-cutter, a pipe. There was nothing. It had been picked clean.

She faced the front of the house, her eyes glued to the threshold for Donator. Then she saw something that sickened her.

Drops of her own blood dribbled along the plywood floor, leading to her hiding place. She was bleeding from the shoulder wound. She should have thought of that. She couldn't hide here, she couldn't hide anywhere. She was bleeding, making her own gruesome trail of crumbs.

Then she realized. She hadn't heard a gunshot in a while, and that was the only thing worse than hearing a gunshot. It meant that she didn't know where Donator was.

She rose silently, trying to slow her heart, quiet her breathing. Maybe he was out of bullets. Maybe he'd given up. Maybe he'd gone back to his car.

Suddenly she heard a shuffling behind her, and she turned.

Chapter Sixty-three

"You bitch!" Donator roared, running at Jill, his hands reaching for her throat.

"No!" Jill raised her arms, but he was already upon her. His strong hands caught her, pushing her off her feet, crushing her Adam's apple under his thumbs.

She gagged. She tried to breathe but couldn't. She tried to pry his fingers off but they closed tighter. She tried to kick him but he kept coming, knocking her off-balance.

She lost her footing. He dragged her backwards by her neck, scraping her heels across the plywood floor. She couldn't breathe, he'd sealed her windpipe with his hands. Still, she kept hitting, prying, and kicking, fighting for her life. Her shoulder exploded in agony.

"Give it up!" Donator yelled, his face crimson with rage. He bared his teeth like an animal. She fell backwards, her head hitting the floor, her arms flailing at him. Donator fell on top of her, tightening his grip, strangling her.

She felt dizzy, she saw stars. She was out of oxygen. She writhed and twisted, trying to wiggle away. She tried to knee him but he weighed her down. She tried to move but couldn't.

Her strength started to desert her. Her arms fell backwards.

Her shoulder was agony. Her legs flopped open. She couldn't fight anymore. She couldn't form a single thought. He had choked the life from her.

"Good girl," Donator whispered, his hot breath in her face, his grimace an inch from her lips. He was killing her and he was enjoying it, she could see. Then she didn't want to see anymore.

Jill closed her eyes. She heard her own, final choking sounds, pathetic and fading.

Then, she heard nothing.

The last sound she heard on earth would be her own silence.

Chapter Sixty-four

Wham was the sound, then a loud *thud,* and a man's agonized shout.

Suddenly Jill was gasping for oxygen, her chest heaving, her body bucking up and down, her autonomic system kicking into gear, the organism trying to survive before its brain could process what had happened.

Victoria was standing at her feet with a two-by-four, and Donator wasn't on top of her anymore.

Jill gasped for breath, sputtering, trying to come back, wanting so much to stay alive. She rolled her head to the side, choking and coughing.

Donator lay still on the floor beside her, face up. Dead. His eyes stared fixedly at the exposed rafters. His mouth was open, his lips a shocked circle. His arms lay at his sides. Blood poured from a gaping wound in his temple, pooling on the concrete floor around his head, like an infernal halo.

"Jill? Jill?" Victoria dropped the two-by-four and rushed to her side.

Jill could feel her heartbeat pounding, her gasps wracking her body, and her lungs beginning to function. Her throat hurt so much, and she tried to speak, but couldn't.

Victoria bent over, gathered her into her arms, and hugged her close. Jill looked up into Victoria's eyes, which shone with a tenderness they'd never held before.

"Are you okay?" Victoria asked, with a weepy smile. "Are you hurt?"

Jill shook her head. She managed a smile. She couldn't say a word, but she knew what she thought, in her heart.

I was hurt, before this very moment. I've been hurting since the last time I saw you.

But I'm fine, now.

Chapter Sixty-five

Jill was only vaguely aware of everything that happened next as she faded in and out of consciousness, in and out of pain, in almost continuous motion. There were police, ambulances, then being strapped into a gurney with EMTs looking down at her with concern. They attached her to monitors, an IV bag, and at one point she cleared her aching throat enough to ask what she had to know:

"Can you call, about Rahul?"

"This is no time to worry about the office," the EMT answered, then they were hustling her out of the ambulance and to the ER nurses in their patterned scrubs, all of them looking down at her with even more concern as they whisked her inside through the automatic doors.

Jill kept saying, "Call somebody, please. Please, call about Rahul."

But they didn't listen, either.

Chapter Sixty-six

Jill sat up in the hospital bed, stitched, bandaged, medicated, and finally safe, in the company of real, ID-producing FBI agents, Special Agent Anthony Harrison and Special Agent Gordon Kavicka. The bullet wound to her shoulder wasn't deep, sutured with only a local anesthetic, and some pain meds had made her comfortable enough to meet with the FBI. The two special agents sat in chairs at the foot of her bed, dressed in dark suits, with striped ties and short haircuts. Victoria sat next to Jill on the bed in her torn jacket, and the cut on her cheek had been butterfly-bandaged.

"Can anybody tell me what just happened?" Jill asked, her throat aching. "Who was Donator, where is Cohz, and did somebody reach my office to ask about my patient, Rahul Choudhury?"

Victoria added, "Also, was my father murdered, and what did Brian have to do with it, if anything? Is he really undercover with the FBI, or were they lying to us?"

"Hold on, one question at a time." Special Agent Harrison raised a hand, his expression grim. He was a tall, lean man with smallish brown eyes, deep crow's feet, and a prominent cleft chin. "Dr. Farrow, we have a call in to your office, and we'll let you know about your patient as soon as they call back. Now, as for what happened, I'll answer as many of your questions as I can, on a need-to-know basis."

Jill felt taken aback. "We need to know everything. We were almost killed."

"Let us finish our jobs, then we'll explain everything. You have found your way into an ongoing federal investigation. We're within hours of making major arrests and indictments, and we cannot jeopardize anything. An investigation as large and important as this one requires countless man hours, budget dollars, and hard work."

Jill didn't interrupt him to say how much he sounded like the fake FBI agents.

"For now, we'll tell you only the information you need to know, and we expect you to treat the matter in complete confidence. Beyond this circle, we depend upon you to say nothing to any friends or neighbors, and explain your injuries by saying that you were in a car accident. Dr. Farrow, your fiancé, when he arrives, must also keep it confidential."

"He will." Jill hadn't spoken to Sam, but evidently the FBI had.

Victoria leaned over. "Special Agent Harrison, can you please tell me about Brian? Is he out of surgery, and is he one of you or not?"

Special Agent Harrison cleared his throat. "Brian works with us. He's awake, and we expect a full recovery."

"Thank God." Victoria brightened, and Jill touched her shoulder. "There's good news."

Victoria nodded. "But who is he, really? Is he even a lawyer?"

"I can't answer that, yet."

Jill thought back to the ER room, with the fake FBI agents. "Cohz and Donator knew he was undercover. How did they know?"

"I can't answer that, at this time."

"So who were Donator and Cohz and why did they try to kill us?"

"I can't answer that, either."

"Don't we have a need to know that?" Jill tried to keep her temper, but it wasn't easy. "What if Agent Cohz, or whoever he was, comes back to try to kill us? Or did you catch him?"

Special Agent Harrison hesitated. "Dr. Farrow, the man who told you he was Special Agent Cohz is dead."

"What? How?" Jill asked, shocked. "The EpiPen wouldn't have killed him, even in the carotid. It's only epinephrine."

"Apparently, he had a heart condition, and it caused a heart attack."

"Oh no." Jill flashed on the scene in the car. "I didn't know, he was so young. It wasn't supposed to kill him."

"We've already discussed this with the local authorities, and you won't be charged, of course. Either of you. It was self-defense."

Jill felt stunned. "But I'm a doctor."

"He would have killed you both without a second thought."

"Maybe, but that doesn't make it right, for me. I took an oath." Jill felt a wave of guilt, and Victoria took her hand.

"I killed a man today, too."

Jill looked over, feeling for her. "But you saved me."

"We saved each other," Victoria said, squeezing her hand. "We'll help each other through this, like you said. We'll get through it, together." She turned to Special Agent Harrison. "Was my father murdered?"

Special Agent Harrison pursed his lips. "I can't answer that. I'm sorry. You don't need to know that—"

"The hell I don't," Victoria snapped. "I *do* need to know that. My sister needs to know that. He's our *father.*"

"I'm sorry, but I can't share that information with you at this time." Special Agent Harrison glanced at Special Agent Kavicka, then back at Victoria. "When this is over, you'll see why."

Victoria squeezed Jill's hand. "I don't understand any of this. Why did my Dad have a double identity, and why was Brian undercover? Was it because of my Dad? Was Brian just pretending to be my friend?"

Special Agent Harrison cleared his throat. "Ms. Skyler, you can discuss that with Brian yourself, but not tonight. We need to debrief him."

Victoria turned to Jill, abruptly. "Oh, no, we didn't call Abby. Should we call her and tell her to come home?"

"No, not yet," Special Agent Harrison interjected. "She's safer out of the picture, and you must wait until after we've made the arrests to tell her anything."

Jill thought of Megan, stricken. "Is my daughter in danger? She's with a friend of mine."

"We know exactly where she is, and she's in no danger. We have a team stationed at the Feehans' house to protect her."

"How do you know where she is?" Then Jill realized something. "Have you been following me? Are you the ones with the black SUV?"

Special Agent Harrison shook his head, his lips a flat line. "Again, I can't explain that to you, at this time. When everything is resolved and things become public, all of your questions will be answered."

Jill couldn't take no for an answer, not after today. "Did Nina's husband really kill her? Or was she murdered by Cohz and Donator?"

"Again, after the grand jury meets and the indictments come down, I will meet with you and explain everything."

Jill felt sick at heart. "Did I lead them to Nina, can you tell me that? Did I get her and her husband killed?"

"Again, I can't answer."

Jill had too many questions that couldn't wait. "Let me tell you what I figured out, and maybe you can confirm or deny. My ex-husband, William Skyler, also known as Neil Straub, was getting inside information from Nina D'Orive about upcoming Pharmcen recalls and selling it to a man named Joe Zeptien, who sold the stock short and made a ton of money." Jill glanced over at Victoria, whose face was downcast, her emotions clearly in turmoil. "They did it on the Deferral and Riparin recalls and they were about to make a fortune on Memoril. But somehow it all fell apart. Why? Why kill anybody? How?"

"I won't confirm or deny. You don't need to know."

"But it's all in the laptop, oh, wait." Jill remembered, with a start. "The laptop and my notes are inside my car."

"Don't worry, we've already obtained the laptop. It took some doing, out of the wreck, and we think we can get it operating again."

"Good." Jill looked over at Victoria, but she sat slumped on the bed, crestfallen. Jill turned back to the FBI agents. "Special Agent Harrison, can't you tell us if William was murdered, and who did it and why? It may be a case to you, but it's Victoria's life, her family. She *needs* to know, in the truest sense of the word." Jill heard herself talking and realized that she was talking about herself, as well. "She's going to spend years trying to figure out who her father was. That process is healing, but if she doesn't know the truth, she can't heal. I know, I've lived it."

Special Agent Harrison paused, his dark eyes shifting to Victoria, his expression less guarded. "Ms. Skyler, I'll make you a promise. As soon as this is over, I'll explain everything. You lost your father, but there are other victims, and more potential for danger. Look at what happened today, to you both. Let us finish our job, and it will all become clear."

"Okay," Victoria said, after a moment.

Jill gave in, only reluctantly. "But what about our safety? Are you protecting us all?"

"Absolutely. We already have a team outside your house."

"How do we know that? Will we see them?"

"No, not if they're doing their job correctly. Trust me. We have you covered."

Suddenly there was a knock on the door, and a young FBI agent stuck his head inside the room. "Special Agent Harrison, sorry to interrupt you."

"What is it?" Special Agent Harrison turned to him.

"You wanted to know if a call came in about Dr. Farrow's patient, Rahul Choudhury." The young FBI agent held out an open cell phone. "This is it."

"Yes," Jill answered, her heart in her throat. "Please, let me have that phone."

Chapter Sixty-seven

"Is it someone from my office?" Jill held her out her hand and tried not to notice it was trembling.

"No, it's a woman," answered the young FBI agent. "She's crying, and she has an Indian accent, so it's hard to understand."

God, no. "Please give me the phone."

"Okay?" The young FBI agent looked at Special Agent Harrison, who nodded, annoyed.

"Give it to her, would you? It's her call." Special Agent Harrison rose and walked to the door, and Special Agent Kavicka did the same, following him. "Dr. Farrow, we'll leave and give you some privacy."

Victoria looked over. "Jill, should I go, too?"

"No, please, stay, it's okay." Jill took the phone. "Dr. Farrow speaking."

"Oh my God, oh my God," said a woman, talking fast, her voice choked with tears.

"Who is this?" Jill asked, stricken. "Who am I speaking to?"

"Oh my God, it's Arami, Rahul's auntie, oh my God, oh my God!"

Jill braced herself. "What happened to Rahul? Please, tell me."

"Rahul is at the hospital now, Padma didn't take the flight."

Arami cried happy tears. "He's in stable condition, now. He'll recover from his infection. He'll *live*."

"Thank God." Jill felt a gratitude and joy spreading through her very bloodstream, a sensation she couldn't medically explain.

"Yes, yes, Padma is with him, she just called me. My sister, her mother, is fine, too, in Mumbai."

"What happened? Did Rahul's grandfather reach Padma?"

"No, no, no one could reach her, she had turned her phone off, for the plane." Arami started to calm down, her words slowing and her tears subsiding. "Padma boarded the plane with Rahul and the boys. They were going to take off!"

"Who stopped them?"

"Someone went to the airport, they *drove* there. They got pulled over for a speeding ticket, then they got a *police escort*. They got Padma and the baby off the plane, right before it left for Mumbai."

"Who did that?"

"Your office manager, Sheryl."

"*Sheryl?*" Jill asked, astounded.

"She's wonderful woman, that Sheryl. A *wonderful* woman."

"She is?" Jill caught herself. "I mean, yes, she is."

"I must go, talk to you later. Thanks again, so much."

"Thanks for calling, and please tell Padma to call me, if she wants." Jill hung up just as there came a knock, on the door.

Chapter Sixty-eight

"Honey, are you all right?" Sam gathered Jill in his arms, and she hugged him back, her eyes brimming, her heart full of love.

"Yes, I'm fine."

"Don't cry. I'm here now, it's okay now." Sam held her close, and Steven stood behind him, looking like a mini-Sam, complete with thick hair, sharp blue eyes, tortoiseshell glasses, and tan Dockers.

"Thanks for coming home." Jill wiped her tears and got in control, and Sam released her, his pained gaze appraising her injuries.

"What did they do to my girl? My God, it looks like it hurts, so much."

"No, it's not too bad."

"I've got nothing left to kiss."

"My lips are fine," Jill blubbered, but the words weren't out before Sam gave her a soft, sweet kiss.

"I love you," he said softly.

"I love you, too." Jill realized suddenly that she hadn't introduced Victoria and Steven. "Victoria, this is Steven Becker. Steven, Victoria Skyler." She hesitated. "Stepson, meet ex-stepdaughter. Oh, whatever. Kids, meet each other."

Victoria smiled. "I'm not an ex-stepdaughter, I'm a stepdaughter."

Steven snorted. "And we're hardly kids."

Sam laughed. "You're both kids, to us. Forever." He turned to Jill, leaned over, and kissed her again. "Let's go home."

"Yes." Jill thought they were the sweetest words ever. "Let's."

"Victoria?" Sam straightened up, turning to her. "You're coming home with us, I hope. We can all have dinner and try to decompress. I'm sure Megan would love to see you again."

Jill felt tears brimming again. She appreciated that Sam made the offer, but she was old enough to know they were still at an impasse. Sam would feel the same way, and it remained to be seen if they could agree on how to make a new family. If they couldn't, there wasn't going to be a wedding. Jill had come to understand that love didn't answer the question of whether they should marry, but merely asked it. Love wasn't the end, but the beginning.

Victoria was beaming at Sam. "Thanks, but what do I do about school? I have class tomorrow."

"I think we can get you a doctor's note," Sam answered, with a crooked smile, then looked down at Jill.

"Done," she said, smiling back. She felt an overwhelming yearning to see Megan again and get everybody safe under one roof, her roof.

On second thought, her greatest wish would be that someday, it would be *their* roof.

Chapter Sixty-nine

Jill was cleaning up after take-out pizza, in the kitchen with Sam, Steven, and Victoria, all of them waiting for Katie to bring Megan home. It was raining hard outside, another spring storm, making Beef shudder on his bed. Victoria had showered and changed into an old T-shirt and sweatpants that belonged to Megan, and Jill had on a pink cotton sweater, jeans, and clogs. Except for the bruises, bandages, and pain meds, she felt like Mom again.

"Mom?" Megan called from the entrance hall, then entered the kitchen in her yellow sweats, gasping when she saw Jill's face. "Mom! What happened to you? Your eye and forehead? Mom, oh my God!"

"Come here, I'm fine." Jill smiled, opening her arms for Megan, who came running to her like when she was a little girl.

"Are you okay?" Megan hugged her tight. "What happened? Katie said it wasn't that bad, but it is. You look like you got really hurt."

"I'm fine, and so is Victoria. We had a long day, but now it's over."

"Nice face, Jill," Katie said with a smile, coming into the room. She met Jill's eye, and in one look, told her that she loved her.

"Back at you." Jill smiled. She had already told Katie everything on the phone. Not even the FBI could come between best friends.

"Hello and good-bye, all." Katie waved to everyone. "I gotta go. Much love!"

"Bye and thanks, honey." Jill kissed the top of Megan's head as Katie left. "Want some pizza? I can microwave it."

"No, I ate." Megan looked up, shaken. "Nothing can ever happen to you, Mom."

"It won't." Jill knew what she meant. "I love you."

"I love you, too. So what happened? This is so weird! It's like everything's gone crazy all of a sudden."

"Go and sit." Jill let her go, and Megan went to her stool at the kitchen island, setting down her cell phone. Sam and Steven stood by the counter, and Victoria sat next to Megan on the island.

"Megan, it's so good to see you," Victoria said, giving Megan a hug. "I missed you."

"I missed you, too." Megan smiled, worriedly. "Does your head hurt? Did you get stitches? This is so random. Jeez!"

"I'm fine. We both are."

"Mom?" Megan turned back as her phone chimed a text alert, but she ignored it. "What happened to you guys? Tell me, I can't even deal!"

"The bottom line is that Victoria and I met up with some criminal types, and we got a little hurt, but we're fine."

"What criminal types? Did they steal from you, like you were mugged?"

"No. It was about William, but I'm not sure how yet." Jill poured Megan a glass of water and set it down in front of her. "The police know all about it, and we'll know more in a few days."

"Did somebody kill William?" Megan asked, then seemed to stiffen, bracing herself for the answer.

"Honestly, I don't know. The police will tell us as soon as they can."

"Where's Abby? Why isn't she home? Does she know?"

"No, and she'll be home soon."

"Jeez." Megan turned to Victoria, touching her arm. "I know you feel sad about your Dad. I'm sorry."

"Thanks, and I'm sorry about the way I behaved at the memorial service. I know you loved him, too. We're in this together, now." Victoria offered her hand, and Megan accepted it, with a smile. Her cell phone chimed again, but she still ignored it.

"I love you, Vick."

"I love you, too, Mega."

Jill watched them, touched. "One last thing, Megan. We have to keep this a secret. If anybody asks, we have to pretend that I was in a car accident and that's how I got hurt. Don't go into school tomorrow, and I'll write you a note."

"I have a meet this weekend, on Saturday, but maybe we shouldn't go." Megan's brow furrowed suddenly, and Jill thought her reaction was strange.

"No, we can go. Don't you want to? You've never missed a meet."

Megan hesitated. "Mom, there's something I have to tell you." Her phone chimed again, but she ignored it again. "You can't do anything about it, though. Anything you do will only make it worse."

"Okay," Jill said, surprised. "Tell me what happened."

"That boy I liked from swim club, Jake? He asked me to send him a picture of myself, so he could show his friends at his school. He said I was his *girlfriend*." Megan picked up her water glass and took a gulp. "So I sent him a normal picture that Courtney took of me, but he photoshopped it to make it look like I was naked, like I sexted it to him."

Jill felt anger flare, but kept a lid on it. "How did he do that?"

"He cut out my head and put it on a naked body and he sent it to all the guys on the boys team, and then all the girls got it, and now the whole club thinks I'm a slut."

"No, they don't, honey." Jill felt terrible for her. "No one thinks that."

Victoria added, "What a douche."

"I know, right?" Megan turned to Victoria. "Sorry, I feel so bad for you, about your Dad, and I have all this dumb stuff going on. It's not as important, and I'm just so, well, lame."

"No, you're not lame at all." Victoria smoothed back Megan's hair. "I can't believe he did that. We're in this together, right? We just said."

Megan looked back at Jill. "Mom, I'm too embarrassed to go to the meet because everybody knows. It's a big, big mess, and I can't even go back to the team. And they need me to win."

Jill was trying to get the facts. "Wait. When did this happen?"

"Sunday, right before the meet. I think that's why I had the panic attack, but I just didn't want to tell you. I knew you'd want to call his parents or Coach Stash, and that would make everything worse. I'm sorry, I know you were all worried about me."

Jill blinked. She had assumed the panic attack was because of William's death, Abby's reappearance, and her own absence, but she had misdiagnosed her own daughter.

"What do I do, Mom? I can't go to the meet, and I can't *not* go to the meet."

"I can't talk to Coach Stash?"

"No, you can't. It's embarrassing. The more you do, the more it's a bigger deal, and the naked picture will go everywhere and everyone will think I'm a *total* slut."

Jill cringed for her. "But if I call his school—"

"No! That only makes me look dumber, don't you see?"

"Yes," Jill answered, because she did, finally. It was a no-win.

"I have to deal with it myself, and I hate myself for hiding and running away. It *sucks, I suck*! I'm the best swimmer on the team and I almost *drowned* because I'm so *stupid and lame.* I don't want to be *that girl* anymore!"

"You're not that girl, honey."

"Yes, I *am*!" Suddenly Megan jumped to her feet, almost knocking over the stool, and before anyone knew what she was doing, she ran out of the kitchen. Beef lifted his head from his paws, and Jill started to go after her, but Victoria rose and put a hand on her arm.

"Jill, wait. Let me go. No offense, but sometimes you don't need a mother. Sometimes you just need a friend."

"You're right. Go." Jill knew it was true, and Victoria left the kitchen and hurried upstairs.

Sam came over to Jill and embraced her, gently. "This, too, shall pass," he said, his voice deep and soft at her ear.

Jill was about to respond when she heard someone calling her outside, in the storm. She looked up at Sam, wondering. "Do you hear that?"

"What?" he asked, but Beef was already up and scampering to the front door, his toenails clicking on the hardwood floor.

"You know who that sounds like?" Jill let Sam go and hurried from the kitchen just as the doorbell rang. Sam and Steven were right behind her, and she opened the door wide.

Standing at the threshold was Abby, next to Special Agent Harrison, who held a pet carrier.

"Abby!" Jill cried, throwing open her arms.

Chapter Seventy

Jill, Victoria, and Megan embraced Abby as Beef ran around them all in excitement and the entrance hall became a whorl of hugs, wet eyes, and wagging tails. A smiling Sam and Steve stood wisely off to the side, next to Special Agent Harrison, who set down the pet carrier on the floor.

"I'm so happy to see you all again," Abby said, with a teary grin. "I missed you guys!"

"We missed you, too." Jill grinned, but she was bewildered. "What are you doing with Special Agent Harrison? Did he pick you up at the airport?"

"No, he's my new best friend, along with Special Agents Tella, Leonard, and Palumbo." Abby counted off on her fingers. "I've been living with FBI agents for the past week."

"*Real* FBI agents?" Megan's eyes popped. "Like on TV?"

"Better," Abby answered. "They're women FBI agents and they even make quilts, for fun. They call themselves the Needle & Gun Club, and they meet every Monday night. How cool is that?"

"What? Why?" Victoria asked, confused, and Special Agent Harrison turned to Jill.

"We picked Abby up for her own protection. We've had her in

a safe house with some of our female agents." Special Agent Harrison paused, glancing at Megan. "This may not be the right time for details, but I will fill you in."

Abby turned to Victoria. "I'm sorry, you were really worried about me, weren't you?"

"Of course I was." Victoria's eyes brimmed, too. "I love you, you idiot."

Jill was slowly coming up to speed. "Abby, does this mean you weren't in L.A.? And there's no Brandon?"

"Right." Abby nodded. "None of that was true. But you believed it, right?"

"Yes," Jill answered, secretly relieved.

Victoria nodded. "Totally."

Abby pursed her lips. "I knew what you'd expect to hear, so I said it, and you know what? It taught me something. I don't want to be like that anymore."

"Aw, Abby." Victoria embraced Abby again, and Jill held Megan close to her side.

"Anyway," Abby said, "know what I decided? I'm going back to college, to study criminology. I really loved the agents, and it might be weird to say now, but I think I'm good at it."

"That's wonderful, honey." Jill felt bittersweet, sensing why Abby had made that choice. "I'm so proud of you."

Sam came over, putting his arm around Abby. "Great idea, kid. If there's any way we can help you, let us know. We're here for you."

"Thanks, Sam." Abby grinned. "You guys are the best, and I think I'll be fine."

Victoria smiled. "Of course you will. We already decided we're all going to be fine. We have each other."

"Right," Jill added. "Family is forever, and so are pets." She gestured to the pet carrier. "And that, I bet, is Pickles. I knew it was strange that you didn't mention him."

"Oh, I almost forgot!" Abby bent down and opened the wire door, and out of the carrier flew an adorable corgi puppy, scampering around like a bunny rabbit out of hell. Everybody laughed as Beef gave chase, barking.

"Wait, don't I know that puppy?" Jill asked, astonished. "It looks like Nina D'Orive's dog."

"It is." Special Agent Harrison nodded. "We were on the scene that night, and I noticed the puppy. The locals wanted to bring it to a shelter, but I knew my wife would love it, except that our son turned out to be allergic."

Abby smiled, sadly. "So I took her, and I call her Hobo, short for Hoboken. I named her in memory of Nina."

"Way to go." Jill patted Abby on the back, touched. "I'm proud of you."

"Thanks. Now here's Pickles." Abby went over to the carrier, cooing, and just then an orange tabby crept out, meowed loudly, and bounded off. "Great. Good-bye, Pickles."

Special Agent Harrison turned to Victoria. "Ms. Skyler, I made you a promise that I'd answer your questions, and I always keep my promises."

"I remember." Victoria turned to him, her smile vanishing. "I'm ready, if you are."

"Let's all go have that talk, shall we, folks?"

Chapter Seventy-one

A thunderstorm raged outside, but Jill, Sam, Victoria, Abby, and Steven were safe and warm, if not exactly happy, in the family room, gathering on soft couches and chairs with Special Agent Harrison, watching the eleven o'clock news. The screen showed men in suits being led in handcuffs from an office building on Wall Street.

The voiceover was saying, "The FBI made arrests late today in Operation Hedge Clippers, for alleged acts of insider trading and securities fraud by an individual and a manager at Piper, Flanagan, one of the largest hedge funds on Wall Street. The Justice Department says that the indictments will begin to clean up illegalities on Wall Street, in the wake of the Galleon Group case and wave of Occupy Wall Street protests. And in other news . . ."

"Okay, we've seen this twice now." Jill aimed the remote to turn off the TV and put her arm around Megan, who sat with her, Victoria, and Abby on the couch. "Special Agent Harrison, can you explain what's going on?"

"Of course." Special Agent Harrison straightened up. "Before I begin, you asked me to confirm or deny your theory in the hospital, and now I can confirm it. You didn't have the whole picture, but you had a piece. Nice work, for a doctor."

Sam winked. "That's my girl."

Abby smiled. "She's Dr. Watson."

Megan looked up at Jill, her eyes shining. "Wow, Mom."

Jill waved it off with a smile. She hardly felt like celebrating, after all the people who had died, including William.

Special Agent Harrison continued, "Operation Hedge Clippers started a few years ago, when the SEC notified us that Piper, Flanagan was showing a suspicious trading pattern, short-selling Pharmcen stock before recalls of two drugs, Deferral and Riparin. We investigated whether Piper, Flanagan was engaging in insider trading, and we learned that the trades in question were made by the same fund manager, Skip Priam, who was indicted today. We investigated and were able to gather sufficient evidence that Priam was trading on the information that he bought from Joe Zeptien."

Jill asked, "Was Zeptien a drug rep?"

"No, he's a former stockbroker." Special Agent Harrison turned to Victoria. "We then were able to connect Zeptien to your father, as a result of visual surveillance at Zeptien's homes and electronic surveillance on Zeptien's cell phone. We gathered evidence that Zeptien was buying the inside information from your father, whom he first knew as Neil Straub. Zeptien was paying your father with money he got from Skip Priam."

Only Abby seemed calm, maybe because she had been living with the truth. Victoria's eyes glistened, and Megan remained quiet, her lips over her braces. Jill suspected that Megan wasn't understanding much, except that it was bad for William.

Victoria shook her head. "Our Dad really did this? So it's true?"

"Yes. You may be wondering why your father didn't trade on the information himself, and we believe the answer is, because he wouldn't have made as much money that way, as he obviously lacked the capital that a hedge fund can commit, and also, it wouldn't have been possible to hide it from the IRS." Special Agent Harrison paused. "In addition, by merely selling information, your father wasn't technically in violation of federal securities laws, because insider trading is only unlawful if the trader is a fiduciary. The classic case, as you may have learned in law school, is of someone overhearing a tip in a bathroom. The listener can trade on that information, legally."

Victoria nodded, and so did Jill.

Special Agent Harrison shifted in his red-checked chair. "We were uncertain, however, as to how your father was obtaining the information, and we didn't as yet have his New York apartment under surveillance. We needed to learn more, so we placed Brian as a securities lawyer at Creed & Whitstone, because it represents Piper, Flanagan, and at the bar downtown that night, in order to meet you, Victoria."

Victoria looked stricken, her hands clenched together in her lap. "Why me? I'm not the one who lived with Dad. Why not Abby?"

"Frankly, Abby already had a boyfriend, at the time. You introduced Brian to your father, and they began to meet, without your knowledge, and they developed a relationship."

"Why did my Dad do that?" Victoria shook her head, dazed.

"Your father wanted to expand. He knew that Pharmcen could only have so many drug recalls, and he told Brian that he wanted to find other hedge funds to which he could sell inside information about other drug companies." Special Agent Harrison tempered his tone, knowing he was on difficult emotional ground. "Nor did your father want to be tied to Zeptien. The two men disliked each other, and we know this because we have Zeptien telling Priam as much. Zeptien told Priam that he suspected your father would eventually go off on his own and find other middlemen and other hedge funds."

"You know that by wiretap, on Zeptien's phone?" Victoria asked.

"Yes. So Brian offered to serve as the new middleman and let your father know that he had significant contacts at other hedge funds and investment banking houses."

Jill could imagine how much the prospect would appeal to William, and she realized that he wasn't evil incarnate. That gave him too much credit, and power. Ultimately, he was merely an opportunist, and he denied the harm that he caused as a result.

Special Agent Harrison continued, speaking mainly to Victoria, "That plan would have cut out Joe Zeptien, and we believe he may have found out about it, or that the friction between the men became too much. We know Zeptien feared losing control of your father, whom he viewed as a potential loose end, and we believe Zeptien murdered your father." Special Agent Harrison paused, and the family room went silent. "Unfortunately, we can't prove that, so we didn't include that in the indictment. We didn't have your father's house in Philadelphia under visual surveillance that day, or from the start. Your father did an excellent job keeping his identities separate, and our best information is that even Joe Zeptien didn't know he was William Skyler, until a little over a year ago, which is how we learned it."

"But how could you not know that?" Victoria gestured to Jill. "She figured it out in a week."

Special Agent Harrison leaned forward. "You have to understand the way we really work. Like any government agency, we're tasked with a mission, in this case, to investigate a Wall Street hedge fund. We have resources and budgets to expend toward that mission, but they're not infinite. On the contrary, they're limited, especially now, in view of the sluggish economy and the demands of domestic terrorism. So we direct all of our resources toward our mission. Piper, Flanagan was our priority and we started there. We maintained visual surveillance on Skip Priam's office and his homes in the Hamptons and Greenwich, Connecticut, as well as on Joe Zeptien's office in New York and his homes in north and south Jersey."

Jill understood. The FBI couldn't be everywhere at once, but it wouldn't be easy to explain that to Victoria.

Victoria's eyes narrowed. "So my Dad falls through the cracks? And Zeptien gets away with murder?"

"No, not at all." Special Agent Harrison frowned. "Joe Zeptien is going to jail for a long, long time. Our case against him for insider trading and tax evasion is rock solid. Believe me, he'll be punished, and we don't need to make a deal with him, so we won't."

Abby turned to Victoria, shaking her head. "He's right, Victoria. Zeptien will rot in jail, and that's all I care about. I wish I knew how he did it, but I saw how hard the FBI works, with my own eyes."

Sam looked over, from his chair. "It's like those Mafia cases, isn't it? The government doesn't charge mobsters with murder, it charges them with tax evasion. Either way, they're in jail for decades."

"Yes, exactly." Special Agent Harrison turned to Victoria again. "In addition, you have to put this in a proper time frame. Your father was killed only a week ago. No murder case gets put together that quickly, even if we weren't involved. In fact, we did liase with the Philadelphia police, and they still don't believe it was a homicide."

Victoria nodded, mulling it over. "Okay, I guess I see your point."

Jill felt the same way as Victoria, vaguely unsatisfied, but she kept that to herself. "Special Agent Harrison, I have a different question. Did Zeptien kill Nina and her husband, or did Nina's husband really do it?"

"Neither," Special Agent Harrison answered. "We believe that Zeptien and Skip Priam hired contract killers to do it, named Richard Deyaz and John Hutcheson. Deyaz and Hutcheson were the ones who posed as Special Agents Donator and Cohz."

Victoria glanced over at Jill but said nothing, undoubtedly for Megan's sake.

Jill turned to Special Agent Harrison. "Did I lead them to Nina?"

Special Agent Harrison shook his head. "No, they already suspected she was the source. We knew it, too, by that point. It took us some time, because your ex-husband dated a number of women as Neil Straub, and he and Ms. D'Orive had an interest in keeping their relationship under wraps."

Jill thought that made sense. "Did you indict Zeptien and Priam for those murders?"

"No, to be precise, the indictment against them would have been for conspiracy to solicit, because they didn't commit the murders themselves. But, again, we kept the indictment as clean as possible, with only the insider-trading allegations, and of course, Deyaz and Hutcheson are dead."

"Who was following me, all this time?"

"Deyaz and Hutcheson, and we were, too. That's why we all came together today, in Parkertowne. We think Deyaz was following you in a black SUV until you spotted him in Manhattan, then we believe he switched vehicles."

Jill masked her shudder. "Why follow me, at all?"

"We theorize that Zeptien got wind that Abby was asking questions about her father's death. We believe that he thought she was a loose end, so he hired Deyaz and Hutcheson to follow her. When she came to your house, they started to follow you. They were together in the silver car that tried to run you off the road."

Jill was processing the information. "Deyaz and Hutchison told us that Brian was undercover. How did they know that?"

"They saw him. Brian blew his cover to save you, and that's why we indicted so quickly tonight, before Piper, Flanagan started erasing computer files and shredding documents. The Bureau tends to move slowly, like any government agency. We at the Philadelphia office call it Eastern District time." Special Agent Harrison smiled, briefly. "We were going to take Mr. Skyler's computer when we picked up Abby, but she had already given it to you. You actually helped us, though you were at great risk."

Megan nestled against Jill's side, and Jill gave her a reassuring pat.

"Piper, Flanagan made $75 million short-selling Pharmcen stock over the past three years. If Skip Priam decides to cooperate, which we believe he will, we'll likely issue an indictment against the top dogs at Piper, Flanagan." Special Agent Harrison leaned back in a final way, as if he were about to conclude. "We're trying to clean up Wall Street, to bolster the nation's economy and get the public investing again. That's what Operation Hedge Clippers was about, from day one."

Victoria raised her hand half-way, almost as if she were in class. "I have a last question. Did Brian pretend to be my friend? Because of my Dad? Is that the way you work, undercover?"

Special Agent Harrison puckered his lower lip, slightly. "Brian's job was to get close to your father, but his friendship with you was genuine. He felt conflicted about having to deceive you, and he'll explain that to you. You can visit him tomorrow in the hospital, if you wish."

"But who is he, really? Is he even a lawyer?"

"Yes, he is, and it aided us immeasurably in this operation. His real name is Brian Prendergast. We usually choose a name close to the original, in case he gets recognized on the street."

Abby looked over at Victoria with a sly smile. "And guess what? He doesn't really have a girlfriend in Paris. They made that up, because he wasn't allowed to get in a relationship with you."

"Oh, *there's* a silver lining." Victoria rolled her eyes. "Brian's a liar, but he's single. Count me out." She returned her attention to Special Agent Harrison. "Why did my Dad have a double identity?"

"I'll tell you what I know, because you may find it some comfort." Special Agent Harrison's expression softened. "He told Brian that he wanted to protect you and your sister, in case things went wrong. He wanted you completely screened off from trouble. He loved you both and he didn't want you in danger."

Victoria's face fell, and Jill got a lump in her aching throat, not knowing if it were true but sad just the same. For a minute, nobody said anything, giving William a moment of silence, all of them lost in his or her own thoughts. Megan looked down, playing with her fingers, and Victoria sat motionless, her eyes filming.

Sam was the one who broke the silence. "We'll help each other through this, as a family. That's *my* promise," he said, simply.

Chapter Seventy-two

Jill was in her nightshirt, listening at their bedroom door, which she'd cracked open so she could hear what was going on in Megan's room. Victoria and Abby were in there with Megan, and the girls hadn't emerged except to let Beef join them. Jill couldn't help but wonder what was going on.

"Honey, they're fine." Sam was in bed, reading, his glasses perched at the end of his nose.

"But what are they doing in there?"

"I think they're dealing with it, and they'll be fine."

"This is the week from hell, for Megan." Jill stayed at the door. "And I haven't been the most attentive mother."

"Megan knows you love her."

"Now she's the one who needs triage." Jill felt achy, bruised, and tired. "I can't believe I was wrong about her panic attack. I blew that, big-time."

"No, it was all of a piece. She had everything going on, all at once. The text photo was only a part of it."

"Not to a thirteen-year-old."

"Come here, love. Come to bed." Sam took off his glasses and set them and his book on the nighttable, and Jill shut the door, went to bed, and slipped under the covers, lying on her good side.

Sam reached for her, stroking her arm. "How do you feel? Does your eye still hurt?"

"A little." Jill edged over, giving him a kiss, then another, sweeter one. "I love you."

"I love you, too, and I have something to say." Sam met her eye, growing serious, and Jill sensed it was time for their reckoning.

"I guess we have to figure this out, huh?"

"Yes, and one of us already has."

"Okay, go ahead," Jill said, trying not to be nervous.

"I'm sorry I acted like a fool. It's not that I don't want the kids, it's that I wanted more of you. You see the difference?"

"Yes." Jill felt touched. "I'm sorry, too. I should have talked to you more. I don't want it to be about the kids twenty-four/seven, either. I really don't." She gestured down the hall. "I'm not listening at Megan's door, for example. That would be *crazy*."

Sam laughed. "Good point. That's progress."

"See?" Jill smiled, then it faded, and it was her turn to get serious. "But what are we going to do about Abby and Victoria? You see them, they're down the hall, one door from Steven, and I like it. I *love* it. All of us, under the same roof. This is going to happen, from time to time, if I have things my way. What do you say?"

"You know what, I'm fine with it."

Jill scoffed. "Come on. Really?"

"Really." Sam nodded, apparently happily. "I'm fine with it now. I'm educable, for an academic."

"What changed your mind?"

"A few things. First, losing you. It scared me, to think about losing you. It put everything in perspective. All the fighting, and all the disagreements, they're stupid. Life is short. Too short." Sam touched her cheek. "And second, and more importantly, I finally understood what you had been saying about Abby."

"How so?"

"Remember when you said that if something happened to me, and Steven needed you, what would I want you to do?"

"Yes."

"Well, that wasn't the hypothetical that convinced me. The hypothetical that convinced me just happened." Sam paused, his jaw working, and even the trace of a smile vanished. "Because if something happened to you, if I lost you, I realized that I would never stop being there for Megan. I realized that I'd always love her and I'd always feel like her father. No matter what, no matter who. Forever. I'm *hers*."

Jill could have cried with happiness. "Sam, that's lovely."

"You taught me. Of course, you almost had to get killed to teach me, but I came around." Sam smiled, touching her face. "So. Again. Will you marry me?"

"Yes. Please." Jill kissed him softly.

"Good. Thank God that's settled. I can't function. You should've seen me, in Cleveland. Worst paper I ever gave."

"I doubt it."

"No, truly. Lee put me on the plane. He practically said, good riddance."

Jill laughed.

"Now, let's get some rest. You must be exhausted. I'll get the lamp." Sam reached over and switched it off, so the bedroom was dark and still. The only light came from the moon outside the open windows, and a cool breeze ruffled the sheers. The rain had stopped, having washed the world, and the air smelled fresh, clean, and most of all, like home.

"This is nice." Jill shifted over and fitted her body to his side, finally exhaling.

"It sure is. We made it. We *survived*."

"Yes, and all that is over now."

"Yes it is, all over now," Sam repeated, and Jill lay still while he fell asleep, not five minutes later.

But she didn't fall asleep. She couldn't. Her head pounded, her throat ached. Her shoulder bandage made it hard to get comfortable. She tossed and turned, but couldn't shut out her thoughts. So much had happened in such a short time, and her mind crackled as if it were electrified. She'd been in two different ERs in one day, as a patient, not a doctor. And she'd quit her job at Pembey Family.

I'm not an employee, I'm a doctor.

Jill didn't regret her words, rash as they were. Even if Pembey wanted her back, she wasn't going. She was already thinking she might try to get a job in an ER at a children's hospital. She could put her triage mentality to good use there, and maybe she'd work full-time, now that Megan was older. Maybe the next chapter of her life wouldn't be so bad. The future could be better than the past. Maybe, after all, there was a forever.

She turned over but still couldn't sleep, so she got up and went downstairs. The house was dark and quiet, except for the sound of crickets and bats coming through the screens. Jill turned on the kitchen lights, went to her laptop, sat down, and moved the mouse to wake it up. Its bright screen light made her squint, but her eyes adjusted, and it was still open to the last document she'd worked on, the file she'd made of her notes from William's laptop. She'd copied all of his files, too.

Nice work, for a doctor.

Jill couldn't feel pleased with herself, not after such a bitter-sweet day. After all the people who died, and at the end of the day, the ones she felt sorriest for were the girls. Victoria would need time to understand her father, and Abby had her work cut out for her, starting over in school. Jill thought of Megan, with a pang. They would have a lot more conversations before she understood what had happened, and Jill felt terrible for being wrong about her panic attack. It's true that more than one thing could have caused it, but she'd lost touch with Megan this week. She'd been guilty of diagnosis momentum, with her own daughter.

Jill mulled over the events of the day. The only bright spot was Rahul. That hadn't been an easy diagnosis, and she thanked God that she hadn't stopped asking what was behind Rahul's ear infections. That's where the truth lay. Behind. Under. Hidden.

Jill's gaze fell on her laptop screen, aglow with the all the files William had made, about tons of drugs. He had made tons of money, too, but he wanted more, and that had gotten him killed. She eyed the screen. Something felt wrong, but she couldn't put her finger on it. And she found herself wondering.

What's behind this?

Chapter Seventy-three

"Sam, wake up," Jill whispered, giving him a quick kiss on his grizzled cheek. She'd showered and dressed as if on fire, then made him a mug of black coffee, and its aroma scented the air. "Wake up, I have something to tell you."

"What?" Sam shifted over, groggy. "What's got into you?" He glanced at the clock, its digital numbers glowing in the dim bedroom. "Babe, it's five o'clock in the morning."

"I know." Jill rubbed his back in the thin T-shirt. It was still dark outside, but dawn was on the way and there was no time to lose. "We have to hurry. We have to leave."

"Okay, okay." Sam edged up in bed, blinking, his hair ruffled. "What's happening?"

"I figured out something. The diagnosis is wrong." Jill switched on the lamp, and Sam squinted against the light, putting up a hand to shield his eyes.

"What are you talking about?"

"We stopped asking, what's behind this? We mistook the first answer for the right answer."

"What diagnosis? Wrong about what?"

"Okay, well, here goes." Jill handed him his coffee and launched into telling him what she'd figured out last night, and he drained his cup while she finished. "And now that I know the truth, I'm going to do something about it. This morning. Are you with me?"

Sam blinked. "You really want to do this?"

"Yes. Absolutely."

"Then I'm with you, all the way." Sam smiled, shaking his head. "I figured us out, you know. I'm a thinker, and you're a doer."

"So what are you waiting for?" Jill smiled back. "*Do!*"

Sam threw off the covers, and Jill ran for his clothes.

Chapter Seventy-four

Jill approached the Pharmcen building, walked through the glass entrance, and strode past the security desk to the granite reception banquette, with its phones and monitor screens. The pretty young receptionist was the same one as yesterday, and she hung up the phone, recognizing Jill.

"May I help you?" she asked, already wary.

"Yes, hello, I don't need an appointment, but I have some documents for Elliott Horton." Jill handed over a manila envelope, which contained copies of a few of William's emails to himself, without the identifying information. "Can you get these to him, as soon as possible?"

"Yes," the receptionist answered, but her attention shifted to the right, and Jill guessed that the security guard was coming up from behind, so she turned around and saw that he was the same one, too, with the funny soul patch.

"Hello, Barry," Jill said, with a smile.

"How may I help you today, Miss?" he asked, coldly.

"I'd appreciate it if somebody could take these documents to Elliott Horton."

"Documents?" The guard eyed the envelope with suspicion. "What kind of documents?"

"It's only paper, and he'll want to see it." Jill lifted the flap, showing him. "Okay?"

"Fine." The guard nodded at the receptionist, who extended a hand, and Jill gave her the envelope.

"Thanks so much. Please give those to Elliott as soon as possible. I'll be leaving now." Jill turned and walked to the entrance, with the security guard on her heels. He stood watch outside the building while she went to Sam's Lexus, got inside, and drove away.

She had reached the first traffic light on Weehawk Boulevard before her cell phone rang. She checked the screen. She didn't recognize the number, but she knew exactly who was calling her.

"Hello, Elliott," Jill answered, bracing herself.

Chapter Seventy-five

Jill waited on a wooden bench in the corporate park behind Pharmcen, with her purse and BlackBerry beside her. The park was beautiful and quiet, a several-acre tract of open space for company picnics and softball games, bordered by willow trees, boxwood, and hedges. There was a man-made pond on the left, and a mallard duck landed on the pumped-in water, its wings extended, showing bright blue stripes. The only other people in the park were a young man and a woman a few benches away, their heads bent together.

Jill straightened up when she spotted Elliott Horton entering the park. He came stalking toward her across the grass, his head down and his thin, white-blond hair catching the sunlight. He looked to be in his forties, tall and skinny, in a white oxford shirt and dark blue pants, and he was frowning deeply. He hadn't even reached Jill before he started firing questions at her.

"Is this some kind of joke?" Elliot's voice was on the high side, and his diction precise. "Who are you and where did you get that information?"

"Sit down and I'll explain."

Elliott remained standing. "That information is confidential, the property of Pharmcen. It's a massive breach of company security."

"Yes it is." Jill thought a minute. "Yet you came to meet me alone, and it couldn't have been easy to get away this morning, with Pharmcen in the news. The government indicted the biggest hedge fund on Wall Street last night, for insider trading in Pharmcen stock, specifically with respect to recalls. I would think somebody would want to interview you." Jill cocked her head. "Come to think of it, how did you get away?"

"Our PR department handles all that, and I didn't think this would take long. Now who are you, and where did you get that information?"

"Oh, I guess I was wrong. I was thinking that your bosses and maybe some security types told you to come out and meet me, to see what I wanted."

"No, not at all." Elliott's eyes widened slightly, a wan blue. His skin was as pale as a lab rat's. "Now answer my question. Who are you, and how did you get our data?"

"My name is Jill Farrow, and my ex-husband was William Skyler, who was Nina D'Orive's lover. That's how I got the data, from my ex's laptop. You might not know who I am, but your bosses do. I've been to Pharmcen twice this week, I talked to the security guard both times. Barry Whatever, with the soul patch." Jill met Elliott's eye. "Your bosses aren't leveling with you. They're playing you. They know who I am. You're the only one who doesn't, and oddly, I'm the only one on your side."

"I don't know what you're talking about." Elliott lowered himself onto the bench, his bony fingers linked in his lap.

"You know, somebody's going to have to take the fall for what just happened. Poor Nina passed on some very valuable information, and you were her boss. You even promoted her to VP." Jill rested her bandaged hand on the back of the bench. "I know it's not fair to blame you. You oversee fifty employees in Pharmacovigilance, and you can't be accountable for everyone."

"How do you know all this?"

"They will ruin you, Elliott. Not in the foreseeable future, while they still need you. But in the end, you'll get fired, and you'll have a helluva time getting a job anywhere else, given the scandal. I know that part, I lived that part."

"What do you want?"

Jill could see he was choosing his words carefully. "First, let me tell you how I figured out what was really going on. My ex's scheme started about three years ago, with Deferral. How'd that sell, by the way, before it was recalled?"

"None of your business."

"Okay, I'll tell you. It sold well. I saw online, it was used by two million allergy sufferers in the U.S. alone. My ex also sold information about Riparin, a diuretic that interacts with enzymes in the digestive track. How'd that sell, about the same?" Jill didn't wait for confirmation that she wouldn't get. "Both Deferral and Riparin had about the same number of complaints, and they were re-called."

"How do you know that?" Elliott raked his thinning hair. "The number of complaints per drug isn't public information."

"I know. My ex got the raw data from Nina. I gave you only some of it, like an appetizer."

"That can't be true." Elliott shook his head, and filaments of his fair hair caught the sun.

"It is. You may have noticed that none of the raw data I gave you is in the federal indictment. The government doesn't know it yet. That's why I said I'm on your side." Jill shifted toward him. "Now, as I was saying, the next drug up is Memoril, but now, there's a twist."

"What's the twist?"

"Correct my facts, because all I had to go on was the Internet. Memoril is a new Alzheimer's drug, and about five million people in the U.S. have Alzheimer's. Other major diseases like stroke, breast cancer, prostate cancer, even AIDS, they're all on the de-crease. But not Alzheimer's. It's up 66 percent."

"Yes, I know all that. Alzheimer's is huge."

Jill winced at his callousness, but wasn't surprised. "Memoril was approved a year ago, and it has great potential, given that there are so few drugs like it on the market. I even knew a woman at my old group, Mary Fitzmartin. She was on Memoril, with good results."

"What's your point?"

"I studied the data that Nina was supplying my ex, and I found the same proportion of complaints for Memoril as for Deferral and Riparin. In fact, the men who were indicted were waiting for Memoril to get recalled or withdrawn, but it wasn't, and I know why." Jill met his eye, calmly. "Pharmcen isn't reporting those complaints to the FDA. They're deep-sixing them. They're covering them up to keep a very lucrative Alzheimer's drug on the market."

Elliott's eyelids fluttered. "That's not true."

"Oh, please. I'm on your side, Elliott. The government believes that those Wall Street types killed my ex because he was trying to expand to other hedge funds and middlemen, but I thought there was something else behind it, and there was." Jill tried to collect her thoughts. "The complaints on Memoril were coming in, but they were being covered up. By you, at your bosses' behest. Nobody at your level does that alone. They told you to do it, and they used you. They played you. I think my ex-husband figured it out, because he had the raw data from Nina, and I think he tried to blackmail you. And you killed him."

Elliott recoiled.

"Am I right or am I wrong?"

"You must be crazy." Suddenly Elliott reached over and yanked on Jill's sweater, almost tearing the neckline, but she made herself stay calm, raising her hands.

"Frisk away. I'm not wearing a wire. Go ahead, you're a doctor. Kind of."

"You don't know what you're doing." Elliott patted down her sides, then her chest, his eyebrow twitchy. His gaze fell on her bandaged hand. "Let me see that hand."

"Fine, allow me." Jill unpeeled the gauze, showed him her purplish cut, then covered it back up. "Satisfied?"

"Give me your purse." Elliott grabbed her purse, rummaged inside, and tossed it aside, then rose to go. "This is ridiculous, I'm leaving."

"I wouldn't do that yet. You didn't hear how I'm on your side, and you're going to wish you did. Because, sooner than you think, you're going to have no job and no money and no career. Or you're going to end up dead. Either way, you're going to wish you'd stayed."

Elliott turned, then sat back down, saying nothing.

"Your bosses aren't very nice people, Elliott. The government thinks that the Wall Street guys hired two killers to kill Nina and her husband, but I think your bosses did it."

"No, that's wrong." Elliott blanched, shaken. "Nina's husband killed her. He was abusive. We all know that."

"Did you really buy that? It looks like you did. No, your bosses had Nina and her husband killed, I assume so there wouldn't be any loose ends. Then *I* became a loose end, and they sent the killers after me. But I guess they kept all this from you, for some reason." Jill eyed him, wondering. "Oh, did you like Nina? That's too bad." Jill let it go. "Well, to get to the point, your bosses sent you out here, so they know what I have and they can guess what I want. Money. I just quit my job, and it'll come in handy."

"How does that benefit me?"

"You know there's a fortune in that building, Elliott. Enough for us both, and we're not as greedy as they are. Tell them I want to be paid, but let's share it. We can set the figure together. I say five hundred grand? Six?" Jill paused to let it sink in. "Let them pay us, and we'll split the money. You collect it from them, and deliver half to me. Three for you, three for me. No one has to know but you and me. I want to be paid, and I'll keep quiet about your lousy drug."

"Memoril's a *great* drug," Elliott said, suddenly animated. His light eyebrows flew upward, and his cheeks mottled, with new emotion.

"Not if there's that many complaints about it."

"You don't know the first thing about Memoril. All you did is read our website." Elliott snorted. "You have no idea how much

R&D, clinical trials, time, money, and superb chemistry went into that drug. It was *nine years* in the making."

"All for naught. Memoril's a terrible drug, Elliott. Admit it, it doesn't work."

"Yes, it *does*. You said so yourself, it helped someone you knew."

"Until it kills her. Memoril doesn't work if you have to lie to keep it on sale."

"I *don't* have to lie." Elliott flushed, angering. "The regs don't require me to report a complaint to the FDA unless it's serious, life-threatening, or unexpected. They're open to interpretation, and I interpret them. That's my job."

"Oh, please. You don't *interpret* anything. You find the wiggle room in the terms to prop up your bad medicine. You fudge the data. You *cheat*." Jill could see he loved his drug and he was protecting it, like a mother did a child. Or even like Megan, who didn't like it when people said Beef was fat. Suddenly, Jill knew how to get to him. "It's a bad drug and a bad plan. Pharmacists can report adverse effects directly to the FDA. So can any consumer, online. It's only a matter of time before the world finds out that Memoril is *poison*."

"No, you're wrong," Elliott shot back. "The numbers will be far lower if we don't report, and it's the total numbers that trigger their attention."

"They're the FDA, not the IRS." Jill forced a cocky smile. "They go by the severity of the adverse event, too. Deferral and Riparin were only Class III recalls, but Memoril works on brain chemistry, so it's probably causing strokes, even fatalities."

"Who can say that any given death is linked to Memoril, especially in a geriatric patient? They get so decrepit, they would've died anyway, from a myriad of causes." A cruel smile curled Elliott's upper lip, and Jill felt her stomach turn over.

"You can't hide those complaints forever."

"I can, and I *have*." Elliott lifted his chin, defiantly. "Memoril helps more people than it kills. It's a true scientific advance."

Jill realized he'd just shown his hand, but she couldn't stop now. "You're making a monumental mistake. If you don't get me that money, I'll go to the media and I'll sell them the story. I'll tell them all about Memoril and what you're doing."

"Don't you *dare*." Elliott jumped to his feet, leaning over her, his features contorted with anger. "You and your ex are two of a kind. You think you know everything. Well, did he know everything? Where is *he* now?"

"You don't scare me, and you can't stop me." Jill could see he was about to explode, so she provoked him. "I'll get my money one way or the other. I'll *kill* your drug."

"I'll kill *you* if you do, and don't think I'm not capable of it!" Elliott's eyes flashed with a zealot's madness. "I killed your ex-husband! He was easy to fool. I let him think we were going to pay him, told him I was coming over to negotiate the deal. I told him he drove such a hard bargain, I needed a drink. It only takes a second to dump a test tube in a drink. You think I don't know how to mix drugs in solution? Add a masking agent, for flavor? I'm a *chemist!*"

Jill didn't know what to say, and suddenly she didn't have to say more, or get Elliott to say any more.

"FBI, hands up!" shouted a squad of FBI agents in dark wind-breakers, racing from the treeline, lead by Special Agent Harrison. "FBI, get your hands up!"

"Don't shoot!" Elliott froze, raising his hands, his eyes popping as Special Agent Harrison and the other FBI agents grabbed him, patted him down, and handcuffed him.

Jill hustled away, as she'd been instructed, and the man and the woman sitting on the bench, both FBI agents, sprinted toward her and whisked her aside.

"Great job, Dr. Farrow!" The female FBI agent thrust out her hand. "I'll take the device now."

"Here you go." Jill handed her the BlackBerry, which had been specially outfitted as a recording device. "Thanks for protecting me."

"Jill!" Sam yelled, and she turned to see him running toward her, his sport jacket flying open. The sight lifted her heart, and she hurried to meet him.

"Sam, he admitted it, did you hear? Did they hear?" Jill met him, and Sam hugged her close.

"Way to go, babe. They've got the murder charge against him ready to go, and next they're going after Pharmcen." Sam smiled, looking into Jill's face with love. "I hope this gives the girls some real closure, too."

"So do I." Jill hugged him, finally at peace. "*Now,* it's over."

Chapter Seventy-six

It was dark by the time they got to Shood Memorial, and Jill and Sam exchanged looks as they walked down the glistening corridor. Megan and Abby were behind them, chatting with Steven, and Victoria brought up the very rear, her head down, her thoughts to herself. It had been Jill's idea to visit Brian tonight, but neither she nor Sam knew which way it was going to go, between Brian and Victoria. Victoria had confided in Jill that she was nervous about seeing Brian again, but she'd wanted to go, so Jill felt some trepidation as she led everybody into the hospital room.

"Hello, Special Agent Prendergast." Jill smiled, relieved to see that Brian was well enough to be sitting up in bed, reading a sports magazine. A bandage was wrapped around his head, making his brown hair puff in odd directions, and an older-looking pair of glasses perched on top of the gauze over his ears.

"Hello, hey, nice of you to come, Dr. Farrow, everybody." Brian grinned gamely, setting down the magazine. His color was good, but his face showed a few cuts and some bruising. His blue eyes were weary, but they came to life when Victoria finally walked in. "Vick, it was nice of you to come, too."

"It wasn't my idea," Victoria shot back, standing stiffly at the foot of the bed, and Jill stepped over to his bedside, to smooth things over.

"Brian, meet my fiancé, Sam Becker, his son, Steven Becker, and my daughter, Megan." Jill gestured at them, and Sam came over to shake his hand.

"Good to meet you, Brian."

"You, too." Brian nodded, acknowledging them all with a smile. "Hi, everybody. Good to meet you. Hey, Abby."

"Hey, Brian," Abby said, walking over. "How are you feeling?"

"Fine, thanks. Nothing's broken. I lucked out."

Jill felt her throat thicken as she thought about what she'd come to say. "Brian, I want to thank you for saving my life. I don't know how to say thank you for something that huge, other than just to say it, so thank you, so much, from the bottom of my heart." She managed to hold back her tears. She didn't want it to become about her. "I owe you, everything."

"No, you don't." Brian smiled, modestly. "It's my job."

"Maybe so, but it's quite a job, where you risk your life for other people." Jill flashed on the memorial at the police station in New York, with the plaques to the officers who fell on September 11. "I think you deserve at least a thank-you, a commendation, or whatever medal they give you. To me, you're a hero."

"To me, too," Sam said, nodding gravely.

"Yep," Abby added, and Megan nodded, staring at Brian, thrilled to be in the presence of a real FBI agent.

"Well, thank you, all." Brian turned to Jill, cocking his head. "By the way, Dr. Farrow, I heard you were quite the undercover agent today. Wearing a wire, the whole nine? Way to go, rook."

Jill blushed, still too moved to laugh, but next to her, Sam chuckled.

"I know, my wife is 007 now. You should've seen her. She kept him talking like a pro."

Jill nudged him, embarrassed. "Hardly, Sam." She gestured at Brian. "*This* man is a pro. He tried to drive bad guys off a road, at a hundred miles an hour. I'll never forget that day. I've never driven that fast in my life."

"I have, except for the tree." Brian laughed, and so did everybody else, except Victoria. "Doc, you're a tough cookie when you want to be. I tried to warn you off, remember? When I threatened you with the restraining order?"

"Oh." Jill smiled. "That only made me madder."

Brian laughed, turning to Sam. "Dude, you've got your hands full. Good luck."

Sam burst into laughter. "You can say that again."

"What's the secret, with these women, bro?"

"It's easy. Do what they say, when they say it."

Everyone laughed, except for Victoria, again. An awkward silence fell, with everybody wondering about the elephant in the room. Brian looked over at Victoria after a moment, clearing his throat.

"Vick, I'm sorry for deceiving you, I really am." Brian winced, and it wasn't from the scratches on his face. "It's part of my job, too, but it's, hands-down, the *worst* part of my job."

"Then congratulations on a job well done." Victoria's tone was heavy with sarcasm. "Way to go, Operation Hedge Clippers."

"Go ahead and yell at me." Brian frowned, his regret plain. "I deserve it, and you know you want to."

"Yell at you? I wouldn't stop at yelling. If you weren't already in a hospital, I'd put you in one."

Jill cringed, looking down.

Brian said, "Victoria, I really am sorry."

"You made friends with me just to meet my father."

"But then we became friends, you and I. The time we spent, that was real. We're real friends."

Victoria scoffed. "No, we're not, not anymore."

Jill stiffened, uncomfortable, but she didn't interfere, as much as she wanted to. She knew it wasn't her place, and since she'd been deceived herself, she could understand Victoria's reaction. On the other hand, she felt for Brian, who was only doing his job, and was obviously crazy about Victoria, job or no.

Abby rested a hand on the bedrail, her young face falling into prematurely sad lines. "Brian, I'm not mad at you. I got to know some of the other FBI agents and I understand why you did what you did, with Victoria. I even get it, about Dad. I love him and I always will, but I know that he was the one doing wrong, not you."

"Thanks, Abby." Brian frowned, in a sympathetic way. "I know this is hard for you, for both of you, and just so you know, your Dad talked about you guys all the time. He loved you both." Brian turned to Victoria, again. "Victoria, I really am sorry. I'm sorry I deceived you. I want you to know that I mean that, whether we stay friends or not."

"We've known each other for a year, and you lied to me every day." Victoria shook her head. "You lied about what you were doing, where you were going, even who you are. What am I supposed to do about that?"

"I had a job to do, and I did it, but I'm really sorry."

"But still." Victoria exhaled, frowning, her eyebrows sloping down, as anger gave way to hurt. "It's just that you lied to me about everything, even your name."

"Not everything. I care about you, that was real."

"How do I know that?"

"I'm telling you, now."

"But you told me before, when you were lying." Victoria tilted her head, pained. "And what about your imaginary girlfriend, in Paris?"

"I had to say that, it was part of the cover. What can I do to convince you?"

"I don't know. That's your problem, not mine."

"What if I proposed?"

Victoria blinked. "What?"

Brian smiled, a new smile, one full of feeling. "Will you marry me, Victoria? I love you, you have to know that."

"What?" Victoria asked, astonished.

"Please, marry me. I don't have a ring and I can't get down on one knee, but I love you, and I've loved you every day for a year." Brian's voice thickened, suddenly. "And when I thought I might die in that car, you were my last and only thought. *You.* Marry me. Please. That is, if you love me, too."

Victoria's mouth dropped open. Her eyes filmed, but she didn't say anything.

Everybody held his breath, all equally amazed. Sam and Steven exchanged glances. Jill felt tears on the way. Megan's eyes popped with delight.

Abby interjected, "Yes, yes, yes! She loves you, she's crazy about you! She told me she wants to marry you, a million times! Yes, already!"

Victoria burst into teary laughter, rolling wet eyes. "Abby, shut up, please, and let me think."

"Victoria, say yes! You know you want to!"

"Abby, please. This is my business, not yours."

"Tell him!" Abby gestured at Brian. "He's waiting!"

Jill couldn't believe these girls. She stepped in and separated them, smiling. "Girls, don't fight, not now, okay? Abby, please be quiet. Victoria, you have the floor."

"Thank you, Jill." Victoria turned to Brian, trying to compose herself. Her eyes filled with tears, and she pursed her lips, but she didn't answer.

Brian's eyes stayed glued to her, a steady blue, but his face began to fall, and his smile slowly faded. "Vick?"

Victoria smiled sweetly, her lower lip a little shaky. "Brian, please understand, I love that you asked me. But don't you think we should go on a date before we get married?"

Brian laughed, a little sadly, then he nodded. "Okay, if you want, I guess we could do it that way. It's somewhat conventional, but I can work with that."

"Wonderful." Victoria smiled, her eyes shining, and she stepped over to his bedside. "But I can tell you this, I love you, too."

"You do?" Brian asked, grinning again.

"Yes, I do, so much." Victoria leaned over and kissed him, once, then again.

Sam and Steven clapped, and Jill burst into happy laughter, proud of Victoria.

Abby squealed, and Megan chanted, "Victoria's in love! Victoria's in love! Victoria's in love!"

Victoria straightened up, breaking into a huge grin. Her face flushed with happiness, and she turned to Megan. "Mega, can you wait a little longer until we go dress-shopping?"

"Yes! Yes! Yes!" Megan squealed, running into Victoria's arms. "Yes!"

Chapter Seventy-seven

Saturday afternoon swim meets always drew the biggest crowds, with parents home from work and siblings off from school, and the pool gallery was packed to bursting, with the crowd talking, laughing, and joking around. The meet was held at Sequanic High, and the last time they were here, Megan had had that panic attack. Jill prayed that today wouldn't be an instant replay as she and Sam made their way down the row to Victoria, Abby, and Steve, who had driven separately in Steve's rental car, taking Megan.

Jill and Sam waved hello to the Cohens, the McGraths, and Bill Roche and Jenny Zeleny, then sat down on the hard wooden bleacher, where Jill turned to Victoria. "How was Megan on the ride over?"

"Fine, and we gave her lots of support."

"It has to be hard for her to see that boy again. I hope she'll be okay."

"I know she will. We gave her a pep talk in the car."

Steve turned to Jill, grinning warmly. "I drove and pretended not to hear anything."

"Way to go. I do the same thing, all the time." Jill smiled, then caught sight of the boys' team, grouped on the far side of the pool, against the sunny window. She squinted at the swimmers. "Which one is he?"

Victoria pointed. "The blond in front."

Jill spotted a skinny kid with curly blond hair, and almost growled. "Is his mother here? Can I deck her?"

"Down, girl." Victoria looked over. "Megan's stronger than you think. After all, she's her mother's daughter."

Jill smiled, then eyed the pool deck for Megan. A flock of yellow bathing suits and matching swim caps clustered behind the starting blocks with Coach Stash, and Megan stood at the periphery, looking up at the bleachers the way she always did. Jill raised her bandaged hand. "Hey, honey!"

Megan broke into a grin, waving back. "Hi, Mom," she mouthed, which she had never done.

"She looks happy," Sam said, waving.

"She really does." Jill felt a rush of relief.

"Jill, Jill!" Rita motioned from down the row to Jill, who leaned over. "Victoria and Steven told us about your car accident, in Jersey." She gestured at the bandage. "Are you okay?"

"Fine, thanks," Jill answered.

"I heard what that little jerk did to Megan. How is she?"

"She was upset." Jill knew it had to be the talk of the swim moms, but they'd all be on Megan's side.

"She's fine, you'll see," Victoria said, smiling mysteriously.

Jill turned to her, puzzled. "What, is something going on?"

"Yes, and it was all Megan's idea. Watch."

Jill and Sam craned their necks at a sudden commotion, taking place poolside. Coach Stash had walked away with his clipboard, and Megan and the rest of the girls swarmed like yellowjackets, flying toward the boys' team. Megan grabbed the blond swimmer by his one arm while Courtney nabbed his other.

"What's she doing?" Jill asked, confused. Sam and Steve looked over at the scene, and Victoria and Abby pointed in delight. Heads turned in the gallery as Megan, Courtney, and the rest of the girls whisked the boy to the edge of the pool and pushed him into the water.

"Yay! Yay!" Megan, Courtney, and the girls burst into laughter, applause, and cheering. The boys doubled-over with laughter, shoving each other in glee.

Victoria, Abby, and Steven cheered, and the Valley West parents stood up, clapping, as the blond swimmer swam to the side of the pool. The girls crowded around a grinning Megan, jumping up and down, hugging her.

"Way to go!" Sam laughed.

"Good for you, Megan!" Jill stood up, clapping loudest of all. Her throat caught as she realized that her daughter was growing up, right before her very eyes.

And it was a beautiful sight.

Acknowledgments

I've written eighteen novels, and in each one, my goal is to write something that's true. That doesn't mean true in the literal sense, at all. It means emotionally true. A novel doesn't connect unless it's emotionally true, and when it's emotionally true and does connect, what happens is magic.

To write a novel that's emotionally true, I have to go within. For it to reach your heart, it has to come from mine. I dug deep for *Come Home,* because in my own life, during my second marriage, I was a stepmother of three girls, in addition to my own daughter. The first point I need to make here is in the nature of a disclaimer: the stepdaughters in this novel aren't my real stepdaughters, nor are they based on them, in any way. The characters herein are completely fictional, and the same is true of the second husband in this book. But the emotional truth of being a stepmother, and an ex-stepmother, I know that. I lived that, and so I'm free to write about it, and I hope it informs the novel and gives it an emotional truth.

That said, you don't have to be a stepmother or even a mother to recognize the feelings or have them strike a chord in you, because that's the way it is with truth. It rings true, for everyone.

And, of course, the other point to be made is a big thank-you to my (former) stepdaughters, for the years we spent together, and for letting me into their lives. I love all three of you, and always will.

Now to the thank-yous, where I get to thank all of those experts who helped me, and make clear that any and all mistakes herein are mine.

I needed a dynamic duo of pediatricians to help me understand how they think and work, and for this, I am indebted to Dr. Carol Actor, in private practice in Phoenixville, Pennsylvania, and Dr. Eileen Everly, of the Children's Hospital of Philadelphia. Both women took valuable time to answer all of my questions, and I could not be more grateful to them for their kindness, expertise, and guidance—and more important, for all they do for children.

For the intricacies of the Federal Bureau of Investigation, I turned to my dear friend and former special agent Linda Vizi, and thanks so much to her. I am so grateful to Linda for her time and expertise, as well as all of the years of service she gave to the FBI to take care of us all. And yes, there really is a Needle & Gun Club of female FBI agents, and I'm proud to have one of their quilts hanging in a place of honor in my home.

Thanks to the police officers at the Sixth Precinct in Philadelphia, as well as the police officers of the Sixth Precinct (a coincidence) in New York City, for their help, and again, their service to us all. Special thanks and a big hug to Detective Kenneth Baker of the NYPD for answering all of my questions.

Thanks to Tom Melvin, genius accountant, who helped me with the financial details herein, as I have math anxiety. Thanks to Mary McMahon, swim mom extraordinaire. Thanks to Danielle Bersch, Elaine Gondek, and Veronica Mendina, too.

Thank you to the gang at St. Martin's Press, starting with the terrific John Sargent, Brian Napack, Sally Richardson, Matthew Shear, Matt Baldacci, Jeanne-Marie Hudson, Brian Heller, Jeff Capshew, Nancy Trypuc, Kim Ludlam, John Murphy, John Karle, Sara Goodman, and all the wonderful sales reps. Big thanks to Michael Storrings, for an astounding cover design. Also hugs and kisses to Mary Beth Roche, Laura Wilson, and the great people in audio books. I love and appreciate all of you.

I want to take a special moment to thank my editor, Jennifer Enderlin, to whom this book is dedicated. I came to Jen when my writing life was well-established and my habits somewhat entrenched (if not ossified). But getting to know her, to listen to her suggestions, and to watch her approach to my work has opened my eyes, and heart, in so many ways. A great editor has the talent and power to bring out the best in a writer, and I feel Jen doing that for me, encouraging me to go deeper, and truer, with each book and even each sentence. Jen, I can't thank you enough, and this dedication is only a start.

Thanks and big love to my incredible agent and friend, Molly Friedrich, who has guided me for so long now, with her expertise, brilliance, humor, and heart. Thanks, too, to the amazing Lucy Carson and Molly Schulman, for all of their comments on this manuscript. Thanks and another big hug to my dedicated and wonderful assistant and best friend, Laura Leonard. She's invaluable in every way, and has been for over twenty years.

Thanks, too, to my girl pack of Nan Daley, Rachel Kull, Paula Menghetti, and Franca Palumbo. We're all moms of daughters and they're all we talk about, and always will be. Thanks, ladies, for being yourselves, and for helping me, every day.

This is a long way of saying thank you very much to my amazing and brilliant daughter, Francesca, a wonderful writer in her own right, to my mother, Mary, and to my late father. I love you all, and you've taught me everything about everything.

Thank you, always and forever.

KEEP QUIET

Dedicated to the memory of the incomparable Matthew Shear,
brilliant publisher, beloved friend, warmest heart

Making the decision to have a child—it is momentous.
It is to decide forever to have your heart go
walking around outside your body.

—Elizabeth Stone

Chapter One

Jake Buckman knew his son had a secret, because his wife told him so. They didn't know what it was but they suspected it was about a girl, since Ryan had been texting non-stop and dressing better for school, which meant he actually cared if his jeans were clean. Jake wished he and his son were closer, but it was probably too late to turn it around. Ryan was sixteen years old, and Jake couldn't compete with girls, friends, the basketball team, Facebook, Call of Duty, Xbox, Jay-Z, Instagram, and pepperoni pizza. No father could, least of all an accountant.

Jake drummed his fingers on the steering wheel, waiting in front of the multiplex for Ryan, who'd gone to the movies with his teammates. The rift between father and son began five years ago, when Jake lost his job. The accounting firm he'd worked for had gone bankrupt in the recession, and he'd been out of a job for almost a year. They'd lived on his unemployment, his wife's salary, and savings, but he felt ashamed at the brave smile on Pam's face, the snow globe of bills on the kitchen table, and the endless rejection from jobs for which he was overqualified.

He shuddered, thinking back. Since he hadn't been able to

get a job, he'd done something he'd always wanted to do, start his own financial-planning business. He named it Gardenia Trust for Pam's favorite perfume and he'd dedicated himself to getting it off the ground. He'd worked days and nights at a rented cubicle, cold-calling everyone he knew to drum up clients. He'd said yes to every speaking engagement, keynote or not. He'd given seminars at retirement villages, Rotary Clubs, and libraries. In time he became one of the top-ten ranked financial planners in southeastern Pennsylvania, but it had taken a toll on his family. He and Pam had fixed their marriage with counseling, but in the meantime, Ryan had grown up. Only Pam believed Jake could still fix his relationship with Ryan before their son left for college. She'd encouraged him, even tonight.

Go pick him up at the movie, she'd said. *He's expecting me, but you go instead.*

The movie theater was wedged between Best Buy and Nordstrom, and cars idled out front, their exhausts making chalky plumes. Jake wondered if some of the other parents were in the cars, but he wouldn't recognize them anyway. He'd only attended one or two parents' nights, a National Honor Society induction, and assorted basketball finals, because Ryan played varsity. Pam went to all of Ryan's games, having more flexibility in her work schedule, and Jake had told himself that her being there was the same as his being there, as if he could parent by proxy. He'd been wrong. He'd made himself superfluous in his own son's life. His wife was the keynote.

A crowd flowed from the multiplex, lighting cigarettes, checking phones, and chatting as they passed in front of his headlights. Jake looked over to see Ryan push open the exit door with his shoulder and roll out of the theater with his teammates, whose names Jake had made a point to memorize: Caleb, Benjamin, and Raj. They were all tall, but Ryan was the biggest at six foot five and 225 pounds, the scruffy tentpole of a shuffling group of shaggy haircuts, black North Face jackets, and saggy pants—except for the two girls.

Jake shifted upward in the driver's seat, surprised. He hadn't known Ryan and his buddies were going to the movies with any girls and he was pretty sure Pam didn't, either. One girl was a redhead and the other a long-haired blonde, who stood near Ryan. Jake wondered if the blonde was the mystery girl and if he could get a conversation going about it with Ryan on the way home. Pam always said her best conversations with him happened spontaneously, while they were driving around. If so, Jake would plan his spontaneity.

The girls waved good-bye, and he waited for Ryan to notice the Audi. He'd texted to say he was coming, but Ryan hadn't replied, so he couldn't be sure the text got delivered. Jake didn't honk, wave, or do something else dorky, so as not to embarrass himself or suburban fathers in general.

Jake saw Ryan slide his iPhone from his pocket and flick his bangs back, so that the phone illuminated his son's face. Ryan had large, warm brown eyes, a long, thin nose and largish mouth, his handsome features framed by wavy, chestnut-brown hair, which he kept longish. Everybody said Ryan was the spitting image of his father, but Jake knew that was true too many years and twenty-five pounds ago. Jake was forty-six years old, with crow's-feet, graying temples, and a starter paunch to prove it. He always said that Ryan got his size from his father, but his brains from his mother, which was the best of both.

Jake watched as Ryan looked up from his iPhone, spotted the Audi, and jerked his chin up in acknowledgment, then slapped Caleb's palm and came toward the car. Jake unlocked the passenger door, and Ryan opened it and slid inside, his jacket sliding against the leather seat.

"Where's Mom?" he asked, eyebrows lifting.

"She was busy, so I figured I'd come. How was the movie?"

"Okay. You left Moose home?" Ryan kept an eye on his iPhone screen.

"Oops, yeah." Jake hadn't thought to take the dog, though Pam carted him everywhere. He disengaged the brake, fed the car gas, and headed for the exit.

"I get you didn't want him to come. This car is too awesome." Ryan kept his head down, his thumbs flying as he texted, growing the blue electronic bubble on the phone screen.

"No, it's not that. I forgot. I'll bring him next time."

"Don't. He'll drool on the seats. We must keep the machine pristine." Ryan paused as he read the screen. "You mind if I keep texting? I want to stay with this convo."

"It's okay, do your thing." Jake steered around the back of the King of Prussia mall, where the lights of JCPenney, Macy's, and Neiman Marcus brightened a cloudy night sky. Cars were rushing everywhere; it was Friday night, the busy beginning to the weekend. It should have been colder for February, but it wasn't. A light fog thickened the air, and Jake remembered something he had learned tonight from the pretty weathergirl on TV.

Fog is a cloud on the ground.

He turned the defrost to maximum and accelerated toward Route 202, heading for open road. Ryan texted away, his hip-hop ringtone going off at regular intervals, punctuated by the Apple-generated swoosh. Jake wondered if his son was talking to the mystery girl. He himself remembered racking up huge phone bills when he first dated Pam, at college. He'd fallen for her their freshman year at Pitt and felt unbelievably lucky when she married him. She was a great wife, and he gave her total credit for Ryan being so well-adjusted and popular, despite his naturally reserved manner. He was earning A's in AP courses, got solid SAT scores, and was already being recruited by college basketball programs, some Division I.

Jake switched into the slow lane, heading for the exit. He

wanted to ask Ryan about the girls, but he'd warm up first. "So, how was the movie?"

"Good. Like I said."

"Oh, right." Jake forgot, he had asked that already. "How's Caleb? And Raj and Benjamin?" He wanted to show he remembered the names.

"Fine."

"Everybody ready for the finals?"

"Yep."

Jake was getting nowhere fast. He still wanted to know about the girls, and according to Pam, the trick with Ryan was to act like you didn't care about the answer to the question you'd asked, or you'd never get an answer. So he said, offhandedly, "By the way, who were those girls at the movie?"

Ryan didn't look up from his phone, his thumbs in overdrive. Pink and green bubbles popped onto his phone screen, so he was texting with more than one person, like a conference call for teenagers.

"Ryan?" Jake tried again. "The girls at the movie, who were they?"

"Girls from school."

"Oh. Friends?"

"Yeah." Ryan still didn't look up.

"Nice." Jake let it go, an epic fail, in the vernacular. He pressed a button to lower the window, breathing in the moist, cool air. The fog was thickening, softening the blackness of the night, and the traffic dropped off as they approached the Concordia Corporate Center. They passed glowing signs for SMS and Microsoft, then turned onto Concordia Boulevard, which was lined with longer-stay hotels. He'd eaten enough of their reception-desk chocolate chip cookies to last a lifetime, because even his out-of-town clients were in the suburbs, the new home of American business.

Jake returned to his thoughts. His own office was in a nearby corporate center, and he spent his days ping-ponging between his corporate center and his clients' corporate centers, after which he drove home to his housing development. Some days the only trees he saw were builder's-grade evergreens, planted in zigzag patterns. Lately he felt as if his life were developed, rather than lived. He was a financial planner, but he was coming to believe that too much planning wasn't natural for trees or accountants.

Fog misted the windshield, and the wipers went on to clear his view, and Ryan chuckled softly. "Dad, this car is *sick*. I love how it wipes the windshield automatically."

"Me, too." Jake grinned, feeling the spark of a reconnection. They both liked cars, and last year, when Jake's old Tahoe hit 132,000 miles, he'd bought the Audi, mainly because Ryan had lobbied for one. Jake was a born Chevy guy, but Ryan had built umpteen online versions of the flashy Audi on the company website and designed what he called a "dream machine"—an A6 sedan with a 3.0 liter engine, Brilliant Black exterior, Black leather interior, and Brushed Aluminum inlay on the dashboard. They'd gone together to pick it up, and Jake had given Ryan a few driving lessons in it, when Ryan had the time.

"Dude." Ryan shifted forward, sliding the phone into his jacket pocket. "We're coming up on Pike Road. Can I drive?"

Jake checked the dashboard clock, which read 11:15. "You're not supposed to drive after eleven o'clock. You only have a learner's permit."

"But Dad, I've had it for five months already. I only have one month left before I can get my license. I did fifty-five out of the sixty-five hours, and all the nighttime driving hours and bad-weather hours. And you're with me, you're an adult."

"It doesn't matter, technically."

Ryan deflated. "Oh, come on, there's never traffic on Pike, not on the weekends. I can do it, Dad. You know I'm an excellent driver."

"We'll see when we get to Pike. If there's people around,

no." Jake wanted to keep the conversational momentum going, especially when Ryan's ringtone started up again. "So. It sounds like you're in demand tonight."

"I'm blowing up." Ryan smiled.

"Is something going on, or is it just the usual women beating down your door?"

Ryan snorted. "Yeah, right. I'm a chick magnet."

"Nobody's a chick magnet, buddy. That's why God invented cars."

"Ha!" Ryan slapped his hands together. "*That's* what I'm talking about! Agree!"

Yes! Jake realized he'd said the exact right thing, and Ryan shifted around to face him, with a new grin.

"When I get my license, you'll lend me the machine, right? I won't have to drive the Tahoe all the time."

"I will." Jake smiled.

"Awesome! Dad, guess what, I'm so stoked. I might have a date tomorrow night."

Bingo! "Really? Who?"

"Wait. Whoa. Hold on, it's Pike Road, we're here. Please, please, pull over." Ryan gestured to the right side of Pike, where the asphalt ended without a curb. "Right over there."

"Relax, remain calm." Jake braked as he approached the street.

"Please let me drive. We're almost home. Look, the place is dead." Ryan waved toward the corporate center. The follow-up ringtone sounded in his pocket. "Can I drive?"

"We'll see." Jake cruised to a stop, letting an oncoming truck pass, then made a left and pulled over, so he could scope out the scene. Pike Road was a long street that ran between the woods on its right and the Concordia Corporate Center, on its left. It was used mainly as a shortcut to the corporate-center parking lots, and during the week, corporate running teams and athletic teams from Jake's high school used it to train. There was no traffic on the weekends.

"Dad, *please.*" Ryan leaned over, his eyes pleading, and Jake didn't want to ruin the mood.

"Okay, let's do it."

"Sweet!" Ryan threw open the door and jumped out of the car. Jake engaged the parking brake, opened the door, and straightened up, but Ryan was already running around the front, slapping him a strong high-five. "Thanks, dude!"

Jake laughed, delighted. "Speed limit is forty, but watch out for deer."

"Gotcha!" Ryan plopped into the driver's seat, and Jake walked to the passenger seat, got in, and closed the door behind him. He didn't have to adjust the seat because they were the same size.

"Now. Hold on. Before you go anywhere, adjust the mirrors, outside and in."

"On it." Ryan pushed the button to rotate the outside mirror, then reached for the rearview, and Jake watched him line it up, with approval. His son was careful and methodical, a perfectionist like him. Ryan even enjoyed practicing, especially basketball. Once he had told Jake that it took two-and-a-half hours to shoot a thousand foul shots, and Jake didn't have to ask Ryan how he knew.

"Don't forget your harness."

"I wasn't going to." Ryan fastened himself into the seat with a *click.*

"I have the low beams on. For this street, with no lights, I recommend the high beams."

"Agree." Ryan peered at the dashboard and switched them on.

"Take a second and look around." Jake looked down the street with Ryan, the high beams cutting the light fog. Pike Road was a straight shot the length of the corporate center, then took a sharp curve to the right. Tall trees lined the road, their branches jagged and bare.

"Good to go." Ryan released the emergency brake as his phone signaled an incoming text.

"Don't even think about getting that text. No texting while driving." Jake himself had stopped texting while he drove unless he was at a stoplight, and he talked on the phone only if he had the Bluetooth.

"I know." Ryan fed the car gas. The follow-up ringtone played but he stayed focused on his driving. "That's just Caleb, anyway. He's hyper tonight. He likes one of those girls we were with, the redhead with the white coat."

"I saw her." Jake relaxed in the seat, since Ryan had everything in control.

"Anyway, this girl I might go out with tomorrow night? She's new." Ryan smiled as he drove, warming to the topic. "Her family moved here over the summer from Texas. She rides horses. Barrel-racing. How baller is *that*?"

"Baller." Jake knew *baller* meant good. They passed Dolomite Road on their left, which ran behind the corporate center. "Was she the other girl at the movie? The blonde?"

"Yes." Ryan burst into an excited grin. "Did you see her? Isn't she *mad* cute?"

"I did see her. She's very cute."

"Yo, I'd be so lucky to be with this girl! She's short, but it works on her, you know?"

"Sure. Short is good. I like short. Your mom is short." Jake smiled. Pam was only five foot three, and his mother had called them Mutt and Jeff, back in the days when people knew who Mutt and Jeff were. Jake's mother had died ten years ago of blood cancer, and he still missed her every day. He didn't miss his father at all, though his father had outlived his mother by six years, which proved that not only was life unfair but death was, too.

"Her name's kinda weird, not gonna lie. Janine Mae Lamb.

Janine Mae is her first name. You have to say both names." Ryan maintained his speed as they approached the curve, marked by a caution sign with an arrow pointing right.

"I don't think that's a weird name. I think it's pretty. Feminine." Jake made approving noises to keep up the good vibe. The car's headlights illuminated the caution sign, setting its fluorescence aglow. "Lower your speed. It's a blind curve."

"On it." Ryan slowed down.

"So what's she like, personality-wise?"

"She's funny. She has a Texas accent. She says pin when she means pen."

"Accents are good. Accents can be adorable."

"Agree!" Ryan beamed as they reached the curve, and Jake felt happy for him.

"So you're going out with her tomorrow night? Why don't you take her someplace nice, on me, like a restaurant?"

"A *restaurant*? Dude, we're not *olds* like you!" Ryan looked over in disbelief as he steered around the curve, and Jake met his eye, bursting into laughter.

But in that split second, there was a sickening *thump*.

They jolted as if they'd hit something, and Ryan slammed on the brakes, cranking the wheel to the left. The right side of the car bumped up and down, fishtailed wildly, and skidded to a stop.

And then everything went quiet.

Chapter Two

"What was *that*?" Jake threw an arm across Ryan, but the accident was over as suddenly as it had begun. The noise had come from the passenger side of the car, toward the front.

"Dad, I'm sorry, I hit something, I think it was a deer." Ryan shook his head, upset. "I didn't see it, I was looking at you. I hope I didn't hurt it or the car."

"It's okay. Don't worry about the car." Jake hadn't seen anything because he'd been looking at Ryan. The car sat perpendicular on the street, its headlights blasting the trees. The airbags hadn't gone off. The windshield was intact. The engine was still running.

"If it's a deer, maybe it's not dead. Maybe we can call the vet. Dr. Rowan is a good guy. He'd come, wouldn't he?"

"Hmm, I don't know. It's kind of late to call him." Jake twisted around and checked behind them. The back of the car had stopped short of a tree and a yellow stanchion sticking out of the ground with a sign that read GAS PIPELINE. He shuddered to think how much worse it could have been.

"Maybe the emergency vet then? Can we call them?"

"Let me go see. You stay here." Jake patted Ryan's arm, opened the car door, and got out, steeling himself for the sight. He'd hit a deer two years ago and still felt guilty. He looked to the right, where the sound had come from. Something dark and lumpy lay off the road, in the raggedy fringe of brush bordering the woods, bathed in the red glow of their taillights.

Oh my God.

Jake knew what he was seeing, in his heart, before his brain let him accept the reality. He found himself racing toward the dark and fallen form. It wasn't a deer. It was a human being, on its side, facing away from him. It couldn't be anything else from the shape. And it was lying still, so still.

Jake threw himself on the ground beside the body. A woman runner in a black jersey and black running tights lay motionless on her side, her skinny body like a limp stick figure.

"Miss, Miss!" Jake called out, frantic. She didn't reply or moan. He pressed her neck to see if she had a pulse, but didn't feel anything. He couldn't see much in the dim light. The woman was petite. She had long hair. Dark blood flowed from a wound near her hairline. Her features glistened, abraded by the asphalt. Road dirt pitted her nose and cheek.

"Miss!" Jake leaned over her chest, trying to hear a heartbeat, but he couldn't hear anything. He turned the woman over on her back to begin CPR and put an arm under her neck to open her airway. Her head dropped backwards. He realized with horror that she was dead.

"Ryan! Help! Call 911!" Jake shouted, horrified. He'd left his phone in the car. He knew CPR. He'd been an Eagle Scout. He prayed the protocol hadn't changed. He bent over and began CPR, breathing into her mouth, willing oxygen into her lungs, counting off breaths in his head. Her lips were still warm, but she didn't respond.

"Dad! Oh my God, oh my God!" Ryan came running up, his

hands on his head, doubled over in shock. "It's a *lady*! *I hit a lady*?"

"Call 911!" Jake stopped breathing for her, shifted position, linked his fingers, and pumped the woman's chest, counting off in his head, praying to God he could resuscitate her. He had to bring her back. She couldn't be dead. This couldn't be happening.

"What are you doing? Tell me she's alive! She's alive, isn't she? No, this can't be! She has to be alive! I'm calling 911!" Ryan shook his head, edging backwards. His breaths came in ragged bursts. He pulled his phone from his pocket, but dropped it, agitated. "Dad, she . . . doesn't look like she's alive! She's alive . . . isn't she? She can't be . . . *dead*!"

"Stay calm, pick up your phone, and call 911." Jake pumped her chest, counting off the beats, trying to stay in emotional control. The woman still didn't respond. He kept pumping.

"Dad . . . no it *can't* be true!" Ryan cried out, bursting into an anguished sob. "I have to call . . . my phone! They can help her!" He dropped to his knees, frantically looking in the dark for his phone, crying and crawling around the street. "She can't be dead . . . where's my phone? I can't find my phone!"

Jake kept pumping on the woman's chest. His efforts became futile, grotesque. He was abusing her body. She had become a corpse. He couldn't believe it. He didn't understand. It was inconceivable. She had been alive a minute ago, running around the curve. Now she was dead. They had killed her.

God, no.

Jake stopped pumping and leaned back on his haunches. Tears came to his eyes. His hand went to his mouth, reflexively stifling himself. He looked down at the woman in the dim light. The sight broke his heart, and he knew it would be seared into his brain for the rest of his life. He bent his head and sent up a silent prayer on her behalf.

"No, no! Where's my . . . *phone*?" Ryan sobbed, scrambling

for his phone on all fours. "I *killed* . . . a lady, I *killed* . . . a lady, I wasn't looking . . . it's all my fault!"

"Ryan, she's gone," Jake whispered, his throat thick with emotion.

"No, no, no, no, she's not *gone* . . . she's not gone . . . what did I *do*?" Ryan fell over, collapsing into tears, his forehead on the asphalt. "Dad, I killed her . . . no, no, no!"

Jake rubbed his eyes, dragged himself to his feet, and half-walked and half-stumbled to Ryan.

"No, no, no!" Ryan cried, his big body folded onto itself, racked with sobs. "I can't . . . believe this. I . . . *killed* someone, I *killed* that . . . lady!"

"We'll get through this, Ryan." Jake gathered him up and hugged him tight, and they clung to each other in a devastated embrace.

"I *killed* . . . that lady . . . *I killed* . . . *that lady!* I wasn't . . . *looking!*"

"I didn't see her either. I'm at fault too, we both are." Jake held him close, then spotted Ryan's phone glinting in the light, by the side of the road.

"*I killed her!* Oh no oh no . . . what did I do?" Ryan wept and permitted himself to be held, and Jake's thoughts raced ahead. He'd call 911, but if he told the police that Ryan had been at the wheel, Ryan could get a criminal record, since he'd been driving after hours on a learner's permit. It would jeopardize his college admissions, basketball scholarships, everything. And Pam would never forgive him for letting Ryan drive or letting this happen. The open secret of their marriage was that his wife loved their son more than she loved him. Jake reached a decision.

"Ryan, listen to me. We need to call the police, but we can't tell them the truth. We're going to tell them that I was driving, not you. Got it? We'll say I was the driver, and you were the passenger."

"No, no . . . I did it . . . *I killed that lady* . . . she's *dead*!" Ryan sobbed harder, his broad chest heaving. Tears poured down his cheeks. His nose ran freely, his mucus streaming.

"Ryan, look at me. Look at me." Jake put his hands on his son's tearstained face. They had to get the story straight before they called the police. They had no time to lose. A car could come along any minute. "I need you to listen to me."

"I killed her!" Ryan kept shaking his head, hiccuping with sobs. "Dad—"

"Ryan, listen, try to calm down—"

"I can't, I can't!" Ryan shook his head back and forth, almost manically, out of control. "I killed her, I killed her!"

"Ryan, listen!" Jake shouted, only because Ryan was becoming hysterical. "We're going to tell the police I was driving the car, do you understand? I was driving the car and you were the passenger. Got it? I'll do all the talking, you keep quiet. You can do that, can't you?"

"No, no, no, I . . . *killed her!*" Ryan shouted back, his words indistinct, his tears and mucus flowing.

"Ryan, stop. We're going to tell the cops *I* killed her. Do you hear me? You *cannot* contradict me, no matter what they ask you. I'll do the talking, you keep your mouth shut."

"Dad . . . no!" Ryan lurched out of his arms, scrambled backwards, and staggered to his feet, shaking his head. "No, no, Dad. No!"

"Yes, do what I say, it's the only way." Jake got to his feet, hustled to the phone, and picked it up to call 911.

"No, no, wait . . . look. Wait." Ryan plunged his hand into his pocket, pulled out a plastic Ziploc bag, and showed it to Jake, sobbing. "Dad . . . I . . . bought this . . . today. What do I do with it . . . when the cops come?"

"What is it?"

"I'm sorry . . . it's weed . . . I'm sorry—"

"*What?*" Jake asked, aghast.

"I smoked up . . . with Caleb . . . after practice." Ryan wept, his hand flying to his hair, rubbing it back and forth. "But I'm not . . . high now, I swear it . . . I'm not, I'm not."

"You *smoke dope?* Since *when?*"

"I don't do a lot . . . I swear. I did it today . . . but I'm fine now . . . that's not why I hit the lady—"

"Give me that!" Jake grabbed the bag from Ryan's hand. It was a quarter full of marijuana.

"I killed that lady . . . she's dead!" Ryan dissolved into tears, holding his head, falling to his knees. He rocked on his haunches, back and forth, becoming hysterical. "She's dead . . . because of me . . . Dad, what do we do? I killed her . . . I killed her . . . I killed her!"

Jake had to make a split-second decision, wrestling with his conscience. A woman was dead, horribly, but that couldn't be changed. If Jake called the police and told them the truth, then two lives would be destroyed—hers and Ryan's. And Ryan was too distraught to maintain any lie to the police. Even if Jake tried to claim that he himself had been driving the car, the cops would question them both. He couldn't be sure Ryan wouldn't blurt out the truth about who was driving, and if Ryan did, the cops would test him and find marijuana in his blood. They would convict him of driving under the influence and vehicular homicide. He would go to jail. There would be no college, no future, no nothing. Ryan's entire life would be ruined—and all because Jake had let him drive.

Jake's mouth went dry. He couldn't bring himself to look back at the poor woman lying off the road, lifeless. He had no more time to ponder. He was a family man, and he'd lived his whole life being good, moral, and honest. He'd never broken the law in any way. So he knew he was making the absolute worst decision of his life when he stuffed the cell phone and Ziploc bag into his pocket, grabbed Ryan by his coat, and pulled him to his feet.

"Get back in the car, son," Jake said, grimly. "Hurry."

Chapter Three

Jake entered the kitchen to face his wife ahead of Ryan, according to plan. He felt sick to his stomach with guilt and horrified at what they had done. All he could think about was the dead woman, but he had to keep it together for Ryan's sake, to get past Pam. He'd been able to wipe the blood off his face and hands in the car, and he'd hidden his blood-stained parka in the garage. Pam wouldn't think it was strange that he didn't have a coat on because he often left it in the car, since their garage was attached. On the way home, Jake had pulled over and quieted his weeping son, even as he'd laid down the law.

Ryan, don't tell Mom. Never, ever.

I . . . never ever would. Are you . . . insane?

I mean it. No matter what. You know what she'd do. She'd have to.

I swear . . . I won't tell Mom . . . I won't tell anybody.

"Jake, what took you so long?" Pam was standing at the sink and turned toward him, a petite, naturally pretty woman with intelligent blue eyes, an upturned nose, and a small mouth with a perfect smile. She had her horn-rimmed glasses on, and with her long brown ponytail, gray hoodie, and jeans, she looked exactly like what she was, the smartest girl in the class, his vale-dictorian wife.

"Ryan was starving, and we stopped at the diner." Jake tried to mask his emotions and avoided her eye, while Moose trotted over and began sniffing him, wagging his feathery tail harder than usual. The golden retriever must have been smelling the blood he hadn't been able to wipe off his jeans, because it had seeped too quickly into the fabric. He hoped Pam wouldn't notice, since there wasn't much and the denim was dark blue, but Jake felt repulsed at the very thought. He never would have imagined himself being responsible for the death of an inno-cent woman, much less leaving her body by the side of a road.

"Why didn't you call?" Pam shut the dishwasher door with a solid *clunk,* then looked past him for Ryan, as if she was already sensing something amiss.

"Sorry, I should have." Jake put his hands on her shoulders and gave her a quick kiss on the lips, feeling like Judas himself. He had never lied to her, except to tell her that he liked all the wacky things she did to her hair. Highlights, lowlights, whatever, she was beautiful to him. He loved her.

"So why didn't you call?" Pam pulled away, with a slight frown.

"Fill you in later," Jake whispered quickly, as if he were try-ing to say it before Ryan came in. He pressed Moose's muzzle away from his jeans, but the dog wasn't giving up, so he reached down and scratched the dog's head, as if he wanted him close.

"Okay." Pam's forehead relaxed, and Jake could see that she had put a wifely checkmark in the box next to Explanation Pending. He glanced at the TV, which showed the local news, playing on low volume. He couldn't bear it if a breaking news report about the accident on Pike Road came on, with a lurid HIT AND RUN banner. Every time he'd seen a hit-and-run report on the news, he'd wondered to himself what kind of person would do such a hateful thing. And now he knew. He'd just become the guy he hated. In fact, he'd just become the guy every-body hated. He turned off the TV, his hand shaking slightly.

Pam looked over when Ryan entered the kitchen and she flashed him a warm grin. "Hey honey, how was the movie?"

"Okay," Ryan answered, his voice sounding almost normal.

Jake turned around to see what his son looked like in the bright lights of the kitchen, and his eyes were predictably red-dish and puffy, his fair skin mottled. Jake's heart broke for him, because he knew how guilty and anguished Ryan was feeling. Yet at the same time, Jake was relieved that they had their story in place, because any mother could tell that the boy had been crying, especially as good a mother as the Honorable Judge Pamela A. Buckman, of the Superior Court of Pennsylvania.

"Only 'okay'? The reviews were excellent." Pam folded her arms and leaned a slim hip against the kitchen island, getting ready for a conversation, but Ryan kept walking through the kitchen to the hallway, precluding any question-and-answer, as planned.

"Mom, I'm going up, I'm beat," Ryan called out, tugging Moose away by the collar, on the fly. "See you in the morning. Good night, guys."

"Oh, okay, sleep tight, honey." Pam shifted her gaze to Jake, lifting an eyebrow.

Jake called out, "Good night, Ryan!"

They both watched as Ryan crossed the entrance hall and climbed the stairs, followed by Moose, wagging his fluffy tail. As soon as their son was out of sight and Jake was alone with Pam, he felt the tension level rise, as if their kitchen had a barometric pressure of its own. He had to tell Pam a convincing lie, but all he could think of was the woman he'd left dead, in the darkness. He'd driven away, too appalled and disgusted with himself to look in the rearview mirror. Her face had glistened with dark blood, slick and black as tar, covering her features so completely that he couldn't see what she looked like or how old she was.

"So what's going on?" Pam asked, mystified. "Was he crying? It looked like he was crying."

"He was, but he'll be okay, you'll see." Jake crossed to the sink and turned on the faucet, thinking about the dead woman. He felt stricken, knowing that she had been somebody's mother, wife, or even daughter.

"Why was he crying?" Pam followed him, tucking a strand of hair into her ponytail.

"We had a fight after the movie, but we worked it out." Jake pumped overpriced hand soap into his palm, lathered up, and began washing his hands of the poor woman's blood. He didn't see any telltale pink water going down the drain, and the very notion made his stomach turn. He felt as if he were in a waking nightmare, walking in the shoes of someone else entirely. A murderer, a criminal, a liar, or all three.

"But you guys don't fight. You don't talk enough to fight."

Jake reddened, but it gave him an idea for a better story. He'd been about to tell the story they'd made up in the car, involving Ryan getting mad at Caleb, but his new idea didn't involve a third party. He kept rinsing his hands, as if it would cleanse him of his guilt, like some villain in Shakespeare, he couldn't remember which. "Well, we fought this time, a bad one."

"Really."

"Yes, believe it or not." Jake kept his head down and his eyes on the water. The image of the woman's face reappeared. He could feel the warmth of her lips, when he was trying to get her breathing again. Maybe he shouldn't have given up so soon. Maybe he should have kept trying. He couldn't bring her back to life. She was really gone, and they had killed her.

"So what was it you fought about?" Pam folded her arms. "And why do I have to take your deposition? Tell me already."

"I am telling you." Jake realized she was right. He was stalling. He didn't want to lie to her. Once he did, the nightmare would become real, and there would be no going back. He didn't know if he could lie to her anyway. He hated lying to her, and he hated telling her the truth. It was a night of no-win decisions.

"Jake, you're beating around the bush."

"No, I'm not."

"Yes, you are. Honey, what is *going on*?"

Man up! Jake willed himself to get a grip. There'd been no going back the moment he'd left the scene. He twisted off the faucet, reached for the dishcloth, and started drying his hands, but he still couldn't make eye contact with her. "Okay, you're right, maybe I am. I don't feel that great about it, is all." He thought fast, realizing that his obvious discomfort could serve his story. "I mean, think about it from my point of view. I go to pick him up at the movies to get closer to him, and we fight and I make him cry, pushing him further away. I tried to do a good thing, but it turned out wrong." His throat caught when he realized that he was telling the truth, in a way. All of the emotions were real, if not the facts. "So now I'm home, and I have to tell you what happened."

"Aw, honey." Pam's voice softened, and she rubbed his back lightly. "I didn't mean to be sharp. I'm so tired. The weeks we sit *en banc* are a bitch. I'm sorry."

"No need to apologize." Jake knew that when the Superior Court sat *en banc,* the entire court would come to Philadelphia to hear oral arguments. There was a lot of preparation, and Pam worked extra hard, drafting opinions into the night to keep up with her regular caseload. Still, she wasn't so tired that she wasn't peering at him, intently.

"So tell me what happened."

"Okay, but it won't be easy for you to understand, because you guys have such a good relationship." Jake folded the dishcloth and set it in its pile by the paper towels, more deliberately than necessary. "Plus I'm worried that, the way I handled it tonight, I blew it. I'll never get in sync with him now, not before he goes to college."

"Aw, yes you will." Pam rubbed his back again. "So what happened already, ya big lug?"

Jake cringed inwardly, because he loved when she called him that. Pam liked his size because she said it made her feel safe, and he always thought he could protect her and Ryan—until tonight. He never would have guessed there'd be a jogger around the curve. He never would have foreseen they'd hit her. He told himself to get back on track and tell the story. He said, "It was silly, a little thing that got to be a big thing."

"That happens." Pam nodded in an encouraging way. He'd seen her do the same thing in the courtroom, trying to put a lawyer at ease during oral arguments. *Counsel, don't let us intimidate you,* she'd say. *Judges are people too. Just smarter.*

"Well, we were driving home from the movie, and I was trying to have a conversation with him, but he was texting the whole time."

"I don't let him do that in the car." Pam's lips pursed. "It's the same rule as at mealtimes. The principle is the same, whatever the location. He doesn't get to ignore his parents or people around him. It's just plain rude."

"Right, I think so, too, but I didn't want to lower the hammer—"

"Oh, be honest."

She knows. Jake reddened, stricken. "What do you mean? Honest about what?"

"You wanted to be Fun Dad." Pam snorted. "That's why you didn't lower the hammer."

Jake tried to recover, but she was right. That was exactly what had happened. He never should have let Ryan drive. He'd made the classic mistake. He'd acted like a friend, not a parent. Pam would never have made such a terrible decision. He sighed heavily, feeling the weight of his conscience. "I know, you're right. I know, I know, I know."

"Honey, enough. Don't beat yourself up."

Jake couldn't help it. If she only knew. He tried to return to the story, to spit it out. "So anyway, I didn't tell him to stop texting. My plan was to win him over, to see if I could engage him on my own. Make it volitional, not a rule."

"I hear you." Pam regarded him impatiently behind her glasses. "And so . . ."

"And then, well, to go back a minute, when I picked him up at the movie, I noticed that there were two girls they were talking to."

"Girls?" Pam lifted an eyebrow.

"Yeah, so while he was texting, I started to ask him about them, who they were and how they came to be at the movie. I was trying to make conversation, to get something going." Jake was making it up as he went along, but Pam's manner had changed from impatient to intrigued.

"So what did he say? I didn't know there were girls going to the movie, or that they were meeting girls there."

"I didn't get an answer. But wait"—Jake caught himself—"if I tell you what happened, you can't talk to him about it."

"Why not?"

"If you say anything, he'll never confide in me again, and that would defeat the purpose of my going to pick him up in the first place." Jake realized suddenly that if he could get Pam not to bring up the subject with Ryan, then the boy wouldn't have to lie to her. "Let us work it out, him and me. I think we did by the end, so let me keep at it."

"Okay, Coach." Pam rolled her eyes, amused. Her hands went to her ears, fingering the diamond studs he had given her, checking the backs to make sure they stayed on, a nervous habit. "So, as you were saying . . ."

"Well, all he would tell me about the girls was that they were from school and . . ." Jake stopped short, not wanting to tell her about the girl from Texas that Ryan had asked out. "Anyway, when I asked him another question, he kept texting, and I heard him mutter under his breath, 'It's none of your business.'"

"That is so disrespectful!" Pam's mouth dropped open. "He gets that from Caleb, you know. I *hate* that kid. He's a bad influence."

Jake bit his tongue. Pam was more right than she knew. "Ryan says he didn't say it, but I swear he did, and we got in a fight. I told him I thought he was being fresh and entitled—"

"Hoo boy." Pam's eyes flared.

"—and he told me that he was too old to be reporting his personal life to his father, and he shouldn't have to account for everything he did, and we yelled at each other."

"And he *cried*? He *never* cries."

Jake told himself to remain calm. Pam may have been a Ryan expert, but she didn't know he smoked marijuana and she would disapprove heartily. He had tried pot in college, and she hadn't even tried it. His wife took seriously the fact that she was a judge and had sworn an oath to uphold the law. Plus she believed marijuana turned kids into underachievers, which in her mind, was practically criminal. Jake reminded himself to get back on track with the story. "He cried from the stress, I guess. I shouted at him. I lost my temper."

"*You?*" Pam blinked. "You never lose your temper."

"I do sometimes."

"Okay, whatever." Pam shrugged, but Jake didn't want to remind her of the night he'd lost his job, when he'd thrown his laptop across the kitchen and cracked the screen. It wasn't even under warranty.

"Anyway, he pushed my buttons."

"Did you call him names? Remember, you're not supposed to call names."

"Of course not, I don't call names." Jake knew from therapy that name-calling was against the rules, like the Geneva Convention of marriage.

"I don't understand something. Was this in the car or the diner?"

"Was what?" Jake lost his train of thought again. He kept thinking of the woman, how horrible she had looked, lying there.

"The fight," Pam was saying. "Did you have it in the car or the diner?"

What diner? "In the car."

"After a fight like this, you went to the diner?"

Jake realized it sounded implausible. "Yes," he answered anyway.

"He went along with that?" Pam recoiled, surprised. "I would think he'd be embarrassed. He'd been crying. What if he ran into someone he knew? Everybody knows who he is, from the team. You can't miss him, he's built like a lighthouse."

"That's what he said, but I insisted on it. He cleaned himself up in the car. I always have those Wet Wipes in the console, for when I eat in the car." In truth, Jake was the one who cleaned up using the Wet Wipes. There had been blood on his face and hands. He'd driven away from a hit-and-run, thrown away the Wet Wipes and the marijuana in a Dumpster, and taught their son that dishonesty was the best policy. Jake didn't know himself anymore. This wasn't him.

"Why'd you want to go to the diner? You mean Mason's?"

"Yes, Mason's." Jake realized he'd just trapped himself. He was a terrible liar. His heart beat wildly in his chest, as if it wanted to escape his very body.

"But you hate Mason's. Every time I ask you to go, you say no."

"I know, but you and Ryan love it, and I thought we could sort things out better there."

"In public?" Pam didn't look suspicious, merely critical. "Why didn't you come home? I could've helped."

Think! "I know, that's the problem. If we came home, we would have looked to you to settle it, like Judge Mom. I didn't want that. We had to do this on our own, just the two of us."

"Really." Pam nodded, with a new half smile. "So you went to Mason's because I wasn't there?"

"Honestly, yes. I have to find my own way with him. That's the goal, right?" Jake felt he had turned a corner, inadvertently saying something that made complete sense, however false. Still it brought him no satisfaction or relief.

"Exactly."

"You keep saying you can't *facilitate* my relationship to him. The therapist said that too."

"True."

"So I tempted him with a cheeseburger, and we got over it."

"Wow." Pam brightened, genuinely happy, which only made Jake feel horrible.

"So it's over. We solved it."

"You *resolved* it."

"Whatever, I'll take it." Jake managed a shaky smile, and Pam patted him on the back.

"You're a good guy, Jake. That's why I knew we'd be fine. Back when, you know."

Jake's throat caught. She meant when he'd lost his job and they had their rough patch. She'd dragged him into marriage counseling. It wasn't his way, with his old-school, close-mouthed, working-class Scottish upbringing, from the other side of town. But like everything else he'd learned growing up, it had been 180 degrees wrong. Pam had taught him that, and now he was lying to her face.

"You're reliable, and kind, and you try. You really do." Pam smiled, sweetly. "You know what my mom always said about you."

Jake couldn't even fake a smile back. It was something they always said, a marital call-and-response, but the words soured on his tongue. "I'm Husband Material?"

"Ha! Don't say it that way. Yes, you are." Pam gave his back a final pat, like a period at the end of the sentence, then turned to go upstairs. "Okay, let's go up. This week needs to end."

"Right behind you." Jake followed her from the kitchen, flicking off the lights. He should be relieved that he'd gotten away with lying to Pam, but it made him sick to his stomach.

He trudged upstairs behind Pam, leaning on the banister and hanging his head. He tried to unravel the night in his mind, to unspool the hours, to undo all the times it had gone wrong. He wished he had told Pam the truth. He wished he'd called the cops at the scene. He wished he hadn't distracted Ryan while he was driving. He wished he hadn't let Ryan drive in the first place. He wished he'd never even gone to pick Ryan up. Most of all, he wished that that poor woman was alive and well, back from her run, happy and at home, with her family.

But she wasn't.

Jake had committed himself and his son to a course, and he had to see it through. Even though the notion filled him with dread.

And the deepest, deepest shame.

Chapter Four

Jake turned over, facing away from his sleeping wife, and opened his eyes. The bedroom was pitch dark because Pam liked to keep the blackout shades down, and it made the green digital numerals in his alarm clock glow even brighter. It was 2:45 A.M., and he'd been tossing and turning since he'd showered and gone to bed. He knew he would never fall asleep, replaying the night in his head, starting with him being parked outside the movie theater and ending with his avoiding his rearview mirror, so he couldn't see the broken corpse of the woman vanish into blackness.

Jake tugged the covers up over his shoulder. In his mind, he went over everything he did and everything he said, then everything Ryan did and said, again and again, trying to see how it could have come out differently, or how he could've reached a different decision. But he kept coming out in the same horrendous place, reaching the same unthinkable conclusion.

Anguished, Jake felt like it was a no-win situation from the moment they hit the runner, or maybe from the moment he found out about the marijuana, or maybe from the moment he let

Ryan drive. His guilt and remorse drove him to keep trying to parse his decisions and sent him into another spiral of what-if reasoning, *what if I hadn't gone to pick him up, what if I hadn't let him drive, what if I had paid attention to the road, what if, what if, what if.*

Jake squeezed his eyes shut, keeping tears at bay. He slept on the side of the bed closer to the door, because he was supposed to protect everybody, the Daddy-dragon guarding the Dutch Colonial. The thought made him cringe, after what had happened. He'd protected his son into a nightmare. And if he was having a sleepless night, he could only imagine that Ryan had it worse.

He eased off the covers, got up quietly, and padded down the hallway to Ryan's room. He turned the knob carefully, opened the door, slipped inside, and closed the door behind him. The bedroom was dark, and moonlight came through the striped curtains. Ryan made a large mound under his comforter, and Jake could see his head on the pillow, but couldn't make out his face. Moose was curled up on the bed, his head resting on Ryan's feet, and the golden retriever didn't stir.

"Dad?" Ryan whispered, and Jake crossed to the bed and sat down on the edge.

"How are you doing?"

"Horrible. How are you?"

"Horrible, and worried about my boy." Jake's eyes were adjusting to the light level, and he could see the shadows of Ryan's young features, the hollows of his eyes and cheeks, and the dark waves in his hair. "Are you getting any sleep?"

"No."

Jake sighed heavily. "I know, I'm sorry. I'm so sorry that it happened."

"Me, too, I'm sorry, so sorry. Everything is my fault, all of it."

"That's not true."

"It is, you know it is. I was the driver. I'm the one responsible."

"No, it was an accident. That's why they call it an accident. Accidents happen." Jake had been giving himself the same speech for the past hour. "We weren't doing anything really wrong, it just happened."

"Come on. I *was* doing something wrong. I wasn't watching the road."

"You happened to look over for a minute, a second, even a split second. You were having a conversation with me, and that happens every day, in cars all across this country."

"But, Dad—"

"You weren't texting or talking on the phone. In the fraction of a second you looked away, we hit a blind curve, and a runner was in the street. Who knew that she would be running that time of night? And she didn't have any reflective gear on, either."

"It's not her fault she got hit."

"I didn't mean that." Jake realized he was lying then, too. He did mean that. He had just blamed an innocent victim for getting herself killed. He must be losing his mind. A wave of guilt washed over him, so profound he had to close his eyes until it passed.

"Lots of people run late at night."

"I know, but it's not your fault that you hit her. That *we* hit her."

Ryan moaned. "No, *I* hit her, you just said it."

"Ryan, we're in this together, and we will get through this together." Jake stroked Ryan's hair back from his face, a gesture he did without thinking, then realized that he couldn't remember the last time he'd done it. He felt his throat thicken. "I love you, do you know that?"

"I love you too."

"You're a smart and able kid, and you're stronger than you think." Jake swallowed hard, not really knowing what to say. "By the way, everything went okay with Mom. But I didn't tell her the story about Caleb and you getting in a fight. I told her that you and I got in a fight about texting in the car."

"What?" Ryan asked, a new note of anxiety in his voice.

"I changed the story."

"Why did you do that? We decided on the Caleb story."

"I know, but this is better."

"No it isn't."

"I think it is." Jake hated himself, fussing with his son over which lie was better. "It makes more sense because it keeps everything between us and doesn't involve Caleb. We don't want her to start talking to Caleb's mom, do we?"

"Oh, no, because of the weed," Ryan answered sadly.

"That wasn't what I meant. I was just saying that I don't want any chatter between the moms about tonight, and also I told her that she shouldn't bring it up with you. If she does, just say you don't want to talk about it."

"You think that'll work?"

"For you, it'll work. For me, no chance in hell."

"That's a random thing to say, Dad." Ryan fell silent, then pulled out his iPhone. Its home screen glowed in the dark, show-ing a funny photo of Moose rolling on his back, his four big paws in the air. Ryan started to scroll to the Internet. "I looked online, but the news doesn't have anything about the lady. Does that mean they didn't . . . find her yet? Does that mean she's . . . still lying there?"

"Not necessarily. Maybe they found her but haven't released it to the public yet. They have to inform the next of kin."

"That means her family, right?"

"Yes."

"But she must live with her family. They would know that she didn't come home from her run."

"Maybe she lives alone."

"Do you think she does? Could you tell . . . how old she was?"

"No, I couldn't." Jake shuddered, flashing on the woman's abraded face.

"Also it's going to rain all night. Do you think she's out there . . . in the rain?"

Jake hadn't known it was raining. Pam's blackout shades muffled sound, too. "I don't want you to think about that anymore. What's done is done. These first few days are going to be hard, I know, because you're a good kid and you feel terrible."

"I do, I feel *terrible.* I keep wondering who she was. I keep thinking about her."

Jake squeezed his shoulder. "I know, but we need to stay the course. Keep it to yourself, and obviously, don't say anything to any of your friends or anyone on the team."

"I wouldn't, Dad. I'm not stupid."

"I know, but you're feeling bad and you could open up to people"—Jake didn't know where he was going with this, so he let it go—"anyway, enough said. We did the right thing, in the circumstances."

"*What?* You really think we did the right thing? I don't."

"Listen, I'm your father and my job is to protect you. I feel horrible about what we did and if I could bring her back, I would. I tried to. I made the best decision I could on the spot, and in that moment, my first concern is always you."

Jake's chest tightened as he tried to explain the inexplicable.

"Look. If there were any chance of saving her life, I never would've left. But she was gone. It was an accident, I don't know what purpose would have been served by your going to jail for a long, long time. Then two lives would have been destroyed, instead of one."

"So you think it was the wrong thing, too."

"Okay, yes, right."

"It was the wrong thing. We did the wrong thing."

"Yes, we did. Well, I did the wrong thing, for a good reason."

"What does *that* mean?"

"Forget it." Jake raked his hand through his hair. He had done the wrong thing. He had acted too fast. He should have called the cops and taken the blame himself. Maybe Ryan could have held it together under questioning. Maybe Ryan could have run home, though it was miles away. Or hid in the woods. Or whatever. He hadn't had time to think, on the scene. Either way, it was too late now.

"So then, maybe, we could change our minds. Could we do that?"

"No, we can't," Jake answered, more sharply than he intended. Moose lifted his head, then thumped his tail on the comforter, *whomp whomp whomp*.

"No, Dad, listen to me. I was thinking, couldn't we go to the police now and tell them that we left, but we're sorry we left . . . and tell them all about what happened?"

"No, we couldn't, no." Jake had been second-guessing himself, too, but he kept coming out in the same place. "Once we left the scene, we left the scene, and if they were to test you, they would find marijuana in your system. I think that stays in your system for days."

"I know, they give us random drug tests on the team. They just tested us yesterday for the playoffs. That's why we figured it was okay to smoke."

"It ends now, Ryan. No more smoking."

"Yes, agreed, of course, but maybe if we explained to them that I wasn't high when I hit her, that it was a blind curve, they would—"

"Understand? Let it go? It doesn't work that way, buddy."

"No, I know they wouldn't let me off or anything, but maybe I would get probation, or I wouldn't go to prison for that long—"

"No, this was the right thing."

Ryan scoffed. "Dad, it's *not* the right thing. Stop saying that."

Jake cringed. "Fair enough. But it's the only thing we could do, and if it makes you feel any better, please remember it wasn't your decision. It was my decision, and I think the thing to do, from here on out, is for you to live your life. It's going to be hard in the beginning, but then it will get easier, I promise."

"Why will it get easier?" Ryan asked, incredulous.

"Time changes things. It makes things easier."

"Dad, I *killed* that lady. That's wrong, like, forever. Time doesn't change *that*."

Jake felt a stab of sympathy for him, so deep it felt like a knife wound. He had no immediate reply, because Ryan's reasoning was logical, and in fact, he sounded just like his mother. Meantime, Moose had awakened and was stutter-stepping to them on the bed, then he plopped his feathery butt down and opened his mouth, so that his tongue lolled out. Jake decided to change tacks with Ryan. "So what are you doing tomorrow?"

"I don't know. After this, I feel—"

"No, what were you going to do tomorrow, before this happened?"

"Well, it's Saturday. Chemistry, Algebra. You know, homework." Ryan shrugged, and Moose lay down, tucking his muzzle between his meaty front paws.

"Okay, so do your homework. Do everything you would do. Go out on that date, with that blonde, Janine Mae—"

"Dad, are you serious right now? That's not possible."

"I know it's not easy, but it's the only way, and we did this so you can have a life. So live your life."

"Is that why we did it? For me?"

"No, well, for us both."

"No, for me." Ryan's voice softened, pained. "Tell the truth, Dad. You did it for me. You were going to tell the cops that you were driving, for me, before you even knew about the weed."

Jake waited, not understanding or not wanting to answer, or both. "Is that a question?"

"Yes."

"Then yes."

"That's, like, so unselfish of you."

Jake felt a surge of emotion that constricted his chest. "Son, I love you and I'd do anything for you. It's as simple as that."

"I love you, too." Ryan paused. "Dad, what are you doing tomorrow? Are you going to the office?"

"No, I'm—" Jake caught himself. "I told your mother I'm going in early, but I have to take care of the car."

Ryan gasped. "Oh no, I forgot! What about the car? Is there blood on it? Is it dented?"

"I'll handle it." Jake had found a dent on the front bumper and on the undercarriage. "I don't want you to think about this anymore. Let me handle everything. These are my decisions, not yours. The less you know the better, as a general matter."

"Can I go with you?"

"Where?"

"To the body shop."

"No. Now lie back, and go to sleep. In fact, make sure you sleep in. You always sleep in on Saturday mornings, and your mother expects that, so don't change anything." Jake sensed it would be safer if Ryan wasn't alone with his mother, in the short run. The boy was too fragile right now, and Pam could cross-examine a rock.

"Dad, how am I gonna sleep late? I can't sleep now."

"Stay in bed anyway. I'll be back before noon, and I'll come get you. Okay? Don't worry, let me handle everything. Now lie down and try to rest." Jake gave him a final pat on his shoulder, then rose to go. "I'll be down the hall in my office."

"Why?"

"I have some work to do." Jake realized he'd just told his third lie of the night and resolved to stop counting. "Try to get some sleep. I love you."

"Love you, too."

Jake went to the door, taking one last look at Ryan, who was hugging the dog in the dark. He flashed on his son as a child, cradling Moose as a fuzzy puppy, just brought home from the shelter. The memory was completely fresh, and for a moment, Jake felt stunned by its appearance, the sweetness of the past clashing so horribly with the anguish of the present.

Jake thanked God he had a son to put to bed when he knew somewhere there was a family, right now, waiting for someone who would never come home. Jake felt a wave of new shame. Then he slipped out of the bedroom, closed the door behind him, and padded down the hall to his office.

He was a planner, and he needed a plan.

Chapter Five

Jake slipped into his office, flicked on the overhead light, and closed the door behind him, so he didn't wake Pam up. He blinked while his eyes adjusted to the brightness and crossed the room, making a beeline for his desk, a cherrywood computer table facing the wall between two windows. He moved the mouse to wake up the computer, then sat down while it fired up. He wanted to know the penalty for vehicular homicide in Pennsylvania.

The large monitor came to life, and onto the screen popped his screensaver, which was their official family portrait, posed for his firm's website and brochure, to show that he was a good family man. Jake felt his chest constrict at the sight. The photograph was taken when Ryan was only in middle school, and both father and son were wearing identical blue oxford shirts that emphasized how much they looked alike, except that Ryan was all unruly hair and big goofy grin, with orthodonture for miles. His son said the same thing, every time he saw the photo:

Quite the grille.

In the picture, Jake stood beaming next to Ryan, and in front of them, seated on some ridiculously ornate chair, was Pam, who wore a light blue shirtdress, her legs crossed demurely at her ankles. She'd chosen the color to complement their outfits and the cerulean backdrop, which was meant to be clear blue sky but came off like a Tiffany's box, more upscale than anybody intended. Pam had been running for judge at the time and had made her unhappiness known to the photographer.

Don't you have a different backdrop? We elect judges in this state, and I have to get votes from normal people. I'm not running for Queen.

Jake went online and typed his search request into Google. He clicked through the first few websites and found himself reading one DUI site after another, featuring the crassest sort of brochureware with glossy photos of grave-faced lawyers in three-piece suits, troubled kids in handcuffs, and a six-pack of beer, with one spilled out. He'd wanted to read the actual law, but the DUI bar had evidently bought the neutral-sounding website names. One DUI firm had a pop-up showing a smiling man on the telephone, **NEED A DUI LAWYER?** above **Click Here!** or **No, Thanks!**

Jake kept searching and finally found a website that cited Pennsylvania statutes regarding the juvenile system. He read that if Ryan were charged as a juvenile, he'd go before a judge and there would be a trial that would send him to a juvenile facility for six months, then he'd be under court supervision until he was twenty-one. It was lighter punishment than Jake had thought, but then he saw a sentence that chilled him to the bone: **Call now to avoid serious ramifications, such as your child being charged and tried as an adult!**

He knew vaguely that the district attorney had discretion in deciding whether to charge a juvenile as an adult, and it could go either way with Ryan. It was certainly possible that Ryan could be tried as an adult, because the crime was serious enough, resulting in death. And Pam's status as a judge could cut either way. Either the district attorney would do her a favor and keep Ryan in the juvenile system or he might want to make an example of him, showing that Ryan didn't receive preferential treatment.

Jake didn't know the penalties if Ryan was tried as an adult, so he went back to the search engine, plugged in **Pennsylvania vehicular homicide DUI,** and got his answer in a nanosecond:

Under 75 Pa. Cons. Stat. § 3735, the criminal offense of homicide by vehicle while driving under the influence (DUI) is punishable as a second degree felony. A conviction for this offense can result in a prison sentence from three to ten years and/or a fine up to $25,000.

Jake felt his gut clench. A three-year sentence would derail Ryan's future, and a ten-year sentence would obliterate it. If they hadn't left the scene, Ryan would've ended up a convicted felon. It was the worst-case scenario, and as a financial planner, Jake was supposed to make a living out of estimating the downside risk and preventing worst-case scenarios. He felt heartsick thinking about it now, too late. If he'd been considering the worst-case scenario on Pike Road, he never would have let Ryan drive and that woman would still be alive. He'd underestimated the downside risk, and a human being had lost her life.

He leaned back in the chair, his stomach in a knot. A woman was dead, and he was responsible, as surely as if he had been driving. He was the adult, and he should have known better. He would carry his remorse with him forever; he felt it to the marrow, as if guilt were seeping into his very cells. He never should have left the scene, but that wouldn't bring the woman back. He wished he had called the cops, but that wouldn't bring her back either. He hadn't wanted to destroy two lives, one of them his own beloved son's. It would kill Pam.

Jake swallowed hard, thinking of his wife, sleeping down the hall. She would know DUI law, because as an appellate judge, she had a general overview of all state law, which governed the nuts and bolts of real-life, from premeditated murder to employees who stole trade secrets. He tried to remember if Pam had written any significant opinions in any DUI cases, but couldn't. He was too distraught and exhausted to think clearly, and his heart kept returning to the dead woman.

He palmed the mouse again and navigated to the local news site to see if her body had been found. He scanned the front page, then the next few, but there was nothing except an upcoming snowstorm and articles about budget cutbacks in the township. He was surprised that the police still hadn't found her, and he wondered if she didn't have any family or if it just hadn't found its way into the news yet.

Jake rubbed his cheek, slumping back in his chair. His gaze traveled around his plush home office, taking in the beige sofa, matching chairs, and tasteful cherrywood shelves filled with books and awards. He didn't deserve an office like this, he was every inch a fraud. He found himself looking out the window, framed by beige curtains handpicked by his discerning wife.

This is the perfect color, see how it picks up the sisal rug?

Jake had laughed. *Is sisal the same as straw? Because to me, this rug is straw.*

Outside the window, a steady rain came down, running in rivulets on the windows and graying out the houses across the street, identical to his own. It was raining hard, and Jake knew it would be turning cold, with the snowstorm coming. He couldn't bear to think that the woman was still lying on the street and wondered why it was taking the police so long to find her.

He turned back to the computer, palmed the mouse, and clicked REFRESH, but nothing had changed on the news page. Still he refreshed another time, and the only sound in the quiet office was the *click* of the mouse and the thrumming of the rain outside the window. He and Ryan were the only people who knew that the woman was dead, and as far as the world was concerned, no crime had occurred and she was alive and well.

Jake wished he and Ryan could live inside that reality, in the very interstices of time, tucked under the comforter of not-knowing, sleeping as soundly as they used to, the Before the same as the After. But even so, he couldn't wait another second for the woman to be found, gathered up, lifted onto a gurney, and taken from the horrific scene, out of the rain, away from him and Ryan, and finally safe.

The horror of what he had done brought new tears to Jake's eyes. He clicked REFRESH again and again. He wanted to know the precise moment that After began.

But by morning, when it still hadn't happened, he got dressed and left by the kitchen door.

Chapter Six

Jake hurried into the chilly garage, holding his jacket over his arm and carrying his empty traveler's mug. He was dressed for work in an old wool sweater, jeans and sneakers, the way he always did on a Saturday; he'd worked at least one day of the weekend for as long as he could remember, because it was the quiet time he needed, to think without phones and interruptions.

He checked his watch—6:15 in the morning, which was when he usually left. He'd gotten ready quietly enough for Pam to remain asleep and he was doing everything the way he always did, just in case she woke up. He hadn't checked on Ryan because that would've been out of the ordinary; the Saturday routine was for Jake to go to work early, Pam to get up around eight o'clock, let the dog out, and leave for the gym around nine thirty. Ryan would stay in bed until eleven o'clock or so, if he didn't have a game or practice.

Jake hustled to the car, stopping to double-check the damage to the front bumper. It was too dark to see well because the only illumination came from three small windows in the garage door, but he wouldn't normally turn on a light, so he didn't now. He straightened up, chirped the car unlocked, opened the door, and jumped inside, throwing his coat on the passenger seat and screwing his travel mug into the console.

He buckled into his harness, hit a button on the rearview mirror to open the garage door, and while he waited for it to *ca-chunck* upward, he surveyed the front seat and floor of the car, scanning for any errant napkin, sign of blood, or anything from the accident scene or his efforts to clean up. Everything looked in order, and there wasn't any sign of blood or anything else on the front seat, dashboard, console, or steering wheel.

He twisted on the ignition, reversed out of the garage, and cruised down the street. It was too early for any of the neighbors to be out starting their Saturday errands, and he cruised past the darkened houses that sat silently behind the blue recycling bins and rolling trash cans. He fed the car some gas, switched on the heat, and turned right, heading for the office. He didn't breathe any easier once he left their street, but on the contrary, felt more nervous, either because he was leaving Ryan alone with Pam or because of what he had to do next.

What about the car?

Jake tried not to think about it as he drove through their development, the only car on the curvy, man-made streets with their oddly high curbs, taking the perimeter road, past the mandatory forestation and specimen plantings required by the township zoning board. The trees in the front row were the builder's-grade evergreens, planted in that telltale zigzag for maximum privacy, and though they'd grown and filled out, Jake remembered when they'd been only four feet tall, shaped like gumdrops the same height as Ryan. He'd taken a photo of Ryan with one of the trees, and they had the picture in the house somewhere, Pam would know where.

Jake steered past the Chetwynd Springs sign at the grandiose entrance/exit of the development and flipped on the radio. It was tuned to the local news channel from last night, but it was weather on the nines. He didn't need a meteorologist to tell him it was a crummy day, under a sky opaque with thick gray clouds.

Fog is a cloud on the ground.

Jake hit the open road and joined the line of sparse traffic, his thoughts shifting into gear at the task that lay ahead. He had a plan and he knew where he was going. He knew what he had to do and what he had to say. He had done the research he needed on the computer. He told himself to stay calm, and that he had to see his plan through, as dreadful as his purpose was, it was the only way to protect Ryan. He drove on autopilot, listening to the radio and waiting for the news as traffic got heavier, with people getting the jump on the day, ready to check off items on their things-to-do list. They'd run to Acme and Whole Foods in pre-snowstorm panic, stocking up on salt.

Suddenly, he heard the announcer change on the radio, and the news began, "In headline news, the victim of a hit-and-run driver in Concord Chase last night has been identified as sixteen-year-old Kathleen Lindstrom. A junior at Concord Chase High School, she was struck while jogging. Police are asking anyone with information regarding this incident to please call the main tipline, at number . . ."

Oh my God, no.

Jake gasped aloud, in horror. His fingers clenched the steering wheel. He almost ran into the maroon Subaru in front of him. He slammed on the brakes, setting his ABS system shuddering.

No, no.

Jake shook his head, shocked. He clung to the wheel as if it were a life raft and he a drowning man. His heart thundered. He broke a sweat under his shirt. He couldn't believe it was possible. The revelation stunned him.

I killed a kid. Kathleen Lindstrom.

Jake didn't recognize the name, but now it was a part of his DNA. It would echo in his head for the rest of his life. New tears brimmed in his eyes. He couldn't fathom that she was so young. He'd thought she was petite but she was just a *girl*. A teenager, only sixteen years old. Her life was just beginning, and now she was gone.

God, forgive me.

Jake flashed on her face, covered with blood. She had been somebody's daughter. She had parents, waiting for her to come home from her run. They would wait and wait, until they got the call that every parent dreads. They would never see her alive again. Their daughter, their child. His heart broke for them.

Jake felt shaken to his very foundations. Kathleen was the same age as Ryan. She was a student at the same high school. Jake realized, aghast, that Ryan probably knew her. Concord Chase High wasn't that large, only about a thousand students.

He killed his classmate.

Jake found himself reeling, stopped at a red light. This news would kill Ryan. His son wouldn't be able to bear the guilt; it would be unsupportable. He didn't know how Ryan could go to school, ever again. Ryan's classmates, and all of the faculty and staff would be mourning a girl that he knew he had *killed*. It would be impossible, untenable. Ryan was too sensitive a kid to get past this, ever. Jake feared for his son's sanity, maybe even his very life.

The horn of a car behind him blared, startling Jake out of his reverie. The traffic light had turned green, and he fed the car some gas, following the Subaru mechanically. He felt sick to his stomach and fought the impulse to call Ryan, but it was too risky, with Pam at home. Then he had another, darker thought. What if the news would send Ryan to Pam, to spill his guts?

Dad, I swear, I won't tell Mom. I won't tell anybody.

Jake couldn't process the information. He wanted to pull over but there wasn't time. He felt his gorge rising, but swallowed hard. He had to stay on plan. He blinked his tears away and tried vainly to ignore the pain in his chest. He drove ahead, past clapboard Cape Cods, new brick split levels, and a Dutch Colonial with white stucco, wondering if Kathleen Lindstrom lived with her family in a house like one of these. Pike Road was only ten minutes away.

Jake gritted his teeth, trying to recover. The stretch of road he was looking for lay just ahead, a two-lane street lined with houses, trees, and a strip mall that held a Chinese restaurant, a Wawa convenience market where he always stopped for coffee on the way to work, and the auto body shop he'd used for years. He'd given plenty of free financial advice to its owner Mike Ayanna, and Mike owed him a favor, but Jake wasn't about to depend on Mike, favor or no. The police would undoubtedly be investigating the local body shops, and Mike would be compelled to turn over his records.

Jake put on his right blinker when he spotted the Wawa sign, glowing a corporate red, and slowed as he approached its parking lot. It was the side entrance to the store, with a line of parking spaces under a white sign, NO IDLING—DIESEL POWERED VEHICLES OVER FIVE TONS. The parking spaces ended next to a bundle of cardboard recycling, a stack of flat boxes, and a green metal Dumpster. The side lot was completely empty, which is what Jake would've expected this early in the morning.

He turned into the parking lot and aimed at the Dumpster. He hit the gas, steering slightly to the right, knowing that the damage would obliterate the dents from last night. The Dumpster raced forward to meet him.

Jake braced himself for impact, feeling that if anything went wrong, he deserved to die.

Kathleen, I am so very sorry.

Chapter Seven

The Audi slammed into the Dumpster, and Jake jolted forward, caught by his shoulder harness. His airbag exploded, hit him in the face, and pushed him backwards. The odor of plastic and a chemical powder filled his nostrils.

Abruptly the airbag deflated, imploding in a pile on his lap and draping over the steering wheel. The engine was still running, and the windshield was cracked but intact. The hood had buckled and his right front bumper crumpled into the Dumpster. No one would ever see the dent again.

Jake realized he'd succeeded, but he still felt sick to his stomach. The collision reminded him of last night, a memory embedded in his very body. He moved the airbag from his lap, his muscles stiff from shock, not of the accident, but of the revelation.

I killed a kid and left her dead. To save my own kid.

Jake was alive, but he didn't deserve to be.

"Jake, Jake!" someone called out, near the car. It was Christopher, a Wawa clerk, hurrying toward him. They knew each other because Jake always stopped here on the way to work.

Christopher appeared at the driver's-side window, his young face creased with concern. "Jake! Are you okay?"

Jake nodded, collected his phone and jacket, opened the door, and got out of the car, his knees suddenly wobbly. "Christopher, My God—"

"You look white as a ghost, Jake. Stay still, I'll call 911. My phone's in my locker, 'cause we have to lock it up during work." Christopher turned to hurry off, but Jake touched his arm.

"No, no, stay. I'm fine."

"For real?"

"Yes." Jake tried to recover. "I'm just a little . . . upset is all. I surprised myself. It's kind of a shock."

"Sure, I get it. You gonna toss 'em? You look it."

"No, I'm fine. Don't call."

"You sure you don't wanna go to a hospital? My manager might want you to." Christopher frowned, scanning him with worried eyes.

"Nah. I'm fine, thanks."

"Coulda been worse, I guess, huh?"

"Right." Jake dusted the airbag powder off his clothes. "I thought I hit the brake, but I must've hit the gas instead."

Christopher shrugged sympathetically. "You didn't have your coffee yet."

"Right." Jake walked to the front of the car, leaned on the hood, and surveyed the damage. He was thinking of Kathleen, her body broken in her running gear. It was too awful to comprehend. There was so much death and destruction, all of a sudden. He shuddered to his very bones, eyeing the car. "Damn, I really messed up, didn't I?"

"You never know. Mike next door can fix it."

"I'll let him take it, it's not drivable with that windshield anyway. My wife will pick me up." Jake slipped into his jacket, put his cell phone in his pocket, and gestured at the Dumpster, which had a large dent in its middle. "It looks like I did a number on your Dumpster, too. Sorry about that."

"Oh, forget about it." Christopher waved him off, but that was the wrong answer for Jake. He felt bad manipulating the kid, but it couldn't be helped. That was why he'd damaged their property. They would be required to make a police report for liability purposes, and he needed everything to be documented, so there would be no questions later.

"No, make a report, so my insurance will pay."

"But it's just a trash can. Who cares?"

"The store doesn't own the Dumpster, the hauling company does. See?" Jake gestured at the Waste Control logo on its lid. "The store will have to pay for the damage, and you shouldn't be in that position. I'll put in a claim, but we'll have to call the police."

"Let's see what Donna says. She's my manager." Christopher turned toward the store just as a ponytailed employee came hustling around the corner. She was heavyset and wore wire-rimmed glasses, her face a mask of worry.

"What happened? Are you hurt, sir?"

"I'm fine, thanks." Jake had seen her before but he didn't know her, and he could tell from her expression that she was thinking the same thing about him. "I'm Jake Buckman, I always stop in here before work. I hit the gas instead of the brake and crashed into the Dumpster."

Beside him, Christopher nodded. "He says he doesn't need to go to the hospital."

"That's lucky. The police will be here any minute, I already called them." Donna's forehead relaxed, and she eyed the car and Dumpster. "Any accidents on our property need to be reported. I hope you understand, sir."

"Yes, of course, please call me Jake."

"Jake, are you sure you weren't injured in any way?"

"I'm fine, thanks."

"Okay then. I'll have you sign some paperwork, if that's okay. Come with me. I have the file in the office." Donna started walking to the front of the store, and Jake and Christopher fell into step beside her.

Christopher looked over with a smile. "How about we treat you to a cup of coffee?"

"No thanks," Jake answered, with a twinge. Donna went to the door, yanked it open, and led them inside the store.

Christopher split off. "Okay, Jake, see you later. I gotta get back to the register. Let me know what Mike says about the car."

"Will do, Christopher. Thanks for the assist. I owe you one." Jake followed Donna past stacks of bound newspapers, shelves of blue antifreeze jugs, and a refrigerated case of prepared salads and hard-boiled eggs. A customer in a down jacket and sweatpants stood at the lineup of bronze plastic coffee canisters, where the air smelled of hazelnut flavoring and Lysol.

"This way," Donna called over her shoulder, leading him around the hoagie counter, down a short hallway, and into a cramped office that contained a box of paper towels, a cluttered gray desk, and a cheap black chair. A bulletin board held shift schedules, OSHA notices, and a cluster of kids' school pictures, next to a black metal shelf with a trio of security monitors, one of which had a red Phillies cap sitting on top.

"Go Phils," Jake said, nervous. He hadn't counted on the security monitors, and he could see that the one in the middle overlooked the side parking lot.

"Are you a baseball fan?" Donna fetched a manila folder from a tan file cabinet against the wall.

"Who isn't?" Jake couldn't stop looking at the security monitor. Its resolution was remarkably good, in full color, and he could clearly see the Audi's far side embedded in the Dumpster. He'd caught a lucky break in that the view of the camera was on the driver's side of the car, so it wouldn't have picked up the dent on the passenger side when he'd pulled in. Still, he wondered if Donna had seen the accident as it occurred or if there was a digital copy or videotape.

"Here we go." Donna set a few forms in front of him. "These say that you had an accident here and that you declined to go to the hospital. Would you sign them? We have to have it for the lawyers."

"I understand." Jake picked up a pen and started signing the forms, preoccupied with the security camera. He gestured to the monitor. "Look at that. My God, it looks like the car is growing out of the Dumpster."

"It kinda does, doesn't it?" Donna eyed the screen. "I'm sorry for you. That's a really sweet car."

"Thanks." Jake flipped to the next page of forms. "That monitor is good quality. Do you get a lot of detail?"

"Yes. We have it in case we get held up, but that hasn't happened yet. Knock wood." Donna rapped her knuckles on her head. "I tell my mom, it's Concord Chase. The worst thing that happens here is minors trying to buy cigarettes. Still, she hates my working the night shift. She worries."

"That's what parents are for, to worry about their kids." Jake cringed inwardly. He finished signing the forms and pushed them across the desk to her. "Here we go. Do you ever watch the monitor?"

"Mostly I'm busy on the floor."

"So you didn't see my accident?"

"No, sorry. I just heard the noise and covered the floor while Christopher ran out."

"Of course." Jake let it go. He didn't want to arouse her suspicion or provoke her into playing the video. "When do you think the police will get here? I should call my wife and give her the heads-up that I'll need a ride later."

"They said they had a car nearby."

Suddenly the door opened, and Christopher stuck his head inside the office. A tall, middle-aged police officer stood behind him, and Jake's mouth went dry. Christopher said, "Donna, look who's here, Officer John!"

"Yo, Officer John!" Donna burst into a grin, went to the door, and threw her arms around the policeman, who hugged her back.

"Hey, good to see you, girl!" he boomed, releasing her. He had a broad smile and friendly blue eyes under a black CTPD knit cap. A silver badge gleamed from his black nylon jacket, and embroidered white block letters over his right breast, which read McMULLEN.

"You, too! When did you get back?"

"Yesterday." Officer McMullen grinned back at Donna. "I'm back in the pink and all healed up. I have rehab for a coupla weeks, but I'm good. How have you been?"

"Fine, thanks." Donna's gaze shifted to Jake. "Mr. Buckman, Officer John just recovered from hip replacement. Don't think it was anything cool like a gunshot wound."

"Oh." Jake managed a smile.

"Donna, I got a metal hip, I'm Robocop!" Officer McMullen shot back, and the others laughed, then the policeman faced Jake and extended a hand. "Sir, are you the gentleman who had the accident?"

"Yes. Jake Buckman." Jake prayed his palm wasn't sweaty and shook the officer's hand. "Thanks for coming out."

"It's no bother, sir. First things first. I understand you declined medical treatment?"

"Yes, I'm fine, really. I want to do whatever needs to be done for you and for the insurance company, then my wife will come pick me up."

"I'll need to take a statement and I won't keep you too long. Where do you live?"

"The Chetwynd development."

"Sure, I know it, about fifteen minutes away. I'll give you a lift home."

"No, that's okay. I'll call her, I hate to put you out." Jake hid his alarm. The last thing he wanted was to ride home with a cop, and God forbid that Ryan saw him pull up in a police cruiser.

"It's no trouble. I'm happy to do it."

Donna burst into laughter. "Of course he's happy to do it! Officer John gets lonely tooling around in his copmobile, since his partner got reassigned. He'll talk your ear off. The siren's the only thing that shuts him up."

"Ha! Very funny, Donna." Officer McMullen laughed again, then motioned Jake forward in a way that was suddenly authoritative. "Come with me, sir. I'll make an incident report, then I'll give you a lift home. I insist."

Chapter Eight

Jake followed Officer McMullen to his cruiser, a black-and-white muscle car with a massive chrome grille and a sleek modern lightbar on the roof. CHETWYND POLICE, read gold reflective letters on its jet-black door. Jake had managed not to be nervous when he'd given Officer McMullen his statement about the Dumpster accident because Donna had stayed with them, interrupting with chatter. But now that Jake was alone with the cop, he felt anxious about the ride home. He could have handled it before the news about Kathleen Lindstrom, but not now. It was as if he had too many emotions to hide.

"Mr. Buckman, there is no room for you up front. Don't take it personally. My duty bag takes up the whole damn passenger seat. See?" Officer McMullen motioned to the front seat of the cruiser, where a gray nylon messenger bag filled the passenger seat next to a laptop mounted over the console, tilted toward the driver's seat. A large black AK-47 was mounted upright between the two front seats, its butt down and its lethal muzzle facing up.

"I see," Jake said, trying to get his act together.

"There's not much room in this car, that's the problem. We got these new Dodge Chargers with a hemi. We love 'em because they're so fast. But they're not that comfortable and the seats are small. Sometimes I miss the old Crown Vics." Officer McMullen opened the back door. "Here you go, sir."

"Thank you." Jake climbed into the backseat, which had no cushioning, but was made of molded gray plastic and separated from the front seat by a metal barrier and a thick plastic panel, with a sliding window in the middle.

"Buckle up, sir." Officer McMullen shut the heavy door, which made a solid sound.

"Thanks." Jake reached for the shoulder harness, buckling himself in. He felt as if he deserved to be where he was, in the backseat of a cruiser. He should be under arrest, brought to justice to pay for the death of Kathleen Lindstrom.

"How you doing back there, sir? Could you be any less comfortable?" Officer McMullen climbed in the front seat, slammed his door closed, and buckled in his shoulder harness. He reached back and slid aside the window between the front seat and backseat, making a foot-wide opening.

"It's fine, thanks," Jake called back, miserably.

"Let's roll." Officer McMullen started the ignition, reversed out of the lot, and headed for the exit. "It's a shame about your car."

"It sure is." Jake pulled out his iPhone and checked the time. It was almost nine o'clock, so Pam would be up. He prayed Ryan would still be in his room asleep, so he didn't know about Kathleen yet.

"My brother-in-law has an Audi. They're fast, aren't they?"

"Yes. Excuse me, I'll just text my wife and tell her we're on the way." Jake composed a text to Pam. **Had a minor fender bender. Cop giving me a ride home.**

"Good call." Officer McMullen cruised ahead, talking idly over his shoulder. "I'm married twenty-six years. My wife likes it when she knows what's going on. Women, they like to know things."

"Right." Jake added, **See you soon.** He hit SEND and held the phone. He looked out the window at the passing scenery, his heart aching.

"Kind of a busy morning, this one. Everybody's over at a scene on Pike Road, a hit-and-run. That's where I was when the property-damage call came in, for you. My supervisor told me to go."

Oh God. Jake kept his expression calm, so he didn't look suspicious in the rearview mirror. He hadn't anticipated that McMullen would've been at the scene, but Pike Road and the Wawa were both in Whiteland Township, which was small. It wasn't unlikely that the cop who came to the Wawa would also have been on Pike Road.

"I'll tell you this, it wasn't pretty." Officer McMullen slowed the cruiser to a stop at a red light. "The victim was a high-school kid, a jogger. Female."

"What a shame." Jake swallowed hard, feeling a wave of regret so powerful he almost confessed. Then it could all be over. He would be punished, he would pay. But so would Ryan.

"They were gathering evidence when I left. No suspects yet, in case you were wondering."

Jake should have been wondering, but he was still thinking about Kathleen. He flashed on her bloodied face, for the umpteenth time.

"We got a crack team on the case. We call in a team of accident-reconstruction officers who are specially trained to investigate a hit-and-run. We share them. We don't have the payroll to justify them, or the need, but we borrow them from Pikeland Township."

Jake nodded, but Officer McMullen didn't require encouragement to keep talking.

"They're crackerjack, five full-fledged accident-reconstruction specialists. Most of our guys were active-duty law enforcement, so they have a lot of experience too. We call it the total station."

"I see." Jake had to get it together. As anguished as he felt about Kathleen, it worried him to think of how expert the police could be. He felt his gut wrench, caught between feeling guilty and not wanting to get caught, for Ryan's sake.

"They go out there with equipment, like surveyor's equipment with the scope, and they triangulate the scene. They measure everything. They look for skidmarks, any damage, any trace evidence or other physical evidence, like pieces of the headlamp or any part that came off the car." Officer McMullen kept his eyes on the road, and they looked flinty in the glare from the bright gray sky. "They collect that evidence, log it in, and bag it, and they can run down exactly what car it was, make and model, the whole nine."

Jake's phone signaled an incoming text, and he looked down. It was Pam, saying, **Oh no, are you okay?**

"It's all up-to-the-minute technology, those guys are something else. They come back and upload all the data into the computer and they can completely rebuild the accident. They can tell you exactly how it happened."

Jake texted back, **I'm fine, don't worry. Go to the gym if you want to. Don't wait for me.**

"This poor kid was knocked out of her shoes, her sneakers. Most pedestrians who get hit, they get knocked out of their shoes. I bagged her sneaker myself."

Jake couldn't hide the revulsion he felt inside and he didn't try. He was the lowest form of life on the planet.

"A few months ago, I worked a scene, this is kind of gory, but we got body parts, like the skull. We put that in these cans, looks just like a regular paint can, gallon size. That's for evidence that can decompose. We get all the evidence we can and we comb the area for debris. You never know what'll pay off."

Jake's phone signaled a text. Pam replied, **Not going to the gym. Ryan's sick.**

"And that's only the beginning. We knock on doors, we ask the neighbors what did you see."

Jake guessed Ryan must have found out that their victim was his classmate. He texted quickly, **what's the matter?**

"Plus normally we can usually get good tapes from the cameras on the street, like the red-light cameras and such. They're usually a real help."

Jake felt panic tightening his chest. He hadn't thought that street cameras or red-light cameras could have spotted them the night of the accident, and evidently, Ryan was awake and talking to Pam.

"Unfortunately, we got no red-light cameras on Pike Road. There's nothing on that street. You know where else we get good evidence, usually?" Officer McMullen glanced in the rearview, waiting for an answer.

"No, where?" Jake asked, lightly. The text alert sounded on his phone, and Pam responded, **God only knows. Ttyl.** ☹

"The Wawa, like where you were. They have the best cameras around. The resolution is awesome. Any hit-and-run, we check the local Wawas for their cameras. We get lucky about half the time."

Jake realized he could've made a colossal blunder, going to the Wawa.

"You want my opinion, the driver was probably drunk. That's why people hit and run. To avoid detection because they're drunk."

Jake nodded, texting to Pam, **hang in, home soon**.

"Drunks usually stop for a hoagie or something to eat. They've been drinking and they get hungry. Wawa has cameras in the parking lot out front, too, so we can see the cars pull up. We even get a good view of their license plates. It's unreal how often we luck out." Officer McMullen snorted.

"Anyway, I'll go back to the scene after I drop you off. The rest of my platoon is still there, and I bet the body will be, too."

"Really?" Jake blurted out, appalled.

"Yep. I've had bodies lie for a while in this county." Officer McMullen's upper lip curled with distaste. "You have no idea. I've had bodies lie bleeding through the blanket and I had to change the blanket."

Jake flashed on Kathleen, bloodied in his arms last night.

"Problem is the coroner is in East Chester and he's not always in his office, because he doesn't have to be, and he's the only one who's allowed to pick up the body. He makes the declaration, then he takes the body to the hospital for the post. Postmortem, that is." Officer McMullen steered the cruiser onto the road leading to the Chetwynd development. "People think the coroner does the post, but he doesn't. He's an elected official, and so's the deputy coroner. They're not even doctors. They could even be dentists. That's why he's not in the office half the time. Between you and me, it's political." Officer McMullen shook his head. "I guarantee the body's still there."

Jake's stomach did a backflip, and another wave of guilt engulfed him. He knew he couldn't hide it, so he turned his face to the window, where the police officer couldn't see.

"So anyway, the post gets done at Paoli Hospital by a forensic pathologist, and unlike the coroner, he's the real deal. He gets the trace evidence off the body, like hair, fiber, any prints, evidence like that. Between what he finds and what we find, we'll get him."

Jake spotted his house at the end of the street, not a moment too soon.

"It could be a woman, too. Remember last year, that socialite who hit that kid on a skateboard?" Officer McMullen eyed him in the rearview mirror. "Did you read about that case?"

"Yes, I did." Jake edged forward, hoping that Ryan was nowhere near a window to see a police car pulling up.

"We caught her in the end, and we'll catch this one, too. It might take us a week, a couple of months, or even a year, but we'll get him. It's only a matter of time." Officer McMullen glanced over his shoulder. "What number did you say it was again?"

"My house? Two thirty-six, with the black shutters." Jake scanned the façade of his house, relieved nobody was at the windows. "Officer, thanks so much for the lift."

"No problem, sir." Officer McMullen steered the cruiser to the curb, slowed to a stop, and got out to open the back door. "Good luck with your car."

"Thanks," Jake said, fleeing the cruiser.

Chapter Nine

"What happened, honey?" Pam asked, meeting him in the entrance hall. Obviously, Ryan hadn't confessed to her, because she looked like her normal self—sweet, loving, and concerned about him. But she must already have been in Ryan's room, because Moose trotted up behind her.

"It was nothing, really. I hit the Dumpster at the Wawa. I clipped the edge." Jake gave her a brief hug, so he didn't get any residual airbag powder on her clothes. She was dressed for the gym, in glasses, ponytail, and a long T-shirt over her black yoga pants, but worry was etched into the lines of her lovely face.

"How did you do that? You weren't on the phone, were you?"

"No, I hit the gas instead of the brake."

"Really?" Pam recoiled, puzzled. "You're a better driver than that."

"I know."

"So how did it happen?"

"God knows. I needed my coffee." Jake let her go and shrugged it off, or tried to. He'd been too preoccupied on the ride home to make up a detailed story about the accident. "Mike's is right there, and I don't think it's totaled, so it's a nuisance, but that's all."

"Thank God." Pam's intelligent blue eyes searched his face from behind her glasses. "What's that powder on your sweater?"

"From the airbag." Jake brushed it away, but Pam lifted her eyebrow.

"The airbag went off? How fast were you going?"

"Not that fast."

"But you have to be going a certain miles an hour for the airbag to go off. You must've been going kind of fast."

"I didn't think I was, but whatever. We're insured, and I'm not going to sweat it. I have to rent a car." Jake looked around for Ryan, masking his anxiety. "So what's up with Ryan?"

"I don't know, he seems really sick." Pam raked her nails through her hair, which had a ridge from her ponytail. "He's thrown up twice and he looks terrible."

"Oh no." Jake let his concern show.

"And he hardly slept last night. He didn't want to tell me because he knows he can't be sick now. The game's Sunday. It's the playoffs, remember?"

"Right." Jake had forgotten. He didn't know how Ryan would bear up under the pressure. It was getting worse and worse.

"He could have something, like a bug, but he was hiding it from me. I heard him in the bathroom and went in. He's miserable, but there's no fever. It could be the flu, there's something going around."

"That's probably what it is. The flu." Jake's heart went out to his son. It sounded as if Ryan was distraught over the news about Kathleen, which was just what Jake would have expected. Ryan had to have known Kathleen, at least to say hello. And she had died at his hands.

"Wait a minute." Pam frowned. "Did you tell me he had a

hamburger last night, at the diner? I should call Sal right now and make a complaint."

Think fast. "No, he didn't have the burger. He only had ice cream." Jake had to prevent her from calling Sal, who would tell her that he and Ryan hadn't even been in last night.

"But you said he had a burger." Pam frowned, more deeply. "I remember because I was surprised. He'd been saying he wants to eat less meat."

"He ordered the burger, and I ordered a sundae, but when the food came, he thought mine looked better and we ended up switching." Jake knew this was believable because everybody coveted his ice-cream sundaes, but he was the only one who ever ordered them.

"Oh, okay. Then it wasn't the meat. Good." Pam cocked her head. "Hmmm. It could've been that cheesy crap with the nachos, at the movie."

"Right." Jake wanted to talk with Ryan alone, which would be a problem now that Pam wasn't going to the gym. But he knew how to make that happen. "Meanwhile, I didn't get any breakfast. I didn't even get my coffee yet."

"I can fix you some eggs, if you want."

"I'd love that, thanks. I'll change and stop in and see him." Jake went to the stairwell.

"Okay, I'll call you when they're ready." Pam went to the kitchen with Moose following her, his toenails clicking on the hardwood. Jake hustled upstairs, knocked on Ryan's door, then slipped inside his room.

"Dad!" Ryan looked pale and drawn, and there were dark circles under his eyes. His hair was a rumpled mess, and he was sitting up in bed in his sweats. His laptop, notebooks, and an open textbook lay scattered around him. "Did you hear? It was *Kathleen Lindstrom.* She's in my *class.* She goes to my *school.*"

"I know." Jake hurried over, scooped Ryan up, and hugged

him close. He could feel his son slump against his chest, as if there were no strength at all in his young, athletic body.

"She's *my age.*" Ryan's voice sounded hoarse, about to give way to tears. "I didn't know her, but a lot of my friends did."

"I know, I know." Jake held him closer, rocking him a little, reflexively. For a second, he didn't know who was comforting whom, because they both felt so guilty and heartsick, bound by remorse.

"Janine Mae, that girl, the one I was going to go out with tonight, they were *best friends.* They both ran track. Dad, she even has MacCabe for homeroom. Remember Mrs. MacCabe?"

"Yes, of course, I'm so sorry."

"God, it's so horrible." Ryan pulled away, his face a tormented mask and his weary eyes glistening. He yanked his laptop over, his movements suddenly frantic. "Look, you should see on her Facebook page, they already made it a memorial and everybody's posting how they're so sorry and how could somebody do such a thing, to leave her to die in the street, and she was so nice, she had to work after school—"

"Oh, this is just awful." Jake glanced at the memorial Facebook page, which showed a photo of a grinning Kathleen Lindstrom, but he didn't have the heart to read the posts. He realized he'd have to set aside his own anguish to help his son, and be strong for him.

"I told Mom I was sick, but it's just that I feel so terrible, and you should see, everybody's posting about it, how sad it is, and it made me throw up, and the only reason I stopped was there was nothing left. Dad, I already got a text from Janine Mae saying she's so upset, and like, she was so cute, everyone on the boys team wanted to take her out." Ryan's words sped up, and he started scrolling through Facebook, tapping the trackpad. "Look, Dad, I think her mom and dad are divorced, and look at this, the track coach said on our Facebook page that nobody's allowed to run on Pike Road anymore. Caleb says on his page the school is going to stop all the teams from running there—"

"Ryan, please, I know how you feel, but maybe you shouldn't look at the computer anymore." Jake kept his hand on Ryan's shoulder. "It's making it worse—"

"But I killed Kathleen, I killed her—"

"Lower your voice, please." Jake glanced toward the door, though Pam couldn't hear from the kitchen. "Son, I'm worried about you—"

"Dad"—Ryan interrupted, tapping the trackpad in an agitated way—"they're all talking and texting and posting about her, and how could this horrible person kill her and leave her, and they all mean *me,* but they don't even know—"

"Ryan, we did it, we're both responsible, but you need to try and not get too focused on this." Jake tried to calm him down, but he could see that Ryan was hardly listening.

"Dad, no, you know what, I was thinking, if we tell them how it happened, we could explain that I wasn't high at the time—"

"Tell who?"

"The police."

"No, we couldn't," Jake said firmly. "If they test you and find out you smoked, you would be guilty of a DUI and vehicular homicide. If you got tried as an adult, which is distinctly possible, that could be a ten-year prison term. We can't go to the police. Don't even think about that. I know we did the wrong thing—"

"No, it was all my fault. *I* hit her—"

"Ryan, we can't keep going over and over this, around and around in circles." Jake had to tell him about the car accident at the Wawa, because it would look strange to Pam if he didn't. "Listen, I just had a fender bender that will cover the damage in the car."

"*What?* How?" Ryan's eyes widened, glistening and bloodshot.

"I don't have time to give you the details, and it doesn't matter."

"Don't forget your coat in the garage—"

"I'll take care of it, and I didn't forget." Jake knew what to do with the coat, but the car had taken priority. "I knew as soon as I heard that it was Kathleen, how you would feel, but you need to let me handle—"

"I just can't believe it. I hate myself, I hate this—"

"I know how you feel, but we have to keep it together." Jake squeezed his shoulder. "This is the time to stay calm. Let me handle everything. I know what's best for you, I really do. I love you."

"You said that I could get ten years in jail if they charge me as an adult, but what if they don't?" Ryan began to calm down and met his gaze evenly. His bloodshot eyes were still wet, but he was no longer on the verge of tears. "What if they decide I'm a kid, a juvenile? I went online and did the research—"

"You can't find an answer like that online." Jake didn't add that he'd tried.

"But I found these websites for lawyers, and if I go in the juvenile system, it looks like a lot less time—"

"No website can tell you whether you'll be tried as an adult. Considering who your mother is, they might want to make an example of you."

"But you don't know that, you can't tell that for sure. What if we went to a lawyer?"

"No, we need to keep it to ourselves—"

"We could go to a lawyer together and tell him what happened, and see what he said." Ryan seemed to recover, sitting up straighter, his voice strengthening. "Maybe there's a way we can still make it come out right. We could go to the police and make them understand."

"No." Jake stiffened. "There's no way."

"But if we could get, like, an expert opinion—"

"I know what I'm doing, son."

Ryan blinked, and Jake knew he was remembering the year that his dear old dad got laid off, rejected for every job he applied to, dressed up for interviews that got canceled. Pam and Ryan had seen him every morning, leaving the house for his rented cubicle, wearing a tie and jacket like a costume. It had been the year that his family had learned Dad wasn't infallible. Jake felt as if he could never live it down, but he had to try.

"Ryan, I do know what I'm doing. You have to believe me."

"But the lawyer on one of the sites said that anything clients tell him is confidential. Is that right, that he can't tell anybody?"

"Yes."

"So then why can't we go?"

"How are we going to go see a lawyer together? What do we tell your mother?"

"She doesn't have to know. She has that dinner tonight, remember, for whatever? She has to go, she's supposed to give a speech."

Jake had forgotten that, too. He was so preoccupied with Kathleen and Ryan.

"Dad, what if she goes to the dinner, and you say you have to stay home with me because I'm sick, then you and me can go to a lawyer?"

"No, I don't want to do that." Jake's every instinct told him to contain the information. Any lie he told, like the one about the hamburger, not only led to other lies, but greater exposure. "I'm not even sure you should go with me if I see a lawyer. Then we can't tell him that I was driving."

"Why not?"

"Because if we tell him that I was driving and it's not the truth, he can't represent to the court that it is."

"How do you know that? You're not a lawyer."

"I know a few things, Ryan."

"That makes no sense." Ryan frowned in confusion. "You

mean it's okay if he keeps it secret that we committed a crime, but it's not okay if he keeps the details secret, like who was driving?"

"Yes." Jake realized it didn't make sense, either. "Look, I admit, I don't know the niceties, but I don't like the idea and I doubt that we could get a lawyer that quick anyway."

"What if I already got us one?"

"*What?*" Jake asked, dismayed. He could see Ryan's life exploding, flying into a million pieces, right before his eyes. "What did you *do?*"

"Don't be mad—"

"I'm not mad, I'm *scared,* for you! What did you do?" Jake tried not to raise his voice. Panic gripped his heart. "Ryan, this is a secret. Once it's out, it's out, and you can't put it back."

"Don't worry—"

"Ryan, did you call? Did you use your cell phone?"

"No, I sent an email, but I made up a second new Gmail account under a fake name, John Kane. I didn't use my own name. It's safe."

"Ryan, they can still find out it's from your computer, if they trace that. You know every computer has its own ISP address."

"The lawyer's not going to look it up, and nobody else is either. You don't have to go if you don't want to, but I want to."

"Wait, hold on." Jake had to slow him down. "Tell me what you did. What did you tell him?"

"Nothing. All I said was that I needed to talk to an expert."

"You didn't tell any of your friends, did you?"

"No."

"You swear?" Jake's fears started to run away with him. "You didn't tell anybody on the team, or this girl you're supposed to go out with?"

"No, Dad, I swear, I didn't, I only emailed the lawyer and he emailed back."

"What were you thinking?" Jake reached for Ryan's arm.

"Don't you realize how serious this is? You can't tell anybody what happened! You can't play games with this!"

"I'm not playing games. I want to see if there's another way—"

"You can lose your whole life over this, Ryan. I'm not going to let that happen, and we're not going to see any lawyer."

Ryan pursed his lips. "Dad, I want to see a lawyer. All I did was write an email."

"Show it to me."

"Here." Ryan grabbed his laptop, hit a button, and swiveled it around, and Jake read the lawyer's response, which came up first:

> **Dear Mr. Kane, I am available for a confidential consultation entirely free of charge, anytime this evening starting at seven o'clock. I look forward to hearing from you. Sincerely, Morris**

Jake read down to see Ryan's email. He felt himself losing control of the situation, which terrified him.

> **Dear Sir, I have a confidential question about a DUI law. Are you available tonight? Sincerely, John Kane**

Jake looked up, stricken. "Who is this lawyer? Where is his office?"

"Westtown, but he could meet us wherever we wanted. It doesn't have to be his office. I bet it could even be in a car."

"Ryan, this guy can put two and two together. If he gets an email like that and he's in Westtown, he'll know there was a hit-and-run sometime last night, and that you're probably—"

"Dad, don't be mad, please, don't be mad." Ryan's brow furrowed deeply under his messy hair. "I'm just trying to do the right thing."

"I'm not mad at you, I'm worried for you. Worried sick."

"But I would feel better if I knew it was the only thing left to do, like, we really tried to see if we could do the right thing, but we just couldn't, in the end." Ryan's voice turned pleading, his eyebrows sloping down plaintively. "I'm just trying to deal with it, and if the lawyer says this is the right thing, the only way, then I think I would feel better."

"You're being naïve, son. You don't know how bad this can get, and I'll be damned if I'll put your life into the hands of some second-rate DUI lawyer."

"He went to Yale."

"He's a stranger. He doesn't know you or care about you, or love you like I do." Jake had to get Ryan in control. "We already decided. There's no going back. What's done is done. It's *done*."

"Can't we just go, to make sure? For me?"

Suddenly, there was a commotion in the hallway, and Moose burst through the door, bounded into the room, and jumped on the bed, landing in the middle of Ryan's worksheets and knocking into the laptop.

"No, buddy!" Jake faked a laugh, grabbing the dog by the collar.

"Whoa, Moosie!" Ryan moved the laptop out of harm's way and closed the lawyer email.

"What are you two up to?" Pam entered the room, puzzled. "Jake, I called you twice. Your eggs are ready."

"Sorry, babe. We've been solving a mystery. You were right. He had the cheese nachos."

"I knew it!" Pam smiled in triumph, then looked at Ryan. "Honey, nachos in a movie theater? Really?"

"Sorry, Mom," Ryan said, with a sigh.

Chapter Ten

Jake climbed into the passenger seat next to Pam, for the trip to pick up the rental car. He'd changed his clothes and eaten, only so Pam wouldn't get suspicious. It had taken everything in him to swallow each bite, because he'd felt so terrible, thinking about Kathleen. His gaze strayed to the metal shelves along the garage wall and the white jugs of Roundup weed killer that hid the nondescript brown bag with his parka, covered with Kathleen's blood. The lifeblood of a young girl was on his hands.

"You and Ryan looked like you were having quite the bonding session." Pam set her purse on the console, disengaged the emergency brake, and twisted the key in the ignition.

"We were just talking." Jake tore his gaze away from the hidden parka, for fear of tipping off his wife. He tried to put on a calm expression but he couldn't. He'd known Ryan would be devastated when he heard about Kathleen, but he hadn't foreseen that his son would start contacting random DUI lawyers. Jake hated leaving him alone, not knowing what his son would do next.

"What were you guys talking about?" Pam glanced behind

her before she put the car into reverse. She drove a black Mercedes SUV, which had a camera in the dashboard that showed a full view behind the car, but she never trusted it. She wasn't the kind of woman who delegated the important things in life. She wouldn't have made any of the decisions he'd made. She never would have let Ryan drive. She never would have left the scene. She believed in the law, in what was right and moral. So did Jake, but that was Before. Now, in the After, he was a hypocrite. He turned to the window, instinctively hiding his face, ashamed of himself.

"Jake?" Pam asked. "Did you hear me?"

"I'm sorry." Jake had let his thoughts get away from him. "We talked about how he was feeling, like that."

"He seems kind of upset, don't you think?"

"Throwing up will do that to you."

"But it's more than that." Pam frowned as she put the car in forward gear and gave it some gas. She steered down the street, flipping down her visor against the glare of the cloudy sky. "It could be the playoffs, you know. There's a lot of pressure on him. His job is to make a three, and he knows that Coach Marsh and Dr. Dave count on him."

"I think I know what's on his mind, and it's not the playoffs." Jake suppressed a twinge of annoyance. Coach Marsh ran the basketball program at school, and Dr. Dave Tolliver was Ryan's shooting coach, a parent volunteer on the team whose son had graduated a while ago. Jake felt that both men had too much influence over Ryan's life, or maybe he was just jealous that they saw him so much.

"What do you think it is?" Pam glanced over, her blue eyes frank. They drove through their development, where neighbors were unpacking groceries, heavy bags of salt, and new Backsaver snow shovels from their SUVs, their hatchbacks open like so many gaping maws.

"I think it's about that girl. This is only a guess, but I think

he was supposed to go out with her tonight. He was just starting to tell me when you came in, this morning."

"Damn!" Pam hit the steering wheel with her palm. "I wonder
who she is."

"I'm not sure, but I think he asked her out on a date."

"My God, that would be his first real date! Our baby's growing up." Pam puckered her lower lip, mock comically, but Jake
knew she wasn't kidding. He'd inadvertently stumbled onto a
good way to change the subject.

"We're going to have to cut the cord sometime."

"I know, I know." Pam let her voice trail off. "I don't know
what I'm going to do when he goes to college."

"What am I, chopped liver?" Jake managed a smile.

"You know it's nothing against you, right? It's just that as a
mother, it's hard to let him go."

"I understand," Jake said, meaning it.

"Cheryl and Jamie say the same thing, we all do. If you have
a great kid, it's hard to let them go. The world is a dangerous,
dangerous place. Anything can happen."

"I know." Jake was thinking of Kathleen, with a new wave of
guilt. He turned toward the window, again.

"I mean, it's not easy being an empty-nester. Jamie's already
on antidepressants. It's just sad. It's a loss. I know you feel the
same way, honey."

"I do." Jake knew she said it out of a sense of parity. "Anyway, as far as this alleged date goes, I got the impression that
something about it bummed him out."

"What?"

"Two possibilities. Either he asked her out and she said no,
or she said yes, but now he can't go because he's sick."

"Oh no." Pam's shoulders fell. "That sucks. I hope she didn't
reject him, but either way, he can't go out tonight."

"Agree."

Pam shook her head. "What a shame."

"The course of true love never did run smooth."

"Was he studying when you went up there?"

"I think he was trying to, but cut him a break, he's sick."

"That reminds me." Pam looked over, suddenly businesslike. "You know we have that Eldercare Services dinner tonight, that benefit? I have to go. I can't get out of it, they're giving me some kind of award. Can you stay home with him?"

Jake hesitated, for show. "Sure."

"I think you should. If he keeps throwing up, he's going to get dehydrated, and I think we need to keep an eye on him."

"Fine, right. What time do you think you'll be home?"

"Late. I speak after dinner, and that's when they present the award, so I'll be there 'til the bitter end. Probably be home around midnight. Call me if he takes a bad turn, so will you?"

"Of course. Hopefully, he can get some sleep. I wouldn't mind taking it easy tonight, myself. I started the day off with a bang, after all."

Pam looked over. "So you have a good excuse for missing the rubber chicken."

"I don't mind the rubber chicken. It's the weird black rice I hate."

"That's wild rice, and it's classy."

"Rice gone wild?"

Pam smiled. "Exactly."

"Yuck. I like my girls wild and my rice tame. Is that so much to ask?"

Pam laughed, and Jake felt his heart lift. She had a great laugh, and he loved to make her laugh. He loved her, and he would lose her if she knew what he had done to Kathleen, and their son.

"So fill me in on the schedule," Jake said, because he had some planning to do. "What time do you have to leave for your gig?"

"It's at the Wyndham downtown, but there's a VIP reception

before the dinner, so I have to be there by five." Pam glanced at the dashboard clock, which read 11:15. "I have to leave the house by three thirty, just to be sure. What are you going to do today?"

Jake had to think of a lie, because the truth was appalling. "Work."

"You're not going into the office, I hope?"

"No."

"You're not feeling too good, are you?" Pam patted his leg, and though Jake felt the softness of her touch, it gave him no comfort. He turned back to the window. After putting on a false front for the Wawa employees, the cop, and Ryan, he was running out of energy to put one on for Pam. He couldn't wait to be alone, apart from her and anybody else, so he didn't have to pretend anything anymore, so he could let the grief and guilt come.

"I'm just tired, is all," Jake told her.

"Could you be having a delayed reaction to the crash?"

"No, really."

"Should we go to the emergency room?"

"No, no." Jake eased his head onto the headrest and closed his eyes.

"Did you get whiplash or anything like that?"

"Honestly, no." Jake turned to her, trying to smile. "What kind of idiot has a car accident when there's nobody around to sue?"

"An honest one," Pam answered, smiling back at him, with love.

Chapter Eleven

Jake went about his task with grim purpose and he didn't have much time. Ryan was sleeping in his bedroom, and Pam had just left for her benefit dinner, made up, perfumed, and sparkly in a slim black dress with sequins at the neckline. She'd come to his office to say good-bye, her face alive with excitement and a black lace shawl over her arm, which matched her lacy black high heels. Jake knew his wife well enough to guess that she had coordinated even that subtle touch.

Pretty damn sexy for a member of the judiciary, he had told her, kissing her on the cheek.

Don't be silly, she had said, but he knew she was pleased when she kissed him on the lips, then hurried off.

Jake had made sure Pam was gone, when he'd locked the dog in the house, hurried out to the garage, and started looking for bits of plywood. He'd muddled his way through his share of home projects and had plenty of random lumber around, for when the table leg needed shimming or the window air conditioners had to be braced on the windowsill.

He collected a few pieces of wood, then rooted through the

storage shelves and found some old soiled towels and rags. He grabbed some to-be-recycled newspapers, his bloody jeans, and the brown bag that held the bloody parka, then hustled out of the garage, glancing around to see if any of his neighbors were watching. Only his neighbor across the street, Sherry Kelly, was out, but she was already walking up her front walk, her back to him, so the coast was clear. Even so, Jake was about to do what plenty of suburban daddies did on a Saturday, which was burn some trash in a burn pile. Technically, he needed a permit, but the law was honored only in the breach.

He went down the side of the property, then let himself past their gate and into their yard, screened from view by their privacy fence. It was six feet tall, and it enclosed their backyard on the east and west sides, but left it open in back to the woods that surrounded the development. They owned a two-acre parcel, and neither he nor Pam had seen any reason to cut themselves off from the forest, a decision that would work to his benefit right now.

He hurried past their swimming pool, covered with a stretched green tarp for the winter, to the back where he kept his burn pile. He worried about a neighbor's wandering by, or the off-chance that the police decided to start enforcing the law, or Pam's having forgotten something, but he had prepared for all of those eventualities as best he could, using the other trash for cover.

Jake dumped the brown bag, rags, and wood on the cold ashes of the burn pile, where the lumber landed with a clatter. He bunched up the newspapers, reached into his pocket, pulled out the pack of matches, then struck the match. The newspaper began to burn, smoldering at the ragged corner at first, then catching fire gradually, curling the front-page headline BUDGET DEFICIT WIDENS before it burst into flames.

He glanced reflexively over his shoulder, but no one could see, and he reminded himself again that even if they could, nothing would look amiss. He burned trash all the time, probably once a month, and gray smoke rose from the burn pile like it always did. It didn't even smell funny. A sharp-eyed neighbor might have noticed that he was standing closer to the pile than usual, but no one was watching.

Jake grabbed a stick and stirred the pile, encouraging the flames to creep over the plywood, and when it began to catch, he tossed the stick aside, bent over the paper bag, and rolled out his jeans and balled-up parka. He fed the parka to the fire, starting with the front, where the blood had been. He couldn't get close enough to see the stains, but he knew they were there. The black nylon was stiff where the blood had dried, making shapes that reminded him of a map of the continents, so when the jacket finally caught fire, the entire globe was aflame.

He stood there, watching, waiting, and tending the fire, then threw in the bloody jeans and burned them, too, until wood, rags, newspaper, and incriminating evidence had been consumed, and all that remained were chunks of charred wood and the melted plastic zipper of his jacket, lying on the glowing ashes like the molted black skin of a snake.

Jake turned back to get the hose. Luckily, it was getting dark out and the risk of detection was miniscule, if not nil. Still, he wasn't about to take any chances. He planned to put out the fire, gather the ashes, and dump them. Oddly, he felt no relief now that the jacket had been destroyed, and if anything, he felt worse than before. Now, if all went right, or dreadfully wrong, neither he nor his son would ever pay for the young life they had taken.

Smoke clung to his sweater and filled his nostrils, and he took a few deep breaths as he strode toward the house. He reached the hose and was about to turn on the faucet, but he looked around, yet again, to make sure no one was watching. But this time, there was a silhouette in the window on his own second floor, at the back of the house. It was Ryan, motionless, then he vanished.

Fifteen minutes later, Jake was driving a white Toyota Corolla, the "intermediate" rental car. He was hoping to make quick work of disposing of the soggy ashes and melted zipper, which he had scooped into a large coffee can and stowed in the trunk. He cruised through his development, avoiding his neighbors' eyes, even as he scanned their trash cans. He couldn't take a chance of being seen disposing of the ashes. It was dark, but there were still too many people around, unloading their cars.

He hit the road, heading for the first gas station, but bypassed it when there were too many people in line waiting to fill up. He cruised ahead and figured he'd stop at the Wegman's, but as he steered into the landscaped entrance, he spotted the boxy security cameras on the stores. He decided against, curved around the turnaround, and navigated out the exit.

He hit the gas and found himself surveying every stoplight for a camera meant to catch traffic violations, but which could also catch him. He tried to think where he could dispose of the ashes. He needed a place where there was no development, but developments surrounded him, commercial and residential. There was only one place he could think of that would have no cameras, because it was still natural. He'd grown up here and always thought he'd move away, but when he met Pam, she liked the hominess of the area, so they'd stayed.

Jake pulled up to the quarry and parked next to a lighted sign that must've been new. **FUTURE SITE OF LIMEKILN CORPORATE MEWS**, it read, and underneath that, **BURNER CONSTRUCTION COMPANY, WILL BUILD TO SUIT.** He got out of the car, not completely surprised. It was the site of an abandoned limestone quarry, typical of the kind that pockmarked the Lehigh Valley. He and his family used to picnic on its far side, the three of them spreading raggedy bathtowels on the hard rock, with only one beach chair, a faded plastic lattice affair that his father commandeered as the head of the family, if not its bread-winner.

Jake shook off the memory, which wasn't a good one. William "Bucky" Buckman couldn't hold a steady job but he'd acted like a king on a throne, placing the plastic chair on the flattest rock he could find, where it would nevertheless wobble uncertainly, representing one of the many trials his father had to endure. The open secret of the Buckman household was that his mother's secretarial job was the one that put food on the table. Still, Jake and his mother would be relegated to the rocky ground, while his father would sit in the chair and complain about how unappreciated he was by his family, his various bosses, and the universe in general.

Story of my life, his father would always say, in his sad-sack way. Or, *just my luck.*

Jake hurried around the car in the light from the sign, popped the trunk, grabbed the can with the ashes. He hustled through the rubble and overgrowth toward the quarry, then slowed his step out of caution. He could barely see where he was going because the lighted sign was behind him and the night was moonless. He wasn't sure where the edge of the quarry was, but it was several hundred feet down to the water and the last thing he needed was to fall in.

Story of my life.

Jake tried to ignore his father's voice. He and Pam had come here once or twice when Ryan was little, but by then, swimming had been prohibited, for which Jake was grateful. He had too many bad associations with the quarry and had vowed long ago never to become his father, which was only one of the reasons why he'd taken losing his job so hard.

Just my luck.

Jake almost tripped on some black netting on wooden stakes, but stepped over it, guessing he was approaching the edge. The underbrush reached to his knees, scratching his jeans, but he took a few more steps and stopped. He was close enough, and the undergrowth anchored his feet. He took a deep breath, and the air smelled the way it used to, fishy and vaguely gritty, as if it were still leavened with limestone silt.

Construction of the new corporate center must have begun, because klieglights glowed on the opposite side of the quarry, and Jake could make out job trailers and the hulking outlines of backhoes, dump trucks, and Dumpsters behind cyclone fencing. He couldn't see anyone walking around, and it was too great a distance for anyone there to see what he was up to. He gazed into the massive crater, dark as night, with the water below glinting like pooled ink.

The sky above him was black, the water below him was black, and he stood at the edge of an abyss that he tried not to see as metaphorical. He couldn't fathom how he had fallen so low, so fast. He had killed a young girl, left her in the street, and counseled his son into a nightmare. He was no better a man than his father; on the contrary, he was far worse.

He raised the can and dumped the ashes and melted zipper into the quarry. It was too dark to see if it all came out, so he tossed the entire can into the water.

Then he turned around and hurried back to the car.

Chapter Twelve

Jake showered and came out of the bathroom, a towel around his waist, surprised to find Ryan waiting for him in his bedroom, fully dressed in a white polo shirt, jeans, and sneakers, and sitting in one of the chairs. He had a good guess about why Ryan was dressed up, but he wasn't sure.

"Ryan, feeling better?" Jake asked, concerned.

"Not really. Where were you?"

"Out."

"Did you burn the jacket?"

"The less you know the better." Ryan's eyes were puffy, but his mouth a firm line.

"Don't treat me like a baby, Dad."

"I'm not, I don't mean to, but we had this conversation already." Jake padded to the dresser, leaving wet footprints on the rug. He pulled open the drawer and grabbed a fresh pair of boxers. He usually felt so good after a shower, but not tonight. He felt miserable, depressed, and guilt-stricken. He couldn't come to terms with the notion that they'd hit Kathleen. A classmate of Ryan's and so young. Her life had been cut short before it had even begun. In the shower, he kept thinking about her mother and her father. They would never see their daughter again. They would know she had died alone, and violently. That knowledge and burden would be with them every minute, every day they woke up and every night they went to sleep. It had to be hell on earth.

"Are you not telling me to protect me?"

"Exactly." Jake went to his bottom drawer, pulled out a pair of jeans, then closed it and went over to the bed to put them on. The room was warmly lit by crystal lamps on their night tables.

Ryan fell silent, then asked, "Do you guys ever even use these chairs?"

"Not really." Jake slid off the towel and into his boxers, even though he was still a little wet.

"Then why do you have them?"

"Your mom likes them. Sometimes, she uses them." Jake stood up and put on his pants quickly, feeling strange being naked in front of Ryan, oddly vulnerable and exposed.

"What for?"

"To sit down, when she puts on her shoes." Jake sensed that Ryan was trying to pick a fight, but he didn't take the bait. He went back to his dresser, opened a middle drawer, and pulled out a plain blue T-shirt. He slipped it on, standing there. He was getting dressed for staying home, not going to any lawyer's office.

"I don't know why you need chairs and a table in the bedroom. Like, what exactly is the purpose of this?" Ryan gestured to the sitting area that Pam had created in front of the fireplace, a decorative upgrade that didn't work. She'd covered its surround with Delft tile and bought a soft chair and a reclining couch in a yellow-and-blue flowered pattern, for either side. She'd finished it off with an antique pine table, its surface only large enough to hold another small crystal lamp and a stack of hardback books.

"I think your mom wanted it to be a reading area."

"Does she ever use it for that?"

"No." Jake finger-combed his wet hair into place, eyeing himself briefly in the dresser mirror. He had to bend at the knees to see his face, which didn't look good. His eyes were bloodshot, and his expression showed the strain. He could still smell traces of smoke on his skin and hair. "You must be hungry. Why don't we get some dinner?"

"Dad, I really want to go see this lawyer."

"I said no."

"I want to, I have to. Kathleen was in my class, Dad. I want to know if there's anything we can do, and what my options are—"

"No, it's too risky." Jake palmed his wallet on the dresser and tucked it into his back pocket.

"Dad, please."

"Tell you what." Jake sighed. He knew how Ryan felt but he couldn't let this happen. "Let's go downstairs and talk about it over dinner. We'll feel better when we've had something to eat."

"We don't have time." Ryan stood up. "I already wrote him back. He's expecting us to meet him at his office at seven o'clock."

"Are you *kidding me*?" Jake turned in disbelief, and Ryan drew himself up to his full height.

"I'm going, whether you go with me or not."

"What are you *talking* about?"

"I need to see a lawyer," Ryan answered, almost preternaturally calm. "I did something horrible, something criminal. I need a criminal lawyer, so I can decide what to do."

"We already *decided* what to do." Jake started to lose his temper, more out of fright for Ryan than anger. "We already did what we did. There's no decisions left. There's no going back."

"Maybe there is."

"There isn't!" Jake grabbed Ryan's arm, more roughly than he needed to, but he had to shake some sense into the kid. "I'm trying to keep you out of prison. I'm trying to save your life, your future."

"I know, you're trying to protect me." Ryan's eyes filmed, but he didn't cry. "But I want to know my rights."

"You don't have any!"

"Yes, I do. I'm going to see the lawyer, whether you come with me or not."

"How are you going to get there?" Jake stopped just short of saying, *You gonna drive?*

Ryan blinked, hearing the words that Jake didn't say, and for a split second, father and son eyed each other, wounded and hurting in front of the pretend fireplace.

"I'm sorry." Jake grabbed Ryan, just as his son pulled away.

"No, no, I'm sorry, it's all my fault."

"Ryan, come here!"

"No!" Ryan jumped aside and batted Jake's hands away, but Jake went after him, grabbed him, and struggled mightily to muscle him closer, into an embrace. The days were over when he was stronger than Ryan, and Jake didn't know if he could still take him. He flashed suddenly on Ryan as a little boy and remembered that they used to race each other in the driveway, then down the sidewalk, and his heart broke to think of those sunny days, now consigned to Before.

"All right, down, all right, you win," Jake heard himself say, shaking his head. "We'll see the lawyer. We'll get your questions answered and we'll see what he says. But we won't let him make any decisions for us, and we'll do it my way."

"What's that mean?"

"You'll see."

Chapter Thirteen

Jake sat at the head of the polished conference-room table with Ryan to his right, waiting for the buzzer that would signal the arrival of Morris Hubbard. Jake had decided it would be safer to have Hubbard meet them at his office, because if they were spotted at Hubbard's office, it would be obvious that they were consulting a criminal lawyer. Here, they were unlikely to be seen by anyone, and even if they were, it would look as if Hubbard were consulting Jake, and there was nothing suspicious about that. Jake met plenty of clients after hours, and, presumably, even a sleazeball DUI lawyer needed financial planning.

Ryan looked over. "Dad, you look worried."

"I'm not," Jake answered, modulating his tone. "How are you? You okay?"

"No." Ryan sipped water from his white styrofoam cup. "I talked to Janine Mae. I told her I was too sick to go out, but she was too upset anyway."

"Oh no." Jake felt a deep stab of pain, thinking about Kathleen. Her death would traumatize everyone she loved, her friends at school and her parents at home. Suddenly the buzzer sounded, and Jake came out of his reverie. He rose, stiffly. "I'll get it, and remember, let me do the talking."

"You said I can ask questions."

"Yes, but we're not hiring anybody tonight." Jake went to the door of the conference room, then stopped. "This is a consultation and discussion only, agreed?"

"Right," Ryan answered, and Jake left the room, strode down the hall, and crossed the reception area to the front door, which he opened.

"Come in," he said, ushering Hubbard quickly inside. "I'm Jake Buckman."

"Mo Hubbard." Hubbard extended a hand, and Jake shook it. Hubbard looked to be in his early thirties, on the short side, with a bulky build in a black fleece pullover and baggy jeans. His gold wire-rimmed glasses, a head of frizzy brown hair, and a thick beard and mustache made him seem like a throwback hippie.

"This way," Jake said, gesturing, and they strode down the hall.

"Nice offices," Hubbard said pleasantly.

"Thanks." Jake opened the door to the conference room, and at the end of the long mahogany table his own beloved son rose, standing to meet his lawyer, like an adult.

"Hi Morris, I'm Ryan Buckman. I'm the one who wrote you the emails."

"Oh, you used an alias. Very clever." Hubbard smiled as he entered the room and shook Ryan's hand. "Call me Mo."

Jake gestured Hubbard to a chair opposite Ryan. "Please, sit, Mo. You want some water or anything? Coffee?"

"No thanks." Hubbard unbuttoned the top few buttons of his fleece to reveal an old-school blue work shirt, then sat down heavily. "How can I help you?"

"Well," Jake said, sitting down at the head of the table, "before I explain the situation—"

"Excuse me, I thought it was your son who contacted me," Hubbard interrupted, turning to Ryan. "Who am I here for, you or your father?"

"Both of us," Jake answered quickly. "My son Ryan is a minor, sixteen years old, and I can explain why we wanted to meet with you."

"Fair enough." Hubbard folded his pudgy hands in front of him on the table. He made no move to take notes or reach for one of the fresh pads and pens from the center of the table.

"First," Jake began, "am I correct in assuming that anything we tell you in this consultation is privileged and confidential?"

Hubbard nodded. "Yes."

"Does that mean, if you were to hear information from us that might be incriminating in some way, you couldn't go to the authorities and tell them what you heard. Is that right?"

"Correct. Not only am I not obligated to do so, I am obligated *not* to do so. Let me explain something." Hubbard cocked his curly head, seeming to address Ryan, mainly. "The way I think about this is simple. My job is to help you. There are rules about how far I can go in helping you. For example, I can't ethically assist you in covering up wrongdoing, and I wouldn't. But the way the American system works is that the prosecution has to prove that somebody did something wrong. That person, called the defendant, doesn't ever have to help them do that. You get to remain silent, just like they say on TV. That right is guaranteed to you by the Constitution. Understand?"

"Yes," Ryan answered, his tone quiet.

"I represent people accused of crimes. My job is to represent my clients fully and zealously, to the best of my ability. I don't involve myself with their guilt or innocence. I don't even ask my clients if they're guilty. You understand?"

"Not really." Ryan frowned. "Doesn't it matter to you if they're guilty or not?"

Listening, Jake felt secretly proud of his son. Ryan didn't

understand because he expected the law to lead to justice, not thwart it.

Hubbard nodded, acknowledging the question. "It doesn't matter to me because I'm not the judge. I'm the defense lawyer. My job is to represent you. I make sure that you have the array of protections the law affords you. The Commonwealth has a lot of resources at its disposal that you'll never have, no matter who your father is. Or your mother."

Ryan blinked, and so did Jake, both of them getting the message. Hubbard was telling them he knew who Pam was, and he had probably already guessed that they had called him about the hit-and-run on Pike Road. And Hubbard's subliminal message—whether Ryan was getting it or not, Jake couldn't tell—was that he distinctly did *not* want to be told who was driving the car that night, so he could maintain deniability. In fact, Jake realized that Hubbard could be assuming Ryan was alone in the car.

Hubbard turned and faced Jake, his eyes small and dark blue behind his glasses. "Now, would you like to fill me in?"

"Certainly." Jake chose his words carefully. "To make a long story short, we left the scene of a car accident, without calling the police or 911, after we had ascertained that the pedestrian was dead and unresponsive to CPR. We were wondering what our legal obligation was, at this point."

"Are you asking me if you have a legal obligation to turn yourselves in?"

"Yes."

"No, you do not. You have no such legal obligation."

"I see." Jake shot Ryan a glance. He had guessed correctly that there was no legal obligation, only a moral one, which paradoxically, wasn't the same thing.

"As your lawyer, I would be under no obligation to counsel you to go to the police. My sole inquiry would be, what can I do for you, legally. I would begin by asking if you had an alibi—"

Ryan interrupted, "But what if we *wanted* to go to the police and tell them everything? What would the police do? Can we explain what happened?"

"Ryan—" Jake started to say, but Hubbard waved him off.

"Ryan, that's a good question. I'm happy to answer it. You're always free to go to the police. But, if that was something that you both decided you wanted to do, I would make sure that before you did it, we arranged a plea bargain." Hubbard spoke slowly, without judgment. "Let me explain what a plea bargain would be in this case. Under 75 Pennsylvania Code Section 3744, an adult who strikes and kills someone with a car, and does not remain at the scene, call the police, and give information, is guilty of vehicular homicide and leaving the scene of an accident. That's a felony of the second degree, carrying a five-year prison sentence—"

"It wasn't an adult who killed someone, it was me," Ryan interrupted again, and Hubbard pursed his lips in his dense beard.

Jake felt his heart sink, but he didn't want to upset Ryan by telling him that he'd just said the exact wrong thing. "Ryan, let Mr. Hubbard continue, then you can ask questions later."

Hubbard nodded. "Ryan, let me finish. I think I'll be answering your question."

"Dad, no." Ryan shook his head. "I don't want him to think you did anything wrong. You were just in the car. I want him to know *I* was driving and *I* was the one who hit her."

"It's okay, buddy." Jake turned to Hubbard, and the two men locked eyes, both of them tacitly understanding that Jake's cover story, in which he was the driver, was now blown. "Mr. Hubbard, you were saying?"

Hubbard relinked his short fingers. "So in the case where the driver is unlicensed and—"

"I have a learner's permit," Ryan broke in.

"Okay," Hubbard continued, "the driver has a learner's permit. But he's driving outside of the restricted hours, yes?"

"Yes."

"Dad is in the passenger seat, presumably having permitted son to drive, correct?"

"Yes," Ryan answered, but Hubbard turned to Jake.

"Jake, are you aware of the doctrine of negligent entrustment?"

"No," Jake answered, but he could figure out the gist. "I'm at fault because I let him drive, right?"

"Correct, but it's more serious than that, in the event of a fatality. It's criminal."

Jake swallowed hard. "I didn't know that."

"Most people don't, and I can see that you've been more worried about your son's legal responsibility, than your own." Hubbard's expression softened. "I understand, I have a son, myself. You thought of him first."

"What's my legal responsibility?" Jake asked, feeling his heartbeat quicken.

"You would be charged with permitting violation of title, in breach of 75 Pennsylvania Code Section 1575, and you would be charged as an accomplice to involuntary manslaughter for negligently entrusting an underage driver to drive. The penalty can be up to five years in prison."

Ryan gasped. "*What?* My dad would go to jail? But he didn't *do* anything!"

"He would be charged with an F2, a felony of the second degree."

Jake absorbed the information, momentarily speechless. He had known it was wrong to let Ryan drive, but he never would have expected it had legal implications, much less a prison sentence.

"*No!*" Ryan started shaking his head, agitated. "Mr. Hubbard, really, my dad just *sat* there, in the passenger seat! He didn't do anything *wrong*!"

Hubbard nodded calmly, in Jake's direction. "Yes, he did. He let you drive. You're an underage driver. As such, if your father permits you to drive and you have a fatal accident, your father is legally more culpable than you. He is a person in a position of authority over you and he was supervising you. The law views him as running the show, not you."

"That's not fair, I was *driving*!" Ryan cried out, and Jake reached over and put a hand on his arm.

"Ryan, let him tell us the law and we'll sort it out later."

"No!" Ryan shook his head vehemently. "Mr. Hubbard, let me just ask you this, if we went to the police right now, and we told them I was driving and my dad was in the passenger seat, what would they do?"

"Without a plea bargain?"

"Yes, without a plea bargain, if we just went and told them the truth, *everything,* even that I smoked up before the movie, because that's why my dad didn't call the cops. He wanted to call 911, he told me to, but he knew they'd test me. Are you telling me they'd put him in *jail*?"

"Yes, they would," Hubbard answered. "To reiterate, your father would be charged with involuntary manslaughter and sentenced to five years in prison. You, as the driver, would probably be charged as a juvenile and enter the juvenile system."

Jake heard that one glimmer of hope. "So Ryan wouldn't be tried as an adult?"

"Probably not, if they had you. If he were charged as an adult, which is always possible, I would move to decertify and have him tried as a juvenile. Still I couldn't guarantee I would prevail. He's so big and well-spoken. He doesn't come off like a child. He comes off like an adult."

"But he's sixteen. That's young."

"It's in between, these days. He *looks* like an adult. I call it 'the falsehood of physicality,' but it hurts him in court. I know from bitter experience." Hubbard inhaled briefly. "Let me explain the differences between the juvenile system and the adult system."

Ryan fell back in his chair, his hand covering his mouth, and Jake said nothing, needing to understand the law.

Hubbard continued, "The purpose of the prison system for an adult is punishment. But in the juvenile system, the purpose is rehabilitation. If you were to tell the D.A. that Ryan was driving, he would be sent to what is called 'placement,' a euphemism for juvenile prison."

Jake began to understand the implications, with a growing sense of dread. If he and Ryan turned themselves in, they would *both* be sent to prison. Even if they got some sort of plea deal, they would both serve some length of time in prison. Their legal position was even worse than he'd thought, and he'd thought it was awful.

"Most of these placements are up in the mountains, in facilities like Northwestern or Glen Mills. You, Ryan, would live and go to school there with other juvenile offenders. If you told the D.A. that you were driving under the influence, you would be evaluated and treated for substance abuse."

Ryan recoiled. "I'm not a *drug addict*. I barely smoke. You can check it, they test us on the team."

"Nevertheless, in three to six months, Ryan, your case would be reviewed. You would go before a judge, and you would have to show that you're making good progress. You could conceivably be free in two years, but the system retains supervision of you until age twenty-one. You will have a criminal record."

Jake tried to imagine the implications. Ryan's life would be ruined, and Pam would be devastated. She couldn't even deal with Ryan going to college, how would she deal with him going to prison? She would lose them both at once. She would never forgive Jake for ruining Ryan's life and for destroying their family. She would divorce him. She would step down from the bench.

Hubbard raised his finger again. "One last point. The DUI. Even if they tested Ryan's blood for marijuana, or THC metabolites, the D.A. couldn't prove that he was under the influence at the time of the accident, or that his level was above the statutory minimum, which is .5 nanograms per liter of blood. The DUI charge drops out, which reduces the sentence from ten years to five."

Jake tried to understand what he was being told. "So by leaving the scene, we evaded the DUI charge."

"Correct, but they'll offer you a worse deal. You don't win, either way. I would advise you, in the strongest possible terms, to enter into a plea deal." Hubbard glanced at Ryan, who looked numb with shock, pressed back in his chair, his eyes glistening. "If you decide to turn yourself in, that is."

"What is the best deal you could get us, if we were to turn ourselves in?" Jake asked, reaching out to touch Ryan's arm.

"The best, I think, is four years for you, and two for your son, with him sentenced as a juvenile."

"So Ryan would be considered a juvenile?"

"If he goes in with you, there's a better chance. If he goes in alone, probably not."

Jake didn't try to process the information, just to gather more. "Who makes the decision about whether he's tried as a juvenile or as an adult?"

"The first assistant district attorney, usually. In this case, given the circumstances, the D.A. may weigh in, too."

"Which way does that cut?"

"My sense is, against you. They would want to avoid any appearance of favoritism."

"And if I went to the police alone, without Ryan, saying that I was the driver?"

"No, Dad!" Ryan blurted out, stricken. "You can't, I won't let you. I'll go, I'll call them, I'll tell them the truth. You won't be able to stop me. I'll tell them you lied and I was driving."

Hubbard answered as if Ryan hadn't spoken, "Mr. Buckman, your going in alone may not be tenable, if Ryan isn't going to let you, and in that event, I can't represent you. I can't suborn perjury, that is, I can't ethically sit there and remain quiet while I know you're lying to the court."

"Understood." Jake was about to ask his last question, but Ryan leaned over across the table to Hubbard.

"Mr. Hubbard, what if I went to the police, and let's say, like, I told them that I borrowed my dad's car and took it out by myself? In other words, like, that I was alone in the car, and I hit Kathleen. My dad wasn't in the picture at all. What would they do?"

Jake recoiled, looking over at Ryan. "I wouldn't let you do that in a million years."

Hubbard glanced from father to son. "Ryan, your father would have to support the story, and it looks as if he wouldn't support your story, just as you wouldn't support his—"

"I absolutely wouldn't," Jake shot back. "It wouldn't work anyway, not with the facts."

Ryan groaned. "Why not, Dad?"

"Son, the timing wouldn't work, and the police would be able to figure that out. The accident happened after I picked you up from the movie, which you went to with your friends. The police could figure out that there wasn't enough time for us to get home and for you to go back out again."

"But how would the police even know I was with my friends?"

"They'd investigate, Ryan—"

"Even after I go in and tell them what happened?"

"Of course, they don't just take your word for it."

Ryan turned to Hubbard for verification. "Is that right? Would the police go talk to my friends, even after I say what happened?"

"Yes, they would."

"Ugh!" Ryan smacked the table, in frustration.

Jake had a final question, so he addressed Hubbard. "One last thing, of a more practical nature."

"Certainly." Hubbard nodded.

"If we didn't turn ourselves in, what are the odds?"

"What are the odds that you'd get away with it?"

Jake winced at his bluntness. "Yes."

"I can't counsel wrongdoing, and I'm not, and I cannot advise you or help you make a decision. I'll tell you the relevant facts so you can make your own decision. Do you understand the distinction?"

"Yes."

"The police in this county investigate thoroughly. They have accident-reconstruction specialists work up the scene, check for debris and tire marks, and physical evidence, like DNA."

Jake felt relieved that Hubbard didn't go into gory detail, because he could see Ryan fidget in his chair.

"They also knock on doors, talk to the local businesses, check local body shops and auto parts stores. I don't know if you read the case, but a man was arrested in Upper Darby last week for a hit-and-run, eight months after the fact. Delaware County police tracked him down via a headlamp he ordered to repair the Toyota 4Runner he was driving when he struck the victim."

Jake didn't interrupt him, running over a grim checklist in his mind. Burned parka, check. Crashed car, check.

"They also visit local hospitals and doctors. They examine red-light and convenience-store tapes. They post it online and solicit tips. Tips are a major factor in hit-and-runs. In all crime, really. People have a tendency to tell their friends."

Jake didn't dare look over at Ryan.

"These things happen rarely in this township, and the local police have expertise, but not experience, unlike places like Coatesville."

Hubbard paused, in thought. "In addition, it was raining last night, and water on the road prevents skidmarks from forming. Also the accident scene is out of the way. There are no street cameras in its vicinity, only in the corporate center."

Jake hadn't told Hubbard that the accident happened on Pike Road, but nobody was kidding anybody at this point.

"By the way, the statute of limitations on leaving the scene is seven years."

Jake blinked, surprised. "I assumed there was no statute of limitations."

"No, that's only for murder. This would be manslaughter, not murder. Do you have any other questions?"

"No, thanks." Jake understood. Hubbard was telling them that the odds were they wouldn't get caught.

"No, thank you," Ryan answered miserably, looking up.

"Well then." Hubbard pushed back his chair and rose. "I'm sorry for your trouble. Please feel free to call me."

"Will do, and please do bill me for this time." Jake began to stand up, but Hubbard waved him back into his seat, heading for the door.

"Please, stay here. I can show myself out. There's no charge for a consultation. Best of luck to you both."

"Thanks." Jake eased down into the chair and patted Ryan's hand, after Hubbard left the conference room. "You okay?"

Ryan hung his head, then looked up with anguished eyes. "I don't want you to go to jail."

"I'm not going to jail."

"But you would, if we go to the police." Ryan rubbed his face, leaving a welt on his fair skin. "I never should have asked to drive. I never thought anything like this could happen."

"Neither did I." Jake got up, went to Ryan, put his arms around him, and gave him a long hug, then held on, as if to support them both. "It's on me. I'm the adult, like he said. I ran the show, not you."

"But you didn't know about the weed. I should'nt've had the

weed." They clung to each other, sad and resigned. "I hardly ever smoke, I swear, Dad."

"I know. It really is my fault, not yours." Jake gave him a final hug, then released him. "I took it too lightly. I didn't think it through. I underestimated the downside risk."

"What?" Ryan looked at him, bewildered, and Jake straightened, standing in the conference room as he had so many times before, explaining to his clients.

"It means that whenever you do something, you have to understand that the worst-case scenario happens, even to good people." Jake hoped Ryan accepted that explanation, even as he realized that that was only part of what had gone wrong. He'd wanted to be Fun Dad, so he hadn't said no. He'd wanted to be closer to his son, so he'd been a buddy, not a parent. It was a mistake he would regret the rest of his life.

Ryan rose slowly. "At least we know what to do. I never would've thought *you'd* have to go to jail, I thought it was just me. If I go forward and turn myself in, they'll get you." He met Jake's gaze directly. "So I won't turn myself in. I won't say a word. I'll shut up."

"Oh no," Jake said, but it came out like a moan. "That's not a given, Ryan."

"Yes it is, no doubt." Ryan's tone grew determined, and he stood up straighter. "There's no other way. I'll never tell, *ever.*"

Jake felt sick to his stomach, even though he was getting what he wished for, or maybe because he was getting what he wished for. "We can talk this out at home."

"Dad, there's nothing to talk about. Like you said, it's a done deal. I can't let *you* go to jail, just like you couldn't let *me* go to jail." Ryan smiled sadly, cocking his head. "You protected *me,* now I'm going to protect *you.* Guess I'm my father's son, huh?"

Jake felt his heart lurch, at the irony. "But it's my job to protect you. It's not your job to protect me."

"That made sense when I was a kid, but not now. I told you

I'm not a baby anymore." Ryan's forehead eased, and his expression turned oddly accepting, almost peaceful. "I wanted an answer and I got one. I'm not going to let anybody else be punished for something I did, least of all, you. I love you, Dad."

"I love you, too," Jake said, and they faced each other, eyeball to eyeball, but not as they had before, in his bedroom. There was no confrontation now, and nobody was spoiling for a fight. Ryan wasn't trying to declare his independence, and Jake wasn't trying to hold on to any primacy he used to have as a parent.

They were both exhausted, trapped, and full of remorse. They were bound together not only by blood and love, but by guilt and lies. They were father and son, but they were also partners in crime.

Ironically, they had never been closer.

Chapter Fourteen

It wasn't until he got home that Jake had a chance to eat something. He stood at the granite counter and spread lumpy strawberry preserves onto semi-frozen Ezekiel bread, glancing up at the television. A cop show was on, so he looked away and finished making his sandwich. He checked the over-the-counter clock. It was 10:58 P.M., and the local news would be on any minute.

"Mrfh!" Moose barked, his round brown eyes looking hopeful, the way they did whenever peanut butter was in the vicinity.

"Here, buddy." Jake slid his index finger along the butter knife, swiped off some peanut butter and jelly, and offered it to the dog. Moose licked it happily, his tail swishing back and forth on the floor like a windshield wiper, reminding him of last night in his car.

I love how these wipers go on automatically! Dad, this car is sick!

Jake wished to God he had said no. If he had, none of this would have happened, Kathleen would be alive, and his son would be happy and carefree. As it was, Ryan was upstairs hiding in his room and getting ready for bed, so he'd be asleep by the time Pam got home. It was the only way he could avoid her cross-examination about the flu, his homework, or how he'd spent the evening.

Suddenly there was a commotion at the front door, and Moose scampered off, barking toward the entrance hall. Jake worried that it could be the police and hurried from the kitchen.

"Honey!" Pam burst through the front door, alive with excitement. She tossed her car keys, little purse, and black shawl on the console table, and Moose wagged his tail frantically.

"Hey, hi!" Jake tried to recover. "You're home early."

"Why didn't you answer your phone?" Pam closed the door behind her. "I've been calling and calling!"

"I didn't hear it, sorry." Jake must have forgotten about his phone in the rental car. "What's up? How come you didn't park in the garage?"

"I didn't bother, I'm in a rush! Where's Ryan?" Pam was already heading for the stairwell, her high heels clacking on the hardwood. "Ryan, come down! Come downstairs!"

Jake didn't like what was going on. This wasn't the way he planned it at all. "He might be asleep, honey. He wasn't feeling well—"

"Oh please. He's been on the phone for the past hour." Pam took off her high heels and placed them on one of the steps, to be taken upstairs. "Enough with the shoes. Showtime's over."

"Mom, what do you want?" Ryan called from his room upstairs.

"Come down, right now!"

"I'm in bed!"

"Come down, this is important!" Pam rolled her eyes and looked at Jake with a knowing smile. "He must be talking to the girl. I checked online and he's on G-chat, too. Did he do his homework?"

"Some of it, I think." Jake began to worry, wondering who Ryan was talking to on the phone and online. "He didn't feel well."

"He has a French vocab test on Tuesday, so he has to study in advance because of the playoffs."

"Aw, cut him a break. He's sick. He slept most of the evening." Jake marveled that his wife always had Ryan's schedule in the back of her mind, running on a parallel track with her own.

"Were you born yesterday?" Pam snorted good-naturedly. "He may have been in his room, but if he was on the phone and G-chatting, he wasn't studying or sleeping."

"It's hard to focus when you don't feel well."

"Mom, what's going on?" Ryan appeared at the top of the stairway and walked down slowly, running his hand along the banister and blinking against the bright lights of the hanging fixture in the entrance hall. His hair was messy, and he was dressed for bed in a maroon Chasers Nation T-shirt and pajama pants.

"Come down, I want to talk to you and your dad." Pam beamed up at him, but Ryan avoided her eye as he descended the stairs, and Jake wanted to give him the heads-up.

"Ryan, Mom says you've been on the phone, but I thought you were asleep. You playing possum, buddy?"

"Nah, sorry." Ryan looked away, and Pam threw open her arms when he reached the floor and gave him a big hug.

"I'm sorry you don't feel well, honey. But humor me and come into the kitchen. I really need to talk to you and your dad."

"What about?" Ryan asked, his tone offhand, as Pam released him from her embrace, took him by the arm, and led him into the kitchen in her stocking feet, with Jake and Moose behind.

"I have amazing news, truly amazing."

"Great, Mom," Ryan said, but Jake looked past his son's shoulder to the TV on the counter, where the local news had just begun and the top story was being reported. STUDENT

KILLED IN HIT-AND-RUN, read a lurid red banner across the screen, and an attractive African-American anchorwoman was saying, "A tragic story is first up tonight. A teenage jogger identified as Kathleen Lindstrom was struck and killed in Concord Chase last night, while running on Pike Road. Police believe the vehicle struck the jogger, then fled the scene . . ."

Jake crossed the kitchen to turn off the TV, but Pam grabbed his arm, beaming.

"Honey, sit down. Ryan, you, too. You have to hear this."

"I was just about to turn off the TV—"

"I can't wait another minute!" Pam motioned them into their tall stools at the granite countertop and hustled around the other side, standing in front of the oven and the television. Jake and Ryan sat down in their seats and faced a delighted Pam, against the backdrop of the news report of the heinous crime they had committed together.

The anchorwoman continued, "Lindstrom was a junior at Concord Chase High and she had just moved here from Seattle with her mother, Grace, but the duo had already made fast friends with neighbors like Dylan Paolucci, who lives next door." The screen switched to footage of an older man standing in his threshold, saying, "I'm still shocked. I just finished talking to her. She was a good kid. Her mom is a doll. I cannot believe somebody would hit her and not even stop the car."

Pam took a deep breath, barely able to contain her excitement as she looked from Jake to Ryan, and back again. "Guess what?"

"What?" Jake asked, but Ryan's attention was riveted to the TV screen, which had returned to the anchorwoman, who was saying, "Police have no suspects at the present time, but they are looking for the vehicle, which is likely to have damage to its passenger-side fender and undercarriage . . ."

"Ryan!" Pam barked, with a mock frown. "May I have your attention? What does it take! Sheesh!"

"Sorry." Ryan straightened up, and the TV screen changed to a remote report by a male reporter in a logo ball cap and windbreaker, standing on an otherwise darkened Pike Road, at the blind curve. He was saying, "The heartbreaking death of young Kathleen Lindstrom has brought new attention to this deadly blind curve on Pike Road, which residents have been complaining about to the Township Board of Supervisors for years. Traffic accidents happen routinely here, usually involving walkers, cyclists, and joggers, but last night's was the first fatality . . ."

"Boys." Pam made a drumroll sound, her blue eyes shining with happiness. "Tonight at the dinner, I found out that there's about to be a new vacancy on the federal district court!"

"Really." Jake could see in his peripheral vision that the TV screen had returned to the anchorwoman in the studio, but the enlarged photo behind her grabbed him by the throat. It showed Pike Road as a crime scene, with yellow plastic tape, red flares, and a black body bag being lifted on a gurney. The voiceover said, "If you have any information on the crash or the location of the alleged hit-and-run vehicle please call Concord Chase police at . . ."

"Guys, what?" Pam scowled, hurt. "Why are you being so rude? What's so damn interesting?"

"Nothing, honey," Jake answered, and Ryan swallowed visibly, but Pam whirled around to face the television, then watched the end of the news report, shaking her head.

"Oh. That *is* sad. Everybody was talking about it tonight. What's the matter with people?"

"God knows." Jake put an arm around Ryan, while Pam turned back to face them.

"Ryan, are you okay? You don't look good. Do you have a fever?" She reached across the table and put her hand on his forehead sideways. She always had an uncanny ability to tell if he had a fever, so they called her The Ther-MOM-eter.

"No, Mom, I'm fine." Ryan pressed her hand away. "Tell us your news. Please."

Pam brightened again, nodding energetically. "Okay, anyway. Judge Medova is going to step down and become managing partner at Ringman Tesher."

"Oh, interesting." Jake didn't know where her story was going, but he was finally able to listen, since the TV news had moved on to a dorm arsonist at Temple.

"And guess who's the front runner to fill the vacancy?" Pam's eyes lit up. "Me!"

"Wow," Jake said, astounded.

"Can you believe it?" Pam squealed in delight.

"What's this mean?" Ryan blinked dully, and Pam reached across the island and took his face in both of her hands.

"It means your mother is going to be a *federal judge!*"

"Great!" Ryan said, mustering up the requisite enthusiasm.

"Oh my God, honey." Jake felt happy for her, went around the island, and hugged her hard. "Congratulations, I'm so happy for you, babe."

"Thank you, thank you, thank you!" Pam hugged him back. "Can you believe it? Can you even believe it?"

"Sure, I can. You deserve it."

Pam giggled delightedly. "The state court judges are always overlooked for the federal bench, except for Judge Spaeth, who was even considered for the Supremes. But since him, I don't think there's been anybody. Isn't it amazing?"

"Absolutely amazing," Jake said, meaning it. He leaned over and turned off the TV.

Ryan rose, placing a hand on the counter. "Can somebody explain to me what this is all about?"

"Sure." Jake's heart went out to his son, trying to rise above the circumstances for his mother. "Pam, tell your son what a big deal you're about to become."

Pam smiled, pleased. "There are two systems of justice in the country. There's a state system, which I'm a part of, and it rules on questions of state law. State judges are appointed for a term of years, and they're elected, which you've heard me say is totally ridiculous. Pennsylvania is one of the few states in the country that still elects judges, instead of having them appointed based on their qualifications and merits. It's like a judicial popularity contest, and a corruption of the law—"

"Mom." Ryan rolled his eyes. "Please don't start with that again."

Pam burst into laughter. "Okay, but as I was saying, the other system of the judiciary is federal, which decides questions of federal law."

"Is one better than the other?" Ryan asked, sitting back down.

"Well, more important matters come before the federal bench. Questions of antitrust law, banking law, constitutional law, and First Amendment law, all sorts of big, complex questions." Pam grinned. "Really cool stuff."

"So it's a big deal," Ryan said, with a shaky smile.

"Yes," Pam answered, beaming. "And another cool thing about it is that federal judges are appointed under the Constitution, for *life*. I never have to run for election again. That means no more county fairs, no more funnel cakes and hot dogs, no dairy and goat shows, no more sucking up to every petty potentate so I can do some good in this Commonwealth."

Jake felt happy for her, but it was still hard to smile. He kept thinking of that news photo, with the body bag. Inside was Kathleen, whom they had killed. He tried to get his act together.

"But guess what, there's no pay raise. On the contrary, I have to take a pay *cut*." Pam snorted. "You know how you've heard me say Pennsylvania judges are among the top paid in the country? Believe it or not, a federal district judge makes fifteen grand *less* than I make now."

"Really?" Jake was surprised. Pam made good money as a Superior Court Judge, but they didn't talk salary in front of Ryan, so he didn't ask her for an exact number. He didn't care anyway, not really, not anymore. He was a financial planner who was learning that money wasn't as important as he'd always thought. "So what happens now?"

Pam smiled up at him. "They nominate me, then I have to go before a Senate committee."

"Mom, you mean like in *Washington, D.C.*?" Ryan asked, surprised. "That's baller, G."

"Yes, exactly." Pam chuckled. "It's a federal appointment, and it has to go through the Senate. It's a long process, like years, and it's very political, but in the end, I'll be there forever." She leaned over the counter to Ryan. "But listen, honey, you can't tell anyone. It's confidential. Don't say anything to any of your friends, the team, or your teachers."

Jake cringed at the irony. Ryan was keeping a wonderful secret to protect his mother and an awful secret to protect his father.

Pam continued, "Monday or Tuesday, they'll press-release that Judge Medova is stepping down, but they won't announce that I'm on deck until the preliminaries are wrapped up. The FBI has to come interview me and you guys, too. They do an in-depth background check of the family."

Jake felt his heart stop. He had no idea what that would involve, but he was instantly worried about Ryan and he could see the blood draining from his son's face.

"Mom, the *FBI*? Why do they have to interview *me*?"

Pam chuckled again. "Don't worry, honey. It's just procedure. You'll do fine."

Ryan's lips parted. "But why do they have to investigate us? And what do they do, like, exactly?"

"Honey, don't sweat it. It's more for Dad and me. The FBI

wants to find out if we do anything illegal, like hire illegal aliens or pay the cleaning lady under the table. But we don't do that, and we never would."

"But what do they do?"

"They talk to you, is all." Pam waved him off, airily. "They do it for security reasons, and to avoid any surprises that might come up during the confirmation process, embarrassing everyone and putting a kibosh on my nomination."

Jake put on his best reassuring smile. "Ryan, there's nothing to worry about."

Pam bubbled over, beaming. "Of course there isn't, honey. I say we celebrate! Your father and I are having champagne, and you can have a ginger ale."

"Great idea." Jake winked at Ryan, trying vainly to lighten his mood. "I'll get the champagne."

"I'll get the ginger ale." Pam crossed to the refrigerator, glancing back at Ryan. "Don't be such a nervous Nellie. We'll pass with flying colors. After all, it's not like we have anything to hide."

Chapter Fifteen

Jake locked the front door, turned off the entrance-hall light, and walked to the staircase in darkness, heading up to bed. It was after midnight, and Pam had already gone upstairs, after Ryan and Moose. He and Pam had polished off a bottle of champagne, but it had only depressed his mood further. He started to climb the stairs, almost tripped over her high heels, then grabbed them on the fly and went up, leaning heavily on the banister.

He reached the second floor and bypassed the closed door to Ryan's bedroom. His son needed sleep, and so did he. He made his way to his bedroom, slipped inside, and closed the door behind him. The room was empty, and he knew Pam was in the bathroom by the faint buzzing of her electric toothbrush. He brought her shoes to her closet, where he dropped them on the rug, catching a glimpse of her at her sink.

Pam's back was to him, and she was bent over, rinsing her mouth, in a lacy black bra and tan bikini panties. His eyes traveled her shapely body, from the exposed nape of her neck to the cleft of her back, taking in the dimples above the lacy edge of her panties and coming to rest on her ass, which was perfect. In any other mood, Jake would have been turned on, but tonight he felt like the lowest of the low. Only hours ago, he'd met with a criminal lawyer and made a corrupt bargain with their son.

What are the odds that you'd get away with it?

Pam dried her face, spotting him in the mirror when she replaced the towel. "Caught you looking, honey."

"Oops." Jake faked a smile. He felt like an intruder in his own bedroom, a pervert peeking at his own wife. He had become a stranger to himself.

"Like what you see?"

"You're amazing," Jake answered, meaning it. She was too good for him. He was unworthy.

"Hold that thought." Pam walked to him, raising her arms and reaching up for him. She had that cool look in her eye, and he knew she wanted to make love. He couldn't refuse her, he never had, and he leaned down and embraced her, on Husband Autopilot. She parted her lips to kiss him, covering his mouth, tasting sexy and familiar, like champagne and Colgate. Her body was soft and warm in his arms, and he found himself kissing her deeply. He felt a vague stirring in his pants and wanted oblivion. He didn't want to think about Ryan, Mo Hubbard, or Kathleen, anymore. He didn't want to think at all.

He slipped his free hand into the back of her panties, cupped her cheek, and lifted her onto him, pressing himself between her legs. She kissed him back with a soft, throaty moan and wrapped her thighs around his waist, pushing herself against his zipper, holding on to his T-shirt in back as he carried her to the sitting area by the fireplace. He stopped kissing her only to lower her onto the chair, where she sat, eyes closed, arching her back, her breasts straining against the dark lace of her bra cup. Her arms fell to her sides, her legs parted, and he knelt between them to yank his T-shirt off over his head.

Do you guys ever even use these chairs?

Ryan's voice popped into his consciousness, unwanted and unbidden, and Jake froze. He didn't even know why he'd taken Pam here, and not the bed. They'd never made love here.

You protected me, now I'm going to protect you. Guess I'm my father's son, huh?

Pam's eyes fluttered open after a moment, in muzzy confusion. She whispered, "Jake?"

No, he thought, deflating. He wasn't Jake. He didn't know who he was anymore. He was the man who left a young girl dead by the side of the road. He was the man who ruined his own family. He was the man who destroyed their wonderful son.

"You okay, honey?"

"No, sorry, I'm just tired." Jake sighed. "It's the booze. It must be."

"So . . . you don't want to?" Pam frowned, blinking.

"Let's just call it a day," Jake answered, leaning down to kiss her, one last time.

Chapter Sixteen

Jake opened his eyes, vaguely aware that Pam was trying to wake him up. He squinted against sunlight pouring into the bedroom, because they had forgotten to pull down the blackout shades last night. His wife's face came into focus, and Jake could see that she was back to business, already made up and ponytailed, in her contacts, maroon Chasers Nation sweatshirt, and jeans. She smelled like face wash and things-to-do lists.

"Honey, wake up." Pam stroked his arm. "The game's at one o'clock. You're coming, right?"

"Yes, right." Jake's head was pounding, and he had a major hangover. He'd been hoping he could keep reality at bay, but it came rushing back to him, leaving a bitter taste in his mouth that had nothing to do with alcohol. "Is Ryan up?"

"Of course. He's already out shooting."

"Is he sick or okay?" Jake heard the rhythmic bouncing of the ball outside on the driveway, the sound of rubber hitting cold asphalt, echoing in the quiet Sunday morning.

"He seems better. Get up and shower, please. I thought it would be nice if we all had pancakes together."

"Pancakes? Ugh." Jake felt his stomach turn over. "How can you eat?"

"I'm fine, and Ryan likes pancakes on game day. Can you be down in half an hour? We have to leave by ten o'clock."

Jake glanced at the clock, which read 8:07. "Why ten, if the game isn't until one?"

"The team has to be there early, and I have carpool, so we're picking up Jerome and Baird, so that adds forty-five minutes. Plus it's an away game, at North Mayfield, and that will take another forty-five minutes extra . . ."

Jake closed his eyes against the familiar rat-a-tat of the schedule, his wife expertly counting backwards. She'd timed everything so they wouldn't be late, because she still lived in the world where the worst thing that anyone in their family could do was to mess up the schedules of the other overscheduled families.

"Now get up and I'll see you downstairs." Pam ruffled up his hair, rose, and left the room, while Jake threw off the comforter, eased himself into a sitting position, and rubbed his face, as if that would ease the pain in his head, or his heart. He got up and walked around the bed, pausing to glance out the window, which offered a parallax view of the basketball hoop, in the driveway in front of the garage.

There was a cold sun in the sky, and Ryan was shooting a foul shot in his black parka and team sweatpants, wearing his earphones, his hair ruffling in the wind. The ball *thwapped* loudly on the grimy white backboard, spun into the basket, and tumbled through its frayed rope netting. Ryan rebounded without missing a beat and shot a layup, which he missed, but he retrieved the ball, again without missing a beat, his iPhone wire jumping around as if electrified. He pivoted perfectly on the ball of his sneakers then hopped into the air to shoot the three-pointer, his right arm high, his long fingers spread, releasing at just the right moment, and the ball swished through the net.

Yes! Jake cheered for the kid silently, though Ryan didn't stop. He went after the ball as he had before and took another shot. He wasn't smiling, and his forehead knitted, focused, and as Jake watched him, he sensed that his son was losing himself in the drill, using it to black out what had happened on Pike Road, like Jake himself had tried to last night, in the booze and sex. He realized that basketball had become a coping mechanism for his son, as well as being part of his identity; Ryan was the quiet kid who was famous as being a shooter, most comfortable on the court, where action substituted for conversation.

Jake watched him, thinking that he'd never been able to decide if Ryan was having fun when he played basketball, even when the boy was younger. Jake had never played basketball, even as a teen, because he had to work after school, as a bagger at the Giant. He'd never pushed Ryan into basketball just because he was tall; Jake had grown up with everybody asking him, *Why don't you play basketball,* and it was Ryan who had taken to the sport himself.

Jake eyed Ryan and could remember him as a little boy, shooting baskets on the driveway, no matter the season or temperature. Everybody in Chasers Nation said basketball was a passion, and they were right, but Jake knew that as soon as Pam saw the passion in their son, she had nurtured it with characteristic drive. She got him into the neighborhood leagues in elementary school, then the school and traveling teams in middle school, and the right basketball camps by the summer of seventh grade. They were called "exposure" or "showcase" camps, run by professional players or people with connections to recruiters, and the most talented players went there to be seen.

Jake remembered what a scene that had been, when he and Pam visited a summer tournament on one weekend. The kids were in ninth grade, still in orthodonture, but a lineup of Division III and even Division I coaches had sat in the front row, notebooks in hand, and by Sunday, the "impact players" had been identified. Ryan had been one. College basketball was big business, but recruiting started before puberty.

Ryan made another three-pointer, and Jake projected forward into his son's future. He didn't know if the boy would be happy at a Division I school, where he'd have to live the game, twenty-four/seven. Jake doubted that he was good enough to play professionally, and Ryan was more than just a basketball player. He had a real interest in environmental sciences, and Pam would rather have Ryan use his basketball prowess to get into a better school academically, in Division III. Jake felt the same way, although now he would settle for Ryan going to any college at all, outside of a juvenile detention home.

Suddenly, Jake noticed that Ryan stopped shooting and was looking toward the garage. Pam was coming out, talking to him, and hugging herself to keep warm. Jake couldn't hear what they were saying but he left the window to get ready. He didn't want to leave Ryan alone with Pam any longer than necessary.

Later, Jake found himself sitting on the hard bleachers at North Mayfield High School gym, which reverberated with the talking, laughing, and shouting of several hundred high-school students, teachers, and families. Little kids ran up and down the stairs between the bleachers, and cheerleaders practiced their splits and dance moves on the sidelines. School bands ran through their fight songs, complete with tubas, trumpets, and drum solos. Student booster groups—the Chasers Nation for Concord Chase and the Cardinal's Nest for North Mayfield, dressed in matching T-shirts and face paint—tried to drown each other out, cheering from opposite ends of the gym. Jennifer Lopez sang "Let's Get Loud" over the loudspeaker, and its throbbing bass ricocheted off the corrugated-metal ceiling.

Jake sat alone on the row, which was still mostly empty. Pam had gone to the ladies' room with some other Chasers' moms, leaving their parkas, scarves, and knit hats in a perfumed clump.

He exhaled a relieved sigh at having gotten Ryan through the morning. Over breakfast, they'd talked about his English homework, and though Ryan had seemed subdued, it was nothing that couldn't be chalked up to normal stress levels before a league playoff. Once they'd picked up his teammates, the boys plopped their game sneakers in their laps, plugged into their iPhones, and chattered away, reliving the plays from their last victory, a sixty-one to thirty-five drubbing of Great Valley. Ryan hadn't contributed much to the conversation even when he was its subject, and the others crowed about his twelve buckets, eight rebounds, and five blocks, with a dunk in heavy traffic. The consensus was that they would win today against North Mayfield, and the only time Ryan spoke was to remind them not to take anything for granted.

Game time was getting closer, and families started to fill in the remaining seats in the bleachers, mixing the Chasers' and North Mayfield fans. A heavyset woman in a hooded parka gestured to Jake. "Sir, are you saving this seat?" she asked, before entering the row.

"No, it's all yours."

"Thanks." The woman sat down at the aisle seat and took off her parka, revealing an I Heart My Corgi sweatshirt, then a short man came up behind her, a Sunday newspaper tucked under his arm.

"Sir, excuse me, is that seat taken?"

"No, you can sit down," Jake answered, gesturing, and the man sat down next to the woman and put his newspaper in his lap. A folded crossword puzzle was on top, and Jake spotted the headline that read, **NO SUSPECTS IN CONCORD CHASE HIT-AND-RUN.**

"I'm Lewis Deaner. My son plays for North Mayfield." The man extended a hand, and Jake shook it. "Are you from Concord Chase? You don't look familiar."

"Yes. Jake Buckman."

"Nice to meet you. I don't go crazy at games, even in the playoffs. I tell my son, I make up for the fathers who sit in the anger-management section." Deaner smiled tightly behind his wire-rimmed glasses, his thin lips stretching like a rubber band. His hair was light brown, thinning at the crown, and he was on the slight side, barely filling out his blue parka and baggy jeans.

"What position does your son play?"

"He's a guard, a sophomore. He's only a substitute, so I doubt he'll see any minutes today. But I come anyway." Deaner slid a ballpoint pen from his parka, uncapped it, and looked down at his crossword puzzle, which was half-completed. "I'm divorced, so I make the effort. That's the lay of the land."

Suddenly the crowd noise surged, and the Chasers trotted onto the glistening wood floor, a moving phalanx of maroon long-sleeved shirts and sweat suits. The coaches jogged alongside them in order of rank; Head Coach Ronald Marsh and his uniformed assistants, then Dr. Dave running next to Ryan.

Deaner looked up from his crossword. "That's my son, on the sideline, about to come on the court. The short one with the glasses. Number 16. Steve."

Jake spotted who he meant, in a pair of plastic wraparound glasses. "Good-looking boy."

"Which one's yours?"

"The one toward the back, number 22." Jake watched Dr. Dave put a hand on Ryan's shoulder and felt a flare of jealousy, even though it was his own fault that Ryan was closer to his coaches than his father. The crowd noise surged again, and the Cardinals hustled onto the floor in their bright red warm-ups. The Cardinal's Nest cheering section rose as one, flapping its arms, and singing a fight song that was unintelligible.

Jake looked around for Pam and her friends, but didn't see them. Ryan fell in line behind his teammates, and they ran a drill, jogging up and down the half-court with their knees high. The Cardinals did the same thing at their end of the court, and the crowd yelled, cheered, and called the players' names, getting more excited. One of the North Mayfield moms on the other side of the aisle produced tiaras from a white Dollar Tree bag and gave them out to her girlfriends. The music over the loud-speaker segued into "I've Got a Feeling."

Deaner watched the Chasers' warm-up session. "Your team came to play, eh?"

"Yours, too." Jake spotted Pam and her friends on the floor, hurrying toward him.

"What do you do for a living, Jake?"

"Financial planner." Jake leaned over, slid out his wallet, ex-tracted a business card, and handed it over, reflexively. "How about you?"

"Technical writer, freelance." Deaner glanced at the card, then slipped it inside his parka. "I can't afford you, I can tell. I bet you drive a nice car, like an Audi."

"Ha! Does it show?" Jake forced a smile. It was a lucky guess, but it rattled him.

Deaner capped his pen and tucked it inside his parka. "You know, my apartment's not around here, it's in Concord Chase. Not far from Pike Road, where that hit-and-run was. You prob-ably read about it. A junior from the high school was killed. A girl."

"Oh, yes." Jake kept his eyes on the court, where Ryan and the Chasers had started a new drill, lining up on both sides of the half-court, taking shots and rebounding for each other.

"I'll come by your office tomorrow morning, and we can have a talk."

"What about?" Jake asked, his tone casual.

"I think you know. I think you know exactly. Make sure you're there." Deaner rose. "Enjoy the game, Jake."

Chapter Seventeen

Jake watched, stunned, as Deaner made his way down the stairs, reached the floor, and vanished into the crowd. His thoughts raced. It had been such a bizarre conversation.

I bet you drive a nice car, like an Audi.

Jake felt a bolt of panic. It was too much of a coincidence. The Audi, the mention of the hit-and-run, even the newspaper headline. What if it was all intentional? What if Deaner *knew*?

Jake told himself not to jump to conclusions. He had to stay calm. He spotted Pam and her friends, climbing the steps and heading toward him. There had been no one else around that night on Pike Road. The corporate center had been empty, there were no houses. But if Deaner didn't know anything, why was he coming to Jake's office? Was Deaner still at the game?

Jake scanned the crowd, but didn't see Deaner. Was he coming back? Why did he leave? What had just happened? Who the hell was this guy? Jake slid his smartphone from his pocket, got online, and typed in **Lewis Deaner freelance technical writer**. Instantly a group of links came onto the tiny screen, and he clicked the first, but it was from a man in Huntsville, Alabama.

Jake reformulated his search request and typed in **Lewis Deaner freelance technical writer PA,** but he got no responses. So either Lewis Deaner wasn't Deaner's real name or the man wasn't a technical writer. He plugged in **Lewis Deaner Concord Chase PA,** but it came back no responses. He tried to compose himself.

"Don't work so hard, honey." Pam was sitting down, handing him a bottle of water and a soft pretzel wrapped in transparent paper. "Want a snack?"

"No, thanks." Jake slipped his smartphone back into his pocket.

"How's he doing?" Pam craned her neck at the court and watched Ryan, who was in line to shoot.

"Fine," Jake answered, though he didn't know. His attention went to the kid with the glasses on the Cardinals, Number 16. The kid took a jumper, and Jake wondered if Number 16 was really Deaner's son. The Cardinals didn't have their last names on the back of their jerseys, neither did the Chasers. Jake could have IDed Number 16 from the Cardinals website, but not in front of Pam, who was introducing two moms in Chasers Nation hoodies, filing in behind her and sitting down.

"Honey, meet Melissa and her sister Gwen. Melissa is Baird's mom. You know him, he's a forward, a senior. He's going to Princeton next year and he'll be playing for them."

"Oh, great, right. Hi." Jake couldn't focus, replaying his conversation with Deaner.

"Nice to meet you," answered Melissa and her sister Gwen, in unfortunate unison, then they laughed. They both had short strawberry blond hair and their smiles were similar, though Gwen looked older, with reading glasses on a multicolored lanyard.

Chasers Nation parents started to find seats in this section, mixing in with the red-shirted North Mayfield parents. He masked his thoughts, which were in overdrive. Maybe Deaner really wasn't a team father? What if he was a cop, digging for information? Working undercover?

"Jake, look, here come Katie and Sean, and Chris and Vanessa with the kids." Pam motioned to a Chasers-clad group, and they waved back, grinning. The moms had maroon basketballs painted on their cheeks, like forty-year-old Raggedy Anns, but Jake found himself eyeing the Cardinal moms with the tiaras, at the end of the row.

"Hello, ladies. Pam, excuse me a minute." Jake rose, setting his water bottle and soft pretzel on the bleacher. "I'm going to the men's room before the game starts."

"Okay, hurry back." Pam patted his leg, but Jake was already walking down the row, returning the smiles that everyone flashed at him and waving back to the other Concord Chase parents.

"Excuse me, sorry," he said, moving down the row, stepping over sneakers and handbags, and finally reaching the aisle, where the tiara moms sat in a rowdy row. "Ladies, can I ask you a question about the Cardinals?"

"Sure," answered the first tiara mom.

"Do you know Number 16, that player with the glasses?" Jake gestured to their half-court, where the team had finished its warm-up and were stripping off their jerseys and sweatpants and handing them to their manager, who stowed them in a red laundry bag.

"Sure, that's Mikey."

"Mikey." Jake's heart began to thump in his chest. Deaner had said his son's name was Steve. "What's Mikey's last name?"

"Murcio, why?" shouted a stocky man from the row behind them, in a Cardinals T-shirt and glasses so thick that Jake took a calculated guess.

"Are you Mikey's father?"

"Yeah. Mike Sr." The man rose, extending a beefy hand. "Why?"

Jake shook his hand, introduced himself. "I think your son

came to the job fair last year and talked to me. I wanted to know if he followed up with the financial planning firm I told him about."

"I don't think so." Mike Sr. looked at the woman sitting next to him, a short redhead. "Babe, did Mike go to some job fair last year and see a financial planner?"

The wife shrugged, with a smile. "Who remembers? I don't even remember yesterday. Don't ask me where I put my car keys."

Mike Sr. chuckled, facing Jake. "Sorry."

"No worries, he's a nice kid." Jake had gotten the answer he needed, which only worried him more. He didn't know who Deaner really was. He kicked himself for giving him a business card.

"Good luck, bro." Mike Sr. lowered himself onto the bleachers, and the tiara moms started to cheer.

"Go, Cardinals, go! Go, Cardinals, go!"

Jake hurried down the bleacher steps, reached the gym floor, and threaded his way through the crowds hurrying to get to their seats before the game. He looked for Deaner on the floor and in the stands, but didn't see him. He followed the signs to the men's room and hurried inside.

The room was empty, and he hustled to the sink, stuck his hands under the automatic faucet, and splashed cold water on his face. His heart raced, his head pounded. He felt like he was having a panic attack.

I bet you drive a nice car, like an Audi.

Jake leaned over, bracing himself on the sink. He had to get it together. Pam would begin to wonder if he was gone too long. He could hear the crowd outside surging again, and the announcer's over-amplified voice welcoming everyone to the game.

He reached for a paper towel and dried his face, barely recognizing the expression on his face, one he'd never seen on himself. It was a mixture of bewilderment and dread, as if he were permanently aghast.

The crowd started cheering wildly, and it brought Jake back. He hurried to the door and pushed it open, only to find Dr. Dave in the hallway. "Oh, hi, excuse me."

"Jake, I don't know if you remember me. I'm Dave Tolliver, Ryan's shooting coach? We met last year at the championship dinner?" Dr. Dave smiled quickly, showing even teeth. He was of average height, much thinner than Jake, and his jet-black hair was cut close to his head, with sideburns too long for anyone not in a rock band.

"Right. Yes. Of course. I knew that. Dr. Dave." Jake extended a hand, which Dr. Dave shook.

"Right." Dr. Dave grinned, looking ready for *GQ* in a charcoal suit jacket of some sleek Italian cut, which somehow coordinated with his hip, graphite glasses.

"Thanks for your help with Ryan."

"It's my pleasure." Dr. Dave's eyes were dark brown, and for some reason, oddly serious. "I was looking for you, and Pam said I might find you here."

"Oh?" Jake said, taken aback.

"Got a minute? It's about Ryan."

Chapter Eighteen

"Sure, but the game's about to start." Jake gestured to the gym, where the announcer was introducing the Cardinals cheerleaders. The crowd responded with cheering that echoed harshly in the corridor, painted white cinderblock with a wide red stripe.

"This won't take long." Dr. Dave slipped his hands inside his pants pockets. "I'm concerned that Ryan seems off tonight. He's going to have a rough game."

Oh no. "He's been sick." Jake felt his chest tighten. "But he wanted to play, and don't sell him short. He'll have a good game."

"He didn't warm up well. I'm concerned that something's wrong with him, and it's not physical."

"Of course it is." Jake tried to shrug it off. "He was throwing up all day Saturday. He had some bad nachos. He's only playing today because he'd never let the team down."

"Jake." Dr. Dave paused, lifting his eyebrows slightly. "I'm a practicing child and adolescent psychologist, for twenty-five years. I know the difference between a teenager who's got food poisoning and one who's got something on his mind."

"No he doesn't. He's just sick."

"Seriously, it's more than that."

"How do you know this?" Jake tried not to sound skeptical, just interested.

"He's *off.*"

"Off?"

"Yes, off. He's not focusing. He's out of sync. He didn't walk in the way he always does, the way he did last week. He's a shooter, and a shooter is a creature of habit. Basketball grounds him. It keeps him centered—"

"I know that." Jake was in no mood to be lectured about his own son.

"Then you know he has a system that works for him. He keeps his warm-up exercises and his warm-up routine the same. He takes the same number of shots, in the same way. His work in the gym is always focused and purposeful—"

"I know. He's my son."

"—but tonight he's shooting flat. He's not getting enough lift on the ball. He's not releasing it high enough, so he's pushing it instead of throwing it—"

"He'll be fine."

"No, he won't, you'll see. We'll win, but Ryan's an impact player and he won't help the team today."

"Why are you telling me this?" Jake asked, unable to keep the impatience from his tone. "What do you want me to do about it?"

"Fine, I'll come to my point." Dr. Dave pursed his lips. "I get the impression that you're riding him, and I'm asking you to back off during the playoffs. Ryan's hard enough on himself, and it's a critical time."

"I'm not riding him," Jake blurted out, surprised. The crowd had started hollering again, and the announcer called the Cardinal cheerleaders onto their floor, to their music, "Brick House."

"Jake, please don't be defensive."

"Then don't make me defend myself. Don't tell me I'm riding my son when I'm not."

Dr. Dave put up a hand like a Zen traffic cop. "I should explain. I spend a lot of time with Ryan. I know him very well. He tends to tighten up when you come to a game—"

"So what am I supposed to do, not come to my son's game?" Jake felt his anger overcome his worry, bollixing him up. "I don't need to stand here and listen to you tell me about my own son."

Dr. Dave emitted a sigh. "When I asked Ryan, he said nothing was wrong. But Pam told me that you and he had some sort of fight on Friday night—"

"*What?* Why are you talking to my wife about our son?" Jake felt panicky. Pam couldn't be so open with Dr. Dave about their family business. It was too dangerous, after Pike Road.

"I talk to Pam all the time about Ryan. That's my job."

"What job?" Jake heard his tone sharpen. "You're a volunteer. What are your qualifications?"

"You're angry, so you're challenging me." Dr. Dave exuded a professional calm. "You don't really want to know my qualifications."

"Try me." Jake hated being told how he really felt, especially by people who had no idea how he really felt.

"As I said, I'm a child and adolescent psychologist. I have a small but growing specialty in adolescent sports psychology—"

"What does that have to do with basketball? You're talking about 'impact players' and 'lift on the ball,' but you're supposed to be a shooting coach."

"I played varsity basketball for three years at Penn, then I played professionally in Italy and Brazil before I got my degree." Dr. Dave emitted another small sigh. "But, this isn't about you and me. This is about you and Ryan. Pam said that you fought, because you didn't like something he said—"

"It wasn't that big a deal." Jake had a story, and he had to stick with it. "It was about texting."

"You asked him to stop texting?"

"Yes, and what parent hasn't?"

"The fight wasn't really about texting. You asserted your authority, and Ryan was unwilling to recognize or credit that authority, which you can understand, given the history of your relationship."

Jake bristled. "You're out of line."

"I'm trying to help."

"I don't need your help."

"What if Ryan does?"

"He doesn't."

"Jake, you needn't feel threatened by me. I'm not trying to replace or supplant you. There's room for us both."

"No, there isn't. Butt out." Jake turned away, strode down the corridor, and turned the corner into the noisy gym just as the Chasers were being introduced. Ryan was second in line, shifting his weight from one sneaker to the other and eyeing the bleachers where they'd told him they'd be sitting. Jake waved at him, but Ryan didn't see, so he hurried down the sidelines behind the team benches, which were separated from each other by a long metal table that held reporters sitting in front of open laptops.

He reached their bleacher section, which had filled in completely, with parents, kids, and students sitting shoulder-to-shoulder. He scanned the crowd for Deaner, and made his way to Pam, who was standing up with everybody else, clapping. He took his place to stand beside her, and she gave him a kiss on the cheek.

"Perfect timing!"

"Yes, right." Jake had to put a stop to her talking to Dr. Dave, game or no game. It was too risky, especially today. "Honey, Dr. Dave found me."

"Good. Did you talk to him?"

"Why did you tell him that Ryan and I had a fight?"

"He's worried about Ryan." Pam kept her eyes on the court, but leaned over and answered, to be heard over the crowd noise.

"Ryan's sick, that's all. There's nothing to worry about."

"Dr. Dave thinks it's more. He asked me if there was anything that happened recently that could have bothered him, and I told him about the big fight you guys had."

"It wasn't that big a fight."

Pam scoffed, keeping her attention on the court. "You made him cry, Jake. He never cries. So it was a big fight."

Jake couldn't believe the irony. He was getting in trouble over a fight he didn't even have. "Don't you think that's something that should be kept between us?"

"No, why?" Pam glanced over, puzzled, then turned back to the court. The Cardinals had been introduced, and the announcer was asking everyone to face the flag for the national anthem.

"It's our business, not his."

"Don't be silly. It doesn't matter if he knows. Parents fight with kids all the time." Pam put her hand over her heart when the anthem started playing, and she began to sing loudly, in her characteristically pretty soprano.

"It matters to me." Jake put his hand on his chest, sang the national anthem, and when everybody burst into applause, he leaned over to Pam. "Honey, do me a favor. Don't encourage Dr. Dave's snooping into our personal life."

"He's not snooping." Pam looked at him like he was crazy, then faced the court, where the team captains, referees, and coaches were gathering at the center.

"These things aren't any of his business."

"He's a friend of ours, a friend of our family's." Pam stopped clapping, and Jake could see he was getting her attention.

"Please, let's keep the conversation with him to basketball, not our family life. We already had therapy. We don't need more."

Pam frowned. "What did you say to him?"

"I told him Ryan was fine and I could handle it."

"What does that mean?"

"I told him to butt out."

"You *did*?" Pam's lips parted in dismay. "You said that? Jake, how could you? Why?"

"He's telling me that Ryan gets tense when I come to games. That's out of line."

"Ryan wants your approval, you know that. He wants to play well when you come. He doesn't need you to get him in bad with the coaches. God, they talk to the recruiters all the time. You want to queer it for him? What were you thinking?" Pam shook her head, missing the jump ball that started the game.

"Pam, I'm his father—" Jake noticed the Chasers' moms sneaking a glance at them, so he kept his voice low. "And I don't want you talking to any third party about something as personal as my relationship to my own son—"

"Oh, please." Pam rolled her eyes. "Don't be such a control freak."

"It's our business, my business—"

"You're just *jealous,* and you have absolutely no right to be. Nature abhors a vacuum, Jake, and Dr. Dave stepped in to fill a void that was created by *you.* He didn't go looking for Ryan, Ryan went looking for *him.*" Pam's fair skin flushed with resentment. "Now you've decided to step back in, and good for you, but don't expect everything to be just the way you want it, right away. It takes time. You have to *earn* your way in."

Jake regretted bringing up the subject here. Chasers' and Cardinals' families were eyeing them, even though the game was in full swing. "Pam, relax—"

"No. You can't just snap your fingers and make people do what you say, or feel what you want them to feel. I hope you didn't piss Dr. Dave off." Pam craned her neck, scanning the sidelines of the court. "You should go see him right now and apologize. He usually sits in the front row behind the bench. Do you see him?"

"I have nothing to apologize for, Pam."

"Then I will." Pam pointed. "There he is, by Coach Marsh."

"Pam, really?"

"Absolutely." Pam rose and made her way down the row, then the stairs, toward the court.

Jake lost sight of her, then gave up. He felt eyes boring into his back, but he had bigger problems than being the subject of gossip. He had Lewis Deaner on the brain. He didn't know who the man was and if he knew something or was bluffing. Jake felt his gut clench and tried to get into the basketball game. The lighted scoreboard read **Home 10, Away 4.** The Chasers were behind. There were nine minutes left in the first quarter, so there was plenty of time to catch up. Ryan stole the ball and dribbled it down the court, his hair flying.

"Go, Ryan," Jake shouted, making a megaphone of his hands.

"Ryan, Ryan, Ryan!" chanted the Chasers' student section.

"Shoot, Ryan! Shoot!" called a Chasers' mom in back.

"DEFENSE!" bellowed one of the Cardinals' dads.

Ryan stopped with the ball, his sneakers squealing, faced the basket, and took a jumper from the outside, like he had in the driveway this morning. The crowd shrieked as the ball hit the transparent backboard, bounced onto the rim, and dropped outside the hoop, missing the basket. Ryan seemed to stall, as if rooted to the shiny wooden floor.

"Follow your shot, Ryan!" somebody shouted in back.

And Jake's heart sank, because he knew what he was seeing. *He's off.*

Chapter Nineteen

Pam drove home because they'd taken her car, and Jake rode in the passenger seat, in suburban exile. They'd barely spoken for the remainder of the game, and he didn't know if she'd talked to Dr. Dave, though he assumed she had because she'd been on the warpath. Jake's thoughts kept circling to Lewis Deaner, and he'd spent the rest of the game looking for him in the crowd. He'd even checked the parking lot after the game let out, but no luck.

Pam braked when they came to a red light and glanced in the rearview mirror at Ryan, who sat in the backseat, plugged into his iPhone, listening to music. The Chasers won, forty-five to thirty-eight, but Ryan had been benched for the second half, unprecedented in his basketball career. He'd scored six points instead of his usual fifteen or so, and missed every three-pointer. He hadn't played good defense either, and the ball had been stolen from him twice. After the game, he'd come out of the locker room with his head down, stone-faced and atypically apart from his teammates, who'd emerged laughing, talking, and slapping five after the victory.

"How are you feeling, honey?" Pam asked, to the rearview mirror. The sky around them was gray-bright, thick with a winter cloud. The air smelled damp and chilled, like snow was coming.

Ryan didn't reply. Jake glanced back, but he couldn't see Ryan, who was sitting behind him.

"Ryan? You okay?" Pam repeated, louder, though it was obvious that Ryan was avoiding conversation. He knew Ryan had to be dying inside, the least of his worries being the way he'd played.

"Ryan!" Pam said, more sharply, because she knew when she was being avoided, too.

"I'm fine, Mom."

"Honey, don't beat yourself up. Everybody's entitled to a bad day, and you've been sick. Your body can't recover that fast. You're probably dehydrated." Pam squinted into the rearview. The traffic light was still red. "Don't you have any water with you?"

"No."

"We could stop at McDonald's or Dunkin' and get you some. You want to?"

"No thanks."

"But they're on the way home, and you must be hungry. Don't you want to stop and get something to eat? It might perk you up."

"I don't want anything."

"What did Coach Marsh say?"

"Not much."

"But what?"

"He said, next time to tell him if I'm not feeling good."

Pam frowned. "Okay. But what would he have done differently?"

Ryan shrugged.

"He didn't say?"

"No."

"He would have played you, no matter what. You've never not started."

Ryan said nothing.

"Did you talk to Dr. Dave?" Pam glanced sideways at Jake, who knew that she wanted to know if Dr. Dave had said anything about their argument.

Ryan didn't reply.

The traffic light turned green, and Pam hit the gas. "Ryan, did you talk to Dr. Dave?"

"Yeah."

"What did he say?"

"Nothing."

"Ryan, he didn't say *nothing*," Pam shot back, her tone exasperated. "Can't you fill me in? Do I have to pull teeth here?"

"Mom, watch your driving!"

Jake cringed. "Ryan, please don't talk to your mother that way."

Ryan gestured to the road. "Dad, she's not looking where she's going. She didn't even see that Subaru, turning left."

Pam frowned in annoyance. "I saw it, Ryan. It wasn't anywhere near us."

Jake didn't know what Subaru he was talking about, but anxiety was plain in his son's voice. "I'm sure she did, Ryan. Just watch your tone."

Pam's head snapped toward Jake. "Thanks, but I can talk to my son myself. I don't need you to intervene."

Jake let it go. He knew she was only blowing off steam and he wasn't about to fight with her. Instead he looked out the window, and his gaze flitted restlessly over the strip mall with its CVS, Subway, and Rita's Water Ice, a sight he found oddly comforting. He'd heard people complain that the country had become so homogeneous, with the same chain stores everywhere, but he didn't have a problem with that. The chains were a part of his daily routine: he got his coffee at the Wawa, his turkey hoagies at the Subway near his office, and his chocolate-covered doughnut at Dunkin' Donuts drive-thru, right before he hit the on-ramp. The sameness of the stores and their food implicitly reassured him that everything would always be the same in his life, at least until recently.

I bet you drive a nice car, like an Audi.

Pam straightened up. "Ryan, I know you feel disappointed about the game, but you don't have to sulk like Achilles in his tent. I'm trying to talk to you because I love you. It's a good problem to have, that you have a parent who cares enough about you to ask you how you're feeling, okay?"

Ryan groaned. "Mom. You're not asking, you're nagging."

Jake kept his face turned to the window, feeling a pang. He knew that Pam would be hurt by that dig and that Ryan was hurting inside, too, which was why he'd made it. Jake didn't say anything because he'd been warned off, so he kept his own counsel. Pam defaulted to silence, but she fed the SUV some gas. He felt the lurch of its angry acceleration and watched the scenery go by faster; the Acme, the Cold Stone Creamery, the Walgreens, and the Pottery Barn blurring into one neon streak of commercialism with convenient parking, open on Sundays and taking all major credit cards.

They traveled in silence, then crossed into Concord Chase, and Pam steered onto Concordia Boulevard. They passed another Wawa and a massive Wegman's, then she put on her left blinker and moved into the left lane. Jake realized with dismay that she was going to take the shortcut home, via Pike Road. They'd go around the same curve on which they'd struck and killed Kathleen Lindstrom.

Jake had to do something. He couldn't put Ryan through the pain or take the chance that the boy would throw up, cry, or react involuntarily, showing their hand.

Jake waved her off. "Honey, don't take Pike. Why don't you just go straight?"

"Why?" Pam glanced over, frowning. A truck was barreling down the oncoming lane toward them, and she stopped before she turned onto Pike to let it pass.

"This is where that girl was killed. Let's not go this way."

"Since when are you such a sensitive flower?"

"Pam, really." Jake knew that she was punishing him for fighting with Dr. Dave, but she didn't know she was punishing her son as well.

"Don't be silly."

Jake turned away. He didn't have anything left to say that wouldn't tip her off and he was suddenly tired of the bitterness between them, the back-and-forth. He missed the Pam of last night, the one who wasn't keeping score. The truck rumbled past, its big muddy tires spraying gravel, and Pam took the left turn, driving onto Pike.

Jake kept his face to his window, to avoid looking down the road and reliving everything that happened before the curve. Ryan remained silent in the backseat. The car grew so quiet that Jake could hear the tinny beat of the music through Ryan's earbuds and wondered how he could listen to such loud music, then realized the boy must've cranked up the volume. He prayed Ryan could keep it together when they reached the blind curve.

"It's just that it's so much faster to take Pike," Pam said, her tone gentler. "Plus I want to get Ryan home. He's not feeling well."

Ryan said from the backseat, "I'm fine, Mom."

"Well, good," Pam said, lightly. "Glad to hear that, honey."

Jake looked out his window. He wondered if Ryan was sending him a message, saying he was fine and telling him not to worry. The SUV cruised forward, and he started wondering about Lewis Deaner again when they approached the Concordia

Corporate Center sign, with a sign that listed businesses in the B section: Marble Fabricators, Lee Security, Ltd., Tropical Technologies, Inc., Cryotechnics, and a few others.

Jake considered it. Lewis Deaner could have been employed by any one of those companies, in any capacity. The closest office building in section B wasn't far from Pike Road, maybe a hundred feet to the left, due north, and someone could have been working late on Friday night, in any one of those buildings. Jake hadn't seen any cars in the lots along Pike Road that night, but there was a large interior parking lot in the corporate center. Deaner could've parked there and all he would have had to do to see the accident was to look out the back window of one of the offices.

Jake felt his gut clench, trying to guess how much Deaner knew, if anything. Jake thought back to the accident; he had gotten out of the car first, and Ryan had come later, from the driver's seat. They were both tall and they looked alike. It would be hard to tell who was driving, from a distance. Maybe Deaner didn't know who had been driving, whether it was him or Ryan.

Dad . . . I killed . . . that lady . . . I killed . . . that lady.

The SUV traveled down Pike Road, and Jake remembered what Deaner had said about having an apartment near Pike. He surveyed the woods to the right, and to his surprise, he spotted some buildings through the trees, in the distance. There were a series of red brick low-rises of an older, boxy design, and they looked like an apartment complex, situated on the other side of the woods. Jake hadn't known they were there, but he used Pike Road only as a conduit, and the apartments wouldn't have been visible from Pike during most of the year, when the trees were in full leaf.

The SUV closed in on the blind curve, and Jake tried not to think about what had happened that night. Instead he eyeballed the distance from Pike to the apartment buildings and estimated it to be about the length of three basketball courts. That would be too far away for Deaner to see any details of the accident unless he had been using binoculars, which made no sense. But it wasn't impossible that Deaner had seen the Audi or could identify it at that distance, because the car's frowny headlights were a well-known design feature, recognizable to anyone who knew anything about cars and easily visible at night, even in the fog.

Pam slowed as they approached the blind curve, and Jake mulled over the possibility that Deaner could have seen the accident from his apartment and could identify the Audi. Still, how could Deaner have identified Jake, much less found him? Had he seen the Audi's license plate? How? Or if Deaner was an undercover cop, maybe someone else had seen it and called it in as a tip.

Pam reached the blind curve, and Jake reached for the door handle, reflexively bracing himself for a collision that had happened days ago. A forlorn memorial had been set up by the roadside—a motley clump of plush teddy bears, grocery-store flowers, thick Yankee candles, and sympathy cards, next to a maroon singlet from the track team and a handmade sign that read **Chasers Pride! We miss you, Kathleen! Xoxoxo**

Pam cleared her throat. "I guess this is where the hit-and-run was."

Jake didn't say anything, and neither did Ryan.

"It's a dangerous curve, so I could see how it could happen. But how could he not stop?" Pam *tsked-tsked*.

Jake didn't answer, and he prayed Ryan stayed quiet.

Pam steered around the curve, staying in her lane. "Sorry we came this way," she said softly.

"S'okay." Jake felt his anger ebb away, if not his shame. The SUV powered forward as Pam accelerated, and he scanned the dirt shoulder of the road, checking. There was no shard of glass, no piece of heavy plastic, not even a skidmark to incriminate them.

Dad . . . I killed . . . that lady . . . I killed . . . that lady.

Jake found himself sending up a silent prayer, asking forgiveness for himself and Ryan. And yet, at the same time, he watched the apartment buildings recede in the distance, wondering what Deaner really knew about the accident, who Deaner was, and what he wanted. If Deaner was a cop, then he wanted Jake and Ryan, truth and justice. But if he wasn't, Jake had a good guess what he wanted. He'd find out tomorrow, for sure.

Chapter Twenty

Jake stood in the doorway to Pam's home office, where she was at her desk on the cell phone. She motioned him inside, and he entered and sat down in the pink flowered chair opposite her. They had achieved an uneasy truce during dinnertime, then Ryan had gone to his bedroom to do homework and she had retreated to her home office to make calls to the powers-that-be about her judicial nomination. He'd come in to see her to find out any details about the FBI interviews, so he could prepare Ryan. Lewis Deaner had to settle for the backburner, for now.

Pam held up an index finger, flashing him the one minute sign, and Jake looked idly around her office. It was smaller than his, but it had a cozy feel, which was why she always called it her nest. The two windows on the wall had a sunny southern exposure, but they were dark now, and red oriental-type lamps gave off a soft, homey glow. He liked her office, but it was very feminine, with pink walls, a maroon, red, and pink Heriz rug, and pink-and-red curtains in a pattern that had colonial people standing in front of thatched huts.

Toile, Pam had said, of the curtain pattern. *It's called toile.*

How do you spell that?

T-O-I-L-E.

Like toilet?

Pam had laughed. *You're useless, completely useless.*

Jake tried to relax in the chair, but couldn't. He was facing an entire wall of her framed diplomas, admission certificates to the Pennsylvania and New Jersey bars, and documents that admitted her to practice law in the Supreme Court of Pennsylvania and the Third Circuit Court of Appeals. They stared him in the face, setting into stark relief the paradox of their different positions. His wife was sitting behind a cluttered desk, trying to become a federal judge, one of the highest positions in the country in which to make and to enforce civil and criminal law. He sat opposite her, as if diametrically opposed, having committed the worst crime imaginable and concealed it from her and the authorities, in a conspiracy with her own son.

"Sorry if I was testy today." Pam hung up the phone, excited and happy.

"No worries. I'm sorry too. How's it going? Anything new?"

"Actually, yes." Pam leaned excitedly over the messy papers. "This is really happening fast. They're going to make it public later I think. My name is definitely going up the ladder to the White House, to be nominated."

"Honey, that's amazing! Congratulations!"

"I know! Isn't it so great?" Pam's eyes lit up, then she seemed to check herself. "But I can't count my chickens before they're hatched. There's a lot that has to happen between now and then, and you know these vacancies can be open for years."

Jake liked the sound of that. Ryan needed a few years to get past the accident. "So then they're not going to investigate you for a few years?"

"No, you misunderstand me. They do the investigation now and the nomination happens, then there's the Senate hearings, but you have to wait to be confirmed. That's the part that takes years."

"Oh, too bad." Jake hid his alarm.

"Patty Shwartz still hasn't gotten on the Third Circuit and she was nominated over two years ago, for a seat that was vacated two years *prior*. She had her hearing and she *still* hasn't been confirmed." Pam shook her head. "It's classic hurry-up-and-wait."

"So when does the investigation start?"

"Right now."

"But your nomination isn't public yet—"

"No, to be precise, I haven't been nominated yet. It's the president who does the nominating." Pam's voice turned professorial. "There's a questionnaire I have to answer and hand in next week, so if that goes smoothly, then it becomes public and starts officially."

Jake tried not to panic. It was too short a time for Ryan to have any emotional distance from the hit-and-run.

"The way it works is first, I get nominated by the president, then I have to submit the answers to the questionnaire to the Senate Judiciary Committee within five days from the date of the nomination."

"Five days? Wow."

"They make my answers public for three weeks and the hearing is scheduled anytime after that."

"So this is all happening this month?" Jake masked his dread.

"They emailed me all the questionnaires and information, and I printed it out. I ran out of paper, you believe that?" Pam gestured happily to the stacks on her desk. "I have to answer all of it *this week*. I can't believe how extensive it is." Pam flipped through a thick packet of papers, bolted at the top with a heavy metal clip. "This is only one of the questionnaires. It's sixty pages long!"

"Let me see." Jake held out his hand, and Pam gave him the packet, which he began to flip through. He passed headings for Education, Employment, Bar and Court Admissions, Public Statements, and Published Writings. He didn't see the part about the FBI. "It's a lot of work here."

"I know, right? And you see where it says I have to give the names of the counsel in these cases? They contact them, all of them. They interview them."

"Who does? The FBI?"

"No, the FBI investigates me and you, personally. The Department of Justice, the ABA, and the Senate Judiciary Committee investigate my career and finances. But they do overlap, not surprisingly. It's a bureaucracy. There's multiple questions that basically cover my judicial career, with an emphasis on any personal wrongdoing."

Jake shuddered. "Wrongdoing? You? How absurd."

"Obviously, but they have to ask. There's tons of questions that require disclosure of any violations of the law since I was eighteen years old. It even asks whether I've been accused of violating any county or even municipal regulations or ordinances." Pam snorted. "The only criminal questions that aren't covered are traffic violations for which a fine of fifty dollars or less was imposed."

Jake managed a smile. "You don't even have that."

"I know. I'm such a good girl. They ask about tax liens, collection procedures, or any kind of civil-law violations or state-bar proceedings. It's all public, except our financial records. The financial stuff will take forever." Pam rolled her eyes. "Will you do that part for me?"

"Of course. Is that for the FBI, too?"

"No. Those questions come from the Justice Department and the office of the Attorney General. They want to make sure there's no financial conflicts of interests, and they want our tax returns, for God-knows-how-many years."

"That's okay, I can deal." Jake wasn't getting anywhere beating around the bush. "Tell me about the FBI. How does that work?"

"They assign a special agent, or sometimes two, to investigate us. I was on the phone with Michael Rizzo just now, and he told me that over a three-week period, he had twenty-four hours of face-to-face interviews with the FBI."

"Really?" Jake's mouth went dry. "That's a lot longer than I thought."

"You and me both." Pam cringed. "Worst job interview ever."

"How long did they question his family for, did he say?"

"He said they spent an entire day with his wife, because she had a lot of financial ups and downs they had to sort out. But we don't have that. Anymore."

Jake knew what she was referring to. "How about his kids?"

"They don't have any. And they asked him for phone records, old passports, case files, and even some old school records."

"Do you think they'll ask for Ryan's school records?"

"I don't know."

"Will they interview Ryan alone or with us?"

"I don't know that either. He has nothing to worry about, but I bet they'll spend a lot of time with you and ask questions about your finances. But we don't have anything to worry about though. We do everything by the book."

"How about Ryan? What could they possibly ask him?"

"I have no idea. We're as clean as a whistle, really." Pam shrugged. "And they really do talk to the neighbors. Rizzo told me that the FBI contacted twenty of his friends and classmates all over the country, even the world. He said they really do go up and knock on the neighbors' doors. They asked his neighbors if he and his wife got along well with everyone, fought excessively, drank excessively, or were ever seen doing anything suspicious or unusual. Can you imagine that?"

"Sheesh." Jake had a sick feeling in the pit of his stomach, praying that no one had seen him burn the parka the other day.

Pam plucked some papers off the desk and handed them over. "Here, can you take a look at this? It's the financial part. Go to page fifty-nine."

"Sure." Jake flipped to the page, which was headed **Deferred Income/Future Benefits.** He skimmed the question. **List all the sources, amounts and dates of all anticipated receipts from deferred income payments, stock, options, uncompleted contracts and other future benefits** . . . "Boy, they aren't kidding."

"No, they're not. And go down to item number 22, which is source of income."

Jake read down to the paragraph. **List sources and amounts of all income received during the calendar year preceding your nomination and for the current calendar year, including all salaries, fees, dividends, interest, gifts, rents, royalties, licensee's fees** . . . "I get the idea."

"It's a nightmare."

Jake didn't bother to correct her. He knew exactly what a nightmare was and he was living it. "I can answer this for you. I'll do it tomorrow at the office."

"Thank you, thank you, thank you." Pam picked up another set of papers and handed them over the desk. "They also need a complete and detailed statement of our net worth, which goes back before the nomination, and the worst part is, since there's always a delay between the nomination and the hearing, sometimes three and four years, we have to keep updating the information, on a quarterly basis." Pam threw up her hands. "It's like doing your taxes every quarter for the next five years!"

Jake smiled. He wished he were living in Before, too, back when the only thing he had to worry about was paperwork. "Don't worry, we'll get through it."

"I wonder if I'll even make it." Pam flopped back in her cushy chair. "They said one of the reasons my name came to the front was because I'm a registered Independent. I'm the most apolitical, but that's not always the best thing."

"Sure it is. You're about the job, not about the politics."

"Ha! Well, of course, it being the federal government, there is a document that actually gives you the precise qualifications for the job." Pam searched around her desk, located some papers, and held them up. "Here we have a form. Presto!" She read aloud. "I'm paraphrasing, but the first requirement is, I have to be a citizen."

"Check."

"I have to have a reputation for integrity and good character."

"Check," Jake said, but that would disqualify her if anything about the accident came to light.

"I have to be fair and unbiased."

"You are."

"I have to be of sound mental and physical health."

Jake smiled. "Mental health? You can't win them all."

"Very funny." Pam grinned and returned to her document. "I have to be committed to equal justice under the law, have an outstanding legal ability, and competence and a willingness to manage trial proceedings."

"You have all that. You'll get it."

"But the fact that I'm not political means that nobody really backs me from either party."

"Or conversely, it means that neither party opposes you and your nomination sails through."

"Thanks. I try to do the right thing, every case. I try to follow the law." Pam raised her hand like the Statue of Liberty. "I stand for the law!"

"That's my girl!" Jake masked his emotions, feeling like a total fraud.

"I'm also supposed to think about why I really want to be a federal judge." Pam paused. "Let me remember how Rizzo put it. He told me I'm supposed to engage in 'critical self-reflection.'

I told him don't worry about that, I'm a woman. I wake up in critical self-reflection."

Jake smiled. "You want it, right?"

"More than anything."

Jake got up, walked around the desk, and gave her a big hug. "Then you shall have it, my love."

Chapter Twenty-one

Jake was at work the next morning by six o'clock, watching the parking lot through the floor-to-ceiling windows of his office and wondering if Lewis Deaner was going to pull up. Jake would be the first to see Deaner enter the building, whether or not Deaner parked in the spaces designated for Gardenia visitors. His office was three floors up, on the corner of the rectangular building, the corporate equivalent of the castle built on high ground. But it was still dark outside, and the lot was almost empty, so all Jake could see in the window was his own troubled reflection.

Still he kept an eye out, ignoring the flop sweat under his shirt. His tie felt like a noose. He'd barely slept last night, but he'd come to the office on time, always the first one in. He'd kept his door closed to signal no interruptions, but he still hadn't gotten anything done. He couldn't focus. He'd tried to do the things he had to do—check his email, then the markets in Japan, London, and New York—but all the while, in the back of his mind, he'd been worried about Lewis Deaner.

Jake caught sight of the treeline beyond the parking lot, and the jagged branches looked like so many hunting knives, cutting into the sky. He wondered for the umpteenth time if Deaner lived in the apartment building near Pike Road or worked in one of the businesses in the Concordia Corporate Center—or if he really knew anything about the accident, at all. Last night, Jake had searched online for information about Deaner or the accident, but found nothing new. He'd told Ryan not to confide in Dr. Dave, and Ryan had agreed, still shaken from driving down Pike Road again. When Jake had left him, Ryan was beginning to tackle his homework, his *American Pageant* textbook open next to his laptop. He was studying the American Dream, and Jake ignored the irony.

He saw his own troubled reflection ghosted in the window, but checked the parking lot again. Cars began to enter, but no sign of Deaner. In time a frigid sun climbed the sky, and cars arrived one by one, first among them his ace office administrator, Amy Carlino, who parked her maroon Acura next to his rental Toyota. She got out, gathered up her big purse, and eyed his car, undoubtedly worried about why Jake had a rental. He felt touched, wondering how disillusioned she would be if she knew about Pike Road.

Jake watched the Gardenia lot fill up, and his employees emerged from their Nissans, Jettas, and SUVs, their phones to their ears, juggling travel mugs, cigarettes, purses, and tote bags. None of the spaces was officially reserved or assigned, but the employees knew where each other parked, like seats at a dinner table. So far, no sign of Deaner.

His attention turned to the farther sections of the lot, scanning it for an unfamiliar car. The lot accommodated five other companies, all of them bigger than Gardenia, so any car could have belonged to Deaner. He checked out the drivers, but none was Deaner. In the meantime, he could hear the noises outside his door as Gardenia filled up with all sixteen employees, which included five portfolio managers that reported to him, as well as specialists in banking, fixed income, research, sales, and marketing.

"Jake?" said a voice behind him, and Jake startled, then swiveled his chair around. Amy stood in the open doorway, puzzled. "I knocked, but you didn't hear me."

"Amy, sorry." Jake tried to get his head in the game. A cold sunlight filled his office, which had a side wall of light wood shelves, and a beige leather couch and matching chairs across his desk. His desk had a glass top that matched the one on a round conference table. Mullioned panels flanked his doorway.

"Mrs. LeMenile is out in reception. A new client, remember? She's on your calendar for ten o'clock. You ready for her?"

"Sure. Yes."

"You okay?" Amy searched his face with large, espresso-brown eyes. "You don't look well."

"I'm fine, thanks." Jake couldn't remember the last time he'd lied to Amy, except for her surprise birthday parties, which he lied to her about routinely. "By the way, I had a fender bender over the weekend, so expect the insurance company to call."

"I was wondering." Amy frowned with concern. "Meanwhile, did you hear about that hit-and-run on Friday night? The girl went to Concord Chase? Did Ryan know her?"

"No." Jake forced himself not to show any reaction. "Also, we may get a visit from a guy I know, named Lewis Deaner."

"Okay, I'll go get Mrs. LeMenile. Be right back." Amy left and returned a few minutes later with a handsome older woman. "Jake, this is Mrs. Guinevere LeMenile," Amy said, before she slipped out, closing the door.

"Hello, Mrs. LeMenile." Jake rose to greet her, extending a hand, which Mrs. LeMenile shook, her grip surprisingly strong. She had sleek silvery hair, which was clipped back off of her lined face, and she was tall, weathered, and lean in a camelhair jacket, jeans, with brown boots that lent her a horsey air. Her hooded eyes were a lively gray-green, alert and sharp, set off by a green silk scarf.

"Jake, call me Guinevere. Wonderful to meet you."

"Please, sit down." Jake gestured to his conference table and sat down opposite her. "Can I get you some coffee or tea?"

"No, thanks, I haven't much time." Guinevere set her leather bag on the floor and plunked down in the chair, crossing her legs. "I'm here because my friend Helen Weissman recommended you. She can't say enough good things about you and you made her a significant amount of money."

"Thank you, and I think the world of Helen."

"I'm a widow, and my husband died two years ago, leaving me with an estate of $5 million." Guinevere's manner was authoritative, and she didn't pull out any bank statements, notes, or scraps of paper like many of his first-time clients. "Two million of that are the proceeds from his life-insurance policy, one is our combined savings, 401(k), and pension fund. I live in our home, which is worth two. My money is currently in short-term Treasury bills and I'm making nothing, but I've become very dissatisfied with the fees I'm paying my current financial planner. Even though I negotiated them down from 1 percent to .5 percent, it still seems utterly ridiculous for what is essentially a liquid asset, don't you agree?"

"Yes," Jake answered, because she was absolutely right. Suddenly his attention was drawn away by activity at Amy's desk, but he could only see part of what was going on through the mullioned windows.

"I think I'm ready to put that money to work for me, so I've come to you. Why don't we begin by your telling me about Gardenia?"

"Sure. Right." Jake wondered if it was Deaner at Amy's desk, which would be odd. Guests had to wait in reception before being sent back. "We have almost a hundred . . . million dollars under our management." Jake felt himself falter, distracted.

"We look for high-quality stocks from established companies, ones that pay dividends, and—"

"I read that on your website." Guinevere waved him into silence with a wrinkled hand. "I'd rather you explain how you make your investment decisions, exactly."

"I would be your portfolio manager, but here we make our investment decisions as a group." Jake tried to look past Guinevere to see what was going on, but couldn't. "The investment committee, which I head, uh . . . meets three times a week and we share our expertise. We invest only in quality growth stocks, er, and there are only approximately thirty to forty of those."

"Like which ones, for example?"

Jake had to think a minute, though he'd picked the stocks himself. "Disney, IBM, Eaton Corporation, Qualcomm, Exxon-Mobil, Johnson & Johnson, and Chevron, to name a few."

"That list could use some tweaking, don't you think?" Guinevere sniffed. "It doesn't include the biotech companies, which are a very good buy right now."

Jake could tell he was losing her, by a new distance in her demeanor. He tried to get his head in the game. "That brings me to an important point about Gardenia. We don't follow trends or crazes. If you read the biotech companies are hot, that doesn't cause us to rebalance your portfolio."

"Why not? You'll miss out. Rather, I will."

"Our view is long-term." Jake felt his mouth go dry when he saw Amy getting up. He caught a glimpse of her talking to someone, but couldn't see whom. "A bubble can burst and a fad stock . . . can turn out to be a dog, and we don't want you in that position. We diversify where appropriate to lower your risk."

"Well, obviously."

Jake couldn't get back on track. He couldn't have Deaner out there, on the loose, saying God knows that. "Nor do we . . . churn your portfolio. Our turnover average . . . is 15 to 25 percent over a year, much lower than the typical 75 percent."

"But your fees are higher than a place like Vanguard."

"That's true, but . . . we charge nothing to manage Treasury bills or similarly liquid assets, and we charge 1.5 percent on stocks and 1 percent on—"

"That's not insubstantial." Guinevere lifted a graying eyebrow. "It's higher than Vanguard, which is essentially offering its services at cost."

"You're comparing apples with oranges. They administer index funds, which are—"

"I know what an index fund is." Guinevere frowned, a fissure deepening between her bright eyes. "Please don't condescend to me."

"I'm sorry, I didn't mean to." Jake swallowed hard. Amy left her desk, and people were milling around in the area. "Vanguard has $2 trillion under management . . . and 28 million clients—"

"What difference does that make?" Guinevere's eyes narrowed. "They told me that at my asset level, they would assign me to an asset manager, just like you."

"But we have a more personalized approach . . . not only in the stocks we select, but in the . . . uh . . . ancillary services we offer." Jake couldn't focus. He didn't know where Amy was. "We view your portfolio . . . er, as merely one part of the whole that we will provide for you or your loved ones—"

"My husband and I had no children. There's just me. When I die, my money goes to Thorncroft Equestrian Center."

"Okay, then we can help you find an accountant and an estate lawyer—"

"I have an estate lawyer, and my will is in place, as is my living will and power of attorney."

"Good, well, then." Jake was kicking himself. He knew she'd have her ducks in a row. He reached onto the middle of the table, picked up a Gardenia promotional folder, and offered it to her. "This sets forth all of our ancillary services. For example, in the event of your incapacity or illness, we will step in and liaise with your estate lawyer. We can even pay your household bills for you—"

"In other words, you do a lot of hand-holding." Guinevere set the Gardenia folder aside. "But I don't need my hand held. I have a horse and a pony and I'm perfectly capable of taking care of both. In fact, they're provided for in my will. So why do I need Gardenia?"

Jake found himself shifting in his chair, to see the hallway better. Amy still wasn't back, and for a second, he felt a bolt of fear that Deaner could have done her harm. Anything was possible.

"Jake, that's it! Am I *boring* you? Because you keep looking over my shoulder. Hmph!" Guinevere reached down and grabbed her bag. "You know, I had been worried that I was a rather low-net-worth individual for Gardenia. I saw on your website that many of your clients have assets of $10 million and up, and I'm concerned that my account wouldn't get the attention I deserve."

"Guinevere, wait, I assure you that $5 million is a lot of money by any measure, and it's a lot of money to—"

"I'm sorry, but I've just made my decision." Guinevere stood up and tucked her bag under her arm. "Thank you for your time. I'll be on my way."

"No, wait." Jake jumped to his feet. "Hold on, please reconsider. I can assure you that here, you would get kid-glove, personalized treatment."

"I'd rather save the fees." Guinevere charged for the door, with Jake on her heels.

"But if you would—" Jake followed her out, only to find Lewis Deaner standing with Amy, in front of her desk.

"Jake?" Amy turned to him, in confusion. "Mr. Deaner says

you asked him to stop by this morning, but I told him you were in with Mrs. LeMenile. I asked him to wait in reception, but he doesn't seem to want to—"

"Hello, Jake." Deaner's eyes bored into Jake, from behind his wire-rimmed glasses. "Did you forget about our appointment?"

"Hmph!" Guinevere said, striding past the desk. "Just as I suspected. You double-booked the appointment. You're worse than my gynecologist!"

Chapter Twenty-two

"What the hell is this about?" Jake folded his arms, standing against the windows while Deaner's light blue eyes flitted around, taking in the glass desktops, watercolors pressed between glass panes, and crystal awards. It struck Jake for the first time that almost everything in his office was breakable.

"Jake, you should ask me to sit down." Deaner met his gaze coolly. "Isn't that what you do with clients?"

"You're not a client. Tell me why you're here."

"Then what am I? Or more accurately, what are we going to tell your employees I am?" Deaner spoke quietly, and his tone was reasonable. He had several fine lines in his forehead, so he must have been older than Jake had thought at the game, maybe in his fifties. "Because if Amy doesn't think I'm a client, you're going to have to explain who I am and why I'm here. Unless you want me to."

"Sit down, then." Jake hated that Deaner knew Amy's name. He must have gotten it off the website.

"You should sit opposite me, shouldn't you? Play your part,

Mr. Financial Planner." Deaner unzipped his parka, and lowered himself into the chair.

"Tell me what's this all about." Jake stood his ground, behind the chair.

"Shouldn't I look like I'm taking notes? That's what clients do when you talk, isn't it, Jake? They write down what you say?" Deaner slid a pad and pen from the center of the table, wrote something, and flipped it around to show it to Jake. It read, **Go, Ryan, go!**

Jake's heart thudded in his chest. "Why are you here? Who are you? What's your real name?"

Deaner didn't reply, but set down the pad and picked up the Gardenia promotional folder. He slid out a brochure, which had a photo of Jake in shirtsleeves, smiling confidently. "Nice tie."

"Answer my question."

"Slick materials. Very upmarket." Deaner waved the brochure. "No one would ever guess where you and Ryan were Friday night."

Jake froze. He forced himself to stay in control. Not to confirm or deny. Deaner could be bluffing, or he could be an undercover cop or a private investigator, even wearing a wire.

"Now, sit down. You'll need to."

Jake lowered himself into the chair. His chest tight, his mouth dry.

"I figure you make almost a million bucks a year." Deaner set the Gardenia folder aside. "Your house is probably worth about $550K, and I bet it's paid off. You're not a flashy guy. You live below your means. You're cheap, which means you have a ton of dough in savings, pension plan, 401(k), college fund for Ryan. I'm guessing almost a million, and you trade your own account. You're trying to grow it. How'm I doing?"

"Get to the point."

"Fine. I know what happened Friday night." Deaner pushed

up his glasses with a finger that had a bitten-off nail. "Ryan was driving your car and he hit the jogger. You both got out of the car. You switched seats with him and drove away."

Jake felt his world explode around him. The glass tops, the crystal awards, the massive windows. Shards of glass flew everywhere. He didn't know how he could put it back together again. It was all gone, falling away, shooting through space.

"Yes, I know it all. I saw it. You threw yourself on the sword for your son, good for you. *Dad.*"

Jake struggled for self-control. The worst-case scenario had just gotten worse.

"What was it that Ryan had in his hand? You were about to call the cops, after all. I heard you yelling."

Jake reeled. He had no idea how Deaner had seen or heard them. The apartment complex, the corporate center. Somewhere, somehow.

"You gave her CPR. Was she dead when you left her, or did you leave her to die?" Deaner shook his head. "You're not a monster, right? You're basically a decent guy, but you slipped up. Hey, it happens."

Jake didn't reply. He couldn't. Emotion churned in his gut. Inwardly he raged at Deaner, then at himself. It was his own actions that brought him to this point. But he had to shift into damage control or all was lost.

"You're wondering if I have proof, and I do. Take a look-see." Deaner reached inside his parka, pulled out an iPhone, hit a few buttons, and showed the screen.

Jake almost gasped. The photo was an enlargement of Ryan and him at the accident scene, in front of the headlights, their faces grainy but visible. The photo was dark, but Deaner must have enhanced it somehow.

"But wait, there's more, as they say." Deaner took the phone back, then swiped the screen a few times. "Let me show you the video. The parting shot, as it were. Here." Deaner held the phone up, and the video started.

Jake watched himself kneeling in front of the body, then running to Ryan and saying something, and the both of them hustling to the car.

Deaner half-smiled. "The audio isn't great but I can fix that, and I will, if I have to. So can the cops. Wait for the last shot. It's priceless."

Jake watched the last shot, which was a close-up of his own license plate, taken as the Audi receded down Pike Road. The video ended, the screen froze, and a white arrow ghosted over the darkness of night.

"The End." Deaner emitted a dry laugh.

"Where did you get that?" Jake asked, finding his voice. He had a million questions.

"None of your business."

"Do you live in those apartments near Pike Road? Or do you work at the corporate center?"

"None of your business."

"Who are you? What do you do?" Jake's face felt hot and damp. He told himself to get a grip but couldn't.

"I told you."

"You lied. Why were you there that night? What were you doing?"

"Who said I was there?"

Jake recoiled, confused. "You said. You said you saw what happened."

"I meant on the video."

"So if you didn't take the video or the photos, who did? How did you get them? Who gave them to you?"

"Also not your business."

"How did you find me? Did you follow me that night? Was it from the license plate?"

"Now to my point, as you put it." Deaner put the iPhone back into his pocket. "I'll go to the police tomorrow unless you wire $250,000 to this account by eleven o'clock."

"So you're blackmailing me." Jake felt the blood drain from his face. He didn't know what to do. He couldn't believe this was happening.

"Obviously." Deaner slipped his hand into his other pocket and extracted a yellow Post-it packet, then tore one off the top and pressed it onto the glass tabletop. "This is the bank you wire it to."

"You want me to wire blackmail money to a *bank* account?"

"It's offshore, a numbered account. Not that hard to set up, interestingly. When I get the confirmation that the wire transfer went through, I'll send you the video and pictures."

Jake's mind raced. He didn't know how to react. He couldn't process it fast enough. "You won't go to the police."

"Try me."

"I'll bring you down with me." Jake knew the best defense was a good offense.

"No you won't. You'll have no credibility. You'll only make it worse for your wife and son. Bigger news, bigger headlines. Scandal. Yikes."

Jake's stomach turned over. Deaner knew about Pam, too. He had no leverage, not a card to play. "How do I know that if I pay you, this is where it ends? Or that whoever took the video won't want to get paid, too?"

"You don't."

"Plus it's a digital file. You have other copies. How do I know you'll give me all of them?"

"Again, you don't. You don't know anything." Deaner shifted back his chair, getting ready to leave. "You only know what happens if I don't get paid. A world of pain for your son."

"But I can't get that much money that fast."

"We both know you can. You have the dough. Liquidate stocks in no time. Cash one of those client's checks you must have lying around. You're a financial planner, so plan some *finances*." Deaner stood up and crossed to the door. "You have until eleven o'clock tomorrow."

"I can't do that." Jake felt his blood pressure rise, pounding at his temples. "I'd never do that. I never have. It doesn't work that way, anyway."

"I don't think you're taking me seriously, Jake. Good-bye." Deaner opened the door and said loudly, "Thanks so much for the meeting. I'll be in touch."

Jake watched him walk down the hall and nod good-bye to Amy, who got up from her chair and came over.

"Who was that guy?" she asked, blinking.

"A possible new client. I met him at Ryan's game."

"Did you sign him? Should I send him some papers and open up a file?"

"Not yet."

"Don't look so worried, Jake. You'll reel him in, sooner or later. You always do." Amy smiled under her headful of curls, and Jake could barely manage to smile back.

"Thanks."

"Funny, I never would've pegged that guy for having money, and my paydar is pretty good."

"Paydar?"

"Yeah. Like gaydar, only with dough. I can usually pick 'em, even when they dress down. But that guy fooled me."

"Gotta get back to work." Jake went back into his office, where he closed the door and hurried to his desk. He got on-line, went to the website for his bank, and signed in to check his accounts. **Interest Checking, Savings,** and **Money Market,** read the blue virtual folders, and he thought back to what Pam had said last night, about the financial disclosure required for her nomination.

It's like doing your taxes, every quarter for the next five years!

Jake leaned over to get his messenger bag, tugged out the

forms that Pam had given him, and flipped through them frantically. The questionnaire asked for the "**sources and amounts
of all income received during the calendar year preceding your
nomination and for the current calendar year, including all
salaries, fees, dividends, interest, gifts, rents, royalties, licensee's fees . . .**"

Jake couldn't see any way around the questionnaire. Even if he
wanted to pay the blackmail, he couldn't take $250K out of their
accounts without its showing, and if the money didn't appear in
another account, canceled check, or trade receipt, the FBI
would find out. They would get caught. It would scuttle Pam's
nomination, if not send them both to jail.

Jake tried to think, his temples throbbing. Even before the
FBI would find it, he knew Pam would. She was always going
online and checking their household balances. She might not
check the money market, but he couldn't take the risk.

Cash one of those client's checks you must have lying around.

Jake's gaze traveled the office and came to rest on the crystal
awards. He'd gotten a check for $321K from one of his longtime
clients last week. It was still in the company safe, waiting to be
deposited because it had come in too late on Friday. It was due
to be deposited today. He racked his brain to think of a way
he could use the check, borrow the $250K, and replace it later,
somehow, after the FBI interviews were over and Pam's judgeship was in the clear.

Jake stopped his thinking in its tracks. Was he seriously
thinking about stealing? He couldn't, ever. He loved his clients,
and he loved Gardenia. It was his baby, he'd raised it from in-
fancy. He had personal integrity; he had morals and pride. He'd
worked hard to gain the trust of his clients, and he had a spot-
less, unimpeachable record. He was a Good Guy, so when had
he turned bad? Then he knew the answer, on Pike Road.

Jake considered another option. He could try to stall Deaner
until after the FBI interviews. Then he could take the money

from his personal money market and replace it before Pam realized it had gone missing, or he could sell some stock, which she checked far less often. Suddenly his cell phone started ringing on his desk, vibrating next to his keyboard.

Jake looked over, and the call was from Ryan. The screen showed a candid photo of his son, grinning on their driveway with a basketball tucked in the crook of his elbow. Jake reached for his phone and hit ANSWER. "Hey, pal, what's up?" he asked, keeping his tone casual.

"Dad!" Ryan sounded hysterical. "Dad! You need to come get me at school, now!"

Chapter Twenty-three

Jake pulled up around the back of the school, outside the cafeteria, which faced the student parking lot. He spotted Ryan hurrying toward him without a coat, hunching his shoulders against the cold. Jake leaned over in alarm and opened the passenger-side door. "Ryan, what's the matter?"

"Dad, drive." Ryan jumped into the car, pulled up his long legs, and slammed the door closed. "Hurry. Just go."

"Where? Why? What happened?" Jake hit the gas, glancing over. Ryan looked distraught, but hadn't wanted to tell him why on the phone.

"Drive away. Where nobody can see us. Please." Ryan gestured quickly, pitched forward on the seat, and Jake drove through the lot, past cars with **Go Chasers** painted in maroon on the windows.

"What about school? Did you cut class?"

"No, they don't know I'm gone yet. It's A Lunch." Ryan raked his bangs in agitation. "Dad, for real, class is the least of my worries right now. Something really scary is going on. Really scary."

"Okay, calm down. Relax. Whatever it is, we can handle it." Jake steered out of the student lot and on to the winding road that led to Lincoln Avenue, where he made the green light, then took the left fork and entered the Stone Hills neighborhood, so named because the homes were made of an indigenous tan-and-brown fieldstone.

"Is anybody following us, can you tell?" Ryan peered at the mirror outside the car.

"No, of course not," Jake answered, but he checked the rearview mirror anyway. There was nobody behind him except a FedEx truck. "Why would somebody be following us? Ryan, what's going on?"

"Pull over." Ryan stayed glued to the outside mirror.

"Okay, relax." Jake heard his phone ringing inside the breast pocket of his suit jacket, but he'd get it later.

"I don't know." Ryan scanned the street, shifting in his seat. "Do you see anything random? Is anybody following us?"

"No. Relax, I'll park." Jake pulled over at the corner and put the car in park, leaving the engine running for the heat.

"Do you think it's safe here?"

"Of course it is." Jake looked around, and the street was quiet and still. A young mother pushed a stroller, her ponytail caught on the hood of her parka.

"I'm scared shitless. I went to my locker and checked my phone before lunch. Look." Ryan slid his iPhone out of his pocket, opened the text function, and showed Jake the text in its bright pink bubble.

i am crazy 4 u

"What, Ryan? Some girl has a crush on you." Jake exhaled, relieved.

"Right, that's what I thought. At first I thought it was from Janine Mae, but it isn't." Ryan started talking fast, running his words together. "She's in my phone and if it were from her, it would come up with her name. I don't know that number. It's not in my Contacts. See?"

Jake looked at the phone number from the text, which had a 999 area code. "So? Somebody has a crush on you. Somebody you don't have in your phone already."

"Totally, that's what I thought, too. I got stoked, thinking some girl liked me. I'm so stupid." Ryan scrolled to the next text. "Look at this."

Jake read, **ur an awesome player**

"Wait." Ryan scrolled down to the next pink bubble, which had been delivered a minute later. "It gets worse, a lot worse."

Jake read the text, beginning to get a bad feeling. **i watch u all the time** "Okay, kinda creepy."

"That's nothing, compared to the end. You look at the rest. I can't. It makes me want to hurl." Ryan thrust the phone at him. "My phone number's not that easy to get. It's not on Facebook, and anyway, I have all my privacy settings on. The school has it, so it could be someone who works in the office. It's on the team portal, but only the team can get in. You'd have to hack it. I don't think I have it anywhere else."

Jake scrolled down through the line of pink bubbles, reading: **i wish i cld b w u**

ur soo sexy
ur soo cute
ur soo tall
ur shredded
i love ur hair
u have gr8t eyes
I love ur smile
i think of u all the time
i dream abt u
i see u
i watch u

"How many are there?" Jake asked angrily. It had to be Deaner. Deaner must have gotten Ryan's cell-phone number. Or the texts were from whoever made the video, if it wasn't Deaner.

"Like fifty or so, I stopped counting. They came one after the other, like seconds apart." Ryan kept shaking his head, his fair skin mottled. "Keep reading. It gets worse. *Way* worse."

Jake seethed, reading.

i kno everything about u
i follow u everywhere
u can't get away from me

Jake scrolled up and checked the time of the first text, delivered at 11:02. That would have been minutes after Deaner had left his office. Jake had thought that Deaner would go after him, but he'd gone after Ryan instead. Jake scrolled down again and read more texts, delivered only seconds apart.

we shld b 2gether
we belong 2gether

"Oh no." Jake reminded himself to stay in control. He had to keep calm for Ryan, who was almost hyperventilating.

"Do you see this? Do you *see*? Keep reading to the end!"

Jake read on: **we r meant to be**
i am ur destiny
i see u at lunch
i see u in algebra
i see u in english
i see u in western civ
i see u in French
i see u in chemistry

"Dad, she knows my schedule! She knows everything! Or it might not even be a girl, who knows? They musta hacked the student portal, too. Whoever this is, a boy, girl, or whatever, they're crazy!"

"I know, I can tell." Jake felt his temples pounding again. He wanted to get ahold of Deaner and beat the living hell out of him. He kept reading. **i see ur games**

i see u at practice
u cant get away frm me
no one loves u like me
u have 2 be w me
u will be w me
u cant get away
u killed me
u deserve 2 die
dont u feel guilty?
dont u feel bad?
dont u feel sad?
kill urself
kill urself
kill urself

"Oh my God." Jake gritted his teeth, enraged.

"Keep going. You're almost there."

Jake scrolled down.

kill urself on pike rd
die & join me
you know who i am

"Bastard!" Jake exploded. "I'm going to kill this guy!"

"What guy? How do you know it's a guy, and do you understand what this means?" Ryan grabbed his arm. "Whoever sent this knows what happened. They know it's *me*. What are we going to do? They *know*. Look at the next one, it's a picture."

"Okay, try and stay calm." Jake looked at the screen, which showed a thumbnail photo of a young girl. He tapped it to enlarge it, though he could guess who it was. A school photo of a beautiful young girl popped onto the screen, and she had long, dark hair with large, dark brown eyes, and a wide, sweet smile. The caption read, **I'm Kathleen Lindstrom.**

"That's the last one." Ryan twisted around in his seat, frantic.

"Dad, whoever sent this, they *know*. This *is not* a lucky guess. This is *not* a troll. Somebody *knows* I did it. Somebody is *stalking* me. He could be watching us *right now*."

"No, not really." Jake had to cool him down. He patted Ryan on the knee, which was drawn up to fit his long legs into the cramped Toyota. "He's just trying to scare you. Don't give him the satisfaction."

"Who? Why? Why's he trying to scare me?"

"You have to let me handle this." Jake looked over, and Ryan's eyes went wide with disbelief and fear.

"What are you *talking* about? Do you know who this is? What's going on?"

"Please, let me handle this." Jake would have to come up with the money for Deaner. There was no other way. "You have to go back to school. What time is lunch over?"

"Dad, I can't go back to school. What if it's somebody at school? Is it somebody at school?" Ryan went wild-eyed with bewilderment. "How do they know I play basketball? *What's going on?*"

"Trust me, it's better if you don't know."

"You have to tell me." Ryan shouted, jabbing the air with his index finger. "It's *me* they're after. It's *me* they want. I'm the one who did it! I have a right to know. It's *my* life!"

"We're not going to discuss this now. You have to get back to school." Jake checked the dashboard clock, which read 11:50. His phone rang again, but he'd have to get it later. "Tell me what time lunch is over."

"12:10. I'm supposed to be in Western Civ at 12:15, but Dad, I'm not going. I'm done for the day! Tell me what's happening!"

"Listen to me. You have to let me handle this." Jake disengaged the emergency brake. "The only way to deal with this is if you do what you're supposed to do. Go to class, then practice, then come home. I'll explain everything."

"Dad, *get real*!" Ryan exploded, distraught. "I can't go to class!

What do you think, I can sit there and listen? Take notes like nothing's wrong? You don't know what it's like at school today! All the girls are crying, all the teachers are upset. They're going to do a memorial for her tonight. They're planting a tree out front. The girls track team went around the homerooms to collect money for a scholarship fund." Ryan gestured, his arms flailing wildly. "*Janine Mae* was tight with her, she was *popular*! You saw, she was supercute, Dad. She had tons of dates. I killed her, and this *guy* knows it. *Who is he?*"

"Ryan, work with me. We can talk about this at home tonight. Nothing's going to change between now and then. You give me your phone and I'll get you a new number." Jake put the car in gear and was about to give it some gas when Ryan's phone signaled an incoming text. They both looked down at the screen.

"Oh my God! It's another picture!" Ryan tapped the thumbnail on the touch screen, and it opened to the photograph that Deaner had shown Jake this morning, of Ryan and him arguing in the headlights, next to Kathleen Lindstrom's fallen form. "Oh no! No!"

"Ryan, don't panic. I have this under control—"

"Oh my God!" Ryan dropped the phone. His hands flew to his head. "He has a picture! There's a picture! Oh my God, what are we going to do? He has *proof*! That's *proof*! Dad, I don't want you to go to jail!"

"Ryan, you have to keep your wits about you. I have this in control. I saw that photo already. I know what to do about it." Jake started to put a hand on Ryan's arm, but he batted it away, angry.

"What are you *talking* about? You *knew* about this? Why didn't you *tell me*?"

"Take it easy, I just found out this morning." Jake kept his tone reassuring and put the car back in park. "But you don't have to think about it anymore. It's going to go away."

"What do you mean? How did you see that picture? It can send you to jail! Tell me everything!"

"Okay, relax. I'll tell you but you have to be calm. I'm handling it." Jake had no choice but to level with him. "Bottom line, a man came to my office today and he's blackmailing us."

"*What?*" Ryan's hands flew to his face and stayed there, cupping his own cheeks. "Are you *kidding* me? Are you *kidding* me right now, Dad?"

"You have to calm down. It's as simple as that."

"You mean we're getting *blackmailed* like on *TV*? Like *a movie*? Did he have *a gun*? In your office—"

"I'm not telling you another thing unless you calm down, and you have to go to class after this."

"Oh my God! What are you talking about? Are you crazy?" Ryan threw up his hands, bursting into mirthless laughter. "Are you blackmailing *me* now?"

"Stop." Jake felt his temper begin to give way, his anger at Deaner and himself spilling onto Ryan, scattershot. "You said you weren't a baby, so stop acting like one. You need to rise above this, Ryan. You need to ask more of yourself."

"How?" Ryan dropped his hands. "What?"

"Calm down. Get a grip."

"But I'm *scared*! I'm scared for *you*!"

Jake felt a deep pang of guilt. "I know that, but the best way to help me—to help us both—is to stay in control. In charge."

"Okay, okay. Okay, I'm calm." Ryan took a breath. He picked up his phone and held it in his hand. "Okay, I hear you. I'm calm. Just tell me what the guy said, and I'll go to class. Who is he?"

"I don't know who he is. I don't know any more than I'm telling you." Jake put the car in gear again, fed it some gas, and pulled away from the curb. "All you need to know is that the man is asking for money. Luckily, we have money, and I'm going to give it to him. After I give him the money, it's done. Period. Do you hear me? It ends."

"How do you know he won't go to the police anyway?"

"Because it's not in his interest. If he goes to the police, he goes down, too."

"Why?"

"Because blackmail and extortion is illegal," Jake answered, off the top of his head. He had no idea if that was the proper name for the crime and he didn't care. He had to end this conversation. He drove past the lovely houses of Stone Hills and the young mother pushing the stroller, feeling surreal talking about blackmail and thugs.

"So you're going to pay him? How do you know he won't try asking for more money? That's what they do in the movies."

"I don't, but you don't have to worry about that because I have plenty of money. If he asks for more money, I'll give him more money."

"But where does it end?"

"We have the money, Ryan. It's not an issue. We live within our means, you know that. We all say I'm cheap, and it's paying off."

"How much money did he ask for?"

"Ryan, why do you have to know the details?" Jake turned left, heading back toward the high school. "The details don't matter. It's really better if you don't know everything."

"Please, just tell me."

"He asked for $25,000."

"Oh my God. Oh my God. That's, like, a *year* of college tuition."

"Don't even worry about it. I have it in savings. It's worth the money to me."

"But what will Mom say? She'll notice that, for sure."

"No, she won't know." Jake got ready to tell another lie. He kept his face forward, looking through the windshield as they were approaching Lincoln Avenue, heavily trafficked during the noon rush. "We have separate checking and savings accounts, in addition to the joint account that we use to pay our bills. I don't ask her questions about hers, and she doesn't ask about mine."

"Why do you do that?"

"Have separate accounts? You've heard her say that she thinks every woman should have her own money. She likes it, too, because when she buys me a present, I don't see how much it costs. I feel the same way." Jake was making it up as he went along, getting away with it only because he'd never talked to Ryan about their family finances. Maybe Ryan had been right, that Jake treated him like a baby. "Plus when I trade some stocks, I don't like her to see the losses. I want her to think I'm smart." Jake looked over and flashed a smile, trying to cheer him up, but it wasn't working. "Trust me, everything is going to be all right. This has turned into a business deal, no more and no less. I do these every day. I got this."

"Oh man, I can't believe this happened." Ryan moaned, his forehead dropping into his hands. "I'm so sorry, Dad. I screwed this up so badly."

"No you didn't. I did."

"Get real. It's on me." Ryan's tone had softened, and his shock and anger had gone, but Jake wasn't sure it was an improvement.

"Stop, son. Let it go. We're almost out of the woods." Jake drove across Lincoln Avenue, entered the Concord Chase campus, and headed for the road that led to the student parking lot. He glanced at the dashboard clock, which read 12:05. "Good, we're right on time. Where should I take you? Around the front or the back?"

"The front. It's closer to Western Civ."

"Okay." Jake drove on the road, bypassing the student parking lot and leading to the main entrance. "Just stay cool for the rest of the day, and I'll fill you in tonight. Try to put this out of your mind."

"I'll try," Ryan said, just as his phone signaled an incoming text, and they both jumped.

"Don't look at it," Jake said quickly. "It'll upset you. He's trying to upset you. Give me the phone."

"No, *I* got *this*." Suddenly, Ryan raised his phone and slammed it down on the dashboard, again and again, until it went silent.

Chapter Twenty-four

GARDENIA TRUST, read the polished plaque on their wooden door, and Jake powered through into the office. He tried to look and act the way he always did, but he was sweating under his suit jacket. He was on fire after reading those texts and he knew it had to show. He strode through the empty reception area, with its sky-blue patterned couch, walnut end tables, and brass lamps, and it was the first time in his career he'd been happy there were no clients.

Jake plastered on a smile as he approached the reception desk. Debbie Tarkington had been with him since she graduated from community college, and her unflappable nature made her the perfect choice for the front desk. Not all of Jake's clients were easy to get along with, and he knew that money didn't guarantee good judgment, starting with the man in the mirror.

"Jake, hi." Debbie smiled, a welcoming grin that creased her pretty face. She was African-American and had large eyes and short hair, which she wore natural. She handed him a packet of pink phone messages. "Here's your calls. Everything go okay?"

"Yes, thanks." Jake thumbed through his phone messages, to avoid meeting her eye. He hadn't explained where he was going when he'd left, which he knew was unusual. "Sorry I ran out. I had to take care of a few things for Ryan. He was sick this weekend, but he went to school today."

"I hope he feels better. By the way, Martin wants to see you and so does Ramon. They both said it was important, so you can pick your poison."

"Okay, thanks." Jake didn't have time to talk to either of them. Martin Niemeyer and Ramon Ramirez were two of his best portfolio managers, but they would have to wait. "I'm not taking calls this afternoon. I don't need interruptions."

"Gotcha. Also there's leftover pizza in the coffee room."

"Thanks." Jake walked down the hall just as Martin popped out of his office and came striding down the long hallway toward him. A bright young refugee from Lehman Brothers, Martin still looked very Wall Street, with his moussed brown hair, frameless Swiss glasses, and charcoal pinstriped suit.

"Jake," Martin called out, in his characteristic bark. "We need to talk about Disney. I'd like to buy a block for Bob Cadison and I need to—"

"Martin, do whatever you think is right." Jake patted him on the shoulder and kept walking down the long hall, which ended in his office. "I can't talk now."

"But you know how he is. He second-guesses every pick, even Disney."

"Then call and explain it to him."

"I know, I know," Martin called after him, wearily. "Like you always say, 'It's his money, not mine.'"

"Right." Jake cringed, inwardly. He kept going toward his office when he saw Ramon lumbering down the hallway on the right, an unmistakable figure because the man was built like a refrigerator. Ramon had played right tackle at Harvard and still managed to graduate at the top of his class, the antithesis of the dumb jock.

"Boss man!" Ramon called out, with a broad smile. His silk tie flew as he walked and his white shirt and dark suit pants strained at the seams because he was so supersized. "You didn't answer my email."

"Sorry, but I can't talk now." Jake couldn't remember the last time he checked his email. He reached Amy's desk at the same time that Ramon did.

"I know, but I need your okay on the Shamir trust. Remember, for the kids? I sent you an email about it."

"Ramon, sorry, I didn't get a chance to look at it. You decide. I'm wall-to-wall this afternoon."

"Appreciate the confidence." Ramon clapped him on the back, then went back down the hall, and Amy looked up worriedly.

"Jake, how's Ryan? Is he feeling better?"

"Yes." Jake had mumbled something before he left about Ryan's not feeling well. "He thought he might want to come home from school, but he decided to stick it out."

"Good, Pam was worried."

Jake hid his surprise. "Pam?"

"Yes, she called here. She said she called your cell, but you didn't answer and she needed to talk to you."

"Oh damn." Jake remembered the phone calls that had come in when he was with Ryan. He had forgotten about them, completely preoccupied on the way back to the office. He reached into his breast pocket, slid out his phone, and saw the screen banner that showed two missed calls from Pam.

Amy blinked under her dark curls. "She said call her back as soon as you get a chance."

Jake was in real trouble, because he'd have to explain what

was going on with Ryan. "I'll call her right back. Will you hold my calls for the afternoon? I really need to focus."

"But you and Ramon have an appointment at 3:30 with the Marchman Group, remember?"

"Oh, right." Jake had forgotten that, too. The Marchman Group was one of his corporate clients, and he needed to see them, but this was no time to meet with anybody. "Do me a favor and cancel it. Apologize profusely. I have a ton of work and I didn't get enough done this weekend."

"Gotcha." Amy picked up the phone, and Jake hurried into his office and closed the door behind him. He hustled to his desk, woke up his computer, and logged onto his bank program, then he called Pam, multitasking.

"Honey?" Pam said when the call connected. "What's going on? You went to school? Is Ryan okay?"

"Yes. Sorry I missed your call." Jake watched their accounts pop onto the computer screen.

"So what's going on?"

"He was queasy again after lunch and he thought he might want to come home." Jake knew that Pam's real question was why Ryan had called him, not her. It was unprecedented in their family history, so Jake knew he had to address it up front. "He didn't want to bother you, so he called me."

"He could have called me. It's no bother, he knows that."

Jake had to think of something to help the story. "He heard us talking in your office last night, about your nomination and all the work you have to do, the questionnaires and everything. He tried to cut you a break."

Pam moaned. "I want him to feel like he can still call me, though. He's my priority, no matter what. I mean, how much longer do I even have with him? I'll call him after school and tell him—"

"Don't honey. This is the way we want it to be, right?" Jake fell back on his default, best-defense is a good offense. "Ryan is learning that he can lean on me sometimes, too. Like we said in therapy, you want him to know he can turn to me. Don't call him and make him feel like it's strange. You're relegating me to the junior varsity."

"Sorry, I know, you're right." Pam sounded convinced, if miserable. "So what did you two decide? Is he at home or at school?"

"We decided together that he was feeling well enough to finish school and go to practice."

"So did he miss class?"

"No, we met during lunch, we talked, and he went to Western Civ on time."

"Well, aren't you guys so smart?" Pam still sounded unhappy. "He has a test today, and it's a bitch to make them up. He'll never have the time, and the makeup tests are always harder. Well done."

"Thanks," Jake said, as if he could take pleasure in any decision he'd made recently.

"I tried to call him but he doesn't answer his phone. I know it's probably in his locker, but I wanted to leave him a message telling him that I was thinking of him. But he hasn't called me back yet."

"I'm sure he will when he can." Jake flashed on Ryan breaking his phone on the dashboard. "In the meantime, we handled it together, just fine. Now. What did you call me about?"

"Bad news. My questionnaire has to be finished by Wednesday now, because we have to get an accountant to look it over before I turn it in. I already have a call in to Ellen."

"Why can't I do it?" Jake had to buy time and the last thing he needed was their accountant Ellen poking around. "I'm an accountant, we don't need another one."

"Michael thinks we need to have an independent accountant review everything. He thinks it would help if Ellen wrote us a letter, too."

"A letter saying what?"

"That our finances are in order, like an official stamp of approval."

"There's no such thing."

"Jake, it's just window dressing."

"We don't need it. I'm as official as it comes, I do our taxes. All Ellen has to do is sign her name to the return."

"Don't get all bent out of shape, honey. We might be gilding the lily, but if it helps me get nominated, why not? The issue isn't the accuracy of our record-keeping, but whether we're up to shenanigans."

Jake shuddered.

"You can't give a stamp of approval to your own bookkeeping or tax returns. It has to come from someone independent. If it's too much work, Ellen can do everything. Is that better for you?"

"No, I want to do it," Jake answered quickly. "Don't worry about it, I'll get the papers together and have them FedExed to Ellen for Wednesday morning. All she'll have to do is write her phony-baloney letter, okay?"

"That would be great, thanks. I love you."

"I love you, too."

"Talk later. I'll be home late tonight. The powers-that-be want to powwow about the nomination. Can you deal with dinner for Ryan?"

"Sure, take care," Jake said, hanging up. He found himself staring at their online bank account, which had logged him out. He had to pay the blackmail or Deaner would keep torturing Ryan.

Jake sweated under his jacket, thinking about that check in the safe.

Chapter Twenty-five

Jake clicked through the Gardenia Trust spreadsheet on his computer, trying to figure out how to get the money from company or client funds, but he couldn't find a way. The check in the safe couldn't be used because it was made out to Gardenia, and even as the company's principal and sole owner, he couldn't cash it or deposit it into his own account. It could only be deposited into Gardenia's holding account, and from there, it couldn't be wired to any personal account, much less offshore. Gardenia's bank, Pennsylvania National Bank, would simply refuse to do it, because it would run afoul of FDIC regulations, which was only one of the layers of rules and regulations. Gardenia was also a state-chartered trust company, so they were also governed by FNRA and the SEC, because they were also an RIA, an alphabet soup of laws.

Jake rubbed his face, trying to understand his position. He couldn't use his personal funds because the FBI would see, and he couldn't use Gardenia money because he couldn't get it. The problem was that the FBI would be able to see the balances in any existing accounts, but that gave him an idea, because it meant that they couldn't see the balances in any accounts that didn't exist right now.

Jake reached for his phone and scrolled down to Harold Ackerman, his banker at Pennsylvania National, in charge of all of Jake's personal accounts, as well as Gardenia business accounts. He pressed in the number and Harold picked it up after the first ring. "Harold, I need a favor. Confidentially."

"You got it. How can I help?"

"I need a personal line of credit for $250 grand to be opened today."

"No problem, Jake. You have the balances to back that up. You want it in your name, or yours and Pam's?"

"Just mine, and I need it wired to an offshore account by eleven o'clock tomorrow morning, at the absolute latest." Jake knew it would be an unusual request, but he also knew that Harold wouldn't ask any questions. Anybody who dealt regularly with high-net-worth individuals knew that they had expensive secrets like gambling debts, mistresses in fancy apartments, and the occasional cocaine habit. Jake hated the thought that Harold would believe one of those things were true about him, but his reputation didn't mean more to him than Ryan's life.

"I can do that. A wire transfer takes fifteen minutes, if I set it up now. The money's not the problem, the paperwork is. You know how it goes."

"Tell me about it." Jake understood. It would've sounded topsy-turvy to anybody who didn't know how banking worked, but he knew better. Harold could put his hand on $250,000 faster than he could get the stack of forms through the bank bureaucracy.

"I'll set it up, and get it out first thing tomorrow morning. Wire room's open at nine. It'll be done by nine fifteen."

"Okay. Thanks much." Jake pressed END, relieved. It was a good plan and he thought it would work, at least in the short run. Since the personal line of credit didn't exist until now, it wouldn't show on his and Pam's current bank statement, which they would be disclosing to the FBI. Jake would have to replace it by their next quarterly tax return, but he could do that with some gains from stock dividends or other trading. It would take fancy footwork, but he wasn't a financial planner for nothing.

Jake's phone started ringing in his hand, and he looked at the screen. It showed a picture of Pam again, the photo taken on Myrtle Beach, in happier times. He picked up and pressed AN-SWER. "Hi, honey. You forget something?"

"I'm worried." Pam sounded tense. "I thought you told me that Ryan went to Western Civ today."

"He did."

"No, he didn't."

"How do you know that?" Jake asked, dismayed.

"I checked the Parent Portal."

Jake cursed the Parent Portal, which was an online program by which Concord Chase parents could log in and check on their kids' daily assignments, tests and paper grades. Pam checked it as often as she checked their bank balances or her carbohydrate count.

"Jake, he was absent from class. He missed his test."

"Are you sure?"

"Of course. The Portal doesn't lie."

"It could be a mistake."

"No it couldn't. The information comes from the teachers themselves. Mr. Nelson even made a note on the Portal that Ryan has to contact him to schedule a makeup exam."

"Mr. Nelson might've made a mistake." Jake knew it was lame the minute he said it. He couldn't think of something better to say. It was exhausting, all this lying, putting out fires.

"Jake, come on. If Ryan's not in class, you notice. He could be really sick." Pam's voice sounded thin with anxiety. "I called the school nurse, but she's at another school on Mondays. I called the office, but they don't answer after four o'clock."

"Don't get all worked up, honey." Jake logged out of the Gardenia accounts and cleared his Internet history, just in case. "Did he go to the class after Western Civ?"

"He doesn't have class after that. He has Study Hall, last period of the day on Monday."

Jake didn't know Ryan's class schedule, but Pam had it memorized, every year. "I'm sure he's fine."

"Don't minimize it, Jake. He could be really sick."

"I'm not minimizing it," Jake said, though that was exactly what he was doing. "He's not a hundred percent, but I'm sure he's fine. He was fine when I left him."

"How do you know that? You didn't feel his forehead, did you?"

"No, but he looked fine." Jake got up from his desk and went to get his coat from the back of the door. He had to find Ryan, either at practice or at home, and see what happened.

"How he looks doesn't mean anything. You're taking this too lightly. You never think anything can go wrong, but it can."

"I'm not taking it lightly." Jake couldn't believe the irony. No one knew better than he that things could go wrong. He opened his office door and hurried into the hallway.

"I called his phone again but he still doesn't answer, and I know he usually checks it after school, before practice. That means he didn't return my first phone call."

"He told me he broke his phone, I should have mentioned that." Jake looked around but Amy wasn't at her desk. He didn't leave her a note because he didn't want her to blow his cover again.

"I assume he went to practice. But what's he up to? It's not like him to cut class. If he's not sick, something went wrong with your plan."

"I understand, and I'll take it up with him as soon as I get home." Jake hurried down the hall toward reception.

"Good. I'm not going to be home 'til ten or so, maybe later, but you should be the one to get to the bottom of this, anyway."

"I agree. I'll take care of it."

"Jake, remember, if he's not sick, he lied to you. You have to call him out on that, even though you're Fun Dad."

Jake couldn't remember ever wanting to be Fun Dad, much less having any fun. He passed Debbie and he pointed to his phone, so he had an excuse for not telling her where he was going. "Got it. Don't worry about it. Good luck with your meeting, and I'll see you when you get home."

"Text me and let me know how he is."

"I will. Love you." Jake flew out of the office, bypassing the elevator and jogging toward the stairwell.

"Love you, too. See you later. Bye."

"Bye." Jake hung up on the fly, banging through the exit doors, off to go find his son.

Chapter Twenty-six

"Ryan?" Jake opened the bedroom door to find his son asleep on top of the comforter in his practice sweat suit, his hoodie pulled over his head and his ears plugged with his earbuds. His arm was flopped over Moose, who was asleep, amid an open laptop, textbooks, and school papers.

"Ryan!" Jake said, louder. He was still in his suit jacket, breathless. He'd raced home, but traffic had been terrible. He approached the bed, but only Moose woke up, thumping his tail on the comforter and raising his head slightly.

Jake sat down on the edge of the bed, gave the dog a quick pat, and tugged one of the earbuds from Ryan's ear. "Ryan, wake up."

"Dad?" Ryan's eyelids fluttered, and Jake rubbed his arm, in the cottony sweatshirt.

"How are you doing, pal? Are you okay?"

"Yeah," Ryan answered, weakly.

"Why don't you wake up? We need to talk."

"Leave me alone. Can't I sleep?" Ryan's eyes closed again.

"No, we need to talk." Jake rubbed his arm again, to get him going. "Why didn't you go to Western Civ? Your mom found out from the Parent Portal that you missed your test."

"Don't worry about it, Dad. I'll tell her that I was throwing up again."

"No, you can't do that. Because I told her that I saw you during lunch and you seemed fine."

"What?" Ryan frowned, opening his eyes. He rose sleepily and propped himself on his elbow. "Why did you do that? She never had to know."

"I didn't tell her. Amy did. Mom called my office."

"Oh no." Ryan rubbed his face, leaving reddish streaks, and sat up.

"Why didn't you go to class? You said you were going to."

"I *was* going to." Ryan met Jake's eye, pained. "I went to my locker and got my books, and I was about to go in, but I just couldn't stop thinking about the pictures and that night, and now someone's *blackmailing* us. It's just so bad. It just keeps getting worse and worse."

"I know, I'm sorry." Jake squeezed him on the shoulder. "I know, it's a lot to deal with, but that's why you have to let me deal with it."

"What happened with the blackmailer guy?"

"It's all in order. I have the money and I'm giving it to him tomorrow."

Ryan's eyes flared in alarm. "Dad, be careful. Are you meeting him somewhere? He could have a gun."

"He's coming to my office, and I'm in no personal danger." Jake squeezed his arm again. "Don't worry about me. Worry about yourself. You have to do your thing at school. You can't be missing these classes. It's not good for you and it's too hard to explain. You went to practice, didn't you?"

"Yes, but I screwed up there, too." Ryan shook his head. "I sucked so bad. It's like I forgot how to shoot."

"Oh no." Jake's heart went out to him. It killed him to think that his son was getting so derailed. "It'll come back. You're just upset now, is all."

"I don't know. I don't even know if I'm going to start next game. It's a shit show."

"Watch your language," Jake heard himself saying, out of an impulse to control something, somewhere, to hold a line against chaos, but misplaced. "It's okay."

"No, you're right." Ryan slipped off his hood and rubbed his hair front and back. "I gotta man up. Coach is starting to look at me funny, and Dr. Dave's all up in my grille."

"Dr. Dave? What does he have to say?"

"He thinks I'm depressed."

"Did he say that?"

"No, but I can tell. He hints around."

"You're not depressed."

"I know that. I told him that." Ryan shook his head. "If he knew what was going on, believe me, he'd understand."

"Yes he would. But he can't know what's going on."

"I know that, Dad." Ryan hit a key on his open laptop and the screen came to life, showing the front page of the local newspaper. "I was reading about Kathleen and her mom. The mom got her a job at this IT company where she's a web designer, and they seem really close." Ryan scrolled down, so a photo of Kathleen appeared next to one of her mother. "They're both really pretty, aren't they? They have the same smiles and eyes, like the shape is the same." Ryan pointed at the photos. "See what I mean? I think they had a hard life. Janine Mae told me Kathleen's mom and dad got divorced last year, and there was a big custody trial over her, that's why the mom moved here from Seattle."

"Ryan, I don't think it's a good idea to be thinking about her, so much."

"This is the company where they worked." Ryan scrolled down to a group photo. "So many people liked her and her mom.

They interviewed them in the paper, you should see the stuff they said. They were super tight and they were always laughing, and the people they work with put up their own money for the reward and the company matched it, even this little company of, like twenty-five people, they put in their own money—"

"Ryan, stop." Jake glanced at the laptop. "I don't want you to keep researching her online."

"I know, but I can't help it, Dad. I try not to, but I just can't help it. It's all anybody at school's talking about." Tears brimmed in Ryan's eyes, which were bloodshot. "Janine Mae was crying in school, Dad. She was crying about her best friend from the track team, who I killed. What if she found out it was me? She would hate me, *I* hate me—" Ryan's voice broke, and Jake leaned over and gave him a hug.

"Ryan, no, don't. I know it's hard now, but it's going to be okay. We're going to get through this together."

"Dad, I don't know, it's like she's always on my mind. I keep thinking about her, like that blackmailer said, like she's my destiny or something."

"No, no, don't think that way. She's not your destiny." Jake felt his chest seize. "That guy was just making up those texts. He was trying to get to you. Don't let him get to you."

"No, but some of the stuff he said, it's *true*." Ryan pulled away, his expression anguished. "Like when he said that you can't get away from me, I *feel* like that. I feel like I can't get away from her."

Jake felt terrified for him. "No, you just feel guilty. You're a good person and you feel guilty. But that feeling will diminish in time."

"No, no, I don't think it will. It's only getting worse, Dad."

"Don't say that!" Jake said, urgent. "If you keep saying things like that, you'll make it true, and it doesn't have to be true, not at all."

"But I'm obsessed with her, *obsessed*." Ryan shook his head in bewilderment. "Like no matter what, I'm thinking about her, and like, we're studying that if you tell yourself not to think about something, the more it makes you think about it. That's why I couldn't go to Western Civ. I was walking to the door and I started to get so freaked, and I saw Caleb, and, he said, 'What's the matter with you, dude?' He knew right away. I mean, I couldn't get in control."

"Caleb?" Jake asked, worried. "You didn't tell him anything, did you? Wasn't he the guy who sold you the dope?"

"The weed? Yes, right." Ryan's expression changed suddenly, as if a mask came over his unguarded features and he seemed to catch himself.

"Ryan? Did you tell him?"

"No, no, no way." Ryan shook his head in a newly jittery way, and Jake could see he was hiding something.

"What? What happened? You're a terrible liar, Ryan. I can see it all over your face. Did you tell him something? Anything?" Jake tried to control his fear, but it was impossible. "If you did, tell me now and we can deal with it. Don't hide it from me. We're in this together."

"I didn't tell him anything."

"I don't believe you."

"I didn't say anything, not a word!" Ryan raised his voice, but Jake could see that he was protesting too much.

"Then what is it? What's bothering you?"

"We smoked up, that's all, Dad. I'm sorry—"

"You got *high* at *school*?" Jake asked, appalled.

"Yes, I'm sorry." Ryan raked his hair back with a shaking hand. "Caleb told me it would help me mellow out for practice, and it really did. It did. It got me back in control."

"No!" Jake practically cried out, feeling suddenly like everything was circling the drain. "Ryan, I did this to help you. It defeats the whole purpose if you start to fall apart. If you start to cut classes. If you start getting high. That's not you. That never was and never *can be*—"

"I know, Dad, I know, I'm sorry—"

"You can't do this to yourself, you *can't*." Jake found himself grabbing the open *American Pageant* textbook and smacking the page, so loudly that Moose woke up, blinking. "Ryan, *this* is what you need to think about. *This* is what you need to focus on. Your *schoolwork*. Your *game*. Your*self*." Jake picked up the laptop. "Not this. Not Kathleen Lindstrom. Not her mother. Not how nice they were." Jake was about to put down the laptop when he glanced at the screen, and did a double-take. The group photo that had been on the screen was larger, because he must have hit a button when he picked up the laptop. The enlargement enabled him to see something in the company photo he hadn't seen before. He looked closer and couldn't believe his eyes.

"Dad? What is it?"

"Nothing," Jake answered, but he was lying through his teeth. He set the laptop on the bed and struggled for emotional control. In the back row of the group photo stood a line of employees, and on the end, half-hidden by the row in front of him, was a face that Jake recognized instantly.

It was Lewis Deaner.

Chapter Twenty-seven

Jake left Ryan in his bedroom, then hurried into his home office and closed the door, stricken. He felt the situation ebbing away from him. He flashed-forward on Ryan's becoming depressed, obsessed with Kathleen, spiraling downward, letting his grades and the team fall by the wayside. It could end in suicide, as if Ryan was doomed by the very actions set in motion to save him. Jake wasn't about to let that happen without a fight.

He hustled to his desk, logged onto the Internet, sat down, and typed in the name of the company he had seen on Ryan's laptop. The company website popped onto the screen, and it read GreenTech Enterprises in kelly-green letters. Directly below that was a candid photo of Kathleen Lindstrom, sitting at a laptop on a desk, evidently at the GreenTech office. The photo was framed by a black memorial border, and next to it was a paragraph:

GreenTech mourns the passing of Kathleen Lindstrom, who was the victim of a hit-and-run accident last Friday on Pike Road in Concord

Chase. Kathleen was the beloved daughter of web designer Grace Lindstrom, and Kathleen worked for us part-time, impressing our entire office with her intelligence, charm, and beauty. She even started us running at lunchtime and we lost a total of 76 pounds combined! She will be profoundly missed, most especially by her devoted mother, but by all of us whose lives she touched. GreenTech and its employees are posting a $10,000 reward for information leading to the arrest of the person responsible for her death, and if you have any such information, please call the authorities . . .

Jake looked away, because he didn't want to focus on Kathleen now. He wanted to focus on Deaner and understand how Deaner was connected to her. Jake hadn't realized that they could have known each other. He scanned the left side of the website, which listed categories for several different pages; IT Support, Web Design, GreenTech Web Hosting, GreenTech Consultancy, About Us, and Contact Us.

Jake skipped to About Us and clicked the link. Onto the screen appeared the group photo that had been on Ryan's laptop. It showed about thirteen employees lined up in three rows, and the last person in the last row on the left was Deaner. Jake clicked on the picture to enlarge it, double-checking, and it was definitely him: a short, slight, and bespectacled man, his appearance as nondescript as blackmailers ever got. It must've been a recent picture because he had the same thinning hair, wire-rimmed glasses, and oddly controlled expression.

Jake hit a button to return the picture to normal size, then read the caption below, which contained the employees' names. He scanned them quickly to reach the name of the man he knew as Lewis Deaner, but the first name on the row wasn't Lewis Deaner, but Andrew Voloshin. Jake blinked, absorbing the information. So Deaner's real name was Voloshin and he wasn't a freelance writer, but worked at an IT company.

Jake returned his attention to the photograph and spotted

Kathleen Lindstrom in the second row, only two people away from Deaner/Voloshin. Kathleen was standing next to her mother Grace, an attractive woman with curly brown hair. They had their arms around each other, the both of them smiling happily at the camera, wearing almost identical outfits, an artsy T-shirt and skinny jeans.

The photo stopped Jake in his tracks. He could see how close Kathleen and Grace were from their body language; they looked like a mother and daughter who were best friends. Tears brimmed in his eyes, and he felt the deepest ache welling up in his heart. He couldn't imagine how grief-stricken Grace would be, bereft over a beloved daughter that had been taken from her, so young and so violently. Jake was the one who had taken her young life, as surely as if he had been at the wheel himself, and he felt the full weight and agony of his guilt. He knew how much he had compounded his sin, by lying about it every day since then and by compelling Ryan to lie, too. He'd traded Kathleen's life for Ryan's future, and he would never, ever forgive himself. He'd played God, so he couldn't even ask God himself to forgive him.

He wiped his eyes with his arm, and tried to swallow, but couldn't. He refocused on the screen, trying to get his thoughts back on Deaner. It was obvious from the photo that Deaner knew Kathleen and her mother. It was a small company, so it couldn't have been otherwise. Jake wanted to know what they did for GreenTech, so he scrolled down and scanned the company description, which read:

Our offices are in Shakertown, and we're one of the few companies in the Delaware Valley who offer greener computer services—including solar-power, low-power and low-material-use computer systems, IT support, and green-web-design services. We've been in business over ten years and we're growing! Call us anytime for an estimate to meet your IT needs, in a way that helps you, your business, and our planet!

Jake considered it, vis-à-vis Andrew Voloshin. It seemed consistent with Voloshin's manner and appearance that he was some kind of IT guy. He logged back into the search engine, then went to White Pages, and plugged in the name Andrew Voloshin and Concord Chase PA, because Deaner had said he lived in an apartment in Concord Chase. The screen changed and read, **your search has yielded no results,** so Jake tried again. Voloshin worked in Shakertown, so Jake plugged in Andrew Voloshin and Shakertown PA. The screen changed, showing the question, **Did you mean this Andrew Voloshin?** Underneath was an address with the phone number:

> Meadowbrook Mews
> 37 Meadowbrook Lane
> Apartment 2C
> Shakertown, PA

Jake grabbed his phone from his pocket and dialed Voloshin's number. He felt a darkness come over him, a sheer malevolence he'd never felt in his life. He was about to talk to the man who had terrified Ryan. The man who could drive his son crazy, even to suicide. Jake felt in his heart, for the first time ever, that he was capable of committing murder. If he were ever in the same room with Voloshin again, the little man wouldn't get out alive.

"Jake?" Voloshin answered, his tone surprised, but Jake didn't let him get out another word.

"Who the hell do you think you are, scaring my son? I'll kill you for that. Do you hear me? You leave my boy alone!"

"You weren't taking me seriously." Voloshin seemed to recover. "I had to show you that I—"

"We made a deal. You'll get your money. It'll be there by eleven, and you better send me the copies of that video and photos. The deal is between me and you. You leave my family out of this or you'll get nothing. *Nothing!*"

"Oh, I don't know about that—"

"Don't test me. It's killing my kid to keep this secret, so if it's not going to help him, I'll blow it wide open. I'll go to the police myself. We both will. I'd rather have my son sane and in jail than crazy and outside of it." Jake heard himself yelling and realized that what he was saying was true. "So don't press me. Don't test me. You don't know me."

"Now who's the tough guy?"

"I am," Jake growled, and this time he meant it. He could feel it, a bile and fury inside, bubbling. "If you ever, *ever* contact my son again, I'll come after you. I know where you live. I have your phone number. I know where you work. You'll never get away from me. I'll find you *wherever* you go." Jake heard himself threatening Voloshin, an eerie echo of the very texts that Voloshin had sent to Ryan. Suddenly Jake started to wonder about something. He'd just learned that Voloshin knew Kathleen, so maybe the way Voloshin had gotten the photos of the hit-and-run wasn't because he lived or worked close by, at all. "Wait. You live on Meadowbrook Lane, but that isn't anywhere near Pike Road. GreenTech isn't in the corporate center, either. It's in Shakertown, three towns over. You didn't happen upon the accident scene and take that video. You didn't see it from a neighboring office or an apartment complex. I'm onto you. I have your number. You were on Pike Road yourself. You were there *already*. You were *stalking* her."

"What? No, that's—"

"Don't bullshit me. It all makes sense. Kathleen was a young, beautiful girl who works in your office. Her mother gets her a summer job there. You're a lonely, single nerd, the dweeby IT guy who codes all day."

"You don't know what you're talking about. I'm friends with her mother. Kathleen was the daughter of my good friend, that's all."

"Oh, please. You started out friends with the mother, but

you're not blind. A beautiful young high-school girl comes into your world, and you fall head over heels. You think about her all the time." Jake sensed he was right, even as he said it. "You took those pictures and that video, no one else. That's how you got the pictures. That's why you were so close. That's how you got such a great video, even in the fog. You found out where she runs, where the track team runs. What were you doing? Hiding in the bushes? In the woods? Waiting for her to run by? Did you know her running schedule? Her route?"

"We were just friends. She was my friend's daughter. I was a friend of the family—"

"Give me a break!" Jake burst into laughter, but it wasn't mirthful, just a release of pressure. "You were *friends*? A man your age is *friends* with a gorgeous sixteen-year-old girl? Who're you kidding? Did you hit on her or just fantasize? You're a sick freak! You're a *predator*!"

"It's not true—"

"If you were such good *friends,* then why are you capitalizing on her death?" Jake realized it was true the moment he said it. "You're such great *friends* with her that when she gets killed by a car, which you witness, you don't go to the police? You don't say to them, these people killed my *friend*? You don't even give your other good friend—her *mother*—the information?" Jake could hear Voloshin had gone silent. "Instead, you sneak around and try to blackmail my son, who had an accident? You try and make money from the girl's death, the daughter of your very good friend? You *disgust* me!"

"I don't need to listen to this."

"Neither do I," Jake shot back. He pressed END, hanging up. Suddenly he heard some noise downstairs, the slamming of the front door, then someone coming upstairs.

"Jake! Ryan!" It was Pam, and she sounded furious.

Chapter Twenty-eight

"I'm up in my office!" Jake got off the computer, erased his Internet history, and got up just as his door flew open.

"Jake, we have a problem." Pam stood frowning in the doorway, still with her trenchcoat over her suit. She hadn't even kicked off her black pumps. "Where's Ryan?"

"In his room, resting."

"Resting! Very good!" Pam spun around on her heel and stalked down the hall toward Ryan's room, her coat billowing behind her. "I'm getting to the bottom of this, once and for all."

Oh no. Jake hustled after her. "What's going on?"

"Wait until you hear this," Pam called over her shoulder.

"Why are you home so early?"

"Because no meeting is as important as this." Pam flung open Ryan's door and entered his bedroom, which was empty except for Moose. The golden retriever stood up in the bed unsteadily, wagging his tail, but Pam crossed the room and knocked on the bathroom door. "Ryan? Ryan, come out of the bathroom."

"Mom?" Ryan called from inside the bathroom. "I'll be out in a little bit. I'm about to take a shower."

"Honey, give him a break." Jake tried to calm the waters. "I already discussed it with him. He wasn't feeling well, and that's why he didn't go to class. He made it to practice though."

"Ryan!" Pam tried the doorknob, but it was locked, then she banged on the door. "Come out of the bathroom, right this instant!"

"Honey, relax." Jake had never seen her this upset. He started to worry about what she knew, or what she thought she knew.

"Don't tell me to relax! I was right, all along. I knew it. I knew something was going on." Pam banged on the door again, and from inside the bathroom came the sound of a toilet flushing.

"Mom, chill." Ryan opened the door and came out of the bathroom, looking more put together than before, with his hair combed back and his hood off his head.

"Don't you tell me to chill!" Pam grabbed his arm, pulled him toward the bed, and made him sit down. Moose licked Ryan's face and wagged his tail harder, thinking this was some new game. "Where were you during Western Civ?"

Jake stepped in. "Pam, I already discussed this with him. You don't have to—"

"The hell I don't!" Pam put her hands on her hips. "Ryan, I asked you a fact question, as the lawyers say. Where were you during Western Civ?"

"I didn't feel well—"

"I didn't ask you how you felt. I asked you where you were."

"I was with Caleb," Ryan answered, not meeting his mother's eye. "I didn't feel well, and he had a study hall, so we hung out."

"And what did you do?"

Jake couldn't take seeing Ryan twist in the wind. "Honey, don't yell at him. He doesn't deserve to be yelled at."

"Yes, he does." Pam ignored him, still glaring at Ryan. "He deserves that and more. You don't know what he's done."

Jake shuddered inwardly. He went over and put his hand on his son's shoulder, to steady him. "Pam, whatever it is, yelling at him won't help. Why don't you talk to him and we'll sort it out in a civilized fashion, instead of screaming questions at him?"

Pam folded her arms, pursing her lips tightly. Suddenly she became very still, searching Ryan with her eyes and not saying anything. The room fell abruptly silent, except for the dog's excited panting. Jake told himself to stay calm while Ryan glanced up at his mother, then looked down, hanging his head. Somehow the ferocity of Pam's angry, loving gaze seemed to break Ryan down, and his strong shoulders slumped. His hands fell to his sides, and Moose nudged his nose under Ryan's palm, which was the dog's favorite bid for attention.

"Pam," Jake said, trying to get control of the situation. "Why don't you tell us what's on your mind, and Ryan can respond?"

"No," Pam answered, almost sadly. She kept her eyes on Ryan's bowed head and folded her arms in the bunchy trenchcoat. "I don't want to tell Ryan what I know. I want Ryan to tell me what he and Caleb were doing, because I want to find out if I raised a liar."

"Pam." Jake was still trying to defuse the situation. "He's already told you the truth. He admitted he cut class and hung out with Caleb."

"Ryan?" Pam looked down at Ryan, still ignoring Moose on the bed. "Did I raise a liar?"

Jake swallowed hard. "Pam, don't call him a name. You know we're not supposed to do that."

"Oh, Jake, shut up. You hate that crap as much as I do." Pam returned her attention to Ryan, who had hunched over, resting his elbows on his knees, in collapse. "Ryan, did I raise a liar?"

"Yes," Ryan whispered, almost inaudibly, without looking up. "It's not your fault, but I am a liar."

Jake felt his heart break, rubbing his son's back. He didn't want Ryan to think of himself as a liar. "Buddy, that's not true."

"Yes, it is, Dad."

"No, no that's not true." Jake squeezed Ryan hard, avoiding Pam's gaze. He could feel his son shaking just the slightest, as if the truth had a pressure of its own and was trying to force its way out of his very body. Jake couldn't let that happen, because if Ryan spilled his guts now, Pam would make them go to the cops for sure. It would ruin them all. Suddenly, he got another idea. "Ryan, why don't you tell your mother what you told me, that you and Caleb were smoking during class." Jake looked up at Pam, whose lovely features were fixed so grimly that they could have been etched in marble. "Pam, Ryan told me the truth. So if that's what you're talking about, you didn't raise a liar."

"Really." Pam heaved a quiet sigh, and her blue-eyed gaze shifted from Jake to Ryan and back again. "So he told you the truth."

Jake nodded, relieved. "He told me everything. He told me that he's never going to smoke again, and he knows it's bad for him and illegal."

Pam sucked in her cheeks, unplacated. "Was he going to tell me?"

"We both decided it might put you in an awkward position, being a judge. It's enough that he told me, isn't it?" Jake didn't press his luck. "How did you find out?"

"Dr. Dave told me that he suspected it today at practice." Pam kept her eyes on Ryan, even though all she could see was his crown. "So I called Caleb's mother. She found marijuana in his drawer, a fair amount of it. It turns out he's been selling it, too."

"That's terrible," Jake said, keeping his arm on Ryan, who was still trembling.

"Ryan?" Pam asked, her tone gentler. "I was so disappointed to think that you would do something unlawful, not to mention stupid. I don't care if everybody else does it, I disapprove completely of smoking marijuana. I told you already, everybody I know who smoked dope in college just got dumber and dumber. And that's only the ones that didn't go on to worse drugs."

Jake didn't interrupt her, because he could see that they had dodged a bullet. He kept his arm around Ryan, praying that the trembling would subside.

"Ryan, I know you feel stressed and bad about what happened at the game, but your reaction to negative emotion can't be to reach for a drug. Or alcohol. Or anything else. Do you understand?"

Ryan didn't answer or even move, except to tremble.

"Ryan?" Pam paused. "I hope you don't need me to tell you what could happen if any of the coaches from these college programs found out that you were smoking, especially during school hours. Division I is too competitive, and they want players who not only make an impact, but who are assets to the program."

Jake kept his mouth shut, but all this talk of impact players made him sick to his stomach.

"If you get a bad reputation with these recruiters, you can jeopardize not only any scholarship possibility, but your entire future. I don't mean to sound like that D.A.R.E. program in elementary school, but it's true, and they never should have discontinued it. The choices you make now have huge implications for the rest of your life—"

"Mom, I know," Ryan said hoarsely, staring at the ground, and Moose beat his tail on the bed at the sound.

"He knows," Jake added, hugging Ryan closer and jostling him just the slightest, to signal that they were about to end the conversation. "Pam, I gave him that lecture, times ten. You don't have to worry about that. I worked him over, and he gets it. Really."

"Good." Pam cocked her head, trying to see Ryan's face. "Ryan? Tell me that your dad's right and I don't have to worry about it.

Tell me that you'll always tell me the truth and that you'll do the right thing, no matter what anybody else says is right. Only you know what's right, and you have to answer for that, always."

Ryan kept his head down. Moose thumped his tail on the bed.

Jake jostled Ryan again, feeling the tension build in his son. "He knows."

"Jake, don't answer for him. I'd like to hear him tell me himself." Pam frowned, her head still cocked as she tried to see Ryan's face. "Ryan?"

"Ryan, answer your mom." Jake looked over, then held his breath.

Ryan looked up at Pam, his eyes filmed and his expression agonized. After a moment, he cleared his throat. "Mom, I killed Kathleen Lindstrom on Pike Road."

Chapter Twenty-nine

The next few hours were pure agony, and if Jake expected the truth to be cathartic, it didn't turn out that way. Ryan became too upset to tell the story, and Jake took over and told her every detail, including their meeting with the lawyer Morris Hubbard, the blackmailer texts, opening of the line of credit to pay the blackmail, the transfer to be delivered by eleven o'clock, his phone conversation with Andrew Voloshin, and his suspicion that Voloshin had been stalking Kathleen Lindstrom. Pam had listened in horrified silence, easing herself into Ryan's wooden desk chair, still wrapped in the cocoon of her trenchcoat. She kept her pumps on her feet, like a soldier who wanted to die with his boots on. She had said nothing except to ask questions, and Jake felt more and more tense, waiting for the proverbial sword to fall.

"So that's it," Jake said, when he had finished. "I'm sorry, honey. I feel horrible about this, and so does Ryan. You know that, you can see that. And I'm so sorry for what this does to you, that it puts you in an awful, awful position—"

"Hold on a second." Pam raised a hand, weakly, and her voice was pained. "I'm trying to understand how the man I married would leave a young girl dead on the road."

Jake took it on the chin. "It's like I explained, honey. I made the best decision I could at the time. I only had a second, I had to react. I've replayed it over and over, I know it was wrong. I didn't know what to do, I just reacted, to protect Ryan."

"Mom." Ryan sniffled, sitting next to Jake on the bed. "He thought he was helping me, and he was. He was about to call 911 when I told him about the weed. He woulda called if I hadn't smoked up. It's not his fault, it's mine."

Jake patted Ryan's leg, touched. "It's okay, I can take it. Your mom is right, it was a terrible decision. I knew it was when I made it, the moment I made it."

Ryan shook his head, distraught. "But Dad, would you make it differently if you had to do over again? You saved us both from prison." He whipped around to Pam, who was slumped sideways in his desk chair, leaning on his desk. Behind her was a lineup of plastic *South Park* figurines and a Funny or Die poster of Will Ferrell. "Mom, what would you have done? Don't be a judge, be a person."

"I'm not being a judge," Pam shot back, shaking her head.

"Then what would you have done, if you were Dad?" Ryan raised his voice, his nose still stuffy from crying, so he sounded oddly like himself as a young boy. "Let's say you were the one that night on Pike Road. Would you have called the cops and sent me to jail?"

"*I* never would've been in that position!" Pam shouted, suddenly. "*I* never would've let you drive!"

"Mom, I can get my license in a month. What difference does it make? It's arbitrary!"

Pam's eyes flashed with anger. "All time limits are arbitrary, but that doesn't mean they're not limits. The law is made up of time limits. I've thrown people out of court because they missed a month-long time limit to file an appeal. And when you get older, try to file your tax return on April 16! It's not acceptable under the law. You shouldn't have been driving, and your father shouldn't have let you drive. He admitted as much. This is *all his fault!*"

"Agree, I agree." Jake nodded, dry-mouthed. Pam sounded so angry that she'd passed through the heat of that emotion into a cooler disgust, or worse, disrespect. He wondered if they'd be able to keep their marriage together, but then again, after she went to the police, he'd be in prison and they wouldn't be a family anymore, anyway.

"No, Dad! Don't let her put it on you! She's acting like a judge, and nobody has a right to judge us, even her! Nobody was there but us! Nobody knows what it was like but us!"

"Ryan, are you crazy?" Pam rose, her eyes flashing with anger. "What you did was unlawful and morally wrong. You should know that, and so should your father. I fault him more than you. He's the adult. He's the one who's culpable, not you—"

"Mom, no!" Ryan shouted at her, and Jake put a restraining hand on Ryan's arm, because he could see the hurt cross Pam's face. She'd wanted father and son to become closer, but not allied against her, especially in these circumstances.

Pam faced Ryan, agitated. "Ryan, you're naïve. You don't know what you're talking about. The fact is, the law judges you. A court will judge you. A judge will judge you. I'm just the sneak preview."

Ryan threw up his hands. "You think I don't know that? You think I don't know that I'm sending my own father to jail? That I'm going to jail? But right now I don't need a judge, I need a *mother.*"

Pam gasped, then shut her mouth, stricken. Her fair skin looked suddenly tinged with pink, as if she'd been slapped in the face. Ryan was watching her, his eyes glistening, and before

Jake could realize what was happening, Pam had come forward and opened her arms to her son, and Ryan had gotten off the bed to meet her.

"I'm so sorry, Mom. I'm sorry, I'm really sorry. I feel so bad about everything, and about her. Everybody at school is so upset, they have grief counselors and everything—"

"I understand, I'm here. No matter what, I'm here for you and I love you." Pam held him close even though she was so much shorter, and Ryan found a way to lean his head sideways on top of hers. She hugged him, then rocked him, just the slightest. "We'll figure this out together."

"Just don't blame Dad. It's not his fault, please."

"Okay, enough fighting for now." Pam released Ryan from her embrace, walked him over to the foot of the bed, and sat down beside him, putting her arm around him.

Jake caught Pam's eye, and he knew his wife well enough to know that she was only tabling the discussion. She hadn't forgiven him. She would never forgive him. She would blame him always, and he deserved it. He would blame himself forever, too.

Pam sighed heavily. "Well. I know what we have to do next, like it or not."

Jake looked past Ryan to Pam. "Pam, listen, please. I know you want to go to the police, but let me just explain why we shouldn't."

"Before we get to that, hold on." Pam held up a hand, without meeting Jake's eye. "I know a way to make this easier, immediately. First I'm going to withdraw my name from consideration for the judgeship."

Ryan moaned. "Mom, no. I'll get my act together when the FBI talks to us, I promise. I can do it. I'll just answer the questions. I know how to put it out of my mind, if I have to."

Jake realized Pam was saying that because she'd never get nominated or appointed, after he and Jake had been convicted. "Pam, please, don't withdraw. Don't give up. We can get through the investigation. The line of credit will be paid back by next quarter, if not next month. Voloshin will be paid off, which buys me some time to think about how I will explain the transaction later."

Pam shook her head, her lips pursed. "No, it's all right, I'm fine with it. We have bigger problems right now."

"Mom—"

"Pam, please. Why?"

"It's too much to deal with right now. Enough said." Pam waved them both into silence, her expression stern. "We're in a crisis, and we have to get through it. Jake, call off the line of credit, or take it back, or do whatever you have to do. Will you do that, first thing tomorrow morning, or better yet, call Harold tonight?" Pam spoke without even looking at him. "Tell me you'll do that for me. It's the very least you can do."

"I will," Jake agreed, reluctantly. "But Pam, as for what to do about going to the police, just hear me out—"

"No, my mind is made up," Pam said firmly.

"Listen," Jake said anyway. "I hate keeping this secret, and I hate that Ryan has to keep it, too. I know you're a judge and you believe in the law. I know that." Jake tried to make his argument as logically and rationally as possible, as if he were a litigant before her bench. "But Hubbard was right on the legalities, wasn't he? If you go to the police and tell them the truth, Ryan will be convicted of vehicular homicide and sent to a juvenile detention center. No college, no basketball, no future. Even if you're mad at me, if you go to the police, you'll be punishing him. Neither of us wants that."

"Mom, here's what I think," Ryan started to say, but Pam cut him off with a chop.

"Hush. I don't want to know what you think, because I don't want you to have any responsibility in this. This situation wasn't created by you, and you're not going to weigh in on it, one way or the other."

"Mom, no," Ryan shot back. "That's treating me like a baby."

"Oh please." Pam waved him off. "That crap may work with your father, but he didn't give birth to you. You may think you're large and in charge, but I see through that. You may not be a baby, but you're still a kid. You leave wet towels on the bed. You don't know how to fill out a check. You'd wear clothes with *mold* if I let you. I'm not going to let you have a say in decisions that are this important. I wouldn't let you make a decision about whether or not to go to college, would I? You're going to college, whether you like it or not, because that's what's best for you. So I'm not going to let you make a decision about whether or not to go to prison. It's simply not your decision. It's a decision I make for you. Because *I'm your mother.*"

Jake saw his opening. "But, Pam, what if we disagree? You shouldn't trump me. I'm his father, and I have an equal say. I will not stand by and see him go to prison for this. Not for something that was my doing."

Pam met Jake's eye, for the first time, but there was no love there, only controlled fury. "Jake, at this point, you're right. We have no choice now. You made sure of that when you left the scene. You turned an accident into a crime."

"I know, I'm sorry, but—"

"So Jake, you pay that blackmailer from our savings or money market. I'm not going to the police, and my son isn't going to jail."

Jake couldn't believe his ears.

"This is a secret we're going to keep, as a family."

Chapter Thirty

Jake went into his home office while Ryan took a shower and Pam escaped to her office down the hall, to make the phone calls that would end her becoming a federal judge. He flopped miserably into his desk chair and buried his face in his hands. He couldn't think, he could only feel, and what he felt was abject misery. He didn't see any way out of the situation, of his own making. He had wanted Pam to agree to keep their secret, and he'd gotten what he wished for, but it was only the lesser of two evils. He felt a creeping dread that it had only increased the pressure on all of them, tying their family together in a corrupt bargain, each one tethered to the other in a way that doomed them not to survive, but to sink.

Jake straightened up and tried to shake it off. He could hear Pam talking through their common wall, but he couldn't make out the words she was saying, and he felt awful for her. She'd stormed out of Ryan's room right after she announced her decision, and he hadn't had a chance to talk to her alone or to say how sorry he was, again. He knew she'd unload on him later, saying all the things she couldn't say in front of Ryan, and he hated being betwixt and between, living in that hell reserved for married people, who had to postpone their fights for not-in-front-of-the-kids. But no couples fought about things like this, ever.

Jake tried to focus and make himself do things, so he called Harold and instructed him to stop the line of credit and wire the $250K from their money market and savings account. Harold agreed, no questions asked, of course. Then Jake went online, plugged **Andrew Voloshin** into the search engine, and tried to find out more about him, but couldn't. Voloshin wasn't on Facebook or any of the other social-networking sites and belonged to no professional organizations or alumni groups. Jake felt too distracted to keep looking, much less to answer any emails from work, and when he heard Pam finally get off the phone, he rose, left his office, and went down the hall to hers, knocking gently on the door.

"Pam, can I come in?"

"Yes," she answered, and Jake opened the door, not surprised to see her teary-eyed at her desk. Her eyes were puffy, her hair undone, and she held a crumpled Kleenex in her hand. She slumped in her chair, framed by the soft pink walls and the red-and-pink toile curtains. All the feminine appointments of her office reminded him there was still a girl inside his wife, and he knew her heart was broken.

"I'm so sorry, honey." Jake started to come around the desk, but Pam stopped him with a hand, her soft features hardening.

"Don't even think about it."

"I'm sorry, I really am." Jake stopped in front of her desk. "Are you okay?"

"Do I look okay?" Pam tossed the Kleenex in the wastebasket.

"What did you tell them?"

"That I wanted to spend more time with my family." Pam chuckled, but it was without mirth. "I don't know how you could do it, Jake, I really don't. You've ruined everything, you know. You've ruined our lives. Above all, you've ruined Ryan's life. He's never going to be the same, ever. This secret, it will ruin him."

"I'm sorry," Jake said again, because she was right and it was all he could say.

"It's such a joke," Pam said, disgusted without batting an eye, though she never cursed. "You finally decide to pay attention to your family. You want to step back in and reestablish a relationship with your own son, your only son. So I say, like an idiot, go pick him up at the movie. And what do you do? You decide it would be a great idea if he drove the car!" Pam raised her voice, throwing up her hands. "What a great decision! Wasn't that a *great* decision? Wasn't that one of your greatest, all-time decisions *ever?*"

Jake didn't reply. She needed to blow off steam, and he deserved every word.

"Fun Dad evidently is the last one to know that a father is supposed to be a parent, not a friend. It's Parenting 101, but you didn't get the memo. It's every magazine article, or on every Dr. Phil or Oprah episode *ever.*" Pam scoffed. "That's right, she went off the air, so it's her fault. It's *Oprah's* fault! Because it's not your fault, right, Jake? It can't be! I have a son blaming himself, but really it's *your fault.*"

"I admit it's my fault. I know it's my fault."

"I know that, too, but that doesn't do us any good, because Ryan doesn't know it's true. Ryan was properly brought up, by me I might add, which means that he has a conscience. He knows the difference between right and wrong, as do I. Only *you* don't know the difference between right and wrong."

Jake didn't say anything. She was right, and there was nothing to say.

"You'll never convince him of anything else, ever," Pam said, louder. "Even though the law would apportion the lion's share of the guilt to you, he'll still feel guilty. And now he feels guilty because you would be the one to go to jail and not him. The kid can't win!"

"I tried to explain it to him—"

"I don't know who you are, frankly!" Pam jumped to her feet. "You leave a young girl on the road, *dead*? You crash your own car? You burn evidence? You lie to the police? You lie to Amy, and to Harold? You lie to *me*!" Pam snorted. "What a bunch of bull! You made me feel bad because I questioned you with Ryan! You made me feel like I was hurting your getting close to him! You backed me down, you manipulated me, and you lied to me every step of the way! I didn't raise a liar, but I sure as hell *married one*!"

"Pam, I know, I'm sorry—" Jake said, then fell abruptly silent when the door opened and Ryan was standing there, his hair wet from the shower, dressed in his gray T-shirt and sweats.

"Mom." Ryan stood in the threshold, his hand on the doorknob. His eyes were dry, and his forehead smooth and untroubled under bangs so wet they dripped on his shoulders, like raindrops. "You need to let it go now. Dad said he was sorry, and you need to get off his back."

Jake's mouth went dry. He knew Ryan was trying to help, but it would only upset Pam more if Ryan intervened and took Jake's side. "Ryan, it's okay—"

"Ryan, please, go." Pam waved him out, agitated. "This is between your father and me. I'm sorry if you heard, but this is between us."

"I disagree." Ryan looked from her to Jake, oddly calm. "You were talking about the hit-and-run, and that's not just between you guys."

"Ryan, I—" Jake started to say, but Pam cut him off with a chop of her hand.

"Jake, why don't you let *me* answer our son? Ryan was speaking to me and questioning what I was doing, and he deserves an answer from me, not you."

"Fine," Jake said, tense.

Pam continued sternly, "Ryan, in point of fact, we weren't talking about the hit-and-run. We were talking about our relationship, about the importance of honesty in our relationship, in our marriage. So you see, it wasn't something that includes you. It's not the same issue."

Ryan blinked, unusually unfazed. "Mom, you sound so much like a judge tonight. Why don't you let it go? I think you've ridden Dad long enough."

"I don't."

"I do."

"Oh really?" Pam shot back, her tone sharpening. "Ryan, it's not your place to tell me how to talk to my husband, even if he's your father."

"I can have an opinion."

"No, actually, you can't."

"I can't have an opinion?" Ryan snorted. "Are you serious right now?"

"Okay, you can have an opinion, but it's not one I need to heed or even hear. You have no standing."

Ryan pursed his lips. "Mom, why are you being such a hypocrite to Dad?"

"I'm not being a hypocrite!" Pam glared at Ryan. "How dare you say such a thing to me!"

"Mom, if you think honesty is so important in a marriage, then why don't you tell Dad about Dr. Dave?"

Jake wasn't sure he heard Ryan correctly, for a second.

"Ryan!" Pam barked, angry. "What are you talking about?"

Jake held his breath, betwixt and between again, knowing and not knowing.

Ryan gestured, grandly, toward Jake. "Go ahead, Mom. Tell

Dad about Dr. Dave. Tell him the truth. I could tell him, but I want you to. I want to know if I was raised by a liar."

Jake felt something give way inside his chest. He kept his eyes on Ryan, who stood motionless, because he couldn't bring himself to look back at Pam. He didn't want to know what she looked like right now, being confronted with an accusation. He didn't want to see her deny it, or admit it. It had never occurred to him before, but as soon as it was given voice, he realized it couldn't be otherwise. Because Ryan never lied, not until Jake had taught him to.

"Mom." Ryan hesitated, evidently waiting for Pam to say something, but she didn't. "Honesty is important in any relationship, isn't it? What about your relationship to me? Why don't you tell *me* what happened with Dr. Dave?"

"Nothing!" Pam said, but her tone didn't sound as strong. Jake still didn't look at her.

"Nothing? Really, Mom?" Ryan grew preternaturally still. "Dr. Dave's married, too, you know. So tell me, do you know the difference between right and wrong? Does he? Because I heard you on the phone with him, when you came to pick me up after practice. It was sophomore year, I forgot my French book and I had to go back inside, to my locker. Then I realized I had it with me, so I came around the corner and I heard you on the phone with Dr. Dave. I think it was Dr. Dave, but it was definitely somebody named Dave. Because you said, 'I miss you, Dave. I love you.'"

Pam gasped.

Jake didn't turn around. His body felt suddenly stiff, as if he were getting ready to absorb a blow, his muscles bracing for impact in a collision that had already occurred. It was his own personal hit-and-run, taking place not on Pike Road, but in his very home.

Ryan's face fell, and he looked suddenly sad, but he didn't cry. "Mom, you're right. It isn't my business. It's more important that you explain it to Dad than to me." Ryan faced Jake, with a heavy sigh. "Dad. I'm sorry. I thought you should know. Good night." Ryan closed the door, leaving Jake facing the door, turned away from Pam.

"Jake," Pam said hoarsely. "I can explain."

Jake found himself walking stiffly to the door. He didn't know why. He didn't want to leave but he couldn't stay.

"Jake," Pam said, louder. "It's over, it's history. I ended it last year, before we went to counseling. It didn't last that long, only six months. It was a symptom, and I knew it—"

Jake opened the door and walked out, not sure what came next. For the first time in his life, he didn't have a plan.

Chapter Thirty-one

Jake found himself stopped at a red light, sitting at the wheel of the rental Toyota, without even remembering getting in. He came into the moment as if he'd been pulled into the present from his own subconscious, a black void that matched the darkness around him. He didn't have his coat on but was still in his shirt and tie from work. He was stopped at an intersection, and there were no other cars on the street. The dashboard clock read 9:28 P.M. He'd been driving for two hours.

He checked the street sign on the corner to his right, but he couldn't read it. His eyes were blurry and his nose leaking; he realized he'd been crying. He wiped his nose on his shirt-sleeve, looked around, and saw only the spiky black trunks and branches of trees, silhouetted in the light from the windows and front-door fixtures of the large houses, whose peaked roofs and massive entrances hulked shadowy in the night.

He didn't recognize the neighborhood. He felt dislocated, disoriented, generally out of place. He glanced at the dashboard and determined that the car had a no-frills GPS, but he didn't bother to turn it on. He didn't know where he wanted to go. He had no destination, so he didn't need a route.

When the light turned green, he was in no hurry to hit the gas, but he did anyway, proceeding straight through the intersection without knowing whether he was heading north or south, toward home or away. It didn't matter. It was all uncharted terrain. He didn't know how he had gotten here, not only literally, but to the point where he'd become a suburban husband and father who was driving around aimlessly, in a car that wasn't even his own. He'd worked hard his whole life and followed all the rules. He had risen out of the ashes. He was a self-made man; he had made himself and his business. But the other things he had made were a son who was self-destructing and a wife who had fallen in love with a better suit.

Jake cruised down the dark street, hollow and aching inside, thinking of Pam. He wanted to know when her affair had started, and why. He wanted to know where they did it, how they did it, how many times they did it. Where they did it, which house, which car. If she liked it better with him, if he was a better lover. Who started it, and exactly how it ended. If it ended, why he was still calling her.

The darkness seemed to envelop Jake, swallowing him whole, but still he drove forward into the void. He didn't know what Pam saw in Dr. Dave, other than the fact that he was so frigging helpful with Ryan. Jake kicked himself for not guessing that something was going on between them. There were too many phone calls, too many times she quoted Dr. Dave. Jake began to doubt the whole shooting-coach thing, questioning whether Dr. Dave became Ryan's shooting coach in order to get close to Pam, in the first place.

Jake had never felt so stupid in his life, ashamed that he hadn't realized she was cheating. He'd never cheated on her and had never really been tempted. His sin had been that he worked too hard, not that he ever dreamed of straying. He saw himself in her; they were so much alike that he never imagined she'd break the rules, or break her word, ever. That was why he'd been so surprised tonight, when she'd agreed to keep the secret about Pike Road. He always thought of Pam as the good girl to his good boy, and it was more her style to do what she had eventually done—nag him until he finally went to a marriage counselor. He didn't want to think about her sleeping with another man, underneath another man, with her legs wrapped around him.

Jake spotted another car on the road, driving toward him in the oncoming lane, its high beams on. It was the kind of thing that usually made him nuts, and he would normally blink his lights to signal the other driver to lower his high beams. If that didn't work, he'd been known to turn on his own high beams out of spite. But tonight he didn't do either of these things. On the contrary, he fed his car some gas, and a different idea popped into his head:

He considered crossing the yellow line and driving straight into the lights.

He drove forward and so did the oncoming car, about a hundred yards apart, then ninety, then eighty. He thought of how easy it could be, just to jerk the steering wheel to the left at the last moment. He wouldn't have to think about it, time it, or work very hard to make it happen. It would be just like when he hit the Dumpster. Easy, peasy.

He looked directly into the high beams, and they seared into his eyes. The cars were seventy feet apart, then sixty, then fifty. He hit the gas and stared into the light, forcing himself not to squint or look away, flooding his brain with a brightness that obliterated the houses, driveways, and recycling bins, like the white-hot blast of an atomic bomb.

The other car raced toward him, its unseen driver unaware of what he was thinking, and Jake knew all he had to do to achieve the desired result was to aim his left bumper at the left bumper of the oncoming car and the impact would do the rest.

The oncoming car barreled toward him, its headlamps double-barreled beams of light, and he wondered what the driver's face would look like, just before they crashed. Shock. Horror. Surprise.

The cars were thirty feet apart, then twenty. He gritted his teeth, squinting against the high beams. The cars were ten feet apart, and he squeezed his eyes shut, grimacing, waiting to see what would happen, and when the other car was almost upon him, he realized he couldn't do it.

He opened his eyes and drove straight. He couldn't kill another human being. He couldn't be responsible for the death of anyone else, ever, in the time he had left on earth.

The other car whooshed past him, the driver not knowing what could have happened, and Jake exhaled loudly, emitting a breath he didn't even know he'd been holding. It struck him that he hadn't driven into the other car not only because he didn't want to kill anyone else, but also because he didn't want to die. He wanted to live. He wanted to redeem himself. For Kathleen Lindstrom's tragic death. For Pam's infidelity. For Ryan's depression.

Jake steered down the darkened street, past the windows that looked into family rooms containing happier families. He didn't have a plan, any longer. The time for plans was over. He didn't believe in them anymore, anyway. Pam didn't plan on cheating on him. Ryan didn't plan on killing Kathleen Lindstrom. Nobody planned on the worst, but they got it just the same and had to deal. He knew the saying that "Man plans and God laughs," but he'd learned the truth was exactly the opposite—Man plans and God cries.

His thoughts returned to Pam, without pain. He knew in his heart why she had strayed, but he loved her still. He didn't want to give up on their marriage, no matter what. He didn't know how she felt; he didn't know if he was ready to find out. He hoped they could put back the pieces of their new life, one that they would make together, with Ryan. Their son needed the both of them now, more than ever, and the three of them had to go forward and hang together in a way they hadn't before.

He pulled over to the side of the street, braked, and plugged his home address in the GPS, then pressed START. **Calibrating Route**, said the GPS, with an arrow pointing behind him. He hit the gas, pulled away from the curb, and started to head home, his mind running free. He wanted to go home, talk to Pam, and work everything out, even if it took all night. He wanted her to know that he was sorry she felt abandoned by him; that he hadn't realized it had gotten so bad. He would tell her that he was sorry, and he flashed-forward to a heart-to-heart in their bedroom, that ended with her coming into his arms, crying and asking him to forgive her.

He wound his way through the quiet suburban streets; the GPS had been set on the shortest route, not the fastest, but he didn't bother to reset it. The lighted blue GPS screen showed a right turn, but he'd been too preoccupied and missed it, so he went straight and the GPS screen switched to **Recalibrating Route**. Jake read the screen, realizing that's exactly what he was doing too, in his life. He would be recalibrating a new route, for himself, Pam, and Ryan, too.

He stopped at a traffic light, which bathed the car's interior in a blood-red glow. He flashed on Friday night after the crash, wiping the blood from his hands, then finding it etched in the lines of his palm. He tried to push it from his mind, to recalibrate again. He reminded himself that he was going to go home and try to move forward, with Pam and him putting their marriage back together for their own sakes, and for Ryan's. They wouldn't be able to get through this together unless they acted as a family. Their house, divided, could not stand. He hoped she'd be happy that he still loved her and was willing to forgive her.

So it came as a shock to Jake when he finally got home and pulled into the garage, only to find that Pam's car was gone. Pasted on the garage door was a sheet of legal pad that read:

I will not be back tonight. Don't call or text me. Ryan is asleep. Tomorrow, go to work your usual time. I will come home and take him to school. Leave me alone. Goodnight.

Chapter Thirty-two

The next morning, Jake was in his office as early as usual, showered, shaved, and stiff in a cutaway collar and fresh suit. He looked out his window into the dawn of a new day, another frigid one under a cloudy pewter sky. He ignored the overseas markets, his voicemail, email, a stack of tri-fold correspondence, and pink phone messages on his desk. He wouldn't think of working until the wire transfer went through this morning, and maybe not even then.

Last night he'd hardly slept for thinking of Pam, though he'd followed her directions, not texting or calling her and leaving the house early, so they hadn't run into each other. He prayed she hadn't run to Dr. Dave. He'd thought of calling him, but she would be too angry. He did call the Marriott Courtyard Suites near the house, but they wouldn't tell him if she was there. He'd even called the local hospital, in case she had an accident.

Jake racked his brain, thinking where Pam would have slept. Her best friend had moved to Singapore last year, and though she was close to all of the Chasers' moms, she wouldn't confide in them, given Dr. Dave's status with the team. She was in a book club, but she wouldn't want them to know, and as a judge, she wasn't close with anyone in the bar. She had a secretary, Christine, who was a stodgy sort, and otherwise in her chambers, there were her three law clerks, in their twenties. Pam had no one else but him and Dr. Dave, which worried him.

Jake heard noises beyond his closed door as Gardenia came to life, but he kept his eyes to the window, idly watching as his employees filled in the spaces in the parking lot. Amy parked her car next to his rental, and he took his receiver off the hook, so she'd think he was on the phone and wouldn't interrupt him. She knew him well enough to know that something was really wrong.

Jake's cell phone rang. The screen read **Harold**, and he grabbed it, knowing it would be about the wire transfer. "Hey, everything okay? I was just about to call you."

"Not exactly. We have a glitch, but I trust it won't be a problem."

"What glitch?" Jake asked, his gut churning. "There can be no glitches."

"The woman who usually does our wires, Barbara, called in sick this morning. I just found out. I'm out of the office and I won't be in until later."

"So what does this mean? You can still transfer the money by eleven, can't you?"

"No. I can do it by noon, but not eleven."

"*What?*" Jake exploded. If the money wasn't there on time, Voloshin would go to the police.

"I won't be in. I'm out of the office at a meeting. I stepped out to call you."

"I need it by eleven!" Jake shouted. "I have to have it by eleven! You said you could do it!"

"I know, sorry. It'll just be an hour later—"

"That's too late!" Jake checked his watch—9:02. Voloshin would take the photos and video right to the police. It would ruin Ryan and him, and now, even Pam. She'd kept their secret, a judge who kept quiet about her son's hit-and-run.

"Harold, leave the damn meeting! Where are you, Timbuktu?"

"North Jersey. It's too important, and if I did, it would raise questions."

"But this *matters more*! Leave!"

"Jake. I would leave if I could, but I can't make it back in time anyway."

"Make somebody else wire the money!"

"No. We have another woman in the wire room but it wouldn't be prudent to use her."

"Why not?" Jake heard himself panicking. "All she has to do is push a button!"

"But it's going to an offshore account."

"Harold, don't tell me I'm your only client to wire to an offshore account!" Jake found himself on his feet. "I wasn't born yesterday!"

"I'm not saying that." Harold's voice stiffened. "What I'm saying is that only Barbara handles such transactions. I can't ask anyone else to do it. I'll do it myself as soon as I get back to the office."

"There's *nobody* else? Not even one of your other bankers?"

"No, not possible."

"You can't trust one of your other bankers to send a wire for one of your best clients? Are you kidding? You have all my personal accounts, all of my business accounts, and Gardenia's!"

"Jake, that would be imprudent. Trust me, I have only your interests at heart. I'll be in by noon—"

"Can't *I* go over and do it? I know how to do a wire transfer—"

"Hold on, I got a better idea. Let me go to Plan B. I may have a way to get it done ASAP, but I can't be sure."

"What way?"

"Let me hang up and see if I can make it happen. I'll call you as soon as it's done."

"Call me as soon as you fix it!"

"I will. Talk soon."

Jake pressed END, sat down in front of his computer, and got online and plugged in GreenTech. Blood pounded in his temples. His mouth tasted dry. He had to go to his own Plan B. He couldn't take the risk that Voloshin would go to the cops. The GreenTech site came on the screen, and he clicked to the Contact Us page, found the main number, and pressed the link to make the call.

"GreenTech," answered a woman. "How can I help you?"

"I'm calling for Andrew Voloshin."

"I don't see him. May I tell him you called?"

"Do you know where I can reach him? Is he out of the office?" Jake's heart throbbed in his chest. Voloshin could be on his way to the Caymans. Or sitting outside the police station.

"I don't know. Our receptionist isn't at the desk, and I just happened to be passing by."

Jake felt frantic. "Is there anyone else there who would know where he is? It's really important that I speak to him."

"Why don't you call him on his cell?"

"I wish I could, but I forgot the number. I have it in my business phone, but I left that in the car. I'm calling you from my personal phone."

"I don't have his cell. Hold on a minute. Let me see if anybody knows where he is."

"Thanks." Jake checked the clock while he waited—9:35, then 9:36.

"Hello, sir?"

"Yes. Were you able to find where he is?"

"Sorry, nobody knows. Sometimes he comes in late, if he's been up coding. You can try him at home if you want."

"Fine, thanks." Jake hung up, went online for the White Pages, got Voloshin's home number, and pressed it into his phone.

"Hello?" a man answered, but his voice sounded raspy, unlike Voloshin's.

"I'm looking for Andrew Voloshin. Is he there?" Jake double-checked to see if he'd dialed the correct number, which he had.

"Who's calling?"

"I'm an . . . associate of his." Jake didn't know who he was talking to, so he chose his words carefully.

"What's your name? What's this in reference to?"

Jake decided to stick with the story. "I'm a financial planner that Mr. Voloshin contacted. I need to speak with him."

"What did you say your name was?"

Jake hadn't said. He glanced at the clock—9:42. "Jake Buckman of Gardenia Trust. Is Mr. Voloshin in?"

"Mr. Buckman, I'm Detective Zwerling with the Shakertown police. I'm sorry to inform you, but Mr. Voloshin is dead."

Chapter Thirty-three

"My God!" Jake couldn't process it quickly enough. It should be good news, but it didn't feel that way. His blackmailer was dead. His troubles should be over. Relief flooded his system, but it left him shocked. He was stunned. "But he wasn't old. How did he—"

"Actually, Mr. Buckman, he was murdered. We've notified next of kin, and it should be public."

"When did this happen?"

"Last night. Mr. Buckman, what company did you say you were with?"

"Gardenia Trust." Jake forced his brain to function. The police were at Voloshin's apartment. Photos of him and Ryan on Pike Road were in Voloshin's phone and undoubtedly his computer. The police might have seen them. If so, the police had proof that Ryan was guilty of the hit-and-run. Fear crackled through Jake's body like electricity.

"Gardenia Trust? Is that local?"

"Yes, in Concord Chase." Jake tried to sound normal. He told himself maybe the cops hadn't seen the photo and videos yet.

"Where?"

"In the Bates Mill Corporate Center."

"We'd like to see you, Mr. Buckman. Would you be available in half an hour?"

"Sure, yes," Jake answered, because anything else would be suspicious. Why would the cops want to meet with him, if they hadn't found the photos and video? Would they arrest him in the office? Would they take Ryan at school?

"Mr. Buckman, we'll see you then."

"Okay, thanks." Jake hung up, stricken. His heart thudded in his chest. His first thought was of Pam. He had to tell her about Voloshin. He scrolled to her cell number and pressed CALL, but it rang, then went to voicemail. He left a message, "Honey, call me as soon as you can. It's very important. I love you." He hit END and considered calling her chambers, but remembered the court was sitting this week and she would be on the bench.

He rose and began pacing, trying to collect his thoughts. He told himself he was jumping to conclusions. Maybe the police hadn't collected the phone and laptop for evidence yet. Or maybe Voloshin had password-protected his phone and computer, and the police hadn't looked through them yet. He didn't know what time Voloshin's body had been found or when the police had started investigating.

He paced back and forth. His temples throbbed. He considered calling a lawyer to represent him when the cops came, but it would only make him look guilty. Still it made sense to get some legal advice. He thumbed through his phone log, found Hubbard's phone number, and pressed CALL. The phone rang, then went to voicemail, but Jake hung up, telling himself to remain calm. He had seen enough TV shows to know he shouldn't volunteer any information.

He resumed pacing. He remembered that he had called Voloshin last night from the house. He'd have to make sure to mention that to the police, before they got Voloshin's phone records.

Suddenly Jake stopped stock still, his pacing ceased. If the police had found the photos and the video, then discovered the wire transfer, they could figure out that Voloshin was blackmailing Jake. The police might even suspect Jake of murdering Voloshin. His mouth went dry. His thoughts raced, threatening to run away with him. The blackmail gave Jake a perfect motive for wanting Voloshin dead, and Jake's only alibi was that he was home with Ryan, who was implicated in the same crime. The police could be coming to question him in connection with Voloshin's *murder.*

Jake realized he had to stop the wire transfer. His gaze flew to the desk clock—9:59. The police would be here in no time. He had to get ahold of Harold and reverse the instructions. He raised his phone and pressed Harold's cell number. The call rang once, twice, then three times and went to voicemail.

Jake heard the beep and left the message, "Harold! Change of plans. *Don't* send the money to the account. Do you understand? Call me as soon as you get this message, but in *no* event should you send the money to the account." Jake wanted to make sure Harold got the message, so he scrolled to the text function and typed: **Harold, Major change of plans. Do NOT send the wire transfer. Call me ASAP.** He hit SEND, but still wasn't satisfied. He pressed the number for Harold's office at the bank.

The call was answered, "Hello, this is Pennsylvania National's Wealth Management Group. I'm Marie DiTizio, how can I help you?"

"Hi Marie, it's Jake, and I have a problem." Jake knew Marie but he didn't know if she had been told about the transfer. "I need to reach Harold. He called me this morning, and I know he's in a meeting. You know where he is?"

"Yes, of course, but our clients are confidential, as you know—"

"I don't care who the client is. Call him for me. Not on his cell, but at the client. Somebody has to put a note in front of him right away and tell him to call me. It's very important."

"Interrupt his meeting?"

"Yes, Marie, I wouldn't ask you if it weren't an emergency."

"May I help you instead?"

Jake hesitated. "Did Harold discuss anything with you about one of my accounts yesterday or this morning?"

"No, but if you update me, I'm sure I can help—"

"Then no, thanks. I need you to call Harold, get a note in front of him, and tell him to call me immediately. Have them write on the note that he should *not* do what we discussed. You understand?"

"I suppose I could do that," Marie said uncertainly. "That he should *not* do what you discussed."

"Yes, exactly." Jake glanced at the clock, feeling time slipping away. The police would be here soon. "Call me right back after you've made the phone call."

"Of course. I'll attend to it right now."

"Thanks, good-bye." Jake pressed END on the phone and checked the clock—10:06. The police were on their way. Phone in hand, he hurried to his office door, flung it open, and hustled to Amy's desk. "Hey, we had some terrible news this morning."

"What's going on?" Amy focused her warm brown eyes on his face, her concern immediate. She had on a funky multicolored scarf and dangling silver earrings with bright red stones.

"Amy, do you remember that prospective who dropped in yesterday morning? Lewis Deaner?" Jake leaned over, lowering his voice, even though the closest desk wasn't within earshot. "I just got a call from the police, and he was found murdered in his apartment."

"Oh my God." Amy's hand flew to her mouth. "That's terrible."

"I know, and the police are going to be here in about twenty minutes."

"Here? Why?"

"I assume they want to investigate and ask what we met about yesterday." Jake tried to remain composed. Over Amy's shoulder, he spotted Ramon heading his way.

"How did they know that you met with him? Is that who you were on the phone with?"

"Yes." Jake saw Ramon, trying to flag him down. "I called Deaner at home to follow up with him, and the police were there. They're on the way over now."

"So what do we do?"

"Will you make sure the big conference room is available? Obviously, we'll keep this between us."

"Sure thing." Amy nodded quickly, so her curls bounced and her earrings swung. "Ramon has the Janoviches coming in this morning, but I'll move them into the small conference room."

"Good, thanks. Also please meet the police in reception when they come in and take them into the conference room. I don't want them identifying themselves at the desk, in front of the clients."

"I'll be smooth." Amy smiled, but Jake couldn't.

"I'm expecting an important call from Harold at Pennsylvania National." Jake glanced at her desk clock, a comical plastic cat—10:08. "I'm hoping he'll call on my cell before they get here, but if he doesn't, I want you to put him through to me immediately, even if I'm in with the police. Okay?"

"Gotcha."

"Jake!" Ramon called out, reaching the desk. "Can we sit down and go over the Brady trust—"

"No, sorry," Jake interrupted him. "I don't have time right now."

"But I can't set up this trust without your approval and I can't meet with them without the trust being set up. I sent the documents to you Friday, remember? I followed up on Sunday, when I didn't hear from you."

"Ramon, I'm busy," Jake snapped, tense.

"But they're coming in this afternoon to review the documents and sign the papers."

"Then put them off."

Amy pursed her lips, looking from Jake to Ramon like a child in a custody battle.

"I can't do that." Ramon shook his head, bewildered. "Brady is impossible to get a meeting with. He's a surgeon, and you know how they are with schedules. If I don't have the papers ready, he'll be pissed."

"Then he'll be pissed!" Jake exploded. "I'm busy, how many times do I have to say it? I'm busy! Don't you get it?"

Ramon's dark eyes flared, and Jake stalled momentarily, taking in Amy's tight expression, and the other assistants, frowning in surprise. They'd never seen conduct like it from Jake, and he edged away. He realized that what he was seeing in their faces wasn't even a fraction of their reaction if they knew what he had done. That the police could arrest him for a hit-and-run, maybe even for murder. They could take him away in handcuffs this very morning.

Jake felt himself edge backwards. Gardenia would have to close. Some of his employees had been with him since the beginning. He would do to them what his old company had done to him. They would lose their jobs, this very morning. Their lives would turn on a dime, and so would the lives of their spouses, their kids, and the people who depended on them.

Jake turned on his heel and fled down the hall to the conference room, checking his watch on the fly. He'd prayed Harold or Marie called before the cops got here. He couldn't take the call in front of them. That would take nerves of steel, which he was fresh out of at the moment. His cell phone waited in his breast pocket like a bomb ready to explode.

Jake hustled through the reception area and into the conference room, hiding from everyone.

Even himself.

Chapter Thirty-four

Jake turned to see the conference-room door opening and Amy ushering in two men, one middle-aged and the other in his early thirties, both dressed in dark suit jackets and slacks.

"Jake," Amy said, calmly. If she was upset with Jake from his outburst, she was too professional to let it show. "This is Detectives Zwerling and Woo, from Shakertown."

"Thanks. Welcome, gentlemen. I'm Jake Buckman." Jake approached them with a false smile and an outstretched hand. He couldn't tell from their impassive expressions whether they had seen the photos and videos, much less suspected him of Voloshin's murder.

Amy returned to the door, then paused. "Jake, they didn't want coffee or anything, so I'll go."

"Thanks." Jake nodded, and Amy slipped out, closing the door behind her.

"I'm Bill Zwerling," said the middle-aged detective, who had a raspy voice and smelled vaguely of cigarette smoke. He was a chubby five foot seven, with wavy gray hair, slack jaws, and a bulbous nose. His paunch popped through his unbuttoned jacket as he gestured to the younger detective. "This is my partner, Rich Woo. We showed our ID to your secretary, I mean, assistant. But if you want to see—"

"No, that's okay. Hello, Detective Woo." Jake extended his hand to Detective Woo, who was tall and lanky, and his grayish suit fit him perfectly at the waist, as if he worked out.

"Good to meet you." Detective Woo flicked back his glossy black bangs, which flopped longish over his forehead and ears. "My father always says I should see a financial planner. Invest what I've saved."

"Your father's right. Detectives, please sit down." Jake gestured them into chairs, giving them the view facing the window. "I'd be happy to advise you, Detective Woo. It's never too early to start saving for retirement."

"Problem is, you have no idea what my pay grade is. There's not a lot left over, if you follow."

"I hear that, but you have to start somewhere. You're young, and I wish I knew then what I know now." Jake met Detective Woo's gaze, but still couldn't tell what the police knew or if they suspected him of Voloshin's murder. He sat down at the head of the conference table, which he hoped would reinforce his credibility.

"How much money do I have to have to use your services, Mr. Buckman? Do you have a minimum?"

"Please call me Jake, and no, not at all. We'd be happy to put you in our Gardenia mutual fund, which contains the same blue-chip stocks that we put high-net-worth individuals in." Jake checked the walnut clock on the credenza against the far wall. It read 10:28. That transfer had to be stopped or he was dead meat.

"What's the cutoff, money-wise, between me and high-net worth?"

"Those with assets over $500,000. I'd be happy to meet with you, anytime."

Detective Zwerling cleared his throat, as he pulled a slim spiral notepad from inside his breast pocket and flipped open its cardboard cover. "Let's get this show on the road, shall we? We have a busy day ahead of us."

"Fine." Jake forced himself to stop checking the clock so often. He didn't want to show his hand to the cops, like he had Guinevere LeMenile. "I'm very sorry to hear about Mr. Voloshin's murder. That came as a shock. We don't have many of those in Concord Chase."

"He lived in Shakertown, the north end. Trust me, it happens." Detective Zwerling shifted in the chair, his belly lipping the table.

"How was he killed?" Jake wanted to make sure he asked any questions that seemed appropriate.

"He was stabbed to death. Another tenant found him in his apartment, because he left his laundry in the washer."

"Ugh, that's terrible." Jake didn't have to feign repugnance. "Do you have any suspects or is it too soon?"

"*Way* too soon. It's not like TV, where the body hits the floor and they already cleared the case." Detective Zwerling curled his lip in a way that suggested he'd given the lecture before. "Me, I'm a big *Dexter* fan. They get at least a few episodes to solve the crime."

"I wonder why somebody would kill him. He seemed like a nice, harmless guy."

"The details of our investigation are confidential, but his valuables appear to be missing. Wallet, laptop, phone, like that."

"How sad." Jake clucked unhappily, though relief surged through him. If Voloshin's laptop and phone had been stolen, the police probably didn't know about the video and photos incriminating him and Ryan. Still he couldn't be certain, and if the wire transfer wasn't stopped, it could blow everything. He checked the credenza clock as discreetly as possible—10:34.

"Mr. Buckman, Jake, you don't mind if we tape this, do you?"

Detective Woo slid a handheld tape recorder from inside his pocket, pressed a button on the side, and set it down on the table between them.

"No, I don't mind at all. So how can I help you?" Jake hadn't anticipated the meeting would be recorded, but his answer appeared to be moot anyway.

"We have a few questions." Detective Zwerling clicked the back of his pen with a chubby thumb. "Jake, just tell us something about yourself. Family? Residence?"

"I'm married, and we have one son, in high school." Jake didn't supply any names, to keep them out of it. "I live in Concord Chase."

"For how long?"

"Twenty years, and I've had the business the past five."

"You own it?"

"Yes."

"Good enough." Detective Zwerling took notes. "Tell me how you came to meet with Mr. Voloshin."

"I was at my son's basketball game at North Mayfield, last Sunday afternoon. He sat next to me."

"You're a big guy, Jake. Did you play hoops in high school?"

"No."

"College?"

"No. I worked."

"Okay." Detective Zwerling took notes. "Why was Voloshin at the game, do you know?"

"Yes. He was with North Mayfield and was watching his kid, a sophomore." Jake decided to stick with the story Voloshin told him, because it was too risky to improvise. He didn't want the detectives to know that he knew Voloshin had lied about his name, family, job or anything else. He doubted the police had asked Amy any questions, because she knew Voloshin as Deaner, and he doubted the police would go find the tiara moms.

"Did Voloshin tell you what he did for a living, at the game?"

"He was a freelance writer."

"How long did you speak with him?"

"About five minutes."

"That's all?"

"You know how these games are. You end up sitting with people, trying to make conversation or drum up business. Network. I told him I was a financial planner, I gave him a business card, and he said he'd come see me." Jake heard himself volunteering too much, out of nervousness. "To make a long story short, he came by my office Monday morning and we met."

"Where, here?" Detective Zwerling took more notes on his pad.

"Yes, but not in the conference room. In my office."

"For how long did you meet?"

"Fifteen minutes."

"So, short?" Detective Zwerling took another note.

"Yes."

"Is that typical?"

"No."

"Why did it end so soon?"

"He seemed like he'd heard enough." Jake swallowed hard. "He ended it."

"Did you make notes during the meeting?"

"No."

"Do you, usually?"

"No." Jake sneaked a look at the credenza clock—10:40. He could hear it ticking in his brain.

"What did you talk about?"

"I told him about the company and our investment philosophy, like I do with any new client."

"You were hoping to get his business?"

"Yes, I was hoping to sign him." Jake kept his answers short. He wasn't about to take any chances, in case the detectives had somehow seen the photos or video.

"What do you mean, sign him?"

"We have an agreement that new clients sign, called an Investment Advisory Agreement."

"Did he sign it?"

"No, I didn't offer it to him. We didn't get that far." Jake remembered that he ought to mention his phone call to Voloshin, to preempt any suspicion when the police found Voloshin's phone records. "By the way, I called him on Monday night, to see if he had any questions or if I could help him further, but he said no."

Detective Zwerling made a note. "What time did you call him?"

"About nine o'clock or so."

"After business hours?"

"Yes." Jake tried not to look at the clock and to keep his focus on Detective Zwerling, in a natural way.

"Is that typical for you to call a client, a prospective client, outside of business hours?"

"Sure, especially if I want his business." Jake wasn't lying. "I'm self-employed, so I work all the time."

"But he turned you down, so why did you call him?"

"To follow up, to make sure."

"What did he say?"

"That he was thinking it over."

"I see." Detective Zwerling made another note. "So then why were you calling him at home, this morning?"

Oops. "I'm persistent."

"Did he tell you how much money he had?"

"No."

"But you still tried to sign him, as you say?"

"Yes."

"You tried that hard to sign him, but you didn't even know how much money he had?"

"Yes." Jake could see he wasn't buying it.

"You must really have wanted his business." Detective Zwerling frowned so deeply, three lines creased his brow.

"I really want everybody's business." Jake could see he had to convince him. "To be frank, five years ago, I lost my job. It turned out okay, I founded Gardenia, but I never want to go back there again. It's a mentality."

Detective Zwerling blinked. "How typical is it that a client doesn't tell you how much money he has?"

"Very typical."

"How so?"

"Clients like him, who aren't referred to us by an accountant, estates lawyer, or a banker, aren't well-versed in what we do. Like Detective Woo." Jake gestured casually at the younger man. "Not everybody in that situation wants to disclose their assets. They're concerned about confidentiality. They don't understand, or really trust, that all of their financial information is confidential. We're very careful about that here."

Detective Zwerling made another note, then looked up at Jake, cocking his head. "Did Mr. Voloshin tell you where he worked as a freelancer?"

"No."

"You didn't ask?"

"No."

"Did he tell you his salary or anything about his finances?"

"No."

"Again, you didn't ask?"

"No. I don't want to come off as prying, too early in the relationship. I never begin a relationship with a new client by asking them about their assets, because as I say, they regard it as prying. I give them my sales pitch and explain how we can tailor their portfolio to meet their investment goals." Jake gestured at Detective Woo again. "As I told you, the truth is, it doesn't matter how much money someone may have. I know I can grow it over time, no matter how much it is, and that's the point I make at the outset."

Detective Zwerling didn't seem impressed. "Did he tell you where he kept his money? What his bank was?"

"No."

"You didn't ask him that either?"

"No."

"Why not?"

"Same deal."

Detective Zwerling lifted an unruly eyebrow. "Let me get this straight. When you talked to Mr. Voloshin, you had no idea if he even had the money to invest?"

"Yes that's right." Jake stole a glance at the credenza clock—10:54. He began to sweat under his starched shirt.

"How do you know he wasn't wasting your time?"

"I don't, but most people don't come in if they don't have the money or close to it. In any event, I think long-term. They may not have it now, but they could someday."

"Did Voloshin seem wealthy, to you?"

"I never make an assumption about how much money anyone has by their appearance or their manner. My assistant Amy calls it paydar, and my paydar is terrible." Jake smiled when Detective Woo did, though Detective Zwerling didn't. "Mr. Voloshin wasn't an ostentatious man, but I know from experience that someone like that could have a fortune socked away, or they could be a waiter."

Detective Zwerling frowned again. "You mean a waiter, like in a restaurant?"

"No," Jake answered, grasping for purchase on the terra firma of shop talk. "In my profession, a waiter is somebody who's waiting for an inheritance. They live on the interest of trusts during most of their adult life and many of them live very frugally. They tend to look and act like Mr. Voloshin."

Detective Woo clapped his hands together, smiling. "You mean they're *waiting* for their parents to die? Oh, that's *cold*."

Jake flushed. The clock read 10:56. "I didn't make up the term. We all use it. I guess it is harsh."

"*Waiters!*" Detective Woo laughed.

"Enough, Richie." Detective Zwerling pursed his lips. "To get back on track, Jake, did Voloshin tell you that he expected to be coming into money?"

"No, he didn't."

"Did he ask you about setting up an offshore account for him?"

"No, he didn't. In point of fact, we're not a bank, so we don't set up any bank accounts, offshore or otherwise. We're an investment company and we invest our clients' money in stocks, bonds, and the like."

Detective Zwerling hesitated. "We did find evidence that would suggest Voloshin had set up an offshore account, himself. We're trying to understand where the money to fund it would be coming from. Do you have any information about where Voloshin was getting the money?"

"No."

"None at all?"

"None."

"Where do your clients usually get money from?"

"What about inheritance?" Jake shrugged, casually.

"Don't think so. He has a mother and we notified her as NOK, or next-of-kin. But she's upstate in a nursing facility, with insurance footing the bills. Did he mention anything to you about a girlfriend?"

"No."

Detective Zwerling frowned. "He didn't mention a girlfriend?"

"No." Jake wondered if Voloshin had a girlfriend, because the detective's tone sounded surprised.

"There was no talk of providing for anyone?"

"No, no beneficiary or anything like that."

"Didn't you think that was strange, since he had told you he had a son, and an ex-wife?"

"No, because as I say, he didn't give me much information at all. He played it close to the vest, and I pitched him."

Detective Zwerling pursed his lips as he took notes. "So he didn't say anything to you about a woman."

"No."

"Did you see what kind of car he drove?"

"No."

Detective Woo shrugged, glancing again at Detective Zwerling. "Give it up. I'm telling you, I'm right."

"Give what up?" Jake sneaked a glimpse of the credenza clock—10:59.

Detective Woo answered, "One of the tenants heard Voloshin arguing with a woman last night and saw a brunette leaving his—"

"Richie," Detective Zwerling interrupted. "Enough."

Detective Woo fell silent, and Jake remembered that Kathleen's mother was a brunette. Maybe she had found out that Voloshin was stalking her daughter. But he didn't know why she would kill him.

Detective Zwerling returned his attention to Jake. "To move on, Voloshin was never married. He had no ex-wife. No kids either. This isn't confidential, it'll be in the newspapers."

Jake faked a confused frown. "But he said he was watching his son at the basketball game."

"That wasn't true."

"So he's not a dad? He doesn't have a kid on the team?" Jake recoiled in fraudulent shock. The clock read 11:00. Either the transfer was stopped, or he was dead. The realization stressed him to the max. His heart beat wildly, throwing itself against the inside of his chest, as if it were trying to escape his very body.

"You say that financial planners don't set up offshore accounts?" Detective Zwerling set down his notebook, laying his pen on top.

Jake tried to recover. "No."

"So why did he want to meet you?"

"I don't know. Maybe he thought we did, mistakenly."

Detective Zwerling narrowed his eyes, making his crow's-feet look even deeper. "But you said he didn't ask you if you did."

Jake felt his mouth go dry. "Maybe he decided against it, after he saw the offices or something."

"But why did he come to you, in particular?"

"Because we met at the game." Jake struggled not to choke on his words. "I pitched him. I wanted him to come in."

"Then why would he lie to you about the son, and the ex-wife? It doesn't make sense."

"I don't know. Maybe to fit in, to make himself seem more normal, more like one of my clients?"

"But why? Why you? Did he go to the game to meet you?"

"I don't know. I am one of the top ten independent financial planners in the region, rated by *Barron's*. The other top guys are in Philly and Pittsburgh."

"So why not just come to your office, like any other client? Why make up some story and meet you at the game?" Detective Zwerling shook his head, his dissatisfaction evident.

"Maybe he didn't want to wait until Monday."

"But how does he even know you'll be at the game?"

"My son's a well-known high-school basketball player, in the newspapers all the time. It's a logical assumption I'd be there." Jake didn't elaborate. He wanted to keep Ryan's name out of it altogether.

"Do you go to his games?"

"Not all of them, but this was the playoffs. I go then." Jake saw a way out. "So maybe Voloshin made it a point to run into me. Maybe he thought he'd feel me out at the game, then he listened to my pitch and decided to come in, but saw that we don't do the kind of thing he was interested in."

"Why didn't he ask you about it then?"

"An offshore account? Would you, if you saw this place?" Jake gestured at the conference room. "We're obviously not the kind of place that deals in shady offshore accounts. We don't even breathe that word around here."

"Hmph." Detective Zwerling paused. "Anyway, so he expected to come into money. But I don't know where he expected to get it from. Do you have any idea?"

"No."

"In your practice, or whatever you call it, how do clients generally come into money?"

"Inheritance, gift, stock windfall. He could've even won the lottery. I have two lottery winners among my clients."

Detective Woo's face came alive. "The *lottery*? Whoa! That's incredible! What's it like to win the lottery?"

Detective Zwerling snorted. "It ruins your life, right?"

Detective Woo laughed. "Come on, Bill! Only *you* could find something wrong with free money! It's the best thing *ever*!"

Detective Zwerling snorted again. "Be careful what you wish, grasshopper."

"Winning the lottery can be a wonderful thing," Jake jumped in, relieved to change the subject. "I've seen it change lives for the better."

"Tell me!" Detective Woo leaned forward. "What do they do when they win? Give a party? Buy a Lamborghini? If I won, I'd take all of my buddies to Cabo!"

"Not on my watch." Jake managed a smile. "We'd discuss it, but I'd invest you consistent with your goals, and I'd refer you to an accountant, a private bank, and an estates lawyer."

Detective Zwerling scowled. "And a shrink, because you'll need one."

Jake let it go, and the clock ticked to 11:02. Suddenly his phone signaled that a text had come in. He rose and reached for his pocket, looking for an excuse to end the meeting. It had to be Harold or Marie, calling with the best or worst news of his life.

"Detectives, excuse me, I was waiting for that text and I need to make a call. We're finished here, aren't we?"

"Well, yes, I suppose we're done." Detective Zwerling flipped his pad closed. "For now."

For now. Jake fled for the door, glancing at his phone screen. The text wasn't from Harold or Marie, but from Pam, and it read:

Don't worry. I took care of Voloshin.

Chapter Thirty-five

Jake pressed in Pam's cell-phone number, hurrying back through the reception area to his office. He'd been expecting to hear from Harold, not his wife. What did she have to do with Voloshin? And last night? It struck him suddenly that Pam could be the brunette that the detectives were talking about, who had been spotted at Voloshin's apartment complex.

Oh my God.

Jake hustled down the hall and caught Amy's eye. Pam wouldn't have *killed* Voloshin, would she? It was almost unthinkable, but she was the best mother on the planet. Would she have killed Voloshin to protect Ryan?

Jake waited for the call to connect while he motioned to Amy that he was finished with the detectives and she should see them out. He slipped into his office and closed the door behind him. "Babe?" he said, as soon as Pam picked up. "What did you—"

"I *told* you not to call me." Pam's voice sounded thick with frost. "If I wanted to speak with you, I would've called you. I spent last night and this morning cleaning up after your mess.

Plus I stopped by the mall, bought Ryan a new phone, then dropped it off at school. Now I have to get to work and I can't take the time—"

"Pam, what did you mean by that text?" Jake hurried across his office to his window, so that he could see when the police left the building. His heart was pounding in his chest. His shirt was damp with flop sweat. "We have to talk—"

"The hell we do, and I'm driving. The traffic is terrible and I'm not about to get killed because you want to kiss and make up—"

"It's not about us, it's about your text. What did you do to Voloshin?"

"I handled the situation. I don't think it's wise to talk about it over the phone."

"Why not? Pam, what did you do?"

"Trust me. Not over the phone and not now." Suddenly Pam gasped. "*Damn* you! I almost hit that truck! Haven't you caused enough trouble? I'm hanging up—"

"No, don't! Pam, the police were just here." Jake was about to explain when he heard his phone signal that another call was coming in. He prayed it was Harold or Marie. He glanced at the screen, which showed Harold's cell-phone number. He had to find out whether the transfer had been stopped. "Pam, where are you?"

"In Fraser, about to get onto 202."

"Meet me at the quarry, there won't be anyone around. I'll be there in fifteen minutes."

"The quarry? What quarry?"

"Where we used to go, you know, when Ryan was little. Go in the entrance we used to use."

"Why? What's going on?"

"See you there. Good-bye." Jake pressed END and picked up Harold's call, breathless. "Harold, did you stop the transfer?"

"Yes, but what the hell is going on—"

"Thank God!" Jake almost shouted with relief. He leaned for support against the large glass window, leaving a sweaty handprint. Outside, the police hadn't yet appeared, leaving the building. "Harold, you're *sure* you were able to stop the transfer?"

"I'm positive."

"Absolutely sure?"

"It's done."

"Does it leave any trace that it was attempted, electronically?"

"No, but this isn't like you. First it's top priority that it goes through, then it's top priority that it doesn't? Are you okay?" Harold's tone softened. "I'm asking you as your friend, not as your banker. We've known each other ten years, through thick and thin, you remember. We go back."

Jake remembered. "No, I'm fine," he answered, firmly. "Thanks."

"So where do we go from here? What do you want me to do?"

"Forget the whole thing. I'm fine, and I appreciate your jumping on it when I needed you to."

"No problem." Harold's voice snapped back to business. "Then I'd better go. I left the meeting to call you."

"Thanks again. See you." Jake pressed END just as the two detectives emerged from the building entrance below. He couldn't leave the building until they were out of sight, so he watched them walk toward the front row of parking, reserved for Gardenia visitors. Two of the spaces were filled by a Volvo and a Jaguar, which Jake figured belonged to the Janoviches and the Warners, but next to them was a Crown Victoria, an older model in a dull navy blue. He assumed it belonged to the detectives, confirmed when they made a beeline for the sedan. But then they stopped suddenly, turned around in unison, and looked back at the building.

Detective Zwerling shielded his eyes, and they both squinted up at the building's façade, their heads together in conversation. Evidently, they were trying to locate his office window.

Jake edged away from view, shuddering. He didn't know why they were looking back at him, if they didn't suspect him of something. He realized that they hadn't asked him where he was last night, to see if he had an alibi, so maybe they didn't suspect him at all. Or maybe they didn't want to tip him off. Maybe they were playing games with him, doling out their questions as they continued their investigation. What was it that Detective Zwerling had said?

I suppose we're done . . . for now.

But it was Pam he was worried about. Had she killed Voloshin? It seemed unthinkable. She was a sitting judge. Jake knew Pam to the marrow and he never would have believed her capable of murder. But then again, he never would have believed she would cheat on him, either. Or that she would keep the secret about the hit-and-run. Or give up a federal judgeship that she had wanted forever. What other sacrifices would she make for Ryan? Where did she draw the line?

Still, he couldn't wait to see her.

The simple fact was, Jake loved his wife.

No matter what.

Chapter Thirty-six

Jake arrived at the quarry, the gravel popping under his tires. He cut the ignition and parked, but he didn't see Pam. He got out of the car and checked around to make sure, but she wasn't there. The only activity was on the far side of the immense quarry, at the construction site. Workers walked this way and that, backhoes toed the ground, and oversized trucks dumped loads of soil. The rumble of the equipment echoed off the rock walls of the crater.

Jake found himself worrying briefly if the construction workers could see him and checked around for security cameras. He knew he was being paranoid but he couldn't help himself. He'd driven here with an eye on the rearview mirror, checking to make sure that the detectives weren't following him.

Jake breathed in deeply, trying to relax. The air carried the familiar grit he remembered from his childhood, making it hard to breathe, but that could have been his memories. He glanced inside the enormous crater at the greenish brown water below, slightly choppy in the wind off the surface of the deep cliffs. A jagged vein of darker rock ran around the circumference of the quarry, a high watermark like the dirty rim of a bathtub, and his gaze traveled upward, over the strata of the limestone, its streaks of gray, tan, and brown formed over centuries.

It struck him that he was looking at a cross-section of time itself, if not his own personal history. His childhood would've started somewhere in the grayish streaks near the top, forty-odd years ago, and his father's and mother's would have started an inch below that, almost a century into the past, as if the layers of the limestone were the pencil lines they used to draw on the kitchen doorjamb when he was growing up, to chart his height. He and Pam drew the same lines on their kitchen doorjamb to mark Ryan's height, the only tradition of his family's worth keeping.

Jake realized with a deep pang that his mother would weep if she knew that her son had just been questioned by the police, after he'd left a young girl dead on the road. He also knew what his father would say.

Just my luck.

Jake swallowed hard, eyeing the strata of rock in the sun, which spilled into the countless crevices on the face of the cliff, illuminating even the tiniest of crevices, indentations, and faults, making shadows everywhere. The quarry kept no secrets, hiding nothing, but lay bare every buried sin, exposing it to light and air. Jake sensed he was looking at his own history, in which his decision on the night of the hit-and-run would become the blackest vein, a fault line that would render him and his family unstable, forever.

Story of my life.

There was a noise behind him, and Jake turned to see Pam driving up, on the phone. He wondered if she was talking to Dr. Dave, which brought him a stab of pain. He couldn't read her expression because she had designer sunglasses on and she was dressed for work in one of those jackets-over-a-dress combinations that she favored. She turned off the engine, hanging up, then threw open the car door, jumped out, and let it slam behind her.

"Pam." Jake walked toward her, raising his arms to embrace her, but she stiffed-armed him.

"Why am I here?"

"What happened with Voloshin last night?"

"I told you, I took care of it." Pam slipped the phone into her blazer pocket and folded her arms. Her tone was cold, and her hair blew in the wind off the quarry. "I cleaned up your mess."

"You didn't kill him, did you?" Jake had thought of nothing but that question on the drive here.

"*What?*"

"Andrew Voloshin is dead. He was found stabbed in his apartment last night. Two detectives were just at my office questioning me. They said one of the tenants saw a brunette leaving the complex last night. He was also heard arguing with a woman. Kathleen's mother is brunette, but so are you. It wasn't you, was it?"

"Are you serious?" Pam asked, sounding for the first time like herself. She tore off her sunglasses, revealing a horrified expression.

"You would never kill anybody, even for Ryan, would you?"

"Of course not." Pam's eyes flared in disbelief. "I don't know what you're talking about! Voloshin's not dead, he can't be. I just saw him."

"He is dead. Murdered." Jake's thoughts raced ahead. "If you didn't kill him, who did? And why?"

"I just saw him," Pam repeated, shaking her head.

"What time? Where did you see him?"

"Around ten o'clock, at his apartment."

"You went to his apartment?" Jake asked, dumbfounded. "Why? What were you doing? How do you even know where he lives—"

"If you let me explain, I will," Pam snapped, her eyelids

fluttering briefly. "I looked him up online, like you did, and I found his address. I decided to go over there."

"Why?"

"Why not?" Pam shot back. "You drove us straight into a ditch. You kept everything from me and you instructed Ryan to keep everything from me, so I had no say in what was going on. But once I found out, did you think I was going to sit around and do nothing?"

Jake didn't interrupt because she was on the warpath.

"I used to be a pretty good litigator, remember? I still have sharp teeth and I'm not without resources. I decided to go over there and give him a piece of my mind. I wanted him to back off of Ryan and I wanted him to know that he wasn't getting any more money after this initial payment. I wanted him to know that I wasn't about to be blackmailed into bankruptcy." Pam paused. "Wait, what about the transfer? Did you pay him?"

"I stopped it in time. It never went through."

"Good." Pam rubbed her forehead irritably, leaving pinkish welts with her nails. "So I drove over and knocked on his door. The apartment complex is one of those with townhomes stuck together, only two stories. Duplexes, and it's kind of run down. His apartment is on the second floor of one of the townhouses. His name was on the mailbox. I went in the downstairs door behind the first-floor tenant—"

"The tenant let you in? Just like that?"

"Please, he's an old man and I gave him a big smile."

"Did you tell him that you were there to see Voloshin?"

"What's the difference?"

"I'm thinking about the police. I'm wondering if you're the brunette that they were referring to or if the old man can identify you—"

"Of course he can't. It was dark. He could barely see me through his trifocals, and anyway, I didn't explain anything to him. I just walked in behind him, smiled, then went upstairs."

Pam threw up her hands, with the sunglasses looped around her thumb. "Honestly, Jake! What are you so worried about?"

Jake let it go. He didn't want to tell her what he was so worried about, not yet.

"Anyway, I went upstairs, and Voloshin's apartment door was open partway. I knocked and called for him, but it swung open all the way."

"He leaves his door open?"

"It was the only apartment on the floor, so I assume he wasn't worried about it. I went in. He came up later with a basket of laundry. I guess he'd been in the laundry room, wherever that was."

"So he came into his apartment and found you there?" Jake was trying to imagine the chronology.

"Yes, but not before I did some snooping."

"What did you do? What did you see?"

"Hold on. When he came in, I explained to him who I was and why I was there."

"What did you say?"

"I told him that I was Ryan's mother and a judge, and that he was the lowest form of life on the planet. I told him that if he ever breathed a word of what he knew or bothered us again, then I'd go to the police myself."

"Did you raise your voice?"

"Of course. That's my forte."

"Did he?"

"Not really. He asked me to leave, but I wasn't about to go until I said my piece. Then I left."

Jake couldn't hide his dismay. "The police said one of the tenants overheard a woman arguing with him."

"That would be me. That little bastard, he's the worst kind of bully. A coward." Pam paused. "It's too bad he's dead, murdered that way, even if it means he can't blackmail us anymore. I mean, I wouldn't wish that on anybody."

"The killer made it look like a burglary, or it was an actual burglary. But Voloshin was alive when you left him?"

"Of course. He threw me out. Walked me to the apartment door."

"And you went downstairs. Did you see anybody on your way out?"

"No."

"What about the old man? The first-floor tenant?"

"No. I didn't see anybody. Why are you asking me all these questions?"

"I want to know. Then what did you do?"

"I went to the car and left."

"Were you wearing your sunglasses?"

"Of course not. It was nighttime."

Jake tried to imagine it. "Did the place have a security guard, like a gatehouse at the front?"

"No, you just drive in."

"Did you see any security cameras around or any security guards?"

"There was no security guard, and it was too shabby to have any surveillance cameras."

"How long would you say you were there?"

"Talking with him? Five minutes. Before that, snooping around? About ten minutes. I took pictures."

"You took pictures inside his apartment?"

"You're not going to believe what I saw." Pam looked at her iPhone, and Jake came over as she thumbed through to her camera roll, a multicolored grid like an electronic mosaic. She looked over at him, then edged backwards again. "Forget it. I don't have time to look at them. I have to get to work."

"You're not even going to stand next to me now?"

"You think everything is fine, just like that?"

"No, of course not, but—"

"Nothing's fine, nothing. You got us into this mess. You ruined our lives. You ruined our *son*."

"Honey—"

"Don't 'honey' me. I don't want to talk about it now. I have to get to work. If I get in any later, people will start asking questions."

"Can I see the pictures?"

"You can't see them in the sun, anyway." Pam waved the iPhone at him. "He keeps a bulletin board over his desk and it has lots of pictures of Kathleen. He was stalking her. You were right, okay? Is that what you need to hear?"

"So you took pictures of his desk." Jake wondered if her fingerprints would show up anywhere. "Was his computer there?"

"Yes, a laptop. I took a picture."

"The police said that whoever killed him took his laptop and phone. Did you see a phone anywhere?"

"No, I assume he had it with him. Maybe it will show up in the photos. You can look for yourself." Pam hit a few buttons on her iPhone. "I'll email—"

"No, don't email—"

"Why not? I just did."

"Pam, think about this." Jake realized that she hadn't thought it through, probably because she'd been so upset. "The police are looking for a brunette who had an argument with Voloshin right before he was murdered. They suspect he had a girlfriend, but we know that woman is you, unless another brunette came by later, like maybe Kathleen's mother, but still, I don't know why she would—"

"So what?" Pam checked her watch. "Could you speed it up?"

"So after you leave Voloshin's apartment, sometime during last night, he turns up dead. If the police figure out that you were the brunette, they could suspect you of his murder. They could come question you, like they did me, at your chambers or at home."

Pam stood stunned, blinking. Behind her, a shadow crossed the quarry from a passing cloud.

"You were the last person to see Voloshin alive, and the photos you took are proof that you were in his apartment last night. Now that you sent them to me, and even if you delete them from your phone, we can't delete them from the email server." Jake could see her withdrawing, recoiling as it dawned on her. "Your picture is in the newspaper from time to time, so one of the tenants could have recognized you. Or even if you hadn't been seen, a security camera or even a traffic-light camera could've taken your picture. If the police come to question you, you're done for, and so are we all."

Pam's lips parted, but she still didn't speak.

"Honey, are you okay?" Jake asked gently, reaching for her arm, but she jerked it away, dropping her sunglasses and iPhone. They both bent down to retrieve the items, but she reached them first and snatched them up from the gravel and dirt, then held them to her chest in an oddly protective way.

"Jake. That's not possible, what you're saying." Pam frowned, shaking her head and backing away, her voice softer. "That's impossible. Nobody would think that of me. The police would never think that."

"They could, honey. They came to my office today because I called Voloshin this morning, telling him the transfer would be late. His murder hadn't hit the news by then, but it probably has now—"

"That's why the police came to you? What did you tell them?"

"I told them that Voloshin came to me as a prospective client but that I didn't sign him. I did the best I could, but I couldn't really explain why he sought me out at the basketball game." Jake could see she was getting more upset, backing away from him and shaking her head. "If they get his phone records, the police will see that I was the last person to talk to him last night, but I think I explained that. They didn't ask me if I had an alibi, but they still could. And you, what's your alibi?" Jake didn't ask because she was so distraught, but what he wanted to ask was, *Is Dr. Dave your alibi?*

"Oh no. Oh no." Pam closed her eyes, still clutching her phone and sunglasses. "I put myself on the hook, didn't I? I went over there. I argued with him, loudly. I didn't try to hide. I didn't wear sunglasses or anything. Anyone could have seen me. Anyone could've heard us arguing. Anyone could've seen my car or my license plate. I didn't know someone would *kill* him. Who would *kill* him—"

"Honey, don't worry. We'll figure this out, together." Jake took a step toward her.

"No, leave me alone, I have to go." Pam turned away, hurrying toward her car.

"Pam, please!" Jake hustled after her and caught her arm, but she wrenched it back, tears filling her eyes.

"Don't touch me! Leave me alone! I hate you! You ruined everything, everything, everything!"

"Pam, no—"

"Stay away from me! Stay away from our house!" Pam reached her car and flung open the door. "I'm going home tonight, not you! You won't live there, ever again! It's over, Jake! *We're over!*"

Chapter Thirty-seven

Jake sped away from the quarry, as if his guts had been kicked out of him. He turned onto Concordia Boulevard, its four lanes of traffic beginning to congest with the coming noontime rush, and he steered the car toward home. He wasn't going back to the office and he wanted to look at the pictures from Voloshin's apartment, then figure out if he could delete them from his email server.

We're over!

Jake tried to put Pam's voice out of his mind, but couldn't. He looked through the windshield at the traffic light, but all he saw was her tears. His fingers curled around the plastic steering wheel, but all he could feel was the warmth of her hand under his palm. He had taken that touch for granted. He was trying to wrap his mind around the fact that she had cheated on him, but now it was beginning to sink in that she could really be in love with Dave, and that he had lost his wife forever.

A horn blared behind him, and Jake came out of his reverie, checking the rearview mirror. A massive construction truck was flashing its lights for him to move out of the fast lane. He hit the gas, powered through a yellow light, and reached for his phone, pressing the buttons on-the-fly to call the office.

"Hey, how are you doing?" Amy picked up instantly.

"I'm fine, thanks. Amy, I'm not going to be back to the office for a couple of hours. Can you deal?"

"Totally." Amy paused. "But what's going on? You seem so—"

"I thought I'd work at home. I got nothing done this morning and I don't need any more interruptions."

"Is there anything I can do?"

"Hold the fort and I'll give you a call as soon as I know what my schedule is. Take care."

Jake turned left off of Concordia Boulevard, got home in no time, and hit the house running, letting the door slam closed behind him. Moose waddled out of the kitchen, his fluffy tail wagging slowly.

"Hey buddy," Jake called to the dog, then hurried up the stairs, taking them two at a time, his tie flying. He reached the second-floor landing, slid out of his jacket, and hurried into his home office, where he tossed his jacket onto the couch, plopped down in his desk chair, and hit the mouse to power up his computer.

He opened his email, watched his incoming pile onto the screen, and scanned the countless client emails for Pam's name. Moose trundled into the office, panting from the effort of going up the stairs, in his characteristic *huh-huh-huh*. The golden lumbered over to the desk, and Jake palmed his big head before the dog could start his nudging routine.

Jake found Pam's email, scrolled to the attachments, and clicked OPEN. There was a list of ten photos and he opened the first one. The photo must have been taken from the door to the apartment, and it showed scenes of a tiny galley kitchen next to a small living room, with an old black futon and a wooden coffee table. There was no other furniture in the room, nor were there any books or newspapers. Two windows on the far wall had broken blinds and between them, oddly, was a poster series of tennis player Anna Kornikova.

Jake opened the next few photos, scenes of Voloshin's apartment, messy and nondescript. The following few photos were of a massive black monitor affixed to the wall and surrounded by a floor-to-ceiling entertainment center, also in black, with plastic video games shoved every which way in its crammed shelves. There was a photo of large black speakers and consoles that lined the top shelf, mixed with an array of weird pornographic figurines.

Jake shuddered. He opened the next photo, which was of a black laminate desk cluttered with Red Bull cans, cellophane Tastykake wrappers, and bags with multicolored Skittles strewn amid a dark tangle of joysticks, headsets with microphones, controllers, wires, a mouse, and a large silver laptop.

Jake eyed the laptop, wondering if it had contained the pictures of him and Ryan on Pike Road. Either way, he assumed the killer had taken the laptop. The right edge of the photograph showed a doorjamb that must have led to a bedroom, but that wasn't what caught Jake's eye. What he noticed was the brownish cork edge of a bulletin board on the wall, which must've been the one that Pam mentioned.

Jake clicked open the next photograph and sat back in his seat, trying to absorb the shock. It showed the bulletin board full of curling photos of Kathleen, which looked like they had been printed from the computer; Kathleen at work, company picnics, and softball games, hitting the ball, eating a chili hot dog, or smiling with her arm around her mother, who sported an identical grin. Jake cringed at one of the mother-daughter photos, in which both Kathleen and her mother were wearing matching bunny ears.

"I'm so sorry," he heard himself say, realizing he said it aloud only because Moose nudged his leg. Jake could never begin to imagine the depths of that mother's pain at losing her daughter, and he knew he could never forgive himself for his responsibility for Kathleen's death. Everything that had happened since the hit-and-run followed as inevitably as one domino knocking down another, except that the dominoes were the people he loved the most in the world and the mess was their life as a family.

Jake told himself to get a grip. He scanned the photos again to see if he'd missed anything, but he hadn't. It only confirmed that Voloshin had a crush on Kathleen and that both mother and daughter trusted him as a friend, or they never would've posed for the pictures.

Jake clicked on the last attachment and opened the photo. It showed the left-hand side of the bulletin board, and oddly, it was different from the right-hand side. The pictures were darker, printouts of photos taken at night, and they showed Kathleen running alone or with the track team down Pike Road. In the background was the corporate center and the road that came off of Pike, Dolomite Road. A few of them had thumbtacks in the corner and photos underneath, as if they were a series. One of the photos was taken at twilight in the summertime, with the girls running back toward the school in sweaty Chasers singlets and skimpy shorts, a sight that must've given Voloshin quite a thrill.

Jake noticed two photos on the far right, mostly hidden under the others. They had also been taken at nightfall, but there were no runners in the foreground; one had a woman with a ponytail getting into the passenger side of a dark car parked along the brush on Dolomite Road, its back bumper facing out. The second photo showed two figures sitting in the same car, the driver taller than the woman with the ponytail, more the height of a man. Their heads bent together as if they were kissing, indistinct silhouettes in the front seat.

Jake didn't get it. He moved the mouse and clicked on the photo to enlarge it, but couldn't see the people in the car, whose backs were to him. He squinted at the license plate, which was a Pennsylvania plate, and he could make out only the first three letters, HKE, and none of the digits. A red plastic thumbtack in the corner of the photo suggested, as before, that it was one of the series, but it got Jake wondering.

Who were the people in the photo?

He thought about it, and tried to reason it out. This was a bulletin board about Kathleen, so if Kathleen wasn't one of the people in the car, that would be the only photo *not* of her. So did it mean that Kathleen was meeting a man in a car? Jake enlarged the photo on the screen, trying to read the rest of the license plate, but he couldn't. He scrutinized the silhouette of the man, but couldn't see anything other than he was in the driver's seat and seemed to be of average height and build.

Jake squinted at the car, which looked long enough to be a four-door sedan of some type, and it was navy blue or black because it blended with the background. He enlarged it further, and after a few clicks, was able to read some chrome lettering on the upper left side of its trunk—535.

It was a BMW.

Jake thought about deleting the photos, but hesitated. He was already planning his next move.

Chapter Thirty-eight

Jake turned left onto Pike Road, approaching it from the opposite direction than he had the night of the hit-and-run, when Ryan was driving. There was no car on the street, which ran single lanes in both directions, and no police, runners, or dogwalkers were in sight. His dashboard clock read 1:30, so he was assuming that most of the employees at the corporate center had already gone back to work, and there were no students out yet because school was still in session.

Jake decreased his speed short of the blind curve ahead, with its makeshift memorial. The flowers, candles, and sympathy cards sat in a forlorn pile by the side of the road, and he felt a familiar tightness in his chest at the sight, but he pressed his emotions away. It was strange and risky to return to the scene of the crime, but he wanted to see if he could figure out what Voloshin had been up to, as well as the identity of the people in the BMW sedan.

Jake braked, getting the lay of the land. The blind curve was probably five hundred feet up ahead, then Pike Road jogged to the right, then the left and continued straight. Dolomite Road ran perpendicular to Pike Road, about a hundred feet down from the blind curve, and from where he sat, he could see the corner of Dolomite and Pike Roads. He couldn't see beyond that, farther down on Dolomite Road, because he was at too oblique an angle.

He picked up his iPhone from the passenger seat, scrolled to the camera roll, and retrieved the photo of the sedan from the bulletin board, which he'd enlarged before he left the house. The picture was too dark and unfocused to reveal anything going on inside the sedan, but it did show the sedan's location and orientation on Dolomite Road, which was all Jake needed.

He drew an imaginary line from the back of the sedan, across Pike Road, and into the brush on the left side of the road, working on the assumption that its trajectory would point to Voloshin's location when he took the photo. The only thing on the left side of the road was overgrowth and trees, but he had a theory to test and there was only one way to find out if he was right.

Jake took one last quick look around, turned off the engine, slid the keys out of the ignition, and got out of the car. He reached the undergrowth in four feet, then started making his way through the brush, using his arms to shove aside branches and tangled vines. He worked as quickly as possible because he didn't want to draw any attention to himself. He began to sweat, wishing he'd brought pruning shears.

Jake powered steadily forward, walking a straight line by orienting himself by one of the apartment buildings in the distance, a sandstone low-rise that he kept ahead of him, like the North Star. Twigs snapped under his shoes, and nettles clung to his pants. He consulted the iPhone picture and the sandstone apartments as he kept moving through a grove of evergreens that had grown together in natural tangle.

He passed one tree and behind it found a large area where the grass had been flattened, but it was a large circle, made by resting deer. He kept going, sensing that if he didn't find any-thing soon, he'd missed his guess. He fought his way around ivy that clung to one of the evergreens, and suddenly came upon another flat area, but this one had clearly been man-made. Tree limbs had been pruned back, and sucker vines had been cut. The undergrowth had been flattened but the area wasn't a large circle like deer made. He stood in the middle of the flat area, turned around with his back to the sandstone building, and faced Dolomite Road.

Bingo.

Jake felt his heartbeat quicken. There was a raggedy break through the trees, all the way to the blind curve and to a sec-tion of Dolomite Road. If Voloshin had stood in this spot, he would have had a perfect view—the same view as the photos of Ryan and him that had been taken, exactly where the hit-and-run accident occurred.

Jake's stomach twisted. Voloshin had aimed his camera as if it were a rifle and he'd managed to catch Ryan, Jake, and now, Pam in his crosshairs. And the evergreens would have screened Voloshin from view, and the little pervert would also have been free to spy on Kathleen and photograph her whenever he wanted, especially if he knew her schedule and worked from home often enough that he didn't have to account to the office for his time. Voloshin had set himself up like a hunter in a blind, wait-ing for the girls to run by.

Jake looked down, and a few white berries caught his eye, oddly bright in the brownish underbrush. He bent down, moved the undergrowth aside, and picked up the berries, examining them. They weren't berries at all. He flashed on the photo of Voloshin's desk, with its bags of Skittles. The white berries were candy, their coating washed away by the rain, probably dropped by Voloshin during one of his stalker sessions.

Jake hurried back the same way he came, keeping the sand-stone apartment building directly behind him, moving tree limbs and vines out of his path until he reached the edge of the woods. He stalked through the grass at the edge of Pike Road, hustled to his car, jumped inside, and started the engine. Luckily, there was still no one on the street.

He hit the gas and cruised forward, approaching the blind curve. He glanced over at the memorial as he passed it, sending up a silent prayer for Kathleen, then took a right. His destination was Dolomite Road and it lay just ahead, at a ninety degree angle to Pike. He turned right onto Dolomite, orienting himself, slowing his speed and taking in the surroundings.

The street was quiet and still, with no cars or foot traffic. On its left side was the parking lot that surrounded Concordia Corporate Center, which was screened from the street by thick landscaped hedges and zigzagging evergreens. On the right side of the street were more overgrown woods and trees, the parcel evidently unused.

Jake drove down the street and noticed that the left side of the street stayed the same, with the thick landscaped greenery that screened the corporate center, but on the right side, the woods stooped for a clearing of a few homes, newish clapboard colonials, one of which had a FOR SALE sign out front. He drove to the end of the street, which veered left and led to one of the remote parking lots of the corporate center, where a group of black Goren's Janitorial vans were parked.

Jake turned around and cruised back up Dolomite Road, heading toward Pike Road. He passed the houses on his left and slowed his speed when he got to the place where he thought the BMW sedan had been parked. He braked, cut the ignition, and got out of the car.

"Sir!" said a man's voice. "Stop right there! Sir!"

Jake froze. It had to be the police or security for the corporate center. He didn't see anyone. The voice came from beyond the hedges.

"What are you doing, sir? You hold on! Right there!"

"Okay, sure." Jake's mouth went dry, and there was a rustling in the evergreens and movement of the limbs as an older man emerged, dressed in an insulated purplish-blue jumpsuit, with a white patch that read CONCORDIA CORPORATE CENTER. His face was a network of wrinkles, his bifocals slid down his bony nose, and he was as lean and worn as the rake he carried.

"Where do you work, sir? You got the bulletin, didn't you? I was told all the tenants got the bulletin!"

"I don't work here." Jake crossed to his car door, but the old man held up a gnarled hand.

"There's no more parking back here! I don't know when you people are going to learn!"

"I wasn't parking here." Jake thought fast. "I was thinking about buying that house at the end of the street. Do people park here a lot? Is that a problem? If it is, I don't want to buy the house."

"Oh, beg pardon." The old man seemed to stand down, leaning on the rake. "You don't want to buy a house on this street, not unless you like a peep show. This is a lovers' lane, that's what we used to call it. Everybody comes here to park 'n spark."

"You mean from the high school?" Jake's ears perked up.

"Hell, no! I mean our tenants! From these businesses." The old man gestured back to the corporate center. "They got so many women working here now, and there's all kinda tomfoolery goes on here at lunch. You'd be surprised what I find in these bushes this time o' day! Cigarette butts, beer cans, *rubbers*! Disgusting! They have a *damn* good time in these cars! Every morning, too, from partyin' that goes on after work!"

"I bet." Jake opened his car door. "I'll be going now. I appreciate your giving me the information. It doesn't sound like a great place for the kids."

"No sir, no way! Nice talking to you. Bye now."

"Take care." Jake started the engine, steered down Dolomite, and turned right on Pike Road. He felt like he was getting closer to something, but he didn't know what. He assumed for a minute that it was Kathleen in the photograph of the BMW sedan, because if it hadn't been, Voloshin would have no reason to put it on his bulletin board with the other photographs of her. If Voloshin had been in his duck blind, watching Kathleen on one of her nighttime runs, he could have discovered that she wasn't running, but meeting someone on Dolomite Road.

Jake took a right turn, preoccupied. His theory made sense because it answered some of the questions he'd had earlier, like why was Kathleen running alone so late at night? Maybe it wasn't unusual for the track team, but what if Kathleen was using running as a pretense to get out of the house at night? What if she was going to Dolomite Road to meet someone, in a car? But who was she meeting? Someone whom Kathleen was keeping a secret, probably from her mother, if she was meeting him in a car.

Jake turned right and joined the traffic on Concordia Boulevard. Ahead lay the manicured main entrance to the corporate center, with its varietal grasses in mulched beds, around the brown sign that read CONCORDIA CORPORATE CENTER, HOME TO AMERICAN BUSINESS! Underneath that was a listing of corporate tenants; Brej Construction Management, Moxico, LLC, Valley Tech, SMS, Goren's Janitorial, Branson Hospitality Services, with a subhead that read FORTUNE'S 100 BEST COMPANIES TO WORK FOR! He scanned the list as he approached, thinking that the most likely person to know about the lovers' lane on Dolomite Road was someone who worked at one of these businesses. He reached the entrance and on impulse, turned right into its campus.

If he got lucky, he'd spot a dark BMW with an HKE license plate.

Chapter Thirty-nine

Jake cruised the parking lot and scanned a row that held a gray Toyota, a lemony VW Beetle, a white Acura, and an older brown Honda, his thoughts churning. If Voloshin had discovered that Kathleen was meeting a lover, he could have become jealous, even angry. What if Voloshin had tried to blackmail her lover, the way he tried to blackmail Jake? Voloshin could have threatened to tell the man's wife, if the man was married, or to tell Kathleen's mother, or even the authorities, because Kathleen was underage. The lover would be guilty of statutory rape if it came to light that he'd had sex with Kathleen.

Jake surveyed the parked cars, cruising past the bumper stickers and decals. MY CAT CAN BEAT UP YOUR HONOR STUDENT, a navy blue Nittany Lion, a white circle for Academy of Notre Dame de Namur, an oval 13.1 decal, and a puzzle piece for Autism Awareness. He didn't see the BMW yet, and his head was full of questions. What if Voloshin had tried to blackmail the BMW driver, but unlike Jake, the man hadn't come up with blackmail money? Or what if the man in the BMW had been the one who murdered Voloshin?

Jake's fingers clenched around the steering wheel, and he drove down one line of parked cars, then the other. The police would have seen the bulletin board in Voloshin's apartment, unless the killer took it. He assumed for a moment that the killer took the bulletin board, along with the laptop and phone, then he rejected that as highly unlikely. If the killer were a burglar, no burglar would take a bulletin board, and it would attract attention to be hurrying from the apartment with a large, unwieldy bulletin board.

Jake spotted BMWs, but they were the wrong color, too, so he drove on, mentally testing his theory. The killer could have gotten away with taking only the photo of the sedan parked on Dolomite Road, but that was unlikely too. The photo was half-hidden and someone who committed murder would be in a hurry to escape. Jake drove preoccupied past USPS mailboxes, FedEx, DHL, and UPS drop-offs, and the endless signage that replaced trees; THIS IS A TOBACCO FREE WORKPLACE, SPEED LIMIT 10, UNAUTHORIZED VEHICLES TOWED AT OWNER'S EXPENSE, ADDITIONAL PARKING ON OTHER SIDE OF BUILDING, ALL VISITORS PLEASE CHECK IN AT 200 CONCORDIA PARKWAY.

Jake navigated to another section of the parking lot and surveyed the cars, but they seemed to recede into the background as he realized something awful. If the killer looked inside Voloshin's computer and phone, then he would know what actually happened the night of the accident on Pike Road, that he and Ryan were responsible for Kathleen's death. And the killer would also know that Jake was being blackmailed, too. The police had said that they had seen evidence that Voloshin was setting up an offshore account.

Jake felt a new tingle of fear, and another set of questions rushed at him. If the killer had feelings for Kathleen, he could want revenge on those responsible for her death. What if the killer decided to come after Ryan? Or him, or Pam? Jake had to find out who killed Voloshin, so he could protect his family.

His troubles weren't over with Voloshin's death, they were just beginning. Whoever the killer was, he was a lot more dangerous than Voloshin.

Jake headed down another aisle of cars and checked each one, redoubling his efforts. Who was the killer? How did Kathleen find him? If her mother didn't know about him, did any of her friends? How could such a nice young girl be mixed up with somebody ruthless enough to stab a man to death? Suddenly his phone started ringing, and he checked the screen. It was Pam calling, and he picked up. "Yes?"

"Listen, I don't have much time. We're on break during oral arguments." Pam's tone was clipped and professional. "I just spoke with Ryan. He called me."

"Okay, what's up?" Jake sensed Pam was telling him that Ryan called her, not him, as if they still were playing tug-of-war with their son.

"There's a memorial program tonight at school for Kathleen. The team is going, and he has to go with them."

"Oh no." Jake pulled over and parked, so he could focus. "That'll be tough for him. Can't he get out of it? Can't we say he got sick again?"

"No. He has to go. We have to go, too. He'll need the support. You have to leave work early. The program starts at six thirty."

"Okay, fine." Jake didn't bother explaining that he wasn't at work. "But honey, listen, we have to settle this. I can't move out now. You have to let me stay home."

"No I don't. Get a hotel room. No one has to know. We'll keep it a secret. You're good at that."

"Pam, I don't think you and Ryan should be alone in the house right now. It's not safe."

"You're just saying that because you don't want to break up."

"That's not true. I'm saying it because you could be in danger. So could we all. The more I think about it, the more I worry that whoever killed Voloshin could come after us—"

"I thought you were worried about the police. Now a murderer's coming after me? What is this, scare tactics?"

"No. It could happen, babe. I looked at those pictures you took and I figured out that Kathleen was meeting someone in secret. I'm thinking he's the guy who killed Voloshin—"

"So what are you saying? I need a bodyguard?"

Jake hadn't gotten that far in his thinking. "You might—"

"Oh, great! Of course we can't go to the police, or Ryan goes to jail. My son goes to jail!"

"That won't happen."

"What do we do then? Got any ideas?"

"We can talk about it tonight. I need you to be careful. Keep an eye out when you're driving or when you—"

"Jake, if you're trying to scare me into staying in this marriage, it won't work. You don't understand the damage you've done. You don't get it."

"We can fix it. I can fix it."

"No we can't," Pam shot back. "I didn't go outside the marriage because I wanted to, I went out because I had to. I'm not proud of it, but it is what it is. And we gave it a shot, which you totally destroyed. I'm making myself crazy, going over it and over it in my head. If we had broken up, you wouldn't have been in the car Friday night with Ryan. None of this would have happened."

"You can't think that way. You don't know that—"

"Yes, I do. Get your head out of the sand, Jake. It's over. It has to be. We can't go back, we just can't. I can't. I'm *done*. I can't forgive you, ever. I want a divorce."

"Babe, listen, I love you, and no matter what problems we're having, we have to get through this together. Even tonight, we have to put up a united front, for Ryan's sake."

"You're saying that for you, not for him."

"No, I'm not. You know this is killing him, and we have to

make sure he keeps it together. He's cutting classes, getting high, messing up in basketball. God knows what he could do next. He needs us both—"

"You're shameless! Since when are you so sensitive to our son? Since he started taking your side? Since he decided *I'm* the bad guy?"

Jake told himself to remain calm. "Pam, you said you don't have time to talk, so let's not waste time fighting."

"It's so unfair to me, Jake!" Pam raised her voice. "This is unfair to me *and* him! You're the one who put us in this impossible situation! You're the one who told him it was okay to drive in the first place!"

"We've been over this—"

"But somehow, I'm the one who's a murder suspect, and now, a *target*! That girl would be alive if not for you!"

Jake felt the truth in her words, and her contempt for him, like a knife to the chest. "I know that, believe me, I know that every minute. But as far as we go, you and me, please just let me live at home, at least for the foreseeable future."

"Damn you! Damn you for doing this! You're putting me in a corner!"

"No, I'm trying to make the best of it. We have to stay together. You want to kick me out later, fine, but for right now, let's agree to disagree."

"I'll be *damned* if I'll pretend that everything is fine!"

"You don't have to."

"You're damn right I don't! This is awful, Jake, all the way down—"

"I know that—"

"It's awful and it's all your fault. Now you're telling me we're in *danger* and all of it is *your fault*!"

"Honey, I'm sorry, I've said it a thousand times, and I mean it—"

"Wait, hold on." Pam lowered her voice, as if someone had come into the room. "See you at home by six fifteen. Don't be late."

"Okay, bye," Jake said, but Pam had already hung up.

Chapter Forty

The sky was beginning to darken, and an early chill came on. Jake had searched the parking lot at the corporate center over an hour, with no luck. He'd found three black BMWs, but one had a New Jersey license plate and none had a plate with HKE. It was still his theory that the killer worked at the corporate center, though he kept it open as a possibility that the killer worked elsewhere and used Dolomite Road to park, finding it on his own.

Jake parked in his driveway and walked to his front door, glancing over his shoulder to make sure he hadn't been followed by the detectives or anyone else. Nothing on their street was amiss, and there were no cars he didn't recognize. The houses stood quiet because nobody was home from work yet.

Jake unlocked the door and let himself in, but Moose didn't greet him. He stopped, feeling a glimmer of worry, but heard voices talking in the kitchen and one of them was Ryan's. "Ryan?" Jake called out, puzzled. "You're home?"

"Hey, Dad! We're in the kitchen!"

We? "Hi! Be right in." Jake tossed his keys on the console table and slid out of his jacket, noting that his sleeve had tiny tears from the thornbushes. He set the jacket on the chair and walked to the kitchen, where Ryan was sitting at the table with a girl Jake didn't know. Soda cans, an open bag of hard pretzels, and crumpled napkins covered the table, next to an open laptop and two stuffed backpacks. Moose sat next to Ryan's chair, sniffing the pretzel bag, his tongue lolling out of his mouth.

"Dad, this is Sabrina, from the track team." Ryan flushed, gesturing at the girl, who looked tall and wiry, and her long, dark red hair was tied back in a floppy double ponytail. She had on a gray dress, whose short sleeves showed the ripped arms of a runner. Her eyes were grayish, and tiny freckles dotted her largish nose and cheekbones, which were pronounced, even a little gaunt, like someone with zero body fat.

"Hey, Mr. Buckman." Sabrina half-smiled, showing a row of Invisalign braces. "Nice to meet you."

"Hi, Sabrina." Jake crossed to the refrigerator, opened the door, and slid out a can of Diet Coke. He wished he could talk to Ryan alone and see how he was doing, because he seemed subdued and disheveled, with his bangs in his eyes and his blue polo shirt wrinkled.

"Dad, did Mom tell you about the memorial assembly tonight for Kathleen Lindstrom?"

"Yes, that's why I'm home early. How was school?" Jake avoided Ryan's eye while the awkward moment passed. He had no idea how his son would get through such a difficult evening, knowing what they had done and having to put on a false face for all of his classmates.

"Fine, good." Ryan met his eye briefly, then looked away.

"What happened to practice?" Jake leaned against the counter. He didn't like the fact that Ryan was alone in the house, with God-knows-who watching.

"They canceled it because of the assembly tonight. The whole athletic department's going."

"I see. How did you get home?"

"Sabrina's mom dropped us off. We can take her to school with us, after Mom gets home. That's okay, right?" Ryan's expression looked guarded, and Jake knew he was giving him the heads-up.

"Sure, great. So what are you guys doing? Homework?"

"No," Ryan answered. "Sabrina has to give a speech tonight at the assembly, and I'm helping her. Rather, I'm supposed to be helping her, but we're not doing so great."

"I'm sure you're helping." Jake cringed inwardly, on Ryan's behalf.

Sabrina frowned at the laptop, tucking a strand of long red hair behind her ear. "I suck at writing. I freeze up. Ryan's one of the best writers in the class, that's why I asked him to help me. I don't know how to do this, especially this, like, a eulogy. It's too hard."

Jake felt a stab of guilt. "I'm sorry about your loss. Was Kathleen a good friend of yours?"

"Not really, because she just came this year, so it wasn't like I had that much time to get to know her. I'm team captain, and Coach wants me to do it . . ." Sabrina faltered. "I just can't believe Kathleen's really gone. It's so . . . weird."

Ryan looked away.

Jake nodded, pained. "I'm sure it's difficult. I know."

Sabrina kept shaking her head. "I'm supposed to give this speech, but I don't know what to say and I don't want to say the wrong thing. I can't speak in front of all of those people. Kathleen's mom is going to be there and her father, and my parents and everybody in the school will be there, waiting for me to say something, and I mean, *everything* I write sounds lame." Sabrina deflated, and her gaze returned to the laptop. "But I still have to write this speech, and I don't know what to say. I don't have that much time left and what I wrote so far really sucks."

"No, it doesn't." Ryan motioned at the laptop. "You have a good start."

"Argh." Sabrina moaned. "No I don't, and Coach said it has to be, like, three hundred words. I only have forty words so far, and I worked on it the entire study hall. I can't do it. Mr. Buckman, can you help?"

"Sure." Jake faked an encouraging smile.

"I'll read you what I have so far." Sabrina hunched over the laptop. "First, and this doesn't count for the words, I have to introduce myself and say thank you to everyone for coming, like to the faculty and families. Right?"

"Right."

"Okay. Then, I say," Sabrina read from the laptop, " 'The Lady Chasers and Concord Chase High School in general suffered an extremely tragic loss when Kathleen Lindstrom was killed last Friday night in a horrible hit-and-run accident. Everybody loved Kathleen, who was friendly, outgoing, an asset to our team, a great hurdler, and fun to be with.' " She looked up. "Mr. Buckman, what do you think?"

"That's a great start." Jake was trying to say something helpful, but the words practically lodged in his throat. "Keep going."

"But I don't know what to write next. I'm sucking. I can't do this." Sabrina buckled her lower lip. "It's so horrible that she died and it's even worse that the guy didn't even stop and see if she was okay. People like that should be *shot*. I should say that, I should give a speech about *that*."

"No, just keep going. You can do it. Write what you feel."

"I *can't* write what I feel. I feel sad and weirded out, that's all. We all are, so *sad*. I don't know how we'll run without her. We'll lose to Methacton for sure. Nobody wants to run. I think we should cancel the meet. We just cry, like, all the time. Her wake is tomorrow, and we're going in uniform, like a tribute to her."

Jake felt terrible and he knew Ryan did, too. "Then write about Kathleen. Write about what she was like, as a person."

"That's what I tried to do, but I can't." Sabrina sighed again. "That's why I said she was friendly and nice and everything, but I didn't know her that well, and we weren't that friendly, then she got tight with Courtney and Sarah and Janine Mae. I'm not good at giving speeches, anyway. I can't do this. I should've told Coach that I can't do it and it's really too important and I'm failing at it, epically."

Ryan shook his head. "No, you're not. You're doing fine."

"I'm not, I *suck out loud*! I'm going to let everyone *down*!"

Ryan shrugged. "Why don't you tell a story about her? Sometimes if you tell a story about somebody, that tells the audience something about them. Like we studied about in *The Great Gatsby*. People tell stories about Gatsby before you even meet him."

"Great idea," Jake said, grateful. "It will cheer them up, too."

"Och." Sabrina dropped her chin into her palm. "There's a lot of stories about her, but I don't know if they're good enough to tell."

"Like what?" Ryan asked, swallowing visibly.

"Like she really liked to sing on the bus, and she had a good voice, but that's not good enough." Sabrina cocked her head. "Well, also, she was superhot and all the guys on the boys' team really liked her, but that's not a good story to tell at something like this, either. Right, Ryan?" Sabrina turned to him, knitting her forehead. "Like remember when Sam and Caleb, they both asked her to the Halloween dance? That's not a good story, is it?"

"No." Ryan flushed.

Jake stepped in to rescue him. "Sabrina, I think Ryan means you should tell a story about her, about something she did."

"Oh, right. Totally." Sabrina thought a moment. "She was really good with computer graphics, and she made an awesome website for the travel track team. It had animated gifs and everything." Sabrina brightened, straightening in her chair. "In fact, oh, I have a good story, a better one. There was the time she raised the money to buy shirts for the travel team, that's a good story. We all had the same singlets, but our gym bags and

T-shirts didn't match. We never looked as good as the other travel teams, like Great Valley always looked awesome. They even had matching scrunchies, blue-and-white."

Ryan nodded, with a shaky smile. "Good. Then tell that."

"But that's not the story. Your dad said tell a story about her, like something she did. That doesn't tell what she did. I didn't get to that part yet."

"Okay." Ryan pursed his lips, and Jake could see that was the last thing he wanted to know. He prayed Ryan could get through tonight and the next few weeks. Jake would never forgive himself if Ryan tried to hurt himself. He'd quit Gardenia and go on twenty-four-hour suicide watch, if that's what it took.

"Anyway, Kathleen got everybody together and she got this idea where we would stuff envelopes for free to get the money for the T-shirts, and we all worked together and we had the money in, like, four weekends, all because of her." Sabrina brightened. "And the coolest thing was that we all had fun, like we weren't doing another stupid bake sale or standing out in front of the Acme, begging for money in front of an oaktag sign, like we were Brownies or something. It was like we worked for our T-shirts, all of us together, the way a team should be. It was a really different idea and she thought it up herself." Sabrina stopped abruptly, her smile fading. "Except she won't even get to see the gym bags. They didn't come in yet. We got the T-shirts and the scrunchies, but the gym bags take longer. She'll never get to see them . . . now."

Ryan paled. He didn't say anything, and neither did Jake. The only sound in the kitchen was the *huh-huh-huh* of Moose's panting.

Sabrina looked over at Ryan, her eyes shining. "Ryan, what do you think? Is that a good enough story?"

Ryan sighed heavily, but couldn't even muster up a smile. "It's great, Sabrina. Just great."

Chapter Forty-one

Night fell hard and cold, and White Springs Road was congested with stop-and-go traffic, heading to the high school for the memorial service. Jake sat in the passenger seat, tense, while Pam drove them in silence. They'd exchanged pleasantries for show at home, putting up a false front for the kids, and she'd freshened up, drained a cup of coffee, and changed her shoes. She drove without looking at him, sitting ramrod-straight, her eyes fixed on the road.

We can't go back, we just can't. I can't. I'm done. I can't forgive you, ever.

It hurt Jake to be so close to her, in the familiar intimacy of her car, while she walled him off. He knew that she had to be dreading going to the service tonight, and she felt all the guilt and shame he did, but with an overlay of anger and resentment. He wished he could comfort her, but he was the cause of her pain. Their coats touched, but they couldn't. He could smell her perfume, but he couldn't kiss her. He was married to her, but she wanted a divorce. She had slept with someone else, maybe even last night. He felt heartbroken and furious, both at once.

The kids rode in the backseat, their heads bent over their iPhones and their ears plugged with earbuds. Ryan didn't text at all, but listened to music, and Sabrina rehearsed her speech, whispering to herself like a nightmare voiceover, ". . . a tragic loss for the track team and the Concord Chase High School community as a whole . . ."

They stopped behind a long line of cars, plumes of exhaust floating into the air like ghosts. Jake tried to tune Sabrina out, but wasn't succeeding. She was whispering, ". . . and she had so many talents and hobbies, for example, she was excellent with computer graphics and made a super-professional website for . . ."

They were almost at the high school, which was just around the corner. A dark van inched beside them in the right lane, and Jake looked over. Inside the van was a couple just like them, except the man was driving. A younger kid played a handheld video game in the backseat, his face wreathed in eerie green-blue light. Jake had checked every passing car to make sure it wasn't the dark BMW, the detectives, or otherwise suspicious.

The traffic eased, and Pam steered right around the corner onto Racton Hill Road. Flashing police lights sliced through the black night, from cruisers out in force, parked on the curb. Cops grouped on the sidewalk, and Jake realized that they were just directing traffic to the high school. One motioned the cars to keep moving, waving a flashlight with an orange cone.

Jake thought of the detectives and worried if they would interview him again. Would they just drop in or call first? Did he need a lawyer? Did Ryan? Should he call Hubbard? Jake hadn't gotten a chance to talk to Pam alone yet. She would get a lawyer, probably a separate one from him and Ryan. And she'd get a divorce lawyer, too.

"We're late," Pam muttered under her breath.

They were only at the middle school, and Jake could see the high school ahead on the left, a long, two-story box of red brick, its continuous panels of windows ablaze with light. "Not very."

"That's not the point. Late is late."

"So will everybody else be, in this traffic."

"Again. Not the point."

Jake let it go. He was trying to make it better, but that was impossible. They were going to the memorial service for a young girl they had killed, and they were ruined, guilty, and afraid. A corrupt family, bound by a secret crime. Bankrupt, despite the money they had. Nothing could be made better.

The traffic eased, and the car began to move forward. Pam exhaled. "Finally."

Jake didn't say anything. He could hear Sabrina whispering, like a prayer, ". . . Kathleen was an extreme loss for the Concord Chase High School community in its entirety . . ."

"How'd your Western Civ make-up go, Ryan?" Pam asked, tilting her mouth up as if she were talking to the rearview mirror.

"Fine," Ryan answered, after a moment.

"How do you think you did?"

"Fine."

"Really?" Pam arched an eyebrow, edging up in the driver's seat.

"What, did you look on the Parent Portal?"

"Yes. Did you?"

"No. He graded my test already?"

"Yes."

"What did I get, Mom?"

"Don't worry about it. You'll do better next time."

Ryan didn't reply.

Sabrina whispered, ". . . Speaking as the captain of the track team, I can assure you that Kathleen will be sorely missed by every . . ."

Jake turned to Ryan, who looked crestfallen. "Don't sweat it, buddy."

Ryan didn't say anything to him, either.

Jake turned back around, pained. He didn't want to think about what would happen to Ryan if he and Pam divorced. His son was already depressed and guilt-ridden. It wouldn't help that he'd ping-pong back and forth between their houses. Jake would become a weekend father, if that. Everything had gone to shit because of his decision on Pike Road. In trying to be a good father, he'd been a terrible father. In trying to save his son, he'd destroyed him. He'd driven his wife away. He'd lost everything.

Story of my life.

Sabrina said, ". . . there are so many cool stories about Kathleen, like that she sang the loudest on the bus, and that everyone on the guys team wanted to take her out, but there is one main story I know that will tell the audience about her . . ."

Jake felt his chest tighten as they reached the lighted brick CONCORD CHASE HIGH SCHOOL sign and turned into the entrance, where another cop directed them to keep moving toward the back, behind the school.

"Damn." Pam sighed. "They're sending us to the lot by the tennis courts. It'll be a long walk." She shifted up to the rearview mirror, slowing the car. "Ryan, Sabrina? You guys want to get out here, since we're running late?"

"No," Ryan answered, after a moment.

"But honey, you won't get a seat."

"The team will save me one."

Sabrina said, "I'll stay. I'm good."

"Okay." Pam fed the car some gas, and they approached the entrance doors on the right, then they stopped again in the line of traffic. A thick crowd thronged under the lighted canopy that covered the entrance doors, and at the perimeter, a TV news crew filmed a pretty anchorwoman raising a bubble microphone to a tall, well-dressed man with dark hair, talking in the bright white klieglights.

Pam snorted. "I can't believe TV people are here. They're

vultures. Have they no shame? Does the world really need another man-on-the-street interview?"

Jake felt his heart sink, on Ryan's behalf. He could see for himself that Kathleen's death shocked the entire school community, and he had underestimated how difficult this would be for Ryan. His son lived in this world and he'd have to deal with it, every day, all day at school. Jake glanced back to check on him again, but Ryan was looking pointedly away from the TV cameras.

Sabrina leaned forward. "Mrs. Buckman, the guy they're interviewing is Kathleen's dad. I saw his picture online, asking if the community could help him find who killed Kathleen."

"Poor man," Pam said quietly, and Jake realized that the only thing they shared tonight was guilt. He eyed Kathleen's father talking in the klieglights and realized he was just another father like him. Jake had taken that man's child, in trade for his own.

Pam drove along the road, which continued between the school on the right and the main parking lot on the left. She seemed distracted by something in the parking lot, and Jake craned his neck to see. It was Dr. Dave, getting out of a white Prius and chirping it locked. A woman in a black down coat stood with him, presumably his wife.

Jake gritted his teeth. She had a pretty face and a sweet smile, and her short brown hair ruffled in the wind. He wondered if she knew that she had been cheated on, or if she was as naïve as he had been. The couple left the parking lot and crossed the road with the crowd, right in front of their headlights.

Jake itched to get out and beat Dr. Dave to a pulp, but Dr. Dave walked straight ahead, acting as if he didn't recognize Pam's car. Jake looked over to see Pam's reaction, but she stared straight ahead, too. Just then he noticed a car in the parking lot, sitting a few rows back, to the right—it was a black BMW sedan, with an HKE license plate.

My God. "Pam, hold on, be right back," Jake blurted out, reaching for the door handle.

"No, Jake, please don't." Pam turned to him in alarm.

"It's not what you think." Jake flung open the door. "I see a client I need to talk to. See you inside."

"Wait a sec, there's a space," Pam said, but Jake was out the door, hitting the ground running.

Chapter Forty-two

Jake hurried through the parking lot, going against the crowd heading toward the school entrance. One of the mothers looked over at him curiously, so he slowed his pace as he made a beeline for the BMW. He didn't want to draw attention to himself. He hadn't thought about the possibility he'd see the BMW here, but he'd been focused on Ryan and Pam.

Jake threaded his way through the crowd, squeezed sideways between parked cars, and finally reached the BMW. It was the correct model, a 535, and its Pennsylvania plate read HKE-7553. It had to be the same car as the one in the photograph. His heartbeat quickened. So Voloshin's killer was at Kathleen's memorial service. It seemed risky, unless the killer was someone who would have been conspicuous by his absence, the way Ryan would have been if he hadn't come.

Jake glanced around and ascertained that no one was watching him, so he walked to the driver's side of the car and tried the door handle, but it was locked. He peeked inside the front seat. The car had a black interior and it was hard to see in the dark, but it looked empty and gave no clue as to the driver's identity. He peered in the backseat, but it was also empty. He walked around the trunk and checked for the car dealership, or anything to give him more information about the driver, but there wasn't one listed. The license plate had a chrome surround, but it read BMW, with no dealership.

Jake slipped his hand in his pocket, took out his phone, and snapped a picture of the car's license plate, then turned away and hurried back to the school entrance, adrenalized. So the BMW driver would be at the service tonight, and the more Jake thought about it, the more credibility it lent to his theory. The driver had known Kathleen, maybe even loved her, and he could have killed Voloshin because Voloshin was blackmailing him about their relationship—or maybe in a fit of rage, when he went to Voloshin's apartment and saw that Voloshin was stalking her.

Jake joined the crowd going into the entrance, turning his head away from the TV cameras and scrutinizing the people around him. The killer could be any one of the dads, who looked just like him—a moving mass of crow's-feet, expensive haircuts, and Patagonia jackets slipped over shirts and ties, because nobody had time to change after work. They tossed away forbidden cigarettes, checked their email, or talked on the phone, making their last calls.

Jake caught snippets of their conversations—*you have to be kidding me, Tom, you didn't file it yet?*—or with their wives—*I don't have time to call the roofer, can you?*—or their kids—*so how was school, buddy?* None of them sounded or seemed like a killer, which made Jake suspect all of them, everyone around him. Then he realized he wouldn't have to play guessing games anymore. He could leave the memorial service, stake-out the BMW, and see whoever came to claim the car.

Jake's heartbeat picked up, and he thought of a new plan. He would confront the killer and warn him to stay away from Ryan and Pam—or risk exposure to the police. It would be piling one corrupt bargain on top of another, but it would keep Pam and Ryan safe. He reached the entrance doors, went through, and crossed the threshold into a large, tiled entrance area leading to the administrative offices and the auditorium.

CHASER PRIDE, read a poster-painted banner, and the crowd flowed in two messy lines to the auditorium doors, which had been propped open. Suddenly it struck him that Pam and Ryan were here, unprotected. The killer would know who they were, but they wouldn't know who he was. The killer could be following Ryan or taking a seat next to Pam, this very minute.

Jake pressed forward, looking for Pam or Ryan, but he didn't see them anywhere. He didn't know if they'd gone inside, but assumed they had, knowing that Pam was in a hurry and she'd seen that parking space. He shifted to the right, went around a large family, and joined the other line into the auditorium, which was moving faster. Still, no Pam or Ryan.

Jake finally got inside the auditorium, which was standing room only in back, and wedged his way through the standees to find Pam and Ryan, but they weren't there. He scanned the audience for Pam and Ryan, but there were so many people it was impossible to see them. Faculty, staff, parents, and younger kids filled the seats, walked down rows, tilted their heads together in conversation, checked smartphones, opened programs, or hoisted toddlers onto their laps. Many of the female students were crying, their arms around each other. Mothers wiped tears from their eyes, and fathers craned their necks toward the front, where the program was beginning.

Jake defaulted to looking for Ryan because he was so tall and would be sitting with a very tall group, the basketball team. He began methodically, noticing that two aisles ran the length of the auditorium, dividing the seats into three sections. He checked the leftmost section for the basketball team, but no luck. He checked the middle section, but didn't see them there. He shifted to the rightmost section and finally spotted a tall bunch of scruffy boys on the far right section, at the middle.

He edged forward and looked for Ryan, but he wasn't sitting with the team and there was an empty seat at the end of the row. Jake swallowed hard, beginning to be afraid. What if Ryan and Pam were still outside? What if the killer had intercepted them on the way in? He didn't want to leave and go see until he was sure they weren't in the auditorium.

The crowd quieted, and Jake sensed the program was about to start. He glanced at the stage, a sleek maple curve framed by maroon curtains, and a middle-aged woman tapped a microphone on the lectern. Next to her were the flags of the United States and the Commonwealth of Pennsylvania, then a row of brown folding chairs with some students and school-administration types, and finally, an easel that held an enlarged photograph of Kathleen, framed in black.

Jake's throat caught, but he looked away. Then it struck him that the speakers were supposed to be seated on the stage and that Sabrina was slated to be a speaker. He looked again at the folding chairs, but Sabrina wasn't there. And one folding chair remained empty.

"Welcome, ladies and gentlemen, faculty, students and family. I am Pamela Coleridge, principal of Concord Chase High School, and I thank you for coming this evening to celebrate the life of Kathleen Lindstrom, a lovely young woman who was taken from us cruelly, and too soon . . ."

Jake tuned the speaker out, his heart thudding in his chest. The empty chair on stage was proof that Ryan and Pam must still be in the parking lot, unless Sabrina was sitting with her team.

". . . this program will be brief, and time won't permit us to acknowledge all of the special people here tonight, except that I would like to take a moment to acknowledge Kathleen's mother Grace and her father William, both of whom are with us, at this impossibly difficult time. They're seated in the front row . . ."

Heads turned this way and that as everybody tried to see Kathleen's parents, and murmurs and sniffles rippled through the crowd. Jake tried to find the girls track team, but there was nothing to distinguish them from any other female students.

". . . our first speaker will be Ms. Talia Kelso, who teaches computer science and runs our computer lab, which, as you may know, was Kathleen's home away from home. Ms. Kelso, please come up . . ."

Jake noticed on the stage that one of the teachers, a petite African-American woman with a thick braid, was getting up from the folding chair and crossing to the lectern. He had to find Ryan and Pam, or Sabrina, so he kept scanning the crowd. He surveyed the rows for them, getting more worried by the minute, as the speaker continued her speech.

". . . Kathleen had a remarkable aptitude with computers, but it was her happy, upbeat way that all of us loved. I will never forget Kathleen and neither will any of my teaching assistants in the computer lab. Thank you, and now I would like to introduce our next speaker, Janine Mae Lamb, a junior who was a very good friend of Kathleen. Janine Mae?"

Jake paused, recognizing the name of the girl that Ryan had wanted to date before the accident. He watched as a pretty, petite girl in a black dress rose uncertainly on stage and walked to the lectern with her head downcast, her long blonde hair obscuring her face. Ms. Kelso hovered behind the lectern as Janine Mae reached it and grasped its edges for support. When the young girl raised her eyes to the audience, Jake could tell, even from a distance, that she was crestfallen and already teary.

"Hi, everyone," Janine Mae said, her voice shaking, her drawl pained. "Kathleen's mom and dad, Mr. and Mrs. Lindstrom . . . I know how much you loved Kathleen . . . and I'm so sorry about your loss . . . and I wanted to, uh, speak about her tonight . . . I don't know if I can, but . . . I'll try . . . for her."

Jake swallowed hard, and the audience fell into an anguished silence, holding its collective breath at the rawness of the girl's grief.

"I'm up here because I just really want everyone to know Kathleen . . . the way I did." Janine Mae wiped her eyes with a small hand. "We met, uh, the first day of track, and since we were both new to Concord Chase . . . and, uh, neither of us knew anybody . . . we bonded, like, uh, instantly." Janine Mae sniffled, and her shoulders began to shake. "You never would have known that Kathleen was new . . . she was so friendly and open-hearted . . . and she trusted everyone. We only knew each other for a few months . . . but we really got super close . . . and . . . we told each other . . . everything." Janine burst into a sob, making a heartrending hiccup into the microphone. "Kathleen was my best friend . . . and now she's . . . she's gone . . . and I can't believe it . . ." Janine Mae broke down, and Ms. Kelso stepped forward, cradled the girl, and walked her offstage while the crowd murmured and sniffled anew.

Principal Coleridge hurried to the lectern, adjusting the microphone. "Thank you, Janine Mae, for your very heartfelt words. You said all that you needed to, and I know we all agree. Our next speaker is Christopher Slater, who is president of the Concord Chase Chamber of Commerce . . ."

A tall man in a suit rose and strode to the lectern, but Jake resumed looking for Pam, Ryan, or Sabrina. He migrated to the left to change his angle on the audience and get a view of the rightmost section, in front.

". . . I'm honored to be here tonight to speak about Kathleen," the speaker was saying. "I was so impressed with Kathleen when she came to my office on behalf of the travel track team. She was trying to raise money for new uniforms, but she didn't simply ask . . ."

Jake realized the speaker was telling the same story that Sabrina had told them, and tuned him out. He wedged his way through the crowd, excusing himself, and managed to get to the left side of the auditorium, which gave him a better view of the rightmost section. Still no luck.

". . . Kathleen proposed that the track team would work on the weekends, stuffing envelopes for the Chamber of Commerce, and donate their pay to the team itself. Kathleen further proposed that the Chamber should match the funds and sponsor the team . . ."

Jake couldn't wait another minute. Pam and Ryan weren't in the auditorium, and anything was possible. He made his way to the exit, squeezing through the standees.

". . . in a world where too many people expect things to be given to them, Kathleen was willing to sing for her supper. My wife and I have three young daughters, and we hope that they grow up to be as exemplary as she . . ."

Jake had reached the exit door when he noticed movement on the left side of the auditorium. A side door opened in the wall, and Pam ducked inside, followed by an obviously flustered Sabrina, then Ryan, who hung his head.

". . . I must say, I agreed with Kathleen on the spot, and my fellow Chamber members and I are proud to sponsor the team. My colleagues on the board and I are thrilled to see our name and logo on the team shirts, hats, and the gym bags . . ."

Jake exhaled with relief, feeling his every muscle relax. Pam and Ryan stopped and stood by the side door, leaning against the wall, and he knew they would be there for the program, safe and sound in plain view. Sabrina hurried down the aisle, climbed the steps to the stage, and scooted behind the speaker, who kept talking.

". . . I will never forget the times that Kathleen and her merry band of runners invaded my offices, to stuff envelopes for the Chamber of Commerce. We keep a very professional atmosphere, even on the weekends, but Kathleen brought her own brand of youthful energy to the place. She shook up even the staid Concordia Corporate Center . . ."

Jake's ears pricked up at the mention of Concordia Corporate Center, and he took a second look at the speaker, who was a handsome man, probably in his forties, with lanky blond hair. He wore a stylish dark suit, and his smooth, confident manner bespoke a born salesman. Jake wondered who he was and glanced at the open program of a woman near him. The program read, CHRIS SLATER, PRESIDENT, CONCORD CHASE CHAMBER OF COMMERCE; PRINCIPAL SHAREHOLDER, CS REAL ESTATE DEVELOPMENT, LLC.

". . . Kathleen came to the office many times, to get the job done, and I came to know her well. Of course, being a budding graphic designer, she told us what was wrong with our Chamber website, which you can imagine, didn't please my conservative old board very much . . ."

The audience smiled and sniffled, and Jake began to put two and two together. Slater was a charming, attractive, and successful man who knew Kathleen well, had met with her several times, and helped her find corporate sponsorship for the travel track team. A man like Slater would be catnip for a young girl, especially one who needed a father figure. And Slater's offices were in the Concordia Corporate Center, so he knew about Dolomite Road.

". . . I've gone on long enough, although in my own defense, I had been asked to stall to give our final speaker, Sabrina Moravia, a chance to arrive. So thank you for your attention tonight, and again, my wife and I, together with the Chamber of Commerce, offer our deepest sympathies to Kathleen's mother and father. We share your grief. Now, I will yield the floor . . ."

Slater flashed a charming smile, strode from the lectern, and sat down. Kathleen was a gorgeous young girl who could have tempted even the most married of men, and Jake got a hunch.

Maybe the killer wasn't in the audience, at all. Maybe the killer was on the stage.

Meanwhile, Sabrina took the lectern, gripped the sides, and cleared her throat. "I am the captain of the Concord Chase girls' track team, the Lady Chasers, and I thank you all for coming tonight . . ."

Jake tuned out her speech and mulled it over. Voloshin could have been stalking Kathleen, seen her and Slater together in the BMW when it was parked on Dolomite, then tried to blackmail Slater the same way he tried to blackmail Jake. Slater had a wife and kids, so he would have wanted to keep any relationship he had with Kathleen quiet, which made him a good target for blackmail. Plus Slater was obviously successful, so he had the money to pay. And Slater's motivation for killing Voloshin could have been that either he didn't want to pay the blackmail or he didn't trust Voloshin.

Sabrina was saying, "Mr. Slater told the same story about Kathleen that I was going to, but I can tell it from a different view, *her* view, which will tell you more about her. We were all so worried about going to his offices and meeting this important businessman, but Kathleen told us not to worry, that he was a normal guy and we should believe in ourselves . . ."

Jake began to feel as if his hunch was sound. All he had to do to verify it was get to the BMW before Slater did. He focused again on the stage, where Sabrina was finishing her speech. The principal was getting up from her seat to conclude the service, so it was time for Jake to go. He made his way to the back door, slipped into the empty entrance hall, and made a beeline for the exit.

"Jake, that you?" a voice called out behind him.

Jake turned around, and his mouth went dry. Standing in front of a display case with sports trophies was the last person he wanted to see.

Chapter Forty-three

"Jake!" It was Detective Zwerling, standing alone. He was in his dark suit with no overcoat. "What's your hurry? Trying to beat the traffic?"

Jake slowed his pace, busted. "No, I have to make a phone call."

"Good, I'll walk you out." Detective Zwerling hustled toward him, sliding his leather shoes on the tiled floor, then he fell into step, and they walked to the doors together. "So what brings you here?"

"You know, the memorial service." Jake told himself to remain calm. The service must have ended, because the crowd filed out of the auditorium doors and surged into the entrance hall, wiping tears, checking phones, and zipping coats.

"Did Ryan know Kathleen Lindstrom?"

"Pardon?" Jake asked, blindsided. He didn't remember mentioning Ryan's name to Detective Zwerling. "Uh, no, he didn't. He came with the basketball team."

"You came alone, with your son?"

"No, my wife came, too," Jake answered, hating to bring up

Pam. He didn't know if Detective Zwerling was making conversation or interrogating him, but it felt like the latter. They
reached the doors, left the school, and stepped into the cold
night air. Jake glanced toward the parking lot, but the BMW
was too far away to see in the dark. The crowd flowed noisily
around them, and he looked for Slater, but didn't see him. It
would take longer for Slater to get out, since he'd been on the
stage. At the fringe of the crowd, the TV klieglights flicked on
and cast a pool of light onto the pretty reporter, who raised her
microphone and started saying something that Jake couldn't
hear.

"I'd like to meet your wife." Detective Zwerling half-smiled,
his slack jowls draping the corners of his mouth like fleshy curtains. Close-up, his skin looked slightly greasy and he had a five
o'clock shadow. "I understand she's a judge. Where is she?"

"She's still inside, undoubtedly talking. I wouldn't wait if I
were you." Jake hadn't mentioned that Pam was a judge, so they
had been investigating him. He prayed it would take her a while
to get out of the auditorium, so Detective Zwerling couldn't see
she was a brunette, much less *the* brunette. Then he wondered
if Detective Zwerling knew that already.

"It's nice you both came."

"We wanted to show our respect for the family."

"How do you know them?"

"We don't. We came because of the school, the community.
To show respect, generally." Jake tried not to sound nervous,
but he kept saying the wrong things. The crowd filled the sidewalk, crossed the road to the parking lots, and scattered to their
cars. He sneaked a glance at the lot for the BMW and at the
crowd for Slater, but no luck. The TV reporter collared a passing mom for an interview, positioning her in the klieglights that
filled the area under the canopy with artificial light.

"Sad case, isn't it?" Detective Zwerling reached into his breast
pocket and pulled out a pack of Merits, with a blue Bic lighter

stuck in the cellophane. "I hate to see those girls crying. They're just kids."

"Yes, it's very sad." Jake slid his phone from his pocket. "Excuse me, I'd better make that call—"

"You can't take a minute to talk? I'm starting to think you don't like me." Detective Zwerling made a mock-wounded face as he shook out a cigarette and palmed the lighter. "You like my partner better, don't you?"

"No, not at all." Jake forced a smile.

"Come on. Now I *know* you're a liar. Everybody likes Woohoo better." Detective Zwerling laughed abruptly, then plugged his mouth with the cigarette, which flopped around while he spoke. "Hell, so do I."

Jake forced another smile, tense. He scanned the crowd for Slater, who would be easy to spot, tall and blond. The BMW seemed to be in the same parking space, a dark line in the far section of the lot.

"I can't figure it, can you? What kind of person hits a young girl and doesn't even stop?"

"I have no idea." Jake felt guilt-stricken, but told himself not to let emotions get the better of him. The night echoed with the hoarse noise of engines starting, and white and red taillights flashed as cars left spaces in all sections of the lot.

"At first I thought the driver was a drunk." Detective Zwerling lit his cigarette and blew out a cone of acrid smoke. "Usually is."

"I bet." Jake had to shake Detective Zwerling but didn't know how.

"They turn themselves in after they sober up. First thing Monday morning, we get a call. They're lawyered up by then."

"Really." Jake glanced again at the section of the parking lot with the BMW, but still couldn't see it. Cars were leaving the lot where the BMW was parked, but he thought it was still there, in its dark line. Slater wasn't among the crowd, which kept spilling out of the school, so Jake still had a chance.

"We can't prove anything that late and they know it. Standard operating procedure for degenerates."

"That's terrible."

"But we didn't get any call yesterday morning. Still haven't. I checked. Lindstrom's not my case, but we're a small department." Detective Zwerling's hooded eyes watched Jake through the cigarette smoke. "Concord Chase is a small community. I didn't realize how small until today. After we saw you, we went to Mr. Voloshin's place of employment. He worked at a company called GreenTech. Did he mention that to you?"

"No." Jake felt a bolt of panic, but tried not to betray himself. More engines started, and headlights sliced through the darkness as cars swung onto the road leading to the exit.

"It turns out that Kathleen Lindstrom worked at Green-Tech, too. Part-time. Her mother got her the job. She's the web designer there. Are you sure Voloshin didn't mention it to you?"

"No, not at all." Jake swallowed hard. The crowd kept flowing to the parking lots, and the TV reporter moved closer and collared another parent to interview. The klieglights followed her, casting a bright halo that Jake couldn't see around. If Slater left the building and walked behind the lights, Jake could miss him.

"What's up, Jake? You looking for someone?"

"My wife and son, when they come out."

"Oh. As I was saying, the employees at GreenTech were all upset. It's like a one-two punch, if you think about it. Last week they lost Kathleen in the hit-and-run. Last night they lost Voloshin in the murder." Detective Zwerling spoke casually, as if he were thinking aloud. Cigarette smoke leaked from between his thin lips. "Quite a coincidence, don't you think? It's a small company, and they lost two employees in a matter of days. What're the odds, eh?"

"God knows." Jake masked his panic. If Detective Zwerling was making a connection between Kathleen's death and Voloshin's murder, he could have been here scanning the crowd for Voloshin's killer. And the trail could lead to Slater, or to Pam. Maybe even to Ryan.

"Kathleen's mother is very upset about Voloshin's murder." Detective Zwerling took another drag of his Merit. "She considered him a friend of the family. He took a real interest in Kathleen. Taught her coding, Flash, animated gifs. Whatever that is. I'm no techie expert."

"Me, neither." Jake couldn't see the crowd beyond the TV klieglights. Cars were leaving the lot where the BMW was parked, and he couldn't tell if the BMW was still there. He felt his chances slipping away and he couldn't let that happen.

"I'm a detective twenty-two years. That's my expertise and—"

"Excuse me." Jake brandished his phone like a weapon. "I really have to make that call."

"Right." Detective Zwerling cocked his head, blowing smoke out to the side. "Why don't we reconvene tomorrow morning? You free at nine? I'll come by the office with Woohoo."

"No, I'm busy."

"When are you free? I'll work around."

"I'm not sure." Jake knew he needed a lawyer. He'd call Hubbard ASAP. "Tomorrow's not good for me, but I can give you a call, maybe Thursday."

"Too late." Detective Zwerling pursed his lips, his cigarette forgotten. "Jake, I gotta say, I believe you know more than you're letting on."

"No, not at all." Jake felt his mask start to slip. He remembered the photo of the BMW's license plate he had in his phone. It would be so easy to show it to Detective Zwerling and tell him everything. It was Jake's last chance to do the right thing.

They could catch Voloshin's killer together, whether it was Slater or not.

"Really?" Detective Zwerling eyed him through the flimsy curtain of smoke. "You sure? You're jumpy."

"Don't be ridiculous," Jake answered, getting a grip. He couldn't come clean without exposing Ryan, himself, and Pam. He used to care about justice, but now he cared only about his family. He used to know the difference between right and wrong, but all he knew now was that he loved Pam and Ryan, above all else. And he had to get to the BMW before its driver did.

"I'll call you tomorrow."

"Fine," Jake told him, turning away. He walked toward the BMW parking lot and got close enough to see that the BMW was still there, though cars on either side of it were gone. He pressed a button on his phone for show and held it to his ear, as if he were talking. Detective Zwerling would still be watching him, though for all the detective knew, Jake could have been walking toward his own car. Suddenly red taillights went on in the back of the BMW, and the sedan began to pull away.

"No!" Jake heard himself say, holding the phone to his ear. He couldn't run after the car. He couldn't do anything that looked suspicious. He must have missed Slater or whoever it was when they passed on the far side of the TV klieglights. Then he realized he could still get a glimpse of the driver, when the BMW turned around and joined the line of traffic to the main exit.

But it didn't.

Jake gritted his teeth as the BMW drove away, straight across the emptying parking lot toward the exit at the middle school, one of a slew of other drivers who wanted to get out faster.

"Damn it! Damn, damn, damn!" Jake turned around to see Detective Zwerling, standing alone under the canopy among the crowd of families. The TV klieglights reflected off the cigarette smoke that wreathed him, reducing him to a blurry silhouette.

Jake didn't see Slater in the crowd, but he couldn't wait any longer. His plan was blown, and he needed damage control. Detective Zwerling would be wondering what he was doing. Pam's car was parked nearby, and he walked to it casually, while he scrolled to the text function on his phone and texted Pam:

I'm at ur car. Take Ryan out back door. Cops out front. Talk to no one! BE CAREFUL!

Chapter Forty-four

"Ryan, how are you doing?" Jake asked, as soon as Sabrina had gotten out of the car and closed the door behind her. Pam reversed slowly out of the driveway, stalling until Sabrina got inside her house safely, but Jake was really worried about Ryan. The ride had been mostly silent, with Pam keeping her eyes on the road, Sabrina texting with her friends, and Ryan looking out the window, plugged into his white earbuds.

Ryan didn't answer, so Jake twisted around in his seat to see if he was texting. He still wasn't, oddly. He had pulled his hoodie on and seemed almost immobile, except for the jostling of the car as it bobbled over the Belgian blocks that marked the end of Sabrina's driveway. His iPhone sat ignored in his lap, and his face remained turned to the window, though there was nothing he hadn't seen before, only older stone Tudor homes that lined Baird Road, in the exclusive Chase Run neighborhood that served as the model for their development.

"Ryan? You okay?" Jake asked again.

"Let it go," Pam snapped, then her lips resealed shut.

"I want to know how he's doing." Jake kept his tone soft.

"How the hell do you think he's doing? Does he have to spell it out?"

"Fine," Jake said after a moment, then faced front in the passenger seat. He didn't want to bug Ryan, and Pam had been looking daggers at him from the moment she met him at her car. He didn't have to ask why. The memorial service must have been awful for them both. He hadn't had a chance to explain why he'd texted her because the kids had been there. He'd have to fill her in when they were alone, assuming she wasn't leaving him.

Just my luck.

Jake tried to shoo his father's voice from his head, but he wasn't succeeding. He turned his face to the window in the silent car, idly watching the beautiful homes passing darkly. Warm, golden light shone from within, through iron lattice on arched windows, illuminating spacious family rooms behind tall leafy oak trees. It was a clear night and the moon was almost full, a jagged hole shot through a black sky, glimmering on the SUVs below.

Pam seemed to accelerate, driving faster than usual through the winding streets, and Jake reached instinctively for the hanger strap, as if it could tether him to the world he knew and loved. He could lose his wife tonight, and his son was too upset to talk to him. His family was slipping through his very fingers and the only thing in his hand was a fake plastic strap.

He couldn't remember when he had felt this low, and the answer was never. Not even when he'd lost his job, because he still had Pam and Ryan. All he had lost then was money, but he still had a family and that was everything, at the end of the day. It struck him then that he really wasn't like his father, after all. Because his father had always had his family, but no money, and thought that was nothing. But Jake knew better. He had seen it from both sides, and he knew what he was losing. Everything.

Jake flashed on Detective Zwerling and felt a new bolt of fear. He would need to get ahold of Hubbard and get some advice right away. He didn't know what to expect from the police or how to react, and he couldn't afford to slip up and arouse suspicion that would up the ante on an investigation. He would have to explain to Pam about the BMW and his suspicions about Slater, as well as how he had blown it when he had a chance to catch the driver.

Jake, Pam, and Ryan made it home, got out of the car, walked to the house and unlocked the door, still without saying a word to each other. They piled into the entrance hall, a tense and sorrowful threesome, tossing jackets and purses onto the chair beside the console table. Only Moose was his usual happy self, trotting from the kitchen to greet them, smiling with his tongue lolling out of his mouth and wagging his feathery tail.

"Ryan, you all right?" Jake tried again, but Ryan lumbered past him to the stairwell, his head still covered by the hoodie and his ears plugged with the earbuds.

Pam interjected, "Jake, please, let me talk to him—"

"Honey, I can talk to my own son. You can't be my proxy, remember?" Jake hurried up the stairway after Ryan. Moose joined the chase, delighted at the new game, his toenails clicking on the hardwood stairs.

"I don't want to talk." Ryan kept walking upstairs. "I want to be alone."

Pam hurried up after Jake. "Jake, stop, you're going about it all wrong."

Jake ignored her. "Ryan, unplug those things from your ears. Please, let's—"

"No." Ryan kept going, and Jake caught up with him, placing a hand on his shoulder as they both reached the landing.

"Ryan, I know you feel bad—"

"Dad, stop, you don't know." Ryan whirled around, yanking the earbuds from his ears. "I'm not blaming you and I'm not mad at you, that's why I don't want to talk right now. But I can promise you one thing for sure—that you do *not* know how I feel, either of you."

Jake's heart broke at the anguish on Ryan's face, but there was a new tone in his voice, stronger.

Pam reached the top of the stairs, her fair skin flushed with emotion. "Ryan, please, just listen—"

"No, Mom. *I* was the one who killed her, not Dad and not you." Ryan stabbed his finger into his chest with conviction. "*I* was the one everybody was hating on tonight, the one who took her from her friends, from Janine Mae and the rest of the team. And from her computer teacher and her *mom,* and her *dad,* and they both loved her so much they were in this big custody fight over her—"

Pam moaned. "Ryan, I know, but I'm worried about you—"

"Mom, it's not about me. It's about her. You want me to be happy, but can Kathleen? Can she? She's not going to prom or the meet against Methacton. She won't be going to college. She won't even see the *gym bags* she wanted so bad. It's not about me, in the end. I'm *alive.* She's not. She's *dead,* and *I killed her.*"

"But not on purpose—" Pam started to say, but Ryan cut her off with a hand chop.

"What difference does that make, Mom? Did you see her picture on the stage? And the one in the program? *I killed that girl.* So I want to feel *horrible,* I deserve to feel *horrible.* That's fair, right? Me feeling *horrible forever,* because she's dead forever." Ryan paused, dry-eyed, seeming to gather strength from his own words. He backed toward the door of his bedroom, and Moose trotted beside him, his tail still wagging merrily. "You always tell me to take responsibility for my actions, and I am. I'm trying to. I can't do it in public without Dad going to jail, but I can do it privately. So don't freak out because I'm not happy. I'm *not supposed* to be happy. I'm supposed to feel exactly how I feel. It's the least I can do. For *her.*"

Jake felt frightened. He had never seen Ryan this way, determined to self-destruct.

Pam sagged against the banister, stricken. "But Ryan, Caleb's mom said that you were saying something about dying, that sometimes you felt so bad that you wanted to die."

Jake turned to Ryan, horrified. "Is that true? Did you say that?"

"Of course." Ryan almost smiled. "*Of course.* Honestly, I wish I were dead, not her. I wish I could give up my life for hers, right now. Maybe I can. Maybe I will. Nobody gets away with murder. *Nobody.*"

Pam gasped. "Ryan, no. It wasn't murder—"

Ryan snorted. "How is it different, Mom? I'm not talking about some stupid legal definition. She's dead, and I killed her. I deserve to die. I wish I were dead."

"No, Ryan!" Jake cried out. "Don't say that. Don't ever say that!"

"Leave me alone, go away." Ryan reached his bedroom door, fumbled with the knob, and then turned back to face them. "Also Mom, tell your boyfriend to leave me the hell alone." Ryan turned back, went inside his room with the dog, and closed the door behind him.

Jake faced Pam, angry. "What is he talking about, 'your boyfriend'?"

"Jake, not now." Pam raked her manicured hand through her hair.

"Yes, now. Tell me."

Pam sighed, weary. She couldn't meet his eye. "Dave wants to start seeing Ryan, professionally. Caleb told him what Ryan said, too. Dave thinks Ryan is becoming depressed and it would help to talk to him, as a therapist—"

"Are you *kidding* me?" Jake exploded. "Dave said that to Ryan?"

"To both of us, before the service. He's only trying to help him—"

"Doesn't that violate some ethical code? He was *sleeping* with you! Or *is*!"

"No, it's over, I told you."

"Then where were you last night? Did you go to him?"

"No, I stayed in a hotel—"

"Thank God for small favors!" Jake charged down the stairs. "The *balls* on this guy! *Enough!* I've had enough of Dr. Dave! I want him out of my life! Out of my family!"

"Jake, what are you doing?" Pam called after him. "Don't go over there. You can't. His wife is in town."

"So what?" Jake hit the entrance hall and grabbed the car keys from the console table. "It's between me and him!"

"Jake, don't do anything crazy!"

Jake flung open the door and rushed outside.

Chapter Forty-five

Jake's blood boiled as he drove along Dr. Dave's street, a single lane that snaked through dark woods, filled with towering evergreens and oak trees. There were no other houses on the street, much less painted mailboxes, holiday flags, or recycle bins that had to be rolled away by nightfall. Of course Dr. Dave lived in the Pendleton Tract, a beautiful hundred wooded acres under easement to the county, never to be developed. Jake hated that the man who cuckolded him had evergreens that weren't planted in a zigzag pattern.

He turned onto Dr. Dave's driveway and parked behind his Prius, in front of a house that was predictably spectacular, an ultramodern series of glass-walled boxes with concrete edges and flat rooflines, situated on at least six wooded acres. Jake cut the ignition, blood pounding in his ears. He'd had only a single second thought on the drive over, which was about Dr. Dave's wife. He didn't want to tell her that her jerk of a husband was cheating on her. That would hurt her the way he'd been hurt, so he'd have to make sure she was out of the way, to avoid collateral damage.

He got out of his car and slammed the door behind him, which echoed in the woods. He stalked up a flagstone path, bordered with tiny lights to show the way through the trees. The air smelled fresh and clean, which infuriated him all the more. His enemy even had better oxygen.

He glanced at the floor-to-ceiling window on the left of the house, which looked into a showplace living room, with black leather sofas and chairs. A set of gauzy curtains muted the view, but the living room was empty. He reached the front door, also of glass panels, and he was about to pound on one hard enough to break it when the door opened.

Dr. Dave stood in the threshold, blinking calmly behind his hip graphite glasses, and Jake realized that Pam must have warned him that he was coming, which felt like a body blow.

"Dr. Dave, tell your wife to get lost. She's not going to like this conversation."

"She left for the airport. Come in." Dr. Dave opened the door, standing aside politely. Classical music played in the background, from a crystal-clear sound system. "So what are you going to do, Jake? Punch me in the noggin? Go ahead. You're bigger than I am. Displace all the anger you want."

Jake stepped inside. "Hold the jargon. I'm not impressed."

"I was in the kitchen, having dinner. Would you like something?"

"Are you out of your mind, shrink?"

"Suit yourself." Dr. Dave turned neatly away on his thin black loafers and sauntered down a short hall to the back of the house.

"Oh I get it. This is the psychology part. You act very cool when the raging husband comes over." Jake stalked after him into a modern kitchen. Stainless steel appliances lined the back wall, under a large window that was as black as night, reflecting the two men like a dark mirror.

"Not at all, Jake. I'm a therapist, and so I understand the power of a good conversation." Dr. Dave crossed to an island with tall cherrywood stools and a black granite countertop, which held a complete place setting, a plate with a chicken breast and wild rice, next to a glass of wine and an open bottle. Suddenly a little Siamese cat jumped onto the countertop, but Dr. Dave pushed it roughly to the floor, where it landed on its feet.

"You preyed on my wife and now you're preying on my son. I want you to leave my family alone."

"How do you feel about Lambrusco? It's coming back, you know, and this Lini Vineyard produces such a special grape." Dr. Dave lifted the bottle of wine, showing off the label.

"Stick your wine up your ass and listen, I'm talking to you." Jake collected his thoughts. "I'm not going to hit you. I'm not a bully, a thug, or a badass. But I'm not a pushover either."

"I take it that's a no on the Lambrusco." Dr. Dave picked up his glass, swirled the wine around, then took a sip. Meanwhile, the cat walked to the back door, meowed, and sat down, curling its brownish tail around its delicate brown feet.

"I came here to say that I'm trying to save my marriage and my family, and if you can't respect that, then I don't know what kind of a man you are." Jake couldn't hold back his temper. "Put another way, if I catch you anywhere around my wife or my son again, I will beat you to death with my bare hands."

"My." Dr. Dave took another sip of wine, which darkened his teeth. "These are two separate issues, your wife and your son. As for Pam, if your marriage were a happy one, your wife wouldn't have come to me, and I assure you, she came to me."

Jake swallowed hard, suppressing a deep stab of sexual jealousy.

"As for Ryan, I'm his shooting coach, whether you think I'm qualified or not, so it would be quite impossible to comply with your demand."

"Take care of the other kids. Leave him alone." Jake's phone rang in his pocket, but he let it go, guessing it was Pam.

"Are you sure you have Ryan's best interests in mind?" Dr. Dave seemed to be warming up, wanting to spar. He leaned against the counter, palming his glass. "In my professional opinion, Ryan is experiencing situational depression brought on by several factors, such as the conflict between you and Pam, his schoolwork, and the championship. He's been making statements to his teammates that suggest he's having suicidal ideation, which is—"

"I know the term, and you're not qualified to be Ryan's therapist. You were sleeping with his mother."

"I know Ryan very well, and we could work together and have a very good outcome. I'm sure that Ryan would love to work with me. We're very close." Dr. Dave set down his wine, and the cat meowed again, loudly this time.

"I *said,* leave my son alone." Jake didn't tell Dr. Dave that Ryan knew about his affair with Pam, because he didn't want Dr. Dave to know more about his family than he already did.

"Jake, you're making decisions for Ryan that he's perfectly capable of making for himself. Excuse me, this cat won't shut up." Dr. Dave crossed to the back door, twisted the deadbolt, and opened the door. The cat slipped outside, and in the next moment, a motion-detector light went on in the backyard, illuminating a fancy two-car garage.

In front of it was parked a gleaming black BMW 535.

And its license plate read HKE-7553.

Chapter Forty-six

Jake almost gasped in shock, looking out the window. It was *the* BMW. It didn't belong to Dr. Dave, so it must have been his wife's. They must've driven separately to the memorial service.

Jake's thoughts raced. He didn't realize Dr. Dave had known Kathleen, but he must have. Dr. Dave must have been the one who had an affair with Kathleen, not Slater. Dr. Dave would've known about Dolomite Road because that's where the athletic teams ran. Dr. Dave must have killed Voloshin.

Jake turned around just in time to see Dr. Dave pull a handgun from a cabinet drawer, aim it at his chest, and start firing.

CRAK! CRAK! CRAK! went the gunshots. Flames burst from the gun barrel.

Jake dove out of the way, too late. He doubled over reflexively and hit the tile floor. His stomach exploded in searing pain, like his gut caught fire. He curled into the fetal position, gripping his belly. Warm red blood spurted from between his fingers. He tried to get up. Intense pain felled him. He couldn't move for the agony. He tried to scream but could only whisper, "No."

"Wow, you're still alive?" Dr. Dave set the gun on the island. "No matter. You won't be for long."

"No, no." Jake felt sheer terror. Blood sprayed from his belly, spattering the tile floor. He tried to stanch the flow, but he couldn't. He shifted to get up again, but agonizing pain seared through his entire body.

"Sorry, Jake. I'd put you out of your misery, but the trajectory of the bullet would be wrong. It has to be level and face-to-face. I saw on TV."

Blood gushed everywhere, spattering the tiles, running in rivulets in the grout. Jake watched it leak from him, helpless. He began to lose consciousness.

"I had to shoot you, in self-defense." Dr. Dave picked up his knife from beside his dinner plate and crossed to him. "You drove here, enraged about Pam and me. She called and said you weren't the violent type, so I didn't call 911. You and I were talking it over, apparently reasonably, but suddenly you became angry and tried to kill me."

Jake felt dizzy and faint. The pain raged in his stomach.

"You grabbed my steak knife and tried to stab me." Dr. Dave knelt down with the knife beside Jake, picked up his hand, placed the knife in his palm, and wrapped his fingers around the handle. "I managed to get to my gun and protect myself. Unfortunately, by the time 911 arrived, you had bled to death."

Jake pulled his hand away, but the knife clattered to the floor. The pain was so intense it immobilized him. He was going to die.

"Are your keys in your pocket?" Dr. Dave plunged his hand into Jake's pocket, fished around, and pulled out his car keys. "Perfect. The police will find Voloshin's laptop and phone in the trunk of your car. They'll figure that you killed him because he was blackmailing you. After all, he had proof that you and Ryan killed Kathleen in the hit-and-run."

Jake looked around wildly. He couldn't save himself. He

couldn't get away. Dr. Dave was framing him for Voloshin's murder.

"Kathleen was one of my favorite clients, and she was incredible in bed. Trust me, the ones with father issues are the best." Dr. Dave straightened up, hurried to a base cabinet, and took out a Whole Foods bag. A gray computer cord hung out of its open mouth. It had to be Voloshin's laptop and phone.

Jake didn't want to die. Pam and Ryan needed him. Blood drenched the floor. He could barely see as Dr. Dave left the kitchen with the bag, then the front door slammed.

Ring! Jake's cell phone rang again. It had to be Pam. His heart fluttered with hope. It was his only chance. His cell phone was in his right back pocket. He didn't have any time to lose. Dr. Dave would return any minute.

Jake moved his arm toward his pocket. He cried out in agony. He froze. He couldn't move. His body began to shake uncontrollably. He couldn't keep his eyes open. His phone stopped ringing. It was over.

Jake heard the front door slam, then footsteps returning to the kitchen. He roused, opening his eyes to see Dr. Dave knock his dinner plate to the floor, scattering the chicken and rice.

"The proverbial signs of a struggle," Dr. Dave said, half to himself. He straight-armed the wineglass and bottle off the counter, and they shattered on the tile. He upended a cherrywood stool, then another. He eyed the kitchen, putting a finger to his mouth, then crossed to the oven, grabbed a metal frying pan from the stovetop and threw it clanging to the floor. He walked over to the toaster and pushed it over, then the coffeemaker. He swept newspapers off one of the stools, then glanced over at Jake.

"What, you're still alive? Get on with it, man. I have to call 911, but you don't look dead enough." Dr. Dave took the gun off the counter and walked to Jake, cocking his head as if he were thinking aloud. "I bet I could get away with another shot."

"No," Jake whispered, in terror.

"I could say I was afraid you could get up, in fear for my life."

Dr. Dave aimed the gun at Jake.

Suddenly, there was a noise from the front door.

Dr. Dave turned away, toward the sound.

And all hell broke loose.

Chapter Forty-seven

"NO!" Ryan bellowed, barreling into the kitchen with Pam at his heels.

"No" was all Jake could whisper, horrified they were in harm's way.

Ryan took a flying leap at Dave and tackled him heavily to the ground. They both yelled and grunted, struggling for the gun. Suddenly a shot fired. Pam screamed.

Tears of fright sprang to Jake's eyes. He didn't know whether Ryan or Dave had been shot. He prayed to God for Ryan's life. Pam burst into tears, covering her head with her hands.

Suddenly Ryan staggered to his feet, supporting himself on the kitchen island. Pam ran to his side, crying with relief. Dr. Dave remained on the floor, moaning and holding his shoulder.

Jake thanked God. He could've died a happy man at that moment, but Ryan and Pam rushed together at him.

"Jake, Jake!" Pam sobbed, throwing herself to the floor beside him. "Honey, the police will be here! I worried you got in a fight, when you didn't answer! An ambulance is on the way! They should be here any minute!"

"Dad, don't die, please don't die!" Ryan bent over him, distraught. "I love you, Dad! I love you!"

Jake looked up at them, feeling weaker by the second. He wanted to tell them he loved them. He wanted to tell them to be happy without him, that nothing else mattered to him as much, on the face of the earth. "Pam," he tried to say, but it came out fainter than a whisper.

"Honey, stay with us!" Pam embraced him, beginning to sob. "The ambulance will be here any minute!"

"Dad, don't die, please, please!"

Jake could barely hear them. He felt himself slipping away. He flashed on the bag that Dr. Dave had put in the trunk of his car, with Voloshin's laptop and phone. It contained the only evidence that connected Ryan to the hit-and-run. If Ryan and Pam disposed of it, nobody would ever know what had happened. If they gave it to the police, they would go to jail. He tried to say, "Ryan . . . trunk . . ."

"What, Dad?" Ryan bent over him, crying. "The *trunk*? Of the *car*?"

Jake managed a smile, closing his eyes. They would figure it out when they opened the trunk. They would decide what to do.

Jake knew what he would do, if he had a second chance. But he couldn't say, and he'd have to leave the decision to them.

Because he was gone.

Chapter Forty-eight

Jake couldn't keep his eyes open. He was bathed in light, warm on his face, and for a minute he didn't know if he was alive or dead. He squinted around him and realized he was lying in a hospital room. Sunshine poured through the window and fell on his bed, in a glowing shaft of gold. He thanked God he was alive.

The room was empty, and he lay there, feeling horrible, exhausted and weak. His stomach throbbed with pain. He could think only slowly, as if his brain didn't work. His throat felt raw and dry, it was hard to swallow. An IV shunt was taped to his hand, a plastic clip covered his index finger. Monitors glowed next to his bed, and the door to the room was open. He became aware that the hallway outside sounded busy. People were talking and carts rattled, a metallic sound. He could smell the faint aroma of coffee and eggs, mingling with institutional disinfectants. He wasn't hungry.

He closed his eyes against the sun. He tried to remember how he had gotten here. He must be snowed under with painkillers. It must've been last night. Dave had shot him in the gut.

He'd been bleeding, lying on the floor. He remembered Dave pointing the gun down at him, about to fire again. Then Ryan, rushing in. And Pam, crying at his side. His wife and son had saved his life.

Jake thought of something else. The bag of evidence in the trunk of his car. He wondered what Pam and Ryan had done with it, whether they had shown it to the police or gotten rid of it forever. They weren't around, nobody was, so he figured they must have come clean to the cops and gone to prison.

His heart lurched at the thought, but they had done the right thing, in the end. He prayed that Ryan had been charged as a juvenile, not an adult, so Jake would bear the brunt of their punishment. He could accept going to prison, and he understood why it was necessary. He had *lived* why it was necessary. He had to take responsibility for Kathleen's death, and he'd rather live with honesty in prison than live on the outside, in guilt and shame.

Suddenly, there was a commotion at the doorway, and Pam, Ryan, and Detective Zwerling entered the room. Pam closed the curtains against the sunshine, then looked at Jake and did a double-take.

"Babe, are you awake? Thank God!" Pam crossed to his bedside, with Ryan next to her, breaking into a broad grin.

"Dad, how are you?"

"Fine," Jake answered, hoarse. He assumed Pam and Ryan must have been out on bail. They were wearing the same clothes as yesterday, so they hadn't even gone home. Or maybe they were released on Detective Zwerling's recognizance, waiting to see what happened to him. Jake didn't want to jump to the last possibility, which was that Pam and Ryan had hidden the evidence and hadn't told the police, and they were all back at square one.

"Good to see you." Pam smiled down at him, her expression soft, but not completely unguarded.

"You, too," Jake croaked out, but he knew it didn't begin to communicate the power of the emotion he felt for her. He thanked God he was still alive and prayed that Pam would stay married to him, but that was a conversation for another time.

Detective Zwerling was almost smiling. "Buckman, you're tougher than I thought."

Pam took his hand and held it lightly. "How do you feel?"

"Okay."

"Honey, do you want some water, or juice? Are you in pain?"

"No."

"The doctor said you're going to be fine, in time. They did an ex lap, an exploratory laparotomy, and they removed the bullets from your stomach. There was a lot of internal bleeding, because one went through a major blood vessel, the—"

"Wait, first tell me what's going on with . . ." Jake didn't want to finish the sentence in front of Detective Zwerling, but Pam nodded, reading his mind.

"We told the police about the laptop and phone. They found them in the trunk of your car. Ryan and I agreed to go forward, and we figured that's what you'd want to do, too."

"I did, but how did you know?" Jake felt the weight of the world lifted from his shoulders, but he was still confused about what was going on.

"I know you." Pam's expression grew grave. "As for what happened next, I'll leave that to the authorities to explain. Bill?"

"Sure." Detective Zwerling edged closer to the bed, looking down at Jake, and the folds of his face fell into deep lines. "Pam and Ryan gave us a statement about what happened last Friday night. You'll have to give us one, too, when you're feeling well enough. But neither you nor Ryan are being charged with vehicular homicide."

"Why not?" Jake asked, dumbfounded.

"The autopsy determined that the injuries Kathleen sustained as a result of being hit by your car were postmortem."

"What?" Jake didn't understand, struggling through a pharmaceutical fog to think.

"Kathleen was already dead when you hit her. The cause of her death was blunt force trauma to her head. The District Attorney charged Dr. David Tolliver for her murder and the murder of Andrew Voloshin."

"Are you saying that Dr. Dave *killed* Kathleen?" Jake couldn't process it fast enough. All this time, he had thought that he and Ryan were responsible for Kathleen's death.

"Yes, we believe so."

"How? Why?"

"This is confidential, but in the circumstances, I'll fill you in. Kathleen was a patient of Tolliver's, sent by her mother to help cope with the divorce and custody case. Her parents had no knowledge of any relationship between them, outside the client-doctor. Kathleen's friend Janine Mae told us that Kathleen had fallen in love with an older man, in secret. Kathleen didn't tell Janine Mae that the man was Tolliver. She told Janine Mae it was someone she met online."

Jake couldn't believe what he was hearing. His stomach was killing him, but he didn't want to interrupt Detective Zwerling to get more painkillers.

"Janine Mae knew they met sometimes on Dolomite Road, at night. Tolliver probably used his wife's car because the school teams could have recognized his car."

Jake realized he'd been right about that much, but he was too astounded to feel any satisfaction.

"We think that Tolliver wanted to break off the relationship, but Kathleen didn't. We believe that Kathleen threatened to tell her parents if he called it quits, so Tolliver killed her." Detective Zwerling pursed his thin lips. "Tolliver lawyered up and isn't talking, but we have hard evidence against him. Again, confidential, but we have his hair and fiber on Kathleen's body and clothing. We also have her blood in the BMW. We collected

DNA and expect it will be corroborative, but the results aren't back yet. The forensics show that he killed her in the BMW, by slamming her head into the dashboard."

Jake felt a wave of disgust.

"He left her body by the side of Pike Road. He probably thought she'd look like a victim of a hit-and-run, given the blind curve. You and Ryan came by shortly thereafter, maybe even within ten minutes, according to the best estimate of the pathologist."

"Pathologists can figure that out? How?"

"By the location and type of her injuries, during the autopsy. It's about blood loss and so forth."

Jake tried to understand the implications. "Did you know all along that whoever was guilty of the hit-and-run didn't actually kill Kathleen?"

"No, we weren't sure, and the pathologist couldn't be a hundred percent certain. If there had been more time between the time she was actually killed and when her body was hit, he would have been more sure. But it was our theory, and we liked you."

Jake blinked, surprised. "I like you, too, Detective Zwerling."

Pam snorted, with a sly smile. "Jake, in police talk, 'like' means 'suspect.' The police suspected you."

Detective Zwerling permitted himself a tight smile. "We didn't release that information to the newspapers. We were still investigating. Your actions flushed Tolliver out, but we don't sanction citizen involvement. Law enforcement is for professionals, Jake." Detective Zwerling's smile faded, and his jowls deepened with disapproval. "You almost lost your life. You would have, if not for your wife and son."

"I know. Thank God for them." Jake felt a surge of love for his family, and Pam squeezed his hand.

Detective Zwerling straightened up, as if he were becoming official again. "The D.A. will be in to see you, later today. He'll tell you that you'll be charged with leaving the scene of an accident and failing to give information. Those are misdemeanors in the first degree, or M1s. They involve fines and such, but no prison time."

"I'll take whatever punishment I have coming. But what about Ryan?"

"The D.A. exercised his discretion not to charge Ryan as an adult, in view of your efforts in the case. He'll be charged with the same offenses as you, but as a juvenile. He'll get probation and have to perform community service. He'll have no criminal record when he comes of age."

"Thank you, that's wonderful. We're very grateful." Jake felt relief wash over him, momentarily forgetting about his pain.

Ryan said, "Yes, Detective Zwerling, thank you again."

Pam looked from Ryan to Jake with a worried frown. "Even so, there's going to be other repercussions, for all of us. I'm stepping down from the bench."

"Babe, really?" Jake sighed. He could tell from Ryan's resigned expression that it wasn't news to him. "Do you really have to?"

"Yes, of course. My oath is to uphold and defend the Constitution and the laws of the Commonwealth, yet I chose to hide illegality. It's misconduct, and if I stayed, it would damage the reputation of the Court." Pam pursed her lips, but she didn't seem angry at Jake, just regretful. "I already emailed the Chief Judge and my colleagues, so they won't find out from the newspaper. The D.A. plans to hold a press conference at one o'clock. The reporters are already swarming in front of the hospital."

"I'm sorry," Jake told her, meaning it.

"Thanks, but it's not on you, honey." Pam smiled at him, sadly. "It's on me. I made my choice, and I'll take my lumps."

"So you won't be a judge anymore?" Jake felt terrible for her.

"That might be a good thing, huh?" Pam winked, with a crooked smile. "No more Judge Mom."

"But what will you do?"

"I'm not sure yet. Let's not talk about it now." Pam shrugged it off. "Nobody's getting off scot-free. I'm embarrassed and ashamed, so are we all. There'll be gossip and headlines. It won't be easy."

"I know." Ryan nodded, his lips flattened to a grim line. "People are already posting about it on Facebook. I'll lose a lot of friends, I know. Everybody will be talking about it. The big-time recruiters and programs will bounce. Bye-bye, Division I."

"That might be right." Jake appreciated that Ryan was being so realistic. "I guess I'll lose clients. Plus Amy and my employees are going to be disillusioned. But I can deal."

Pam eyed him, her anxiety plain. "What will happen to Gardenia? Do you lose your certification over this?"

"I don't think so. Amy will stay, and I have enough cushion to float the payroll for a while. It's Ryan I'm worried about." Jake turned to his son. "Buddy, can you take the heat?"

"Totally. We both can. Don't worry about it, Dad. We've been through worse, haven't we?" Ryan looked down at Jake, his gaze grown-up. "Here's what I think. It's awful that Kathleen died, the way she died, but I didn't kill her. I didn't kill *anybody*. I don't have that on my conscience anymore. I don't have to lie to anybody or hide anything. I feel, like, so grateful and *free*. Do you see, Dad? I'm *good again*."

Pam's eyes glistened, but she didn't say anything, letting Ryan and Jake have their moment.

"Ryan, you always were good," Jake said, hoarsely, his entire body flooding with peace.

"We'll get through this together."

"Yes, we will." Jake reached for Ryan's hand, and Ryan reached back, and Jake could feel the warmth, strength, and power that flowed between them, palpable in the clasp of their hands, which were large and so much alike.

"I love you, Dad," Ryan said, with feeling.

"I love you, too, boy," Jake told him, and at long last, he could feel the beginning of a reconnection between them, one that had less to do with superficial things like cars and girls, and more to do with something important, natural, and even eternal.

Flesh, and blood.

Epilogue

Six months later, Jake and Pam were sitting on the bleachers at a packed basketball game, watching Ryan. The gym thundered with the clamoring of parents, siblings, and students. Kids ran up and down the aisles. Moms cheered, dads clapped, and Jake felt as if everything was the same as before—except that everything was also different.

The gym was smaller and shabbier, in a tougher part of town. Ryan wasn't playing, but assistant-coaching, and none of the players was very tall, because they were eight-year-old girls. Their ponytails bounced in their matching scrunchies, their purple T-shirts hung to their knobby knees, and their wide-leg shorts flapped when they ran. Jake took a special interest in the kids' gear because he had bought it all. The team was the Gardenia Guardians, named for what was left of his company.

He nudged Pam, pleased. "They look good, huh?"

"What?" Pam kept watching the game, craning her neck.

"They look good!" Jake said, louder, and Pam looked at him like he was crazy, her blue eyes amused behind her glasses.

"What are you talking about? They're losing by seven points."

"The uniforms, I mean."

Pam rolled her eyes. "It still bugs me they're purple. Gardenias aren't purple."

"White is boring, honey."

"Gardenias aren't white, they're ivory, which is a *lovely* color."

"Kids don't want lovely. They want cool, and purple is cool."

"Oh, hush! Watch the game." Pam turned to the court.

Jake half-watched the game, contentedly. Bottom line, he was happy to be alive. His stomach still hurt from time to time, but he'd even started running with Ryan. In fact, he'd already lost two pounds. Well, it was a start.

Jake sensed the worst was over. Dr. Dave had pleaded guilty to both murders and was sentenced to life without parole, thus avoiding the death penalty. The media had moved on almost instantly, though the gossip lingered in their development, at school, in social media, and in the financial-services community. They would forever be the family who had left the scene of a hit-and-run, but they tried to hold their heads high. Jake hadn't lost his certification, and Amy and almost all of his employees stayed with him. His remaining clients were making money, so he hoped that word-of-mouth would attract new ones. If it didn't, he'd stay small or start over. He'd learned there were worse things in life than losing your job.

Pam nudged him, pointing to the court. "Honey, look. Tiffany's going to shoot."

"She'll miss."

"Don't be that way."

"Please. They always miss. The final scores are, like, three to two."

Pam hit his leg playfully. "Aw, but she's so cute. I love that little girl."

"That's true. She's adorable." Jake watched Tiffany shove the basketball two-handed into the air, then it fell to the court, bouncing away.

"Oh well." Pam chuckled, shaking her head. Both teams raced after the ball, tumbling over one another, a rolling mob of flailing arms and outstretched fingers.

"Looks like a shoe sale at Nordstrom's," Jake said, and Pam laughed, which pleased him no end. They were back in therapy, putting their marriage back together, sometimes with Ryan, too. Pam had been depressed for months, but had begun to come around after the headlines died down. The local law firms didn't make her a job offer, so she was working as a contract lawyer, writing briefs for the big, white-shoe firms in Philly. They wouldn't put her name on the papers, but they were happy to have her brainpower. They'd considered moving away from Concord Chase, but decided against it, unanimously. It wouldn't work in the age of Facebook, and they were through with family secrets.

Ryan had gotten through a predictably difficult junior year, with the school and the team in turmoil. The Chasers lost to Lower Merion in the championship, and the basketball recruiters never called Ryan again, though he'd weathered the social storm at school and kept his grades up. The assistant-coaching gig had fulfilled his community service obligation, but he'd already finished the required hours. He'd found a calling in coaching and landed a summer job assistant-coaching in the playground league, for the Concord Chase Rec Department. He was even talking about applying to colleges closer to home. Pam was relieved he wouldn't be leaving the nest completely, and Jake acted like he was happy on her behalf, but he was happy for himself. He loved spending time with Ryan, and it turned out that he didn't have to compete with Call of Duty. On the contrary, he learned to play video games.

Jake watched Ryan calling to the kids on the sidelines, and his heart swelled with pride. He went to all the games, just to watch Ryan, and felt as if he was finally gaining ground with their son. Ryan, Pam, and he spent more time together than ever before, maybe because nobody else would talk to them. Turned out there was nothing like a public shunning to bring a family closer.

The cheering crowd leapt to its feet, and one of the girls on the opposing team blew past a Gardenia Guardian and actually scored a basket. Jake watched as the little Guardian burst into tears, ran off the court, and beelined to Ryan. Ryan bent down, gave her a big hug, then talked to her and sent her back into the game.

Pam let out a sympathetic moan. "Aw, that's Talisa, the poor kid. She feels terrible."

"Yes, but look at our son," Jake said, with a quiet satisfaction. He fast-forwarded into the future, to the time when Ryan became a father to his own child. Jake could see how loving Ryan would be, and how kind. They had both wanted to meet with Kathleen's parents to apologize, but the Lindstroms had declined the meeting, and it had been Ryan's idea to plant a weeping willow in their backyard, as their private memorial to Kathleen. Suddenly Jake's heart lifted, easing a burden that he hadn't realized he was carrying until this very moment. He had made so many mistakes as a father, but in the end, he'd done one thing right. He'd been a better father than his own, and Ryan would be the best father of all.

"Jake." Pam leaned over, excited. "Look!"

"I'm watching, I'm watching." Jake came out of his reverie.

"Not at the game, at the stands." Pam pointed across the court. "Look over there. Do you see what I see? Third row up, in the pink ball cap, with the white tank top. Isn't that Sabrina?"

"Yes." Jake nodded, matter-of-factly.

"What's she doing here? Is something going on between her and Ryan?"

"Well, he was worried she friend-zoned him, but he's taking her out tonight. It's their first date but she texts him constantly from Friends Central camp, where she's a counselor-in-training. She writes funny texts and he likes that—"

"Wait. How do *you* know all this?" Pam looked at him, wide-eyed.

"I'm *baller,* honey. I'm baller *G.*"

"*What?*" Pam burst into laughter, and Jake wrapped his arms around her, kissing her forehead and catching a scent of her gardenia perfume. His wife was the most wonderful woman he had ever known, and he felt so grateful to be her Husband Material.

Just my luck.

Acknowledgments

I usually love to write my acknowledgments, but not this time, because we at St. Martin's Press have just lost our beloved publisher and friend Matthew Shear to cancer. This novel is dedicated to him, because I loved him and owe him so much, in so many ways. Permit me to tell you about him, because he was someone who loved books.

Matthew was simply a warm and wonderful man, with a big heart and an even bigger grin. He was a hugger. If you sat next to him at dinner, you knew you were going to have the best time of anyone at the table. He was honest and real and fun. He had great judgment. He loved life. He was witty, but no snob. He was the smartest guy in the room, but not a show-off. He could talk about books all day long, but he talked more about his wife of thirty-some years, Sabrina, and his two daughters, Hayley and Lindsey. As much as he loved to talk, he was a great listener. He listened intently when you spoke, and anyone who knew him can picture his direct, dark-eyed gaze while he listened as easily as they can recall the distinctive sound of his laugh, which was loud and joyful. It wasn't a musical laugh. Musical is overrated, as far as laughs go.

Matthew was also a brilliant publisher, and if you don't know what a publisher does, the answer is: everything. In my case, when I first came to St. Martin's Press, Matthew took me under his wing and told me that the house would take great care of me, and it has. He read each of my manuscripts and called or emailed to tell me what he liked in each one. He looked at my book covers with new eyes and changed them so they would reach a wider audience. He weighed in on any newspaper ad for my books, tweaking the taglines, and he moved my publication dates around to get my books in stores when it was best. He took me out of mass market paperback, where I had been published for twenty-odd years, and put me into trade paperback, which got a book of mine on the bestseller list for sixteen weeks, a sales record for me. The move was a radical change for a suspense author at the time, but now has become common. Most of all, he treated my daughter Francesca and me with respect and affection, and considered our opinions—as if we were his partners, not merely his authors. He helped develop the careers of so many authors like me, all because he loved our books and us.

Matthew Shear was larger-than-life, and so he will survive death. Those of us who knew him will never forget him. And we will always love him. In time, we will go on, because he'd want us to, and in so doing, we honor him. So I will thank that great group of wonderful people at St. Martin's, all of whom he loved as his office family, most especially, my incredible editor and dear friend, Jennifer Enderlin, as well as our truly fearless leader, John Sargent, the divine Sally Richardson, and the great crew of Matt Baldacci, Jeanne-Marie Hudson, Brian Heller, Steve Kleckner, Steve Cohen, Jeff Dodes, Jeff Capshew, Nancy Trypuc, Kim Ludlam, John Murphy, John Karle, Rob Grom, Paul Hochman, Stephanie Davis, Caitlin Dareff, and all the wonderful sales reps. Thanks to adorable cover designer, Michael

Storrings. Thanks to Mary Beth Roche, Laura Wilson, Esther Bochner, Brant Janeway, and all the great people in audiobooks. I love and appreciate all of you.

Now onto the experts and kind souls who helped me with *Keep Quiet*. Any and all mistakes herein are mine. I'm a former lawyer, but criminal law wasn't my field, and my first thanks go to a supersmart and dedicated public servant, Nicholas Casenta, Esq., Chief Deputy District Attorney of the Chester County District Attorney's Office. Nick has helped me with every book so far, including this one, and I throw hard questions at Nick, at all hours of the day and night, via panicky email. His answers are always spot-on, superbly well-reasoned, and incredibly helpful, and I couldn't be more grateful to him. Thank you so very much, Nick!

Thanks to Binney Weitlisbach, Betty Tafel, and Holly Palermo, of Haverford Trust, who took the time to answer all my dumb questions about financial planning. Thanks to Chief Gene Dooley and Detective Patricia Logic of the West Whiteland Township Police Department, and Chief John M. Narcise, Lieutenant Robert P. Klinger, Detective Stephen Jones, Officer Andrew J. Wahn, and Nancy Sheehan of the Willistown Township Police Department, who took their valuable time to answer my dumb questions about police procedure. Thanks to Dr. Nicole Kimze, who took her valuable time to answer my dumb questions about medical procedures. Thanks to Michael Skinner, Esq.

Thanks to Doug Young of the Lower Merion School District, and his lovely staff. Doug is an amazing young man, who took his time to explain the techniques and Zen of basketball and basketball recruiting to me, as well as what life is like on a great basketball team in a great school like my alma mater, Lower Merion High School. Doug played on the same team as Kobe Bryant, and they are both rock stars to me. Thanks to Aces Nation, for being so welcoming to me, and congratulations to the championship-winning Aces!

Thanks and love to my wonderful agent and friend Molly Friedrich, who has guided me for so long now, and to the amazing Lucy Carson and Molly Schulman.

Thanks and love to my dedicated and wonderful assistant and best friend Laura Leonard. She's invaluable in every way and has been for more than twenty years. Thanks, too, to my great assistant and friend Nan Daley, who helped so much with the research on this book and supports me every way she can.

Thank you very much to my family, and to my amazing daughter Francesca, for everything.

But my final thanks, as my first thanks, go to Matthew Shear. I am eternally grateful.

April Narby

LISA SCOTTOLINE is a *New York Times* bestselling and Edgar Award–winning author. She has thirty million copies of her books in print in the United States, she has been published in thirty-five countries, and her thrillers have been optioned for television and film. Lisa writes a weekly column with her daughter, Francesca Serritella, for *The Philadelphia Inquirer.* Those stories have been adapted into a series of bestselling memoirs. Lisa lives on a Pennsylvania farm with an array of pets.